Immortals
of
New Orleans

Léopold's Wicked Embrace, Book 5
Dimitri, Book 6
Lost Embrace, Book 6.5
Jax, Book 7

Kym Grosso

MT Carvin Publishing
West Chester, Pennsylvania

Editing: Julie Roberts
Formatting: Polgarus Studio
Cover Design: Alivia Anders / White Rabbit Book Design
Photographer Front Cover: Wander Aguiar Photography
Photographer Back Cover: Golden Czermak /FuriousFotog
Cover Model: Jase Dean

DISCLAIMER
This book is a work of fiction. The names, characters, locations and events portrayed in this book are a work of fiction or are used fictitiously. Any similarity to actual events, locales, or real persons, living or dead, is coincidental and not intended by the author.

NOTICE
This is an adult erotic paranormal romance book with love scenes and mature situations. It is only intended for adult readers over the age of 18.

LÉOPOLD'S WICKED EMBRACE

~·❦· *Chapter One* ·❦·~

Léopold's lips curled in restrained amusement. If it weren't for the acrid smell of burnt flesh emanating from his silver-cuffed wrists, he might actually enjoy schooling the wolves in what it meant to fight with a thousand-year-old vampire. When he'd made the decision to confront Hunter Livingston, Alpha of the Caldera Wolves, he'd fought the desire to kill the leader without hesitation. It was true that the death of adults came as naturally to him as piercing the skin of a delectable human on a warm summer night, but even Léopold had hard limits. It was only yesterday that he had pried the small infant wolf out of the arms of the lifeless woman. The sight of the helpless child had shaken him to his core. He'd many times witnessed children die during his lifetime, but the loss of an innocent life never got easier to stomach.

An eye for an eye; he'd considered penetrating the cold walls of their den and ripping out the Alpha's throat without mercy. Yet he'd known his friend Logan, Alpha of the Acadian Wolves wouldn't approve. Nor would Logan's beta, Dimitri. After he'd saved the Alpha's mate, Wynter, it appeared a bond had been forged between him and his newfound friends. Ever since Dimitri had made the long trip with Léopold to Yellowstone to retrieve Wynter's frozen blood, the two had grown closer. Out of respect for Dimitri, he'd grant the Alpha the opportunity to explain before he killed him.

Earlier in the evening, he'd approached the den peacefully, allowing the distrustful wolves to cuff his hands. The sting of the silver was worth enduring for the pleasure he would get from draining the Alpha. Unlike younger vampires, Léopold stood calmly, easily enduring the bite of the poison. His eyes scanned the room, taking in the sight of the growling wolves who'd gathered to watch their Alpha. Had he been any other supernatural being, he should have been concerned. Yet anger flowed through his psyche, not fear.

His patience wore thin as he observed the Alpha transforming into man. Hunter Livingston rose from a crouched position. Reaching above the fireplace, he snatched a silver claymore off the wall. The air in the room crackled with tension as he deliberately stalked toward his prisoner. He growled and his eyes locked on Léopold's. Sweat dripped from Hunter's forehead as he sliced the sword through the air.

Léopold's face remained impassive as the blade seared a trail of blood in its wake across his abdomen. He gave a devious smile a second before he launched himself at the Alpha. The snap of metal was the only sound alerting the wolves that the vampire was freed. Léopold rushed the tall wolf, smashing him against the stone wall. Clutching his right hand around Hunter's neck, he applied pressure with his other until the weapon clanked onto the floor. His fangs descended, scraping against the rough skin of the Alpha's shoulder.

"Where is the child?" the Alpha sputtered, surprised by the vampire's strength.

"Let me be clear, Alpha. It is I who will ask questions. And it is I who shall grant mercy. Nod, if you understand." Léopold fought to keep his rage at bay. Answers would be forthcoming before he sated his desire for revenge.

Dimitri heard the commotion and immediately sensed danger. He exited the shower and tore off his wet towel. Transforming to wolf, he ran toward the source of the melee. As he rounded the corner, he couldn't believe his eyes. Léopold had Hunter jacked up against a painting. Hunter's eyes glowed red; his claws were embedded into the vampire's arms. The pack wolves growled but didn't attack. Even though Léopold wasn't wolf, his attack on their Alpha was seen as a challenge, one that had to be fought alone. But Dimitri knew that whatever was going on had nothing to do with a challenge to Hunter's role as Alpha. He charged the pair to break up the fight, shifting back to human in the process.

"Jesus Christ, Leo. What the fuck are you doing?" Dimitri placed his palms against their chests in an attempt to separate the dominant males. "Alpha. Hunter. Please stop."

"The child," Hunter spat out, never taking his eyes off Léopold.

"Yes, the child," Léopold hissed in return. His fangs descended, readying to strike.

"Fucking stop it. Both of you. Whatever's going on, it's not what it seems. Leo, release him," Dimitri commanded.

Dimitri knew that both the Alpha and vampire could kick his ass, but he wasn't about to let them kill each other. The vampire's gift of life to his Alpha's mate had secured his friendship with Léopold. But he'd known Hunter his whole life, and he'd stake the ancient one before letting him kill the Alpha.

Upon hearing Dimitri's words, Léopold reined in his anger. In doing so, he was taken aback by his own acquiescence. *Since when the hell do I listen to anyone, let alone a wolf? It's official. I've gone soft.* He'd known that the past few days with Dimitri had changed him. It was as if someone had pounded a crowbar into his cold dark heart and poured in warm honey. *Goddammit, this is exactly why I don't have friends.* He'd freely chosen his solitary life, made a deliberate choice to keep both humans and supernaturals alike as mere acquaintances. It was true that he was close to a few vampires that he'd sired, but they weren't friends. Rather, they were relationships borne out of necessity and respect. A growl brought him back to the situation. Resigned to the fact that he needed the Alpha alive if he were to get answers, Léopold tossed Hunter to the ground.

"Fucking wolves," Léopold grumbled. He glanced up to Dimitri and gave him a look of disgust, realizing his friend was once again naked.

"Get over it, asshole," Dimitri growled in return, raking his hand through his hair. "Goddammit, Léopold. Whatever the fuck your problem is, you could have come to me. I realize this concept may be foreign to you, but use your fucking words instead of killing first."

Léopold rolled his eyes at the admonition and shook his head. He didn't want to admit that the wolf was right. But trust wasn't something that came easily to him nor was he used to having someone who would willingly help him.

"And you," Dimitri gestured toward Hunter, who'd pushed up off the floor. "I told you I came out west with the vampire."

The Alpha limped over to the bar and began pouring himself a scotch. He threw back a shot of the amber liquid and slammed the glass onto the bar. "Yes you did. But you didn't tell me everything."

"Blake, take the pack for a run. I'll be fine. Now go," Hunter told his beta. He wasn't about to have this discussion in front of the entire pack. Hunter waited only a few seconds after they'd gone before crossing the room to slam the door.

"Would someone like to tell me what the hell is going on?" Dimitri grabbed a throw blanket off the couch and wrapped it around his waist. He could have cared less if his nudity bothered the vampire, but it was winter in Wyoming. Even indoors, his human form couldn't take the bone-chilling temperatures.

"Last night is what happened. Ask the Alpha." Léopold sighed, staring into the flames that blazed brightly inside the stone hearth. Ironic that even though a mere lick of a flame could easily bring about his demise, he was still attracted to its warmth.

"Last night you were supposed to get the blood that Fiona had buried. Did you take care of it?" Dimitri's eyes darted back and forth between Léopold and the Alpha, who'd already started pouring himself and his guests another drink. "Come on, what the hell am I missing?"

"Un bébé. A girl." Léopold turned to stare into the eyes of the Alpha, who was handing him a glass. He took it, downed the caustic drink and sighed once again.

"What have you done with her?" Hunter seethed.

"A baby? You took a freakin' baby?" Dimitri jumped to his feet and grabbed Léopold by his shoulder.

Léopold's lips tightened in rage, and he seized the wolf's wrist. "Yes, I took the damn baby. She would have died."

"So she's alive?"

"But of course she is." Léopold shrugged him off, turning to Hunter. "Why, Alpha? Why would you allow a human to take the child into the woods? Had you ordered her death?"

5

"Are you fucking kidding me?" Hunter yelled.

"What? Did you not deem her to be perfect?"

"We'd never do anything to harm a child," the Alpha retorted.

"Really? 'Cause I just found one of your pups in the woods. Nearly dead, in fact. Don't tell me that wolves haven't ever tried to kill a child, one they didn't want in a pack. You know it's been done. Exposure. That's what they called it in ancient Rome. An illegitimate child. A sick child. Tossed aside to the elements, they were. A barbaric practice seen in other cultures as well." Rage coursed through Léopold, and he fought to remain calm. "Did you send the human out to do your dirty work? Where are the child's parents? How could you let this happen?"

"I didn't fucking know!" Hunter screamed as he began to pace wildly, rubbing the back of his neck.

"So you deny involvement?"

"I swear to the Goddess that I did not order this...I did not know. I would never do something like that. She's just a baby," Hunter fought back.

"Is she yours?" Dimitri asked.

"No, I'm not even mated."

"Just askin'. But how the hell does one manage to get a pup away from its mama, anyhow?" There was no wolf more protective than a mother.

"Ava's mother is dead. Ava. That's her name. Her mama, Mariah, died during childbirth." Hunter blew out a breath, rubbing his eyes. "She was a gentle hybrid, but Perry knew how frail she was when they'd mated. She could shift, but she couldn't take the cold, couldn't keep up with the pack either. Once she got pregnant, she deteriorated. The pregnancy was rough. And when she gave birth to Ava..." Hunter's voice trailed off, unable to continue.

"What of the human doctors? If she was hybrid, surely they could have helped her?" Léopold inquired.

"She wouldn't hear of it. Beside, her labor came fast. With the blizzard, it could have taken hours to get her there anyway. She hemorrhaged. And Perry, well, he was despondent. With the loss of his mate, he couldn't take care of himself, let alone a baby. Two days after she was born, he went missing. Of course, we searched for miles, but he'd gone. As for Ava...ya know I'm a bachelor. But I took care of her anyway. Hired nannies... I don't know how it happened...why it happened...one of them just took her." Hunter's cheek quivered in the lie.

Dimitri, sensing the untruth, got up off the sofa, approaching the Alpha. "Hunter, what the fuck happened? You and I know that wolves wouldn't just let someone take one of their own, a baby, and walk out of the pack. You can tell me...him too. That vampire over there," he gestured to and locked eyes with Léopold, "he saved the pup. You can trust us."

Hunter sighed and licked his lips in indecision. They'd all known the child wouldn't be all wolf, yet no one had suspected the origins of her human side.

6

"The baby, she's special. Yes, she's at least half wolf. But Mariah, we didn't know what she was. We all assumed she was human and wolf."

"What are you trying to say?" Dimitri put his hand on the Alpha's shoulder to comfort him.

Hunter raised his gaze to meet Dimitri's. "I can't explain it. Ava has this strange energy about her. I could almost handle that, but then I felt something...something worse."

"What the hell did you feel?" Léopold asked, growing concerned for Ava's safety.

"Something dark was out there. No, it was more than that. Something evil. Hell, I don't know what it was."

"A witch?" Dimitri offered.

"I don't know. I mean, come on, guys; we're in the middle of the wilderness out here. It's not like we're in New Orleans. What the hell would someone be doing practicing dark magick in the middle of Yellowstone? It doesn't make sense. Besides, this was more like something watching...waiting. I don't know, it could've been nothin'. I can't explain it. If I didn't know any better..." He shook his head, unwilling to share his thoughts. Even to him, his suspicions were ridiculous.

"Say it, wolf. I need to know," Léopold insisted.

"There were times when her energy felt so strong. I actually thought I saw her skin glow...like a firefly. And things in her room...would be moved."

"Moved? What do you mean?"

"Like objects. Like a stuffed toy. Her pacifier. I never saw her do it but I think she may be able to move things. Like call them somehow." Hunter pressed his hands on the bar and bowed his head, embarrassed to look at their faces. What he was saying made no sense, he knew. "Goddammit, I know it sounds crazy but I'm tellin' you that she's not just a hybrid."

"The baby glowed?" Dimitri laughed.

"I told you it was crazy. Even if that pup's part wolf, she's something else...something besides human."

"Then what is she?" Léopold considered that he'd best call her caretaker as soon as possible. He'd seen all kinds of supernatural beings during his long life. He may not have liked Hunter, but that didn't mean what the Alpha was saying wasn't true.

"I don't know," Hunter admitted. "So Devereoux, I've laid out my cards. Where'd you take the baby?"

"I shall tell you where she is, but let me be clear, I'm not returning the baby to your pack until her safety is assured. The fact that a human nanny was able to steal her from your home and drag her into a blizzard is outrageous. Given that you have so many security measures, one can only assume that the human didn't do this on her own." Léopold eyed the Alpha, walked to the overstuffed chair and sat down, shifting his feet onto an ottoman. He raised an eyebrow at Hunter, who stood silently contemplating his words. "That being said, you don't need to worry about her being with pack. She's with Logan."

"Logan? How the hell did you get a baby to Logan so fast?" Dimitri asked.

"Why would Logan take Ava?" Hunter questioned, doubting the vampire's words.

"He owes me a debt."

"Must be some hell of a debt if you got Logan to watch her," Hunter said with a shake of his head.

"That it was," Dimitri confirmed. "Léopold saved Logan's mate, Wynter. I was there when she died...almost died. His blood runs through her veins."

"Since when does a vampire give his gift to a wolf?"

"Doesn't matter, Alpha. Just know that it does, and she's alive. I went to Logan last night. It's no business of yours as to how." Léopold shot Dimitri a knowing look. He'd show the wolf soon enough. "It wasn't as if Logan had much choice, but he agreed. And Wynter was more than happy to take the baby. She may not have known it before, but she's very nurturing. They know it's not permanent. But they will care for the pup, and she'll be around a pack."

Hunter quietly considered what had happened. He had no explanation for how the nanny had taken Ava from his well-secured home in the middle of the night. And he couldn't be sure if he'd only imagined the dark force he'd felt or if the pressure of losing two wolves and caring for a baby had skewed his senses. While he cared for Ava, he was not her father. He'd merely been foster parent and he'd known that he'd eventually have to find her adoptive parents.

"I agree that Logan is well suited to watch the child, but we still don't know about the baby...what she is. Her mother, Mariah; I didn't know her very well but I know she'd lived in both New York City and New Orleans. Maybe if we could find Perry or track down a relative, they could help us figure out if Ava has any special abilities."

"We're leaving for New Orleans tonight," Léopold informed them. "Tomorrow, we'll meet with Logan to make sure the child is safe."

"I'm going to search Perry's house tomorrow and see if we can find any clues to Mariah's background. I don't understand why someone would want to kill her baby. It makes no sense," Hunter said.

"People kill for all kinds of reasons, Alpha. Spite, love, anger, jealousy...sometimes people kill just for fun. It is a wonder at times there's anyone left on the Earth," Léopold pondered. "I, myself, prefer to kill for revenge. And the next person who attempts to harm Ava will die. I can assure you of that."

Hunter went to his desk, pulled out a piece of paper and wrote down Mariah's and Perry's full names. He extended the note to Léopold. "Perry's local. He met Mariah in New York last year. But I remember him telling me that she hadn't lived there very long. I don't think she even ran with a pack. You know how the hybrids can be…they like to lay low sometimes. Even though he'd mentioned New Orleans, she may not have been there very long either. I don't have an address or anything else to go by."

"She's never been part of the Acadian wolf pack. Maybe she was just passing through or stayed with a friend?" Dimitri suggested.

"We'll find her family and her friends. And we'll find Perry, too. I don't give a damn if the wolf had his heart torn out all over the floor, a man doesn't just walk away from his child," Léopold replied with disdain.

Dimitri didn't answer the vampire, hesitating to agree with him. While the loss of a wolf's mate was devastating, there was no excuse for leaving one's offspring. Dimitri caught Hunter's gaze, expecting the Alpha to argue with Léopold. Instead, deafening silence hung in the air for several minutes until Hunter responded.

"Listen, I don't condone what Perry did and he's not welcome to return, but I agree with the vamp. We've got to find him. Ava deserves better." The buzz of Hunter's cell phone drew his attention away. He clicked it off and took a deep breath. "I'm sorry gentlemen, but I've gotta take this in my office. I'll just be a few minutes."

As Hunter retreated out of the living area, Léopold addressed Dimitri. "Time to go, wolf."

Dimitri rolled his eyes, recognizing the patronizing tone of Léopold's statement. "Yeah, I need to get dressed, first. How the hell did you get here anyway? I told you I'd find my way back to the cabin. Even if you drove the main highway, you'd be hard pressed to make it up Hunter's driveway tonight. Did you walk?"

Léopold smiled coyly at Dimitri. It had been so long since he'd had a friend and now he was about to clue him in on a little secret. Léopold approached him with a small chuckle, closing the distance between them.

"What's so funny?" Dimitri stood with the blanket wrapped loosely around his hips, confused as to what Léopold found so amusing. The hairs on the back of his neck pricked as Léopold raised his hands as if to embrace him. "Come on, man. Let me go get dressed and we can get the hell out of here. We can call the airline on the way back to the cabin and…"

"Ah, mon ami, have I told you how much I've enjoyed the past few days?" Léopold set his palms on Dimitri's shoulders.

"What? Yeah, okay. Good times and all, but we've got to get going." Dimitri cocked a worried eyebrow at the vampire. His gut told him something bad was about to happen; something very, very bad. He looked from side to side at Léopold's hands. Their heavy weight warmed his bare skin. A whisper fell through his lips. "What are you doing, man?"

"First, know that it's going to be okay."

Dimitri nodded, attempting to remain calm.

"Second, we aren't taking a plane."

~⚜ *Chapter Two* ⚜~

Dimitri hit the floor with a thud, his head barely missing what he recognized as a heavy wooden spindle from a four poster bed frame. His eyes flew open and he realized he was in a strange room, but he wasn't alone. Léopold lay next to him, grunting in pain.

"What the fuck did you just do, Devereoux?" Dimitri yelled, unable to gather the energy to get up off the carpet. Confusion fogged his mind as he tried to figure out where he was and how he'd gotten there. A deep rumble of laughter interrupted his growing state of panic. *Damn vampire.* "Jesus Christ. Are you trying to kill me?"

"Yeah, I thought it'd be better not to tell you. You might not agree otherwise. Much faster than a plane, no?" Léopold continued to laugh as he attempted to push up onto his elbows.

He glanced over to Dimitri who was laid flat out on his back, naked as a jaybird. Very few knew of his ability to materialize and very rarely had he pulled someone through with him. But he needed to get back to New Orleans as fast as possible and flying in a plane would have taken hours. Unfortunately, he'd had to bring the baby last night and hadn't fed in a few days. Exhausted, he clasped his hands onto the side of the mattress and used it as leverage to hoist himself off the floor and onto the bed.

As he rolled onto the soft comforter, he groaned in agony. Reaching across his chest, he fingered the torn fabric and ripped open his shirt. The crusty line across his abdomen provided evidence that he hadn't fully healed from the Alpha's blade. The rush of adrenaline must have kept him from feeling the pain, but now the sting tore across his chest.

"Merde," he coughed.

"What the hell is your problem, vampire? Travel arrangements not up to your standards?" Dimitri spat out, trying to get his bearings.

"Don't tell me you're not impressed, wolf. It's a cool trick. Don't try to deny it." Léopold took a deep breath and blew it out.

"Now you see it, now you don't. You'd better fucking tell me what you just did. I feel like you scrambled my brain. Not cool."

"Ah, stop complaining. You'll feel better in a few minutes. Just look at it like shifting. It's a kind of magic, sort of. Or one could say it is the temporary reorganization of mass and energy. Perfectly safe, I assure you."

"Yeah, well, it may be safe, but you could have told me. A little warning might've been nice."

"And you would have agreed?" Léopold choked up blood and his eyes fluttered.

"Probably not, but shit, Leo," Dimitri huffed. He was loath to admit it but Léopold was right; he was beginning to feel well again. He sat up and noticed Léopold sprawled out on the bed, looking unusually pale…even for a vampire. A nasty scab lined his chest. "Hey man, what's wrong with you? What happened to mister, oh so powerful ancient one? You do remember that vampires heal themselves, don't you?"

"Mon ami, even I have my limits. I need to feed. I flashed back here last night with Ava and now again with you. If I can get my phone out…" Léopold kicked off his boots with his feet and began to take off his jacket, searching the pockets. "Where is my damn phone?"

"What're you doing?" Dimitri stood and stretched, looking at his hands, feet and groin, checking to make sure everything was in working order.

"Arnaud."

"Who's Arnaud?"

"He's my, uh, you know, assistant."

"Like your Renfield, huh? Maaassster," Dimitri joked in his best Transylvanian accent.

"He's not sired or bonded, smart ass. But he is well paid. He was supposed to bring me a donor, and you, some clothes. I just need to lay here a minute…find my fucking phone."

Dimitri laughed. "Looks like the great one is definitely loosening up. First the hot tub. Your liberal use of the f bomb hasn't gone unnoticed either. There's hope for you yet."

"What can I say? You're a bad influence." Unable to find his phone, he threw his jacket to Dimitri, who effortlessly caught it mid-air. "Find my cell."

Dimitri quickly rummaged through all the pockets of the parka. "Nothing. You said, Arnaud is supposed to be here? And by donor, I assume you're talking about a human?"

"Oui. Some are paid, some are volunteers."

"Volunteers, huh? You got em' lined up waiting for you to suck their blood? You must be good," he joked as he made his way toward the door.

"The very best," Léopold replied with a smile. But as soon as Dimitri left the room, he moaned, gritting his teeth together. Damn, he needed his sustenance. He should have known better than to try to transport again without feeding but he'd be damned if he spent another minute in the Alpha's home when there was work to be done. He stared at the ceiling, weighing his options. Sure, he could drag his sorry ass downstairs and catch a cab to a local blood club. But the donor should have arrived already. Within minutes, he heard Dimitri returning down the hallway. The distinctive sound of a singular set of footsteps told him that he was alone.

"No one's here yet. But hey, look at this." Dimitri gestured to the dresser which was covered in an assortment of new clothing with the tags still attached. "Jeeves must've gotten one thing right. You mind?"

"Please do. If I have to look at your naked ass one more second, I think

I'll bite my own arm."

Dimitri laughed, ripping open a new package of boxers. He quickly put them on and went to look through the large pile of jeans. He was about to ask how Léopold's manservant would know his size, more than a little creeped out that some personal assistant was trying to dress him, when he heard a hiss from the bed. He sighed, knowing that his next idea was probably not the smartest thing he'd ever proposed, but damn, he felt a little guilty that the big guy had brought him all this way, sharing his 'special travel skill' and now the vampire was having trouble even sitting up in bed.

"Hey, Léopold. How about we take a cab to one of those clubs? What's the name of that place? Mordez?"

"Soon enough. I just need to rest a bit before I go anywhere."

Dimitri crossed the room and sat on the bed, taking in the listless state of the vampire. He observed that Léopold's eyes were now closed, and the wound had started bubbling apart. Before he could stop himself, he'd made the suggestion.

"I'll feed you."

Léopold's eyes flew open, meeting Dimitri's. "What?"

"You heard me. Come on, let's do this thing. You can bite my arm, right?"

"I don't know…I can't ask this of you. The donors, they come to me freely."

"Yeah, well, so do I. Come on. You did this for Wynter. You had her back, I have yours. It's no big deal, right? I mean, it's not like you're going to have some weird bond to me."

"No." Léopold gave him a small smile. "No bonds. No sires or anything. But still…"

"The faster you're on your feet, the faster we can go try to find connections to Mariah's past."

Léopold's lips tightened and he looked away.

"Ya know I'm right. We can't waste any more time. You didn't fly me all the way out here to lie around, did ya?"

"No, but I don't think this is a good idea."

"Well let me put it this way…At some point, possibly very soon, whoever wanted that kid dead is going to realize that she's still very much alive. Then they're gonna go after her again. And since she's staying with Logan, I don't want them going after my Alpha and his mate. So let's go. Come on, just take a little, enough to get you by until we find your donor."

"I won't need much. Your blood; it's strong. You're wolf," Léopold admitted.

"There ya go, then. Let's get to…what do you need here?" Dimitri sat on the bed and considered how best to feed a vampire. *What the fuck am I thinking? Too late now.* He sat cross-legged, and then changed his mind, lying onto his back.

Léopold grew amused at his friend's insistence. Not that he didn't appreciate the offer, but he wasn't accustomed to needing anyone. Dimitri's blood, given in friendship, felt all too intimate, making him uncomfortable. Yet the lancing pain to his gut reminded him of his dire situation. He shifted onto his side, cradling Dimitri's arm in his hands. Slowly he lowered his head to the wolf's wrist. The aromatic scent of blood called to him as he found the strong beating pulse.

"You're sure?" he asked, locking eyes on Dimitri's.

"Yeah, I can take it. Do it now, before I change my mind." Dimitri glanced away as if someone was about to give him a needle.

Without hesitation, Léopold's fangs extended, striking the wolf's arm. He closed his eyes, allowing the pungent flavor to coat his tongue. Deliberately, he suctioned the life-sustaining fluid, releasing his own power into Dimitri's body. Léopold, grateful for the gift, would cause the wolf no pain, only pleasure. He knew Dimitri would resist, confused by his reaction to the bite. Léopold clutched the wrist to his lips, watching as his friend's body bowed off the bed.

As soon as Dimitri felt the pinpricks, his body flooded with unexpected warmth. The tug of Léopold's lips sent a rush of blood to his cock. *What the fuck is happening?* He wanted to rip his arm away from the vampire, but he felt paralyzed to fight. Desire washed over him from head to toe and before he knew what he was doing, his own hand had reached to grip his shaft through the fine cotton shorts. Stiff as a board, he stroked himself, attempting to relieve the pressure. *Goddess, this feels wrong on so many levels.* His mind screamed at him to move, to struggle, yet his lips parted, releasing only a moan.

Léopold licked the wounds he'd caused, and released Dimitri's arm. Thoroughly energized, he sat up, and stared down at Dimitri, whose face had grown tight in both arousal and anger. Léopold laughed, and rolled off the bed. He watched in amusement as the wolf attempted to launch himself off the mattress but fell backwards, clutching himself.

"Fuck me." Dimitri shook his head at the realization of what he'd just said. He quickly took his hand off his groin and glared at Léopold. "No. I didn't mean that. Don't touch me."

"You're fine," Léopold assured him. He glanced in the mirror and finger-combed his hair back into place.

"This," Dimitri gestured to his erection, "is not funny. Goddammit, I need to get laid. Not that you aren't pretty, Leo, but you're not my type. Shit, look what you did."

"You may recall that I told you that feeding from you was not a good idea. But I must admit, your blood is fine. Very tasty." A broad smile broke across his face.

"Really, Leo? What the hell, man?"

"Sorry, but there aren't many choices when it comes to a bite, you know. Would you have rather had pain? I'm not a sadist by nature, but if you'd preferred it…"

"No." Dimitri pushed himself up so that he was sitting on the edge of the bed. His painful erection was finally starting to subside.

"Well, then, you have to admit that it didn't hurt. Go get a shower, see to your need. I'd love to help you but I'm afraid you're not my preference either, wolf."

"Really, so you give hard-ons but no blow jobs? Lucky me. For the record, if I ever am dumb enough to suggest this again, would you please just say no?" Dimitri hobbled over to the bathroom door.

"Hey wolf," Léopold called from the doorway.

Dimitri lifted his gaze to him. "Yeah?"

"Seriously, Dimitri. I appreciate you helping me. I should've paid more attention. I let myself get run down. It won't happen again."

"No problem."

"You need to know that it has been a very long time for me...this friendship thing. This isn't something someone like me does." *Or deserves.* Léopold's eyes darkened and his tone grew serious. "These few days have been quite the adventure, and I suspect there is more to come. I must ask, however, that you keep what you experienced tonight to yourself. Not the bite but the travel. Logan knows as I couldn't hide it from him when I showed up in his house last night. But no one else. It's a special ability...one I'd prefer others not know about. Understood?"

"My lips are zipped." Dimitri sensed sadness in Léopold. As wolf, with his pack, he was never truly alone. Perhaps he underestimated the loneliness that plagued the vampire.

"Well, then...see you downstairs in a few. I've got someone I want you to meet," Léopold commented as he left the room.

Laryssa Theriot carefully controlled her heartbeat and breathing in an attempt to convey indifference. For the past week, she'd felt the energy. She couldn't be sure but suspected a child of her lineage had been born. So rare, she'd never experienced the warmth, the calling of another whose power was so strong. Yet as soon as she'd indulged in her excitement, acknowledging the fact that someone else like her existed, a cold chill had rolled over her skin, emphasizing the reality of her situation.

Sitting at the bar, she crossed her legs, the tight black leather pants caressing her thighs. There was no way she'd ever wear a skirt in this place. Like the humans, she'd be vulnerable to suggestion and the sexual excitement the vampires could induce with a mere look. She kept her eyes low, glancing around, taking in the auras of the supernaturals. If necessary, she'd invoke her powers to protect herself from danger. She'd gone to great lengths to hide herself, to blend into the magical background of the French Quarter.

After nearly thirty lonely years, she'd grown weary of concealing her true nature. The cloak of evil that she'd recently felt brush across her face had reminded her she'd never be safe, freedom to be herself would remain elusive. It hadn't been the first time she'd felt it nor would it be the last.

Laryssa pushed down her sunglasses, shielding her emotions further from the prying eyes of vampires and humans alike. The bartender regarded her for a moment, noticing that her glass was still half full with wine. She'd needed the alcohol to take the edge off her nervousness. *Show no fear.* The supernaturals would detect the smallest infraction of a loss of control. Increased heartbeat. Sweat. Rapid breathing. So many years in hiding had taught her well to mask her abilities. Like an actor in the grand theater, she played her part, meticulously attending to every last detail of her role, a dominant biker chick, looking for nothing more than a drink. Tomorrow, she'd return to her unassuming job in the Quarter, selling antiques, coming and going as she pleased on assignment. But tonight, she looked as if she was the predator; cold, calculating and ready to catch her prey.

She scanned the room, noting the usual spectrum of auras. Excitement. Hunger. Desire. Jealousy. She nervously tapped her fingernail against the glass, waiting for her friend, Avery, to arrive. Avery was the only soul in New Orleans who knew her secret. She'd been her savior, helping her to hide. After sensing the dark ones, she speculated she'd need a stronger witch to find a spell to ward off the evil. The mere fact she could sense it meant it knew she existed as well. She needed someone to better shield her powers, to keep her safe from the hell that sought her soul. Yet the thought of a new child weighed heavily on her shoulders. If what she suspected was true, she wasn't the only one in danger.

A shuffling of patrons alerted her to a new arrival. She turned to face the bar and glanced in the mirror to observe the commotion. Struggling to keep her composure, she lifted her eyes to the reflection. Both men and women appeared captivated by the dark haired, well-dressed man who'd entered the room. The air thickened with palpable arousal, auras flickered to red, with fangs descending in response. The stranger stopped to take in his surroundings, looking over to the bar. Laryssa lowered her lips to the rim of her glass, attempting to look uninterested.

As soon as he glanced away, her eyes were once again drawn to him. He was tall, at least six-four, his lean muscular build carefully concealed underneath his form-fitting black suit. Strikingly handsome, he smiled with a cool arrogance that told her he was a vampire. And he wasn't a neophyte; quite the opposite, he exuded the confidence of a master. He laughed at something his friend said and winked at a passing waitress. The rugged good-looking fellow who accompanied him looked out of place next to the debonair vamp. Casually dressed in jeans and t-shirt, his forearms were painted in tattoos, the stubble of his day-old beard darkened his jaw. She'd be surprised if he was anything other than wolf, as his aura shone in relaxed blues. Like the magnetic attraction of polar opposites, the odd pair seemed inseparable, and she wondered about their connection.

Her curiosity seemed to get the better of her as she swiveled her stool to catch a glimpse of them leaving. Unconsciously, she tugged at her short black wig, pressing a stray hair back underneath it. Her breath caught as the vampire stopped in his tracks and turned to stare over at her. Her traitorous heart sped up slightly in response to the way his gaze caressed her body. Laryssa crossed her thighs together as warmth spread throughout her chest. Like a blushing schoolgirl, she felt the heat rise in her cheeks. Hastily, she spun away from the sight of him, but not before his eyes locked on hers and she caught his broad smile in the mirror.

She wasn't sure if it was his stare or her own confusion, but as she tried to tear her eyes off him, the slippery leather seat gave way. Her cheeks flushed in embarrassment, her hands flailing to reach the bar top. Expecting a hard fall onto the stone floor, she cringed, anticipating the pain. Air rushed from her lungs as strong hands wrapped around her shoulders, jerking her upright. She grasped her sunglasses that had fallen down her nose, revealing her emerald green eyes to her rescuer.

Léopold felt somewhat guilty for throwing the human off her game. As soon as he'd entered the bar, he'd spotted a woman dressed in black leather. Leather in Mordez was hardly unusual, but this woman looked tightly wrapped, like a Christmas present waiting to be opened. He observed the way she tugged at the ends of her short black hair, as if she was pulling a baseball cap down over her face. Interesting, he thought. Try as she may to blend into the supernatural crowd, her vitality licked at his senses the second he sniffed the air.

Although he hadn't come to play, the way her pulse increased, if only for a second, told him she was aware of his presence in the room. He didn't have time to get distracted, but when he noticed her tottering on the barstool, he rushed to her side. Catching her right before she landed on the ground, a rush of desire slammed him as the swell of her restrained breasts grazed his chest. Léopold felt her quiver underneath his touch, but she quickly recovered. He caught a glance of her captivating green eyes right before she shoved the black glasses onto her face, shielding her from his gaze.

"Careful, pet," he told her.

"I'm fine...really," Laryssa stammered.

"But of course you are," he chuckled at her defensive posturing.

Léopold was about to engage her further when he heard Dimitri call his name. *Merde, cock-blocked by the damn wolf.* He was starting to regret the day he'd become involved with the whole lot of mongrels. He nodded to Dimitri, who was staring at him as if he'd grown a second head.

"Take care, mon petit lapin," Léopold commented as he grazed the back of his forefinger down the side of her cheek.

"I'm fine," she repeated. Laryssa had hoped the vampire would leave her alone. Quite the opposite, he'd positioned himself within inches of her body, invading her personal space. His leg brushed hers, and she took a deep breath, her mind warring between sliding her hand down his thigh or running out the door. Lost in her own confusion, she heard someone call out toward their direction. Out of the corner of her eye, she observed his sexy pirate-looking friend give a wave. Refusing to acknowledge the lash of sexual awareness that he'd left on her skin, her fingers tightened around the stem of her glass.

"I'm afraid I must go. Be safe, mademoiselle. This is no place for a single human," he warned.

Léopold hesitated but a second before returning to Dimitri. While nonchalantly guiding them through a sea of bodies, he stole a glance back to the girl, wondering who she was…what she was. Her scent was like lilies on a spring morning, sweet and fresh. But it was her energy that alerted him that perhaps he was wrong about her. When he'd touched her cheek, her smooth skin sizzled underneath his, and he'd detected something otherworldly. Yet he could tell she was neither vampire nor wolf. A witch, perhaps? Maybe, but the look of innocence and fear in her eyes worried him. She didn't belong in Mordez, and his curiosity about her stood to distract him from the entire reason he'd come to the club. He shook the feeling off as he spotted the person he'd come to meet, making a beeline toward him. Lady Charlotte Stratton.

Laryssa breathed deeply, forcing her physical response into submission, all the while despising the way she'd lost control of her equilibrium. Not only had she broken character, she'd fallen like a dumbass, totally distracted by the sexy but dangerous stranger. His touch had scorched her skin through her jacket, leaving her tingling in his wake. As her eyes caught his, she struggled to slow her pulse, to control the power that could easily spill into the room, revealing her true identity.

Although Laryssa had never met the vampire before, a sense of familiarity and desire had washed over her. There was something about him, something driving the rapid fluttering in her stomach that made her want to jump into his arms. The rush of lust threatened to push her into a panic. She forced herself upright, stiffening her spine, and ratcheted down her foolish and dangerous response to him. *Goddammit, I almost revealed my identity.* The warmth inside her was shaken cold when she felt a tap on her shoulder.

"What?" She spun around to see her friend, Avery, smiling broadly, a hand to her hip. Glancing over to where she'd last seen the handsome stranger, she saw nothing but customers quietly engaging in private conversations, but the smirk on Avery's face told her she'd witnessed the embarrassing spectacle.

"Smooth move, girl," Avery laughed and took the seat next to Laryssa. She held up her hand to the approaching bartender, in an effort to get his attention.

"Please tell me you didn't just see what I did?"

Avery laughed harder, nodding.

"Yeah, just call me Princess. Nothing but grace. God, I'm an idiot for coming here." Her face reddened.

"It was kinda funny. But what was really interesting was watching the most powerful vampire on the east coast catch you like a football. He's hot, I'll give ya that. Smokin'." The bartender approached and she cleared her throat. "I'll have two Sazeracs, please."

"What did you just say? Oh sweet Jesus, please. Who was he? No, don't tell me. I don't want to know." It was best she didn't know who he was. If she knew, she'd be tempted to Google him, look him up or otherwise stalk him. She shook her head. This was so unlike her. The man had her rattled and he'd barely even spoken to her.

"Hey, it's not that bad. You did make a nice recovery. His name's Léopold Devereoux."

"How do you know him?"

"I don't really know him, but he's visited the coven house a few times to see Ilsbeth. I heard that he's some kind of a billionaire philanthropist. Rich but deadly. It's rumored that he likes to kill with a smile."

"Nice."

"Well, I suppose you could still date him. Samantha, one of the new witches; she married one...a vampire. Luca. Kade's his maker and Léopold is the grand mac-daddy of them all."

"Shit, shit, shit," Laryssa muttered under her breath.

"Look on the up side." Avery took the drink from the bartender and sipped it up through a pink cocktail straw.

"What could that possibly be?"

"Samantha doesn't seem to be afraid of Léopold. I've seen her with him."

"Yeah, why's that?"

"Apparently he saved her...once upon a time. Long story."

"Does he have a girlfriend?" *Why do I care?*

Avery laughed. "No way. That one there is the epitome of a playboy. He's here often enough...a different woman every time. And he's kinky as hell."

"Kinky, huh?" Laryssa took a deep breath and tried to tone down her interest in the subject. If she let her mind wander, imagining what sorts of things he did in Mordez...no, she wouldn't let herself go there. "Well, he may be hot, but it's not like I'm lookin' to get involved with anyone."

"Go ahead and tell yourself whatever you want, honey, but I know you. That man had you all seven ways to Sunday flustered. Not that I blame ya. I mean, he is seriously a fine piece of man candy."

"Stop it, Avery. Not happening. Anyway, we didn't come here to talk about my sex life."

"Or lack of one?" Avery teased.

"Yeah, that's about it. Seriously, we need to talk." Laryssa looked over her shoulders to make sure no one was listening and lowered her voice. She knew that despite her whispers, the supernatural could hear her and she'd need to remain cryptic.

"No problem. I mean, I'm sorry we couldn't meet at your place but I'd already promised Mick I'd meet him tonight." She shrugged, and swiveled her head toward the dance floor, searching for her boyfriend. "It's date night."

"Does he know? You know you can't tell him."

"Come on, Lyss. I'm not stupid, okay. He doesn't know anything about you. What's going on?"

Laryssa put her arms around her friend in an embrace, and whispered into her ear. "I need help. I need you to up your wards. If you know what I speak of, nod your head."

Avery's face dropped in concern. It'd been years since Laryssa had asked for her help. Her eyes darted from side to side, taking in the vibe of the room before she quietly nodded.

"It isn't safe to talk…not here…not anywhere. I just need you to do what you can, okay?" Laryssa took a sip of her wine and sighed.

"We should've waited until tomorrow to talk. You can come to the coven," Avery suggested. She wasn't comfortable discussing this issue out in the open with so many wolves and vampires within hearing distance.

"No, this couldn't wait. I needed to see you. I need to know that you'll help me." Laryssa couldn't stand the waiting. "I can feel them."

"Do you feel it here?"

"No." Laryssa scanned the room. She'd instantly recognize the dark presence that haunted her outside her home, the heavy feel of the air. Dead, stale pressure pounding into her lungs. Here, the air was tinged with sex and excitement, lust and hunger, but no darkness.

"Listen, Lyss, I'm not discounting what you've sensed, but maybe things aren't as bad as you think. Someone could've been cooking up some black magick just to try it out…you know, things are always a little funky in the Quarter. It's just the way down here," Avery assured with false bravado. She didn't want to worry her friend, but there wasn't a whole lot more she could do to protect her on her own. She'd need the help of her sister witches to provide anything else than she'd already done. Inwardly she shrugged, knowing that her spells had only been temporary.

"I just…I'm not sure how to describe what I feel. Something's off." Laryssa spied Mick approaching and changed the subject. "Hey, I don't want to keep you any longer. Just, uh, stop by my store, tomorrow, okay?"

"I'll do my best." Avery nodded. "I'd better go find Mick, now. If I don't stay with him, the leeches will come crawling out of the woodwork."

"Looks like he found you."

Laryssa pressed her lips together in a tight smile as Mick surprised Avery, wrapping his arms around her waist. Her friend jumped in surprise, giggling in recognition. *Maybe someday*, Laryssa thought. But as things stood now, she knew that she'd be lucky to survive, let alone find love.

It wasn't as if Laryssa hadn't dated. She'd always purposefully chosen humans, since they were considerably safer than supernaturals, and thankfully, clueless to the existence of her kind. She thought about her last boyfriend, David, who in their final argument, had described her as frosty the snowgirl. Despite their uninspired and utterly vanilla encounters, she'd tried to make their relationship work. Granted, he'd been good on paper, someone her parents would have approved of; responsible, held in good standing in the community, well off and practical. So she'd continued dating him, afraid to admit her clandestine, carnal fantasies even to herself. The sex they'd had was like eating bologna sandwiches for lunch. It was okay to eat every now and then, but hardly nutritious or satisfying.

They'd both known the deal, but still, she'd been surprised when he'd finally broken up with her. The past two months since, she'd become entirely too familiar with her purple plastic friend. Regrettably, while he brought relief, the little fellow was no substitute for the intimacy she craved.

Lady Charlotte, the proprietor and owner of Mordez, glided across the dance floor with the grace of a ballerina. Dressed in a dark satin purple corset and matching mini-skirt, she stretched out her hands toward Léopold, beckoning him to come to her. Her long straight black hair was pulled high onto her head in a ponytail. While she looked as if she were in her mid-twenties, she was several hundred years old. The influential vampire, neither sired to Léopold nor Kade, had been rumored to have been a pirate who'd come to enjoy her fortune shortly after the war of 1812.

"Léopold, darling," she crooned over the blaring music.

"Lovely as always," Léopold said with a brief bow.

"Still the sweet talker, I see. This way."

Lady Charlotte gestured to an exit behind one of the bars, and they followed her. As the door slammed, a dull vibration was all that remained of the music. After a dizzying climb up a spiral wooden staircase, they entered a large living room. In the corner sat an oversized mahogany desk and red velvet chair. A sectional u-shaped red leather sofa faced a set of clear French doors that led to a balcony, overlooking the entire nightclub. Charlotte flipped a switch and a small gas lit fire pit blazed to life, instantly warming the room.

Léopold, familiar with his surroundings, strode into the room. "Char, this is Dimitri LeBlanc. He's beta of..."

"Acadian Wolves," she finished Léopold's sentence, slinking up to Dimitri. She flipped her hair, and smiled seductively at the wolf. Her voice grew husky as she let her palm fall onto his shoulder. "Yes, I know who you are."

Dimitri smiled in return, carefully removing her hand and placing a kiss to the back of it. "A pleasure to meet you, Lady Charlotte."

"A gentleman," she commented with a wink to Léopold.

"He's smooth with the ladies," Léopold responded, his voice dripping with sarcasm.

"Clubbing with the wolves these days? My, my, Léopold. Things are changing." She went to the bar and pulled a bottle of aged rum off the shelf.

"Let's just say Dimitri is a special wolf, one worthy of my loyalty and friendship."

"You are a suave one, Leo. You'd better stop with the compliments… they'll say we're fallin' in love," Dimitri jibed. After the blood donation and the set of blue balls he'd nursed, all he wanted to do was go down to the dance floor and find a she-wolf to fuck. But no, here they were in the lair of the very knowledgeable but dangerous Lady Charlotte, and the damn vampire still hadn't explained why they were there. Considering it'd been a long shitty day, he gladly accepted the drink she offered.

"Where's your Alpha, Dimitri?" Lady Charlotte filled another glass and then handed it off to Léopold.

"Logan? He's home with his mate. I'm taggin' along with the big vamp here." He shot Léopold a look as if to say, 'What the fuck are we doing here?'.

Léopold simply smiled and fell back into a chair, making himself comfortable.

Charlotte raised an eyebrow at Léopold and promptly took a seat on the sofa across from him.

"Léopold, you know I love seeing you, but I assume you need something." She crossed her legs and cocked her head knowingly.

"Oui. We both know you have the pulse on this town. I'm looking for someone. Someone special."

"Aren't we all?" she laughed.

"This is a serious matter. I'm not sure who I'm seeking, but I'm looking for someone with certain powers."

"This town is crawling with supernaturals. Frankly, I'm surprised you're coming to me. Kade practically runs this town. Between him and Logan, they could find whoever you are looking for."

"I've already talked to them both. Logan doesn't know and neither does Kade. Neither has heard of the one I'm looking for."

"And who's that?"

"I'm looking for a being who can move objects." Léopold raked his fingers through his hair, reluctant to share too much information about the child.

"A witch?"

"I don't know…maybe. We all know the most powerful witches can make things move but in all my years, it's always taken a spell of some sort. This gift…from what I can tell, involves pure telekinesis. No magic." Hunter had told him that he'd suspected the child had the ability to move objects. Witch or not, a baby wasn't capable of spells.

Charlotte gave a small smile, waiting to see if he was serious.

"It's possible no one knows what kind of supernatural we are looking for. We only know a few of their powers," Dimitri added. Taking a cue from Léopold, he held back information about why they were asking. He knew damn well that if Hunter didn't know what the child was, then it was likely no one knew. Hell, Léopold of all vampires should know. He'd been on the Earth nearly a thousand years, and while Charlotte was a mover and shaker in New Orleans, he couldn't imagine she'd have the answers they sought. He had to suggest something else, something to brainstorm. "Or it could be a hybrid. Maybe a new kind of supernatural."

"Man or woman? Bigger than a breadbox?" Charlotte laughed as she said it, noticing the scowls that crossed their faces. "Come on. Seriously, look at this from my point of view. A vampire and werewolf walk into a bar…"

"This isn't a joke," Léopold snarled.

"Okay, fine. No joke. How the hell am I supposed to know what you are talking about here? Telekinesis? That's all you've given me."

"We don't have much to give." Dimitri rounded next to her and sat down, sighing in frustration. This was not turning out how he thought it was going to go. He stared over to Léopold who pushed out of his chair and approached the French doors, appearing deep in contemplation.

"Forget it, Char. Let me ask you this. Have you noticed anything dark in town over the past few days?" Léopold practically choked on the question, realizing how stupid he sounded. Darkness in New Orleans? The town was the epicenter of both worlds, good and evil. Yet Hunter had told them about the presence he sensed. Léopold shook his head, realizing that he needed to disclose more information. "When I say dark, I don't mean the usual. I'm talking, well, evil…from hell."

"Demons?" she asked in a whisper, not wishing to conjure trouble.

"Yeah, anything like that? Hell hounds, a demonic trace on anyone here in the club, rumors of rituals," Léopold continued, keeping his back to Charlotte, scanning the club through the glass.

"Léopold, I'm not sure what you are looking for or why, but if we're going down this path, I'd appreciate a little more information. Whatever you tell me, I'll keep it confidential. I swear it. But let's not speak more of demons. You know as well as I do that we don't want to attract the evil to us. I may not be a witch or psychic, but even a human can call on hell."

Léopold stood silent a minute, deciding how much information to divulge. "A wolf named Perry. A she-wolf named Mariah. She was a hybrid.

Have you ever heard of them?"

Charlotte bit her lip and her eyes honed in on Dimitri. "Let me get this straight. You're asking me if I know a couple of wolves?"

"They aren't ours," Dimitri offered. He wished Léopold would turn around and give him some indication of how much he wanted to share with the vampiress. Damn it all to hell, what could it hurt to tell her where they were from? "They belong to Hunter Livingston. But they've been here in New Orleans. No one in our pack knows them. All we know is that they've been to the city, but at no point did they check in. But Hunter says they were here."

"Well, now, this is interesting, boys. Sorry to disappoint, but I've never heard of them. And as far as evil, it's been the same ole, same ole. Nothing terribly out of the ordinary." Charlotte blew out a breath and took a sip of the golden liquid in her glass. "I can't say I've heard of pure telekinesis. But the witches…they must know. Have you tried Ilsbeth?"

"I don't think the person we're looking for is a witch, but I'll be calling on her. She may be able to do a spell to help us find the supernatural we seek. I wanted to start with you first because…"

Conversation stopped as a tall lithe blonde entered the room, carrying an iPad. Charlotte quickly approached her and accepted the tablet.

"Camera five. Situation has been handled, my Lady." Focused on her task, the newcomer pointed to the screen.

"Excuse me gentlemen. This is my assistant, Lacey." Charlotte crossed to the staircase, readying to leave the room. "She'll attend to your needs."

Lacey wore a see-through mesh mini-dress, which left little to the imagination. Her black lace panties and rosy nipples were clearly visible through the netted fabric, catching the attention of Dimitri. Clearly in need of female companionship, he smiled and stood to greet the alluring woman.

"Hello, cher. I'm Dimitri," he said.

"Yes, I know who you are. Beta of Acadian Wolves." Lacey smiled.

Avoiding contact with the wolf, she made her way over to the French doors and opened them. A wave of music rushed into the living space, and she pranced out onto the balcony. She closed her eyes and her hips began to sway. Léopold watched as the siren on the ledge crooked her finger at the beta. Dimitri shot him a knowing smile before he joined her, sweeping her into his arms.

Normally, Léopold would enjoy watching the erotic dance of a man and woman sensually moving to a driving rhythmic beat. He'd revel in the excitement, knowing that eventually they'd make love. Perhaps in public or in private. He may even join into a threesome given the right circumstance. But not tonight.

While he found Lacey attractive, his mind drifted to the leather clad woman who'd fallen off her barstool. Perhaps after he finished with Charlotte, he'd call on the lovely little rabbit whose scent reminded him of home. He smiled to himself, slightly confused as to why she held his interest. It wasn't as if she was his type. No, he generally liked his women assertive and ready for sex, ones who weren't looking for a commitment that he'd never give.

Léopold sighed, attempting to dismiss the feelings that had been creeping up on him over the past week. He'd only made one vow in his life to a woman, his wife. At the young age of nineteen, they'd married. Then, the day he was turned, reborn as vampire, he'd sworn he'd never love another. Women were mere distractions in the adventure he called life. In all his years, not once had guilt arisen as he liberally used humans for blood and sex. But ever since saving the Alpha's mate, he'd found himself reminiscing about his first life, the last time he'd felt anything…felt love, alive. Yet every time he allowed himself the indulgence of remembering his wife, a flood of memories of his last hours as a man slammed his psyche, reminding him why he'd never love again. No, love brought nothing but pain, death and despair.

Thoughts of Ava wrapped around his heart, draining his libido. He had to find a clue as to what she was so that he could protect her. He wouldn't allow another child to die under his watch. He could still hear the sound of her cooing as he'd held her tight against his chest. It was as if her own energy had meshed with his, cleaving open the terrifying past he'd worked so hard to keep sealed tight. By the time he'd gotten her to Logan's, he'd felt the bond forming and he cursed it. Ava had clutched on to his fingers, smiling at him as he rocked her softly. Even though she couldn't talk, he knew the connection between them was as real as a father to daughter. When he placed the infant into Wynter's loving arms, a tear ran down his face as he turned away to materialize back to Wyoming. Goddess help him, he'd keep the child in a New York minute if she weren't wolf. He knew it wasn't right for him to raise a wolf. No, she needed to be with her people, her pack. And she sure as hell deserved better than the cold-hearted bastard he'd developed into over the years.

The sound of Charlotte's voice jarred him out of his silent contemplation and he turned to find her still clasping the tablet. A devious smile crossed her face. She'd found something.

"Well, my old friend, you're one lucky fellow."

"Ah, mademoiselle, there's no such thing as luck. Destiny? Perhaps. Fate? Maybe. But I believe we make luck. Besides, you know the universe won't fight with me for long. She owes me." Léopold let it go at that. He wasn't about to share why, but as far as he was concerned, the universe was a diabolical bitch who owed him a debt, one far greater than she ever could repay.

Charlotte offered the iPad to Léopold, stealing a glance at Lacey and Dimitri, who appeared to be lost in their own world.

"Hit track twenty-seven. Interesting little fight we just had in the bar."

"And we missed it?" His thoughts immediately flew to his little rabbit. *Is she okay? Still here?*

He tapped the screen; a grainy black and white video began to play. Anger licked through him as he watched the scene, his eyes widening in disbelief. A large vampire approached the woman in leather, wrapping his arm around her neck, flicking off her sunglasses. As he hoisted her off the seat, her feet began to flail on the floor. With one hand, she clutched the banded arm around her neck and attempted to elbow him with her other arm, but her attacker refused to let go. No one intervened or attempted to dislodge the man. She struggled helplessly as the others told him to release her. What Léopold saw next both amazed and thrilled him. It happened so quickly, he was surprised Charlotte had caught it. He looked to her and back to the screen.

"Telekinesis, no?"

"I think you may have found the being you seek. A woman no less? Play it in slow motion. I almost missed it, but after you'd asked me if I'd noticed anything strange, well, it was remarkable that a human was able to best that asshole. My suspicion was confirmed. I don't know what she is, but she's no human."

Léopold replayed the video, ignoring Charlotte's commentary. Second by second the frames passed and he observed how his little rabbit, held tight by the beast, had glanced over to the bar. A knife that had been used to cut lemons and limes sat on the edge. With the naked eye, it would have appeared as if the object had been within her reach. It was only a few inches, hardly enough movement for anyone to notice. But on the slow motion video, it was clear the knife had slid to her. As her hand wrapped around it, she immediately brought it to her assailant's neck. Locating his carotid artery, she pierced the skin right beneath his ear. If she'd pressed any harder, he'd have bled out, but very smartly, he released her. As she fled, bouncers pounced, taking him to the floor and cuffing him in silver.

"Gotcha." Léopold smiled at Charlotte.

"You do realize that the witch could have caused it."

"The witch? The blonde spitfire yelling at the vampire?" He pointed to Avery on the screen.

"Avery Summers. She's a regular. Belongs to Ilsbeth's coven. The big guy behind her is Mick Germaine. Warlock. Also runs with Ilsbeth's witches. From what I've seen, they're a couple. But your little dominatrix-looking girl, she's new. I've never seen her before."

"Tell me she paid with a credit card. I need a name."

"Sorry, darling. No name, but I do have a way to find her."

"The witch?"

"No, it would take too long. Besides, I doubt she'd tell you...well, not willingly, anyway."

"Stop with the games. If you don't have a card and you haven't talked to the witch, what's her name? Do you know how to find her?"

"Ah, do you doubt me?"

Léopold smiled at her. This is why he came to Lady Charlotte.

"Track thirty-five." Charlotte grinned smugly as Léopold tapped at the screen.

"Well, now, that is surprising." Léopold licked his lips as his rabbit hopped onto a motorcycle that had been parked across the street and took off like a bat out of hell. *Hell.* He sighed, shaking his head. She'd piqued his arousal, but damn it all, she'd better not be some kind of fire-breathing demon. She smelled way too good for that. Pulling his mind away from the memory of her scent, Léopold tapped again on the screen, freezing the image of the bike and used his fingers to enlarge the photo until he had a clear shot of the license plate.

"Welcome to my world, mon petit lapin," he growled. He memorized the numbers; he'd find her by the morning and she'd be his.

~❦· *Chapter Three* ·❦~

Léopold sat in his black Lamborghini outside LT Antiques. The candy-apple-red Harley had been registered to a Laryssa Theriot. Through the painted glass window on Royal Street, he watched a man arranging knick knacks in the window, and he couldn't help but wonder about his relationship to the girl. Was he an employee? A family member? A husband? The thought of her with another man caused a tick in his jaw. He shook it off, aware that it didn't matter either way. This afternoon, he'd get answers.

He half wished he'd brought the wolf with him today to help him focus on his target. Last night, he'd reluctantly left him to Lacey, figuring Dimitri needed a little female loving to offset the awkward feeding situation. When he'd left Mordez, he'd given fair warning that not a single hair on his mongrel friend was to be harmed while he was there or there'd be hell to pay; more specifically, death. Lady Charlotte, while powerful in her own right, knew better than to go against his wishes and had guaranteed the wolf's safety. Dimitri had promised he'd only stay briefly and then go to Logan's to check on Ava.

As Léopold opened his car door and breathed in the cool winter air, his determination to protect the infant grew stronger than ever. He'd called Kade in the middle of the night, unapologetically waking him and Sydney. Sydney had agreed to run the license plate number for him. They'd planned to meet at Logan's later in the day to discuss the best way to keep Ava safe from whomever, whatever had tried to kill her. Léopold refused to leave her security solely in the hands of wolves. No, his people would be on the case, ensuring that nothing happened to her while he investigated.

Léopold confidently approached the storefront and entered. The distinct musky odor of times gone by filled his nostrils. But there was another scent, one far more delicious and enticing that caught his attention. *Laryssa.* As he passed through the crowded aisle of chairs and tables, he noted the feminine nature of the store with its pink floral stencils along the edge of the ceiling. A collection of crystal chandeliers illuminated the ancient treasures. As he made his way past an enormous armoire, his eyes lit up with excitement. Perched precariously on a step ladder, his little rabbit was hanging a mirror on the wall. He quietly observed as she toyed with the wire backing, carefully adjusting the frame so that it hung straight.

His eyes roamed over her body, and he smiled, realizing that she'd been wearing a wig in the club, which had hidden the thick brunette curls that danced to the middle of her back. Gone were the tight leathers, replaced by a form-fitting pencil skirt that accentuated the curves of her hips and bottom.

A pink cashmere sweater clung to her shoulders. She'd casually pushed the sleeves up as if she'd been working for quite a while and Léopold couldn't hide his amusement at the transformation. While he certainly enjoyed the way she'd looked last night, he admittedly favored this softer, feminine attire. He sniffed into the air, catching a hint of mandarin with notes of coconut. She smelled fresh and warm, as if she'd just stepped out of the shower. Shocked at his reaction to the mere sight of this woman, he silently rolled his eyes. It had taken all of fifteen seconds to lose focus. Willing his visceral attraction to Laryssa into submission, he cleared his throat, hoping to get her attention.

Intrigued, Léopold observed her with both interest and annoyance as she fumbled with the mirror. He heard her say that she'd be right with him, and sought to offer assistance when she began to topple off the third step of the ladder. A loud scream filled the air just as he caught her in his arms. He wanted to be angry, but all he could feel was the softness of her breasts under his hands. Instantly, he hardened as her back pressed against his chest. He wished he could stop but before he knew what he was doing his nose was buried deep into her hair. And he'd been correct about the citrus, definitely mandarin.

Léopold loosely held Laryssa, indulging both his curiosity and desire to touch her. *Goddess, what is it about her?* He couldn't help but notice how well she fit against him. Merde, he needed to get this conversation going. But of course she'd fit against him. She was a female after all. Any female would feel good against his body, but it was as if her body melded to his, making him harder than he'd ever been. He moved his legs, unwilling to let her feel the way she'd affected him. His burgeoning erection painfully pressed against the zipper of his pants and he cursed. Setting her onto her feet, he forced his hands away from her and took a deep breath. Never. He'd never feel this for a woman. He'd never let it happen again.

Laryssa had heard the customer behind her, but the damn mirror wire wouldn't seem to catch right. It kept slipping and she cursed under her breath, hoping she wouldn't drop it. If she could just hold it up a minute longer, she could get it to hang squarely on the wall. She fingered the hook that she'd just renailed into the wall and then moved her thumb over to the thin metal string. With a final shove upward, she attempted to flick it into place. But as the wire caught, it sliced into her flesh. A sharp sting threw her off balance, and her pumps began to waver. *Shit. Not again.*

"Oh my God!" Laryssa squeaked as she fell backwards, fully expecting to crack her head open on one of the many sharp-edged desks that sat adjacent to where she'd been working. As she felt strong male hands slide up under her ribcage, grazing her breasts, she gasped. She wasn't sure whether to thank the stranger or call the police, but as she turned her face to try to see him, she immediately recognized her rescuer.

"It's you," she stammered, clutching his arms. Laryssa giggled nervously, realizing how once again she'd foolishly fallen in front of the sexy vampire. And like last night, he'd caught her. She couldn't believe how clumsy she'd all of a sudden become. She tried to relax and find her footing, but her heart was beating so fast that she could barely think. *What is he doing here in my shop? How did he find me?*

Like a story book flipping pages, her mind whirled until she remembered what she'd done last night at the club. She'd fought off the asshole who'd grabbed her at the bar. The feel of his hands around her throat had forced her fear into overdrive. The knife had only been a few inches away, but still too far. Desperation had taken over as her power surged, calling the blade to her fingertips. Jamming it into his neck was as instinctive as breathing. Kill or be killed, she'd always choose the former. She'd run into the alley, refusing to discuss it with management. The only one who knew her was Avery and there was no way her friend would have divulged her identity to the vampire. She'd be more likely to turn him into a three horned sheep before she'd squeal. The only way the vampire could have found her would have been if he'd followed her home.

A brush to her breast reminded her that she was still being held upright by him, and Laryssa felt her face grow red. Arousal licked over her skin. Cautiously, she rooted her shoes on the floor and turned around, steeling her nerves.

"I'm so sorry," she said.

"My pleasure, mademoiselle, but I suggest you avoid heights in the future."

Surreptitiously, she stole a glance at him, which reminded her how incredibly handsome he was. His short dark hair was perfectly coiffed. His white dress shirt hung casually over the waistband of his jeans. Laryssa forced herself to look away, trying not to stare at the masculine features of his face. Straight nose, square jaw and perfectly kissable lips… lips that were smooth talking and way too articulate, teasing her with every word he spoke. Beads of sweat broke out across her forehead. It felt as if someone had turned up the heat, her skin was on fire. She noticed his eyes were no longer on hers and had dropped to her chest. They lingered only a second, and then he met her gaze and smiled. She looked downward and noticed that several buttons had come undone in her fall, revealing the edges of her white lace bra. *Could this day get any more embarrassing?* Laryssa's fingers shook as she buttoned her sweater.

"I'm so sorry. I just…you just…I just…" *Great, first I'm a klutz and now I can't speak.* She bit her lip, paused and then took a deep breath before starting again. "Thank you for catching me."

"Again." Léopold watched her as she adjusted her clothes, wishing to rip the rest of the pearly buttons from their fragile seams. But he refused to let the beast within take what it wanted. No, he'd find out what the hell she was before showing her his true nature. "Yes, thank you…again." She smoothed down her skirt, trying to pretend she hadn't just fallen into his arms and let him feel her up in the process. *Business, think business.* Her pulse slowed and she willed herself to appear nonchalant.

"We met last night, remember?" he pressed. Léopold smiled and ran his hand over the colorful marquetry in rosewood that scrolled through a seventeenth century secretaire. Interesting that she could deliberately control the flow of her blood. It further piqued his concern about her species. What was she?

Laryssa's eyes met his, widening at the confirmation that he knew exactly who she was.

"Yes, yes I do. But I'm afraid I didn't catch your name." *Vampire. Big bad vampire.* Laryssa watched intently as he fingered the furniture, trailing his thumb over the symmetrical scenes as if he was caressing a lover.

"Lovely." Léopold flashed his eyes to hers.

"What?" Laryssa realized that he was toying with her, purposefully trying to make her nervous.

"I said, it's lovely. The neoclassical architectural structures. The white marble top. Doré bronze mounts."

"Is there something specific I can help you with?"

"You get directly to the point?" Léopold had intended to play with her a bit, throw her off her game. Yet his little rabbit wasn't frozen in the field like he'd anticipated. No, she rebounded nicely, and now stood confidently like a wildcat, poised to attack.

"I don't really have time to waste. So yeah, I'd like to know why you followed me from the club. And I really want to know what you are doing in my shop."

Léopold merely laughed and crossed the room to admire a chair and matching settee.

"Circa 1775?"

Laryssa walked over and placed her hand on the elegant Louis XVI chair. "Yes. How did you know? It's a very special piece. It has the mark of Versailles Palace on it."

"Indeed." Léopold sat in the chair, wrapping his fingers around its arms. "Nothing but the best. Fit for a king."

"And I suspect you'd like being a king." She put her hands on her hips, waiting for him to respond.

"Ah, a king I never was. But I've dined with kings, and I can assure you that while they enjoy the extravagances of the rich, they often lose their heads. Easy come, easy go."

"Why are you here?" Laryssa brushed her hair back, attempting to regain her composure. "Are you looking for something specific?"

"Oui, pet. But not an antique. While I do enjoy shopping, this is hardly the time." Léopold lost the smile, allowing his eyes to pierce hers. "So I shall get to the point. What are you?"

Laryssa lost her ability to rein in her pulse and her heart began to fiercely pump hot blood through her veins. Her lips tightened, and she clenched her jaw. How dare he ask about her? What the hell did he want from her anyway? Dear God, she had enough issues with the darkness on her tail and now he was asking about her origins.

"What do you mean, 'what am I?' I'm the owner of this store. Does that answer your question?" Laryssa asked, her voice growing louder. "Who are you?"

"Léopold Devereoux. That's who I am. I can be your angel or nightmare, depending on the day. So listen up. What. Are. You?" Léopold didn't make a move. He sat completely still, anticipating her answer.

"Get out of here right now. I don't have to tell you anything."

Laryssa realized she'd made the classic mistake of turning her back on a predator and within seconds, she found herself backed against the wall. A mixture of fear and arousal flared as he pressed his body against hers. His hands caged her, and he'd effectively pinned her to the wall without ever restraining her arms. She breathed deeply, inhaling the clean male scent that surrounded her, and she sagged against him. *Please God, don't let me be attracted to him. This is wrong.* Even as she told herself that he was nothing but trouble, she could feel the heat grow between her legs.

"What are you?" Léopold whispered into her ear. His lips brushed her hair and he resisted the urge to kiss her.

"Please…I can't tell you," she begged.

"Laryssa…there's a child." Léopold knew no other way to be than honest. He'd swear her to secrecy if he was wrong and she wasn't aware. Deep in his gut, he knew she was the being he was looking for, the one who'd help him save Ava.

"Oh God. It's true then," she breathed into his chest. Her fingers rose to clutch his shirt. *How can he possibly know about what I sensed? A baby? One born like me?*

"You must help me, mon petit lapin. Tell me what you are."

"No. I can't." He couldn't possibly know what he was asking of her. They'd kill her. Hell, he'd kill her. She shook her head but didn't release the fabric curled into her fists.

"You must." Léopold's hand snaked up toward her throat. His mind warred against the urge to fuck her. At the same time, his frustration grew; her determination to withhold information was maddening. The child could die if she refused to help him. He wouldn't let it happen…not again.

"No," she whispered. Laryssa froze under his touch. As his fingertips grazed her collarbone and his thumb settled into the hollow of her neck, she closed her eyes, pressing her forehead into his chest. On fire with fear and the hot need growing in her belly, she relaxed into him, desiring the submission he sought from her. He could break her neck like a twig, but she sensed that he wouldn't hurt her. It was irrational, she knew.

"How can I trust you? I don't know you." A hot tear escaped her eye.

"Tell me, pet. And while you're at it, I'd like to know why you don't fear me." Léopold fingered her throat, holding her fully exposed to him. His fangs snapped down, both in anger and hunger for the woman in his arms. Her breath warmed his shirt, and he rocked his hardness into her belly, letting her feel what she was doing to him. He fisted his other hand into her long hair and pulled her head backward, revealing the smooth skin of her neck. *Was she crazy? Why wasn't she scared of him? She should be screaming, not aroused. Goddammit, she was making him insane.*

"I...I know...you won't hurt me."

"And how do you know this?" He pressed her further against the wall, and she released a small moan.

"I don't know...I just know you won't."

Léopold bent his head forward, grazing his fangs across her delicate skin. He didn't draw blood, but earned a small squeak from her lips. He swore that if she didn't tell him within the next thirty seconds, he'd taste of her blood.

"Please, don't," she cried. "The child."

"Oui, the child," he repeated. In the heat of the moment, he'd lost sight of why he was even there. Having her in his arms had become all that mattered, taking her, dominating her.

"I need to be able to trust you. You can't tell anyone...please," Laryssa pleaded.

"I swear it to you. Now tell me," he breathed. Before he could stop himself, he dragged his tongue from the hollow of her neck up to behind her ear. She tasted like the sweetest tropical fruit. For the love of the Goddess, he had to have her. He settled his teeth once again against her flesh, but didn't break the skin. It was pure torture and pleasure all at once.

"I...I can do things. Move things...by thinking it." She made the decision to tell him this much, but it was too soon to trust him with all her secrets. Still, her instincts told her that she needed to seek his protection. She released his shirt and wrapped her arms around his waist, pulling him toward her.

Not much could shock the ancient vampire, but the feel of her hands around him made him go stiff. *What kind of game is she playing?* She'd just admitted that she could invoke telekinesis. Immediately, he released her, breaking away from the sumptuous vixen who threatened his sanity. Her look of surprise, then disappointment jarred him further. Instead of running, she fell down into one of her antique chairs and wrapped her arms around herself as if she was missing the feel of him on her skin. He spun around, plowing his fingers through his hair, taking a cleansing breath, willing his erection to subside. *What the fuck is going on with her? With me?* She must be some kind of witch to have this effect on him. He needed to get it the fuck together and damn soon. He thanked the Goddess that Dimitri wasn't with him to bear witness to his idiocy.

"You're a witch?" He bit out, and turned to face her.

"No, not a witch. Listen, Léopold." She lowered her eyes, shaking her head and pressing her fingers to her forehead. "I want to trust you. I need to trust someone, but I can't tell you everything. Not yet. I'll say this much, the child you speak of…I've felt her. I can't say how, I just did. But I'm alone. There's no one like me."

"What do you mean you're alone? Surely there must be others."

"No. Just me. I wasn't born this way. I've only met one other person like me, but she's not here. Not in the city. We don't keep in touch."

"But how did you know? About the child? Or this other person?"

"How do you know when you're around other vampires?"

"Scent. The power. I feel it."

"And I feel it too. Like a hum over my skin, in my mind."

"Did someone infuse you with this magic?"

"It's not magic."

"It has to be magic. I've seen it happen with witches and vampires. What are you?"

"It's not important. What's important is the child." *And living. I really like living.*

"What else do you know about the child?"

"Nothing. I just could feel her." She dropped her head into her hands unable to tell him anymore. The dark ones were going to kill the baby. And her. Worse, she wasn't sure how to stop them. Avery had been her only hope of hiding. But the evil was growing stronger. "You need to protect her."

Laryssa's voice sounded desperate and Léopold grew gravely concerned. He slowly approached and knelt before her. She kept her head lowered, refusing to look at him. Léopold put a hand on her knee and with the other, cupped her face until her gaze met his.

"You can trust me. I can help you. But you have to let me in."

Laryssa's eyes began to water. She didn't want to cry, but the warmth of his voice surrounded her in a shroud of security. His piercing eyes had softened, revealing the heart of a protector, a man who felt deeply, perhaps more so than she ever thought possible. She hadn't felt safe in so very long. And here he was offering her trust. She wanted so badly to be able to rely on someone other than herself.

"The dark ones. They're here," she whispered.

"What are you talking about? Who's here?"

"I've seen them…their black eyes. Like angels of death."

Léopold cared, he really did. Clearly she believed what she was saying. But he was skeptical of what she was telling him.

"Ma chérie, it's not that I don't believe in evil. I've seen it first hand, but…"

"Hollow eyes…well, they're not really hollow. They're black, so dark…it looks like there's nothing in the sockets. And it's not just them…there's someone driving them, someone leading them. I know it. It's like they just stand there. Waiting." Laryssa knew it sounded crazy, she really did. But she'd seen them.

"Waiting for what?"

"I don't know. Maybe for someone to give them orders." She looked up and caught his gaze. He didn't believe her. She sighed and shook her head. "I'm telling you the truth. There's something out there."

Léopold paused, trying to think of the diplomatic words that eluded him. It wasn't as if he didn't know that someone had tried to kill the child. The Caldera Wolves Alpha had told him that he'd felt a dark presence. Léopold considered the possibility that perhaps the infant carried the evil within her, but dismissed the idea as soon as it surfaced. No, there had to be another answer. And as crazy as Laryssa sounded, she was his only lead at this point.

"I've lived a long time and seen all kinds of terrible things." *Many done by humans.* "But I've never heard of the beings you describe."

"But they're real," she protested, her eyes begging him to believe her.

"I'm not saying they're not. I'm just saying that I haven't seen them."

"But you don't believe me."

"Someone tried to kill Ava."

"What?"

"I told you she was in danger. I found her in the middle of Yellowstone. There was a blizzard. The nanny tried to kill her, but I saved her. Now she's here."

"In New Orleans?" Her heart began to race.

"Yes. She's safe…for now." Léopold let his hand slip down to the chair, but not before he slid his thumb over her quivering bottom lip. "I think you should meet her."

"You need to get her out of here…away from them. They'll find her….if they haven't already," she insisted.

"Are you sure you could tell if she's like you?" Whatever the hell Laryssa was, she was holding back, denying him the truth. Supernatural, she admitted as much. He needed more if he was going to save the child. He didn't necessarily believe that she'd seen what she thought she saw. But if someone had tried to kill Ava and she and Ava were somehow related, it wasn't a stretch to think that someone was after Laryssa, too.

"Yes." Of course she could tell if they were the same. But if the two of them were together in the same room, she couldn't predict what would happen.

"You're coming with me now," Léopold told her. This was utter bullshit. If she wasn't going to tell him everything, he'd put her and the infant together, see what happened. He wanted the wolves to meet Laryssa. If Ava's mother had been wolf, maybe they'd be able to sense shifter in her.

"No."

"What do you mean, no?" Incensed, he shook his head. First she lets him practically strangle her and now she was going to refuse him? The woman was certifiable. She obviously had no idea who he was or what he was capable of.

"Uh, I think you heard me. I thought vampires were supposed to have bionic hearing or something like that," Laryssa replied, worried that it could be dangerous for both her and the baby if they got together. "Are you hard of hearing? Or just hard headed? No, don't bother answering. The bottom line is that I don't think it's a good idea for me to meet the child. Not only that, I can tell you don't believe me. So there's no way I'm leaving my shop in the middle of the day to go off with you. But I'm going to hold you to your word. You promised not to tell anyone what I am. I may not look like much but if you don't keep it quiet, I'll….I'll…well, I don't know. But I will be really mad and trust me…I can take on a vampire if I need to."

"Are you seriously threatening me? Me?" Léopold's voice grew louder. That was it. Not only was she crazy, she was as mad as a hatter. "Listen to me, pet. You will come with me. I'm not asking you. I'm telling you. You really don't understand who I am, do you?"

"I'm not your pet," she protested under her breath. Laryssa heard Mason in the back room moving boxes, hoping he hadn't heard their conversation. Thankfully, he usually listened to music through his headphones when he was sorting the items. She hadn't told him about her abilities and didn't want him involved. Keeping her voice lowered, she continued. "You need to keep it down. And yeah, I know who you are. If you remember, you just told me. I also know that you are a pushy vamp who thinks he can order people around. And guess what? I'm not one of those people. I just sat here and told you what I knew and you don't believe me. So believe what you want, but I'm right about what's happening in New Orleans. You don't need to protect me. I can protect myself. I'm still alive. I think you should leave."

Laryssa was shaking by the time she got finished ranting. Exhausted and frightened, she needed to go call the witch. The vampire couldn't help her. She doubted anyone could. As she pushed past Léopold, he grabbed her wrist.

"Let me go." Like a power plant, the electrons began to hum, slowly building in her system.

"No. I need you."

"I said. Let. Me. Go."

No longer able to control it, Laryssa's eyes flew to a settee. Calling on her ability, she hurled the large piece of furniture across the room at Léopold, nearly grazing his head. Laryssa gasped, aghast that she'd nearly hit him. Immediately, fatigue slammed into her and she bent over at her waist, trying to catch her breath. Even though it wasn't a surprise that she'd be drained from using her powers, it had been years since the last time she'd moved such a heavy object, and she never imagined that it would be so intense.

"Point taken, mon petit lapin." Léopold jerked to avoid the projectile, but he stood firm, refusing to leave. He was about to yell at her for trying to smash a fine antique, when he noticed her slump in response. Curling his arm underneath hers, he gently set her onto the floor. He knelt, brushing her hair from her eyes. "What's happening to you?"

"I'll be fine. I just need a minute." She wanted to shove his hand away, but couldn't summon the energy to argue. Regret poured through her at the thought that a piece of the wood could have staked Léopold. She hadn't intentionally meant to hurt him. She'd just wanted him to stop pressuring her, to let go of her arm. "I'm sorry. I didn't mean to…oh God, are you hurt?"

"No worries, I'm fine. That was very impressive, but you'll have to do a lot worse to hurt me. Are you really going to be okay? I've never seen anyone move an object so swiftly."

"It was an accident. I can't always control it. I was just so mad. You wouldn't stop."

"I wouldn't let you go."

"No."

"I may never let you go after that little display. You're a strong woman, that's for certain." *A woman who could defend herself against the likes of him?* Well, damn, that was a major turn on if he'd ever felt it. He laughed softly. "Now can we discuss why you won't go with me?"

"Because I don't know what will happen. No, that's not true. What I suspect will happen is that our energies could be like fireworks. People will notice. The dark ones will notice. It's not a good idea. Neither of us will be safe."

"I promise you that I'll keep you safe." Léopold gently took her hand in his. He meant what he said. Even if he didn't believe her, he was confident he could protect her.

"But you don't believe me…why would you protect me?"

"Because it's what's right. Ava. The baby. I can't let anything happen to her. I won't just sit by and fend off another attack. I have to find out who's doing this so she can live a normal life."

"She'll never live a normal life," Laryssa sighed. Ever since she was turned, life had been far from the warm and loving upbringing she'd once known. Now she was a freak, one who'd grown accustomed to her solitary existence.

Léopold's heart constricted. Whatever had driven Laryssa to conceal her abilities had not been kind to her. Her shame was apparent, and he struggled to understand it. Life as a vampire was not always easy by any means, but it did have its perks. He'd chosen not to get close to anyone, selectively turning only a few humans over the years. Kade was the closest thing he had to family, and it had always been enough. But now? After bonding with Logan and Wynter? The wolves had brought forth an upheaval in his desire to be alone.

"The child. I need you to save her. I don't know how. But you're all I've got. Please." Léopold's voice softened.

"Is she yours?"

"No, she's at least part wolf. I cannot raise her." *But I want to keep her as my own.* He'd never admit it to another soul. If things were different…if he weren't such a self-centered asshole, he'd beg the wolves to raise her as his own. He deserved a lot of things in life; money, accolades, but the privilege of raising Ava, a chance at love and family, wasn't one of them.

"Why? Why do you care what happens to us?" It made no sense why a vampire would put his own life in danger to protect her or the child.

"Because she's important to me. She's innocent. She didn't ask for this when she was born into this world. She's in my charge now. I won't fail her. I won't fail you, Laryssa. Please. Please help me." Léopold inwardly cursed at how pathetic he sounded. Dammit, he should just drag her by the hair into his car and make her do what he wanted. Never in his life had he begged. He should resist the temptation, he knew. Yet looking into her soft green eyes, he could not.

Laryssa took a deep breath, studying the vampire. She knew she'd regret her actions but there was a part of Léopold that she wanted to know. He cared about the baby. An ancient vampire willing to protect the life of one human child seemed unbelievable, yet the truth shone in his eyes. And now that he'd held her in his arms, she craved his touch. It was stupid and foolhardy, but she couldn't deny her body's reaction. He was dangerous and altogether arrogant, but the way he talked about the child only made her want to get to know him more. As he dangled the key to the treasure chest in front of her, revealing his feelings for the child, the only word on her lips was 'yes'.

If something happened to the baby, she'd never be able to forgive herself. He said he'd protect her. As she stood and brushed off her skirt, she gathered up the strength she needed. God help her, she'd go with him. She'd meet the child, and do whatever she had to do to help him save the baby, hopefully saving herself too.

"I'll do it." She gave him a small smile, driven out of uncertainty, not happiness.

"Merci, ma chérie. You will come with me now, no?"

"I need to do a few things and close up here before I can leave. Can you give me an hour?"

"I will send someone for you. Please don't disappoint me. I'm trusting that you'll be here."

"I will." Laryssa sighed as he turned his back and walked out the door. She prayed she'd made the right decision.

Léopold smiled to himself as he left her shop. Relief swept over him as he entered his car. Triumphant for only a minute, he reflected on how close he'd come to losing it, to biting her. He couldn't remember the last time he'd been so terrified. His little rabbit called forth emotions he never wanted to feel again. He cursed, dismissing it as lust. It had to be. After all, he hadn't been with a woman in over two months. It had been in Philadelphia with a pair of lovely twins, if he recalled correctly. A lack of sex was a perfectly acceptable excuse for his behavior, he thought. Still, he couldn't risk emotional involvement with Laryssa.

He'd introduce her to Ava and gain her assistance in protecting the baby. He still wasn't sure what she could offer. But something in his gut told him that she was far more important than he could imagine. No matter her powers, she'd underestimated his ability to get what he wanted. Confidence swept through him. Not only would he save Ava, he planned on stripping Laryssa of all her secrets. What was she? And what other powers was she hiding? He was a patient man, determined and perseverant in all tasks. He'd rally every bit of self-control he had, ignoring the desire for Laryssa that grew inside him. It would serve only to distract him. *Mon petit lapin, enjoy your reprieve, for you will reveal yourself to me. And how sweet it will be.*

~⚜· *Chapter Four* ⚜~

Laryssa knew it had been a bad idea to acquiesce to the vampire. But as she glanced over to the imposing wolf in the driver's seat, her anger grew hot. She wasn't sure if she was madder at Léopold or herself for actually looking forward to seeing him again. Like a schoolgirl, she'd hurriedly closed up her shop, nervously fixing her hair right before she locked the door. The wolf seemed pleasant enough, but he was incredibly muscular, almost scaring her with the sheer size of him. She crossed her arms and pulled at her sleeves, willing her nerves to abate. Stealing a glance at the attractive beta, she jumped when he caught her.

"I won't bite, cher." Dimitri chuckled as she gave him a tight smile and looked out the window. He was beginning to think Léopold's nickname for Laryssa was right on target. *Rabbit?* She certainly was skittish when he'd arrived. Sensing her irritation, he reasoned maybe she'd kicked it up a notch, acting more like a feral cat at this point.

He still wasn't sure why Léopold hadn't brought her himself. Why send him to pick her up when it was clear Léopold had showed interest in her last night? He had a suspicion that the vampire was avoiding her, which was disconcerting considering he wasn't exactly the kind of guy to avoid anything, unpleasant or otherwise. Dimitri would never forget the way he'd deliberately challenged the Caldera Wolves Alpha, effortlessly pinning him against the wall in his own home in front of pack members. Surreal as it was, Léopold had let him go, only caring about the baby. It was a paradox he couldn't wrap his head around, but it served to remind him that no matter what kind of friendship they'd forged, he really didn't know Léopold that well.

Dimitri's mind drifted to his Alpha and how the baby had taken over their household. After only twenty-four hours of caring for Ava, both Wynter and Logan had become exceedingly watchful of her. It was as if the baby had set off both their biological clocks. Wynter was demonstrating the fierce protectiveness of a new mama wolf around her cubs. Dimitri laughed to himself, thinking how insane it was that not only had he watched his Alpha change a diaper but now they were hosting a party for the very supernaturals they'd pretty much avoided over the past hundred years. Fangs and fur didn't usually mesh well. Just as he was leaving Logan's home, an entire crew of Léopold's vampires had arrived.

Dimitri could sense Laryssa's fear, and it made him uneasy. It wasn't as if she didn't have reason to be seriously concerned about her safety. She could be in danger of being attacked if she didn't cooperate. Laryssa's unwillingness to disclose her abilities, what she was, didn't bode well. Léopold told him that she could move objects. He'd seen the tape, but he also knew there was a lot of witchcraft in New Orleans, and they weren't all like Glenda from the Wizard of Oz. No, these folks weren't into ruby slippers, butterflies and fluffy bunnies, magick ending in a happily ever after. The witches and mages he'd known were more about skinning the rabbit and eating it with a fine wine. Dimitri prayed Laryssa didn't pose a danger, that she wasn't part of whoever was behind Ava's murder attempt.

Glancing at Laryssa, he had to admit that she hardly looked the part of a bad witch. Her shiny brunette curls complemented her light pink sweater, making her look more like a librarian...a curvy, sexy librarian. She kept crossing and uncrossing her legs, revealing just a hint of her thigh, as if she couldn't get comfortable. Shit, no wonder Léopold liked her.

As Dimitri's eyes roamed over Laryssa's body, and when his eyes met hers, he noticed she was staring back at him. He smiled, well aware he'd been caught. Well, how the hell was he supposed to react to having a beautiful woman sitting next to him? He was a red blooded wolf, after all. Léopold was the one who'd asked him to pick her up and bring her to Logan's. All was fair in love and lust, he thought to himself; however, his smile faded when he realized she was frowning at his ogling. *Smooth move, Romeo.* He considered that maybe instead of undressing her with his eyes that he should try engaging her in conversation. Perhaps he would have better luck than his friend discovering what she was and if she held interest in the baby.

"So, you run an antique store, huh?"

"Yeah," she responded cautiously.

"How long have you been in New Orleans?" He'd known the store had been in existence for at least two years, but he wasn't the shopper in the pack. No, he'd leave that honor to his Alpha.

"Um, around six years. You?" She'd lived in the city for several years but her business was just starting to prosper.

"My whole life." Nearly a hundred and fifty years. "Well, to be honest, I used to live in the back country most days, but Logan prefers the city. Where'd you come from?"

"Las Vegas. Ohio, originally."

"Why'd you move to New Orleans?"

"I just needed a change. Las Vegas was fun, but too hot for me," she explained. *Too dry.* The idea that she thought she could live in the middle of a desert had been born out of denial. That and desperation to escape Ohio, her former life. Laryssa looked out the window, trying to hide the sadness that washed over her face. "Besides, I love it here."

Dimitri sensed that she was blurring the truth. At most, she looked to be in her mid to late twenties.

"Your family? Are they from Ohio? Do they live here with you?"

"No," she responded curtly. She didn't want to discuss her family or her lack thereof. Sure they were alive. They just didn't want *her* in their lives and hardly cared to keep in touch.

"Okay, I get it. Don't want to talk about it, huh?" No, he didn't get it, but he got the message, definitely not a pleasant topic. *Interesting.* But was she related to the baby? Léopold had only told him that she'd admitted having supernatural abilities, that she'd flung an ottoman at him. He would have paid to see that. "So, Léopold tells me you've got some power to your punch."

"I can't believe he told you that. It was…it was private." Laryssa snapped her eyes onto the handsome wolf in disbelief that the vampire had told him what she'd done. "I knew better than to trust him."

"Hey, it's okay. I'm the only one who knows." *Him and his Alpha.* Dimitri hadn't meant to upset her, but now that he was in for a penny, he might as well go for the pound. "Léopold said you think you're in danger too. He told you that we're trying to find out who tried to kill Ava, right? It sounds like you might know why."

"Yeah, I know a few things, but not much. But I told him I didn't think this would be a good idea to get us together. Our energy," she pleaded. Her eyes brimmed with moisture. She was so tired of hiding, of being alone. "I don't know what will happen. I don't want to attract attention."

"What do you mean?" Dimitri pulled the car into the driveway, lowered the window and opened the biometric security pad. He pressed a button, which extended the retinal scanner and waited for the green light. A buzzer clicked and he turned his head to address her. "Whatever it is, Laryssa, you're not alone. Léopold's committed to protecting Ava and now he seems pretty intent on keeping you safe as well."

Laryssa shook her head, unsure whether to trust him. Completely defeated, the pressure of keeping secrets had caught up with her. "Our energy. Well, I guess Léopold told you that I can move things. But that energy is unstable." She blew out a breath and bit her lips, trying to think of how best to explain it. "My ability is strong when I use it. I've learned how to keep it hidden, but it's powerful enough that I still can use it." *To live. Not die an early death.* "And Ava. Well, she's more like a spotlight at the Saint's stadium at times. When she was born, I could feel it all the way across the country. I'm just afraid that if we are together…"

"You'll blow the grid?"

She laughed. "Yeah, something like that."

"And it's like some kind of siren to these folks you're worried tried to kill Ava?"

"I don't know if they feel it, the humans. But there are others…they'll know we're here."

Dimitri pulled the car into the port and switched it off, deciding to warn her about who was waiting for her inside.

"Listen, cher. I'm not sure if or when you'll be ready to trust Léopold and me with what's going on with you, but I've gotta tell you, even though we haven't shared information about you with anyone else, Léopold's friends are here."

"Is this Léopold's house?" Laryssa asked in almost a whisper. She looked at the beautiful three-story corner home and glanced to the pool. She'd been so busy talking and worrying that she hadn't realized he'd turned off the car. Her heart began to race at the thought of seeing Léopold again. She was angry with him for telling the wolf about her powers, but at the same time, there was no denying the heat and attraction she'd felt when he'd held her. She rubbed her arms, remembering his touch.

"No, this is my house. Over there, the carriage house is mine. And the main home belongs to our Alpha."

"Alpha? As in Alpha of Acadian Wolves?"

"Yeah, and like I just mentioned, a few of Léopold's friends are here."

Her eyes caught his. "Vampires?"

Dimitri smiled, trying to put her at ease. "Yep. No need to say more. And for the record, I feel the same way."

"But you're friends with Léopold?"

"Well, yeah, but that's, uh, different." *Different. Unusual. Odd.* Dimitri laughed to himself, realizing that he really was starting to consider him a friend. "We're tight. But I don't know his friends, so stay close. Got it?"

She nodded quietly. Instead of waiting for Dimitri to open the door, she pushed on the handle, but it slipped from her hands. She raised her eyes and her breath caught at the sight. *Léopold.* Before she could help herself, she'd placed her hand in his outstretched palm. God, he looked magnificent. If she hadn't known he was a centuries-old vampire, she would have sworn he was a high fashion cover model.

Her gaze fell from his captivating black eyes to the hard lines of his jaw, eventually landing on his soft lips. Spellbound, she wondered briefly what it would feel like to touch them with her fingers, kiss them. Her face grew hot and she knew she'd looked for a second too long. Her eyes darted to his, and a broad smile broke across his face. *He knew. Oh God, how could she let herself think for one second that fantasizing about a vampire was even close to a good idea?* Hell, it wasn't at all safe; she knew that as well as anyone.

But there was something about him that drew her to him. Like a comet hurling toward the sun, she let him pull her up out of the car, into his arms, and she quietly gasped as his lips brushed her cheek. She closed her eyes, pressing her hands to the fabric covering his chest. For a second she considered sliding her fingertips downward so she could feel the ridges of his abdomen. Enclosed within his wicked embrace, her world stopped, and she realized her life would never be the same.

Léopold knew he should've waited inside the house for Laryssa, but he'd felt her presence as soon as she'd arrived. It had nearly killed him to ask Dimitri to pick her up, but after his fiery reaction to her, he resisted the urge to see her. He'd met hundreds of beautiful women throughout the years, had sex with nearly as many, but he'd long protected his heart from love.

The insidious torment of his wife and children's deaths had nearly killed him. It had ripped through his body and soul, breaking him down to a skeleton of a man. Truth be told, he would have welcomed the loss of his own life. Their violent murders left him questioning not only God but his own humanity. Ironically, his oath to protect his king and God had caused her demise, and yet it was what drove him to keep living afterward, leading to the ultimate death of his mortal life.

As a knight for King Capet, he'd been sworn into service, earning his place in the nobility. During the snowy winter of 988AD, he'd taken up arms in a Parisian skirmish targeted at the weakened king. He'd known the monarch held little power outside the boundaries of his domain, yet he'd held faith that the new leader would unite France. Gallantly he'd fought, successfully defending the king's territory, only to find out that his own home had been a casualty of war.

Returning from the battlefield, he'd trod into his estate, discovering the aftermath of the attack. His family had been slain. Falling to his knees, he'd submitted to his grief, taking in the sight and smell of death. The blood-splattered floors. Their rotting bodies. The maggots and flies that had somehow managed, even in the cold heart of winter, to proliferate. Despite their decomposed states, he'd gathered his wife and children into his arms, screaming a cry of despair into the night.

The very next day, he'd rejoined his brotherhood in what was supposed to have been a celebration of their victory. Drinking himself into oblivion, he languished in his grief. The loss had stolen any sense of self-preservation. So when a fight had broken out at the inn, he readily threw himself into the brawl. Thirsting for death, he'd fought mercilessly and welcomed the final blow that struck him down. Dragged into the alleyway by a benevolent stranger, Léopold spent his last mortal moments lying on his back in the gritty rubble, crying aloud, the name of his wife and children on his lips. Quintus Tullius, a mercenary loyal to no king, had taken mercy on the young warrior that night, gifting him with immortality. Léopold, despite his wish to die, had been reborn. Vampire. Quintus had stayed until morn, only to inform Léopold that he'd been turned. For a sire he was not. While he'd saved Léopold from certain death, he had no desire to mentor another of his kind. Without regret, he'd left Léopold to fend on his own, never having contacted him again.

Over the centuries, Léopold had learned how to compartmentalize the pain, to shove it deep down, disassociating from the horrific nightmare. Most days, it was as if it hadn't happened…until now. Deliberately, he'd avoided relationships, keeping acquaintances and other immortals at a distance. Saving Wynter had been the impetus for his reversal in fate. Watching Logan and Wynter, their love and commitment splayed open, had driven a wedge into his icy demeanor. Perhaps he should have let her die, but in the heat of the moment, he'd breathed life into her. Like dominos, his actions had triggered the memories of his past, leading him to Wyoming, continuing to help Wynter by finding her blood that could have been used to hurt the wolves.

He'd also grown entirely too close to Dimitri in the past few days. *He cared.* And caring was something Léopold generally didn't do. Caring meant feelings. Feelings meant pain. Pain was something he delivered as punishment, not endured. The ancient warrior was far too battle hardened to go soft, yet that is what he feared had happened. Yet there was no undoing what he'd done, saving Wynter, befriending Dimitri. However small, the experiences had pierced his heart and mind, cleaving open a path to emotion. Now within just a week's time, he'd saved a pup and become infatuated with a woman he barely knew.

Looking down at Laryssa, he couldn't help but wonder if she'd felt the shiver of excitement that he'd tried to suppress. So wrong, but undeniable, he simply smiled at her. Shutting out the unsettling thoughts, he released her from his embrace.

"Laryssa."

"Léopold." Laryssa, shaking, looked down to her hands, which he firmly but gently held in his. Léopold's voice wrapped around her like a blanket, calming her racing thoughts. It was as if she could feel his power connecting with her own, filtering it so that she'd relax. She shook her head disbelieving the warmth that ran through her body. There was no way he could touch her energy, let alone control it. She lifted her eyes to meet his, searching for answers that didn't come.

"Ma chérie, don't fret. It'll be all right. You okay?" Léopold asked. Goddess, the woman charged him like no other. She hadn't been lying about her energy. His fangs itched to pierce her creamy flesh, tasting her essence as he fucked her mercilessly. It was wrong, he knew. He had to leave her alone. If he didn't, she'd only get under his skin further, driving him mad with emotions he swore he'd never feel again. As if he'd touched a hot pan, his hands fell from hers. The less he touched her the better, he thought.

"Um, yeah," Laryssa stammered, embarrassed that she'd held onto him like a child. She wrung her hands together, confused that she'd felt a tinge of rejection at the loss of his touch. He must have thought she was either insecure or pathetically weak.

"Come this way," he gestured toward the door. "I'm not sure if Dimitri told you but there're quite a few people waiting to meet you."

"But you said…you promised you wouldn't tell anyone," Laryssa sighed. She gazed into his eyes searching for the truth.

"I didn't tell anyone else," Léopold said with his hand on the sliding glass door.

"You told the wolf," she countered. *Did he think she was an idiot?*

"Ah well, he doesn't count. And the others? They only know that I'm bringing someone who's helping me find information about Ava. They don't know what you can do or what you are. But then again, you haven't told me what you are, have you?" he challenged.

"Point taken. But why doesn't Dimitri count?"

"He was at the club last night. He's seen the video. So he's in on your little secret. He just hasn't had a personal demonstration like the one you gave me." He smiled and raised an eyebrow at her, reminding her how she'd thrown the settee at him. *What a fiery little thing, she is.* "You're ready now, no?"

"No. Yes. No. Ugh, look what you do to me." She took a deep breath and then stilled as he leaned his head toward hers. *What was he doing? Was he going to kiss her?* She closed her eyes as she felt his warm breath on her ear.

"And what do I do to you, mon petit lapin?" Léopold resisted the temptation to go any closer and waited for her response.

"You…you…" He was too close to her, much too close. She couldn't think about anything but wanting to touch him, to sink her body into his.

"Oui?" Léopold smiled, thoroughly enjoying making her nervous, putting her on edge. But when he scented just a faint touch of her arousal, he regretted what he'd done. Slowly, he dragged himself away.

"You make me…I don't know…I'm flustered. Please, Léopold, let's just go in," she said, both relieved and disappointed that he hadn't kissed her.

Léopold turned to open the door and then stopped and faced her. He didn't owe the woman anything, but he was nothing if not forthright. "They're going to know."

"What?"

"They're going to know you're supernatural. I don't know what you did in the club to hide it, but you're projecting. If I can feel your energy, well, they'll know, too."

She sighed and bit her lip. Oh Lord, he was right. Being around Dimitri and Léopold had made her drop her defenses. It just felt so good not to hide it, to go around concentrating on keeping the hum of her aura to an unnoticeable, human level. Anger surged through her as she thought about being dragged into this situation and she quickly realized that she wasn't mad at Léopold. No, she was mad about being in danger, about being turned. The constant watching and concealing, she couldn't take it anymore.

"I don't care," she stated, looking directly into his dark eyes. She hated to admit the truth of it, but there was something about him she trusted. Moreover, she wanted to trust, to finally have an ally. *Why not go for broke?* "I'm not ready to tell you everything about me, so I'm sure as hell not going to tell whoever's behind that door. But I'm tired of hiding. And if you keep your word about my safety, then that's good enough for me. So let's do this thing, okay?"

"As the lady wishes." Léopold smiled at her bravery. Even though her heartbeat revealed her fear, she intrepidly stepped forward.

The delicious scent of Jambalaya floated in the air as they walked into the kitchen. Instead of being attacked by fangs and wolves, smiles greeted them. Dimitri came in behind Laryssa and put his hand on her shoulder. He guided her over to the stove, where a petite lady with frizzy blonde hair busily stirred a pot.

"Hey, gorgeous," Dimitri said, kissing the woman's cheek. "Laryssa, this is Wynter, my Alpha's mate. Where's the big guy?"

"Hey, yourself. Logan's touring the house with Kade. He'll be out in a few." Wynter dipped the spoon into the pan, lifted it and blew off the steam before tasting her creation. As she did so, she caught the look of surprise on Dimitri's face.

"What?" Wynter asked. She suspected that he was worried about Logan allowing vampires in his home. "It's all right. Sydney's with him."

"Okay," Dimitri reluctantly agreed. Dimitri had heard that Kade Issacson kept his vampires on a tight leash and his fiancée, Sydney Willows, was a hard-nosed police detective, who'd recently transferred to the Big Easy.

"They're double checking our security. You know...for the baby." Wynter wiped her hands on her apron and smiled at Laryssa. "Welcome to our den. Sorry it's a bit crazy in here, but we've got us an impromptu party going on. That little lady over there is the cause of the fuss. I know I should be upset with Léopold, but I just can't be. Ava's just so sweet. Like sugar."

Laryssa looked into the family room and saw a couple cooing over a baby. *Ava.* The handsome man wrapped his arm around the red-headed woman, and they both made faces at the little girl then looked lovingly at each other. She couldn't help but think that Dimitri and Léopold had overreacted in warning her about the vampires. They appeared happy and caring, a far cry from the bloodthirsty monsters she'd been expecting.

"She's adorable," Laryssa agreed, feeling drawn to the infant. Ava's tiny energy pulsed like a siren. Overwhelmed with emotion, knowing another one of her kind actually existed, she took a deep breath.

"Can I get you something to drink? Wine? Water? Sweet tea?" Wynter offered, jarring Laryssa from her thoughts.

"Tea would be great. Thanks." Laryssa, disoriented, dug her fingernails into her palms, trying to focus.

"Come," Léopold told her as he took her hand in his. He could tell she'd been as captivated by Ava as he'd been. He guided her over to the baby, intent on introducing her to everyone. "Laryssa, this is Luca Macquarie."

Laryssa nervously smiled. Luca nodded coldly and stood to greet her. She briefly shook his hand. His eyes were cold and dark, and she knew instantly that she'd been wrong about her initial impressions. Death lurked beneath this man's skin. His aura swirled in red and purples, dominance and compassion sliced through the colors.

"And this," Léopold approached the baby, but Luca moved to block him. Before he could protest, the woman stood with the baby and pushed in front of him.

"Hi, I'm Samantha. Please excuse my overprotective fiancé. He seems to think everyone is a danger, but he forgets that I can take care of myself." Samantha smiled up at Laryssa, holding the baby.

Luca's eyes softened and he put his arm around her. "Just taking care of you, darlin'. You can feel it, can't you?"

"But of course I can. She's very strong." Samantha smiled at her, knowingly. "Come sit. Léopold told us that you may be able to help us protect her."

Protect the baby? Laryssa tensed and glanced up at Léopold, who had perched himself above her, sitting comfortably on the arm of the sofa. His lips curled in approval, never taking his eyes off of her. Laryssa felt her heart begin to race. What was he thinking? He shouldn't have faith in her. She hadn't promised him a thing, only that she'd meet the child. Laryssa had barely succeeded in keeping herself hidden, safe. How the hell was she supposed to help them?

As if he'd read the impending dread stirring in her belly, he placed his hand on her shoulder. The tingle of his touch seared through the thin fabric of her sweater. A sense of calm settled over her, leaving her even more confused. What was he doing to her? She searched his eyes for understanding, but he merely looked away to Ava, who gurgled happily at her caregivers.

Laryssa wasn't sure how much to disclose to Samantha. She seemed nice enough, but she suspected that she also wielded powers. Although Laryssa didn't have great knowledge about supernaturals, she'd never heard of a vampire bearing children. Even if she could trust her, Laryssa wasn't used to others discussing her energy. Anyone who'd known about her abilities had shunned her, afraid of what she could do. The strangers had no reason to trust her. She considered her options and decided to partially disclose why she was there.

"I don't know if I can help." She looked again to Léopold for reassurance, and he simply gave her shoulder a squeeze. It would have to be enough. "I felt her…I could feel her being born. And now…"

The baby squealed, and grabbed a pacifier from Samantha's hands.

"That's right, sweetie. See? She feels you, too."

"May I suggest that we get to the bottom line? What are you, Laryssa? And why would anyone want to harm this baby?" Luca asked. He and Léopold had never seen eye to eye, and he grew annoyed that Léopold had involved vampires in wolf business by bringing Ava to New Orleans, putting them all in danger.

Like an insect pinned to a mounting board, Laryssa struggled silently, her thoughts flailing in distress. Revealing herself was not part of her bargain with Léopold. She reached inside herself for the diplomatic words that would both cease this line of questioning and appease the vampire's curiosity.

"Léopold asked me to come here to meet the child, to see if we connected. Do I know who tried to kill her? No. I have no direct knowledge of who did this. In fact, I literally just met Léopold last night." It was the truth. Sure, she had her suspicions. But that was all she had. There was no hard evidence of anything.

"Why is she here, Devereoux?" Luca demanded. He remained seated but his brow furrowed; he looked like a caged animal ready to attack.

"She's here because I asked..." Léopold began, but was interrupted by Laryssa.

"I'm here because unlike you, I can feel her. And when I say feel, I mean she's putting out energy."

"So what? All humans do that. Or wolves in this case," Luca countered.

Léopold watched intently, altogether peeved at the insolent vampire who challenged him, but his anger was tempered by the way his little rabbit had turned into a tigress, not just defending herself but him as well.

"It's not just some kind of heartbeat or pulse or anything like that. It's pure, clean energy. The kind that electrifies the night sky and can move objects. I don't know you very well, so I don't plan on sharing my life story with you, but suffice to say, there's a chance Ava's like me."

"What exactly are you?"

"Don't you mind what I am. You aren't here to protect me. You're here because of Ava. I'll do what I can to help but make no mistake, the only reason I'm helping is because Léopold asked me and I'm doing it for Ava."

Laryssa realized she'd raised her voice at Luca. Silence cut through the room like a knife and her face heated as she became aware that everyone was staring at her. She caught Dimitri's eyes and he began laughing. *What the hell was so funny?* She took note that Léopold wasn't laughing, but he was smiling.

"Luca, dear. Leave poor Laryssa alone," Samantha said sweetly but firmly. Still cradling the baby with one arm, she cupped his cheek. "You'll catch more flies with honey. Be nice. We just met Léopold's friend, and you're giving her the third degree. I can tell she isn't a danger. And she's right about the little one. Y'all may not be able to feel it. But I can. She's very special. Little Ava here, is humming her own tune."

Luca opened his mouth, about to disagree, when Logan walked into the room with Kade and Sydney. As much as he wanted to argue the point further, he didn't want to upset his lovely pregnant wife-to-be.

"Hey, you're missing all the fireworks." Dimitri jumped up and clapped a hand on Logan's shoulder.

"Yeah, I heard some yelling going on." Logan's eyes shot to Léopold. "Why am I not surprised?"

Léopold laughed. While it was true that Logan was paying a debt by watching Ava, he could tell that it hadn't been that much of a hardship. When he'd first arrived, both Logan and Wynter had been fawning over the baby, looking like a picture perfect family. The Alpha and his mate would be wonderful parents, but they all knew the danger the child represented.

"Come, mon ami. Let's discuss our plans for keeping our petit bébé safe," Léopold suggested. "Sydney. Meet Laryssa. She has…how should I say? Similar abilities to Ava."

Laryssa noticed the blonde detective right away and knew she'd been identified.

"Laryssa? Laryssa Theriot?" Sydney approached her and held out her hand.

Laryssa stood and greeted her. "Hello, detective."

Léopold raised his eyebrows, surprised that they knew each other. *How did Sydney know Laryssa? Had she been in trouble with the law?*

"Laryssa here, volunteers on diving assignments. One of the best I'm told," Sydney explained. "We met on a case. Unfortunately, the search and rescue didn't turn out so well."

"The calls on the river are never good news." Laryssa shook off the compliment, fully aware of why they thought she was a good diver. After hours of searching, they'd called off a rescue but she'd stayed on in the murky water, finally finding the missing kid. She shuddered, remembering how the teen had lain listlessly at the bottom, the body stuck under debris.

"A woman of many skills, I see," Léopold noted, giving Laryssa a look that told her he intended to find out more about her.

"Well, we really appreciate your help." Sydney sat down into a chair, and a man came up behind her, putting his hands on her shoulders. "Sorry, I forgot to introduce you to my fiancé. This is Kade. He heads up the vamps down here. They're a wily bunch. I could hear Luca all the way upstairs. A real troublemaker."

Laryssa almost laughed at the casual way the detective talked about the vampires. Luca cracked a small smile at the comment, revealing to her that they all knew each other well.

"I'm Logan," the Alpha said, grabbing his mate for a kiss.

"Hi," Laryssa managed. This was the Alpha of the Acadian wolves? He looked more like a love strewn puppy than a ferocious leader of the pack.

"Les tourtereaux," Léopold shook his head. "Come, sit. Time for business."

Laryssa gave him a puzzled look, not understanding his French.

"Lovebirds," he translated. "It appears the mates can't keep their hands off each other."

She smiled in understanding, but a twitch of yearning for that kind of relationship flitted through her heart. Between the Alpha and his mate and the other couples, she could see the love in their eyes, causing a twinge of jealousy. The odds of finding a man who'd accept her were exceedingly low. Even her family had tossed her out on her ear.

A hand on her shoulder reminded her why she was there, and she gazed up into Léopold's eyes. As if he knew what she was thinking, he brushed the back of his fingers down her cheek and gave a small smile. The gesture caused her to blush, and as much as she wanted to look away from him, she was mesmerized by his eyes.

Léopold was aware that he couldn't keep his hands off of Laryssa. In a day, the subject of his search had gone from a suspect to the object of his desire. If it had been any other woman, he'd already have fucked her, leaving before the bed grew cool. But his little rabbit affected him in a way that was entirely too intense. Not only could he feel the power pouring out of her skin, he was certain he'd been able to reciprocate, calming her when she'd grown anxious. The crease in her brow had smoothed as soon as he'd touched her. Goddess, he'd have to have her soon. Pretending he could deny himself was becoming increasingly difficult as the minutes passed. He hoped like hell that if he assuaged the need, the passing fancy would cease like the wind. For now, he needed to concentrate on why he'd brought her here, why he'd gathered his trusted men along with Logan's. Protecting Ava was paramount.

"Logan and I would like to discuss how we're going to keep the baby safe," he began. "They tried to kill her once."

"And we can't risk another try on her life," Logan added.

"Which is why we're going to take shifts watching over her. It's best we keep her in one location, here with Logan and Wynter. Ava's wolf. She needs to be with pack," Léopold asserted.

"Laryssa can't stay here, though," Samantha commented. "Whatever's after the baby is probably after her too."

"I'll take care of Laryssa. But I need everyone here to work with Logan on the schedule, at least for a few days until we find and eliminate the threat," Léopold told them.

"Everyone except Samantha," Luca said.

"Oui." Léopold nodded.

"Hey, just because I'm preggo doesn't mean I can't help out with the baby. It'll be good practice," Samantha protested.

"No way, darlin'. Too dangerous." Luca placed his hand over her belly.

"But, I..."

"For once, Luca and I are in agreement. Even though I've seen your magic do some damage, we don't want to risk another baby's life." There was no way Léopold would let Samantha stay with the Alpha. He ignored the rolling of Samantha's eyes but was glad she didn't argue. With both Luca and Léopold against the idea, she didn't stand a chance of winning. "What you can do is talk to Ilsbeth. Find out what kind of wards you can set on this place so that she's better hidden."

"Avery's set wards at my place," Laryssa added. "But I'm not sure they're working right. That's why I met her last night, to see what else I could do. She said she'd have to talk to Ilsbeth."

"It's important that we keep Ava under wraps. That means the fewer people who know she's here, the better," Léopold said. "Kade's bringing in two of his people to keep guard."

"Dominique and Xavier," Kade confirmed.

"You sure about Xavier? He was pretty tight with Étienne," Logan asked. Although it had been a few weeks, Logan couldn't shake the memory of the vampire who'd nearly killed Wynter.

"He's a man of honor. You have my word that he'd never hurt Ava," Kade assured them.

"Jake and Zeke also know. They can be trusted." Logan also had seen his fair share of traitors within his pack. Fiona had been a trusted she-wolf who'd plotted against him and tried to kill his mate.

"But no one else can find out the child is here, got it? You're going to need some kind of excuse to keep the pack away," Léopold suggested.

"Wynter and I can come up with something. To be honest, I've been trying to keep the house just for us anyway. They all know we just mated…been kind of busy, ya know. Really busy up until our little visitor arrived." Logan smiled at Wynter, enjoying the blush that painted her cheeks. "Besides, if the pack wants to get together socially, they've got plenty of places to go besides my house. And meetings are held at the pack house. I think we'll be good."

"What about the girl?" Luca asked pointedly, annoyed that Laryssa still hadn't been candid about her abilities. "We've established that she feels energy or she *thinks* she feels it. She's got some kind of special skills. But we haven't seen a damn thing."

"By girl, I assume you're talking about Laryssa? I'm pretty sure she's a woman. All woman from where I'm sittin'. How 'bout showin' a little respect, fang boy?" Dimitri growled. Vampire or not, he was ready to deck him if he said one more derogatory thing about Laryssa.

Luca, duly chastised, stared at Léopold, waiting for an answer.

"Macquarie, I recall a time not too long ago when I saved your ass. So I suggest you take heed of the wolf and watch your words carefully. Laryssa will be staying with me." Léopold suppressed the grin that lingered behind his impassive tone. The shocked expression that Laryssa wore had not gone unnoticed. *Well, I can't tell her everything.* After all, she was keeping secrets as well. And he planned to find out every last one. The only way he could do that was to spend time with her. "We'll go see Ilsbeth. Her spells are nice, but the witch is often more valuable for her information. I suspect she'll have knowledge about why someone would try to kill Ava and possibly even who that person is. Laryssa can explain best what she is, and she will be fully disclosing that information to me soon." *Whether she likes it or not*, he thought to himself.

"So now that that's settled, anyone have anything else they want to lay on the table? I admit we don't have much to go on here, but we've got to find whoever is behind trying to kill the child." Léopold instinctively reached for Laryssa's hand. He wasn't just worried about Ava. No, he had to keep them both safe.

"I'll take first watch. I'm off duty tonight and I want to go over the exits and entrances one more time. We've gotta make sure this place is sealed up tight," Sydney advised. "I can call in extra support from the station."

"I don't think we should go there yet. We don't know if the threat is human or not. No offense, detective, but we can't trust others. This is pack business now. We take care of our own," Logan told her.

"You sure, Alpha?" Kade's eyebrows drew tight.

"Let's just see where Léopold gets with Ilsbeth first. If she thinks we need to do something else to keep Ava safe, we'll do it. The last thing I need is cops crawlin' around here. If anything, we'd call in P-CAP, and I'm not crazy about that idea either." P-CAP, the Paranormal City Alternative Police, was a supernatural-run sector, but Logan didn't trust them, given it was comprised mostly of vampires. He knew that Kade had been involved with them, but if they were in on what was happening with the child, there'd be no way to keep the information about her contained, secret from the rest of the pack.

"We'll hold off on P-CAP for now, but if things heat up, we're going to need backup and Syd can't do this on her own," Kade concluded.

"I hear ya, but if you want this kept under the radar, we've gotta keep this between us. As it stands now, pack is gonna wonder why my place is vamp central. They all know Léopold saved Wynter, so they're okay with him being here. The rest of you...well, I'm afraid that'll take some explaining."

"As long as Sydney's wearin' a badge, she can always make up some excuse about being here. It's not like we don't have crime on the streets," Dimitri noted. "A human officer is welcome. The second you start bringin' in more supes, badge or not, the wolves are gonna know something's not right."

Ava started to cry and Samantha stood, rocking her back and forth.

"Sounds like someone's hungry," Wynter said. "Let me get her bottle."

"Sydney stays tonight with the Alpha and his mate. Any other comments? Suggestions?" Léopold was met with deafening silence. They all knew it wasn't the best plan but they didn't know the danger that was coming for them. Léopold stood and crossed the room, extending his arms to Samantha. "May I?"

"Of course." The witch kissed the fussy infant's forehead and gently placed the baby into Léopold's waiting arms.

Léopold knew they were all watching him, astounded that someone who they perceived to be the hand of death had the capability to show mercy and compassion toward a child. He ignored their stares and focused on Ava. None of them would be able to fathom the excruciating, churning memories that flared within him. The warmth of Ava's tiny body spread through his hands, spearing grief through his dark heart, cleaving it open where he'd sealed his painful past. When he looked into her blue eyes, a spark of healing gave way to hope. *Could I ever have what was stolen from me all those years ago?* He closed his eyes for a second, imagining that his ability to love could be resuscitated, renewed.

As he lifted his lids, he caught Laryssa's insightful gaze. Was it possible that she'd felt his pain? That perhaps he couldn't hide the darkness of his past any longer? Goddess, no. He couldn't afford to acknowledge the sliver of faith he clutched to like a thread at the end of the rope. Awkwardly, he blinked and turned away, trying to avoid the erupting feelings that clutched at his chest. An expert at cloaking his emotions, Léopold smiled at Ava. None of them would find out what lay deep in the recesses of his mind. Like an actor, he'd pull off the grand façade and protect Ava. Then as soon as it was all over, he'd leave for another city, resuming his empty but immortal life.

❧ *Chapter Five* ❧

As Léopold rocked the baby, Wynter and Laryssa stood in the doorway, observing from a distance. They'd set up a crib inside their master bedroom so they could watch over the infant at night. Wynter quietly closed the door to the bedroom so that she could talk to the stranger who'd come to their home.

"Can I talk to you a minute? Um, this is kind of hard to ask, but what's going on with you and Léopold? I mean I thought he just met you. It just seems like there is something there…something more," Wynter stammered, unable to find the words she needed to articulate her concerns. She had no sire relationship to Léopold, but the man had saved her life; his blood ran through her veins. Like her connection to her mate and the pack, it was as if she could sense how Léopold was feeling, which at the moment felt like torment.

"Well, yes. We met last night but it was just…you see, I fell off a stool. I was waiting for a friend and he was there when it happened. And he kind of caught me…both times. I actually fell twice. It was kind of embarrassing." She rubbed her hand over her eyes, wishing she could crawl into a hole. "You're friends, right?"

Wynter laughed. "Yeah, I guess we are friends. You know Laryssa, as much as I only have eyes for my Alpha, I won't deny that Léopold is a really good looking guy. But he's also dangerous. Very, very dangerous," she whispered. "Listen, I'm not going to tell you what to do, but just be careful. I saw the way you were looking at him and…"

"I wasn't looking at him like anything. It's just that he's the only one I know…really, that's all it is," Laryssa lied.

"He saved my life."

"Sorry?"

"Léopold. He saved my life. I was dying…died. He gave me his blood."

"You're a vampire?"

"No. I'm a wolf. But I do have a few side effects from what he did."

"But he saved you? That doesn't sound so dangerous to me."

"Yes, but…" Wynter didn't want to discourage her as much as warn her. "Just be careful, okay? Léopold is not to be messed with. He's one of the most powerful vampires around."

"In New Orleans?"

"Ever, from what Logan tells me. Look, I know he's very smooth and cultured, but he's lethal. Just don't forget it, all right?"

"Okay." It didn't take much for Laryssa to believe that Léopold was dangerous. Even Avery had said as much. But after her interaction with him today at the shop, not only was she desperately attracted to him, she was certain he wouldn't hurt her. Her ability to throw a large piece of furniture at him hadn't undermined her confidence that she'd be able to hold her own if she was wrong.

"Sorry, I know it's none of my business, but I just felt like I had to say something." Wynter had seen, too, how Léopold had been looking at Laryssa. "I'm sure he'll be fine with you. I mean, just look at how he is with Ava. It's unbelievable really. I've never seen him that way with anyone…so gentle. I guess maybe I didn't know him that well, but I never thought I would have seen Léopold Devereoux taking care of a baby." She shook her head in disbelief and cracked open the door.

"He seems so at ease, doesn't he?" Laryssa commented, knowing Léopold probably heard every word they'd spoken.

"Yes, he does. God help me, it really makes me want to have pups," Wynter confided. "I have to go check on things downstairs. Will you be okay here?"

"Thanks, yeah, I'll be fine," Laryssa assured her.

Quietly, Laryssa pushed open the door, and caught sight of Léopold, who was softly singing a French lullaby to the child. She contemplated what he'd told the others…how she'd stay with him. Was he crazy? If she stayed with him…no, no she could not even go there. In the little time she'd spent with him, she'd already told him so much, too much. Like a geyser, the secrets she'd kept buried for so long had begun to spew forth. She wanted to trust him, to tell him everything. But she couldn't. Going to his home was simply not going to happen, yet the words of protest failed to emerge from her lips. She told herself the reason she didn't argue the point was because she hadn't wanted to stir up more trouble with that nasty vampire. But her gut told her it was because she didn't want to say no. She wanted to say yes. Yes, to everything that was Léopold.

Slowly, Laryssa approached Léopold, as he rocked in the chair, the infant finally asleep against his shoulder. Kneeling before him, she rested her hands on his thighs.

"Elle est belle. She's beautiful, no?" Léopold commented. Speaking softly to the infant, he continued. "Mon petit bébé, we shall keep you safe and sound."

"She's so sweet. It's hard to believe someone would try to kill a baby. Sick. Really sick."

"Einstein said, 'the world is a dangerous place to live; not because of the people who are evil, but because of the people who don't do anything about it.' So much evil exists. It's a wonder people even get up in the morning."

"We're going to stop this…whatever, whoever did this."

"That we will, Laryssa." Léopold pressed up out of his seat and gently placed Ava on her back in the crib. Pulling up the blanket, he felt Laryssa's hand on his shoulder. "I've lived hundreds of years. Like immortals, evil never dies. It's almost as if we know this when we're born. Even the newborn babes cry as they're birthed into our world."

"I don't know, Leo. I do believe that there's something bigger than all of us." Unconsciously, if not out of comfort, Laryssa noticed she'd touched Léopold.

"The Goddess? Oui. But hell, I believe, also exists, spawning the evil in both men and supernaturals. It won't have her."

"Evil? Babies aren't born evil."

"That's not what I mean. I mean that whatever is after her is evil, and it can't have her. I swore it tried to kill her that night in Yellowstone. With all I've seen, it makes no sense. There's something bothering me about this…the creatures you've described."

"No eyes."

"If they are real…"

"They are."

"If they're real, I've never seen anything like them. But then again, I've never met anyone like you." He smiled and captured a lock of her hair in his fingers.

Laryssa took a deep breath, slowing the pace of her heartbeat. She was certain he'd heard her talking to Wynter. She sighed in embarrassment. He was so out of her league.

"You are really good with her." She changed the subject, turning her gaze to Ava. "Have you always been good with babies?"

"We've got to go. It's getting late and you need to rest before we see Ilsbeth in the morning. You should get something to eat downstairs," Léopold suggested. Hastily, he strode across the room, away from both Laryssa and the crib and put his hand on the door handle. He didn't want to discuss his feelings about children with anyone. Foolishly, he'd let his guard down around Laryssa.

"What?" she asked, startled by his change in tone. *Is he angry with me?*

"I said we need to go," he responded coldly. Like a vault, he'd successfully closed his heart and mind shut from Laryssa.

Wynter opened the door, surprising them both. "How's she doing?"

"Ah, Wynter. Thank goodness you're here. We can't leave Ava unattended, not even for a minute. Laryssa and I are going to get going. We need to stop at her home to get her things." Léopold was grateful for the interruption.

"I see you got Ava down. I think I'm gonna take a nap while she's sleeping. I'll tell you, you sure seem to have the magic touch with babies, Léopold. Who would've thought? Big bad vampire is a softy," Wynter sang in a baby voice while tucking in the sides of the blanket, making sure Ava was comfortable, and didn't catch the look of disdain that washed over Léopold's face. "Well make sure you get some of the jambalaya I made.

There're bowls out on the countertop. Or you can take some with you to go."

"I'm really not hungry…." Laryssa started to say, upset with Léopold's apparent shift in mood.

"I'll make sure she eats something," Léopold replied and gestured for Laryssa to leave the room. "Come, pet."

"Not a dog," Laryssa snapped, walking past him toward the steps.

"Excuse me?" he asked.

"You heard me."

"I never said you were an animal." He knew full well why she was angry with him. It was better this way. As much as he wanted her, he could never give her what she needed.

"Yeah, right. Next time, I suppose you'll blow a whistle. Better go find a breeder if you're lookin' for a pet."

Léopold snorted in response, but didn't let her see the small smile that he couldn't keep from curling upward. She was a little spitfire, one he knew was going to give him a few burns before the week was done. Damn, he wished he could keep her in his life, but it'd never work. It was better to keep her angry than aroused. Once this was all over, he could leave her with little fallout.

They'd ridden in virtual silence from Laryssa's apartment. She continued to bite her tongue as they pulled into the gated driveway of his enormous lakeside mansion. Struggling with her feelings, Laryssa found it difficult to understand how she'd let the charismatic vampire take over her life within the past twenty-four hours. When she looked into his piercing dark eyes, it was as if he'd reached into her chest and stolen every ounce of self-control she'd ever had. He made her want to do things, very naughty things…to him, with him. She'd never responded so viscerally to any man, let alone a supernatural. Instead of remaining cool and collected, controlling her energy and her body's reactions to him, she'd lost her concentration. She'd let him arouse her, and then anger her, freeing her power, exposing her abilities for the first time.

The way he commanded the others within the Alpha's home left her in awe. They'd both feared and respected him. But it was how he revealed his gentility with Ava that stole her heart. She wasn't stupid. She suspected that he'd killed over the centuries. An immortal didn't live as long as he had without doing so. Yet he fed and rocked the baby as naturally if he was her father. The simple act divulged more about Léopold than anything else he'd said or done. Beneath his hardened exterior, goodness resided. The anger he'd expressed when she'd asked him about having children was preceded by a brief flicker of grief in his eyes. He may not have intentionally shown it, but the fact he couldn't look at her told her that he was hiding something, something that was so painful that he'd reacted like a hurt animal. What Léopold didn't know about her was that she wouldn't accept his refusal. Perhaps she wasn't thinking with her head, but she was determined to get to know her beautiful vampire.

Like it or not, Léopold Devereoux would learn to open up to her, to trust her. There was no other way she could justify revealing her true nature to another soul. She needed to know that Léopold was worthy of her secret, not just seeking to protect Ava. If he was simply after her powers, she'd still help him, but she couldn't risk becoming intimate with him. It would be nearly impossible to resist his charms, she knew, but she sought more than just a roll in the hay. If she gave him her body, she'd have a difficult time protecting her heart.

Laryssa's thoughts were interrupted when Léopold opened the car door for her. *A perfect gentleman,* she thought. So many years on this Earth had certainly taught him about the finer things in life. She ran her fingers over the soft leather seat one more time before exiting. As she reached for her overnight bag behind the seat, Léopold's hands brushed over hers.

"Allow me," Léopold told her, easily lifting it.

"I can carry my bag," she protested.

"Well of course you can, but I insist. You're my guest. This way." Without arguing further, he walked up to the front door and flipped open a biometric security pad. "I usually park in the garage, but since you're here with me…"

He didn't finish his sentence as he twisted the doorknob, gesturing for her to go ahead of him. "I don't have many people over, but you'll be comfortable."

"It's lovely," Laryssa responded, trying to act nonchalant as she entered his home.

It wasn't as if she hadn't toured a Garden District mansion, but Léopold's home was spectacular. A large foyer with a circular staircase led directly into a great room. Spacious and contemporary, cathedral ceilings gave way to a wall of floor to ceiling windows. The kitchen, with its white cabinets and white marbled countertops, separated the area with a large breakfast bar. Modern cream-colored leather sofas offset the dark cherry floors. A two-story white stone fireplace climbed the far wall.

Laryssa couldn't help but think how ironic it was that Léopold's home was so airy and open yet he himself was quite the opposite, mysterious and enigmatic. She wondered if this was how he saw himself or perhaps it was how he wanted to be. Reflecting on his caring behavior with the child, she knew there was more to him than his role as protector and leader. As she entered the great room, she supposed that although the décor was understated, it presented a flair for the dramatic. As she took in the room, she noticed, however, that it also appeared impersonal. Unlike her tiny apartment which was decorated with pictures she'd taken on vacation and places she loved, aside from a few pieces of art, there was nothing to indicate who lived here or what they did. His home was like a floor model, modern and inviting, but still not quite finished.

As she approached the windows, she couldn't help but press her hands against the glass. *Water.* Its call was undeniable. Before she had a chance to ask about the lake, lights flickered outside, revealing a large rectangular Olympic-sized swimming pool with a semicircular wading pool with fountain. Multicolored lights sparkled within the azure water, appearing to dance in the night. Magnificent as it was, it was the prize lying beyond the pool, waiting for her, that captured her attention.

As she tried to contain her excitement, exhaustion washed over her. She felt drained, in need of its healing. If she didn't tell Léopold soon, she'd have to sneak out into the night air to find the restorative liquid. Like air, she needed the lake's water to survive.

"You like to swim? You're welcome to use the pool while you're here," Léopold commented, watching her out of the corner of his eye.

"Swim?"

"The pool. You're a diver. One can only assume you like the water if you dive on a regular basis," Léopold said, taking the takeout container he'd brought from Logan's. He walked into the kitchen, setting it into the microwave. Léopold worked in the kitchen, all the while aware of her every move.

Laryssa's reticence hadn't surprised him during the drive. He'd driven her to it after she'd asked about him having children. His response had been meant to silence her, and now that he'd done what he'd set out to do, he found he missed the sound of her voice. He'd turned on the outside lighting, thinking she'd caught a glimpse of the pool area. But she seemed preoccupied with something else altogether. *This woman, this creature, what was she?*

She was clearly lost in her thoughts; he observed how she was bent toward the window, her hands spread against it. Her pert bottom peeked at him through the pair of skin-tight jeans she'd changed into at her apartment. Léopold shifted his legs as his dick hardened at the sight of her well-rounded ass. He inwardly groaned, picturing himself peeling them off then driving into her from behind while her firm breasts pressed onto the cold glass.

Merde, I shouldn't have brought her here. Léopold shook his head in disgust with his lack of discipline. True, he needed to get laid, but not with her. His instincts told him that there was something about Laryssa that would shake his carefully constructed world, and that simply could not happen. He wouldn't let himself fall any deeper into her spell. Pulling out his cell phone, he tapped out a text to Arnaud. Food and a fuck would solve his problem. If he didn't sate his hunger, it wouldn't be long before he had Laryssa stripped bare, with his cock buried deep inside her.

The microwave beeped, thankfully distracting him from the tempting

thought. He reached in and pulled out the bowl, setting it on the counter.
"Sit."

Laryssa turned her head toward him and glared.

"Sit please," he replied with a sarcastic tone. "Come pet, you need to eat. See? It's Wynter's jambalaya. Smells delicious."

"Are you always this bossy?" Laryssa asked, irritated that he continued to give her orders. She considered telling him to go to hell but her stomach rumbled, reminding her that she truly was hungry "Can't you just say, 'your dinner is ready?' No, I get, 'sit.' Listen, Leo, if you plan on keeping me here, I'll repeat it once more…contrary to your belief that I'm some kind of a dog or servant, I'm neither."

"I can see quite clearly that you aren't. As for being 'bossy' as you put it, I am the boss, no? It is what it is. You cannot change the moon or the stars, nor can you change the man." Léopold sighed. *Oui, maybe I am an arrogant prick. Little rabbit better get used to it, though, because I'm not changing for a woman, especially one who won't be in my life very long.*

"Why am I not surprised that you'd compare yourself to the universe?" she huffed and sat down at the breakfast bar. She looked down and saw that not only had he heated her food, he'd given her a neatly folded cloth napkin, utensils and bottle of water. She closed her eyes and tried to quell the pang of guilt for calling him bossy. Despite his cavalier attitude, he was trying. "Thank you. It smells great."

"Would you like wine?" Léopold selected one of his favorite reds from a wrought iron rack on the wall.

"No thank you," she answered, picking up her spoon.

"Oui, I do think you need some wine. This is a lovely Pinot Noir I picked up in New Zealand a few months ago." Léopold proceeded to retrieve a couple of glasses from the cabinet and opened the bottle. After pouring a generous portion, he slid the glass in front of her and smiled.

Laryssa watched as he completely ignored her answer. *Did he not just hear me say 'no'? But of course he did.* Despite his actions, there was no denying how incredibly sexy she found his confidence. Acquiescing to his suggestion, she shook her head and picked the glass up, taking a sip. As the dark fruity flavors coated her tongue, she closed her eyes, enjoying its excellent pairing with her meal. It had been a God awful day, and she relaxed as the delicious nectar began to take the edge off. Her eyes snapped open and she silently swore. *Damn him. Did he have to be right about everything?* The soft rumble of his laughter filled the room and she knew she'd been caught.

"Good, no?"

"Okay, yes, the wine is wonderful. And even though I said no, and you ignored me, you were right about it. What about you? Aren't you eating?" Laryssa could've smacked herself right after she asked such a fatuous question. *Food for vampires? As in blood.* It wasn't as if she was volunteering, but as she watched his mouth break into a broad smile, she couldn't refute that she desired his lips on her skin.

"Brave one, mon petit lapin." He held his glass up to the light and swirled it. "I do love the finer culinary delights of humanity but I'm afraid only sang will keep me alive. The wine is delectable, but it doesn't suffice."

"And the food…real food?"

"Real food?" Léopold laughed and placed his drink on the counter before catching Laryssa's eyes. "It's all a matter of perspective. Blood…warm blood from a living human is what I require…crave."

"You don't scare me," Laryssa said, willing her hands not to shake.

"It's not my intention. You asked. I'm answering. A simple conversation. Besides," he returned to his wine. "I don't kill to eat. I do, however, prefer live donors. I can afford it, so why not?"

"As in people?"

"It's who I am. There's no denying my nature." Léopold circled around the bar until he was behind Laryssa. He set his glass next to hers and slid his fingers down through her hair.

"But why not just get bagged blood or whatever that stuff is they have at Mordez?" Laryssa asked but didn't really care. The second he touched her, she lost her concentration, falling back into his hands, but stopped short of purring like a kitten.

"Why should I when I can have what I really want? When I want. How I want it," he whispered into her ear. His hands fell to her shoulders. "If you could have what you want, wouldn't you take it? Relish the experience. Just be who you are. No living in fear or shame."

Laryssa could feel her muscles melt as he massaged her neck. *Oh dear God, I'm never going to be able to deny him. What was he saying? Did he ask what I wanted? That's an easy answer; I want him.* Ah, but it was that small detail about telling him who she was that was going to be a bit of an issue.

"I don't know what that's like," she managed to say. Losing herself in his touch, she moaned. "I want to be free, but I can't."

"Tell me what you are, ma chérie. Free yourself."

"Quid pro quo. Tell me why you got upset with me. I asked if you'd always been good with children and you shut me down."

Léopold released her and walked across the room, gazing out the windows. Laryssa jumped up from her seat, following him.

"Oh no you don't. Not again," she scolded. "You expect me to tell you everything about me, but I ask a simple question, and you get angry. Well, I've got news for you. I'm not laying it all on the line unless you do the same. You want me to trust you with something that is really important to me, but you won't even tell me why you're so good with a baby that I'd think you actually had one."

Léopold had a family? A child? Laryssa knew instantly the minute she'd pressed the issue, and he'd gone as stiff as a board. *But why hide it? Were they missing? No, they were dead.*

Léopold said nothing as her words fell through the air, tearing open old wounds. The woman made him crazy. He should have just left her in that damn antique shop. She hadn't given him any reason to think she could really help him protect Ava. He'd never needed anyone, yet he was acting like he needed her. He contemplated grabbing his car keys and driving her right back to the French Quarter where she belonged. He was about to walk over to the door when he felt her hands on his back.

"I'm sorry," she whispered.

"There's nothing to be sorry for."

"Really, I'm sorry. If you'd just told me…"

"Like you've told me what you are and how you got that way?" he snapped, turning to face her.

"That's different. You don't understand. I don't tell anyone. There's been no one. Don't you get how badly I want to trust you? You don't even know, do you?" Laryssa countered. She looked to the floor, wringing her hands. "I can't just tell you what you want to know. I want to tell you but we need to have trust. Bossing me around isn't trust, Leo. I need more."

"More? I've brought you to my home. There are things about me you don't know, Laryssa. I've lived a long time."

"Yes, but when two people are building a friendship, a relationship…" Laryssa cringed at the use of the 'r' word but whether it was romantic or not, it was what she required in order to tell him the truth.

"Relationship?" Léopold threw his head back and wiped his eyes. "I cannot deny that I'm attracted to you, but a relationship? No, I don't do relationships. I'm not who you need. And my past is dead and buried…where it needs to stay."

"I'm sorry for upsetting you, but yeah, I do need to have a relationship with you if I'm going to just tell you everything about me. I get that you have a past, but I have one too, and unlike you, I'm not some ancient badass. I'm just trying to survive. And I'm all alone. I can't do this. If you can't trust me…I don't know." The effects of the wine weren't nearly enough to calm her; moisture filled her eyes.

Léopold saw her tears threatening to spill, and while he'd generally ignore if not enjoy the sight of fear and pain in another being, it felt as if he was absorbing her torment. *Why does she need me to show her my trust?* He didn't want to do it. It was a bad idea, but she looked so defeated and he really didn't want her to go.

"I was a father." Saying the words out loud for the first time in centuries was surreal. He hadn't said them since he'd been turned.

"Leo," Laryssa's voice cracked. He'd trusted her. She closed the distance between them, wrapping her arms around his waist.

"Rosamund. She was four. Maiuel, he was only a bébé…" It felt so foreign to say their names yet it was as if it was only yesterday that he'd held them in his arms. He could hear his daughter's voice calling for him, *'père'.*

"It was so very long ago…" Léopold closed his eyes, his face tensed. *Why was he talking about this?*

"It's all right. I'm so sorry," Laryssa cupped his face in her hands. "I shouldn't have pressed it. I just wanted to know you…"

When his eyes flashed open, the look of grief quickly turned into one of passion. With the exception of Dimitri, there'd been no one he'd shared anything personal with, let alone the death of his children. Laryssa had not only stirred his desire, but had renewed his memories and connections to the human world. It was as if her brief presence in his life had begun to strengthen the delicate fibers that remained of his compassion. He couldn't bring himself to take her blood, but with her in his arms, he could no longer resist her body.

As his mouth captured hers, Léopold knew it was wrong. He didn't deserve her, but couldn't stop as he tasted the sweet innocence on her lips. Self-restraint slid away as he immersed himself in her, his lips deepening their luscious kiss. Reaching into her mane and taking command, he wrapped his fingers around her locks, and held her in place. He needed to have her, be in her. He'd regret it, but as she responded to him, giving herself to him, he couldn't stop. With a gasp, he pulled his lips from hers and began to trail kisses down the delicate skin of her throat. Hungry for more, his other hand slid up her belly, pushing up her shirt until he'd found the swell of her breast. She moaned at his touch, encouraging him. More, they both needed more and fast. Léopold pulled down the lacy fabric of her bra until her swollen nipple released into his fingers.

"Leo, please," she begged.

"I want you," he breathed against her neck. Léopold leaned into her, his rock hard erection jutting into her. "Do you feel that?"

"Yes," she responded breathlessly.

Léopold grasped her chin with his hand, until her hooded eyes met his. "This," his fangs snapped downward and he bent his knees, pressing up into her with his cock, "is what you do to me. You make me lose control."

"You don't scare me," she responded and licked the crook of his neck.

Is there nothing I can do to deter her? Goddess almighty, this woman would be his downfall. He knew it as sure as he was standing there next to her. Léopold gave in and kissed her passionately, allowing his fangs to nick her tongue. A monster, he was. She needed to know he wasn't safe. He'd hurt her just like he'd done to his family.

Laryssa sensed Léopold's hesitation. He'd shown her his teeth to frighten her, and a small part of her was scared. But an even bigger part of her yearned to have his fangs pierce her skin, possessing her, in every way possible. As his tongue moved inside her mouth, she sucked and breathed, letting her own tongue brush over his sharp teeth.

"Off," was all she heard before he'd ripped the fabric of her shirt over her head.

"Stay still," he ordered, holding her upright. He glided his hands over the smooth skin of her back and he turned her body once again, this time so that she was facing the window. With a flick of his wrist, he slipped the hooks out of the eyes and her bra fell to the floor. "Much better, pet."

"No," she protested at the name he'd called her.

"Now." Léopold reached his hand around her neck, and gently but firmly held her in place. His other hand found her breast. "This is what I've wanted to do to you. Lovely."

Laryssa didn't fear his restraint of her body, but instead embraced it, focusing solely on the touch of his fingers as they kneaded her flesh. She wanted to scream and tell him to stop calling her that name, yet it was as if he was playing her like a grand piano. The music resonated throughout her entire being, making her dance to the rhythm he created.

"Léopold," she breathed, seeking more than he gave.

"Patience. You're so soft and ready, aren't you? But you play with fire, no?"

"What do you mean?" She tried to move her head but he tightened his grip, softly stroking the skin beneath her ear.

"Quid pro quo. What are you?" Léopold breathed against her skin, brushing his lips to her nape.

"I can't," she insisted.

Léopold laughed, frustrated, aroused by his little witch. She may not have been magical but she wielded a sexual spell over him like no other woman he'd met. After confessing the names of his children, she thought she could get away without meeting the terms of their agreement? There was so much he would teach her, if he'd let himself indulge. But he couldn't have her, he knew. In this moment, however, she owed him the truth. *Quid pro quo.*

"Oui, you will," he assured her. Sucking the lobe of her ear into his mouth, his hand fell from her breast and she moaned in protest. Slowly, he teased his hand over her belly, downward.

"Please."

"Qu'est-ce que tu veux?"

"I don't understand," she cried in frustration. *Why is he torturing me?*

"Please what?"

"I can't…I can't say."

"You are a stubborn one. So determined yet so fragile. Like the silk of a spider…you're strong but delicate. Both tough and ductile, you fight against what you are but strain to conform to what society expects of you. But what you must learn, Laryssa," Léopold paused before gliding his fingers under the seam of her jeans, "is that even a spider's web can be tested." His fingers slid through her slick folds, grazing her hooded pearl until he heard her moan. "Ah, yes, the web, while strong, it can be tested, flexed. The energy it can absorb is extraordinary in nature, but not limitless."

Laryssa's pussy ached with heat, pulsing in anticipation of his next stroke.

She struggled to move her hips into his hand but he gently squeezed her neck, reminding her who was in control. Her core contracted as he pressed a finger against her entrance and she knew then she would give anything to be with this man.

"I'll tell you, just please….touch me."

"Like this?' He plunged a long thick finger into her, licking her neck as he did so. He kissed along the bottom of her cheek, wanting so badly to taste her lips again.

"Ah," she cried. "Yes."

"Or like this?" Léopold strummed the pad of his thumb over her clitoris, pumping another finger into her wetness.

"Yes," she cried. The tendrils of an orgasm lingered beyond her reach. She couldn't move, couldn't touch herself. She could only wait for him to give her what she desired. Her chest heaved a breath as he flicked over her swollen clit a second time.

"Tell me what you are, everything you can do. No relationships. Just give." He pressed two fingers up into her, eliciting another moan of pleasure. "And take."

"I'm so close…please, Léopold. Not now…just make me feel." As he stilled his fingers, she groaned.

"Yes, you are…so close to getting what you want. I desire you, but we cannot be. I'm not the man for you. Pleasure I can bring you easily, but anything more will cause you nothing but pain."

"Stop talking," she demanded.

"You want it so badly, don't you? I can feel your flesh quivering around my fingers, sweet, sweet Laryssa," he grunted as he ground his cock into the swell of her ass. If she didn't tell him what she was within the next two minutes, he knew he'd completely lose control and take her right there on the floor. Once they made love, he feared he wouldn't be able to let her go. No, he needed information, not complications. He had to break her, get her to tell him how she came to be, what she was. "Tell me now and you can have what you seek, mon lapin. What are you? I can feel it…you want to give in to me…so just tell me. I can't promise you anything but my trust and protection."

As his fingers pumped in and out of her, driving her higher and higher, hurling her toward climax, she could barely hear him speaking. *Trust? Give in? What is he saying?*

"I can't tell you now…please, don't stop," she breathed, resting her forehead against the cool window pane. "It feels so good. Oh my God."

"Tell me now or we stop."

"What?" Laryssa quivered, her orgasm teetering on the edge. She shook her head, refusing to tell him.

"Tell me!" Léopold grunted as his seed began to seep from the tip of his hardness. *Goddammit, this woman is impossible.* Before he had a chance to press her further, the doorbell rang, interrupting them. "Saved by the bell?"

"What?" Disoriented, Laryssa shivered. Falling off the precipice of ecstasy, her orgasm fell out of reach as Léopold pulled his hand out of her panties. *Why was he stopping?* She'd heard the familiar sound of a buzzer. Was someone at the door? She tried to compose herself, reeling from the loss of his touch. She felt him lift her arms, draping the hole of her shirt over her head.

"Dinner's arrived, I'm afraid. Get dressed," he told her as if he'd ordered off a menu and was sitting in a restaurant waiting for his meal to arrive.

"Seriously?"

"Quoi?" he said, smoothing down the fabric. He bent down, grabbing her bra off the floor and brought it to his nose and sniffed.

Coming to her senses, Laryssa twisted away from him. A mixture of disappointment and embarrassment coursed through her, as she realized that she'd let him restrain her. Worse, he'd deliberately baited her, arousing her, bringing her so close to coming and then stopping. Her eyes flared in anger, as he smiled at her with a knowing look. He wanted her to know what he'd done.

"Get away from me." She brushed his hand off her arm.

"A pity, no? So close, yet so far away." He extended his arm, her bra dangling from his fingertip. She snatched it and clutched it to her chest.

"I wasn't that close," she lied. "How would you know anyway? I could have been faking it."

"You don't wear deception well, mon lapin. Besides, I was referring to the fact that I was so close to finding out the truth….de vous. You'll tell me. That was our agreement. I share, you share. I'm afraid you now owe me." Léopold circled her as she stood as still as a statue. Coming up behind her, he felt her jump as he pressed his lips to her hair. "And I intend to collect right after I'm finished."

"Finished doing what?" She heard a door opening, and Léopold paid her no heed as he moved from behind her toward the foyer.

"Excusez-moi. The door…I must attend to our guests," he called out, leaving her behind.

Cautiously following him, Laryssa moved to where he'd put her bag and snatched it up into her arms, concealing her unrestrained bosom. From across the room, she could see a man and a woman push through the entryway. She didn't recognize them from earlier and wondered who they were, what they were doing here. Panic rose in her throat at the thought that Léopold had lied to her, told others about her and her abilities. She watched pensively as Léopold guided the female into the foyer, toward the great room.

"This is my assistant," Léopold told Laryssa, nodding to the strange man who politely smiled at her. "He's brought dinner."

"Hello," she managed to say in a soft voice, but didn't extend her hand.

"Bonjour mademoiselle. Or should I say bonsoir as it's getting late, isn't it?"

Laryssa forced a small smile. Her eyes darted to Léopold, as he escorted the blonde guest over to a chair. The woman appeared to glide across the floor, her heels clicking a soft staccato on the wooden planks. Laryssa silently gasped, noticing that the woman had a mask tied to her face, blocking her eyesight. *What the hell is going on?*

"Um, why is she wearing a blindfold?" Laryssa couldn't contain her curiosity.

"No worries," Léopold cajoled, appreciating the look of worry on Laryssa's face. "This is Sophie. She's quite comfortable, I assure you."

"But…I thought you said your assistant was bringing dinner…we already…" Laryssa's face turned white as her words trailed off into silence. Her brain slowly put together the pieces of the puzzle. No, Léopold would not do this. Not in front of her.

"Arnaud."

"What?" she asked.

"Arnaud. My assistant's name is Arnaud. And while you've already had dinner," Léopold stood behind the woman and put his hand on the top of her head as if he was petting a cat, "I have not."

Laryssa could feel her blood pumping, fear and loathing tearing through her. *Is he serious? Of course he's serious. He's a vampire. Bloodsucker. Parasite.* She bit her lip, trying hard to fight the tears. Only a few minutes ago, she'd almost made love to him, knowing what he was capable of doing, secretly hoping he'd pierce her skin, drinking in her essence. With disgust, she watched as the woman calmly untied the belt that cinched her trench coat, and shrugged out if it, baring her skin. She wore a black satin slip and nothing more, the hem inching up her thighs.

Laryssa's face heated as her anger simmered. She'd heard the rumors about how vampires ate, their bite inciting the most spectacular orgasms. She'd been foolish to think for one second that she could actually have a relationship with Léopold. Unlike her, he'd proudly confessed who he was, what he was. Behind his debonair and seductive exterior, a cavalier man stood before her, no apologies given. *Why didn't I listen to him? How could I have been so stupid as to misread the attraction as something more than what it is…lust?*

Léopold knew this would be the result when he'd texted Arnaud, telling him to bring him a donor. It wasn't as if he hadn't done it a million times. The donors, male or female, were always blindfolded. Sometimes just for the ride to his mansion, sometimes for the entire time until they returned to their residence. Regardless, they were never privy to the whereabouts of Léopold's mansion.

His home was his refuge, the location of which he only shared with Arnaud. He'd planned on inviting Dimitri eventually, once they returned from Wyoming. In a lapse of judgment, he'd brought Laryssa here. For every hour he told himself that he needed to be done with her, get her out of his life, he grew further unable to deny his hunger for her. He reasoned it was purely a physical attraction, but when she insisted on something more, a connection to assure her of his trust with her secret, he'd broken a million of his own rules. First he'd brought her to his sanctuary, and then told her about his children.

Convinced if she saw him in his true light, she'd understand that they could never have a relationship, he'd asked Arnaud to bring the donor, a female for good measure. The look of hurt and distrust in her eyes should have been cause for celebration, for victory. But the joke was on him, because the only blood he wanted was Laryssa's. Not only had he maliciously caused her distress, denied her an orgasm, he was now taunting her with another woman. Conflicting emotions vacillated inside of him for only a minute, before he'd decided he'd done the right thing.

This was who he was and he wouldn't hide it, wouldn't conceal his true identity. Long ago, before he'd been turned, he'd been a gentle man, caring to his wife and children. Hardworking, a knight for the king. But that man had died with his family. The trifling of decency and compassion within his soul could not compete with the savage animal within. No woman would ever love the beast he'd become.

Laryssa hadn't told him what she was, but he could sense the purity within her. Her humanity thrived, and she'd crave a man who cared only for her. She deserved more, not the selfish individual that she lusted for. He told himself that by hurting her, showing her this side of him, she'd give up illusions of friendships, relationships and connections. Their liaison must be based on finding who tried to hurt the baby. No more, no less. But as he spied a tear trailing down Laryssa's cheek, he questioned his motives. Was he feeding out of hunger or protecting his own heart, one he would deny existed?

"Arnaud, please show Laryssa to the guest room," Léopold stated and then gave her a smug smile. "Unless you wish to stay and watch?"

Laryssa glared at him. The man had to eat but it was as if he was being cruel on purpose, taunting her after withholding her orgasm. Yet he had every right to eat or fuck whoever he wanted. It wasn't as if she'd offered to give him her own blood. No, she'd taken pleasure from him, knowing she wouldn't tell him everything. She had no right to the jealousy that swelled inside her. She held Léopold's gaze as he sat next to his donor, who was proffering her arm upward to his nose. She hated him. She lusted after him. None of it mattered because he would do whatever he wanted.

Léopold absorbed Laryssa's stare. It was as if he could feel his lips on her skin, but the woman he held in his hands wasn't her. For every second of anguish he caused to Laryssa, he felt it tenfold, denying and relinquishing his own desire for her. She'd never want him once he demonstrated how cold he could be, his nature. Descending his fangs, he never took his eyes off of her as he licked the inside of the woman's wrist, detecting her pulse.

"Can I take off the blindfold?" Sophie asked.

"No," he told her.

"Do you want me to lie down? I've missed you."

"Do not speak. It's your blood I seek, nothing else," Léopold claimed. While he'd used and had sex with her before, it was all part of their feeding arrangement. Like any other donor, her purpose was merely nutritional. But after meeting Laryssa, he wondered if he'd ever be able to make love to another woman.

"Come, mademoiselle. Let me take you to your room while monsieur has dinner," Arnaud politely suggested.

"Uh, yes, I think that would be a good idea," Laryssa stammered. A sick sense of relief washed over Laryssa as she observed the interaction. *Did the donor expect him to have sex with her?* Perhaps, but he'd refused her, and it appeared as if he was truly only using her for her blood. Sophie placed her hand on Léopold's thigh, and Laryssa thought she'd vomit. The only thing stopping her was the touch on her elbow, distracting her from the scene.

"Yes, a very good idea," Arnaud asserted.

Laryssa gave Léopold one last glance as Arnaud escorted her out of the great room. A long hallway led to two doors, one on the left and one on the right. She caught sight of a second staircase which appeared to trail downward.

"Mademoiselle, this room here is the guest room." Arnaud opened a solid oak door and flipped on a light switch. "The master's room is across from yours."

"The stairway? Where does it go?" she inquired right before they walked into the room. Water. She needed to get out to the lake.

"There's a billiard and exercise area downstairs. Leads out to the pool. You're welcome to a swim, if you want. I can unlock the back sliders for you."

"Swim? Uh, yeah, that would be great." Laryssa glanced around the room. Like the rest of Léopold's home, it was stark white except for a Blue Dog painting that hung on the far wall. Its captivating yellow eyes seemed to follow her. She'd seen the brightly colored canines so many times when she'd passed the gallery in the Quarter but it was the first time she'd seen the artwork in someone's home.

"You a George Rodrique fan?" Arnaud asked, sidling up next to her.

"Yeah, I love it. His work's amazing, huh?"

"Yes, indeed. Monsieur loves his pieces as well." Arnaud walked away, opening the door to the bathroom. "The towels are in here if you decide to go for a dip. I'll go downstairs now and see to the lock."

"Do you live here?" Laryssa asked, glancing at Arnaud. She wasn't sure why she asked other than interest in what sort of person would work for Léopold. She laughed silently, thinking he must have the patience of a saint.

"Me? No. My boss prefers solitude. Besides, when he's in the city, I live just down the street. But I'm available to him twenty-four seven when he's home."

"Home?"

"New Orleans."

"He travels often?"

"Sometimes," he hedged. "He also prefers his privacy. If there isn't anything else I can get you, I need to attend to a few things before I take Sophie back."

Sophie. Laryssa's breath caught, realizing that for a brief second she'd almost forgotten where she was. That and the fact Léopold was with another woman…dinner. As much as she wanted to pump Arnaud for information about his little 'feeding' arrangement, she could tell she'd already crossed the boundary of what he was willing to share about his employer.

"No, I'm fine. Thanks."

"You're very welcome, mademoiselle. Now if you'll excuse me, I'll see to the door."

As Arnaud left the room, Laryssa admired the painting, thinking about how many times she'd considered purchasing a print. She'd often thought of keeping one in her tiny apartment but had decided she wouldn't see it nearly often enough and had decided to display one in her shop so she could enjoy it all day.

Her store, she thought with a sigh. After closing early, she'd forgotten to call her assistant manager to make sure he opened it tomorrow. She reached for her cell in her pocket and realized that she'd misplaced it. Rummaging through her overnight bag, she remembered she'd put the phone in her purse which she'd left in the kitchen. *Dammit.* As much as she loathed seeing Léopold feed, she needed to keep her business running in her absence.

Laryssa discreetly peeked around the corner, glancing down the hallway. Not seeing Arnaud, she kicked off her shoes and quietly padded toward the kitchen. Sneaking around in a dangerous vampire's home was probably not the best idea she'd ever had, but curiosity bit at her, wondering if Léopold did more than *eat* his dinner. As she tiptoed through the foyer into the kitchen, she eyed her purse. By the time she'd snatched her bag off the stool and turned around, movement caught her attention. *Léopold.* His black eyes pierced into hers, while he held the woman's wrist to his mouth. Sophie writhed and moaned his name aloud, much as Laryssa had done when he'd pleasured her earlier. Except unlike Laryssa, she was most definitely climaxing, enjoying the sexual titillation his bite offered her.

A fresh rush of jealousy seized Laryssa's chest at the sight. Unable to watch for a second longer, she ran out of the room, dropping her purse along the way. She stumbled into the guest room, tearing at her clothing, until she wore nothing but her panties. Remembering she'd forgotten to pack a swimsuit, she grabbed a towel out of the bathroom closet. She wrapped it around her as she took off out of the room and down the stairway. Hot tears ran down her face, embarrassed and hurt that Léopold could bring another woman to orgasm after what they'd done together. The splash of reality, that he truly was just using her for her abilities, slapped her. But she'd been so tired of hiding. Even though she'd been scared, Léopold, with his dashing looks and provocative personality, had seemed like he'd be the one person she could finally entrust with her secret. Bathed in confusion and shame, she fumbled through the darkness, guided toward the outdoor lighting.

As she grasped onto the sliding glass door, she yanked at it, easily pulling it open. While she should have been impressed with the elaborate outdoor pool and lounges, it was the vapor from Lake Ponchartrain that drove her onward. Following the patio, her feet eventually touched down upon the cool, dew-covered grass. Even though the yard was pitch-dark, she spotted a small light coming from a dock down by the water. She put one foot in front of the other, quickening her pace until she was awkwardly running, holding the towel in place. No one could stop her from reaching her asylum, she thought. But as she approached the water, the light flickered off, and she heard a low growl. Red eyes glowed in the distance.

"Who's there?" she yelled into the night. Laryssa had never seen the eyes of the dark ones before, yet this had piercing ones that felt as if they were drilling into her gut. The heavy menacing presence she'd felt over the past months was undeniable and all too familiar.

"Laryssa," it snarled, coming into her line of vision. "It's time."

"Time for what?" she asked, terrified at the answer. As it came into view, her chest began to heave as she fought for breath. The creature, covered in black scales, took the shape of a man. Horns curled from its skull, and its blood-red lips drew up in a sickening smile. It extended its claws, stretching and balling its fists.

"Did you think you could avoid me forever? Since you died, you've been mine," it asserted, stepping closer.

"I don't know you." Laryssa's feet inched backward toward the water's edge, but she never took her eyes off of the menacing creature.

"Don't lie!" It snarled, licking its tongue over its lips. "Your soul's mine."

Laryssa frantically began looking around for a weapon. The exhaustion of using her powers earlier had left her weak, but adrenaline could help her to summon it. In the darkness she saw nothing but a boat hanging off its dry dock. Her eyes darted to a log that had washed up onto the sandy beach. It was a small piece of wood. Slowly, she began shuffling toward it, hoping she'd have enough energy left to move it.

"Do you value your life?"

"Get away from me."

"There's nowhere you can go now. Did you really think the vampire could protect you? He has no wards to protect you, little Lyssa."

"What are you?" she asked, focusing on her target.

"Don't you recognize me? It's been many years, I know, but you owe me your soul. And I'll have it."

"You're crazy."

"Sweetheart, you've always belonged to me. But I'd be happy to take little Ava too, if you'd like."

"Fuck you!" she screamed. *How the hell does this thing know the baby's name?* "You'll never get her."

"Oh, I'll get whatever I want. You. Her. And the Tecpatl."

"Tecpatl?" she questioned.

"One week. Bring me the Tlalco Tecpatl or I take the infant."

"I don't know what you're talking about."

"The dagger. You own it, and I must have it."

"Please leave me alone. I can't do this."

"Remember your death, Lyssa? My sweet embrace, taking you home. That bitch stole you, made you into what you are. And now, I'll take you back. We'll be together. I can please you."

The scaly beast transformed into a man. Devilishly good-looking and muscular, it took its cock into its hands, stroking itself. Laryssa felt her lungs cave at the sight. This demon wanted to mate with her? Keep her as its concubine? Shaking, she looked to the broken branch that had washed ashore. If she could gather enough energy to beckon it, she'd have a chance of making it into the water.

"No, no, no, no…" Laryssa repeated, trying to focus on calling forth her power.

She tried to ignore the sight of its growing erection, but found it difficult as the vision of it began to waver from human to demon, and back again. The putrid stench of ash and musk filled the air, making her cringe. It laughed as a greenish fluid began to seep from its hands. The surge of electricity pushed through her cells, singeing her fingertips. As she made her first attempt to bring the makeshift weapon into her hand, the beast lunged at her, its claws extending forward.

"Your skin tempts me. Show me your flesh, little whore," it roared, swiping its talons at her towel.

Laryssa screamed as its red-hot barbs scraped across her chest. The searing pain and horror provoked her power, commanding the log. As it flew into her hands, she swung it at the creature's head, cracking its lip open. The beast snarled and bared its teeth at her but before it had a chance to attack, she jerked her knee up into its aroused groin. Crumpling to the ground in agony, it released a high-pitched wail. Laryssa gasped for breath, faltering down the bank until she reached the water's edge.

"One week," it screeched at her.

Terror brushed her mind as she reached to the gash on her chest. Falling onto her hands and knees, Laryssa crawled into the lake. Letting her body sink into its curative depths, she closed her eyes. Water rushed into her nose and throat, reminding of her of who she was, what she sought to hide. Deliberately she opened her mind to its curative waters, taking in its energy, healing her wounds.

The positively charged ions danced from one molecule to another infusing their energy within her chest, into her bloodstream. As the vital force permeated every cell, her skin began to glow, casting a dim aura around her entire body. Over the years, she'd learned how to control it, retaining the full effect of the water and its illumination. Careening her own strength into focus, she compelled her light. If the creature came at her in the lake, she'd kill it. How she knew she could do so, she wasn't certain. But with every breath of the cold fluid, in and out, the energy built and her confidence in her ability escalated in tandem. Floating down into the lake bed, she rested in quiet apprehension, waiting for her enemy to strike.

<small>⤜⚜·</small> *Chapter Six* <small>·⚜⤏</small>

Léopold immediately stopped feeding after Laryssa had witnessed Sophie in the throes of her orgasm. Remorse, a distant emotion that he'd long buried, burned through him. It wasn't as if he was ashamed to feed off a human, to be nothing more than he was, a vampire. But he'd deliberately hurt Laryssa, aggressively discouraging her from seeking companionship from a man who wasn't capable of reciprocating.

"Leave it on. Arnaud is going to take you home," Léopold told Sophie, noticing that she'd begun to adjust the blindfold, attempting to see, obviously sensing his discontent.

"But I thought we would…"

"We would what? Have sex? We have a contract through the agency, Sophie. I pay for your services as a donor only. If and when I decide we are to go further, it may proceed. The blindfold stays on. We're finished with our business."

"But you always want to…"

"Tais toi. Not another word. We aren't dating. What happens between us is merely a completion of the food chain. Pay per bite, as you will. If you aren't able to live within the confines of said agreement then I suggest you contact the agency when you return."

"You're a bastard," she huffed, fumbling to adjust her negligee.

"Oui," he responded, unfazed. As soon as she left, he'd request that she no longer be sent to his home. As a result of the pleasure he gave, the donors, both male and female, too often began to develop unhealthy expectations as a result of their exchange. Sophie had become increasingly demanding over the past weeks. Léopold met eyes with Arnaud, who was tidying up in the kitchen. "I'm finished. Please get her out of here."

He felt like an asshole for taunting Laryssa with his donor. He'd specifically chosen Sophie, aware that her physical attributes would draw Laryssa's ire. While there was no denying her outer beauty as defined by societal standards, her lack of personality dulled her allure. No, it was Laryssa who drew his fascination. Léopold reasoned it was merely chemical attraction, driven by pheromones combined with the practicality of the situation, that must be driving him mad with desire for his little rabbit. It amused and impressed him that she'd thrown a piece of furniture at him, standing up for herself, undaunted by his dubious reputation and the reality that he could kill her within seconds. He knew he could have shaken it off, called her foolish for doing so. Whether she'd been conscious or not of the explosive power she was capable of harboring and utilizing on a whim, she'd

74

almost clocked him with the ottoman. But it was her caring nature, selflessly agreeing to walk into the Alpha's den and further, challenging Luca that had displayed her true intrepid nature.

Yet, the woman frustrated him beyond reason. Why wouldn't she just tell him what she was, so they could leverage her abilities? It seemed the prudent and rational thing to do. She was driving him insane with need, and forcing him to extreme measures.

Léopold walked over to the windows, glancing down toward the pool. He'd heard the door slam and known she'd gone swimming. Scanning the veranda, he searched for her lovely body, expecting to see her plotting to inflict torture on him or perhaps a slow miserable death. But instead of finding her brooding on a lounge chair, he saw nothing but the calm blue water shimmering back at him. Where was she?

Panic gripped his chest as he spied fiery red eyes near the dock. The horned creature transformed into a naked man, but he immediately recognized it. A demon? Merde, it had been centuries since he'd seen one out in the open. He cursed as he caught sight of it stroking its dick as Laryssa defensively clutched a towel to her body. The barbarian was jerking off in front of her? Jesus almighty. Léopold readied to materialize to them, and saw the creature lunge toward Laryssa. She flailed a branch at it, and then kicked at its gonads, leveling the beast into the grass. Léopold's heart dropped as she fell screaming to her knees. Enraged, his fangs lengthened and he disappeared into thin air, transforming, intending to kill the beast. But by the time he reached the dock, the demon had dissipated. A revolting smell of rotting flesh lingered in its wake.

"Laryssa!" Léopold screamed out into the yard, unable to find her. Met with silence, he scanned the area, but saw nothing. He raked his hands through his hair, devastated at the possibility that Laryssa had been abducted. A roar of frustration tore through his lungs. He pulled out his cell phone, intending to call Dimitri, when he caught a glimpse of the lambent glimmer rolling through the black waves.

"Laryssa! Laryssa!" he yelled, kicking off his shoes.

Léopold dove into the brisk, murky water, exploring blindly with his hands. Unable to find her, he surfaced, gasped for air and called her name again. Returning into the depths, he plummeted deep into the nebulous reservoir. His body troweled through the vegetation in darkness until a luminous aura appeared. *Laryssa.* Léopold could hardly believe what he was seeing. Her entire body was emitting a fluorescent gleam and her chest moved up and down as if she were breathing on land. Like a firefly, she was lit up, glowing from her forehead over the pale skin of her abdomen to her toes.

He reached for her, concerned that she was dying. As his hand brushed her cheek, her eyes flashed open in alarm. Léopold wished he could somehow communicate that he was attempting to help her as she began to claw at his face and kick her legs. He tried to secure her arms, but she easily slipped out, swimming upward and away.

A touch to her face startled Laryssa's bioluminescent meditation. Renewed terror surged through her mind at the thought that the demon was in the water. Her glow faltered as she used all of her energy to escape. Temporarily unable to see, she shoved at the creature. Frantically swimming, she crested up into the night. The water in her lungs spewed forth and she gasped for breath. She treaded water, swiveling her head side to side in panic, searching for the horned demon. *How did it get in the lake?*

A blood-curdling scream released from her lips as it, too, broke through the watery cloak. It clutched at her arms, and she instinctively brought her knees to her chest and then extended her feet, kicking its chest. Unable to get traction in the aqueous environment, her feet slid downward. She twisted her body, squirming to free herself from its grip. Its hands held tight, and she heard it call her name.

"Laryssa," Léopold grunted as she continued to thrash. Goddess, the woman was strong. "Laryssa, stop," he commanded in a strong, dominant tone. "Enough. It's me. It's Léopold."

"Léopold?" she croaked, forgetting how angry she'd been with him. *Not a demon.*

"Oui. You're safe," he lied as they drifted further away from the coast. Perhaps the demon was gone, but he knew that Lake Ponchartrain could be a dangerous place for even the most experienced swimmers. Besides the treacherous tides and currents, the basin was littered with trees, logs and even glass.

"Is it here?" she cried.

"The demon is gone," he assured her.

Exhausted and relieved, she sagged into his arms and rested her forehead against his chest. It was gone.

"You saw it?" she whispered against his skin.

"Oui, I saw it. Come, let's get inside, ma chérie. It's cold."

Using one arm to paddle, Léopold brought them to the dock. By the time they reached it, Laryssa had begun to shiver uncontrollably and wasn't speaking. Léopold held tight to her, pulling her up the steps with him.

"I can walk," she stammered through chattering teeth. Laryssa wasn't sure what was happening. Normally she never got cold. She reasoned it was the shock of the demon that had done this to her.

"I've got you," Léopold insisted, easily lifting her into his arms.

He cursed, realizing that she was naked save for her panties. Cradling her against him, he knew his own body heat wouldn't sufficiently warm her. He was soaking wet as well, laden down with sodden clothes. He should have asked her before he transported them into his bedroom. But she'd never agree, so he'd made the decision without explanation. Léopold was not surprised when she began mumbling into his chest, complaining about what he'd done. He placed a kiss to her hair, intending to explain to her later about his special ability.

"What did you do? Where are we? Please…" Nausea rose in her belly. Laryssa looked around and realized that Léopold had moved her somehow…without walking. "How did you do that?"

"A conversation for another time, love. Take a few deep breaths. You'll feel better in a minute," he assured her, refusing to put her down. "No time for walking, I'm afraid."

"I don't feel so well," Laryssa slurred. She clumsily pushed at his chest. *How did I get in the house?* Confusion and fogginess blanketed her brain. She swallowed and her breath quickened.

"You're a bit hypothermic is all. Nothing severe, though. Let me look at you." Léopold noted her glassy eyes and the pale color of her skin. Her lips were slightly grayish but not blue. He snatched the comforter off the bed and wrapped it around her.

Reluctantly, he set her into his bed so he could get undressed. He stripped, throwing his lake-soaked clothes aside. Walking into his bathroom, he started a lukewarm shower and then returned to her side.

"How're you feeling?" He asked, gently bending down to eye level.

"Help…help me," she stuttered.

"It's gonna be okay. Easy now." Léopold carefully scooped her up in his arms and took her into the bathroom.

"What're you doing?" she asked, aware of the warmth caressing her skin.

"You're just a little cold from the water. Not surprising given that you were under so long." He unraveled the bedspread, dropping it onto the floor.

"I don't get cold."

"Yeah, you do," Léopold disagreed, stepping into the spray.

"I can go in any water," she insisted. "No matter the temperature."

"See that? You're starting to warm up already," he said, ignoring her comment. He bit his lip, resisting the urge to ask her, 'How's that workin' out for ya?' Yeah, not so well. She could go in any water? What the hell was that supposed to mean?

Part of him wanted to scold her. But he knew in her current state, it wouldn't help the situation. Glancing down, he couldn't avoid noticing how incredibly beautiful she was. Her swollen breasts pressed against his own naked skin, her pink nipples beaded into ripe tips. Goddess, what he would give to take one into his mouth, teasing it further into hardness. He closed his eyes and took a deep breath, willing his dick into submission. *Jesus Christ, already, the woman is suffering and I'm thinking about sex?* He knew it was wrong, but his passion was scarcely controlled.

"Léopold," she whispered, tilting her head upward so that her eyes met his. "I think I can stand. Please."

"Careful." Slowly he let her slide out of his hold but kept his hands on her waist.

"Warmer."

"Hmm?"

"The water. Can you make it warmer?"

"Oui." Léopold reached around her, turning the spigot to the right.

"Ahhh," she purred. Laryssa began to remember what had happened by the lake. *Demon. Rejuvenation. Léopold.* But no matter how hard she racked her mind, she couldn't figure out how he'd brought her to the bedroom. She glanced down to her skin. Realizing she was nude, she covered her breasts with her hands.

"Don't," Léopold told her softly. He reached for her shoulders and slid his hands slowly down her arms, bringing her hands to her sides.

"But I don't have any clothes on…" Her voice was weak. Embarrassed but fatigued, she let him guide her.

"Oui. Nor do I. But we're as we were meant to be. Nous sommes naturel." Léopold let his hands fall to her hips and hooked his thumbs over the sides of her panties. With great patience, he tenderly but deliberately dragged them downward. His lips passed mere inches from her bottom as he bent to remove the dripping undergarment.

"I can't…" she began.

"Don't fret, ma chérie. Let me take care of you," he breathed into her ear.

"No one cares for me." She shook her head, still looking down.

"You're wrong. You have me."

Laryssa exhaled heavily as his breath warmed her ear. Whether it was out of need or defeat, she believed his words as truth. Tendrils of steam poured into the air as she nodded in acceptance.

Léopold removed his hands from her skin and reached for the loofah and soap. Laryssa went to turn her head to see what he was doing when his voice stopped her movement.

"Stay," he directed with a smile, aware that she'd be none too happy with his command.

"I'm not a…"

"Oui. I know, ma chérie…not a dog." He laughed. "You're a woman. A beautiful one at that. Someone who needs lessons in trust, I fear. Will you allow me that much?"

Laryssa didn't answer. The man was incorrigible. Simply unbelievable. But as he swirled the sponge over her back, she sighed, conceding that he was right.

"Yes, yes, I'll trust you. Oh God, that feels so good."

Léopold didn't respond. He merely smiled, continuing to brush his fingertips over her slippery breasts, gliding them across her belly. Dipping further downward, he slid the loofah over her mound. His left hand massaged her shoulder, sloshing the bubbles down her back and into the crevice of her buttocks. Craving her touch, he pressed into her, his cock settling against her silky skin. Léopold dropped the sponge into its wall holder and reached with both hands to deposit a dollop of shampoo into his hand. He heard Laryssa gasp as he fingered the solution into her hair, frothing it throughout the wisps of her mane. Working from underneath, he tended to her scalp.

Laryssa shuddered in arousal, angry that she could feel this way for a man who'd treated her the way he had. Only earlier, he'd pushed her away, almost enjoying the way he'd played with his food in front of her. She tried to imagine the donor moaning on the couch, Léopold's eyes boring into her. But as quickly as the picture came to her, it faded as he ground his hardness into her ass. Confusion swept through her. She hated herself for how much she wanted this man to touch her and was almost glad he'd finished soaping her skin. But as soon as his hands reached the nape of her neck and began to gently caress her hair, she melted, losing her fight to remain angry with him.

"We need to talk." She couldn't go on like this, naked with Léopold, craving his touch, without discussing what happened. Laryssa knew she'd risk making a fool out of herself, sharing how she felt, but the words began to spill out of her mouth before she could stop them. "Listen, Léopold, I don't know what's going on between us. One minute we're kissing and the next you withdraw. That woman…God, I must be an idiot. I mean the way she was dressed. You can call her food or whatever the hell you want, but I'm a woman and she wasn't gussied up just for dinner. She was practically wearing nothing for Chrissakes. But kissing you and touching you, it felt so good. I haven't been with someone in a long time but you're like this super-old vampire guy and I'm like…well, I'm not a vampire. And you know I haven't been completely honest with you."

Léopold smiled, knowing she couldn't see his reaction. Articulating was an art, he supposed. And given she'd just been thrust into his world, had an encounter with a demon and almost drowned, he assumed he should cut her some slack and let her get whatever she needed to off her chest. He wanted to hear what she was, after all, and he knew she was precariously close to taking a leap of faith.

"It's not like I get naked with every guy I meet and jump in the shower with him."

"I should hope not." He stifled his laughter.

"I was so mad at you. I have no right…I know that. I mean you have to eat. But you…she…and we'd just…you know what you did to me," she sighed. "And what you didn't do."

"Ah, that." This time he did laugh just a little.

"Were you going to sleep with her? Do you have sex with all your donors? I know we just met but I can't do this with you. What I'm trying to say is that there is something about you…about us. God, I know I must be crazy. We just met but I was thinking if we could get to know each other better we could…"

"Make love," he suggested, continuing to wash her hair.

"If you hadn't stopped upstairs, yeah, I guess that could've happened. But you want to know what I am. And there are things I want to tell you. I want so badly to trust someone. I've been alone forever. Well, I've had friends but that doesn't really count. The only person who really knows is Avery, my friend from the club. And now that thing…"

"The demon?"

"Yes. That."

"You can say the word. It is what it is. When you described the eyeless dark ones, I wasn't sure what you were talking about. Now a demon. Well, I haven't seen many but I have seen them before. Nasty lot."

"I don't want to say it. If I say it, it'll…" Maybe she'd watched the Exorcist too many times or maybe it was her lapsed Catholic upbringing, but she didn't want to say its name. It was as though if she acknowledged it, she'd be asking it to show itself. "I don't want it here."

"Saying the word demon won't bring it to you. What does worry me is why a demon would show itself to you in the first place. It wanted something, I take it? Something besides sex." Léopold had a difficult time erasing the image of the beast touching itself in front of Laryssa, reaching for her.

"Yes," she said softly.

"Do you want to tell me?"

"It wanted me to find something, to bring something to it." She closed her eyes trying to remember what it had told her. She'd been terrified and not exactly taking notes as it threatened her. "It began with a T…Tamo? Teca? No it was Tlalco something. Dammit, I can't think of what it was."

Léopold momentarily stopped moving his hands on hearing the ancient Aztec word, but resumed, squeezing the bubbles out of her hair from top to bottom. He didn't want to alarm her.

"Tecpatl?" he suggested.

"Yeah, that sounds right. Tlalco Tecpatl. Do you know what it is?"

"A Tlalco is a knife. One that was used by the Aztecs." *To perform human sacrifice.* "Tecpatl was one of the Gods they worshipped. I've never heard of such a relic but that doesn't mean it doesn't exist. We're going to have to do some research. I'm not exactly sure why the demon wants it, but whatever the reason, I know it can't be good."

"It threatened to take Ava if I didn't get it. And it wants to kill me." *Keep me.* The demon had said she belonged to it. *Mine.* She shuddered, deciding to tell him about the time constraint instead. "Seven days."

"What?"

"It wants it in a week. Like I can find some ancient knife in seven days," she chortled. "What am I supposed to do? Waltz into the natural history museum and say, 'Hey, you don't know me but could you acquisition an Aztec knife and let me borrow it to give to some demon?' Why in the hell would it need me to get it anyway?"

"My best guess is that it has something to do with what you are," he surmised. Léopold carefully turned her to face him, and brushed the back of his knuckles over her cheek. He waited patiently until she finally raised her eyelids, before tilting her head back into the hot spray. Carefully, he fingered her locks, the bubbles falling away to the floor. His cock jerked as she licked her lips, parting them as if she would drink from him.

"I want to tell you," she responded, returning her gaze to his. Her eyes darted to his chest and abdomen before catching a glimpse of his glorious erection. He was the most magnificent male specimen she'd ever seen, beautiful, every inch of him ripped in muscle. She shouldn't have been surprised by the way his groin had been perfectly trimmed, the enormous length of him straining outward. As she realized what she'd been doing, drinking in the sight of him like she'd been admiring a painting in the Metropolitan Museum of Art, she blinked back up to his eyes in embarrassment. When she caught his gaze, her heart pounded in her chest. Desire washed over her once again.

"It's okay, Laryssa," he said. His voice was low and smooth.

"What's okay?"

"To look." Léopold finally gave in to his own craving, allowing his eyes to wander over her glistening breasts. The water droplets ran down like a stream, a small waterfall spilling off her rosy peaks. "To touch." He reached out to caress her neck, but became alarmed as he moved closer. Four deep grooves sliced across her chest, healed but still pink and tender. His fingertip glided over her wounds. "It did this to you, no?"

"I'm okay now," she piped cheerfully, attempting to hide her fear about what had happened. Laryssa heard him growl in displeasure, and placed her hand over his, sensing his anger. "See? It's almost gone."

"You heal quickly. This is your magic?"

"The water, the lake, it healed me. I can't live without it." *I've tried and almost died.*

"You weren't drowning, were you?"

"No."

"You were glowing."

"Yeah, I was."

"I thought you were dying. I'd told you that I'd protect you. And then when you saw Sophie and ran out...I didn't go after you."

"Did you want her?" Laryssa defensively pulled her hand off of his, expecting him to stop touching her.

Léopold gave a small smile and shook his head. The woman didn't get how much of an effect she had on him, how, in the moment, he only wanted her.

"She's your lover?" she asked, wishing she could take back the question. "I'm sorry. I shouldn't have asked. It's just that...if you want to be with me..."

"She's a donor. If you're asking if I've had sex with her, I won't lie. The answer is yes. But she's not my lover or girlfriend or anything of the sort. I've told you that I don't do relationships but…"

"It's none of my business." She tried to back away, but he inched toward her.

"I want you to know that what you saw today was a physical reaction to my bite. Nothing more. We were created that way. Vampires. If our bite brought only pain, we'd have been killed as a race a long time ago. And for those of us who take mates, wives, we must be able to drink from our partners to complete the bond. Perhaps it's an evolutionary adaptation, but some of us are no different from humans in wanting to find a soul mate to spend our lives with. The bite must bring pleasure, great pleasure if it's to be done during sex, many times a day."

Laryssa swallowed. *Sex many times a day? With Léopold?*

"But my impression is that you don't date. Don't 'do relationships' as you say."

"No, but I must eat. It can be an aphrodisiac."

"Are you going to bite me?" she asked softly, her eyes lost in his.

"No."

"No?"

"You, mon lapin, I could never use for just a meal." Léopold closed the distance between them, his hand sliding over her skin.

"Why not?"

"Because, if I tasted of you, I'd need more. Much, much more," he growled. Léopold felt his cock brush her belly, smiling as his rabbit shivered despite the heat. "If I bite you when we make love, I fear a bond could take place. I can't allow that to happen. It's not fair to you."

"Don't you mean 'if' we make love?" she quipped.

"No. I mean 'when' we make love," he breathed, leaning forward so his lips touched her ear. His hand slid up from her chest so that he could wrap it around the back of her neck, spearing his fingers into her wet hair.

Laryssa's heart pounded against her ribs. He tempted her, seducing her into his entrancing web. She wanted him to finish what he'd started earlier, taking it to new heights. But the man was frustrating as hell. He wanted to fuck her but he didn't want a relationship? He'd made it clear that not only did he not date, he didn't engage 'friends with benefits' either.

She found it puzzling how a man like Léopold could be so threatened by intimacy. Built like steel, a mind like a razor, he seemed invincible, both physically and mentally. Despite his immortality, the man had survived the centuries well. The vampire, who'd seen wars and plagues, had achieved unfathomable wealth, deliberately shunned others, appeared to relish his self-imposed solitude. While his words spoke clearly of his wishes to remain isolated, he had revealed his ability to connect with the infant. His eyes had lit up when he'd held Ava, sweetly singing to her and putting her to sleep.

Even with the other supernatural she'd met at the Alpha's home, she'd observed his interactions, which appeared natural and uninhibited. Whether he'd admit it or not, he cared about them. But perhaps it was because in at least his mind, those were business relationships. There was no pressure or expectations required so he accepted their company more easily.

Kisses to her neck jarred her back to reality. *Shower. Léopold.* She let her hands roam to his chest, trailing her fingers down his firm pecs. Her nipples hardened in arousal, and the ache between her legs grew painful. The temptation was too great for her to resist. She prayed she could do this, have sex with Léopold and walk away unscathed.

"Don't fight this…us," he said, unsure whether he was talking to her or himself. Léopold gave in to his desires, pressing his lips to the softest hollow behind her ear. He was breaking a million of his own rules, he knew. But this woman, whatever she was, he had to have her…to be in her, to possess her. He heard her sigh in response and grazed his cheek against hers.

"Léopold," was all she managed to say before his lips captured hers.

Laryssa gave in to his intoxicating kiss, wrapping her hands around his neck. She could feel her control slip away as his tongue pressed into her mouth. With a demanding fervor, he kissed her, sucking at her lips, tasting her essence. She couldn't get enough of him, needed him closer. Writhing her belly against his cock, she hoped he'd also lose restraint. In response, Léopold dropped his hands to her ass, lifting her upward until she wrapped her legs around his waist.

"More," Laryssa demanded into his mouth. As her pussy opened against his slippery skin, she pumped her hips against his pelvis, seeking relief.

Léopold merely laughed, but never released her lips from his own. He pressed her back against the tiles, holding her still, ceasing her movement. Tightening his grip on her hips, he slid her upward, then down again, her wet folds brushing his abs.

"Oh God," Laryssa moaned, unable to control his actions. All she could do was accept the pleasure he was giving. Every time he pulled her up and then pushed her down, her clit grazed his skin. The sensation was deliciously arousing yet not enough to bring her to orgasm. "Léopold, please."

"You must trust me."

"I'm afraid to," she confessed. He yanked her up hard against him, putting more pressure against her aching nub.

"I'm going to take you every way I want, my sweet. I don't care what you are. I just need to be so far in you that you never forget this night."

"I'm…I'm a…" She sucked a breath as he let her slide away, losing the contact she needed. Laryssa never thought she could come from just a kiss but when his lips teased at hers, her body lit on fire. The energy rose within her and she let it go. She wanted this man, wanted him to know everything about her. No one had ever commanded her sexuality the way he'd done in just a few short hours. God help her, she had to have him in her life.

"Open for me," he told her as his mouth descended on hers.

Thirst rose and Léopold struggled to keep his fangs from descending. Whatever this woman was, he could not resist her. The thought of his cock and teeth buried deep inside of her flashed into his mind, and his stomach clenched in concern. So many years he'd been alone, and for the first time since he'd been turned, the idea of feeding and making love all at once was alluring to him. As she sucked on his bottom lip, the only thing that became important to him was bringing her to climax.

"Ah yes," she cried again into his mouth as he jerked her body against his.

"Tell me you want this."

"I need you...now...in me now." She wasn't usually so wanton, but damn, he'd refused her once and she wasn't about to let him back away again.

Losing all control, Léopold bent his knees, sheathing himself inside of her. A primal instinct took over as he waited but a second for her to accommodate his size before pumping out and back into her. Dropping his head to her chest, his lips found her breast. He took her ripe tip into his mouth, then sucked it hard, making her cry with pleasure.

Laryssa's breath caught at the welcome erotic intrusion. With unbridled frenzy, she thrust her hips into his, urging him to make love to her harder. His teeth tugged at her perky nipple, causing a sensation of blissful pain, something she'd never experienced in all her life. As he pounded up into her, he began to grind into her pelvis, caressing her clitoris in rhythm with her own movements. So close to going over the edge of orgasm, she dragged her fingernails down his back.

As Léopold's fangs elongated, he was forced to tear his lips away from her shimmering peaks. He could hear her pulse beating and it drove him into an animalistic fervor. Struggling to maintain discipline, he groaned. Just one sweet taste of her blood, and he'd begin a bond with this woman. Focusing on the feel of her tight pussy around his swollen flesh, he thrust up into her with long smooth strokes.

"Please, harder," she begged, panting for breath. Each slamming surge inside of her stroked the thin line of nerves within her channel. "I'm coming...I need to tell you."

What is she saying? Need to tell me what? Léopold couldn't concentrate, lost inside her. He increased the tempo, frantically pounding his cock into her pussy. He pressed his forehead to the cool tile, refusing the temptation to sink his teeth into her inviting skin. *No blood. No damn blood. Just fuck her and be done.* His fangs pierced his own lip in the process.

"Leo," Laryssa cried into his chest as her climax claimed her. She could feel herself spasming around him, unable to stop the crushing waves of power and ecstasy that rolled over her again and again.

"Fuck, yes, I'm coming. Ah, Goddess," Léopold grunted as he jerked fiercely. Stiffening, he came hard, grateful he'd restrained himself.

A few minutes passed before Léopold released her from his grip, gently sliding himself from her warmth. He glanced up to her flushed face, her wide eyes pinned on his. Despite not tasting of her blood, he could feel a connection to this woman. *Jesus Christ Almighty, this is what I've worked so hard to avoid.* He was a fucking asshole for taking her this way, brutally taking her in the shower after she'd been attacked. The shame in his eyes was evident but he doubted she'd know how he felt. Determined not to share his feelings, he wouldn't tell her. But he owed it to her to make sure she was all right.

"Merde, I'm sorry." He shook his head and stepped backward out of her reach. "Are you okay?"

"Why are you sorry? I feel great," she said truthfully. It had been so long since she'd had sex and for the love of all that was holy, she'd reveled in her orgasm.

By the way he was looking at her, she could tell he regretted being with her already. She sighed and turned herself into the spray, washing away the evidence of their love making. *Screw him. I'm not about to let some temperamental vampire make me feel guilty or ashamed for what I did.* If he was looking for a one-off, then that's all it would be. But she'd be damned if she'd let him ruin the afterglow for her. At least for her, life was too damn short not to enjoy mind-blowing sex.

"It's just that I told you," he began.

"Yeah, I know, I know. You don't do relationships. Got it, big guy."

"You were just attacked. You need time to heal…we shouldn't have done this."

"Hey." She turned to face him and poked him in the chest. "Don't you fucking tell me that bullshit, Leo. You hear me? This…whatever this was…was consensual and felt amazing. God, you have issues."

Laryssa looked around the open-blocked shower and tried to find the exit through the steam. Refusing to spend one more second with this man, she moved to get away from him, and he grabbed her hand.

"Please, it's not what you think. I'm sorry. I just wanted to make sure you were okay. I shouldn't have been so rough when we made love." Léopold embraced her. "You're right. It was amazing…you're amazing."

With certainty, Léopold knew that he'd been so wrong about her. No, his Laryssa wasn't a rabbit at all. She was a survivor and a fighter, unafraid to call him out on his atrocious behavior. He closed his eyes, allowing himself to feel every surface of their skin that joined. She and the intimacy she laid at his feet terrified him more than any demon. For the first time in his life, he wondered if he'd be able to continue to live within his own restrictions.

·⚜· *Chapter Seven* ·⚜·

Léopold turned on the heat lamp, guiding Laryssa out of the shower. She took in her surroundings, aware that she'd missed them when he'd relocated them from the lake to the bathroom. Italian architecture echoed throughout the space, with its dark mahogany cabinetry and cream marbled floors. Before she had a chance to walk any further, he wrapped a warm towel around her shoulders.

"Let me," he said in a dark low tone.

"But I can dry myself," she protested.

"I insist," he told her, leaving her no quarter for argument. Placing a bath rug on the floor, he knelt before her, bringing the towel from her shoulders with him so that it trailed down her back.

The act of each soft brush of the Egyptian cotton on her skin was the single most intimate touch she'd ever experienced. Laryssa rested her hands on Léopold's shoulders, reflecting on how they had just made love in the shower. They'd been unleashed, utterly wild with desire. Then he'd grown distant. Despite his apology, it was as if he'd turned off a part of himself emotionally. Yet his behavior continued to conflict with the killer he'd touted himself to be.

"What were you going to tell me when I was inside you?" he asked, caressing the towel down her legs. Slowly, he dried each foot, and then drew the terrycloth up her left inner thigh. He repeated the process on her right leg.

"Naiad. I'm a naiad," she confessed. Relief and concern swirled through her mind, but she was soon caught off guard when he glided his fingertips over her mound.

"I love your smooth pussy. Just a little trail of hair here…very pretty," he commented.

"Um, thanks," she laughed. No one she'd ever been with had ever commented on her lady garden, let alone been on his knees in front of her inspecting it like he was looking at a rare flower. "Aren't you going to say anything?"

"I want to lick you until you can't speak your own name. Shall we give it a try?" He glanced up to her, catching her gaze and gave her a naughty grin.

"Okay. Well that sounds really nice and all, but didn't you just say that we couldn't do this?" She pointed to the shower then to her chest and to him. "Not that I'm disagreeing with you. That sounds pretty tempting to me, but you seem to have a problem deciding whether or not you want to be with me."

"Pas de problème, ma chérie. I want you, don't ever doubt that. It's the bond, the emotions that can form. Complications and such. I suppose I am wavering. On my knees before you, the only thing I can think of is how much I want to drag my tongue over your pink lips."

"If you don't stop, I'm going to demand it. Seriously, Leo, aren't you going to say anything? After everything I just told you…about what I am and you haven't said one word about it." As much as she wanted to discuss it, the idea of Léopold giving her oral sex was extraordinarily attractive. She grew wet with arousal again and she knew he'd smell it on her.

"Well how am I supposed to concentrate when I'm so close to you like this? You taste sweet, no?" Léopold leaned forward and darted his tongue through her slit, tracing over her beaded treasure until he felt her shiver into his mouth. He licked his lips like a satisfied cat. "Ah, oui. Délicieux."

"Léopold," Laryssa cried. *What is it with this man? He must be well versed in the fine art of torture.* She couldn't decide whether or not to grab his hair, and encourage him to finish what he'd started or slap him out of frustration. But before she had a chance to make a final decision, he quickly patted her pussy dry and had pushed onto his feet, standing before her.

"A nymph, oui?"

"Kind of…I guess."

"Here, put this on." He handed her his bathrobe. "I cannot concentrate on a single word you're saying when you're like this."

"You mean like this?" She smiled and took the black garment from his hands. Refusing to put it on, she draped it over her forearm and put her hand on her hip, giving him a full view of her body.

"Exactly like that. Now, put it on." He wrapped his towel around his waist and walked out into the bedroom.

"You're very bossy for someone who was just on his knees," she commented flippantly.

"You're a bit mouthy for someone who was just screaming my name," he countered.

"Should I give you the pleasure of being on your knees again, I'll try to keep that in mind." She rolled her eyes and put on the bathrobe. "So what? No questions? No 'what else can you do'? Or does the wise one already know all there is to know about naiads?"

"Come sit." He gestured to a double width chaise that curved on both ends. Lined in copper studs, its brown leather appeared well conditioned but comfortably worn.

Wide eyed and incredulous, Laryssa stared at him.

"Please sit," he drawled.

"See? That wasn't so difficult, now was it?" She sashayed past Leo, trailing a finger over his bare chest, giving him a flirty smile. Sitting down into the lounge, she curled into it like a kitten and laid her head back on the cushion.

"You are a difficult woman, no?"

"Oui," she teased.

"We need to talk, Laryssa." Léopold walked over to a large antique armoire and opened its doors. Pulling out a decanter and two snifters he set them on his desk and began to pour them a drink. "I've met a few nymphs, but I've never seen one do what you do. While they're known in mythology to be dangerous, I've never met one that was. Aside from needing water, drawing energy from water, I haven't ever met one who could move objects. Here," he said, extending the glass to her.

With a small smile, she accepted it. She shook her head, amused, but not surprised that he hadn't bothered to ask her if she even wanted a drink. He was aggravating yet undeniably thoughtful.

"Thanks."

"You're very welcome," he replied, sensing her internal struggle with his dominance. "Now tell me, were you born naiad? It's rumored you are created as goddesses of the rivers. Some say the daughters of Zeus. Others? The daughters of Poseidon. I, however, believe mythology to be just that…a myth. The supernatural world, through magic or perhaps evolution has created splinter races."

"I wasn't born naiad. I'm human…or I should say, was human. Raised in a small town in Ohio…just like everyone else."

"How'd it happen?" Léopold sidled up next to Laryssa, wrapping an arm around her.

"I died. Well, I drowned. But I'm pretty sure I died."

"How?"

"I was thirteen. Mom had told me not to go skating alone, but my friend, Lauren couldn't go with me that day. And as you may have noticed, I'm determined when I want to be."

"Stubborn? Really? I don't believe it," he said, his words laced in sarcasm.

"I prefer the term 'strong willed'. It's an asset, you know?"

"Whatever you say, ma chérie. Go on."

"Long story short, I lied. I told mom Lauren was going when she wasn't. It had been at freezing temps for over a week. The ice should've been strong, but as I found out, it was thin near where the creek spilled into the lake. It was stupid of me, I know. But I was just a kid. I can still remember the loud sound, the creaking. And then I saw the crack. The ice began shifting. I tried to skate off to get to the other side, but I wasn't fast enough. It all happened pretty quickly."

Laryssa took a sip of her brandy. It was such a long time ago, but she'd never forget the helplessness as she slipped into her icy grave. Screaming as she plunged into the abyss, she knew no one would hear her.

"I'm not sure exactly what happened. I just remember panicking, scraping at the sheets of ice, trying to get leverage to pull myself out. I really tried so hard to get out, but the longer I struggled…I got so tired. I couldn't think straight and my hands," Laryssa pulled at her fingers, remembering the way the cold had immobilized them, "I remember slipping into the icy pond, unable to hold on and then gasping for air. And once I was all the way underneath the water, I couldn't stop from breathing it in. The water, it just suffocated me."

Léopold put down his drink on the floor and gently took her hands in his, massaging her palms with his thumbs.

"I don't know…it was dark. But then all of a sudden, it was light. Not like how people describe when they are dying with *the* light…you know, the one they say you'll see when you die. This was different. There was no tunnel or anything. Just this bright light and then this woman was there, and she was talking to me like we weren't underneath the water. She told me she was naiad and that she was giving me her gift."

"And then you woke up?"

"Well, not exactly. I mean, the woman, she was so calm and beautiful. I can still remember she had this flowing, fiery red hair and it was kind of fanned out in the water, like these magical little tendrils dancing. I don't remember much after seeing her. Only that just for a second, right before I woke up, I felt this darkness…kinda how it felt tonight. It all was so fast, though."

"Did they find you?"

"Well, yeah. My friend had called the house while I was out, and I was totally busted. When my parents found out that I wasn't with Lauren, they went to the lake, saw my gear on the edge of it but not me. I didn't regain consciousness until I was in the ambulance. I'd been under for nearly an hour and a half. They called it a miracle…at least until I came home."

"Is that when you realized your abilities?"

"You know, it just seemed like a dream. All of it. Dying. Seeing that woman. The darkness. Waking up and then in the hospital, I was just me. I didn't feel any different. But within a week of being home, I started to notice this energy…my energy. I can't explain it but I became obsessed with the lake. I'd sneak out of my parents' house. At first, I'd just submerge my hands. And then one day, a few months later, I became angry about something. I was in my room and instead of picking up a pillow to throw it, I just thought it, like I was going to grab it but I hadn't. It flew across the room."

"That must have been scary, no? I remember how it felt after I was turned. No one had mentored me either," he mused.

"I was scared to death. I thought I was going crazy but I remembered that one word. *Naiad.* I went to the library and researched everything I could find about naiads, which wasn't exactly helpful because as you pointed out, most of what people know is just mythology. Not exactly reality."

"And your parents?"

"They weren't having any of it. They are very, very conservative. Of course, I hid it at first. But when my mom caught me moving things in my room, the next thing I knew they had the priest at the house. They thought

I was possessed or something. When they caught me a second time, my mother slapped me across the face, grounded me. And the third time...well, they sent me off to live with my aunt in Chicago."

"How old were you?"

"Fifteen. Aunt Mary wasn't too bad but she wasn't exactly the best role model...drank way too much and brought home lots of strange men. The one thing she did teach me was waitressing. She got me a job at her diner. The day after I graduated high school, I left for Vegas using the money I saved."

"Not much water in the Mojave desert."

"Yeah. I never realized how much of a problem that would be. What can I say? I was young and naïve. I just wanted to get away, to disappear. I knew how to waitress and I thought, 'why not Vegas?'"

"Ah, the lessons of youth."

"In hindsight, I should have known it wasn't a good idea. When I was first changed, putting my hands in a pond or a river was enough to satisfy my need for water. Of course, I tried a pool but that didn't work. It's not part of nature. Anyhow, by the time I moved in with my aunt, I'd begun swimming in fresh water at least once a week. I think she knew that I was sneaking out to Lake Michigan, but she never said anything. It wasn't until my sixteenth birthday that I started to realize that I needed the water in order to thrive. If I didn't go, I'd be exhausted, barely waking up or able to go to school. The longer I went without it, the weaker I'd get. When I got to Las Vegas, though, that's when I learned the hard lesson that if I don't have it, I'll die."

"I imagine a water nymph wouldn't do so well there."

"Yeah, I'm not sure what I thought at the time. Have you ever been to Vegas in July? It's hotter than hell. I'd just turned eighteen and was working in this little all-night diner, staying in a fleabag motel." Laryssa swiped her hand across her eyes. "It was awful. But it was the first time that there was no one to answer to about my 'abilities', no one to make me feel bad about what I was doing. In the end, I only lasted a few months. I had to go all the way out to Lake Mead for my water. I was only going maybe once every two weeks. I knew it wasn't enough, but I couldn't find the time with my work schedule. Also, I think I really just wanted to be normal, so I'd convince myself that I didn't need the water. Denial is a wonderful thing...well, until I crashed. One night I went out to the desert with a friend, I almost died. I should've known. I'd been feeling sick all week."

"A boyfriend?" Léopold shouldn't care, he knew, yet an unfamiliar pain of irritation jabbed at his chest. *Jealousy?* He dismissed it as soon as he thought the word. *Possessiveness perhaps?* Yes, that was more his style. Léopold collected, possessed...*things* that belonged to him.

"No. Yes. Well, it was a guy that I'd seen a few times. You know, we'd fooled around."

"Fooled around?"

"Yeah, you know. We dated. Kissed. I think he may have gotten a little further, but we didn't have sex."

"I see." Léopold remained calm and indifferent. But a fire grew behind his eyes as he thought of Laryssa kissing someone else. *No, this can't happen to me. I don't care who she dated.* As she continued her story, he fought to concentrate, disturbed by his own revelation that he didn't think he'd be able to tolerate her seeing other men, not ever again.

"Where was I?" From her position in his arms, Laryssa was unable to see the look of consternation Léopold wore. Taking a deep breath, she continued. "The desert. By the time we got out there, I was so lethargic that I couldn't get out of his car. I felt myself dying. I begged him to drive me to the lake, to put me in the water. God, I can't imagine what he thought. I was like a crazy woman going on and on about needing water. He had to carry and literally dump me in the lake."

Léopold laughed.

"Hey, be nice." She gave him a small nudge with her elbow. "It wasn't funny. So you can imagine what happened next?"

"I'm afraid to ask." He'd seen the way she'd peacefully lay at the bottom of Lake Ponchartrain, but to a human, she may have appeared dead.

"You saw it, didn't you?" Laryssa turned in his arms so that she could look into his eyes.

"I saw you all right. I thought you were drowning…but you were beautiful. You lit up the water."

"The water. It feeds me energy. I don't know the exact science behind it."

"There's science to being a vampire, witch or wolf?" He laughed.

"Point taken. But you have to remember, and you've got to know what this feels like because you were turned, not born a vampire, there is this human part of me that seeks answers. Not nebulous magic fairy answers. Hard facts."

"I do remember, but I've lived a long time. There are some things in our lives that are better left a mystery."

"Yes, but my glowing?"

Léopold smiled as he recalled the sight of her naked form illuminating the entire lake bed. It had startled him, but also had been a spectacular display.

"From a scientific standpoint, it's bioluminescence. It's found in plants, animals, even insects."

"But not humans," he replied.

"Exactly. The guy, I was with in the desert… I think his name was Scott, well, he completely freaked out. Not only did I go into the water, sinking clear to the bottom, I lit up like a Christmas tree. Twenty minutes later when I re-emerged, he was gone. I knew he'd tell everyone at work, so I hitched a ride back to the motel, packed my stuff and drove cross country to New Orleans. It was embarrassing, but it was also a wake-up call. It sure as hell snapped me out of my denial. Once I got here, I worked for a few months before getting a scholarship to the University. I studied art history. After undergrad, I took on a graduate assistantship, got my masters."

"Lots of water, here, that's for sure."

"Yeah, it's a good place for me. I pretty much stick to the river. It's close. Easy access. I don't get out here too often, but the basin works. Bayou, too. The humidity in the air helps."

"When did you first start seeing the dark ones?"

"Pretty much as soon as I got here. My friend, Avery, the witch I told you about, she was my roommate. I needed to confide in someone. Not only was she supportive, but she began right away creating spells and wards to hide me, my energy. I'd go a few years not seeing any of them and then, 'bam', one would show up in an alleyway. Avery would work her magic and then I'd disappear again…like they couldn't see me. When you saw me at Mordez, I was there to talk to Avery."

"I've never seen you there before," he commented, brushing a hair from her face.

"And you would know this how?" she teased. Laryssa inwardly cringed, thinking of what Léopold did at that place. Sex, blood, dancing and pretty much whatever a supernatural craved could be found there.

"I think you know the answer to that," he replied without apology. Not only did he frequent the establishment when he was in town, he'd engaged in about every activity they had to offer. If he told her what he'd done, she'd really know the beast she'd just made love to. The knowledge of his true behavior would sever whatever attraction they had. For the rest of tonight, at least, he'd save her that anguish.

"Avery said she couldn't help me, that she needed to talk with Ilsbeth. I'm not crazy about her telling the leader of her coven, but I'm desperate. That same dreadful feeling that came over me tonight when I talked to the demon… it's been plaguing me for weeks."

"We should've talked with Ilsbeth today. Unfortunately, she's been out of town."

"Couldn't we FaceTime or Skype?"

Léopold laughed. "High tech solutions to low tech problems. Ilsbeth prefers her meetings in person. She wants to read auras, get a feel for the people she decides to help."

"But she's a witch. What does she know about naiads or demons for that matter?"

"Ilsbeth knows lots of things. I find her a bit of an ice queen, but the woman may be able to help us. She's been around longer than you can imagine and keeps her spoon in many pots."

"Why do you think this demon wants Ava?" Laryssa asked.

"Not sure, but I do know it tried to kill her."

"I've only met one other naiad before. She was here for a convention and came into my store. Her energy was so compelling. I couldn't ignore it. So I confronted her, got her to have lunch with me."

"You're tough, aren't you, pet?"

"She described the same type of experience I had. She'd gone swimming in a lake as a child and drowned. She died." Laryssa paused, trying to figure out how the baby was turned. "This might sound crazy but what if Ava died too?"

"But she was alive when I took her from the snow. Trust me, I know dead, and she was very much alive."

"She could have died before you heard her. Maybe she died and then began to cry when she was touched by the woman who touched me," Laryssa speculated.

"Okay, but she wasn't in water," Léopold replied.

"No, but she was in snow. Snow is just another state of water."

"It's not possible. Even if she had died, we have no connection as to why the demon would target her. The Alpha did tell us that she'd glowed before she'd been stolen, and also said something about an evil presence...like you've described. But we still don't know where the father is, if he's alive or not. We only know that her mother died."

"It's not Ava. She's not evil. I can feel her. She's pure and sweet. Her aura was shining brightly when you held her. A lovely yellow color. I guess I forgot the part about reading auras...I think I was around sixteen when I started noticing the colors," she commented.

"And what does my aura tell you?" Léopold asked.

"Hmm...let's see." Laryssa slowly climbed atop of Léopold, straddling him with her legs. Spearing her fingers into the back of his hair, she tilted her head and licked her lips. "Ah yes, I see it now. Your aura shows that you enjoy telling people what to do. You're dominant in all aspects of your life, expecting everyone to submit to the mighty vampire you know you are. You keep people at a distance, pushing them away so you don't have to feel. You've been hurt, maybe? So you run hot and cold with your emotions...well, mostly cold. But beneath the surface of what we all see, you have unbridled passion in your mind and heart. And you're a highly sexual being. One who craves a certain brunette naiad but won't admit he wants to kiss her, to make her yours."

"You're making this up, aren't you?" In a flash, Léopold had her in his arms and tossed her onto his bed. She landed on her back, giggling.

"I think I could make some extra money in Jackson Square telling fortunes. What do you think?" she laughed.

"You lie, temptress," he growled with a devious smile. Léopold leapt upon her. Placing each of his knees to the side of her waist, he tore off his towel. Effectively immobilizing her hips with his own, he adjusted his semi-erect cock so that it lay heavy on her belly.

"I told you. You don't scare me," she taunted.

Laryssa took in the sight of him, hovering above her like a Greek God. Léopold's ordinarily neatly combed hair was messy and damp. His taut muscles strained as he poised to attack. She knew he'd been careful not to hurt her when he threw her onto the sheets, but he left no doubt that he sought to assert his dominance. Even in play, he was forceful, demanding. Like a feral wolf, he flashed his fangs, stalking his prey. Unable to resist the allure of her sexy predator, she reached her hand upward and traced the tip of her forefinger along his bottom lip.

"You like to play with fire, no?" Clutching the lapels of her robe, Léopold jerked it open, exposing her creamy breasts.

Laryssa gasped as the cool air hit her skin. She closed her eyes and took a deep breath. As her hooded eyes opened slowly, a wide smile broke across her face.

"I want to touch them."

"What?"

"I said I. Want. To. Touch. Them." She extenuated every word before reaching up to his mouth.

Léopold could not believe this woman showed no fear. Hundreds of women had flirted with him, attempted seduction but underneath all their acts, they all bled fear as well as blood. As she trailed the pad of her thumb down his fang, he sucked a breath. *Fuck, what is she doing? Does she have a death wish?* The sound of her sweet laughter filled the room as she plunged her finger into his mouth. His lips captured her thumb like a frog catching a fly. Swirling his tongue over her skin, he smiled until he heard her moan. Only seconds passed before he once again took control.

"Léopold," Laryssa cried as he snatched her wrists and pinned her to the bed. She attempted to move but he'd effectively restrained her. The sensation of being trapped beneath him caused her to grow wet with arousal. But as she tried to move her hips, he applied more pressure, further stilling her movement.

"Going somewhere?"

"Let me go," she demanded. Her back arched as he blew warm air over her nipples. The low rumble of his laughter wrapped around her, promising her pleasure. The bare flesh between her legs moistened, and she was left quivering with need.

"Would you like to read my aura now?" He asked as he settled his chin into the hollow between her breasts. With his eyes on hers, he brushed his lips against her hot skin.

"I don't need to read your aura to know that you'll lose."

"I never lose."

"You'll lose your fight to keep your heart closed." Laryssa tugged again at her arms, relishing the tightness of his grip.

"Perhaps I should gag my little naiad. There are many things you don't know about me."

"There're many things you don't know about me either," she countered. Using her feet, she pressed her hips upward, slowly grinding her body into his. "It's true that I tremble, but that's not fear you detect. It's desire."

"Don't test me, pet. Make no mistake, this isn't play." As he said the words, he prayed it to be true. Her arousal was as fragrant to him as an expensive Parisian perfume. The enticing scent permeated the room, driving him mad. She mocked him. She thirsted for him. He should walk away, leave her alone. But as his tongue probed one of her throbbing peaks, he knew in that moment that he had to finish the game. Like every being in the city, she was his to take.

"Ah, but it is you who errs, Leo. I know full well what I'm doing." *Oh God I hope so. This vampire could break my heart.* His lips on her sensitive nipples. His smooth voice in her ears. His colossal strength wrapped around her like a steel band. It was all too much to resist. Hell, she didn't want to even try. She just wanted to feel and have him feel every shiver he caused.

"You're a brave one. Bewitching." Léopold smiled and captured her breast in his mouth, rolling its tip with his tongue. She moaned in response, and he sucked it hard, careful not to nick her with his teeth.

"Oh my God!" she screamed at the pain. Her core pulsed in response. A hot ache grew in her belly, one that only he could satisfy.

"You continue to surprise me, Laryssa. You sass me yet wish to submit?"

"No," she lied. "It's not true."

"Oui. Your body doesn't lie." Léopold pressed her left wrist into her other, shackling both of her arms, freeing his right hand.

"No, no, no." She continued to deny it, shaking her head. "You don't know me. You don't want to know me."

"You challenge me?" If she only knew how wrong she was. Every second he spent with her would make it more difficult for him to let her go. He wanted to know everything about her from what she liked to eat for breakfast to how many strokes it took to push her over the edge of orgasm.

"It's not a challenge. It's just that...well, you've been clear."

"I thought we already established that I want you very much. Do not change the subject. Look at the way your skin flushes, unable to move. You like this, no?"

"I don't...I can't," she whispered. *Why is he pushing me? What difference does it make if I like it or not?* In the morning, he'd leave her. He didn't want her in his life.

"Shall we see?" Léopold reached between her legs, spreading her slick folds apart. He flickered the tips of his fingers at her entrance, not yet penetrating her heat. As he did so, she cried out his name. "So very wet. Ah, you lie about what you desire...you fancy this, don't you? You do. I think you'll enjoy your submission quite nicely."

"It doesn't matter," she gritted out, panting. She squeezed her legs together trying to assuage the growing pressure but he removed his hand and gave a light tap to her mound.

"No cheating. No coming yet, pet. And oui, it very much matters." Slowly, he glided his fingers back through her slippery lips, avoiding her clitoris. He caught her gaze and gave her a sensual smile. "It was you who read my aura. You started this and now I intend to finish it. My fortune teller thinks I'm dominant, no? I may not be able to read an aura, but your pussy tells me all I need to know. Your body doesn't lie, but I want to hear it from your lips. Tell me, ma chérie, do you want me to dominate you?"

"No...yes. I don't know."

Without warning Léopold thrust a thick finger into her, making her groan in pleasure. He could feel her contracting around him, certain she enjoyed it.

"Oh God, yes."

"So willing and submissive when given the freedom to be so." He yearned to break her, to make her want only him.

"Léopold, please. No more games," she cried as he added another finger. Her satiny flesh tightened around him, anticipating every stroke he gave.

"I don't play games."

"Now it's you who lies," she moaned as he continued to draw out the tension, edging her closer toward climax.

"No games. No lies. Do you, little nymph, wish to submit to me? A fantasy, perhaps?" Léopold speculated that she'd spent so many years hiding not only her identity but her wish to explore her own sexuality. Her ragged breaths grew more frequent as he moved deep within her. Pressing his chest against her belly, he brushed his lips against hers.

"Yes. Oh God, yes!" she screamed as she began to convulse at his hand. Laryssa hated that he knew her dark secret, loved that he wasn't afraid to push her boundaries. Rocked by uncontrollable pleasure, a tear of bliss ran down her cheek.

Léopold slipped his fingers away, driving the hard length of his cock inside her in one swift motion. Without haste, he tenderly made love to her. Releasing her wrists, he braced himself with one hand, so as not to crush her, and with his other, cupped her cheek so that he could gaze into her eyes. The moisture brimming from her lids provided evidence of the implications of what they'd done by having sex. Emotions he hadn't felt in centuries welled up inside his chest. Laryssa was so much more than he'd ever expected. There'd be no meaningless fuck with her. No, if given the opportunity, he'd realize his true desire, which was to know everything about her, to make her his. The sweet pain of his epiphany tore at him, knowing that he couldn't keep her.

"You fascinate me, Laryssa. So very, very beautiful," he confided breathlessly, crushing his lips to hers.

Pouring all of the feelings he'd never confess to her, he kissed her passionately as if he'd never see her again. All of Laryssa's thoughts vanished, replaced with nothing but the vampire who held her in his arms. As he swept his tongue against hers, claiming her mouth, she welcomed the intimacy of his onslaught. Kissing, sucking, tasting of each other, their bodies became one.

As their kiss deepened, they moved simultaneously, slowly increasing the tempo of their rhythm. Léopold's hands glided down her sides, finally reaching her hips. Deliberately, he began to circle his pelvis against hers, stimulating her most sensitive flesh.

"You feel so fucking good," he grunted. .

"So close. Don't stop," she begged, tearing her lips away, gasping for air. Laryssa arched her back, rubbing herself against him.

Léopold rocked faster and faster, brushing back and forth against her clitoris. The spasms of her hot core pulsed around his cock, causing him to suck in a quick breath. She shivered beneath him and he could no longer stop the inevitable. With slamming thrusts, he pounded into her as she cried his name again and again.

Seized in ecstasy, Laryssa surged her hips up to meet his. As her release slammed into her, she stiffened against him, milking every spasm. Her head thrashed side to side, her nails digging into his buttocks. As pleasure claimed her, Léopold gave a loud grunt, erupting deep inside her. Together, they lay motionless as the last quivering pulses rolled through them.

Laryssa curled her body against Léopold as he slowly removed his spent shaft from inside her and brought her up onto his chest. Terrified to look into his eyes, she silently wiped at the tears that continued to fall. *How stupid am I to think that I could make love with someone like Léopold and walk away with my heart intact?*

Powerful and charismatic, Léopold had cut through her defenses as easily as a hot knife sliced through butter. If she stayed with him a minute longer, he'd push her to new heights. Not only would she submit to him sexually, she'd give him her heart. And he'd crush it. With a firm resolve, she vowed to herself that this would be the last time she made love to him. Gorgeous and dominant, he was everything she'd ever want in a lover. But he'd been clear about his intentions from the beginning. They had no future.

Léopold felt her trembling in his arms. No words were needed to tell him what they both knew to be true. Making love had been a spectacular, earth-shattering experience, cloaked in satisfaction but also a sense of loss. It couldn't happen again. Staring at the ceiling, Léopold stroked her hair, hoping it would offer her the comfort she needed to let go. But as he did so, he wondered where he'd get the strength to do the same.

ᴓ Chapter Eight ᴓ

"Bonjour, mon ami," Léopold commented as he strode into the great room, giving a wave to Dimitri. "See you got my text. Arnaud saw to your arrival?"

"Yeah, got it last night at around four in the morning. You vamps really don't sleep, do you?" Dimitri asked, taking a long draw of his coffee.

"I rest when I need it. Besides, as you know, I prefer the night. Why today's supernaturals wish to walk in the daylight is beyond comprehension. The night is the mother of our strength. Why subject yourself to being the likeness of a human in the sun when you can be a mighty lion by the moon?"

"Well, I'm with you there. I do love a good moon." Dimitri gave a guttural howl and laughed. Some days he couldn't get enough of teasing the vampire. Most days, actually. "Hey, you remember meeting Jake, right?"

"Oui." Léopold rolled his eyes in response to the wolf's incessant howling. He nodded and passed by them into the kitchen.

"Gotcha a café au lait. It's on the counter."

"Merci." Léopold opened the lid of the paper cup and sniffed. "Nectar of the Gods."

"See, he still acts normal every now and then," Dimitri joked to Jake.

"Doesn't seem right, is all."

"I need blood to survive. Coffee, on the other hand, just tastes good. It's not as if I can't appreciate the finer epicurean delights that life has to offer." Léopold circled the table and sat down.

"I've seen some of your so-called epicurean delights and they all look female," Dimitri noted.

"Pleasure comes in all forms," he smiled.

Dimitri eyed Léopold as it occurred to him that his typically well-dressed friend was wearing nothing more than black pajama bottoms. His disheveled state piqued his curiosity.

"Hey Leo, what's with the shirtless look today?" Dimitri glanced at Jake and smiled. "Or is it that maybe Mr. GQ is finally loosening up?"

"He definitely works out a lot. Makes me want to get to the gym," Jake added, giving Dimitri a grin.

"Must be that all-protein diet regimen."

"Fuck you," Léopold laughed. "You do realize that when we're turned as adults, we stay in that form. But yeah, smartass, I work out."

"How'd you get so ripped? What'd you do in a previous life? Let me guess…a body builder? No wait. A lifeguard?" Jake suggested.

"Come on. Just look at him." Dimitri glanced to Léopold. "Too pale."

"A gym trainer?" Jake teased.

"No way. He's an old man. As in really old. Maybe a farmer…workin' the vineyards of France. Or, uh, soldier. Yeah, that's more like Leo. Some medieval black ops badass," Dimitri guessed.

Léopold smiled broadly and shook his head.

"That's it." Dimitri pointed at him. "I'm close, aren't I?"

Léopold sighed, debating whether or not to disclose his former profession. He didn't make a habit of discussing his life as a human. Too many bad memories. Yet, there was a camaraderie that he missed that existed when he'd served in the king's service, one that was similar to what wolves shared. He knew, though they baited him, they sought to create a connection. Dimitri already had his trust, his friendship.

"Oui. A knight. I served under King Hugh Capet. I was a warrior in his service in exchange for a fief, of course."

"Damn, bro, you've been holdin' out on me. I bet you have some great stories." Dimitri smacked his palm on the table in jest.

"Life was hard, very hard. France was merely coming together on its own when I was born. My stories will wait for another day, though. We should discuss today's agenda."

"You see how he does that?" Dimitri asked.

"Does what?" Jake looked to him and then Léopold, who was smiling.

"Avoids the topic. The man is smooth. Still haven't answered my original question, Sir Leo the vamp."

"What was the question?"

"Why aren't you dressed? I wasn't born yesterday. I know you, Leo. You're the most impeccable metrosexual guy I know. And here you are this morning, hair flying all over and half dressed. For the rest of us, totally normal. For you? Not so much. What gives?"

"Nothing at all. I heard you all jabbering about in my house and came to see what the fuss was about." He smiled coyly and raised his eyebrows.

Dimitri eyed Jake and then glanced to Léopold who silently sipped his coffee. He may not have known the vampire very long, but he knew his habits. Something was off. And then it occurred to him that he hadn't seen Laryssa. There was no way in hell that Léopold would be so casual with a woman in the house unless…

"How's Laryssa?" Dimitri asked pointedly. His eyes darted to Jake.

"She's fine," Léopold lied. He expected that Laryssa was as far from fine as she could get. At some point during the evening, she'd broken free of his embrace. She'd curled onto her side, facing away from him. Despite her ability to do so, she hadn't hidden her racing heartbeat. He'd known she was awake yet said nothing. After an hour, she threw back the covers and left the room, without looking back at him. No words. No kiss goodbye. Cold sheets were left in her wake. He should be happy, he knew. It was what he wanted, yet the loss of her bothered him far more than it should.

"You mentioned a demon. Where'd it show itself?" Dimitri asked.

"Down at the lake." Léopold nodded toward the windows.

"It came to you directly?"

"No, to Laryssa. I tried to get there in time, but she'd fallen into the lake."

"What? Somehow it took Laryssa from your house down to the lake?"

"No. She went down to the lake and it appeared to her there," Léopold told him without fully explaining.

"Am I missing something? I thought you said you were going to be with her," Jake interjected.

"I was with her, but then dinner arrived and well, you know...things became awkward. She was supposed to be going for a swim in the pool, not the damn lake."

"Wait a second. Let me get this straight. You bring a hot woman to your house. Then at some point you invite a donor over...aka hot chick number two. So Laryssa takes off out of disgust for your eating habits. Some people aren't a fan of blood," Dimitri conjectured. "Or she takes off because she's not into threesomes. Maybe jealous? Maybe she wanted one of those sex bites, herself?"

"Enough already," Léopold demanded. "I needed to feed. I will not deny who I am just because I foolishly decided to protect some woman. And just because Laryssa is 'hot' as you've put it, that doesn't mean I'm going to become attached to her."

"So you're telling me that when she left this house, she was a-okay with your, uh, naked takeout girl?"

Léopold sighed and stood up from the table. Glancing out onto the lake, he recalled the previous evening, how angry she'd been.

"No, she wasn't. She wasn't at all happy. But that is neither here nor there. What's done is done. She went to the lake and the demon appeared. It's given her one week to find the Tecpatl. The Tlalco Tecpatl to be exact."

"What the hell is a Tecpatl?" Dimitri got up from the table and placed his empty cup in the trash.

"An ancient sacrificial knife used by the Aztecs," Jake answered.

"How the hell did you know that?" Dimitri stared over to Jake in disbelief.

"I'm a fan of Mesoamerican history," he quipped.

"He's correct," Léopold affirmed.

"Human sacrifice. Gory shit," Jake added.

"You wolves do have a way with words," Léopold mused.

"So, how about Laryssa? Is she okay?" Dimitri inquired, still suspicious of the vampire's unkempt appearance.

"It clawed at her, but she fought it off and then it was gone."

"Did you just say it clawed at her? Is she hurt?" Dimitri approached Léopold so that they stood shoulder to shoulder, taking in the landscape. It was the first time he'd been to Léopold's lake house.

"No, she's fine, but..." Léopold didn't finish his sentence.

"But what? Exactly how does someone get swiped by a demon and be fine?"

"She's healed." While she was sleeping, he'd inspected the wound and not a trace of a scar was evident.

"I take it this has something to do with what she does?"

"Indeed, mon ami. But I promised her that I wouldn't tell anyone what she is, so don't bother asking. It's her story to tell. You can ask her when she comes out. My guess is that after that demon showed up, she'll tell you. But I cannot break my oath to her. I've already done enough to hurt her on my own without digging the hole any deeper," Léopold confessed. Turning to Dimitri, he raked his hand through his tousled hair.

Dimitri leaned toward his friend and sniffed. He shook his head, knowing the answer to the next question he was about to ask Léopold. "You fucked her didn't you? I can smell it."

"Must you be so uncouth?" Léopold replied, blowing out a breath.

"You did," Dimitri exclaimed. "Jesus Christ, Leo. Seriously, man. You can have any woman you want. Why her? You ever hear that expression, 'don't dip your pen in the company ink'?"

"Yes, I've fucking heard it, asshole. But she's just so…I don't know, she's just special. Goddammit, I know, okay? I know I fucked up."

"I don't see what the issue is here. I mean have you two idiots ever heard the term 'consenting adults'. What's the big deal?" Jake asked.

"The big deal is that he just fucking met her. And we need her to help us to keep Ava safe. If she's in danger, so is our Alpha. Laryssa was just starting to trust us, trust him, and lover boy here just can't keep it in his pants," Dimitri huffed, taking a seat at the table.

"He's right. There's no excuse," Léopold agreed. "It's not sleeping with a woman that's a problem, it's the fact that I can't…I won't have a relationship. It's not happening. And now that we've made love, well, it adds complications to our situation. Ones we didn't need."

"It would be one thing if you actually cared about anything besides yourself, Devereoux. But you don't. That's the thing. If you fucking hurt her…" Dimitri began.

"Why do you care about her anyway, wolf?" Léopold's eyes narrowed on Dimitri.

"Because, Leo," Dimitri stared at his friend. "She seemed kind of nice. And she stood up to that asshole, Luca. And for some reason, unbeknownst to me, she seems like she might actually care about you. Why is beyond me. And she cares about Ava too, and she has no reason to. We are the ones who sought her out. Now, not only have we upturned her life, we've brought a demon to her…right here to your goddamn house."

"I think we've established that I fucked up. I just said so. Can we just move on?"

"She's okay with one night? Because I know that you never have women sleepover. You've told me as much."

"I told her that I don't do relationships. I can't become involved with her. But you're correct in that we do need her. We need to find that knife."

"This isn't going to go well, you know that, right? I mean, I don't know Laryssa, but I saw the way she looked at you yesterday, and I have a hard time believing she's a one night stand kinda girl. Could be wrong? But damn, it was as if she had 'innocence' stamped on her forehead," Dimitri said.

"Please stop already. Okay?" Léopold tilted his head backwards, closed his eyes and wiped them with both of his hands out of frustration. "I get it. I'm a dick. I shouldn't have slept with her but I did. I can't take it back. I promise you that I'll do my best to repair this...'relationship' I've irresponsibly put at risk."

He choked on the word. *Relationship. No, no, no.* As if it wasn't bad enough that he was developing feelings for Laryssa, now Dimitri had him filled with guilt for what he'd done. Damn wolves. Damn humans. For a moment, he wished he could go back to not caring about his new friend. But no matter how he tried, what was done was done. *Merde. I'm truly fucked.*

Laryssa heard shouting coming from the great room and thought to give them fair warning she was approaching. Dimitri had mentioned her name, and she suspected that whatever they were arguing about, it had to do with her. As curious as she was, she was still reeling from her night with Léopold.

Earlier, she'd gone to take a shower to wash away the memories of her night with him, hoping it'd make her forget the way he'd stirred passion within her. It wasn't as if she hadn't felt his heat mere inches away from her body as they lay in bed. She'd known that even the slightest brush of her skin against his would have broken her resolve to leave. She'd been awake for hours, sensing that he was watching her. But not a word was spoken, nor a caress exchanged. The heavy tension had strangled her, causing her to flee.

The hot spray of the shower had matched the tears that fell down her face. As a vampire, she'd known that he'd hear her. So with every heaving breath, she stifled the sound. Thirty minutes later, she'd convinced herself that her good old-fashioned cry was due to the stress of keeping her secret for so long. Her intense reaction to making love was simply lust, nothing more. She told herself that she needed to think with her head, not what her heart told her it wanted. He'd been up front about his intentions, unbending in his ways. She supposed she'd just have to accept it. She wasn't foolish enough to try to change a man. It'd never work, she knew.

Still, as she stood drying her skin, disappointment washed over her, as she realized he hadn't come after her. The reality of the situation was that she'd just had a one night stand. Whatever she thought she felt, she swore to bury it so deep that she wouldn't feel a thing the next time she saw him.

But as she walked into the room, her eyes flashed to Léopold's and a rush of excitement tightened in her belly. *No, Laryssa don't.* Struggling to get control over her reaction, she averted her eyes to the two good-looking men who sat at the kitchen table. She remembered the tall man with the goatee and tattoos as the person who'd driven her to Logan's home. Dimitri, beta of Acadian wolves. The other man looked as if he was a soldier, with his square jaw and tightly cropped hair.

"Good morning," Laryssa said loudly, interrupting their quarrel.

"Laryssa," Léopold sighed, giving her a small smile.

"Léopold. Um, hi." Hearing her name on Léopold's lips startled Laryssa. The last time he'd said her name with his French accent in that low smooth tone, he'd been buried deep inside her.

Léopold, at a loss for words, let his eyes roam over Laryssa. With only a touch of light pink gloss to her lips and very little makeup, Laryssa displayed an innate beauty he suspected she didn't realize existed. Loose brunette curls fell unrestrained over her shoulders, complementing the tight white shirt that clung to her curves. Her black jeans with matching leather riding boots gave her a contemporary look, tempting him to run his hands over her hips and buttocks. A hungry smile emerged across his face as he wondered if she'd enjoy a riding crop.

He sniffed into the air, enthralled with the ambrosial aroma of her essence that he'd remembered from the night before. Only now she smelled like soap and almonds. Underneath it all, her natural scent remained ingrained in his mind. The urge to taste her overwhelmed him and his gums tingled in response, his fangs begging to release. He glanced to the wolves, who had been watching him like a hawk. Slapped into reality by Dimitri's grimace, he broke out of his spell, and quickly concealed his reaction to her.

"You remember Dimitri and Jake from yesterday, no? Let's see, I have breakfast for you. Arnaud brought it. I'd texted him while you were sleeping. I hope you like fruit. Some pastries. Let me see what he brought." *Merde, I sound like a love-struck fool.* Léopold cringed at how he was speaking to her in front of Dimitri and Jake. Quickly, he rummaged through his refrigerator, retrieving the items he'd asked Arnaud to bring and set them on the counter. He pulled a plate, flatware and napkin out of his cupboards and placed them on the breakfast bar, away from the wolves. "Here you go. Dimitri brought coffee."

"Thank you," she quietly replied. Giving a small smile to Dimitri and Jake, she sat down on a stool and stared at the feast that was big enough for ten people. "There's plenty here. Maybe we should put it all on the table. Would you guys like some?"

"Thank you, Laryssa," Dimitri said, thoroughly enjoying watching his friend squirm. "At least someone here has manners, huh, Jake?"

"Hey, why didn't you serve us? I'd love some mango," Jake added.

"Because if I'd offered it to you first there'd be nothing left for the lady. Dogs get scraps," Léopold countered.

"Hey, hey, hey. No need to get nasty, bro. We brought coffee. Just sayin'," Dimitri teased.

"Yeah, right." The truth of the matter was that Léopold had simply forgotten about the food. As he pulled out extra plates from a cabinet, he glanced over to see her taking a bite of a strawberry and nearly dropped them. The juice dripped down over her pink lips and she caught it, licking her finger.

"Don't you love fruit?" Dimitri asked, smiling like a Cheshire cat. Léopold had it bad, and it was even funnier that he kept saying that he didn't want a relationship. Maybe this wasn't exactly a relationship, but Laryssa was definitely having an effect on him.

"Tais-toi," Léopold scolded, annoyed that Dimitri and Jake were practically undressing her with their eyes as she ate. The more he told himself he shouldn't care, the closer he was to throwing her over his shoulder and taking her to his bedroom.

"Come on, man. You know I've got this thing about watching girls with food."

Laryssa looked over at Dimitri, hearing his comment and laughed.

"Come sit with me. Please. There's plenty here for all of us. Y'all are making me self-conscious watching me stuff my face." She patted the seat of the chair next to her.

"I'd love to," Dimitri said and obediently sat down. "See how nice your girlfriend is. You could teach him some manners."

"I'm not his girlfriend. We barely know each other," she stated calmly with her eyes pinned on Léopold's.

"Really?" Dimitri inquired. He glanced at Léopold who stood smoldering across the counter.

"Really," Léopold agreed. He detected a flash of hurt in Laryssa's eyes as he confirmed her statement.

Laryssa glared at Léopold then forced herself to look away. There was no way she'd let him see how angry she was, at him, at herself. She'd known she'd set him up when she denied being his girlfriend. She'd told the truth, obviously, because he agreed that she wasn't. What was worse was that it was apparent that her shower had done little to tamp down her attraction to him.

"We have much work to do today. I'm going to go get ready. Can you two conduct yourselves like gentlemen around her while I'm gone?" Léopold asked, walking away toward the hallway.

"From where I'm sittin', I'm not the one she has to worry about." Dimitri laughed as the vampire spun around and gave him a scowl.

"Behave," Léopold ordered right before he slammed his bedroom door.

"He's got issues. Treats people like they're house pets. Seriously," Laryssa noted.

Jake and Dimitri broke up laughing.

"It's true," she smiled, taking another bite of her danish.

"Amazing how you can spend a short amount of time with someone and get to know them so well." Dimitri put some fruit on a plate and began to eat. "I understand you had a run in with a demon last night. How're you feelin', cher?"

"I'm good. The marks are gone." She rubbed her hand above her breast where it'd scratched her.

"Glad to hear you're okay. That's some pretty quick healing, though. Now I know you're not a wolf. Or a vampire. You seem a little like a witch but that's not it either. Maybe a fae?" he guessed.

"Didn't he tell you already?" Laryssa asked.

"No. Despite spitting tacks and needles, Leo's got a sense of honor. He said he promised you that he wouldn't tell anyone."

"A sense of honor, huh?" Léopold had kept her secret. Why couldn't he have just betrayed her? She wanted a reason to hate him, to make her feel anything other than what she was feeling. Not only had he thought of her, getting her breakfast, he'd kept their conversation in confidence.

"He did tell us what happened last night," Dimitri told her, his expression growing serious.

"Everything?" she gaped. *What exactly had he told him?*

"Well, yeah, the bit about you going off to the lake."

"He was busy," she said coolly, recalling how she'd seen him biting his donor, her moans of pleasure. Foolishly, she had given into her own primal urges and she'd been the one making similar sounds hours later.

"Yeah, about that. You do know he's a vampire, right?"

"Hard to forget."

"I just want to make sure because I'm not sure what we're gonna be doin' today or where this is going to lead us, and he is what he is. You can't be runnin' off when he..." Dimitri's words trailed off as he took a few minutes to think of the best way to say what he was thinking. He didn't want to scare her, but not only did he turn wolf, Léopold was nothing short of deadly when he perceived danger.

"When he what?"

"When he becomes who he is. Obviously, you've seen the fangs and well, it just is in his nature. The women and men, the donors...he needs to feed. Now I'm not sure what you think you saw him doing with that woman last night, but he really does try to make his bite painless."

"And you would know this how?" Jake asked, grabbing a donut from the plate. He smiled and walked over to the windows.

"I know, okay?"

"But that woman..." Laryssa began.

"Let's just say that I'm experienced in the way of the bite," Dimitri explained.

"You let a vamp bite you?" Jake laughed.

"Yeah, I did."

"You let *him* bite you, didn't you?" Laryssa inferred, shocked at what he was telling her.

"It was out of necessity. Trust me. He was in bad shape and well, yeah. But believe me, he didn't want to do it. I guess I should've listened to his warning, because the way it felt…"

"Please stop talking," Jake urged. "My virgin ears don't want to hear this. You and Léopold. No."

"Fuck you. We didn't have sex. That is exactly the presumptuous attitude that causes problems. My point is," he turned to Laryssa, "that vampires have two ways to bite. Pain or pleasure. And he's gotta eat. So there ya go."

"I can guess which way he went with you," Jake jibed.

"Shut it, Jake. Can't you see I'm trying to clue Laryssa in on my vast knowledge of the vamp world so she doesn't freak out again?"

"You're a real doctor Phil."

Laryssa laughed.

"Seriously. The guy has to eat," Dimitri argued.

"If she didn't like the sight of his fangs, just wait until she sees yours, wolfman," Jake said.

"Jake brings up a good point….even if he's being kind of a dick." Dimitri glared at him and then continued talking to Laryssa. "I know you have kind of kept yourself out of the supernatural world and I'm sure you have your reasons, but he's right. At the first sign of danger, there's a good chance I'm gonna strip down and go wolf. I may not be able to respond with words, but I'll be able to understand you."

"Did you just say you're going to strip?" A huge smile broke across her face. She looked at Dimitri and then Jake, and couldn't help but picture them naked. Laryssa's face heated and began to turn pink.

"Yeah, we love to go nudie, baby." Dimitri laughed. "Seriously, though, you can't run off when you see my wolf. I won't hurt you. And neither will Jake, here."

"Thanks for letting me know. It's not every day that I see men taking off their clothes and turning into little furry animals," she giggled.

"Wolves. Big ferocious wolves," Jake insisted. "Jeez, this woman knows how to hurt a guy's ego. Maybe she wants a demonstration right now." He began to unbuckle his pants.

"No, no I don't." Laryssa covered her eyes and started laughing even harder.

"Easy, Jake. Keep your pants on. Leo's gonna kill us if he comes out here and sees you showin' your junk to his girl."

"I'm not his girl," she insisted.

"Yeah, whatever you say, cher. Okay we showed you ours…ready to show us yours?"

"Well, I didn't exactly get to see the show," she remarked with a grin. "But I do appreciate you telling me about your wolf thing you do…even if I didn't get to see you change. I will, however, take a rain check on that one."

"Hey, I can show you," Jake challenged.

"Not here. I'm tellin' you both, Léopold will freak. As much as my boy enjoys a good romp in the hay, he's just getting used to the nudity thing." Dimitri had seen the way Léopold was looking at Laryssa. Léopold could think whatever he wanted about his no relationship rule, but there was no denying the possessive way he was acting around her. What happened between the two of them remained to be seen, but if Laryssa was a bone, he didn't want to pick a fight with the big dog in the bedroom who thought it was his.

"As much as I'd love to see you change, and I really would, I think that maybe Dimitri's right on this. Léopold can get a bit cranky." In truth, she'd like to make him jealous, but playing games with his friends wasn't her style. She found herself drawn to Dimitri, though. His honesty was refreshing. It didn't take her but a few minutes to realize that she wanted to share with them what she'd told Léopold. "Okay, I'll show you mine. Ready, boys?"

"Hell yeah, let's go," Dimitri said.

Laryssa got up off her stool and moved toward the center of the great room. Dimitri stood and walked over to Jake, who was intently watching. She smiled at Jake and extended her hand to him, letting her energy focus toward her target. His donut flew straight out of his hand and into her own.

"Got it," she laughed and took a bite. "I'm a naiad."

"Damn, bro, she just took your donut." Dimitri clapped his hand on Jake's shoulder.

"Hey, now. Was that necessary?" Jake said, feigning indignation. He licked his fingers and grinned.

"She's amazing, isn't she?" Léopold appeared seemingly out of nowhere. *Goddess, she was showing them what she was and demonstrating her powers.* Either she was completely unaware of how powerful Dimitri and Jake were as wolves or incredibly brave.

Surprised to hear Léopold's voice, Laryssa jumped when he came up behind her and kissed her neck, his masculine scent spiraling into her senses. The man was dizzying and delicious. For a long minute, she felt herself melt into his embrace, closing her eyes. But Dimitri's cough reminded her that they weren't alone and that Léopold didn't want her. Her eyes flashed open and she turned to face him.

"You're beautiful," Léopold praised, his eyes drifting from hers down to her parted lips. Her alluring kiss lingered within inches. The temptation was so great, yet he knew he shouldn't.

"I, uh, I was just showing Dimitri and Jake what I can do," she stammered. Breaking free of his arms, she recoiled, realizing that she'd almost kissed him. Needing distance, she crossed the room and took a sip of her lukewarm coffee.

"A naiad, huh? Isn't that some kind of a water-being?" Dimitri asked, closing his fists. He resisted the urge to drag Léopold out of the room and have another chat with him regarding his intentions with Laryssa.

"A mermaid?" Jake guessed.

"More like a nymph," Léopold corrected. He brushed past her, twirling his finger into a curl of her hair, then let it drop. "A freshwater nymph."

"Not a mermaid. No tail or scales. Just me." Laryssa's skin tingled from Léopold's touch. She couldn't take her eyes off of him. He smiled at her as he popped a blackberry into his mouth. He wasn't playing fair. Shit, he wasn't supposed to be playing at all. *How am I supposed to ever forget him and our night together if he plans on flirting with me all day?*

"Nice trick with the donut, cher. Can you move heavier things?" Dimitri asked Laryssa.

"Yes, that and more, mon ami," Léopold answered for her, enjoying her eyes on him. Try as he might, he couldn't deny himself. Like a lure, she fascinated him. Watching her enchant the wolves with her engaging personality only made her more enticing. "We can discuss it on the way over to Ilsbeth's. We've got an appointment with a shrewd witch. Best not be late."

Laryssa shook her head at Léopold. The man was impossible. Larger than life, he exuded charisma and magnetism, entrapping her emotions. She glanced over to Dimitri who gave her a sympathetic smile. He knew, she thought. She couldn't decide whether she should feel embarrassed or relieved. Lost in thought, she gasped as Léopold took her hand.

"Come, ma chérie. I promise to look after you today," he whispered in her ear.

As she looked into his eyes, she knew she was in serious trouble. Her heart squeezed in her chest as he ushered her out of his home.

⊸⊱ *Chapter Nine* ⊰⊷

On the short ride into the city, Laryssa had carefully positioned herself as close to the rear side door as she could get in an effort to keep her leg from brushing up against Léopold's. Dressed in an Italian trim-fitting grey suit, he'd casually interject his opinion into the conversation, always giving her a sexy smile in the process. Taking time to undo the top button of his white fitted shirt was the only semblance of discomfort he displayed. Exuding confidence and strength, he'd insisted that he sit with her in the back seat for her protection. Neither Jake nor Dimitri had argued, but simply acquiesced to his demand.

Stealing glances at him, her eyes always found his. It was as if he knew when she'd look, what she'd say, making her feel as if he'd known her for a long time. Her thoughts drifted to the way he'd held her down, forcing her to admit she enjoyed her submission. If she'd allowed herself to think of what Léopold had done to her for even a second longer, they'd all know what she was thinking. Quickly remembering she was in a car filled with supernatural men, she diverted her mind to a less sexually arousing memory: the demon. Its memory brought an unsurpassed surge of fear to her psyche, one that left her praying she'd survive what was to come. One week. It'd given her one week. She took a deep breath and blew it out, attempting to calm her nerves.

"It's going to be all right," Léopold assured her. He'd sensed her arousal, yet as quickly as it had begun, it was gone, replaced with anxiety. In response, he'd placed his hand atop her thigh, seeking to comfort her. The heat sizzled beneath his flesh. She was fully dressed, but she might as well have been bare to him. Léopold despised his growing need for Laryssa yet all he could think about was making her his.

"You sure you can trust her? Ilsbeth?" Laryssa looked into Léopold's eyes, searching for the truth.

"Ilsbeth and I have known each other throughout centuries. She's a difficult woman, but trust her? Oui, I do," he affirmed.

Léopold's touch warmed her leg, and Laryssa continued to have difficulty separating herself from her feelings toward the debonair vampire. One minute he was cruel, agreeing that she was nothing more than someone he'd met. The next, he possessively kissed her. His caring words, the caress to her leg gave her reason to suspect that he couldn't live within his own rules. She sought to squelch the optimistic thought, that he wanted more than just one night, but his actions spoke louder than his words. Unable to withstand the temptation, she placed her hand on his, completing their connection.

After driving through an ornate wrought iron gate, their car circled in front of Ilsbeth's home. As it came to a stop, Léopold exited first, then rounded the vehicle to open the door for Laryssa. Along with Dimitri and Jake, they made their way up a wide slate staircase that led toward the spectacular home. Its second and third floor windows, adorned in rock, stood watch over the meticulously manicured gardens. A pentagram, nearly eight feet in diameter, garnished the apex of a magnificent dormer that sat perched above the main entrance. As they passed through one of the seven enormous stone arches that led onto the porch, Léopold took Laryssa's hand into his.

Dimitri forged ahead of the group so he could announce their arrival. As he went to ring the bell, the door opened before he had a chance to press the button. Laryssa's friend Avery stood in the archway, smiling.

"You're here," she called. With a gleam in her eye, she spied Laryssa and pulled her into the foyer.

"Avery, I hoped you'd be here but I wasn't sure. This place is so..." Laryssa hugged her friend but quickly released her, taking in her surroundings.

"I know, right? It's amazing. Ilsbeth has a place in the Quarter, but this is where we come for special events. It's her home. No one else lives here," she whispered.

Rose-colored plastered walls with ornate crown molding gave way to a cathedral ceiling. Flecks of speckled light danced on the stone floors. Illuminated by daylight streaming through stained glass skylights, the foyer felt spacious yet it had been closed off from all other rooms and hallways. A corner staircase led to a balcony above, where a grand piano sat untouched. As the wooden front door closed, creaking alerted them of side doors being opened and an ethereal presence called Léopold's name.

Laryssa tightened her grip on Avery's hand as the panels disappeared into the walls and a beautiful woman with long platinum blonde hair glided into the room. Petite, dressed in a purple, crushed velvet jacket with matching pants, she exuded a preternatural aura. But as she began to speak, it was clear that she was very much of this world.

"Léopold, so very good to see you again." Ilsbeth gave him a smile, and waited patiently as he kissed the back of her hand.

"Ilsbeth, you're lovely as usual," he complimented, releasing her wrist.

"This is Laryssa," he told her. Laryssa let go of Avery's hand and reached for Léopold's. "Laryssa. This is Ilsbeth. Maîtresse des sorcières."

"Hello," Laryssa said softly, unsure if there was some kind of special witch protocol she should be following.

"The nymph?" Ilsbeth looked to Léopold for confirmation but Laryssa took the lead.

"A naiad. How'd you know? Did Léopold tell you?"

"No need to fret, my dear. Léopold has kept your secret. But as you will soon find out, I know lots of things." Ilsbeth sharply turned her head toward Dimitri and Jake. An imperceptible flash of fury glinted in her eyes. "Dimitri? What are you doing here? Léopold, you didn't mention that you've been keeping company with wolves."

"Hey, cher. I told Léopold you'd be happy to see me. Good to see you again, too." Dimitri grinned and gave her a small wave from a safe distance. He supposed that he should have told Léopold that he'd slept with the witch. Some things were better left as surprises. The witch was as gorgeous as he'd remembered. Their affair had burned hot, but fizzled out just as quickly. In truth, it had been more of an explosive ending. Quite the argument, as he recalled. His eyes darted over to Léopold, who glared at him. Offering a compliment, he sought to smooth over the awkwardness of the situation. "Ilsbeth, you're lookin' beautiful as always."

"I see you haven't lost your silver tongue," she remarked, turning away from him.

"Missed it, did you?"

"Hardly."

"As I recall, you seemed to enjoy my tongue." Dimitri regretted his words as soon as he said them, catching Léopold's look of disgust.

"Tais toi," Léopold chided. *Damn wolf.* Léopold made a gesture as if he was zipping his lips and nodded angrily toward the entrance, urging Dimitri to shut up and follow her.

"Come, we shall chat," she told them. Ilsbeth continued to ignore Dimitri, walking into the other room.

Dimitri shrugged at Léopold, giving him a devious smile. Léopold shook his head, trying to stifle a smile. The wolf didn't need encouragement to get in any more trouble, he thought.

Laryssa followed into the dimly lit room. Candles in assorted sizes and colors flickered atop the fireplace mantle while streams of light poured through thin rectangular floor to ceiling windows. Léopold took her hand in his, and they sat down in a chenille-covered love seat directly across from Ilsbeth, who reclined in a single high-backed chair. Dimitri and Jake made their way to an adjacent sofa. When they were all seated, Ilsbeth nodded over to Avery, who left them in the room, closing the doors behind her.

"What brings you to me today?" Ilsbeth began. "I'm delighted to meet a naiad. Very rare, indeed."

"There's a child, too," Laryssa told her. "I've only met one other like me."

"A child? Interesting." Ilsbeth raised an eyebrow at Léopold.

"Un bébé. I found her in the snow. In Wyoming. Yellowstone," he disclosed. His eyes met Dimitri's before returning to Ilsbeth's. "She'd been stolen from the Alpha's den. Someone tried to murder her."

"Hunter Livingston's pack?"

"Oui."

"Did you find her before or after she died?"

"Quoi? She's alive. Logan Reynaud is providing refuge. Kade and Luca are helping as well. We're the only ones who know of her existence."

"I asked, 'did you find her before or after she died'?" Ilsbeth repeated her question.

"I died," Laryssa told her, realizing that Ilsbeth had confirmed what she'd suspected to be true. "Why do you think Ava died?"

"Because, my dear nymph, this is how you're made. Naiads are not born. They are created, granted the gift of life through the water."

"The baby was alive when I found her," Léopold claimed.

"Touched by the lady, she awakens new. But as a child, she's not fully grasped her powers nor does she need water to survive. When she turns of age, she will blossom like a flower. Her price is water. But this cannot be why you've sought my assistance."

"We appreciate you sharing your vast knowledge, but we have a bigger problem. A demon. It seeks something from Laryssa," Léopold divulged.

"A knife," Laryssa added.

"A sacrificial knife. Tlalco Tecpatl," Léopold told her.

"Ah, I see. It seeks a relic. The Aztec civilization worshipped many different gods, you know. Throughout any given year, sacrifice came in many forms, but human blood was, indeed, spilled. No class of their society was spared in the rituals. Men, women, children, even infants, all died for the greater good," Ilsbeth lectured.

"Or so they believed. Mesoamerican history. It's a hobby," Jake made invisible quote marks with his fingers, "Let's just say not all the 'sacrifices' went willingly on the way up to get their beating heart cut out."

"They tore out their hearts? I thought that stuff was just in the movies." Laryssa cringed.

"'Fraid not. It was done at different times of the year, with specific kinds of victims as a way to give an offering so to speak, sometimes to help the gods do their job. They needed help with survival, their land, growing crops and such."

"What kind of gods would want death?" Laryssa challenged.

"There were many times during the year that human sacrifice was required. It was pretty much a monthly event. As for which gods? You know...the usual suspects. Rain. Sun. Wind."

"And water. Let's not forget the goddess responsible for water." Ilsbeth's mouth drew tight as the others anticipated her next words. "Chalchiuhtlicue. Some say she was married to the rain god. Some say she was the sister. Counterparts perhaps?"

"So with all this sacrifice going on, I imagine that brings about some bad juju," Dimitri surmised.

"Whether these ancient gods and goddesses exist or existed, is of little consequence. What is of importance is that there are beings who revel in death. Torture. Murder. Evil thrives on it. Like spores in a petri dish, the heat of evil cultivates the seed, it grows," Ilsbeth told them.

"Grows into what?" Laryssa asked her. A pregnant pause filled the room. "What does it grow into?"

"Demons," Ilsbeth responded.

"But I thought *demons* were kind of like fallen angels." Laryssa pensively pressed her lips together. She hated even saying the word.

"Indeed, they are lost to the underworld. But demons can be called to the surface by the nefarious intentions of the flesh, by man," Ilsbeth explained. "It is why we do not speak of the one they serve. The heinous act of the taking of innocent lives, through means such as human sacrifice, can summon forth a demon into our world, albeit temporarily. Even while in their netherworld, they seek to steal souls…often during death. More often than not, the soul does not belong to them."

"Death?" Laryssa asked.

"Indeed. Tell me, Laryssa," Ilsbeth stood from her chair. She walked over to an antique oak apothecary cabinet, which spanned an entire wall of the room. Its bottom half housed hundreds of square drawers, neatly labeled and organized, each with its own brass label finger pull handle. Bottles and containers of various sizes lined the five rows of wooden shelves. "What did you see when you died? A light?"

"No, nothing like that. It was peaceful but all I really saw was this lady. She was glowing and then she touched me, sending me back. But…" Laryssa tried to recall the experience. It sounded crazy, she knew. "I didn't see it. I just felt it. Something dark. Like when I see the hollow-eyed people that come after me…the dark ones. I don't just see them. I can feel them, the evil, down to my bones. I guess Avery told you about them. She's been helping me hide for so many years."

"The Lady stole you from the demon. Or at least this is what it perceives. It was there, trying to take you. You did not have a clear death. No, for naiads, they see the Lady."

"But who is she?"

"Some think she is Chalchiuhtlicue herself…giving life or taking it away as she sees fit. A deity of water, she rules the lakes, the rivers. Even childbirth. Or rebirth, perhaps? Others disagree with this hypothesis entirely, calling naiads daughters of Zeus or Poseidon. Whoever the Lady is, she grants life to young women who die within her arms. But there's a price that comes with the breath of life she breathes into her chosen ones."

"The water," Laryssa whispered.

"You can't live without it. Stray too far from her home and you will die."

"Why does a demon want an ancient Aztec knife? And why does it need her to get it?" Léopold inquired, reaching for Laryssa's hand. "It's given us a week to find it. It's threatening to kill the infant."

"All very good questions." Ilsbeth slid open a drawer and pulled out a clothed item. Setting it on the counter, she reached for a small clear glass bottle and uncorked it. "I'm very happy to help you, provide answers to what you seek, but as Léopold knows, I do not assist without remuneration. You see, as a witch, I cast many spells. Spells which require ingredients. Some are quite common. Like castor oil, for example. Or yarrow root. There're things more difficult to acquire, such as, shifter hair. You know, like wolf hair, perhaps freshly ripped from its root." she gave Dimitri a cold smile and continued. "But it is the very rare ingredients that I treasure. Like a scale of a virgin dragon, perhaps. Or the fang of a vampire."

Dimitri's eyes darted to Léopold. He wished like hell his friend could read minds because he knew as sure as he was sitting in the room what Ilsbeth was going to ask…demand. He'd given her his own hair as a peace offering. He offered. She took. He was still waiting on the peace.

"You can see that when I'm presented with such a prize, I must have it. The blood of a naiad. Now that is very rare, indeed."

"No fucking way," Léopold told her, jumping to his feet.

Placing himself between Laryssa and Ilsbeth, he protectively guarded her. The wolves followed his lead, readying for attack. Shocked at the suggestion that Ilsbeth would ask for her blood, Laryssa clasped at Léopold's shoulders, hoisting herself to her feet.

"Tsk, Tsk, Léopold. You were always such an alarmist. Really, it's just a tiny bit of blood I need." She held up the bottle to the light and then set it down again. Methodically, she unfolded the cloth, revealing a simple brass athame. "But it must come willingly or else it shall be tainted. It must be a gift. A gift in exchange for my knowledge and advice. I believe it's a fair arrangement."

"No. There must be another way," Léopold stormed. No way in hell was he letting that devious witch cut open Laryssa, slitting her like a chicken's throat.

"I'll do it," Laryssa volunteered. Her voice was soft but strong as she pushed past Léopold.

Dimitri fell back into the sofa, aware that Léopold was about to go ballistic. He nodded to Jake who followed his actions.

"What the hell do you think you're doing, Laryssa? No way. As in, no way in hell am I letting you do this," Léopold raged, blocking her way.

"I've got to do this," she told him firmly.

"No, you don't. We'll find another way."

"We can't afford to waste time. Ilsbeth can help us. You saw what happened to me last night." Laryssa's eyes brimmed in moisture as she raised her hand to him, gently caressing his cheek. "You must trust me. Please, Leo. I need answers."

Her pleading tore at his heart. *Goddammit.* He knew she needed answers, but why the hell did it need to involve knives and blood? Her blood? It was true; they had little time to find what the demon sought. Perhaps even less time to find a way to kill it. With his eyes on hers, he solemnly nodded in agreement.

"I'll be okay," she told Léopold as he kissed her palm. He held her wrist but she pulled away, walking toward Ilsbeth. "Let's do this thing."

"Naiads are known for their bravery. That is also why some see them as dangerous. Come give me your wrist," Ilsbeth instructed.

Laryssa pushed up her sleeve, allowing Ilsbeth to take her arm. Léopold came up behind her, surrounding her with his strength. She felt him support her forearm, his warm breath on her ear.

"I won't let anything happen to you, ma chérie," he whispered, with a kiss to her neck. His eyes caught Ilsbeth who was watching him like a hawk. "Be gentle with her."

"Léopold, darling. You act as if I'm a novice witch wielding a kitchen cleaver. Would you like a demonstration of my power?" She smiled while busily preparing the bottle with a glass funnel. Ilsbeth found Léopold's fascination with Laryssa interesting. Well aware of Léopold's limited capacity for expressing his emotions, she grew concerned.

"No, I don't. But heed my words. Be careful," he grumbled.

"Can we just get this over with? How bad can it be? Now that we're on the topic, why can't we just do it like they do at the doctor's office? Haven't witches heard of hypodermic needles? They hurt, too, but very efficient. Safe." Laryssa's eyes widened as Ilsbeth held the shiny athame up to the sky as if she were worshipping the sun. *Why the hell did I volunteer to do this again? Oh yeah, scaly demon from hell. Wants to make me his bitch.* Nervously, she bit her lip as the witch began to chant. "Hey, don't you think that you should use alcohol? I don't want to get some kind of an infection."

Laryssa tried to control her racing pulse, but lost her concentration. Her eyes widened as Ilsbeth seized her wrist. If it weren't for Léopold's calming presence behind her, she would have bolted out the door.

"Seriously, I think I might have an alcohol pad in my purse somewhere. Ahhhhh," she screamed as the blade sliced through her skin. Her natural instinct was to pull her arm away, but the damn witch was strong, holding the dripping wound over the funnel. "Shit, that hurts. Fuck. Fuck. Fuck. Okay, I think that is enough. You said you only needed a few drops."

"You're okay, mon amour," Léopold whispered.

Mon amour. Did that arrogant vampire just call me his love in front of all these people?

"Mon amour? Seriously? I thought we just agreed that I wasn't your girlfriend, mister 'I don't do relationships'?" she jibed. Laryssa tried to turn her head to yell at him but he easily held her in place. His laughter filled her ears. "Okay, look, the bottle is halfway full already. I hope someone brought orange juice. Or cookies. Sweet baby Jesus, that hurts."

"I must say, Léopold, this naiad is a live one. Spirited. She'd make a good match for you," Ilsbeth surmised

"Strong-willed. I think that is the term she prefers." The sweet scent of Laryssa's blood filled his nostrils, and Léopold struggled to ignore her bleeding incision.

"All done, now. See how easy that was?" Ilsbeth sang, delighted with her prize.

"Easy? Easy?" Laryssa's voice began to get louder. "What the hell? Alcohol, people. Band-Aids. Anyone here ever heard of first aid?" She looked over to Dimitri and Jake, who were snickering on the sofa.

"Yeah, laugh it up, wolf boys. It's not your blood."

"This," Ilsbeth held up a clear plastic bottle, "is river water. Why give you a Band-Aid when you can easily heal yourself?"

"No, no, no. I really don't think that's sanitary," Laryssa insisted. But as soon as it hit her skin, the energy spread throughout her arm, instantly ceasing the pain. Within seconds, the water flowing from her cut turned from dark red to pink to clear. "Oh thank God. My wrist is healing. I've never tried that. It's worked in the river, but that's just amazing."

"A little trust, please. I do know what I'm doing," Ilsbeth said, handing her a clean towel. "And that, my friends, is the magic of a naiad...among other things."

Léopold took the towel from Laryssa and gently dried her arm and fingers. She gave him a small knowing smile as he did so. *Mon amour. My love. What is it with this man?* For someone who didn't want a girlfriend, he acted differently. He'd been caring, protective. As his eyes drifted from her hands to her eyes, it was as if she could detect a hint of understanding. Whether he'd admit it or not, there was something developing between them. Her heart constricted as he placed a kiss to her small scar.

"I don't mean to interrupt whatever's going on between you two, but you do want to hear more about how to find the Tlalco Tecpatl. Or did you just spill blood to give me a hostess gift?" Ilsbeth put her hands on her hips and rolled her eyes, flicking her long fingernails.

Both Léopold and Laryssa snapped out of their trance, quickly moving to sit back down.

"Oui, let's hear it."

"Naiads have existed for centuries, as have demons. My theory is that this demon was initially brought forth to the surface of our world by the Aztecs. No doubt, there's been much evil and death over time, but since it seeks this particular artifact, it's tied to it somehow. The demon calls it by name as if it belongs to it. Unfortunately, for you," Ilsbeth looked to Laryssa, "it also calls you by name. I believe when you died, it was there. It claimed your soul for itself. It does not matter whether or not it was the demon's to begin with. Demons lie, steal, murder. The interesting thing about this Tecpatl, this knife, it is rumored to be able to destroy those who claim it."

"Why can't the demon just go get the knife itself?"

"Because it can't. It is hidden to the demon. Your sisters before you have documented instances of demons seeking artifacts from them. They've hidden them, cursed them so that even if the demon knew of its location, it could not get it by itself. It needs you to find it, bring it willingly."

"Why does it expect me to just hand over the artifact?"

"Because it will threaten you or kill someone you love, someone you care about. And if you want to destroy it, you'll need to get close enough to kill it by your own hand, Laryssa. Only a naiad can send it back to its creator. You must use the Tlalco Tecpatl to kill it. Do you understand what I'm saying? Only you can do this. No one else. That is the disadvantage of that particular weapon."

"Can we just do some kind of exorcism? Find a priest?" Laryssa asked.

"No, this demon is linked to you. It believes you belong to it. If it gets its way, not only will it get the Tecpatl, it'll have you too. A demon's courtesan, as you will."

Laryssa felt her face grow hot as panic swirled through her mind. How could this happen? She'd been so careful to hide, to keep her powers concealed from others.

"Are you saying that we have to kill this demon with the Tecpatl or it will take her...forever? There must be some other way," Léopold objected.

"She knew this. What did it say to you?" Ilsbeth pressed Laryssa for an answer.

Laryssa nodded slowly in defeat. "The demon...it told me I'd belonged to it since I died, but I just assumed it was crazy or something. It...it began to touch itself. It was horrible. Please, I can't say what it was doing."

"It's preparing for you. Its flesh to yours. It seeks you now that it's seen you're a woman...no longer the girl you once were."

"No, this cannot be happening. Léopold, please tell her. Tell her she's wrong," Laryssa pleaded.

"I wish I could but I tend to agree with Ilsbeth. I saw what it did last night. We must find the Tecpatl and kill it." Léopold wrapped an arm around Laryssa, who fell against his chest. "I swear, I'll protect you."

"We need to find it," she agreed in defeat. In all her life, Laryssa hadn't ever killed anything. Sure, she'd fished, but that was the extent of her great hunting ability. And now she was expected to kill a demon in hand to hand combat? It seemed an impossible feat. Yet she had no choice. Do or die. She'd choose do. She'd kill the beast.

"Your sisters before you and those who remain with us have hidden their keys and secrets away from the rest of us. I do believe that naiads would be stronger as a whole if you'd gather strength together as one. But because naiads are often unaware of their past, they're afraid to come out in the open. Fear can be very motivating. Despite all of this, your sisters have documented what you need in books." Ilsbeth paced the room and picked up a silver candle snuffer off the mantle. "ιστορίες του νερού. Tales of the Water."

"A book? What? Are we supposed to go to the library to find it? Or do you happen to have a copy?" Dimitri asked.

"Not that I was talking to you...because I wasn't," Ilsbeth sneered. "But there are several copies that have been written and rewritten over the years, going back to ancient Greece. To answer the question, a copy of the book always finds its way to a naiad."

"Not me. I think I'd know, right?" Laryssa remarked.

"You own an antique store. Perhaps it's found its way into your hands that way? Is it possible that the book's in your collection and you don't recall it?"

"I guess anything's possible, but I know that I've never seen it. That being said, Mason takes care of most of the smaller items. Books aren't my specialty. I guess I could ask him."

"Within its pages, you will find the key. If you're tied to this demon, then you're linked to its artifact in some way. Only the book will tell you how to find it."

"I can't believe this." Laryssa fell forward and placed her head in her hands. Terrified as she was, she refused to cry. Léopold's hand, rubbing her back, erased some of her tension. When she finally looked up, everyone in the room was looking at her. "What?"

"Laryssa, what lies ahead is not already written one way or another. We shall fight this together. I will not leave you," Léopold promised.

"The vampire is correct. Your destiny is now allied with the men in this room. I'm certain of this fact." One by one, Ilsbeth began to extinguish the flames. "I'm afraid that is all I can tell you for now. Given your extraordinary gift, I will meditate to see if there is any other way I can assist you with your dilemma. Now, if you all would excuse me, I need to speak to Léopold. Alone."

"I think I should stay with her," Léopold began.

"Alone," Ilsbeth repeated, sliding open the hidden doors.

"I'm fine. Really, Leo. You go. I'll stay with Dimitri and Jake. I want to say goodbye to Avery."

"Don't worry, man. I've got her. Come here, cher," Dimitri encouraged, opening his arms.

"Really, you guys. I'm fine. Sure, I got a bit of bad news, but I can handle it," she joked lamely.

"Come on, now. You know you want a piece of the wolf," Dimitri teased, hoping to lighten the mood. Despite Ilsbeth's glower, he suspected she knew that he was only trying to cajole Laryssa.

"I'll wait for you out here," Laryssa reassured Léopold, whose face was drawn tight in concern. She walked over to Dimitri and hugged him. Together they walked out of the room.

"We need to have but a brief chat, old friend," Ilsbeth stated, sealing the room so that she could speak privately.

"Although the mystery is killing me, I do believe we've had enough excitement for one day. Get on with it, then. Say your piece." Léopold crossed the room, staring out the windows into the courtyard.

"The naiad. She's very beautiful, isn't she?"

"Oui, she is. Somehow I don't think you wanted to speak to me about Laryssa's appearance." He spun around, resting his hands on the back of a chair.

"We've known each other a long time."

"Oui."

"I would not exactly call what we have a friendship but more of a mutual respect, would you agree?"

"I believe that accurately describes our arrangement. At times, we've been soldiers for a cause. Warriors in arms, I suppose. Luckily, we've never been on opposing sides."

"The naiad is very special. She does not realize the implications of her powers, a neophyte in a dangerous world. Although she's lethal in her own right, she's vulnerable." Ilsbeth spoke with her back to Léopold as she busily organized her ingredients and cleaned the athame. "She'll need your guidance. The security of your experience. She must be able to trust you in all ways."

"Agreed." Léopold grew weary of the ambiguous conversation. There was much work to be done to find the book. "What is it, Ilsbeth? The day is short. Tell me your concern."

"I see the way she looks at you. And," she turned to face Léopold, catching his eyes, "the way you look at her. You're not yourself. You may fool her and perhaps, even the wolf, but you do not fool me."

"Stop with the cryptic words. What is it that you wish to tell me?"

"You care for her. And she for you. The seeds of love have been planted in that cold dark cavity inside of your chest where you used to house a heart."

"You don't know what you're talking about. It's not possible," he asserted. "Besides, if you've been paying such close attention to me the past several hundred years, you'd know full well that I don't have mistresses or girlfriends. What you suggest is preposterous."

"Deny it all you want, vampire, but I do know you. And I know what I just saw. Frankly I don't care if you ever fall in love. But actions do not lie. A caress. A look."

"This is ridiculous. Is this really why you wanted to talk to me?"

"Do not hurt the naiad," Ilsbeth warned. "You are a bastard, Léopold Devereoux. A trustworthy one, but I still stand by my statement. This woman, she cares for you already, despite not knowing you very long. I don't know what you've done, but I can feel it in her energy, and I can damn well see it in her eyes when she speaks to you. Now, if you want to sit there and tell me with a straight face that you feel absolutely nothing for her, that's your business, but I'm warning you not to play with her emotions. She needs you to survive this quagmire. And above all else, she must be able to trust you. If you plan on hurting her, you might as well slay her yourself, because the demon will have her and her soul."

"You do know that there's part of me that wants to take you by your broomstick and send you off? You're altogether maddening." Léopold blew out a breath, frustrated by the witch's insight. He shook his head, unwilling to make eye contact with Ilsbeth.

"Yes and yes," she laughed. "But I'm right."

"I will not concede your point, but I promise not to hurt Laryssa. This'll have to be enough for now. I fear that is all I'm capable of doing."

"It's not that bad, you know."

"What?"

"Opening your heart. Caring again. Loving someone. You may not think you deserve this gift, but you do. We all do."

"Are we finished?" Léopold smiled, refusing to engage her further. More than anything, he'd love to give in to his desires and believe what Ilsbeth was saying. But at the end of the day, it couldn't be. Because the witch was wrong about one thing; he didn't deserve Laryssa. And she didn't deserve the death and despair he'd bring to her life.

"Be well, Léopold."

"Be well, Ilsbeth." Léopold slid open the doors to find Laryssa laughing with the young witch, Avery.

Oblivious to him, she brimmed with a resilience and confidence that he hadn't expected to see, given the challenges that lay ahead. He gave her a quick smile as she hugged her friend goodbye. Praying he could keep his promise to Ilsbeth, he resolved to protect her from not only the demon who sought her death, but the beast within himself, who yearned to take her for his own.

·❦· *Chapter Ten* ·❦·

"Mason," Laryssa called as she entered her store. Bells rang, alerting her manager that someone had entered the building. "We have a room full of books in the back that we've been working on cataloguing. Got them in an estate sale a few months back. Trying to determine which are worth anything. Most of them we'll end up donating to libraries and schools. The ones we've already determined we'll sell are here in this display. As you can see, there's only a couple hundred."

"Just a couple of hundred," Jake joked. "There's nothing better than spending time going through some dusty old books."

"Good stuff, right?" Dimitri laughed.

"You said the others were in the back?" Léopold asked.

"Yeah, but let me ask Mason first if he knows about it."

A tall handsome man wearing an apron pressed through the swinging doors, polishing a silver ashtray.

"'Bout time you got in. Whatcha been doing, girl? Can't you see how busy we are around here? You're gonna get your ass fired."

"Stop it, Mase." Laryssa slapped his arm. "I, uh, need to talk to you…in the back."

Mason let his eyes wander over the men before raising both his eyebrows at Laryssa. She tugged on his arm, dragging him back behind the doors.

"Stop looking at me like that," she said.

"Like what? I didn't say a word. Not one word." He pushed the shutter open an inch to peek out at them. "Really, Lyss. Didn't know you were so kinky? Three men at once? Or did you save one for me?"

"Mase, I need you to focus. But in the interest of time," she quietly pointed to each of them through the small crack and whispered, "that one there is Dimitri. Beta of Acadian Wolves….as in 'do not mess with him'. I haven't seen it yet but he told me that he strips down and turns into a big bad wolf. So hands off."

"Did you say strip? Oh baby." Mason whistled, and Dimitri turned his head toward the door.

"Stop it. They can hear you," she shushed. "That one there. Also wolf. Military wolf, I think. Again, he falls into the danger category."

"Nice too. Did he show you his gun, girl?"

"No. No he hasn't. Would you knock it off?" She sighed and bit the end of her thumb, looking to Léopold, who'd begun actively looking through the books. "And that one…"

"You mean mister tall, dark and mysterious. Sexy beast," Mason growled.

"Sharp dresser. Love the suit. I can see that one's got expensive tastes."

"Yeah, he does." She glanced at Léopold and then snapped back to her conversation. "He's off limits. Vampire. One with very sharp fangs. Extremely dangerous. As in approach with caution."

"He's totally hot."

"Yeah, I know. They all are, but Léopold's...he's really just...I don't know... like no one I've ever been with."

"Oh my God. You didn't!" he exclaimed with a broad smile.

"Would you be quiet? They'll hear you...as in freaky supernatural hearing. Probably have heard every single word we've said." She blew out a breath, leaned her head back against the wall and closed her eyes for a minute.

"Hmm...hmm...hmm...you've got it bad, don't you? Not that I can't see why. He is yummy."

"Please. Don't say anything else, okay? I'm an idiot. And yes, before you even ask...yes...I did what you're thinking. But it can't happen again, okay?"

"Why not? What's wrong with him? No motion in the ocean? Hey, what about that bite? I've heard that's a surefire way to..." Mason studied her neck for marks.

"He didn't bite me."

"Let me get this straight. Bed but no bite?"

She nodded.

"What kind of a vampire doesn't suck blood?"

"One that's into one night stands, that's who." She shrugged, bending her head from side to side, trying to ease some of the tension in her shoulders. "It's complicated."

"I just bet it is."

"Listen, there's something I need to talk to you about...I'm in trouble."

"What kind of trouble?"

"The kind of trouble that can get a girl killed."

"What are you talking about? If you're in danger, you need to call the police, Lyss, not waste time chattin' it up with me."

"No, what I need is for you to run things for me for a few days...a week tops. Please. I promise to give you a raise if you can just keep the wheels turning while I'm gone." In a week, she'd be dead or have killed the demon. Mason shook his head in refusal but she knew he'd help her. He was a long time trusted employee and friend and could easily keep things afloat in her absence. "And I need your help with one more thing. I'm looking for a book. A rare book. Something that may have come into the shop during one of our estate runs."

"That, I can help you with. Got your back on the shop, too, but I'm tellin' ya for the record that getting involved with vamps and wolves isn't the best idea you've had in a while, no matter how good-lookin' they are."

"Yeah, not much choice. I need them. They're helping me...stay alive that is. Come on, I'll introduce you. I want them to hear what you've got on the book…if anything." Laryssa pushed through the doors, not waiting for his agreement.

"They're helping you? Is that what you call it? Helping you my ass," he mumbled under his breath.

"Hey," Laryssa called to get their attention. "This is Mason. He's my assistant manager. Handles all small store items. Silver. China. Clothing. Books. Mase, this is Dimitri, Jake and Leo."

The men exchanged nods but Léopold never took his eyes off Laryssa. She'd known that he'd be able to hear her conversation, but she didn't care. All of what she'd told Mason was true.

"So I hear Y'all need a book," Mason began. "We've got all kinds here. A whole room full of them in the back as a matter of fact."

"I promise to help sort them all when I get back," she offered, knowing she wouldn't. They each had their own jobs and worked well to stay out of each other's hair. "The title of this book is, 'Tales of the Water' or 'Stories of the Water'…something like that."

"It's most likely written in another language. Greek. ιστορίες του νερού," Léopold added. "Maybe an ancient language such as Latin. I suspect it won't be very special in appearance."

"Well then, why would someone have kept it?" Mason asked, searching through the records on the computer.

"I don't know, really. I just know that it would have come to me…sometime since we first opened the store," Laryssa said.

"That's a long time. You sure it's not upstairs at your place?"

"No, I'd remember if I had kept one of our books…especially a book like that."

"Well, hello there…look at this." Mason moved to the right so that Laryssa could view the screen. He pointed to an entry. "That one there. 'Foreign text' is how it's listed. Looks like we sold it three months ago."

"That might be it. Did they use a credit card? We need an address. A name." She watched as he selected the book and brought up the information.

"Nope. Paid in cash."

Laryssa pinched the bridge of her nose. "Okay. Do you remember who sold it? To be honest, there're days I can't remember what I had for lunch let alone what I sold a couple of months ago."

"Or I could have sold it."

"True. Hey, you have a date on it?"

"Looks like December nineteenth." He tapped on the keys. "Nothing says Merry Christmas better than a book about water."

"Tales of the Water. And I don't think they bought it for the holidays. Any other books sold that day?"

"No, mostly big items. A few knick knacks."

"Let me use the computer a minute, Mase." She moved into position and began typing. "Video. Hold on a sec. I just need to pull up the security video from that day. Here we go....let's see what we've got. Lots of furniture movin' in and out."

"What are we gonna do? Put out a missing person's report? All they did was buy a book. Not exactly a crime."

"If I need to. I met a cop yesterday, and she seems pretty motivated to help us." She smiled over to Léopold and continued, "Maybe we know the person. We get lots of repeat customers. Or maybe these guys might know...wait, there's you and there's a book. Leo, Dimitri, Jake. Come take a look."

As she stepped back, Mason leaned in to study the picture. "Yeah, I do remember that dude. Kept asking what other old books we had. That's pretty much all we sell."

"I know this man," Léopold stated. *Martin Acerbetti.*

"Why does this not surprise me?" Dimitri said, stroking his beard.

"Martin doesn't live in the city. He's got a place outside of Baton Rouge."

"How well do you know him?" Laryssa asked.

"Not very well. He's a bit idiosyncratic. Has a temper." While the eccentric vampire had violent tendencies, Léopold had never known him to actually commit murder within the city limits. Kade had very little tolerance for those who broke his rules. "I don't keep company with him. No matter, though, I'll call him and how do you say...like the Godfather...make him an offer he can't refuse, no?" He smiled over at Dimitri.

"See, I knew you liked that movie," Dimitri laughed, patting him on the back. "That's my man."

"Do you think he knows about the book? About me?" Laryssa inquired. It seemed strange that a rare book meant for her actually made it into the store and then was bought by another supernatural.

"Maybe. Maybe not. It doesn't matter, though, because we need it. It's not like he's a demon. He's a vampire. One I can easily manipulate, kill if necessary." Léopold brushed lint off his sleeve, unaware that both Laryssa and Mason had gone quiet. When he looked up, he caught them both staring. "What?"

"Hey, man, do what you gotta do." Mason held his hands up defensively, shaking his head with a smile. "Um, yeah, I guess I better start working on those books in the back. You need anything else, Lyss?"

"Leo, I know this is who you are. But some of us," Laryssa pointed to her chest and then to Mason and gave a small laugh. "We, uh, don't go around talking about killing people or demons...got me?"

"Humans, always so sensitive," Léopold sniffed. "I speak nothing but the truth. This vampire is not to be trifled with, Laryssa. I'll do what needs to be done to get the book."

"Well, this human has got to get back to work. You take care, Lyss. One week and you better get your fine ass back here." Mason hugged and kissed

Laryssa on her cheek, never taking his eyes off of Léopold.

When he'd gone through the swinging doors, Laryssa turned to Léopold with her hands on her hips.

"Really? Did you have to go all 'I'm a vampire' just now? You freaked Mason out," she informed him. "And to think he thought you were hot!"

"Oh, he's hot all right," Jake jested. "Nothin' like baptism by fire."

"I think Mason will survive. Besides, if you...Lyss," Dimitri drawled out her nickname that he'd heard Mason use, "are gonna hang out with vampires and wolves, he's got to get used to it sometime."

"How to make friends and influence people....yeah, that's what comes to mind when I think of ole Léopold here," Jake jibed.

"He's got the influencing part down right. Don't worry 'bout that," Dimitri teased.

"I swear you've all gone mad," Léopold remarked with a grin.

"Hangin' out? Is this what we're doing? I'll make sure to invite Y'all to book club. Although with the way Mason reacted, I don't think any of you would last ten seconds around them," Laryssa said, walking toward the door. *Did they really expect to become friends when all was said and done?* She couldn't tell, but she had to admit that she did like both Dimitri and Jake. Léopold, she liked way too much. Unfortunately, he'd made it clear that he had no plans to be with her afterwards, let alone have a friendship. "Leo, you scared the bejesus out of him."

"Hey, does this mean you think we're 'hot' too, Lyss?" Jake winked, knowing he was poking at the bear with the fangs. "Because ya know I'm single."

"Yeah, me too," Dimitri weighed in with a broad smile. "You know us wolves are okay with kinky, right?"

"More than okay," Jake added.

"Y'all have big ears. Didn't your mamas ever tell you it was rude to listen to other people's conversations?" Confirming what Laryssa had suspected, they had heard every word of her conversation with Mason.

"If you're finished, we've got a book to go find. Come on, let's go. I'll make the call in the car." Léopold held the door open. As Laryssa went to pass through, he wrapped his arm possessively around her waist and nuzzled his nose into her hair. "For the record, wolves, I think it's best you understand that the only 'kink' Laryssa is going to be having is going to be with me."

Laryssa looked over her shoulder and her eyes met with his. She sought the hidden meaning behind his seductive words, but he merely smiled, leaving her without answers. Her heart caught, remembering their night together. She wanted so much more than he'd ever conceive of giving her. Yet every time he touched her, excitement flickered deep inside her belly. She knew better than to listen to her heart, but with his arm solidly around her, she was lost in all that was Léopold.

⤚✺· *Chapter Eleven* ·✺⤙

Laryssa stood in front of the art deco mirror, contemplating why she'd insisted on going with Léopold to get the book. In the car ride back to his home, he'd called the vampire, who'd agreed to give them the book in exchange for an undetermined amount of money. Léopold had steadfastly refused to tell her how much. Even though she figured he could afford it, she still felt indebted to him. He'd brushed off her concerns, maintaining that he was doing it for Ava. The manipulating vampire had given Léopold one condition in addition to monetary compensation; he'd asked him to attend at a soiree at his home.

They had quarreled when he'd told her he planned on bringing a blood donor with him to the party, as it would be expected for him to do so. Angrily, she demanded that she accompany him to find the book, arguing that it was her life on the line, not some mindless blood bag. After nearly an hour of going back and forth on the issue, Léopold had conceded her point.

The red satin evening gown she wore clung to her curves, streaming to the floor. The V-neck accentuated the swell of her breasts, and the diamond-studded spaghetti straps, gathered into a singular strand, exposed the creamy skin of her shoulders. The revealing contours of the low-backed dress incited both a sense of nakedness and sensuality. Her makeup was subtle and refined. The matching coral lipstick made her lips appear swollen, as if they'd been kissed.

She glanced at her upswept hair and absentmindedly touched her neck. She wondered what it would feel like to have Léopold pierce her flesh. To allow him to drink from her while they passionately made love. A tear threatened to fall as melancholy struck. Léopold, while provocative and flirtatious, had made no sincere attempt at continuing what they'd started. Their connection felt as strong as steel yet he denied any hint of a relationship.

The sound of a door opening stirred her from her reverie. Léopold's reflection stared back at her, his dark eyes piercing her own. She brought a finger to her lashes, hoping to conceal her emotion, but deep down she knew he could sense even the smallest change in her mood. It bothered her that she felt as if he knew her better than she knew herself. The intimacy was too invasive, too seductive.

With the threads of Léopold's restraint growing thin, the spectacular sight of Laryssa left him reeling. *Goddess, she is enchanting.* He'd planned to keep her safely by his side all evening, but he couldn't fathom how he'd be able to stop himself from making love to her. Did she know how much he wanted her? How he'd secretly lost control? The realization that he was considering breaking all his rules, to make her his own, slammed into him like a train. Centuries of never loving another, and out of the blue, he'd become obsessed with his little naiad.

Concern furrowed in his brow when he thought of the implications. Tonight at the party, he couldn't dare let the others know of his intentions. Like a rare exotic flower, she'd attract the attention of the other vampires, leaving them thirsting for her nectar. If they knew what she meant to him, it would further expose them both. They could use her to get to him. He'd never forget that his wife and children were dead because of his actions.

"You're stunning." His dark suave voice left no room for argument. Gently resting his hands on her bare shoulders, he stood behind her.

"Thanks. You look incredible in your tux. So handsome. Like a prince," she said. A hint of sadness tinged her voice.

"Are you worried about tonight? It's not too late to change your mind, ma chérie." Léopold gave into impulse, and brushed his lips to her nape.

"No. I'm going. I was just thinking, that's all."

"I've brought you a gift." Léopold knew he should take her into his arms, refuse to let her go, but they couldn't afford to lose time in discussion. He reached into his jacket and pulled out a velvet box.

"What is it?" *Jewelry?* The man ran hot and cold. He must have an ulterior motive. She knew better than to think he was wooing her with presents. Besides, he didn't have to do a damn thing to draw her to him, she was already captivated. The more time they spent together, the more she desired the impossible. Reaching for the box, she simply held it.

"Open it. It completes your role," he told her.

"My role?"

"As my date. My donor."

"I play my roles well. Don't you remember the first night you met me?"

"Oui. Calm and cool. Your leathers said biker chick, but you did have a difficulty maintaining your balance if I recall correctly."

"It was you," she said.

"What do you mean?" Léopold had to hear it for himself, her reaction to meeting him. His had been the same, he knew.

"You really don't know?"

He smiled, but said nothing.

"God, Leo. Are you really going to make me say it? Okay, fine. I was rather infatuated with this really sexy guy who had just walked into the bar. I became so nervous that I lost concentration and slipped. Those seats are dangerous, you know?" Laryssa paused, feeling the heat rise to her cheeks. She cleared her throat and continued. "You affect me. I think I've lost a good amount of brain cells just being around you the past few days."

"A guy, huh?" He laughed. "Sounds like I have some competition."

"No, I'm afraid that you've already won." Uncomfortable with her admission, Laryssa looked away from him, breaking eye contact.

"Open the box," he insisted, changing the subject.

"It's beautiful." Laryssa did as he asked and gingerly trailed the pad of her forefinger over the diamond-studded bracelet and its matching earrings.

"It's yours. Put it on." Léopold watched as she inserted the earrings. Gently, he took her wrist and fastened the bracelet. He thumbed the clasp. "This here, this little button. Depress it and it'll release a hidden silver chain from its interior. It's a small weapon, but it can be effective."

"Silver?"

"Yes, that's one rumor about us that's true. Like the wolves, we don't do well with silver. I know you can move objects, but this is one more layer of protection in case things go south."

"Thank you. It really is lovely."

"Perhaps we should discuss the rules," he suggested, continuing to touch her.

"You've already told me that I need to pretend as if I don't mean anything to you. I'm a donor, not a girlfriend."

"Mais oui. If they suspect anything more, you'd essentially be exposed as a weakness of mine."

"Are you telling me that none of the people going tonight are lovers?" she asked. What kind of people took someone to a party but acted like they barely knew them? None of it made sense.

"Depends on the definition of lovers. I'm sure there're others in the same predicament but you must understand, it is the nature of the affair that dictates our actions. Martin is a purist. Some would say he's orthodox."

"How do you mean?"

"Take me, for example. Contrary to what you may think, or the wolf," he rolled his eyes, "I'm social with humans, wolves, witches, etc. I conduct business and pleasure with little regard to who is a vampire. But Martin, he leans toward socializing only with vampires. He does this because one, he wishes to be with his own kind, those who understand his needs, and two, because he believes that he's far superior. Tonight, you will see only vampires and humans. His tastes run dark, so while I expect he'll bathe his guests in decadence, you may see things that surprise you. You must remain calm."

"What kind of things?"

"Whatever happens, stay focused. You must act as if it doesn't bother you, understand? As a guest, I'd be expected to bring a well-trained donor or human with me who isn't easily offended. Preferably, I'd bring someone who'd want to participate."

"Participate in what?"

"Feedings. Sex. Games. All out in the open, of course. It's his home so he'll be altogether impossible. You must be wary of Martin and the other guests. He surrounds himself with those of like minds."

"He sounds delightful," she mused.

"I cannot stress the importance of following the rules," he told her. "The rules are for your own safety, mon lapin."

"Please don't call me that. You know I looked that up online, and I'm not a…"

"The rules," he continued with a small smile, ignoring her protest. "First and foremost, never leave my side. Not even to use the bathroom. Female vampires will also be in attendance and have no qualms about taking another woman. In their presence, you must be subservient. I know this isn't something that comes naturally to you….or should I say, you submit when you choose." He caught her gaze, referring to how she enjoyed being restrained. "You'll be my guest. And I'm your master. As such, you will address me as master or sir. You will not address me by any other name."

"Master? I…I…don't," she began to argue but decided against it. All she wanted to do was get the book. "That title sounds pretty vampish to me. Or like some BDSM club thing."

"Oui. It's a bit of both. All you need to know is that you are expected to behave a certain way in order to blend in."

"Is this how you treat all your dates? Or is this just because we are going to this party?"

"This is why I don't attend his parties very often. But since you asked, I don't do dates. And secondly, I think you doth protest too much when it comes to your own sexual preferences. Let us not forget last night. I do recall how hard you came."

"Just because of what happened last night, it doesn't mean that I'm like your donors. Don't get used to this persona we're making up," she insisted, hating that he knew what she fantasized about in the bedroom.

"With that sass, you'll earn yourself a spanking."

"Promise?" She wished she was joking but she'd love the feel of the sting of his hands on her bare bottom. Trying to distract herself from the ache that grew between her legs, she bit her lip and flashed her eyes up to him.

"If you talk to me like that at the party, I'd think nothing of bending you over my knee in front of everyone. I'm sure Martin would enjoy the display. I know I would. Hell, maybe he'd give us the book for free." He watched intently as her face flushed at the mention of a spanking. The scent of her arousal nearly caused him to tear off her dress.

"As if," she teased. *In public, that'd be a no. In private, hell yes.* "Not happening."

"Now that's not very submissive, ma chérie. You must play the role. If not, that kind of behavior will get you in trouble tonight. No, correction, that'll get us both in trouble. On the other hand, if we do this right, we can get in and out…. make an appearance, corner Martin, get the book and leave."

"Easy peasy."

"Hardly. Although Martin has agreed to give it to us, who knows what he'll say when we get up there? He could try to manipulate me further, to hurt you. He cannot be trusted." Léopold's face grew serious and his eyes darkened. "Laryssa, I meant what I said earlier. I'll kill him if he tries a game, puts his hands on you. We must get that book in order to get the Tecpatl, to kill the demon."

Laryssa nodded quietly.

"You need to be prepared for this possibility. At the end of the day, it's my nature to kill. This is who I am, who I've always been, who I always will be. Do not ever think of me otherwise."

She turned in his arms, caressing his freshly shaven cheek with her hand.

"Leo, you're so much more. How you have gone all these years thinking like that, I don't know. I may not have known you for very long, but that isn't you. Last night, I felt you deep inside me...that man is caring and passionate. And that's what's inside your soul. If you're forced to kill tonight, I'll be there standing right beside you. I'm not scared of you or anything you're capable of doing. I can do this. I'm not a helpless damsel in distress. I'm not human, either."

Laryssa rose on her tiptoes, and pressed her lips to his. *I could love this man,* she thought. He was tough, yet incredibly compassionate. Confident but self-deprecating. Vampire did not equate to monster, no matter what he'd seen or done in his lifetime. Resisting the urge to deepen the kiss, she eased back onto her heels and gave him a small smile.

"I'm not worthy of you, mon amour," he whispered, his eyes remaining closed.

"You are," she disagreed, laying her palm to his chest, knowing she'd never be satisfied with one night. Consumed by him, she wouldn't give up on breaking through to him. His battle hardened exterior seemed impenetrable, but she had the will of a thousand warriors. He just didn't know it yet. "Leo, when this is over...It's just that I... I want us...we need to talk."

"Oui. But we can't afford to get distracted now." His eyes opened, burning with fire.

"Later then? Promise me."

"Oui." With a shake of his head, he shoved the emotion back into his chest and returned to discussing the plan. "Tonight, it'll be just you and me."

"What about Dimitri and Jake?" It wasn't lost on her that he'd again changed the topic of conversation.

"I told you, Martin's a purist. No one but vampires are permitted to step foot onto his property. Arnaud will drive us. Dimitri and Jake will follow, but stay parked down the street. I pray they don't have to intervene, but I'm not foolish enough to take you there without backup. Jake inserted a bug into my collar. I'll call on them if needed, but only if we're in dire straits."

"Anything else?"

"When we walk through that door," Léopold glided his hands over her shoulders and down her arms, "you'll belong to me and no one else. You'll be mine in every sense of the word. Your actions. Your body. Even your blood."

Laryssa's eyes widened and her pulse raced. She considered his words, aware she'd no choice but to give in to his will, his rules to stay alive. But for a second, she wondered if she'd do it for him even if her life wasn't on the line. Deep within, she knew the answer, but would never admit it. She'd already gone far over the line, giving him too much power over her heart and he didn't even know it.

"I can do this, Leo. I'm not a fool. I wouldn't be going if I thought you'd hurt me," she told him, holding her chin up high. *My heart, however, is already aching.*

Léopold gave her a small smile and shook his head. She intrepidly trusted him, and he couldn't conceive how such a gentle being could have such faith in him.

"Are you going to bite me?" she asked, catching him off guard.

"I'll avoid it at all costs. I can assure you that we won't make love at the party, so there is virtually no risk of creating a bond if I was forced to bite you. I honestly don't see that happening, but I can't rule it out." Léopold felt the sting of rejection emanating off of Laryssa. *Does she want me to bite her? To bond with me?* As much as he wished to contemplate her wishes, he needed to focus on their imminent task, one he was certain was not going to be as easy as it appeared. "You can back out of this at any time. But the second we step out of the car, there's no going back. Do you understand? I'm going to need you to give yourself over to me without reservation. Tell me, Laryssa. Do you agree to the rules?"

"Yes. For tonight, I'm yours." The words fell naturally from her lips without hesitancy. She'd give him more than one night, a lifetime if he asked. As they walked to the car, she'd never been more confident of anything in her life.

The affair appeared entirely civilized at first glance, but Laryssa knew otherwise. She fought to maintain control of her breathing as she took in the gala's atmosphere. A sensuous blues song filtered throughout the antebellum mansion. As the band played on, couples milled about the ballroom, drinking and laughing. While some guests were dressed for an evening at the opera, in ball gowns and tuxedos, others looked as if they were going to a fetish club, wearing leather and corsets. All eyes fell on them as they entered.

"This way," she heard Léopold say, and gladly followed, terrified to be left alone.

"Drink," he told her, handing her a champagne-filled flute. She hesitated, concerned it could be poisoned. As if sensing her apprehension, he took a sip of his own and coaxed her. "It's delicious."

Remembering her role, she nodded in agreement and placed the rim to her lips. Taking a tiny amount into her mouth, the bubbles danced over her tongue and down her throat. She sucked a deep breath, and she willed herself to calm down. Her temporary tranquility was soon replaced with fear as an imposing man with exposed fangs approached. She struggled to keep the liquid down and squeezed Léopold's arm.

"Léopold Devereoux, my old friend. How've you been? I must say I was surprised to get your call this afternoon, but I'm thrilled I did."

"Merci beaucoup, Martin. I certainly wouldn't pass up such a fortuitous opportunity to enjoy your company and do business all at once." Léopold supposed he was laying it on thick, but he was well aware that Martin enjoyed having his ego stroked, especially in a public forum. "Your home's magnificent. The restoration is impressive."

"Thank you for noticing. But of course, someone of your stature would appreciate the finer things. I've personally overseen all of the architectural detail work," he boasted, his eyes feasting on Laryssa. "You must introduce me, Léopold. Who is this lovely little choice you've brought with you tonight?" He held out his hand to her.

"This is…" It occurred to Léopold that they hadn't discussed whether or not to use her real name. Thinking quickly, he chose a name that he knew would draw her ire, making her focus on him, not her fear. "Jessica. Jessica, this is our gracious host, Martin. Go on, mon lapin. Don't be shy. You have permission to shake his hand."

"Yes, sir," she answered submissively. Her heart raced as she extended her palm toward the imposing vampire. As it occurred to her what Léopold had called her, Laryssa's eyes flared. *Jessica? Jessica freakin' Rabbit?* She caught the smile on his face, realizing he'd done it on purpose to distract her. Tamping down her reaction, she embraced her role. Laryssa lowered her eyes and placed her hand in Martin's, praying he couldn't feel her fingers shake.

Martin gave a devious smile, before capturing her hand and placing his lips upon it. Rather than release her, he held onto it, engaging Léopold in conversation.

"Oh my, she is striking," he crooned. "You must let me taste her."

"Ah, I'm afraid that's not possible. You see, she's in training with the agency. I'm working very hard to teach her the proper manners required of a donor. Please forgive her in advance as she's a novice." Léopold possessively wrapped his hand around Laryssa's waist, pulling her away from Martin, forcing him to release her hand.

"Well, I must say it is very generous of you to do that for them."

"Considering the short notice, it was acceptable. Your observation is correct, though, mon ami. She's quite fetching. I plan to use her in every way possible this evening, make sure she's thoroughly disciplined." Léopold maintained a deadpan tone to his voice as he commented, as if it were nothing more than business.

Martin released a hearty laugh. "Practice makes perfect. But do let me know if you need any help with her. I'd be happy to give her a go."

Laryssa kept her eyes on the floor. *Give me a go? Is this guy serious?* Martin's voice made her feel as if thousands of spiders were crawling over her skin. She rubbed her arms as nausea threatened.

"Merci. Your offer is very generous, however, this one is entirely my responsibility. On another note, I've brought what you've asked regarding our business."

"Very good. We can make the transfer in a bit." Martin grew distracted by a large crowd of new guests filling the foyer. "Will you please excuse me? I'll be but a minute and then we can go to my office." Martin looked again to Laryssa and blew a kiss at her before turning his attention to his new arrivals.

As he walked away, Laryssa felt herself sag against Léopold in relief.

"You're doing very well for a novice," Léopold noted, sipping his drink.

"Thank you, sir," she answered.

"Jessica," he paused and chuckled. "Are you enjoying the party?"

"Yes, sir." *Enjoy the party?* Laryssa wasn't sure if he was serious or not. She briefly considered breaking character but judiciously decided against it. Martin had looked at her like a shark who was about to snap up a seal and she wasn't about to test her theory.

Léopold took Laryssa's hand in his, leading them onto the dance floor. As they stepped out onto the parquet floor, he took her glass and his, and handed them off to a waiter.

"Come," he ordered.

At his demand, the smallest flicker of irritation flashed in her eyes and she lowered her lids quickly, concealing it as she remembered her role. It had only lasted a second. No one gave her a second look, but Léopold had noticed.

"Manners, pet," he warned, reaching up into the back of her updo. Tugging slightly on her hair, he exposed her neck while pulling her flush against him with his other hand. "Or would you like that spanking I promised you?"

Yes. Arousal flooded between the juncture of her thighs at the thought of him doing so. As he pulled her against him, Laryssa's body came to life against his as if they were the only two people in the room. His clean male scent enveloped her as he took control. Her hands fell to her sides, allowing him to guide her to the driving beat of the music. She felt the hard length of him brush against her belly. Involuntarily she released a small moan.

"You are a very dirty girl, aren't you, ma chérie? My, my, my. You do want me to do that to you, don't you?"

"Yes, sir," she breathed into his shoulder. Closing her eyes, she couldn't look at him, to see his rejection as she confessed her desires. "I want it…I want that and so much more…but only with you."

"Jesus Christ," he swore as his cock hardened against his zipper. *Fuck, she's going to kill us both.* She may have been playing a role, but he was certain she meant every single word she said. They were only supposed to seek the book, get out safely. Instead, her actions were ripping him from the inside out. His teeth ached for her skin, for her blood. Any remaining doubt he held that he'd be able to get her out of his mind and his life disintegrated like he'd taken a sledgehammer to a piece of chalk. Once he took her blood, he suspected he'd create the kind of bond that would ensure his centuries of solitude were truly finished.

With furor, he spun her in his arms, slamming her back into his chest. Like a vise, he held tight to her waist, gliding his other hand over her chest until he'd wrapped it around her throat. But the struggle didn't come. No she merely fell into his erotic embrace, digging her nails into the side of his thighs.

"Mon amour, we cannot wish for the inconceivable. Be afraid. Fight me. See me for who I am," he demanded as he ground his erection up into her bottom.

"If it is what you wish, sir," she replied. Lost in the rhythm, she gave into Léopold's demand. No longer playing a role, she reveled in his strength. "But it is you who I seek. Be assured, I see only you."

"Look around you, pet. They all feast upon the sight of your skin, coveting what I have. This, this is my world." *Goddammit. When will she finally see me for what I am? Can't she see the grotesque and treacherous world into which I've brought her?* Léopold may not have been Martin's friend, but these vampires walked within the precarious circles of his life.

Laryssa opened her eyes and noticed that no longer were the other guests dancing. If not otherwise engaged in sex or feeding they had stopped to stare, to observe their impassioned dance. Consumed by the moment, she shook it off, unwilling to care what they thought. This was what vampires did, impulsively acting out their deepest desires, exhibiting their lust and anger.

"Let them look," she challenged, bending at the waist and writhing against his swollen flesh. "Master, I'm here to serve you, not them."

With a jerk, he'd righted her, against him. Was she insane? The charade had gone too far. Léopold considered taking her out to the limo and fucking her senseless, when she placed her hand over his, urging him to take her breast. He slipped his hand underneath the silky fabric, cupping her soft skin. Teasing her nipple into a taut point, he pinched gently until she sucked a breath. But she didn't stop him. No, her arousal filled the air, not a soul in the room misunderstood her intentions.

"Yes, sir."

"How far would you go? Would you let me strip you, fuck you here, in front of everyone?" He couldn't stop himself from pushing her. When would she realize that she was falling for a lethal vampire, who lived off the blood of humans? When would she wake up and see that no matter how badly he wanted her, a life with him would be fraught with vulnerability and danger?

"I would go as far as you needed me to go. Can't you see that? None of it matters unless I'm with you." Laryssa almost lost her composure as she became aware that she'd just professed how she felt about Léopold.

It was not lost on her that others in the room had heard, had been watching. Underneath the cover of her role, she safely revealed her feelings. She'd known that she wasn't supposed to give the impression that she cared for Léopold. He'd be angry with her, she knew, for putting them at risk. She stopped dancing and slid out of his hands, and bowed her head, attempting a recovery of the situation.

"Please forgive me. I have taken advantage of your kindness in training me by letting my physical attraction, my personal lust toward you take priority. I understand if you wish to report me to the agency," she said in a meek voice.

Léopold stood firm, his feet rooted to the floor. If he could have his way, they'd leave right now, but they had to get the book. Cognizant of their errors, he appreciated her effort to rectify what they'd done. As he looked around, the other guests had once again begun dancing, ignoring them.

"See that it doesn't happen again. While I intend to make sure you receive the punishment you deserve for calling spectacle to us at this affair, we shall make the best of it, no?"

Léopold went to usher Laryssa off the dance floor when he spotted Martin making a beeline toward them. No doubt he'd been alerted to their sensual tryst on the dance floor. Going on the offensive, Léopold widened his strides, dragging Laryssa by the hand behind him.

"Martin, I must apologize that my training got a tad out of hand on the floor. This one," Léopold nodded over to Laryssa, whose eyes fell to the floor, "must be reprimanded as soon as possible. She may have difficulty learning to be a donor as it's apparent she confuses the attention of a master for affection."

"Dear boy, I do know the issues involved with finding suitable donors. Like you, I prefer a flavor of the week. Variety is the spice of life so they say. Relationships with donors are an inherent pitfall to the process. Don't worry a minute about the display. My guests," he gestured around the room to several couples who begun publicly having sex, "they do enjoy a good show. Come now, let's attend to business before the party goes into full swing."

Laryssa felt as if the wind had been sucked out of her. Swirling emotions made her feel as if she'd just ridden a roller coaster. But unlike the carnival, there was no respite from the jarring descent. Perhaps she had been confusing her own emotions with the role, but from her head to her toes, her skin burned for his touch.

Breathing deeply, she summoned all her strength, letting the power of the naiad flow through her blood. She forced herself to focus on their mission, the reason why they were at the party. Like a forest animal, she sensed the hunter. Instinctively preparing for the attack, she appeared calm but her storm of energy built. Soon they'd have the book and they could finally leave.

Holding tight to Léopold's tuxedo sleeve, Laryssa followed him down a long hallway. When they arrived in Martin's office, she glanced up and caught an eerie gleam in their host's eyes. She pretended not to notice, hoping he didn't have a death wish. Léopold, sharp and cunning, hadn't survived centuries by embracing naivety. Martin knew this. He'd anticipate the great difficulty involved if he planned on trifling with Léopold, but he'd think Laryssa a weak victim. She could tell by the way Martin eyed her, that he secretly planned a coup. He stalked his prey, luring them into his trap.

Tense, Laryssa went on alert. She strode across his office with a subtle grace, ready to spring at the first inkling of danger. She observed how Martin circled Léopold, engaging him in conversation, his eyes darting over to her every now and then, aware of his quarry. Laryssa scanned the room for objects that could be used as weapons. She approached a plaster statue sitting on a pedestal and was running her fingers over the smooth surface, when she heard Léopold say her name.

"Jessica, we'll be but a minute. Please stand over near the doorway," Léopold ordered, never taking his eyes off Martin. He wanted Laryssa near the exit, far away from the devious vampire.

"Yes, sir," she answered on cue.

Léopold retrieved his cell phone from the inside pocket of his jacket and began to tap the surface. Within seconds, he'd transferred the funds into Martin's account and returned the device. Laryssa's energy slammed into him, and he realized she was close to snapping. With her back against the wall, she stood submissively with her hands at her sides, yet he knew she was ready to strike. They needed to get out as soon as possible.

"The transaction's complete. The book?" Léopold inquired. "I'm afraid we have another engagement this evening and must get going."

"Leaving so soon? How disappointing," Martin commented as he checked his phone, making sure he'd received the payment. Satisfied, he put it on his desk and slowly made his way toward Laryssa. "The book is there on the shelf behind my desk."

Léopold observed the vampire's actions. He spied a single book, which sat next to a crystal vase.

"That one there, with the black spine. I had it rebound. It was a tattered mess."

"Tell me, Martin. How did you come about the book? You never did say."

"I didn't, did I? Not much to tell. A bird put a bug in my ear at a party once. Told me about rare books and mentioned that the ones written in Greek are quite the fetch. I discovered it in this little antique store on Royal, buried with dozens of other old books. I couldn't be sure it was real, of course, but nevertheless I snatched it up for pennies. Stole it, really, considering the profit I just made." Creeping closer to Laryssa, he stopped to lean on the back of a leather chair.

"Lady Luck was with you." Léopold slowly rounded the desk.

"And you as well. This donor you've brought. I beg you to let me show her our unadulterated ways." In a flash, he stood before Laryssa, gripping her chin in his hands. A man of short stature, he buried his nose up into her hair. "Her skin is radiant, like a virgin. Smells pure. Tell me, are you?"

"Am I what?" she asked, her voice filled with feigned tranquility. Laryssa fumbled with her bracelet. Her finger found the nub and tugged at the hidden wire.

"Do not touch her!" Léopold demanded, reaching for the book.

"She's special to you, Devereoux? You've gone soft, I see. After all these years, I wouldn't have believed it. You may fool the others, but not me. Tell you what...I'll keep your secret...in exchange for a taste of the virgin." Martin hooked his fingers around one of Laryssa's spaghetti straps and yanked it downward, exposing her bare breast. With a hiss, his fangs descended and he lowered his head to his prize.

Laryssa screamed as Martin attacked. She'd been certain he would bite her, but instantly, Léopold had leapt to her rescue. He wrapped his arm around Martin's neck in a stranglehold. Enraged that Martin had touched Laryssa, Léopold growled and tightened his grip. But Martin held strong, refusing to let go of her shoulders. Sliding the silver chain taut, Laryssa managed to bend her arms and jammed the chain upward into his throat, scoring his skin. The smell of burnt flesh filled the room and Martin howled in response, allowing her enough time to kick his shin. With a grunt, he released her and Laryssa slipped aside.

"Let this be a lesson to others. Never, ever touch what is mine." Léopold seethed, and sunk his razor-sharp fangs deep into Martin's shoulder.

Léopold held tight as Martin flailed, unsuccessfully trying to dislodge him. He extended his fingernails into claws and pierced them into the soft flesh surrounding Martin's spine. Léopold bore down on his grip, tearing away at the tendons and muscle until Martin's head rolled onto the floor. Within seconds, the vampire's body disintegrated into ashes, leaving nothing but silence in his wake.

The door flew open and one of Martin's guards ran into the room. Laryssa reached her hand toward the statue. Calling on her power, she flung it across the room, catching him in the head. As he fell to the carpet, she slammed the door shut. Léopold, in his furor, realized he'd gone feral in front of Laryssa. He'd revealed the beast. Now, she'd finally see him for what he was...a savage animal. The loss of her in his life would break him, but he'd executed Martin with no remorse. Unable to stomach the taste of him in his mouth, Léopold spat on the floor. As he swiped his forearm across his mouth to clear the blood, he forced his blazing red eyes back to black. The truth of what he was had come to light, and he found it impossible to look into Laryssa's eyes.

"The book? Where'd it go?" Irritated, Léopold focused on the business at hand.

"There." She pointed. In the melee, it had fallen under the desk. Her heart pounded in her chest, expecting that any minute a deluge of vampires would break down the door, seeking revenge for what they'd done.

"Let's get out of here," Léopold calmly said, picking it up off the floor. He slid it under his coat and looked down, disappointedly, to his bloodstained shirt. "Ready?"

"But Leo? What about the others? What if they…" *Kill us.*

"They won't touch me. Or you. Don't be afraid." Not after he'd just killed Martin. Every single vampire on the premises had heard his words: *Never touch what is mine.* They didn't have to see what had happened behind closed doors to know Martin had been killed. But Léopold would not be held at fault. Martin should have known better, did know better. He'd knowingly challenged Léopold and lost. "We're going to walk out of here right now. Our business is finished. Take my arm."

Laryssa wrapped her hand around Léopold, confused as to why she felt no sadness over the death of another human being. But Martin hadn't been human. *Vampire.* If Léopold hadn't stopped him, he'd have bitten her, drained her. As her foot brushed through his dust, she silently wished him good riddance.

⤙ Chapter Twelve ⤚

Léopold threw his head back against the seat in disgust over what had transpired. After making their way safely to the limo, he'd taken off his shirt and jacket, throwing them in the trunk. Arnaud had provided him with clean towels so that he could make quick work of removing the blood and ash from his face and hands. But as he sat bare-chested across from Laryssa, there was nothing that could be done to cleanse his soul.

She'd seen him kill. Not only had he killed, he'd decapitated Martin. He sighed and closed his eyes so he didn't have to see the disdain on her face. Or worse, she'd fear him. Jesus Christ, this was why he didn't fall in love. All he ever did was bring pain to those he cared about. Laryssa was no different. No matter how much he wanted her, they had no future.

When Laryssa had finally reached the back seat, she'd hoped they'd celebrate their victory. Exhilarated that they found the book, she soon found her spirit deflated like a balloon. Léopold had seated himself as far away from her as he could possibly get. A chill settled over them like a layer of frost as Léopold retreated within. Laryssa wondered what was wrong with him. She'd seen his beast, and it had been magnificent. Like a great warrior, he'd taken down his opponent in battle, saving them both.

After fifteen minutes of mind numbing reticence had passed, Laryssa could no longer bite her tongue. Falling to her knees, she crept up between his legs and pressed her forehead to his belly. His hand slid to her hair, teasing out the pins, softly tugging the tendrils free. Still, not a word passed from his lips.

"Leo, please. Let me in," she whispered, rubbing her face into his warm skin.

He shook his head and closed his eyes. *Too much pain.* He couldn't bring this death to her feet, not ever again.

"I won't give up on you. Talk to me," she continued, unwilling to relent.

"I can't," he hissed. "What I did…"

"I saw you tonight. I saw everything. And I'm here. I'm not leaving you." She raised her chin and looked into his eyes. "No matter what you think, I'm not afraid. I'm not repulsed. You were…you were amazing."

"Amazing?" he scoffed. "How can you say that, Laryssa?"

Laryssa reached up to his shoulders, gliding her fingers gently down over his pecs, forearms, finally taking his hands within her own, then pressed his palms to her cheeks.

"Because it's the truth. You're the strongest man I've ever met. Ferocious when threatened. But you're gentle. Protective. Courageous." She kissed the tips of his fingers. "And I want you in my life. One night will never be enough. You've ruined me. There's no one but you."

"Don't you see what I'm capable of?" he asked. His voice faltered. "So long ago…I fought…to keep my family safe. But they killed my wife. My daughter. My son. I left them vulnerable to my enemies. It was no different than if I had sliced my own sword into their necks. When I became vampire, there wasn't a soul inside my chest to be taken. It died with them. For centuries, I've done nothing but kill, ruthlessly climbing my way to the top of the food chain. Those people you saw tonight at the party…this is the danger that surrounds me."

"It wasn't your fault. You cannot continue to think like that, to die this way. What you do is not living…it's experiencing without really knowing, tasting life." Tears brimmed in her eyes, empathizing with the guilt he carried. "I've lived with danger in my life ever since my own death. Every. Single. Day. You are the first good thing to happen to me since I've been reborn. I'll fight for you in my life. But you have to choose me, not guilt. Choose. Me."

"Laryssa," he croaked. For the first time since he'd been turned, someone was offering him the keys to the shackles he'd willingly worn since he'd found his family slain. His prison walls began to crumble. Freedom beckoned. All he needed to do was take it. Goddess, he wanted to open his heart to Laryssa, never let her go.

"Do it, Leo. Believe my words. I saw you tonight. You did your worst. And I am still here…offering myself to you. All you need to do is say yes. You can do it. Just choose me."

Léopold's heart exploded. With her knelt before him, she'd taken an ax to the centuries-old barrier he'd erected. She was everything he'd desired for a thousand years but nothing he'd ever had. Demanding and seductively submissive, at times, she'd witnessed the very darkest he'd become and still sought his attention, his heart.

"Yes." He buried his lips into her hair, raking his hands into her locks. "Goddess, please forgive me, I choose you."

Laryssa let the tears fall as he pressed his lips to hers, pouring all her love and passion into her kiss. Never would he think he was undeserving of her in his life. She'd make sure that he'd know, with no room for doubt, that she was his and he was worthy.

Léopold shattered, releasing the fire he'd held back for so long. Embracing the craving he'd held at bay, he claimed her with his mouth. Sweeping his tongue against hers, he sucked and teased at her lips. His little nymph had torn away his defenses, leaving him splayed open for her bidding. An urgent hunger built in his chest as she moaned into his lips. Tonight, Laryssa would be his.

"Leo," Laryssa panted.

Her hands frantically tore at his buckle and within seconds, she'd unzipped his slacks, taking his swollen flesh into her hands. Stroking his smooth taut skin, she gave him no warning before capturing his cock with her warm mouth. She sucked him hard from the root to his tip, plunging him in and out of her lips. Opening her heavy lids, she caught his eyes and smiled. Swirling her tongue over the plump head, she darted it over its slit, tasting his seed. Twisting his shaft at its stem, she sucked him once, twice then moved her lips over his tightened balls, suctioning them into her mouth.

"Fuck, yes. That feels so good," he grunted. "If you keep doing that, I'm going to…ah, no, no, no."

Unwilling to come in her mouth, he quickly grabbed her by the shoulders, bringing her upward. Recapturing her lips, his hands found her zipper and ripped at the material. He slipped the straps over her shoulders, letting the dress sag at her waist. With a final tug, the fabric left her bare save her panties, garter belt and stockings. Reaching for her breasts, he gathered the soft flesh together. Gently kneading them, he parted his lips catching a nipple, licking and biting at its ripe tip until she screamed with pleasure. Moving from the right to the left, he took his time, lavishing attention to her body.

"You're the most beautiful creature I've ever known," he breathed into her skin.

"I want you so much, Leo," Laryssa managed. As she writhed against his growing arousal, she could feel the length of him through the thin silk barrier. "Fuck me now. I can't wait. Please."

Léopold extended his claws, ripping at her panties until only her stockings remained. Laryssa put her hands on Léopold's shoulders, slowly impaling herself. She threw her head back, thrusting her breasts forward. Léopold held her waist, taking in the glorious sight of his nymph riding him hard. Cupping her breast, he caressed it, altogether aroused by the way she'd got lost in the passion, undulating on him.

"Perfect. You're so goddamned perfect." Léopold whispered as he slid his hand down between her breasts and over her belly.

His fingers descended between their bodies, until he found her slick pussy. He brushed his thumb through her lips, finding her aroused nub. Léopold felt her shiver in response and he knew he'd captured her attention. Letting his other hand slip down her back, he took her ass into his hands. She moaned, rocking against him, surging into his touch. His fingers trailed down the crevice of her bottom.

As he grazed his forefinger over her puckered skin, her eyes flashed to his, but she didn't say a word. Instead she raised her hips, sliding upward, and then rocked him back into her.

"Yes, that's it, mon amour," he reassured her. "Let me have all of you."

Laryssa took only a minute to adjust to the new sensation. She'd never been touched there, but as he continued to circle her anus, she found herself arching her back so he'd increase the pressure.

"Goddess, you're so responsive. I'm going to make love to you in every way possible, Laryssa. There'll be no part of you left unexplored by my touch, my lips," he promised.

"I'm yours to take." She'd given him permission, she knew. Having done so, she trusted him with her pleasure, her life. As he slowly pressed his finger into her tight hole, she quivered, stilling her movement. "Ah."

"Mais oui. Your lips." He kissed her. "Your pussy." He kissed her again. "Your heart. I'll take all of you... as mine. But do you want this, ma chérie? Are you certain?"

"Yes," she cried, as he plunged his finger all the way into her ass. Enveloped in all that was Léopold, she clung to him, her nails dragging down his pecs. Rocking into her orgasm, her chest heaved, desperate for air. "So full. So close. Don't stop. Don't fucking stop. Please, Leo. I'm coming...I'm coming..."

The moment her pulsating contractions took hold of his flesh, he drove himself up into her pussy again and again. Infatuated with her loss of inhibition, Léopold's fangs descended, scraping her neck. Only a whit of suppression kept him from transforming into his naturally feral state. *Feed.* The urge to pierce her sweet skin flourished in his chest. He had to have her. The need for her blood grew unbearable.

"Leo, yes. Do it!" she screamed, her body shuddering upon his. Raptured in climax, Laryssa knew he desired to take her essence. Yearning to have his fangs buried deep in her flesh, she clawed at him, drawing his blood with her nails, becoming the wild mate he rightfully deserved. "Do it. Make me yours."

With an animalistic growl, Léopold exploded, sinking his teeth into her neck. He could feel her buck underneath him in release as her nectar flowed down his throat. It was as if her blood had been created solely for him, and the reality shook him to his core. There'd never be another woman for him but Laryssa. His emotional celibacy had been shattered within days of meeting her and this final act had destroyed the possibility he'd ever return to solitude. The bond he'd fought so long to prevent registered immediately. The memories in her cells meshed with his. He knew she couldn't possibly feel the bond, for it was he who was destined to her for eternity. Waves of ecstasy from her energy filtered into him, and he'd never been more certain of anything in his life. This magical being he held in his arms was forever his.

Chapter Thirteen

Dressed in nothing more than their bathrobes, Léopold and Laryssa sat in silence staring at the pages. After making love in the limo, they'd come home, changed and immediately started working on the book. As much as each of them would have preferred to linger in the afterglow of their lovemaking, the demon's words and the threat of Laryssa's impending death pushed them onward.

For over two hours, each of them had taken turns looking through it, yet they'd found nothing that'd tell them where to find the Tecpatl. Even though Laryssa was unable to understand the Greek language, she'd hoped that because it was her book, it would reveal its secrets to her. Frustrated, she flicked her fingers through the pages one more time before slamming it down on the table.

"I don't get it. Are you sure this is right? There're chapters on sand? Ocean temperatures? Crustaceans? Fish? Even mermaids? But nothing about naiads? Nothing about Aztecs or Tecpatls? It doesn't make sense. Listen, I know you haven't read it page for page yet, but I don't have a good feeling about this."

"You must have patience. There's close to a thousand pages here, all in Greek. You have to give me time to read through the details."

"I guess I just thought that if it was supposed to be my book," Laryssa stood and began to pace, "that it would just…I don't know…that something would just come to me. But no. I put my hands on the pages and guess what I feel?"

"What?" He gave her a small smile.

"Nothing. Absolutely nothing. Zip. How can that be? Shouldn't I feel something? A spark? A tingle?"

"Not sure. Do you always feel something when you touch inanimate objects?" He grinned again, trying to get her to relax. Seldom were things in life as easy as they appeared.

"Well no, but it's supposed to be written by my people, right? If I saw this book on a shelf, I'd have no idea it was meant for me. No wonder it sat there in the store. Hell, I let Mason sell it."

"You've gotta give it some time. We just got home. Apparently, whatever answers it holds, we just haven't found them yet."

The front door opened, and they both looked up at Dimitri. After getting notice that they'd retrieved the book, he'd driven Jake back to Logan's so he could help keep watch over Ava. Dimitri took sight of their grim expressions and crossed the room.

"Hey," he said, sensing the tension.

"Hey, yourself," Laryssa commented. She walked away from the table and threw herself into one of the large chairs and propped her feet on its ottoman. Exhausted, she closed her eyes and put her arm across her forehead.

Léopold looked at him, raised his eyebrows and shrugged.

"So, uh, I see ya got the book. I'm afraid to ask how it's going," Dimitri said.

"Ma chérie expects immediate results, but as you can see," Léopold picked up the book and handed it to Dimitri, "it's a bit of a read. We've paged through it. At first glance, the table of contents reveals nothing unusual, makes no mention of naiads."

"Greek, huh?"

"Oui. Do you know how to read Greek?"

"I know a bit. I'd be happy to look at it." Dimitri glanced at Laryssa. "So what else is up? Is she okay?"

"She needs to go to the water. We ran into some trouble at the party."

"Trouble, huh? Things get rough?"

"Yes," Laryssa mumbled.

"You could say that my offer wasn't sufficient compensation." Léopold's blood boiled with a new surge of anger, remembering how the vampire had attacked Laryssa. "Martin touched her."

"Jesus, Leo. Laryssa, are you sure you're okay?"

"Yep, just tired. Leo's right. I have to go in the water."

"She was spectacular. Gave him a good fight. Then, she hit one of his lackeys with a statue. Sent it straight through the air without touching it."

"That a girl. Damn vampires can't keep their hands to themselves." Dimitri smacked his palm to the table. He raised an eyebrow at Léopold and gave him a small smile. "No offense."

"None taken." Léopold stood and walked behind Laryssa's chair and began to massage her shoulders. "She needs water. And rest. We can look at the book tomorrow."

"What else can I do to help?"

"I want to give Arnaud a call and check on him. He was supposed to bring us food, but he's not here yet." He felt Laryssa tense, but continued. "Laryssa won't feel right until she goes in the lake. When she flung that statue, I'm afraid she used up her energy. Tonight was pretty intense. Would you mind seeing her to the dock? I'll only be a few minutes. I'll come down after I'm done."

"Sure thing. You ready, Lyss?" Dimitri asked with a wink.

"Yeah, thanks," Laryssa responded, thinking about Léopold ordering his *food*. The mere idea of him taking another woman or man's blood, giving anyone the gift of his bite riled her.

Laryssa understood that he needed blood to survive. He was a vampire after all. But the brutal honesty of their intimacy in the car, getting him to accept her, it had led her to believe that they'd agreed to have a relationship. She realized, though, that they hadn't discussed exactly what that meant. Her mind told her it was wrong for her to only know him a few days and expect fidelity, but her heart told her differently. She reflected on why she was so irritated with him and whether it made sense. Rational or not, she knew that she couldn't share him. Not with women or men. Not for sex or food. She wanted a future with Léopold, one where he belonged to her and only her. Stewing in jealousy, she pushed up out of the chair, hiding her face from Léopold. If she caught his gaze, she feared she'd rip into him.

Léopold watched as Laryssa trod down the hallway with Dimitri, refusing to look him in the eye. Like a switch, she'd gone from passionate and loving in the car to seething under his touch in the living room. Though she had no idea, he could feel her jealousy and anger toward him as if it were his own. *Interesting.* But why she was jealous, that he didn't understand. It wasn't as if he'd so much as mentioned another woman. Picking up his phone, he selected Arnaud's number. As the tone rang in his ear, it occurred to him that she may have misunderstood his intentions. *How could she think that I'd feed from another woman after my confession to her? I chose her over all else.* But rather than sharing her concerns, Laryssa became withdrawn, concealing her thoughts from him.

He impatiently tapped his foot as he caught sight of her out the window, walking hand in hand with the wolf. His little rabbit was going to have to learn to trust now that she'd committed to him. *What fun it would be to teach her a lesson,* he thought. He supposed she also was due a reprimand for her behavior on the dance floor. Smiling, he licked his lips remembering the taste of her, anticipating the devious punishment he'd deliver, one they'd both enjoy.

Laryssa's spirit flared to life within the dark abyss. Naked to the cold, she'd stripped in front of Dimitri, no longer worried about being discovered. Like a gentleman, he'd turned his head. In truth, she hadn't cared if he'd seen her. Now that she'd confessed her nature, she felt liberated. Nude and slippery, she breathed in the water, letting the healing begin.

Dimitri sat on the dock with his jeans rolled up and his feet in the water, watching Laryssa swim. Gloriously bared, she dove, exposing her bottom. But when she didn't resurface, he panicked and began to tear off his shirt.

"It's okay," he heard Léopold say.

"No it's not. What the hell? She's drowning. Come on, help me," he snapped.

"Elle va bien. She breathes in the water." Léopold laughed. Still in his robe, he sat next to his friend. "She's amazing, no?"

"Scary is more like it. Dammit, Leo. You could've warned me," he said, blowing out a breath. "Jesus, how does she do that? She's been under for almost five minutes now."

"It's the way of her species. The lake…it heals her. Keep watching."

"Watching for what?"

"Ah, there," he pointed to a faint glimmer, which soon began to illuminate the water within a ten foot diameter. "See. She glows." Léopold chuckled.

"Now that's something you don't see every day. She's like one of those fish…you know, the kind that lights up to lure their prey."

"She's captivating."

"You do realize your girlfriend is lit up like a light bulb, right?"

"Oui."

"Goddamn," Dimitri exclaimed, punching Léopold lightly on his shoulder.

"What's your issue, wolf? I assume you have some good reason for flailing your arms at me?"

"You like her…she's your girlfriend," Dimitri sang.

"Oui, I suppose she is." Léopold's eyes darted to Dimitri, enjoying his shocked expression but quickly focused on the lake again.

"What happened?"

"What are you talking about?"

"Okay, what happened to my dark souled friend, Léopold?"

"My soul has never been dark," Léopold informed him in a serious voice. "My soul died. The day my family died, I died."

"Hey, I was just joking, man. Come on. Lighten up." Dimitri looked to the water and tried not to laugh. "Listen Leo, I'm sorry. Really. And I'm sorry you lost your family all those years ago. But I've always known your soul is in there. And it's never been dark or anything like that. Don't forget, I was there when you saved Wynter. You've just been…I don't know…hurt bad. So you went with tough and alone. Could be worse. You survived."

"Oui, I survived. But as Laryssa pointed out to me this evening, I haven't been living. She makes me want to do that again."

"So, uh, what's the story?" Dimitri asked. "She seemed kinda pissed at you when we left. But look at her now."

"She flourishes. But she must learn that we cannot have secrets," Léopold told him with a smile.

"Can't argue with that….but what happened?"

Before Léopold had a chance to answer, Laryssa broke through the surface with a cry of victory and began laughing. Caught up in her self-induced electrifying pleasure, she'd forgotten about Dimitri. As she glanced over to the dock and saw the men watching her, she rolled onto her back, exposing her breasts. Floating in the water, aglow with energy, she knowingly teased them.

"You've got yourself a live one, bro," Dimitri commented.

"That I do. She's devilish." Léopold shook his head and grinned. "And very disobedient. Look at her taunting us. She knows what she's doing."

"Oh, I'm lookin'."

Léopold gave Dimitri a glare.

"What, man? You know me. I'm not one to pass up the beauty of a nekkid water nymph," Dimitri teased.

"Naiad," Léopold corrected.

"Whatever. Say listen, you mind if I go wolf for a while? I'm planning on stayin' the night given the whole demon business, but I've been crammed in the city for weeks."

"Run wild, mon ami." Léopold's expression was one of pure delight as he watched Laryssa kick her legs and frolic. "You may want to stick around for a few minutes."

"Why's that?"

"Tonight, my little Laryssa came alive on the dance floor," Léopold began.

"I thought you guys were trying to remain inconspicuous?"

"Yeah, we kind of lost sight of that. Let's just say that I do believe she enjoys an audience."

"Really, now? She should be your perfect match, then," Dimitri snorted, recalling how the first time he'd ever met the vampire, he'd been deeply engaged in a public display of affection, having sex in the middle of Mordez. "Well if you're puttin' on a show, I'm down with that."

"Ah, here comes our little fish," Léopold commented, never taking his eyes off Laryssa.

Rejuvenated, Laryssa swam toward the dock, deciding that it was time to talk with Léopold. Taking in the sight of him and his delicious smile, she'd have to resist tearing off his robe and pulling him in with her. As she approached, she kicked her feet up into the air, spraying them both.

"Come in," she called, laughing as they wiped the water from their faces.

"You know, Dimitri, Laryssa and I came to an agreement this evening." While Léopold spoke to Dimitri, he smiled at Laryssa, his eyes locked on hers.

"Yeah. Hmm…what's that?"

"Well you see? I've been quite stubborn about keeping a certain little naiad out of my mind."

"Stubborn? You? Never," Dimitri chuckled.

"Oui, it's true. Our agreement was that I let go of my past, my guilt and choose her. Which I did. Yet for some reason tonight, she thought I betrayed her," Léopold said, his tone growing serious. "But I didn't do any such thing. You see, I was merely ordering food for us…as in human food."

"A girl's gotta eat," Dimitri added with a grin, knowing Léopold was about to do something he'd enjoy.

"Yes she does. But Laryssa thought I was bringing another woman into my home...for me. Now tell me, why would I do that when I've told her she's mine, when I've recently fed from her?"

"Leo, I..." Laryssa stammered. Her heart began to pound as she heard Léopold calmly tell Dimitri what had transpired between them in the car. *Why is he telling him what happened?* Even though she momentarily looked away, she was unable to take her eyes off Léopold. He was smiling. Damn him, he knew. He knew she'd been jealous. "You said you were ordering a meal. You just did that last night and a woman showed up. How am I supposed to know what you mean?"

"Because, mon amour," he crooked his finger at her, drawing her to him until she brushed against his calves, "I made you mine. And you must learn how to trust... to communicate."

"I'm sorry, but I..."

"So you see, Dimitri, she's very naughty." Léopold reached into the water until he'd fitted his hands underneath her arms. Easily lifting her out of the lake, he brought her upward so she straddled him on her knees. He kissed her lightly and continued. "Tonight on the dance floor...she teased me mercilessly, enjoying their eyes on her."

"She did?" Dimitri asked, raising his eyebrow at them.

"Tell me Dimitri, how do you feel about spankings?"

"I do like a good spanking." Dimitri flattened his hands behind him, leaning backward onto the dock.

Laryssa's eyes widened and she tried to push away from Léopold, but he held her firmly about her waist. Slowly he kissed her neck, placing his parted lips underneath her ear. As much as she wanted to struggle, the heat of him wrapped around her caused her to melt. A moan escaped her lips and before she knew what was happening, his lips had found her nipple. Her body lit on fire, and though she caught a glimpse of Dimitri, she soon refocused on Léopold's touch.

Abruptly he stopped and flipped her on her tummy, settling a towel under her head. She knew instantly what he planned to do. Torn between running away and encouraging him, Laryssa squirmed in his lap, putting pressure on his growing arousal.

"Take her hands," Léopold told Dimitri who smiled and turned to oblige. "Now, pet, shall we see what new heights we can reach?"

"Leo, don't do this," she said, feigning protest. Her pussy clenched in arousal as his hands glided over her inner thighs and caressed her bottom.

"I'll stop if that's really what you want. The truth is all I ask. In return, I'll be honest with you. Tonight, after all I'd confessed, you didn't trust me."

"I'm sorry, you know that..."

"Mon amour. Did you enjoy being watched tonight as we danced? Did you like it when I caressed your breast in front of all those people?" Léopold trailed his fingers down the crevice of her ass until he reached the heat of her core and then just as quickly removed his hand. "No lying, now. Tell me the truth."

"No, of course not," Laryssa insisted. She cried out as a sharp slap landed on her bottom. She clutched Dimitri's hands as the erotic sting sent a bolt of desire to her pussy. "Leo, no."

"Did you enjoy being watched? Do you enjoy Dimitri here, watching?"

Laryssa moaned as her hips writhed into Léopold's lap, seeking relief. Her nails dug into Dimitri's palms.

"Please," she begged as another slap landed on her flesh.

Léopold rubbed her reddened cheeks, smiling at how much she enjoyed it yet still refused to admit her penchant for exhibitionism. He slid a hand up her inner thigh and glided his fingers through her wetness.

"Oh God, Leo." Laryssa's orgasm built as his fingers found her clit. She looked up to Dimitri, who was smiling. Embarrassed, she buried her face into the towel and wondered how Leo knew her every fantasy. Things she dared not say. How could he know these things about her after only a few days? He was destroying the secrets she'd kept cached in her own conscience. Suppressing, hiding…it was what she'd learned how to do, but within minutes, he had left her soul unmasked.

"Do you see how difficult she can be, Dimitri?"

"She does seem to enjoy the spanking…but she looks like she wants to come."

"All she has to do is tell me the truth." Léopold slapped her cheeks twice more then plunged a thick finger inside of her, circling her clit with his thumb. Easing off the pressure, he removed the stimulus she needed to come but still held her tension tight. "Do you like this, Laryssa? Being spanked? Being watched? You're safe. All you have to do is say the word."

Laryssa shook her head, refusing to look at either of them, her hips gyrating into his hand. Dimitri played with her fingers and she finally raised her eyes to meet his. With his warm gaze upon her, her excitement escalated. She gasped as Léopold's palm landed on her bottom, causing a renewed gush of her own juices to flow between her legs.

"Say it, pet, or I'll stop," Léopold warned. "I'll let you go right now."

"Don't stop," she pleaded, giving in to his demand. "Yes. Goddamn you, yes."

Tears brimmed in her eyes, her body was shaking, readying to come. At her confession, any last remnants of angst about how she'd felt on the dance floor fell away like seeds in the wind. It killed her that Léopold could make her feel so incredibly open, knowing exactly how to bring her to the precipice of pleasure. Like a ball of string, her darkest dreams were coming unraveled.

"That's it, mon amour. Do not be ashamed. We are what we are." Léopold massaged her ass, while continuing to fuck her with his fingers. Goddess, he wanted to bend her over and make love to her right here on the dock, but he didn't think she was ready for that level of exhibitionism yet.

Increasing the speed and pressure, he added a third finger, pushing her over the cliff. "Let go."

Rocking into his hand, Laryssa lost all touch with reality as her climax claimed her. Soaring high, she shook violently as he stroked the thin strip of nerves inside her core. Unrelenting, his fingers strung out every last spasm. She closed her eyes, gasping for breath, when she felt herself whirl into a thousand pieces. Materializing inside Léopold's bedroom, she fell into the sheets with him.

"What the hell, Leo?" She slapped at his arm, gasping for air. "You have to warn me when you do that. How do you do that anyway?"

"Like your magic, mine is my own," he responded.

"Can other vampires do that?"

"None I've met. But then again, I haven't met any others as old as I am. I wasn't able to do it right away. I suppose I perfected it sometime in the fifteenth century. Nevertheless, I prefer to keep it a secret. The element of surprise is an excellent weapon."

"So why'd you bring me back here? You seemed to be having fun on the dock. I know I was." She winked, still trying to catch her breath.

"Just thought it best we retire in private. As much as I know Dimitri enjoyed your performance, it's not very fair to leave him wanting more. I care for you both, but I'm afraid I won't share you." Léopold disrobed, and pulled Laryssa onto his chest.

"Let me get this straight. Giving me a spanking and getting me off in front of him is perfectly acceptable, but you don't want him to join in? Seems awfully selfish." Laryssa glided her palms over his bare chest, wrapping her leg over his waist.

"Oui. I'm very selfish. Dimitri knows this," he agreed. "I also have my limits. You're mine, no one else's."

"But he just watched you do that to me."

"Spank you? Make you come?" he said with a smile.

"Yeah, that." She rolled her eyes, still coming to terms with what just happened and how incredible it had been.

"It's different. That was for your benefit, not his, mon amour. Exhibitionism, even voyeurism I enjoy. But another man making love to my woman? No. That's not going to happen. Besides, what's the protest? Is this something you want…to make love with another man, a ménage? Because if it is…I don't…"

"I'll admit Dimitri's attractive, but no, I don't want a threesome. Still… about what we just did. Well, that may be normal for you, but for me…I don't do those things. I'm not like that."

"But of course you do and you are exactly like that. Did you not learn a thing from your spanking? You will do those things with me and you'll love it. You're beautiful when you come…so uninhibited. It's an honor to witness."

"It's just so embarrassing. God, Leo." She hid her face in his chest, pressing her lips to his skin. "It felt so good, though."

"No shame. I won't hear of it. Just tell me how it felt."

"When you spanked me, it was just a small sting, but then all the nerves inside me contracted. It made me so hot."

"Go on," he encouraged.

"I don't know. I just loved it. When you put your fingers in me…it felt so good. And I looked up and saw Dimitri watching, knowing he enjoyed watching us. The whole thing was crazy…but liberating." Laryssa pushed up on her arms so she could look at Léopold. "Leo, how do you know these things about me? I've never in my life done anything like that before."

"I may not be able to read auras, but I've had the benefit of time. I'm good at reading people, even when they don't make their intentions explicitly known to me. And now," he stroked her cheek with his fingers, gazing into her eyes, "the bond has begun. Your blood. It's as I told you it would be when we made love and I drank from you. I can feel your emotions projecting at me. Like tonight with the food thing…"

"So that's how you knew…"

"Oui. And if we choose to complete the bond someday, you'll be able to do the same with me." Léopold ran his thumb over her bottom lip. "I have to ask, though, why is it you felt so ashamed tonight? I could feel that too. Even when you came, you still wouldn't just let it go all the way."

"I guess it's just a hang-up. I've been hiding for so long…who I am, how I feel. When I came back from that pond that day, after I died, I had the biggest secret in the world. And when I finally told the people I trusted…my family, they freaked out on me. I mean, look at the lesson I learned when I shared what I was. Pretty much any fantasy, sexual or otherwise, that I've had, I kept to myself. Besides, I already felt like some kind of freak. Being naiad, I can't trust anyone. No one knew about me except for Avery, and even with her, I've kept closed up about all kinds of things. Believe me, it's made for some very lonely nights. My last boyfriend called me frigid. He was right. I just can't open up. It's not easy." Laryssa sighed with the realization that even though she'd accused Léopold of not living, she was guilty of the same. "So then you come along and just kind of sweep me up in this tornado, exposing my fantasies about being watched or held down. I hate it that you can do that. But I love it, too. You are the first person to ever really know all my secrets and accept me for who I am."

Laryssa took her eyes off of Léopold and noticed the room was lit up with candles. What had he done? On a rolling serving cart next to the bed, there was a large plate of sandwiches, cheese and fruit. Two flutes had been filled with champagne. The bottle sat in an ice bucket along with several bottles of water.

"Oh my gosh. The candles. They're beautiful…but how?"

"Arnaud. It's why I had to call him. You need to eat, Laryssa. Especially if I'm going to be feeding from you."

Laryssa turned back to Léopold and pressed her lips to his. "I'm sorry. I should have told you how I was feeling. I just…I don't want to see you with another woman. I know you need to eat, but after having you bite me today…what we shared was so intimate. I know it's not fair of me to ask."

With ease, Léopold flipped Laryssa onto her stomach and she squeaked.

"Oui, I cannot say if our roles were reversed that I'd ever let you do it to another man." Léopold rubbed her shoulders and spoke softly into her ear. His semi-erect cock brushed along the cleft of her bottom. "But we're just getting to know each other, as you've pointed out, and what we are proposing is a…"

"Commitment?"

"Oui. Of sorts." Léopold reached over to a small silver bag next to the food. He pulled out a small bottle, opened it. Pouring the aromatic oil into a palm, he warmed it with his hands before applying it to her skin.

"What is that? Ah, you have magic hands," she groaned with a smile. "Hmm…smells like cinnamon."

"You like? I have more surprises for you, my little naiad. Just wait." Glad she wasn't able to see the devious grin on his face, he worked down the muscles of her back, smoothing out the knots.

"Should I be scared or happy?" Laryssa knew Léopold was up to something. He hadn't even mentioned the food aside from saying she should eat.

"We need to talk," Léopold said, gliding his fingers over her soft globes.

"Hmm…about?"

"Us…how we're going to proceed with our relationship."

She giggled. "Relationship. Yes, Leo, I think that's definitely what we're doing."

"But first, let's talk about toys." Léopold continued to massage her, letting his thumb circle her puckered hole. With his other hand, he dripped oil onto her bottom.

"Toys?" Laryssa tried to lift her head, but as soon as she felt his finger probing, she sucked a breath and dropped her forehead into the sheets. She was afraid to ask, but managed to mumble the question through the linens. "Hmm…what kind of toys?"

"Laryssa, I want to know everything about you from your favorite color to what makes you scream the loudest in bed. I like to play. And I…want to play with you." Léopold pressed his thumb into her anus. Feeling her clench underneath his touch, he held it still, allowing her to relax. "That's right, mon amour. I want to explore all of you. Will you let me do that?"

Laryssa knew what he meant. She hadn't ever done what he was suggesting. Never had a man known her body the way he did, and he was just getting started.

"I've never…I know in the car you touched me there, but I…I'm not sure, Leo," she hesitated.

"How does this feel?" He removed his thumb and inserted two fingers into her, gently pumping in and out of her back hole.

"Tight, so full…but, oh God, why does everything you do to me feel so damn good? You'll be the death of me," she teased. The more he stretched her, the more she wanted him in her. She began to move her hips against the sheets, trying to get leverage as the ache between her legs grew stronger. But as the energy began to build, she felt the loss of his hands. "Don't stop."

"Toys. Remember? I'm going to take you here, too, but we've got to have patience. See?" Léopold held up a bulbous pink device to her eyes, but pulled it away quickly so she didn't have too much time to think about its size. Liberally applying oil to the rubber, he replaced his fingers with its slippery point.

"Leo, I'm not sure that's going to…ah, yes…fit." *God, what is he doing to me?* She was close to coming undone.

"Push back onto it. See, there it goes." Twisting it gently, he pressed it past her tight ring. "Just a bit more."

"Leo, Leo," she cried. A sting of pain was followed by the most delightful fullness that caused her pussy to flood in arousal. "Oh yes, please, Leo…"

"So beautiful. Look at you. I can't wait to fuck your ass." He massaged her bottom, spreading her cheeks apart, then adjusted the plug to make sure it was settled deep inside her. "But now, we must talk."

"What? Talk? Talk about what? Leo, you can't leave me…" she begged.

Léopold gently rolled her over, kissing her protest away. Letting his hands roam over her breasts and neck, he cupped her face and held her in place. Capturing her lips with his, he softly brushed his tongue over hers. Lost in their kiss, he speculated that she'd been created just for him. She was so adventurous. Passionate. He knew what he had planned next would unnerve her, but he was altogether certain she'd come alive when it was done. Sliding his hands over her shoulders, he spread her arms outward, toward the headboard.

The sound of Velcro tearing alerted Laryssa but not nearly soon enough. As she sought to move her arms, she found that Léopold had secured her wrists.

"Leo, what are you doing?" she asked calmly. Strangely, the restraints only served to ramp up her desire. Tugging her arms, she tested them to see if they'd come loose.

Léopold slid his body down hers, placing a kiss to her belly as he went. Securing her ankles, He slid his fingers into the cuffs to make sure they held without being too tight. He pushed out of the bed to admire his work, grinning as he caught the look of annoyance on her face. The glorious sight of Laryssa lying spread-eagle on his bed sent a rush of blood to his cock.

"Do you like it? I think it works quite nicely. It secures underneath the bed, so I don't need to damage the furniture," he grinned.

"Uh, yeah, very nice, Leo. Look what you've done to me," she laughed.

"Okay, fun's over. Let me go."

"Come now, ma chérie. Must we have this conversation again?"

"The one about me saying no?"

"The one where I test your limits. You seemed to enjoy it very much last night, not to mention what we just did on the dock." He leaned over her breast and blew a warm breath on her nipple, smiling as it beaded in response. "And I do believe you are enjoying it now."

"Hey, what about safe words mister fifty shades of fangs? Safety first." She gave him a broad smile, continuing to test the straps.

"You're supernatural, Laryssa. Any confines I place on you are merely ones you allow. At any time, we both know you could move the straps out of place, freeing yourself. Go ahead, do it," he challenged. "I'll take you any way I can get you...I'm not picky. Tie me up, tie me down. Whatever."

She threw her head back against the pillow and groaned out loud, aware that he'd called her out on another one of her fantasies. The subtle feel of surrender felt natural, freeing. "How do you do that?"

"Last night. Your response to me. Every second I'm with you, I know you even better. And right now, I'm thinking that maybe you're hungry. Do you like brie?" He smiled. Naked, he sat on the edge of the bed and prepared it.

"Brie? You're kidding. Please tell me you're kidding."

"No. We need to have a discussion about feeding. So I feed you...open," he ordered with a smile. She made a face, but complied. He popped the tasty cheesy toast into her mouth. "See? It's good, no?"

"Yes. Okay, yes. Once again you are right. God, this really is delicious." She eyed him, noticing that he appeared deep in thought while he was slicing the cheese. "Talk to me, Leo. Why exactly am I tied up while we eat?"

"Because...if we're going to exclusively see each other, which I believe we are, then I'll need to feed from you." Léopold turned to Laryssa and gave her a devilish smile right before he started to spread brie on her nipple. "To be one's food...well that is how you say...a serious commitment. But for us, Laryssa, it is so much more. Not only will the bond grow deeper," he stopped to place a slice of cheese in the valley between her breasts and continued, "you'll begin to crave my bite. Eventually, I anticipate that we'll want to fully bond. And if that happens, you'll want my blood as well."

She opened her mouth to speak but Léopold popped a bite-sized finger sandwich into her mouth. She rolled her eyes in response, but soon made a subtle noise of contentment as she chewed it.

"So before we go any further, we should have a discussion. And I thought...what better way than to use food to demonstrate to you what it is like to be food?" Spreading a small amount of brie on her other bare breast, he smiled. Léopold snatched a couple of grapes and placed them down her belly in a line, clear to her pelvis. Then he lifted a glass of champagne, and brought it to her lips, careful not to spill any on her skin. "I believe in full disclosure. There haven't been many people in my life that I can trust. I need to be able to trust you…to know this is really what you want."

Laryssa swallowed and looked at the food covering her body.

"You're unbelievable, you do know that?"

"So I've been told." He fed her a slice of apple, smiling as she ate it.

"Leo, I do want this. I want to give us a chance. I know normal people…they take months, years to make these kind of decisions. But I also know I'm not normal. And you? Well, just look at me. Far from normal. You helped me to accept myself…to admit it…to be free. And even this," her eyes fell to her brie-covered nipples, "it's a little unconventional, but I know I'm gonna like being dinner."

She wagged her eyebrows at him and laughed.

Like a panther, Léopold stalked around the bed, carefully climbing up her body on his hands and knees until his face was inches from hers.

"You're certain?" he asked, looking into her eyes.

Laryssa nodded as her heart began to pound in her chest. The sight of Léopold, devastating and commanding, made her shiver in excitement. Like a dark prince, he cloaked her in his erotic shadow. As his lips descended on her breast, she sighed in relief that he'd finally touched her. The sweet pain of his teeth caused her to give a ragged gasp. Arching her back, she pressed herself up into his mouth.

"Goddess, woman, you have the most delicious skin." Using his tongue, he cleaned her rose-colored areola of the creamy white cheese. "My hunger for you is insatiable." Capturing her other pink tip, he sucked and laved until it was rigid with need. "Your magical essence is like no other blood I've had. I've never tasted anyone like you." Léopold crawled downward, placing his lips over each grape, replacing it with his tongue.

"Oh my God, please, Leo," she pleaded. Each time he kissed her flesh, the wetness between her legs increased, aching for his attention. As her core pulsated, her bottom tightened around the plug she'd forgotten was there, causing a vicious cycle of arousal to ensue. She attempted to clench her legs together but was unable to move. The cuffs on her ankles held her thighs far apart.

"One must take his time when eating. Savor the flavor," he mused. Rising above her, he reached for the bottle of champagne, letting the ice cold water drip across her chest.

Laryssa thrashed at the sensation, biting her lip. Her body was on fire and the contrast of the icy splash only surged the energy she'd held at bay. She knew that if she wanted to she could release her bindings, yet she resisted. Being at Léopold's mercy was immeasurably erotic and addictive. Being unable to anticipate his actions only added to the excitement of being under his spell.

Settling his knees between her legs, Léopold took his time licking her full peaks, making sure he'd eaten all the cheese and fruit from her body. His tongue glided downward, and he laughed as she bucked beneath him, trying to get him to move faster. Kissing below her belly button, his fingers separated her folds.

"Patience, pet." His lips touched her mound ever so lightly as he spoke. His voice vibrated against her soft flesh, but he didn't go any further.

"Please, Leo. I can't take it…I need you to touch me," she cried. He was torturing her with his lips, she thought.

"Did you know that champagne goes well with just about everything?" he commented blithely, spilling it over her clitoris. He heard her moan in sheer bliss as he licked over her swollen nub, sucking the effervescent delight. Letting the bottle drop to the floor, he plunged two fingers into her satiny core.

Laryssa felt as if she would fly out of the bed as Léopold took to her pussy, making love to her with his mouth. As his fingers pumped in and out of her, she stiffened as her climax splintered throughout every cell of her body. Driving her hips against his mouth, she cried his name out loud, seized by the orgasm. As she tipped the scales, her wrists and ankles wrenched at the unyielding straps.

Léopold held her hip tightly with his hand as she reared up into him. Forever lost in the taste of her, he knew he'd never again drink from another woman. As she tightened upon his fingers, he relished the pleasure he could bring her. The thirst for her heightened and he could no longer deny himself of her heavenly blood. He reared his head up, his fangs distending from his gums. With a savage cry, he pierced the soft skin of her inner thigh,

A scream tore from her lips as she felt him slice into her soft flesh, biting her. A profound wave of ecstasy ripped through her as another orgasm slammed into her. As she gasped for air, she felt her legs and arms release from their bindings.

"Laryssa," Léopold grunted, relinquishing his bite.

Pushing up to his knees, he hooked his arms underneath her legs. With his eyes locked on hers, he fully sheathed himself in her warmth. He watched as Laryssa balled the sheets up in her hands, bracing herself as he retreated and then slammed into her heated channel. Feral with passion, he held onto her hips, pounding into her over and over again. As he felt her contract in climax around his swollen shaft, he screamed her name. Succumbing to his own release, Léopold willingly submitted to the unfathomable rapture, his seed erupting deep inside her.

As the last spasm tore through him, Léopold fell forward onto his forearms, careful not to crush Laryssa. Her flushed face smiled back at him, and he tried to hide the vulnerability that crept into his chest. So many years alone had kept him impervious to heartache. In a few short days, his entire life had evolved. She'd be his weakness, but also his strength. Given no choice but to come to terms with his emotions, he'd protect and cherish her. Laryssa was a gift he'd never expected, a dark horse who'd tame the monster inside.

He eased himself out of her, rolled onto his back and brought her with him so she lay upon his chest. Pulling the comforter up over them, he felt his body meld into hers as they snuggled together. Léopold and Laryssa quietly held each other not saying a word. They'd just committed to each other, all the while knowing they needed to find the artifact. With or without it, she could be dead by the end of the week.

It had been nearly a thousand years since Léopold had last prayed. But as he stroked his thumb along her wrist, he found himself asking for forgiveness and mercy, appealing to the Goddess to give him the power to save Laryssa. It may have been too little too late, he knew, but he'd move heaven and hell to keep her in his life....forever.

·❦· *Chapter Fourteen* ·❦·

The demon's hot breath singed the hairs on the back of Laryssa's neck. Its talons dug into her arms and its acrid stench filled her nostrils. Struggling, she tried to move, but couldn't. Her sticky eyelids blurred her vision. She blinked as tears began to clear her eyes. Red scorched earth cracked beneath her feet, and she knew she'd been taken somewhere far from New Orleans. A bloodcurdling scream tore from her lips. The terror gripped her mind, seizing her muscles. The echo of her voice filled the barren terrain, leaving no doubt she was in hell.

"Welcome home, princess," it growled into her ear.

Hysterical, Laryssa gasped for breath. Dizzy with panic, her knees buckled but the creature held her upright. The hardness of it pressed into her back and the bile in her stomach rose. *Oh God, how did I get here?*

"Tell me, did you find it yet?" Its claws moved from her arms to encircle her waist, reaching under her breasts.

"I don't...I don't have it. Let me go," she yelled. Jabbing an elbow towards its gut, she attempted to wrench free of its hold. Fear boiled over to anger as she realized it'd somehow taken her from her bed. All too real for a dream, her senses told her she was no longer on Earth. It'd somehow managed to extricate her from the warmth of Léopold's arms.

"You'll never escape me now, Laryssa. I broke through your wards...into your mind. Once I have the Tecpatl, I'll travel to the other plane whenever I want. But you," it extended its tongue and gave a hiss, "you shall remain here with me...forever."

"I'm going to kill you," she stated calmly. Numb to her terror, she had no other choice but to fight it. If death was inevitable, she'd face it like a warrior. "I'm going to find that Tecpatl and destroy you."

The demon's dark laughter filled the cavernous space.

"You just do that, princess. Just remember that your king is waiting on you. Tic toc. Tic toc. Do it or the baby will die. Perhaps I'll take a few others if I get the chance to leave here before it's found," it threatened.

"You're nothing to me," she snapped.

"Rylion. My name's Rylion. Say my name, because I'm your master. Soon it's my blood you'll crave. Because I'm generous, I'm going to give you a little gift...something to remember me by." It squeezed her tightly and dragged its claws deep into the smooth skin of her belly until her blood spurted onto the ground.

Laryssa cringed as its long forked tongue wrapped around her neck and traveled down her chest. A new surge of horror speared through her psyche.

Thrashing wildly, she screamed and kicked to get away from the barbed fingers that eviscerated her abdomen. Her feet cut into the sharp gravel, tearing up the flesh. She bit it with her teeth and dug her fingernails into its scaly arms. All at once, the ground broke and she tumbled into oblivion. *Falling. Falling. Falling.* Her deafening screams went unanswered.

The ear-piercing sound of Laryssa's voice launched Léopold into action. Sprinting out of the shower, he found her tangled in the sheets. Her eyes were closed into reddened circles, her whitened face stained in tears.

"Laryssa," he whispered. Gently, he rubbed her arm, and lifted her body into his embrace so that he cradled her like a child. She continued to flail her arms and legs as if she were fighting an invisible enemy. "It's okay, ma chérie. Come now, it's just a dream."

A final scream escaped her lips before her eyes flew open. Seeing Léopold, she clutched at him, gasping for breath.

"Leo," she wept. "It was here."

"No, it was just a nightmare. See, look around you. No one's here. Just us."

Footsteps grew louder and Laryssa jumped as Dimitri flung open the door to the bedroom.

"What's wrong?" Confused, Dimitri looked around the room, finding only Léopold and Laryssa in each other's arms. "What the hell just happened up here? I could hear the screaming all the way downstairs…and it wasn't the good kind, either."

"A nightmare," Léopold told him. But as he adjusted Laryssa on his lap, he noticed a bright red stain blossoming in the linens. "What the…"

"Ow!" Laryssa cried out. Coming down out of her shock, a searing pain pierced her abdomen. "Something's wrong."

"Help me cut this off her. Use your claws," Léopold told him, tearing at the fabric.

Dimitri helped to rip away the fibers until they reached her skin.

"Careful," he said. Her belly, fully exposed, was covered in blood.

"Jesus Christ," Léopold exclaimed. He shot Dimitri a look of concern and then kissed Laryssa's head. "How did this happen?"

"I don't know…somehow…it was here. No, I was there. It…it had me, touched me." She shivered, remembering the feel of its scaly skin upon hers, the smell of it, the wetness of its tongue.

"Dimitri, come here. Take her," Léopold insisted.

"No, don't leave me. Please, Leo."

"The lake. Let me get water. If I take you with me, it'll hurt too much. I'll just be a few seconds," he promised. Remembering how Ilsbeth had used it to heal her wound the day before, he reasoned it would work again.

"Okay," Laryssa grunted as Léopold lifted her into Dimitri's arms. "You promise?"

"I promise." Léopold grabbed the ice bucket and instantly disappeared.

"Hey cher, we're gonna find this son of a bitch. Don't you worry." Dimitri stroked her hair and gently patted the five-inch incisions that dotted her tummy, trying to clot the blood. "Just listen to me...Leo's got this, okay?"

"It hurts." She sucked a breath, trying to focus on Dimitri's voice

Léopold appeared within minutes, and knelt before them. Cupping his hands, he drew up the liquid into his palms.

"The water healed you before. This'll work. Here we go..." Léopold let the water dribble over her open wounds, wishing he could be the one to take her pain. To his relief, his assumption was correct. As it hit her skin, it began stitching her back together. "Look, it's working"

"Oh God," she sighed as the pain began to subside. "We've got to find it."

"The Tecpatl?" Dimitri asked.

"Oui." Léopold knew what she'd meant. He couldn't agree more considering the demon had almost killed her in his own house. If it'd come to her here, it'd be able to find her anywhere.

"I'm going to kill it." Laryssa's face grew serious. A dim sadness flickered in her eyes, but they no longer held tears. The seed of hate had been planted and she planned to let it grow.

"Maybe you need to rest," Dimitri suggested, looking to Léopold for support.

"No, I need to find it. Now." Laryssa paused, glancing to Dimitri and then to Léopold. Her voice never wavered as she spoke with conviction. "I'm going to find that knife and drive it so deep in its heart that it'll never be able to dislodge it. When it's relegated to the pits of hell, it'll spend an eternity wishing it never met me."

Léopold and Dimitri let the silence fill the room, not responding. Everyone knew the situation would come to a head soon. They also knew Laryssa was right. She was the only one who could kill it. They had to spend the day reading the book, researching every last possibility in an effort to locate the artifact. If the demon had found a way to make itself tangible, worldly, able to strike at flesh, Laryssa's days were numbered.

Three days had passed since the demon had attacked Laryssa. Yet as she ran her fingers over her bare stomach, it was as if she still could feel it crawling all over her. Even though Léopold had read the book from beginning to end, he'd found absolutely nothing to indicate where the Tecpatl was located. She'd spent hours on the internet researching both naiads and the Aztec civilization. Calls to experts at the Smithsonian, the Metropolitan Museum of Natural History and several other prominent institutions proved futile. While they all knew of Tecpatls or kept them in their collections, none had been specified as the Tlalco Tecpatl. Even more disheartening, most denied its very existence.

Exhausted, she and Léopold had made love only a few times since the night they'd committed to each other. Laryssa suffered insomnia, worried the demon would call on her again in her sleep. As depression set in, she considered how unfair it was of her to insist that Léopold only feed from her. It was likely that she'd be dead by the end of the week. She'd asked that he choose her, yet what right had she to give herself to him when she knew she would die? The guilt made her want to push him away so he wouldn't care for her, wouldn't miss her when she died. After the devastation he'd endured from the death of his wife and children, she refused to be responsible for killing him a second time.

Returning to the lake had been Laryssa's only refuge. The more time she spent in it, the more she wondered what it'd be like to just live there like a mermaid in a sea. Rising through the water, she glided along the waves, pretending not to notice Léopold sitting in his chaise longue on the dock. She hated the book, the very one glued to his hands. Like a worthless newspaper, she wished she could throw it in the fireplace and light it up in flames. She let the satisfying fantasy float around in her head for several minutes before gathering the nerve to approach Léopold. It tore her apart to suggest that he call on a donor, but she resolved to talk with him....to prepare him for her death. Terrified of his reaction, she swam slowly toward him, keeping her eyes lowered to the water.

"How are you, my beautiful naiad?" he asked, never taking his eyes off the pages.

"I'm okay...I'm wet. Anything new?"

"'Fraid not. Just more of the same jumbled mess of water facts...insane, really. I know this was written several hundred years ago, but seriously, it's nothing but babble."

"Garbage in, garbage out," she muttered.

"Hmm?"

"I said, garbage in, garbage out. Did you ever consider that Ilsbeth just, I don't know, got it wrong? Fucked up? Maybe she's full of shit too," she seethed.

"Temper, temper, ma chérie. We'll figure this out." He took a deep breath and sat the book on his lap, adjusting his sunglasses.

"Yeah, well, you're not the one destined to become the bride of Satan in a few days. No, that'd be me. Lucky, lucky me." Laryssa flopped to her back, moving her hands and legs back and forth, floating on the surface.

"A demon," he corrected.

"What? Did you just seriously say that?" Laryssa lifted her head to yell over at him. "What the fuck difference does it make whether it's a demon or the real king of hell, or not? It told me it was a king. Believe me, where it took me, it was hell…hell for me anyway. Do you know what happens when I don't have water?"

"Oui, I do. And I'm well aware that you're scared. I don't blame you. Don't you think that I'm pissed off that we can't find anything in this damn book? That I'm scared to death that I'm going to lose you? Jesus Christ, Laryssa, I just found you…I need you. But we've gotta keep focused. Keep our eye on the proverbial prize. We can't get distracted. You're letting your fear blur your thoughts." Léopold hadn't adjusted to the trepidation Laryssa had projected since she'd been attacked. No amount of cajoling had helped to alleviate her spiraling descent into hopelessness.

Léopold decided that he was done being nice. He'd push her to the edge, incite her anger. He needed her to fight. Leaning over, he placed his forearms on his knees, holding the book with both his hands.

"Did you hear me? Are you listening, nymph? Because I need you to stop feeling sorry for yourself. This is far from over. I'm telling you that you need to shove all that woe-is-me crap down deep and get with the game. I don't know what's going on in that pretty little head of yours, but whatever you're getting ready to tell me, I know I'm not gonna like it. So what's it going to be? Are you going to just lay back and die? Because if that's the case, we might as well just call the demon now." Léopold thought he may have gone a little too far, but he was getting desperate to shake her out of her funk.

"You, you…" Laryssa saw red. Did he really think she'd given up? Mad at him, angrier at herself, she went on the attack. Her voice got louder as she swam toward him. "You condescending ass! Do you really think I survived all this time to just roll over and let some fucking demon take me? God, I hate this," she screamed. Hauling her palm back into the water, she shoved it forward.

A deluge of cold spray splashed over Léopold. He jumped up and threw off his sunglasses, wiping at his face and hands. In the process, the book fell to the deck.

"And there ya go. That's the spirit," he laughed. Unfolding a towel, he wiped his face.

"You're mean," she spat back at him, finding it difficult not to laugh. The sight of her debonair vampire, hopping up and down as if he'd been doused in holy water brought a smile to her face.

"I prefer the term, 'motivational', no?" He shot her a broad smile before searching for his shades. They, too, had fallen to the ground. As he reached to snap them up, he noticed the book. Its brown leather cover was covered in a speckled glow, similar to the color that Laryssa emanated when she submerged.

"Laryssa, come here," he called, his voice tense. "The book."

"Yeah, yeah," she sighed. But as she pushed up onto the warmed wooden planks, she, too, saw what had captivated Léopold's attention. "What is it? How? It's sparkling."

"No, ma chérie, it's glowing. Glowing just like you. Don't you see? It's the water," he exclaimed. "We should have known."

"What should we do?" Laryssa asked excitedly. Reason quickly set in and her mind began to turn with possibilities. "If it's the water, maybe I should take it in with me. Wait. No. We can't just throw it in the water. The pages are paper. I'm certain of it. There's no way that would work. Maybe brush it on there...carefully or something. But look at it. There're a thousand pages. I mean, how would we know where to start?"

"Come." He patted the dock. She gave him a look, raising her eyebrow at him. Realizing how much she disliked being bossed around, he corrected his words in a sweet tone that told her he understood her perfectly. "Would you please join me?"

He laughed as he said the words aloud, aware of how ridiculous he sounded. Léopold Devereoux didn't ask. He ordered. Sometimes nicely, sometimes, not at all. Being with Laryssa was changing all of that, teaching him a set of manners he wasn't entirely sure he wanted to learn. But as her laughter filled the air, he shook his head, knowing he'd done the right thing. The sound of her joy was becoming the most delightful part of his day.

"Yes, darling," she drawled, smiling up at him. "I do love sitting next to you."

"Mais oui. I'm a catch." He winked and gave her a lopsided grin, chuckling as she shoved on him gently with her shoulder. "Look, it's starting to fade."

Leaning forward, he captured a bit of the water in his hand and flicked it over the cover, but the spots continued to vanish. He blew out a breath.

"Wait. Let's just think. It's my book, right? If anyone could make it work, it would've been discovered already. So maybe," she hesitated, then dipped her fingers into the basin and ran them across the cover. Instantly, it lit up again. A broad smile broke across her face at the victory. "I'm the one who has to do it."

"Excellent. Now....we start at the beginning," Léopold said, flipping the cover open to the first blank page. "The table of contents. Fifty chapters. I'll hold it. Go ahead, touch it," he urged.

Laryssa did as he said, carefully brushing her wet finger across the paper. She shook her head, disappointed nothing was revealed. Léopold carefully pulled over another sheet. Half way down, a line began to appear.

"Leo, look," she whispered, astonished it was working.

"Lucky number twenty-seven." Léopold took out his cell phone as the writing appeared on the page. When she lifted her hand, he snapped a picture. "Calle del Arsenal de las Ursulinas? Mères des filles. La clé."

"The historical signs? Rue des Ursulines. Ursuline Avenue. What does the rest mean?"

"Mères des filles translates to mothers of girls. La clé. The key."

"I was hoping for something along the lines of: 'follow this map to get the knife'. Guess I knew it wouldn't be that easy." She blew out a breath and looked out to the lake, deep in thought. "Mothers. Girls. I don't know. Is there a school on Ursuline? Maybe it's hidden there."

"Filles du' Casket."

"What?"

"Filles du' Casket. The casket girls. The convent on Ursuline."

"You mean the one that tourists visit? Rumors of scary vampires?" She laughed.

"Oui. That's the one. But as you know, my pet, vampires have been around for the millennium. The Ursulines came over in the early eighteenth century. Perhaps the good sisters protected the Tecpatl? They were known to take in young girls, the poor and the like. Maybe a naiad sought safe harbor and hid the relic within the convent walls?"

"But where? I guess we could get in on a tour, but where would we even begin to look?"

"Not worried about how we'll get in...I've got that covered." He shot her a knowing smile. "It's the where that's a problem. The place's fairly large, and the item is probably small. Maybe we should try chapter twenty-seven...to see if there's more."

Laryssa turned the pages, her anxiety rising. *Two days*. It was all she had left to find the Tecpatl. Why couldn't the naiad who wrote the book be direct about its location? She had an inkling of worry that the enigmatic words would only lead them on a wild goose chase, but they were out of options. She shrugged and shook her head in frustration, searching for the chapter. *Let the chase begin*. Again, she dipped her fingers in the water, running them over the wafer thin folio, her eyes widening as more letters surfaced.

"Le waterleaf tombe donne la clé," Léopold read.

"What's it mean?" she asked.

"The waterleaf falls bestows the key...which makes absolutely no sense at all." He sighed and plowed his fingers into the hair on the back of his head.

"Maybe it'll make sense once we get there?"

"Maybe." *It fucking better*, he thought. He'd just spent time trying to convince Laryssa they'd find the Tecpatl, yet the text made no mention of it. "Try the next page, there's got to be more."

She repeated the process, but this time a primitive drawing appeared. A series of lines hovered above what looked to be scales, a fish. Below the fish was a key. Laryssa sighed, unsure of how it tied in with the Tecpatl. Immediately she pictured the river.

"Un poisson," Léopold commented, looking at the picture. "Like you, no?"

"Did you just call me a fish?"

"Oui. But in a good way." He laughed and placed a kiss to her cheek. "Surely this is tied to you? It's a fish. And water. I'm not sure what it means yet but at least we have a clue."

"So, uh, how do you feel about breaking into a convent later?"

"Sounds good. I take all my dates there," he teased.

"Thought you didn't date?" she countered.

"Touché. That was true, but I do now."

"A convent, huh? You sure vampires don't burst into flames at the sight of a cross?"

"Easy there. You're going to insult my delicate ego."

"Delicate ego? Now that's a good one, Leo," she jibed.

"Come now, we must get ready to leave. Sun will be down in an hour. We'll take the car then, you know, pop in," he suggested.

"About that…you promised to warn me first, right?"

"Promise, mon amour," he purred, kissing her neck. This woman would break him, he knew. He had to figure out a way to save her. If she died, he might as well stake himself.

❧ *Chapter Sixteen* ❧

"Nice wheels. Can I drive it?" Laryssa asked, trying to distract herself from the fact that they were about to break into a convent. *Yep, if there is a more direct path to hell, I can't think of one....well, aside from the damned demon.*

"You know I'm very fond of you, no?" Léopold deflected her question, staring at the cream-colored plastered wall that surrounded the old convent.

"So you'll let me drive it?"

"You're the most beautiful little naiad I've ever met."

"I'm the only naiad you've met. Can I drive home?" She smiled at him, realizing he was avoiding answering.

"Well, aside from Ava, that's true. You ready to go inside?"

"I've never been in a Lamborghini before. How fast does it go?" she continued.

"Do you recall me telling you that I don't share?" he countered.

"Yeah, that was about me, not the car. I promise to be careful. Besides, it's just a car."

"Just a car," he sniffed. "You do realize how much this car…"

"No. Don't care. And why's that? Let me see… yeah, that's right, I could be dead in two days. Just checking…no, I don't care how much it costs. But I would like to drive really, really fast." Without equivocation, she reached over and took his hand in hers. Their easy conversation had filled her soul, allowing her to forget, albeit only for seconds, the sobering reason why they were sitting in the car in the first place.

Léopold glanced out the window with a grin and shook his head. He'd give her the damn car and anything else she wanted to make her happy. He knew she was worried…worried they'd fail, that the demon would kill her. Maybe he couldn't change the situation, but he could lift her spirits.

"We'll see, mon amour. I'm not going to let you get us killed speeding before we have a chance to make love again."

Laryssa made a sad face, sticking out her bottom lip and then quickly smiled. "Please…."

"Okay, okay. I'll let you drive it. On one condition." He took the keys from his pocket and held them out to her.

"What is it?" She raised a curious eyebrow at him.

"When all this is done, I want you to move in with me."

"It's kinda soon for that, isn't it?"

"Shall I tie you up again when we get home?"

"So it's just my blood you want?"

"No. It's you that I want. I want you in my home. I want you in my bed.

And I want you there forever." Léopold had deliberately let the bond grow stronger each day, aware that it would only be a matter of weeks before he sought to complete their bond. It had been a conscious choice that at one time he'd thought preposterous, yet he'd never felt more satisfied or alive. Laryssa recognized the serious tone of Léopold's voice. No longer engaging in easy banter, he'd pinned her in place. Her heart sped with the realization that he was genuinely asking her to move in with him. Her mind warred over what she wanted to do versus what she'd been conditioned as a human to think she should do, what was socially acceptable. Despite knowing she was immortal, she had led her life very much as a human. But having a demon slice open her midsection, one who planned on dragging her into its horrific underworld, forced her to set priorities and face the reality of her situation. There was a very good chance she'd die in two days. With no time for a bucket list, agreeing to move in with the man she was falling for seemed to be the most rational choice in the world.

"Yes," Laryssa replied softly.

"Excellent," Léopold exclaimed, pleased with her answer. He extracted the keys from the ignition and dangled them in front of her. "Ride home. You drive."

"Really? You're serious?" She extended her palm and he dropped them in her hand.

"A man never jokes about his car." The corner of his lip curled upward, his eyebrow raised.

Laryssa wrapped her arms around Léopold and hugged him. She could tell she surprised him as he slowly returned her embrace. Biting her lip, she realized that she'd almost told him how she felt. How embarrassing, she thought, that she'd almost used the *love* word. Aware of why they were sitting in the car, emotion welled inside her chest. Fighting the tears she knew would come all too easily, she pressed her face into his shirt. Inhaling his masculine scent, she sought to sear the memory of him into her psyche. From the way he smelled to the way he firmly held her in his arms, she'd never forget him. Whether in heaven or hell, he'd always be hers.

"This is creepy," Laryssa whispered, carefully walking through the darkened convent.

"I promise to protect you from the vampires," he teased, keeping his voice quiet.

"Maybe we should've told Sydney we were breaking in. Or even better, asked if we could come in…you know, legally." She shone her flashlight toward the floor, hoping no one would see them and call the police.

"The police know nothing of our ways," he said with disdain.

"But what about Sydney? Hello? She lives with a vampire, right?"

"Oui. But she's new in town. Besides, she needs to keep Ava safe, not babysit me."

"I'm just sayin'. Would be nice to be able to just flick on the lights and look around."

"I can see perfectly fine. Come this way," he told her.

"You do remember that I'm not a vampire or wolf? I'm very close to being human. Do you think you're going to be able to accept being…" She'd almost said 'married' and immediately swallowed her words, shocking herself that she'd even had the thought.

"Being what?" he said, unaware of what she was thinking. He gestured toward her. "This way, into the living quarters."

"Are you going to be able to accept that I'm kinda human? I know I have some abilities, but I've been less than effective in helping with finding this knife. Look at how long it took us to figure out what to do with the book. For crying out loud, I had it in my shop for two months and didn't even know it," she huffed, following him down a long hallway.

"You're naiad. You just haven't had time to strengthen your powers yet. And eventually," *with my blood…when we bond,* "you'll be able to do even more things. Don't sell yourself short."

"Maybe…if I actually live long enough. Do you see anything? What was the saying again? Something about a leaf."

"Le waterleaf tombe donne la clé. The waterleaf falls bestows the key." Léopold studied the artwork, hoping there'd be some clue or picture of a leaf.

"Ugh, damn cryptic naiads. Waterleaf. What do you think that even means? Are we talkin' lilies or maybe ferns?"

"Not sure. Maybe the book referred to an actual waterleaf. It's a species of plant. Flourishes in the water. Little blue flowers."

"I have to admit that I'm impressed with your knowledge of horticulture." Catching the small laugh he gave, she pressed him. "What? How'd you know that?"

"Wikipedia. Even an old man like me can use the internet, ma chérie," he grinned. "But look around here, there's no plants at all. I still think that it must be in one of the paintings."

"Look at this staircase…it's incredible," Laryssa commented, flashing the light over the wood. The three-story-high spiral staircase curved upward so that you could look down to the floor while you ascended. "You know this is one of the oldest buildings in the city?"

"Oui. The architecture, it's…"

"It's waterleaf," she interrupted, taking notice of the underbelly of the staircase, which had been inlaid with an intricate cream-colored molding.

"Where?"

"Here." She pointed to the edges that were carved with tiny leaves. "This pattern. It's waterleaf. I can't believe I didn't put it together. I've been in so many mansions...see this pattern. Usually it's carved in the crown molding. But this is rare. I mean look at it, it's a huge area. It covers the entire back of the staircase going up to the ceiling."

"Oui." Léopold sighed, assessing the situation. Taking off his suit jacket, he handed it to Laryssa. She took it from him, giving him a look of confusion. *This is not going to be pretty.* As much as he appreciated fine woodwork, it had to go. *Pity.* Without warning, he balled up his fist and punched it directly through the molding. He heard her gasp as splinters flew into the air.

"Jesus, Leo, what the hell are you doing?" she shouted, bringing her hands to her mouth. "You just totally wrecked that wall. This is a historic building. Oh my God...Lord, please forgive this vampire. We're in a fu...freakin' convent, for God's sake."

"Oui, I'm aware of the fact, but we don't have a lot of time. And I don't have patience. I'll be sure to send a generous donation that more than covers the damage." Léopold began to peel the wood away from the back of the stairs.

"But...but..." she stuttered. Altogether aghast with his actions, she shook her head. But as she shined her flashlight into the empty space, curiosity took over her actions. Intrigued, she searched the cavity. "Leo, Leo...do you see that?"

"See what?"

"Stop for a second. Look, that there." She pointed to a small shiny object on the floor. "That's not a key. What is it?"

"Stand back," he ordered. Reaching into the chamber, his fingers brushed over the piece of metal. Leaning a bit further, he was able to collect the small item. Lifting it to the light, they both studied their find. "Un poisson?"

"A fish," she confirmed. "It's brass. It doesn't look like any kind of key that I've ever seen, but that has to be it. Can I see it?"

Léopold deposited it into her palm. The cold bumpy ridges of its scales were rigid, and she couldn't tell if it was an ornamental piece or something else. But as she flipped it over, she noticed the small round bar that ran from its tail to its head.

"Hey, I've seen one of these. Well, not this exact one but a tiger. An antique tiger lock. This one's similar. I think it's a puzzle, though. The key must be inside it." She shook it and it rattled. "There's something in here."

Léopold brushed the dust off his hands, retrieving his coat from the crook of Laryssa's elbow, where she'd been holding it. He slid his arms into the sleeves, and smoothed down the wrinkles. Laryssa glanced up at him, reminded that behind his refined supermodel looks, lurked a ferocious warrior.

"We've gotta go," Léopold said, hearing sirens in the distance.

"But what about this?" Her eyes darted over to the shards of wood covering the floor.

"As I said, I'll make a donation." Léopold put his arms around her waist, attempting to prepare her for their departure. "Ready?"

"Léopold, you can't just leave…" Laryssa lost all thought as he transported them back into the car. They fell into the passenger side seat together. As her head stopped spinning, she took note of her positioning. She sat atop of him with her legs straddling his. She gave him a small smile, and brushed her breasts into his chest.

"Now this I like," he quipped, pressing his erection up into her.

"You are a very bad vampire. Making a mess like that," she scolded, her voice husky. "Naughty boy."

"Is that a challenge? 'Cause you've got no idea how bad I can be," he replied, letting his fangs drop.

"Léopold," she feigned protest. Being so close to him caused her body to flare in heat. "We've got work to do."

"It's true." He nuzzled his nose into her neck, pressing his lips to her skin.

"Why does breaking and entering make me horny? You're corrupting me," she laughed.

"All day long, ma chérie, all day long." He laughed, but knew he was seriously close to tearing off her clothes. Realizing that if they went further, they'd be having sex in a parked car, with the police soon to arrive, Léopold gripped her by the waist and lifted her into the driver's seat. "Now be careful with my baby. Treat her gently. Avec amour."

"Nothing but love, baby," she said with a wink.

Léopold braced himself as Laryssa inserted the key into the ignition, and the engine roared to life. His stomach flipped at the sight of his gorgeous naiad with her hands wrapped around the steering wheel. As she shot him a sexy smile, Léopold knew for certain the experience would be something he'd already guessed. In more ways than one, he was in for the ride of his life.

❧ *Chapter Seventeen* ❧

Sydney patted Ava on the back, while rocking her in the chair. The sweet smell of the baby warmed her from the inside out, and she wondered if she'd ever change her mind about not having children. Even though she and Kade couldn't get pregnant, the possibility of adopting had always remained an unspoken option.

She had to admit to herself that the past four days, living with the Alpha and his mate, hadn't been even close to a hardship. Both Logan and Wynter had shown her what she'd always imagined to be southern hospitality at its finest. Strangely, she found herself becoming close to Wynter. From sunup to sundown, they chatted about everything from recipes to television shows. Granted, their cloistered existence was beginning to wear thin in that they both yearned to get out of the house, but Sydney knew that by the end of the week, something was going to break in the case. God help them all, she prayed that it wouldn't involve death.

Daily, she'd checked the interior and exterior, ensuring that there were no weak links in the physical structure of the house. Samantha had seen to spells, making sure that no demonic forces could cross over into the home. Unbeknownst to the wolves and the vampires, she'd ordered increased police patrols to be set up within a five block radius. Despite having taken every safety precaution, Sydney knew all too well that if a supernatural force wanted to get to a person, they'd never give up on a plan of attack. Even if they had to wait it out, eventually they'd make their move and strike.

Sydney smiled at Wynter, who'd entered the room. She'd thought it was interesting how the Alpha and his mate had taken to the baby. Even if they never found Ava's biological father, Sydney was certain the baby would have a good home. Between Léopold and the Alpha, there was no question she'd be raised with love.

"How's our baby doin'?" Wynter asked Sydney, drying her hair.

"She's good. It's amazing to me how she sleeps so well after her bottle. She's just so adorable," Sydney said. She got up from the chair, and walked to the crib. Carefully laying Ava on her back, she pulled the baby blanket over her.

"She really is, isn't she? You know, I never thought I'd want pups so quickly. But having Ava here...it'll be really hard to let her go." Wynter's eyes teared up as she spoke. She turned back to the mirror and toweled at her hair, attempting to hide her emotion.

"Have you given any thought to what might happen if they can't find her father? I know the priority's been on killing this demon and keeping everyone

171

safe, but at some point, we're gonna have to have the conversation."

"Logan's said he's put out feelers to his contacts...to packs around the country. Léopold. Well, you know him. He immediately hired an investigator. But they've turned up nothing."

"And what happens if that's the answer? There's a chance the guy may have offed himself, ya know. I see it happen all the time."

"The only thing I know is that she'll be raised as pack. Ilsbeth said that Ava's naiad. Even if she's a hybrid wolf, she'll go through the change. She'll shift. She needs to be with pack," Wynter insisted.

"Hey, you'll get no argument from me. I just wondered if you'd thought about maybe adopt..." Sydney went quiet as the hairs on the back of her neck stood up.

"What was that noise?" Wynter whispered loudly. "Did you hear that? It was something...I don't know...It sounded like a wind chime maybe."

Sydney caught Wynter's gaze and held her finger to her lips to shush her.

Wynter nodded as Sydney went to the dresser. She slipped on her holster and gun she'd removed earlier so that she could hold baby. Wynter quickly crossed the bedroom, scooping Ava up into her arms. Sydney looked out the window, noticing a few people walking down the street. Nothing appeared unusual, but she knew better than to believe what her eyes told her. The noise sounded again and she knew something was wrong. She looked over to Wynter and silently mouthed, "Stay here."

Sydney heard Wynter click the lock on as she shut the door. She quietly padded down the stairs, bumping into Jake, who was running toward his Alpha's bedroom.

"Where's Logan?" Sydney asked, her voice barely audible.

"Logan and Dimitri are on their way here. I just texted them. Did you see anything?"

"Nothin', just a few tourists. I'm goin' to go outside and see what's going on...make sure things are still locked up. Cover me?"

"I'll take the second floor and spot you," Jake told her.

"Come lock the door behind me," she responded. "Don't let anyone in this house."

"No one gets in," he agreed, taking out his gun.

"Seriously, no matter what happens, do not leave Wynter and the baby."

Sydney watched as he bolted it shut then went through the archway toward the gate. Even as she walked toward the exit, everything appeared exceedingly calm. The fresh night breeze blew through her hair, and she wondered if maybe one of Logan's neighbors had installed a wind chime. When she reached the gate, she peered through the wrought iron. Seeing nothing, she pushed the handle and guardedly exited the property to check the gate's lock from the exterior. Looking up the street to her left, she caught sight of a pedicab traveling away from her and reasoned that maybe the noise they'd heard could have been caused by it. Glancing to the right, she noticed a well-dressed man standing on the corner, checking his watch. Even though he looked harmless, she kept sight of him in her peripheral vision as she double checked the gate. Then without warning, he turned to walk in her direction.

"Excuse me," she called out using her professional tone of voice, and lifted her badge from the chain around her neck, so that she could easily identify herself as a police officer as he approached. The stranger appeared not to hear her, looking the other way.

"Sir," she said loudly.

Her second attempt caught his attention and he turned to her with a smile. Although the man looked exceptionally handsome, something about him seemed off, not quite right. His smile was too friendly, as if he'd recognized her as a long lost friend. A flash of creepiness clutched at her chest, the kind she'd get when arresting sex offenders. While his looks appeared benign, her instincts told her otherwise.

"Sir, stay right there," Sydney ordered. She reached for her gun and raised it. He deliberately approached her with his arms outstretched. Bracing the weapon with both hands, she held the barrel upward, looking around her to make sure there weren't any bystanders.

"Sir, if you don't stop right there, I may be forced to shoot," she told him. Out of the corner of her eye, she spotted Jake standing behind an open second story window with his gun aimed downward.

"Sydney," the man trilled. His voice sounded freakishly low, as if he'd been using an electronic device to disguise his identity.

She watched in astonishment as his body flickered, revealing an unearthly form. *Scales. Horns.* Without hesitation, Sydney fired into the night. The bullets hit its chest, but sailed through its body without injuring it.

"What are you?" she whispered as it came toward her. By the time it had reached her feet, it had transformed into its true hellish form. Its long talons snapped together on the pavement, the stench of its breath saturating the air.

"I'm your worst nightmare. And I want you to deliver a message," it hissed.

"A message?"

"A message for the naiad. For the wolves. Tell them I was here and I'll be back for the baby if she doesn't return the Tlalco Tecpatl to me by midnight tomorrow. I'll find her."

"Yeah, okay. Well, here's my message..." Sydney unloaded an entire clip into the demon, praying to God it would take him down. When the dust settled, she gasped as it lurched for her, laughing as it did so.

Grabbing her by the throat, it lifted her off the ground. Sydney could hear Jake firing off his weapon yet the creature held tight. Extending its claws, it sliced its entire fist into Sydney's abdomen. Like a red hot poker, its nails pierced clear through from her belly to her back. She released a horrific scream as her organs burst apart at its touch. Blood spewed onto the street as it threw her to the ground. Gasping, her throat filled with fluid. The demon leaned over her wound and spat its acidic saliva into her before dissipating into the night. As the circle of darkness surrounded her, thoughts of Kade danced in her mind. Although she tried to fight, the sweet sensation of death called to her, lulling her to sleep.

⟶⟪❀⟫ *Chapter Eighteen* ⟪❀⟫⟵

Laryssa's stomach lurched with the news that Sydney had been attacked. By the time Dimitri had called Léopold, they'd already driven to the lake. Laryssa had remained silent the entire trip back to the Quarter, her thoughts spinning with dread. Even though it was good news that the demon hadn't breached the wards, it had viciously assaulted the detective.

Laryssa couldn't fathom why they hadn't taken her to a hospital. Léopold insisted that there were no human doctors who would have been able to save her. Her organs had endured systemic trauma and the resulting injuries were catastrophic. No human should have survived. The gash to her abdomen had sliced her open clear through to the other side. Dimitri had relayed that Kade had arrived within minutes of her being slain on the street. Kade's blood had been the only hope, keeping her alive. It should have healed her completely, but she hadn't fully recovered. Still unconscious, she clung to life.

As Laryssa and Léopold slid open Logan's back door, they were met with somber faces. The Alpha's eyes met Léopold's, but he made no move to release his mate from his arms. Samantha sat, holding the baby and glanced up to Léopold with reddened eyes. Rather than engaging in conversation, Léopold merely nodded and waited as Dimitri approached him.

"Hey man," the beta said, putting his hand on Léopold's shoulder. "Laryssa. How's it goin'?"

"We found something. It's some kind of a lock, maybe a puzzle," Laryssa offered. Earlier, they'd filled Dimitri in about the book and how they'd discovered the hidden writing. "We were on our way back to see if we could get it open. We think it'll tell us the location of the knife."

Dimitri nodded. "You'd better not stay long then."

"How is she?" Léopold asked. "Kade?"

"She's alive. But something's not right," Samantha answered from the sofa. She kept her voice quiet as she brushed her fingers through the baby's hair. "The vampire blood should've healed her."

"Jake saw the whole thing. He covered her from the window. Shot it several times...I mean over and over. Nothin' worked." Wynter paused, shaking her head and considering her words. "After it gutted her, it...well, Jake said it spat into her. Blood or something. I don't know. I was in the room with the baby and didn't get close to the window."

"Why would it do that?" Laryssa wrapped her hands around her midriff, recalling the burn of its claws. "There must be a reason."

"Kade thinks the demon did it to tie her to it somehow. It said something about taking her and the baby if it didn't get that knife." Wynter broke free of Logan's arms and nervously walked into the kitchen. She pulled several cups out of the cabinet and checked the pot of coffee she'd brewed earlier. In an effort to keep busy, she arranged the mugs in a row. "Can I get Y'all some coffee? Cream? Sugar?"

"Yeah, thanks." Laryssa felt as if she'd been sucked into an alternate reality. *Would you like cream and sugar with that demon?* Here they all were calmly and politely discussing Sydney's attack as if it was completely normal, a day in the park. Having lived her whole life away from the supernatural world, it was like immersion therapy gone wild.

"You know, it, uh, talked to her before it attacked," Dimitri added. Noticing that Wynter's hands were shaking, he took the pot of coffee from her with an understanding smile and finished pouring.

"Oh God," Laryssa said. She pushed her fingers through her hair in worry.

"It talked? What did it say?" Léopold approached Samantha and ran his hand over the baby's forehead. Ava smiled up at him and cooed in response.

"Same ole with a dash of more. It wants the Tlalco Tecpatl…by tomorrow night. Said it's comin' to you. You're running out of time, Leo." Dimitri's eyes fell on Laryssa. They all knew the consequences if they didn't find it, and they had less than twenty-four hours to do so. "There's one other thing I forgot to mention. This time, Jake said it looked like a man. A human. It didn't last long, but that's how it appeared at first. I don't remember Ilsbeth sayin' anything about that."

"It needs Laryssa to be whole, to cross over to our world whenever it wishes. It's possible that since it attacked her, maybe her blood did something to augment its power," Léopold surmised.

"Gave it extra mojo," Dimitri guessed.

"Oui, made it stronger. Or it may have been able to do it to begin with, no? It's not like a demon's going to tell us its abilities. No, it's going to lie, conceal. It'll do what it needs to do to get the Tecpatl, but it wants Laryssa. That night at the lake…it's more than just her soul. It wants her."

"I agree with Leo. That night…the way it looked at me. This won't end until I kill it or it takes me." Laryssa's voice was shaky as she spoke the words aloud.

"I'll never let it have you," Léopold told her, his eyes meeting hers and then falling to Dimitri.

"Hey, maybe you should go see Kade? We didn't want to move Sydney too far so we kept her here…took her upstairs. Figured the wards on the house are workin' since the demon couldn't get in. But I gotta warn you that Kade doesn't seem to be takin' this so well."

Léopold opened his mouth to tell Dimitri that he would visit, when he heard Luca trample down the stairs and into the great room. With his fangs protruded, Luca rushed toward them. Instinctively, Léopold moved in front of Laryssa, protecting her from an attack. Already aware that Luca disliked her, Laryssa kept quiet and clutched the back of Léopold's jacket out of fear. While she knew that Sydney's mate, Kade, would be devastated by her attack, she hadn't anticipated the ill-tempered vampire's violent reaction.

"Goddamn you, Léopold. This is your fault. You brought that baby here. You knew Sydney would try to protect the child. If she dies, it's her blood on your hands. Yours and that nymph you're fucking," Luca roared. "If you'd just given her over to the demon, none of us would be in this mess."

Before Laryssa or Dimitri had a chance to stop him, Léopold lunged at Luca. Shoving him against the wall, Léopold seized Luca by his throat with one hand. Luca struggled to get free, but his effort to dislodge Léopold's grip was futile. Everyone in the room froze at the sight of the two vampires engaged in battle, one nearly killing the other. Neither Dimitri nor Logan made a move to interfere, as they knew it wasn't their place as wolves to get involved in the dispute.

"Stop it!" Samantha screamed. The baby began to cry, and she quickly handed Ava to Wynter. Despite wanting to break up the fight, she, too, knew not to get close to the vampires. She was pregnant and wouldn't risk the life of her own child.

"This...this...is what separates us from animals, "Léopold seethed, his fangs descending in anger. "If we cannot protect a child, then we are no better than the demons. The detective knew what she was doing. She accepts her oath."

Dimitri caught Laryssa's gaze. He shook his head at her, warning her not to interfere with their argument. Ignoring him, she surged forward. Dimitri caught her hand but she shook him off, running to intervene.

"You will submit, son of Kade. Do it," Léopold growled as Luca choked for air.

"Léopold, stop. You're going to kill him!" Laryssa cried, pushing her way in between the two vampires. She trembled in fear as she did so. They'd both gone feral yet she couldn't let Léopold kill the vampire. She knew that Luca disliked her, but she couldn't imagine that a man expecting a child would be callous enough to kill her in cold blood in front of everyone. Squeezing in so that her back was to Luca, she placed her palms on Léopold's chest. "Please. Stop."

"Get out of the way, Laryssa." Léopold's eyes fell to her, and the sight of her face weakened his fury.

"No, Leo, I won't. Please...for me. Just stop." Laryssa's voice went soft, trying to reach into his soul.

"This doesn't concern you." Léopold pinned Luca with his eyes, letting a renewed rush of rage flow through him. "What say you, Luca? Would you like to die today? Or would you do the right fucking thing and try to save this child?"

"Ssss...orry," Luca hissed, but still Léopold refused to release him.

"Look at me, Leo. Luca could kill me right now, but he's not even trying."

Laryssa glanced over her shoulder at Luca. He may not have been able to bite her but he could have snapped her neck. "Don't do this. He's got a family...he's having a baby. His friend's hurt. He's just upset...like you. Let it go. Please don't let the demon win."

"Merde," Léopold huffed, tossing the vampire to the floor.

Luca stumbled over to Samantha, who caught him in her arms. The tension in the room simmered to a slow boil.

Léopold grabbed Laryssa by the waist and pulled her against him, whispering in her ear. "Tu es folle."

"I don't know what you just said, but thank you for letting him go," Laryssa replied. Her forehead fell to Léopold's chest, relieved he hadn't killed Luca.

"Don't ever do that again," Léopold demanded.

"Someone's gotta make you see reason," she responded. The low dominant tone of Léopold's voice registered in her mind. He wasn't making a suggestion, rather he was ordering her.

Léopold grasped the back of her hair, and tugged her head backward. He loved her bravery, yet it would get them both killed if she didn't listen to him. Looking into her eyes, he felt her shiver against his body. Retracting his fangs, he observed the slight waver of her lips as they parted just for him.

"Never again, Laryssa," he told her. Giving her no time to argue, he kissed her. Deepening his hold on her, his lips took hers, in a show of passion and possession. Satisfied he'd made his point, he reluctantly pulled away. Leaving her breathless, he gave her a smug smile before releasing her from his embrace.

Laryssa panted quietly, trying to catch her breath. Unsure of how Léopold had so quickly turned the tables on her, she tried to slow her heartbeat, which felt as if it was pounding through her chest. Her face flamed and she wished she could run out of the room.

"We're going upstairs to see Kade," Léopold announced as he nodded at Luca.

"Maybe you should go with them," Wynter suggested to Logan. Kade had been despondent, sitting at Sydney's bedside and refusing to talk to anyone. They all knew his blood should have cured her, but her pulse remained erratic. "Laryssa, why don't you stay down here with us?"

Laryssa nodded, feeling as if she needed space from Léopold. The man had a way of compelling her, paralyzing her thoughts and turning her body into fire. As if she couldn't get enough of the drug she was addicted to, she stopped him before he left to go upstairs, and lovingly touched her palm to his cheek. She gave him a sad smile, and then briefly touched her lips to his face. With nothing else to be said, he tugged on a lock of her hair before turning back to Dimitri, disappearing down the hallway and up the stairs.

"Go ahead, Laryssa, sit down. I forgot the coffee," Wynter said.

"No, really, I can get it. You want some?" Laryssa asked.

"Thanks, I'd love a cup." Wynter sat carefully into a recliner and held Ava against her chest, patting her on the back.

"None for me. My little one, here, doesn't do well with the caffeine." Samantha took a deep breath. "Laryssa, thank you…for stopping Léopold just now. I would never recommend getting between two vampires, but if Léopold had…you know, had hurt Luca…" She rubbed her stomach with tears in her eyes. "I just…I know Luca can be difficult, but we're close to Sydney. And he and Léopold have never gotten along well. I'm not trying to make excuses. Well, maybe I am. He's just upset."

"I get that Luca's not my biggest fan, Samantha. Y'all hardly know me. I can't blame him. But I'd never stand by and let Léopold kill him without trying to stop it." Laryssa picked up two mugs of coffee, set one in front of Wynter and then sat down.

"True. We don't know you. And that's why it means even more that you stopped him. Wynter and I both know Léopold and he's…" Samantha looked away, unsure of what to say.

"You don't have to say anything. Really. Léopold is lots of things, but he cares and he's helping me. He saved that little baby girl right there. He didn't have to but he did. And now the demon. He won't stop until we find the knife."

"The demon. I know Ilsbeth doesn't mind speaking of it but maybe we shouldn't," Samantha suggested. "The wards are strong but it knows where we are."

"I have to kill it." Laryssa took a sip and swallowed. When she looked up, both Samantha and Wynter were looking at her as if she'd sprouted an elephant's trunk. "What?"

"How can you say something like that and be so calm about it?" Wynter asked while she played with Ava's toes.

"Léopold's not going to let you go after a demon," Samantha asserted.

"Léopold doesn't have a choice. Neither do I." Laryssa took another drink then continued. "Not sure if Dimitri mentioned it but that thing…that creature…it came after me the other night. It, uh, it scratched me up pretty bad. Somehow, with me dying all those years ago, it thinks I belong to it. The knife that it wants…it's the only thing that'll kill it. Unfortunately I have to be the one to do it, because only a naiad can kill it. Léopold knows. I don't think he wants to face the fact that I may die, but deep down, he knows that it has to be me."

"Speaking of Léopold, I guess that chat we had the other day didn't make any difference," Wynter commented with a small smile.

"I saw it too," Samantha added. "Never thought I'd see the day."

"Me either. The way he looks at her…" Wynter began.

"What?" Laryssa had an idea of what they were talking about but she couldn't bring herself to discuss her feelings for Léopold when Sydney was upstairs fighting for her life and her own life could very well be gone by tomorrow night.

"Like an ice cream sundae with whipped cream on top?" Samantha smiled.

"You really are preggo, girl. No, he looks at her like...you know, like a lion who's about to find his mate. Leo the lion finds his lioness." Wynter's voice became sultry as if she were trying to really sell her story.

"Yeah, I guess that does sound better. You'd think with me being mated to a vampire, I'd know a bit about what he really wants...and I can tell you it's not ice cream."

"I know you warned me about him, Wynter, but we...I'm...let's just say that I care about him a lot. But none of it really matters...I could be dead tomorrow. It's not fair to him." Laryssa set the cup of coffee on the table and raked her hair up into a ponytail, nervously twisting it into a bun. "We probably shouldn't be talking about this when the detective is so sick."

"You've been feeding him," Samantha noted quietly. Her eyes darted over to Wynter and then back to Laryssa. "Have you bonded?"

"Léopold? Bonded? No way," Wynter blurted out, shaking her head. Even though Léopold seemed smitten with his nymph, she found it hard to believe that he'd commit to anyone, given his proclivity for solitude. One glance to Laryssa told her that she'd made the wrong assumption. "Hey, I'm sorry. It's just that Léopold...I never thought he'd bond with anyone. It's nothing personal, it's just that he's, pardon the pun, a lone wolf....vampire."

"He's not how you see him. He's had his reasons. But to answer your question, I have been...feeding him, that is. He said that we've started the bonding. I don't know what to say about it. It's complicated." Laryssa rose to defend Léopold. Her fingers absentmindedly flittered over the bite mark on her neck. With Sydney nearly dead, the realization that she soon would have to face her own mortality was not lost on her. She smiled at Wynter and Samantha who waited for her to finish her thoughts. Her eyes began to brim with moisture, and she pressed a fingertip to her bottom eyelid, in an effort to catch a tear. "I'm sorry. It's just that I don't want to hurt him."

"You? Hurt Léopold? Sweetie, I really don't see how you could do that. Not sure if you noticed but he's usually the one who does the hurting..." Wynter's words trailed off, as she realized how upset Laryssa had grown.

"Listen, I know he's arrogant. Bossy. He's really bossy." Laryssa gave a small laugh. She stood and walked over to the kitchen sink, placing her cup inside it. "But he's caring and he doesn't deserve to lose someone else. Look at what just happened to Sydney. Let's face it, there's a very real possibility that I may die tomorrow. The bond...for his sake, I have to try to stop it."

"A bond with a vampire cannot be broken." Samantha felt Laryssa's pain. Having bonded with Luca, she knew how it felt to have that intense connection with a vampire.

"No it cannot," Léopold asserted, having walked in on their conversation.

Laryssa's face flashed to his, and an overwhelming barrage of guilt surrounded her, knowing what she planned to do. With the bond already set in, it was as if she could feel him touching her soul, reading her innermost thoughts. She attempted to think of something unrelated, altogether pleasant, like how she enjoyed reading a book at the outdoor café while listening to live music. As she did so, the guilt worsened. *Liar.* The word rang in her mind. No, she wasn't really lying, she told herself. Masking private thoughts was her right. Yet as he strode over to her and caressed her cheek, her stomach clenched in shame. She averted her gaze, unable to look him in the eye. They'd talk soon enough, she reasoned.

Stupidly, she'd mentioned her concerns to Wynter and Samantha. Blaming it on her naivety, she'd take responsibility if the conversation went further. Pasting on a passive expression, she glanced to the women who cautiously eyed them from the sofa. She wished she didn't care what any of them thought, yet they'd known her secret and hadn't rejected her. Talking with a wolf and a witch had felt natural, as if she'd finally found other women who were like her. Even though she'd always felt that way with Avery, their hushed conversations were intended to eradicate the evidence of her naiad origins. No longer in the shadows, she could finally openly engage with others.

"How's Sydney? Kade?" Laryssa changed the subject. "That was fast."

"Not much to be said. Sydney's resting. Kade is stronger than people give him credit for. He'll be her rock while we do what we need to do. What he doesn't need is people fussing over him. He can handle this." Léopold crossed the room to Wynter, who stood with the baby. "Ava? She's doing well?"

"Yes. She's adorable. Just the sweetest little girl," Wynter gushed.

"Oui. She's loved here. I never doubt my actions," Léopold observed. "Sometimes the best things in our lives are unexpected, no?"

"True. I swear Logan and I will do everything we can to keep her safe. Promise me, Léopold that you'll get rid of this beast that's after her. Please," Wynter pleaded.

"We," he looked to Laryssa, "will do our very best." He ran his fingers over Ava's back and then turned to Laryssa. "We need to get going."

"Is Dimitri coming with us?" Laryssa asked.

"No, I've asked him to stay here. Where we're going, we'll be safe until we meet up tomorrow. Ladies," Léopold nodded at the women, and walked to the sliding door, opening it, "Good evening."

"Thanks for the coffee," Laryssa said with a small knowing smile, appreciative that Wynter and Samantha hadn't pursued the discussion about her breaking the bond with Léopold.

As Léopold ushered her out the door, she purposefully jammed her hands into her pockets, resisting the urge to touch him. Like a magnet to steel, her body and heart was drawn to him, but if she was ever going to break the bond, she'd need to stay strong, keep herself at a distance. She caught Léopold's eyes roaming over her posture, and suspected that he'd detected her deception. Laryssa had never been in love, really loved another person with all of her soul, enough that she'd sacrifice everything to make him happy. It was in that moment that her heart crushed with the reality that she'd fallen for Léopold. She'd never be able to take away the agony he'd suffered watching his wife and children die, but she'd be damned if she'd torture him all over again. If she could break the bond, he'd survive her death with little consequence.

She looked down to her phone for the time. In less than twenty-four hours, her life would most likely be over. Even if she somehow managed to find the knife, she didn't trust the demon not to take her anyway. Closing her eyes, she shuddered, recalling its tongue on her skin. No, it'd never be satisfied with some little trinket that promised it a free pass to the other side. It wanted what it had tried to take once, what belonged to it. Her body. Her mind. Her soul.

Chapter Nineteen

"Where're we going?" Laryssa asked. The sign to the Lake Ponchartrain marina alerted her that they weren't returning to his home.

"We're getting off the land, ma chérie. This demon. It's grounded to the earth. The water. Now that's where we'll find a bit of peace." Léopold pulled into the yacht club and drove up to the valet parking. Shifting the car into park, he opened his door as the attendant arrived.

Laryssa fumbled the fish puzzle in her fingers. She ran her thumb over the cool metal fins, and tugged, hoping that for once, something would just magically happen…that it would open, revealing its secrets. As she expected, nothing happened. Swirling clouds of worry passed through her mind as she stared mindlessly at the rows of boats. The door hinge clicked, jarring her contemplation, and she jumped in her seat.

Léopold towered above Laryssa, studying her. Before he had a chance to reach for her, she leapt out of the car and wrapped her arms around her waist. She'd been acting strangely ever since he'd returned downstairs to find her talking with Wynter and Samantha. Whispers of broken bonds were all he'd heard, but it was enough to tell him that his little rabbit was readying to flee.

He thought it interesting that although he'd never bonded to another person in his life, how naturally he'd taken to the experience. With her blood in him, he could sense both her thoughts and feelings. Reading Laryssa was becoming as simple as reading a menu. She'd deliberately tried to deceive him, shielding her true emotions with false ones, but he'd known all the while what she'd been doing.

"You okay?" Léopold inquired. He tapped his finger on the top of his car.

"Yeah, I'm fine. Just a little tired."

"I guess breaking into convents will do that to you," he joked.

"A museum. We broke into a museum…to keep evil out of the city. That's my story and I'm sticking to it." She gave a small laugh.

"I knew you'd see it my way. Come, pet. We must get to the boat." Léopold strode down the docks, taking care to make sure Laryssa was in step with him. Whatever storm brewed inside her pretty little head, he planned to calm it and make sure she never lied to him again.

"Here we are," he commented, unlocking the chain. "Ladies first."

Laryssa went to take a step and stopped, realizing the 'boat' was not a simple fishing skiff. In line with everything Léopold, the sixty-foot yacht sparkled underneath a flood of lights. Rolling her eyes at him, she shook her head and smiled.

"Is this yours?" she asked, stepping onto the boarding ramp.

"Mais bien sûr, mon amour," he replied.

"You know I don't speak French, Leo. But I'll take that as a yes."

"Oui. And I do believe you do speak un petit bit. I recall that you don't appreciate being called mon lapin." He smiled and winked.

"So, um, how'd you learn to steer this huge boat of yours?"

"Ah, my sweet Laryssa, you'd be surprised at all I can do. When you're immortal, you have much time on your hands, no? I usually employ a captain to sail it for me. This, however, is not one of those times. We need to be alone." Léopold retrieved a small stainless steel flask from his bag and handed it to her. "There's some water in here. Go ahead inside. See if there's anything you can find in the book to get the puzzle to open, to show us where we need to go to get the knife. Remember, this fish was meant for you, a naiad."

Laryssa heard the anchor drop and was certain that Léopold would soon be down to check her progress. After an hour of looking at the puzzle, she hadn't come any closer to finding the solution. Tracing the pad of her thumb down its underbelly, she could feel small bumps, but they didn't move. *Remember, it was meant for you.* The track of Léopold's words played in her mind. *The water.* Everything, since the day she'd drowned, came back to the water. It was who she was, how she thrived, how she'd continue to survive as an immortal.

Opening the flask, she dribbled the water onto the fish, expecting to see it glow. Disappointed when it didn't, she flipped it over. Trying again, she waited patiently but nothing changed. Only wet metal lay in her hands.

"Come on, dammit. I'm running out of time," she gritted out. Furious and frustrated, she lost her temper, and hurled it across the room. The fish smashed into the wall and tumbled onto the floor.

"It's going well, no?" Léopold said, entering the cabin. He shook his head and picked up the puzzle. "Come now, you must concentrate."

"I can't, Leo. Can't you see? It's not working. Nothing is going to work," she replied.

"You can't give up," he scolded. He tossed the fish in the air and caught it. As it landed in his palm, he felt movement. "Perhaps a little anger goes a long way?"

"What?" She sighed.

"It's moving. It has to be the water. Look…the scales, they're peeling."

"Really?" She jumped to her feet and ran over to Léopold, watching as he thumbed away the scales. Like a fan, they began to spread, until the cavity was revealed.

"A key," Laryssa breathed.

"Yours." Léopold held out the copper object and offered it to her.

Laryssa hesitated, and then reached for the key. As soon as she touched it, her body quivered as if she were a tuning fork that had been struck against metal. The resonance of the key shocked her, searing into the layers of her skin yet her hand wouldn't release it. Tears ran down her face as it burned her palm, her eyes widening with the realization that they'd discovered something horrific. *Death. Torture. Blood. Screaming.* Flashes of the demon flickered through her mind. Laryssa fought for breath, her chest heaving in pain.

She faintly heard Léopold's voice but was unable to respond. Driven by its diabolical energy, she staggered out onto the deck. Evil coursed through her veins and she was helpless to stop its commands. Léopold lunged for her as she teetered on the edge of the stairs, but she thwarted his efforts to catch her by effortlessly causing a chair to fly through the air, nearly cracking him in the skull. Scrambling over the seats, she reached the ledge of a railing. In the recesses of her mind, she fought to stay sane, but the drumming of evil propelled her over the edge into the deep abyss of the lake.

Like water on a hot oiled pan, her body sizzled as it hit the lake. Convulsing, Laryssa lost herself to the dreadful coil of death that had taken her as a child. The water, typically her savior, rejected her as the evil shroud ensconced in the key held her under, searching for its target. She gasped for breath, and her throat flooded with water. Choking, her eyes bulged in terror, but she was helpless to resist its compelling draw. Shackled to the key, she gave in to its will.

By the time she hit the lake bed, she'd embraced the cold darkness that sought to take her. The metal in her hand burned like fire, forcing her to consciously experience the slow torture of drowning. With the demon dancing in her head, she prayed for God to take her, yet she remained awake in her nightmare. As her fist hit the rocks, a single chasm illuminated a few feet away from her. Laryssa's attention was drawn to the small hole. Unable to move her body, she slid her arm toward it. Feeling as if she was ripping the skin from her hands, she pried her fingers open and jammed the key into the rock. The last thing Laryssa saw before she drifted off into oblivion was the brilliance of a white stone blade.

Léopold lay naked in bed, skimming his finger over the flint edge of the Tecpatl. The primitive stone had been chiseled into a razor-sharp point. Bound to the rock with cord, its ornate handle had been carved into a warrior. Decorated in black and red, the soldier bowed on his knees, its hilt bore his horns. Léopold wasn't entirely positive how she'd found it, but was certain her power had somehow summoned it forth. She'd invoked the magic, and it had responded. It made no sense that it would be in the location where he'd anchored the boat, but as he fingered it, he surmised the object was otherworldly in nature. Perhaps at one time it had been of the earth, created by man's hands to slice open the chests of fellow humankind. But at some point, it had taken on meaning to the demon. For however long it had existed clandestinely in the depths of the lake, the enchanted knife had finally returned to a naiad.

Léopold contemplated how Laryssa had been possessed by whatever evil was infused into the key. After she'd fallen into the water, he'd dove in, frantically searching for her. By the time he'd found her at the bottom of the basin, she'd lost consciousness, but still glowed in the blackness of the waves. Curled in her hand was the Tecpatl. As they'd reached the surface of the water and the midnight breeze brushed her face, her eyes flew wide open in horror. He'd tried to comfort her, but she'd batted him away. Wrapping her shaking hands around the ladder, she'd climbed out of the lake, leaving him to hold the knife. Her fear and foreboding was palpable and while Léopold continued his attempts to assuage her, she'd rejected his company. She'd insisted on showering alone, so against his better judgment, he'd ceded to her wish.

Léopold had caught onto her strategy to camouflage her feelings by forcing unnatural thoughts. From desperation to determination, he'd sensed her emotions fluctuating across the spectrum. Even though he'd given her a temporary deferment, allowing her solace in her bath, he quietly calculated his next move. The sound of the water ceased and his heart raced in anticipation of their discussion. He looked forward to enlightening her about having faith in their bond.

Laryssa stood nude in front of the mirror, drying her body. When she'd been torn out of Léopold's home into the demon's pit, ripped apart, she'd told herself that she could survive anything. But the sheer evil that had possessed her entire body left her reeling. It shook her to her core, leaving her numb. Lost in the sensation that had suffocated her in the lake, she closed her eyes and took a deep breath. Slowly opening them, she toweled her hair, taking in a glance at the pearly bumps on her neck. *Léopold.* She'd fallen hard for him. It was as if she could literally feel her heart splintering open, knowing she'd be gone within hours. Never would she be able to have a life with the one man who'd selflessly given her the freedom to be herself, who'd shown her pleasure she'd never known, and the one man on Earth who she'd gladly lay down her life for without a second thought.

He'd fight her, she knew. Their argument would come and go, but it had to be done, she'd made the decision. Regardless of the outcome, it didn't matter. Once the demon had her in its claws, she'd never see Léopold again. She'd put off talking to him as long as she could. Wrapping the towel around her body, she sighed and opened the door.

The spectacular sight of Léopold sprawled on the bed caused her heart to stop. His lips curled upward, as if to warn her he'd gone on the offensive. Perfectly masculine, his powerful frame laid waiting for her. From his well-defined chest down to his steel-hard abs, he defined virility at its finest. His thick cock lay heavy upon his thigh, growing ever larger with each breath he took, his eyes feasting upon her.

Laryssa fought the gooseflesh growing on her skin that was caused by the sight of him. She forced herself to look away from the distraction that was his beauty, but she could still feel his presence surround her in its erotic snare. She pressed her lips together as tears rose in her eyes. *Let him go*, her conscience screamed. *I must break the bond*. It wasn't fair to deny him, to crush him with the loss of her soul.

"Leo," she began, "I know we found the Tecpatl, but the death...the evil, tonight it was in me. It's not going to let me go."

In one continuous movement, Léopold was up off the bed. With deliberation, he set the Tecpatl on the dresser in front of her. He stood close behind Laryssa, mere inches away, but didn't touch her skin. Like the stealth predator he was, he waited for his prey to make her first move.

"We must break the bond. Tomorrow...today, he's going to take me. The knife. He'll use it somehow." Laryssa stilled as she felt Léopold wrap his arm around her chest. Her eyes glanced up to his reflection in the mirror and her breath caught. With his eyes pinned on hers, his mouth tightened in a firm line. Her pulse raced as his fingertips skimmed her chest, her body strung out like a live wire ready to be struck by lightning. "It's not fair to you. You already lost your wife, your kids. The bond, it'll make it worse when I go. Maybe you could get a donor or..."

"Laryssa," he growled. Laced with domination, Léopold's voice filled the room. "Never will I have another's blood. The bond cannot be undone. More importantly, you don't want it undone."

"But Leo, you deserve so much more than what I can give you. I can't bear to hurt you." Her chest heaved as she spoke with despair. "And tonight...what I felt in that knife. In my mind. No, through my entire being. I may kill the demon, but there's a good chance that it's going to kill me."

"So you quit? Jesus Christ, woman, don't you understand how much you mean to me? Who you are to me?" His eyebrows furrowed in frustration.

"What am I? I'm a naiad. And yeah, Leo...I care about you. Can you see how much I care? I don't want to hurt you. It took you a thousand years to get over the death of your wife and just when you decide to live again, to bond with me," Laryssa shook her head, lowering her eyes and whispered, "I'll be gone."

"You have to fight, goddammit. Do you hear me? Fight!" he yelled. Goddess, she was giving up after all they'd been through. Denying their bond? No fucking way would he let her bow out gracefully. She was his and he had no intention of letting her go. "Listen, I don't know what happened tonight with the key, but it's over. It. Is. Over. We did it. At every turn, we've figured it out."

"But, Leo…"

"Look at me," he demanded, his fingers gliding over her throat. "You pushed me when it was impossible to do. Now I expect the same from you. I'm telling you to fight. Fight for your life. Fight like hell for us."

"I can't," she choked. Her eyes flashed to his. "It's impossible. I've felt it…the evil."

"I know you were shaken up today, but you're stronger than the demon. We're stronger. You need to make the choice to trust. Trust me. Trust what you feel inside. Trust us." He took a deep breath, cradling his other arm around her waist. Lowering his voice, he spoke to her heart. "Be mine, Laryssa…always. Choose me. Choose us."

A tear ran down her face as Léopold threw her words back into her face. *God, how did this happen? Doesn't he realize I've already chosen him? That I love him?*

"Mon amour. Choose us," he repeated.

"Yes," she whispered, her eyes closing as she trembled.

"Yes," he repeated, kissing her neck. There was nowhere the demon could take her where he wouldn't find her. "I'll never leave you…ever. Never again will you be alone. Have faith…in us."

"Leo," she breathed. "I want so bad to believe you."

"Bond with me," he suggested. Léopold had thought long and hard about asking her to complete the bond. He sought to mark her as his own, to take her as his mate. The instinct to do so was overwhelming. Denying the urge had become increasingly difficult. He'd known it would happen the first time he bit her. But now with her possible death looming over them, it gave him the excuse to take what he wanted. No regrets, he'd bond with her eternally. "You're mine, Laryssa. You'll never belong to another."

"I…I," Laryssa stammered, unsure of what to say. Forever binding her soul to his was certainly irrevocable.

"No matter what happens, I'll come for you. You'll never belong to another. You've already given your heart to me," he challenged. *Amour.* He'd heard the words that played in her mind, ones she'd never confess aloud. He knew he wasn't playing fair, but there was no other choice. He tugged on her towel until it fell to the floor. His cock brushed against her back.

"You're mine, Laryssa. Say yes."

Laryssa swayed in his arms, his smooth voice like a melody in her head. *Say yes.* Her instincts roared in response, telling her to accept her soul mate. Though their ages spanned centuries, their connection felt older than time itself. Impulsively, she embraced the truth in her heart.

"I'm yours," she said, without hesitation. With her heart in his hands and his skin touching hers, desire flared. She drew a deep breath, inhaling the smell of him into her psyche. A maddening ache grew between her legs.

"Oui, mon amour. That's it," Léopold praised. *Goddess, she is magnificent.*

Like an angel, she'd taught him to live again. He smiled as the scent of her arousal filled the room. Satisfied with her submission, he sought to devour her.

"From this day forward, we'll be together. No fear shall befall us. No demon will separate us. This," his hand moved to her chest, over her heart, and lightly tapped, "is mine only. And my heart is yours. Your body." He slid his hand down over her belly. Gliding his finger into the warmth between her legs, he pressed his middle finger up into her tight channel.

"Ahhh," she cried.

"You give to me freely. Mais oui, ma chérie. Your body blazes for me, no?"

"Leo," she managed, groaning as he withdrew his finger.

Léopold brought his hand to his mouth, licking her cream with his tongue, then cradled her chin with his hand, pressing his coated fingers through her lips. Laryssa moaned in response, tasting herself on him.

"You belong to me...and I," he took her hand and brought it to his cock, "belong to you."

Laryssa's mouth went silent, as she immersed herself in the sound of Léopold's voice. Taking hold of his swollen shaft, she stroked her thumb over its silken skin. As she went to pump him with her hand, he spun her around to face him. Breathless, she reached to put her palms to his chest and Léopold backed her into the dresser until her bottom edged against its cool surface.

"You have no idea how much you mean to me, the gift you've given me," he told her, his voice dark and smooth. Raking his fingers up into the back of her hair, his lips descended on hers. Delivering all the intensity his heart held, he kissed her, his tongue sweeping against hers. No matter what happened, he wanted her to feel the love that was growing inside him, the emotion he could not yet put into words.

Laryssa fell into his arms, consumed by his intoxicating kiss. His lips, soft and strong, claimed hers. She could taste his passion for her as his seductive tongue invaded her mouth, seeking and probing. Losing control, she matched his pace, with the need to have more of him. Biting and sucking, she moaned into his mouth.

She gasped for breath as he pulled his lips away, watching as his eyes went wild with lust, and he fell to his knees. She braced her hands on the bureau as he placed his hands on her inner thighs. Slowly and deliberately, he widened them. She panted in anticipation of how he planned to take control of her body.

"Open your legs," he demanded.

Never taking his eyes off of hers, he dragged the tip of his tongue through her swollen lips and smiled up at her.

"Your pussy is so wet." He licked her again and she moaned. "So sweet." Using his fingers to spread her apart, he lightly sucked her swollen clit. "And mine." Using his other hand, he plunged two fingers into her satiny flesh. Continuing to make love to her with his mouth, he skillfully brought her to the edge.

"Leo!" she screamed, shaking as he pleasured her. Her inner walls clamped around his fingers, and she fought to hold her release at bay. Letting go of the dresser, she plowed her fingers into his hair, drawing his face further into her pussy.

Unrelenting, he flicked his tongue lightly over her clitoris, gradually increasing his tempo and pressure. Reaching his hand behind her thigh, he clutched her hip. She bucked against him. In rhythm with his fingers, she drove her hips to his mouth. As he felt her inner walls begin to quiver around his hand, he took her protruding nub between his teeth, softly biting and then sucked her hard until she moaned in release.

"Yes. Fuck, yes. Oh, God. Leo, Leo!" she screamed as her orgasm slammed into her. Ripples of endless pleasure ran through her, and she felt him lift her onto the bed.

"Hands and knees, now," Léopold commanded, easing her belly upward. In one smooth stroke, he thrust into her.

"Yes!" she cried, adjusting her weight so that her legs were spread for him.

"Merde, you're so tight. Don't move," he grunted as her pussy quivered around his cock. The tingling sensation drove him toward his own climax. With a deep breath, he fought the urge to come.

"Fuck me!" she cried. Her forehead fell forward onto the pillow. She wiggled against him, trying to make him move. A sharp slap to her bottom, intended to punish her efforts, only served to further arouse her tender flesh. "Ahhh...yes."

"You're a naughty, girl, no?" He spanked her again on her other cheek, aware of how much she liked it.

"Please, Leo..." she begged.

"You really have learned no patience, have you? How I look forward to teaching you, ma chérie. Tonight, I will own every part of your sweet body," he promised. Clutching her hips, he began to move an inch at a time. The torturous pace he set would make them both want for more.

"Leo," she repeated as she felt him retreat, then enter her ever so slowly, making her mad with need. "Faster."

"You feel so good...yes," he growled. Filling her to the hilt, he stilled himself yet again. He reached for the bottle of lube under the sheets that he'd planned on using on her tonight.

"Don't stop," she protested. As the cold slippery gel hit her bottom, she'd expected he'd brought the plug with him. Laryssa arched her back into his caress of her bottom.

"I'm going to fuck you here tonight," he warned. "Your ass is so beautiful."

"But...ahhh." Her pussy clenched down on him as he inserted a finger into her back hole. Unlike the time before, it slipped in easily, with little pressure.

"That's it." Léopold smiled, hearing her moan as he pressed in a second finger. He began to pump his hips once again, gritting his teeth as he sheathed himself inside of her.

"Yes, yes, yes," Laryssa rambled, adrift in the sensation. Nothing else existed but their two bodies, joined as one in pleasure.

With a final thrust, Léopold pulled his cock all the way out of her, then coated himself in the lubrication. Circling her puckered flesh, he teased her with his fingers, and pressed the firm tip of his cock into her anus.

"Ah yeah. Take me," he encouraged.

"Leo," she panted. "I don't know....I, yes, don't stop." She shook her long mane back and forth, adjusting to the fullness.

"Yes, yes...feel me in you, see how we're made for each other. Push back on me," he instructed, running his fingertips down her shoulders. Responding to her long draw of a breath, he slowly entered her until he was all the way in, his hips flush against her bottom. Gently, he fisted her locks into his hand. Her tight muscles gripped his cock, massaging every inch of his manhood. "Oh yeah."

Relaxing into his dark intrusion, Laryssa opened herself to him. By the time he'd eased his shaft all the way inside her, she'd exhaled a breath and tried to move. As if reading her thoughts, he gently began to rock back and forth, letting her become accustomed to the sweet pressure. Laryssa rose to meet his thrusts, urging him to go faster, but he took control, forcing them to immerse themselves in the ecstasy of every long stroke. Together, they moved in sync, losing themselves to the moment.

Laryssa moaned Léopold's name over and over again as he stretched her in the most satisfying way. She'd never felt so delightfully out of control in her life. Yet, all the while, she was aware of her power dancing through her blood. With his hand pulling her hair, the delicious sting on her scalp caused her to groan aloud. She felt his other hand slip from her hip around to her waist. Letting him direct her, she arched her back as he pulled her torso upward until she was only on her knees.

Holding her firmly around her midsection, he increased his pace. As his primal need grew, Léopold's fangs descended and he released her hair, letting it fall to the side, revealing the long curve of her neck. Wrapping both arms around her, he found her clit once again. As he surged into her ass, he continued to stroke her hooded pearl.

"Mon amour, so fucking close," he hissed.

"Bite me now," she insisted, asserting her dominance. Her swollen nub pulsated as he applied more pressure and she could not keep from coming. "Leo, please."

So near to his own climax, Léopold released a chuckle at his mate's demand. He'd known all along that her submission would come only in the bedroom, and even then, she'd do so on her own terms. Powerful in her own right, she'd push his limits to places he'd never imagined. Yet that was why he was falling in love with her. She captivated him with her adventurous sexuality and courageous spirit. As he heard her groan in displeasure that he hadn't heeded her, he brought his wrist to his own mouth. A quick slice of his fangs sent his blood dripping onto her back.

"We've chosen each other…my sweet Laryssa…." His words trailed off as he held his arm to her lips. Instinctively, she clutched it, drawing in his sanguine essence. Hissing in ecstasy, he reared his head back and sank his teeth deep into her shoulder.

Laryssa clung to Léopold, her body convulsing as her climax ripped through her. From the second his potent blood touched her tongue, she was slammed with a tsunami of foreign emotions. Centuries of memories and feelings poured over her like a massive waterfall, cleansing her, making her anew just for him. As if his thoughts were her own, they ripped through her mind. *Serenity, that he'd finally found his soul mate. Lust, his mind consumed by an insatiable hunger for only her.* She smiled as his love filled her chest. Hidden behind all of it was rage, simmering below the surface. No one would touch his mate.

Tears streamed down her face. Positively possessed by the intimacy of their bond, she quaked in his arms. Overwhelmed, Laryssa let go of her fears, embracing his warmth. The fibers of their bond tightened around her and she knew that from this day forward, she'd never be alone again. The charismatic vampire had stolen her heart, and she'd always be his. *I love you.* The words flittered through her mind before she could even stop the thought. *Je t'aime de tout mon coeur*, she heard in response and smiled. Even though she didn't understand his words, she knew he loved her, enough to commit to her for eternity. No matter what they faced, she knew with certainty he'd go to the ends of the Earth to keep her at his side.

⟳ *Chapter Twenty* ⟲

After making love in the wee hours of the morning and sleeping all day, Léopold's mind turned to killing the demon. He'd called upon both Dimitri and Ilsbeth to meet him at his home. As soon as dusk settled in, they all stood waiting by the docks. The grass was scorched from the last time the demon had shown its ugly face in his yard, and he expected that's where it'd come again looking for Laryssa. While Ilsbeth had suggested summoning the demon where it had last surfaced in the city, Léopold refused to put anyone else in jeopardy. With the Alpha's home warded and well-guarded, the confrontation had to occur where there were no other innocents. Above all else, he sought to keep Ava hidden.

Ilsbeth reiterated to their small group that only Laryssa, as the owner of the Tecpatl, could send the demon back to its hellish origins. Any other attempts to kill it would be done so in vain. The naiads had hidden the knife, knowing the demon could use it to break the veil of the underworld at will. Only a naiad could send it back to Satan. The witch speculated that at some point, the demon had bargained with the Aztecs, attaching its entity to the knife. Relishing in the human sacrifices, the demon used its influence to feed the killings, possessing the thoughts of those who stabbed the Tecpatl's jagged edge into the sternums of its victims, tearing out the beating hearts of men, women and children with their bare hands. They wouldn't be the first or last civilization to do so. But the demon, whose name was Rylion, had infused its evil into that particular weapon.

It terrified Léopold that the demon sought to take her. Since they'd bonded, he'd felt every memory she'd retained of her attacks and Laryssa was convinced that it wanted more than the Tecpatl. *Rylion*. It had called itself her master. Yet no matter the demon's delusions, Léopold knew for certain no one, not even he, was Laryssa's master.

Léopold gave a small smile to Laryssa, who nervously fingered the Tecpatl's hilt. He was unsure of her ability to utilize the bond, to sense more than his emotions. *No matter what happens, I'll come for you, mon amour,* he thought to himself. Instantly, she smiled in return, letting him know she'd felt him. After years of allowing the loss of his family to define him, to entomb and paralyze him in grief, she'd set him free. Falling for her had been an unanticipated gift. Admitting he loved her, however, saying the words out loud, would not come easily. Slipping his hand into hers, he brought her palm to his lips, accepting that he'd gladly give his life for hers.

Thunder rumbled in the distance, and he glanced down to Laryssa whose expression had grown serious. *Rylion,* he heard Laryssa whisper. Lightning struck, crackling across the atmosphere into the lake. Out of the corner of his eye, he heard Dimitri arguing with Ilsbeth and shot him a glare, warning him to cease their conversation.

"It's here," Laryssa said. She looked side to side, expecting Rylion to materialize out of thin air.

"Behind you," Dimitri called to Léopold.

"Laryssa," the demon snarled.

Both Laryssa and Léopold spun on their heels. The demon cackled, tasting her fear like a fine wine on its tongue. Its long forked tongue slithered out from its parted lips as if it were a snake, scenting its environment. Léopold shoved in front of Laryssa, shielding her from its line of vision.

"You brought it," Rylion continued, boring its eyes into Léopold. "Come to your master, Laryssa. The ancient one cannot protect you."

Laryssa felt her face blanch. Its cold voice sank its icy claws into her mind. Even though she'd spent hours mentally preparing, her fear crept up, causing her stomach to lurch. She pressed her forehead into the back of Léopold's shirt, focusing on their bond. Like a band of steel, it tied them together. Nothing, not even this heinous creature, could tear it apart.

"Rylion," she said. Her voice was soft yet firm as she stepped around Léopold. If she had any chance of killing it, sending it back to hell, she had to get close enough to use the knife. "I have the Tecpatl." *I'm looking forward to giving it to you. Tearing you open with it.*

"Let me see it," the demon demanded. Its form flickered briefly into a human male and then quickly transformed back to its scaly self.

As Laryssa raised the flint blade to the sky, her determination began to amplify. *Fuck this thing. This ends tonight.* Her eyes darted over to Léopold who nodded, sensing her intentions. Instead of him seeking to hinder her, she felt his confidence in her powers. This incredible man would die for her tonight, she knew. But he'd support her independence to fight a battle that only she could win.

"Ah. So many memories….the screaming. Children dying, feeding me their souls," Rylion reminisced. "It's beautiful, isn't it? Bring it to me, my sweet naiad."

Laryssa approached the demon, aware that Léopold had her back. She heard mumblings in the air, and caught a glimpse of Ilsbeth chanting.

"The witch has no say here. The Tlalco Tecpatl is mine, has always been mine. That bitch stole it from me, and now it's back," Rylion told them, falling to its knees. Holding its hands out toward Laryssa, it began to speak in tongues.

Laryssa's heart pounded so hard it felt as if it would break her ribs. The hilt began to vibrate in her hands. At first it was merely a tingle but within seconds it burned the skin of her palm. The excruciating pain only served to focus her on her task.

"Liar!" she screamed at the demon. "This is mine, asshole. If it were yours, you'd be able to get it yourself. But you can't. You need me."

"You must give it to me of your own free will. Do it now." Its red palms curled, calling it. "We make a deal."

"You get the Tecpatl in exchange for renouncing your claim to my soul. Take it or leave it," she told the demon.

"We're not negotiating," Léopold growled, in an attempt to support her. "Laryssa's mine. Surely, even a son of Satan like you can feel the bond. She'll never be yours to own…not her soul, not her body. Take the deal, Rylion. Then disappear." A cloud of uneasiness fell over Léopold as he spoke to the demon. If Laryssa gave it the knife, Rylion would have the ability to pierce the veil of the underworld whenever it wished. It was no secret that demons and other underworldly creatures lied. He glanced at Laryssa, trying to get her to strike the demon first. But her innocence washed over him, reminding him of her naivety. Léopold pricked at her mind again, urging her to stop, but he could feel her unbridled fury as it took over. The agonizing years she'd survived, plagued both in hiding and shame, played in her head. No longer would she succumb to that weakness.

"Say it. Say it. Renounce me," Laryssa demanded, her face hot in rage.

For the first time in Laryssa's life, she summoned every ounce of her power. She held out her hand and tunneled her energy towards a huge oak tree. It ripped from the ground with a thunderous roar, and flew across the yard, landing next to the demon. She hated the creature, hated everyone who had ever made her feel like her life was less than living because of what she was. Now that she had Léopold and had embraced her origins, she refused to relinquish her new life.

"As you wish," Rylion falsely conceded. It nodded toward the ground, concealing the deceitful smile it wore. "Your soul was rightfully mine. It was stolen. But I want the knife."

"Say. It," Laryssa spat. She sensed Léopold's concern for her through the bond. It almost felt as if he was trying to warn her, to discourage her from her mission. *I have to kill it, Leo. Please.* As her hatred for Rylion flooded her psyche, she pictured Ava, the demon trying to kill the baby. Laryssa, certain in her decision, shook off any doubts.

"I have no claim to your soul," it vowed, continuing to claw the air with its fingers. "Your turn. The knife. Give it to me."

A flash of deceit in the demon's eyes was all the warning Laryssa had that Rylion was going to take the knife. She couldn't allow him to stop her. The creature had to be sent back to hell. Lunging at the demon, she aimed at its abdomen. As she did so, Rylion latched its talons around her wrist. Crushing her flesh, it forced her to drop the Tecpatl into its own hand.

"You treacherous bitch. Now, you will know death like you've never known," it jeered, yanking her against its chest. The power of the knife splintered through Rylion, and it convulsed in electrifying force. With a whisper, the demon materialized into nothingness, taking both Laryssa and the Tecpatl with it.

Laryssa's cheek slammed into the acrid dust as she fell to the ground. She didn't need to open her eyes to know where it had taken her. She protectively curled into a ball, flattening her palms onto the ground and pushed up on her knees. She shook her head to break loose of the trance she'd been in, so dead set on killing the demon.

Léopold. She'd felt his concern for her while she'd argued with the demon. It almost had been as if he hadn't wanted her to give Rylion the knife. But he'd known that only she could kill it. It didn't make sense. Confused, she rubbed the bridge of her nose trying to think clearly. Wiping the sweaty dirt from her eyes, she caught sight of Rylion stroking the knife as if it were a baby. *Baby.* She vaguely remembered an image of the baby. Had Léopold tried to communicate a picture through their bond? *But why?* She felt dizzy as her mind attempted to solve the puzzle. The sickening truth began to set in as she coughed out the red particles that had stuck to her tongue. The demon had renounced its claim to *her* soul. But not Ava's.

Muttering to itself, Rylion finally took notice of Laryssa and smiled. Oddly, to her surprise, it didn't approach her. Standing tall, it transformed into a man. Its gorgeous features didn't hide the evil that lingered in its soulless eyes. It smiled, moving its gaze to the hollow-eyed soldiers that hovered on the outskirts of the barren land where it lived. Like a desert horizon, the rocky terrain seemed to go on forever, blocked only by the hundreds of ghosts who stood waiting on its orders. Laryssa's skin crawled as she saw them slithering about like zombies. For years she'd seen them in the streets, stalking her like predators, yet now she understood them for what they were, mindless drones that Rylion had created of its own being. Like a hallucination, they were part and parcel of the demon.

"Do you like my new shell?" the demon asked, stroking its fingers over its pecs and admiring its mortal form. "Finally, after thousands of years, I'll be able to walk again on the Earth. And it's all thanks to you."

"I hate you," she sputtered. Her chest heaved as the hot air burned her lungs.

"Hate. Lust. Deceit. All admirable traits as far as I'm concerned. Don't forget how many deaths I had to bring with this knife to earn this honor." It smoothed back its shoulder-length, jet black hair and then stretched its arms. "I've earned you as well, Laryssa. Or have you forgotten that I'm your master?"

"Fuck you. You gave up your rights. Leo, he will come for me," she asserted.

"Very true. But you see, I didn't give up the right to Ava's soul," Rylion informed her. Its eyes lit up in excitement as it continued. "Your vampire tried to warn you, but your hate burned brightly like a torch. A little trick of mine that always seems to work. You do know that Ava's death came at my hands. And like yours, her soul was mine…stolen."

"No, no, no," Laryssa repeated. She glanced away for a second and it disappeared. Screaming into the vast expanse, she searched for it. "Where are you, you bastard?"

"I'm here." Laryssa felt the air gush from her chest as she heard a baby's cry. *Ava.* She closed her eyes, willing it not to be true. *No. Oh dear God. Have mercy. Not the baby.* Forcing her neck to straighten, she turned toward the sound. The demon stood cradling Ava in its arms, laughing as it did so.

"Behold. My daughter has arrived."

"Open the goddamned veil," Léopold demanded of Ilsbeth.

"You must be patient." She raised her head and shot him a glare as she held her hands to the dirt where the demon had last appeared.

"Leo, man. Just give her a second. We'll find her," Dimitri said.

Léopold felt Laryssa even though the demon had abducted her. As soon as Ilsbeth opened the door to Rylion's lair, he was going after her. His gut had told him that the demon would take her, if not for her soul, then to use as a bargaining chip for something else, someone else. *Ava.*

Suspecting it was true, Léopold pulled out his phone and texted Logan. He sucked a heart wrenching breath as he read his reply.

"Jesus Christ. It took her!" Léopold yelled, throwing his phone across the yard in a rage. "It fucking took her."

"Yeah, it took Laryssa. I know. We'll get her back," Dimitri replied.

"No. It took Ava."

"How the hell..?"

"I don't fucking know."

"The knife. It used the knife," Ilsbeth responded, as she sliced her palm open with the athame. "Stand back. When it opens, you must leap through. Do not hesitate. I'll keep it open."

Léopold stormed in anger, knowing that after all his efforts, the demon had taken Ava. Still, for the life of him, aside from Ava being naiad, he couldn't make sense of why Rylion wanted her so badly. He blew out a breath as the ground began to shake. Dimitri stood at his side.

"You don't have to do this, wolf," Léopold said.

"Yeah, I know. But you throw a good party. You know I love to dance," Dimitri tried to joke.

"Dance with the devil."

"They're playing our song."

"You ready to go kill this thing?"

"Yeah, let's do this shit."

The ground began to shake as Ilsbeth chanted louder and louder. A crack in the earth formed slowly before them, opening to a fiery chasm below. Léopold gave no warning before he hurled himself off the edge into the deep abyss. Dimitri gave Ilsbeth a wink and jumped in after him.

Léopold landed on his feet, bracing himself with his hands. A gust of wind kicked up, and through it, he heard the cry of a baby in the distance. A hundred yards north, he caught a glimpse of Rylion dangling Ava like a carrot, his little rabbit stood lost in consternation. Léopold struggled to hear their conversation. *Laryssa, I'm here. We're coming.* As soon as he'd thought her name, the ground began to swell with whirls of red dust. Slowly, the particles circulated upward into the air, escalating into an opaque wall of gritty earth.

"Follow me," Léopold called to Dimitri, who tore off his clothes and transformed into his wolf. Stumbling through the gusty sheets of soil, they ran forward.

Laryssa felt Léopold in her mind, but kept her eyes on the infant. Forcing an impassive expression, she fought to conceal her shock. *Ava is Rylion's daughter?* She quickly tried to make sense of the ambiguous relationship, but there was no reconciliation. As Léopold grew closer, she sought to distract Rylion with questions.

"How can Ava be your daughter? She was born of a wolf," she challenged.

"Possession is a tricky business, especially seeing as I had little control over my access to freedom. But I was owed a soul... you were stolen from me, after all. The wolf was weak and I happened to get lucky, breaking through and possessing him. I'd had plans for the wolf, but that night with his mate changed everything for me. It was my seed that fertilized the bitch's womb. A soul. A brand new soul...just for me."

"You're sick." Laryssa coughed as Rylion brought forth clouds of debris. She shielded her face and took a step toward it. "So you killed her in the woods...."

"Oh no, I killed her mother with my own hands while she bore the child ...a wolf's hands. Ava died that night too. But that goddamned bitch who creates you water whores stole her from me. Like you, all she needed was the water to do it. Of course, the wolf...well, that didn't turn out so well for him," Rylion explained.

"He knew." Laryssa wiped her eyes, aghast with the revelation.

"The beauty of possession is that they don't know they've been possessed." The demon laughed, and began to pace with Ava crying in its arms. "All Perry knew was that he'd killed his own mate. He left and killed himself." Rylion stopped and paused. "What's so perfect about this is that like the Aztecs, I'm willing to sacrifice my own child. Don't you see, Laryssa? It's always been about you."

"Me?"

"I've watched you all these years and then you hid from me, keeping me from your home, your life. Even when I sent my ghosts to watch over you, you spurned me. Why, Laryssa? You've always known I'm there."

"I don't belong to you. You're wrong," she yelled through the wind.

"Even though you reek of the vampire, you're still mine. And you're going to come to me....willingly."

"Are you fucking crazy?" As shock set in, Laryssa began to shake her head. Catching the sight of movement out of her left eye, she attempted to refocus on Rylion. She suspected that the demon had sensed that Léopold was in its world but she wouldn't give it an inch of help.

"Ava's soul for yours. I'll hand over my only daughter to the vampire and his wolf. I know you're here," it called out into the storm. "All you have to do is say yes. Say the words. Accept your place at my side. Look at me now…I'm a man. I can satisfy your earthly cravings. Tell me…tell me that I'm your master. Give me your soul."

"Put the baby down…over there!" she screamed through the din, pointing to the rock where it'd left the Tecpatl.

"Say it. Accept me as your master. Give me what is mine, Laryssa, and the vampire can have the baby. Reject me and I'll murder her. It'll be on your conscience forever."

"Put her down first," Laryssa insisted.

Slowly, she approached him. The Tecpatl rested only a few feet from her hands. If her abilities worked in the underworld, she could have called the knife to her hand. But no matter how hard she tried, the energy wouldn't respond to her summons. She held her hands upward, exposing her palms to him. *Get the baby. Leo, get the baby.* She prayed like hell that throughout the chaos, Léopold could hear their discussion.

"You accept my conditions?"

"Yes," she whispered, spying the knife.

Rylion moved quickly to set the child upon the dirt, never taking its eyes off of her. Once it'd surrendered the child to the earth, it strode toward Laryssa, a broad smile breaking across its face.

"Say it Laryssa. Say you're mine," it ordered.

Laryssa nodded, feigning submission to its will. *Move.* The command came strong, filling her chest with dread. *Move. Now, Laryssa.* Without thinking, she sensed Léopold was coming for her.

"I'll say it…you are my mas…" Her words fell apart as she dropped to the ground and rolled out of the way. Léopold flew from behind her, smashing into the demon. Dimitri cut through the dust and scooped up the child into his arms, tearing back into the tornado of filth. On her knees, Laryssa crawled toward the rock, to the Tecpatl.

"You're dead," Léopold grunted, shoving his fist into Rylion's face.

The demon's human form disappeared at first contact, allowing it to dig its savage claws into Léopold's arms. Léopold pinned it to the ground and hit it again, but Rylion just laughed, and rebounded out of the vampire's grasp. Continuing his assault, Léopold extended his own claws, slicing a gash across the demon's chest. Rylion stumbled backwards, but never faltered. With his fangs descended, Léopold charged at it, tearing his fangs into its flesh. As he bit into it, he curled his fingers into a point. Spearing his hand into the demon's chest, he perforated its gut, clear through to the other side. Closing his fist, Léopold ripped out the demon's entrails from its cavity.

Rylion careened backwards as Léopold released it. The demon's laughter grew louder, even though its legs threatened to fail.

"You can't kill me, you fool," the demon boasted, its wounds healing before their eyes. "No one can kill me."

"I can, fucker." Laryssa screamed as she charged it from behind. "Go to hell!"

Using all her strength, she plunged the Tecpatl into Rylion's back. The sound of its scales splitting open echoed into the air. The demon screamed and hissed, flailing its arms, but she continued to use every last ounce of her strength to ram the knife through its thick skin. She leveraged the knife to hoist herself upward and wrap her legs around its waist. Laryssa held tight and twisted the blade into its flesh. Rylion staggered back and forth as she plunged the blade up to its hilt. Rylion's soulless warriors swirled into a vortex, returning to the demon's body, but it wasn't enough to save it from the destiny of the Tlalco Tecpatl. Blood gushed from its wound, splattering onto the cracked dirt. As the demon's essence drained from its body, it was sucked back into the infernal netherworld from where it had come, its body toppling over, face-down onto the ground. No longer of this world, it had been sent to hell.

Laryssa screamed for it to die, over and over, obscured within her task. She felt Léopold's hands on her shoulders, heard his voice calling her name, but continued to lie atop the scaly shell of the demon. Afraid to release the knife, she rejected Léopold's touch, shoving a hand at him.

"It's gone." Léopold spoke softly to her, aware that she'd come unhinged. His little naiad was no killer...until now. The storm ceased, allowing him to nod over at Dimitri, who held the baby. The shimmering veil remained, but he needed to get Laryssa to move. "Come, ma chérie. You did it."

"No, no, no," she mumbled, terrified that the demon would return. Laryssa felt Léopold brush her mind and whispers of his soothing words caressed her heart, allowing her to open her eyes.

"That's it. You're okay. It's me. It's Leo." For the first time in his life, he'd referred to himself by the shortened name his mother had called him as a child. Even though Dimitri also addressed him as such, it had been Laryssa, alone, who'd made him own it. The name represented the revolution she'd caused within his soul. Her love for him and his for her. "I've got you."

Gently, he slid his hands under her arms, peeling her off the corpse. Through their bond he sent her all his strength and calm, communicating how incredibly proud he was of her. He almost had her extricated when she tensed. With her hands still frozen around the stone hilt, she refused to let go. Léopold reached around her, placing his hands over hers and jerked the Tecpatl from the crackling epidermis. Once released, she clutched the knife to her chest as if she was protecting a cherished treasure. Aware that she'd been traumatized, Léopold scooped her up into his arms, cradling her. His rabbit was a warrior. But now that the battle had been fought, she'd crumbled into his embrace.

·✦· *Chapter Twenty-one* ·✦·

A week had passed since they'd permanently banished the demon from their world. Laryssa had begun working again in her store, with Léopold insisting she take it easy. While she hadn't told many people yet about her newly owned supernatural status as a naiad, she no longer hid it either. Working to train Mason to take over day to day operations so that she could travel with Léopold was going well and she looked forward to her future.

As Laryssa locked the door, she recalled how ecstatic Logan and Wynter had been when they'd returned Ava to their home. A wolf, the child needed to be raised by wolves, in a pack. A naiad, she needed the guidance to learn how to survive and thrive in the water and to hone her abilities. Hunter Livingston had given his blessing to the New Orleans's Alpha and his mate, granting them rights to raise the child. Laryssa and Léopold had been designated godparents by Logan. Laryssa had been honored and humbled, grateful for the opportunity to be a presence in Ava's life.

Laryssa contemplated the only unresolved matter, which had been Sydney's recovery. While her soul had not been lost to the demon, Sydney would never be human again. It had been true that her injuries from the demon would have killed her if it hadn't been for Kade's vampiric blood. While it had gone unspoken on the night of the attack, Kade had turned her. Léopold had known it but hadn't told Laryssa until a few days after she'd killed the demon. Sydney, although engaged to a vampire, had steadfastly wished to remain human. But what was done could not be undone. Despite Léopold's repeated visits to Kade's house, Sydney had reportedly not accepted her fate, remaining depressed and isolated in their home.

Since Laryssa's terrifying experience in the underworld, she'd been working with Ilsbeth to locate information about how to return the Tecpatl to the water. Ilsbeth, still unsure of how to return it, promised she'd assist her. In the meantime, Laryssa had locked and buried it deep within the lake bed for safe keeping.

True to his promise, Léopold had moved most of Laryssa's belongings to his French Quarter townhouse, where they spent the week. They planned on spending weekends at his home on the lake. In either location, she had open access to the life-giving waters she required for her existence. Earlier in the day, they'd made plans to meet for dinner at a quaint outdoor restaurant a few doors down from his home. As she walked along the sidewalk, she realized that she was no longer scared of seeing the eyeless warriors. They'd been a mirage all along, designed by Rylion to keep her under its watch. Even as the night fell, no longer would she fear darkness.

No matter where she was, Léopold was with her, supporting her, loving her.

The only thing that concerned her was that despite the bond, they still hadn't said they loved each other. Three little words seemed like a minute detail given their bond, yet it was becoming tremendously important to her. She loved Léopold. Not only did she want him to know, she wanted everybody to know. Whenever they made love, she could feel his love slice through her, and while he'd whisper sweet nothings in French, she wanted to hear that he loved her.

Bells rang overhead as she opened the door to the restaurant. The maître d' motioned to her, gesturing with his hand for her to come to him. She giggled and looked over her shoulder, unsure of how he'd recognized her. *Léopold.* Rolling her eyes, she politely smiled at the man and walked toward him.

"Ms. Theriot?" he confirmed.

"Yes."

"Mr. Devereoux is waiting for you. Please follow me." He turned, and walked through the busy restaurant.

Laryssa followed him, complying with his wish. Lilac lights illuminated their path through the darkened restaurant. The host pushed through a glass door, holding it open so she could go first into the open courtyard. Ensconced in bowed branches above their heads, hundreds of tiny lights twinkled in the trees. The candlelit tables were decorated with small vases of fresh flowers. As she walked through the romantic dining garden, she spotted Léopold seated in a back corner.

Her stomach fluttered as Léopold gave her a sexy smile. The twinkle in his eye told her she was in for a surprise. As she approached the table, he stood, briefly touching his lips to hers. Waiting for her to sit down, he signaled for the waiter to pour her a glass.

"Mon amour. Lovely as always. How was your day?" He casually swirled his wine and studied its legs against the light.

"Great. Mason's doing well."

"How soon do you think he'll be ready to take over?" he asked nonchalantly. As the waiter passed, he nodded.

"Maybe another week. I think all that alone time without me really helped prepare him." She picked up her glass and sipped her drink. "Did you get to see our baby girl today?"

"Oui. She's doing well. And Logan and Wynter...let's just say even though I don't think they were in any way expecting a new pup, they'll make wonderful parents. I'm sure they're going to be quite busy."

"I still don't understand how Ava can be Rylion's," she stated with disgust.

"She's not. I believe that, like you, the demon thought it had claim to her."

"Delusions of grandeur is more like it."

"Possession is possession. Even witches can sometimes achieve it. But one thing is certain; it was Perry's body that created Ava with Mariah. After Rylion had killed Mariah, though, and then the baby, it claimed her soul or should I say, tried to. The water of the womb is perhaps the most vital water any of us will know in our lifetimes. The Lady saved her from the demon. No evil taints Ava," Léopold confirmed. "Our little one's going to be just fine. She's going to be the belle of New Orleans someday."

"Do you ever wish…I mean, you're a vampire…" Laryssa's voice went soft and she looked away. His hand on hers caused her to glance up to him.

"I won't lie to you. I've always wanted children, but this life of mine, you see…it all died. And now that I have you, that's all that matters." Léopold sensed her sadness. They'd never discussed children. It was never an option….until now.

"You're all that matters to me, Leo. It's okay, really. I mean I never thought I could have kids, so it's okay."

"But if you could…would you?"

"With you?"

"But of course with me," he laughed.

Laryssa took a deep breath and sighed. "Yes." She hoped he wouldn't be mad at her.

"Luca and Samantha are having a daughter."

"I thought you said that she was a witch. They're very lucky."

"Ilsbeth believes it is a possibility." Léopold gave her a small smile, waiting for her to put the pieces together.

"Us? No," she replied, shaking her head. Getting her hopes up for something that was impossible would crush her.

"Oui. Us. Apparently, like witches, naiad can bring life…with vampires."

"Don't joke about this. It's not funny."

"Not joking."

"I'm not ready to have kids yet but oh my God, if you're serious, I'd love to have your children someday," she confirmed. *I love you so much.*

"You'd make a wonderful mother, ma chérie." He smiled, pleased with her response.

Laryssa was his perfect soul mate. The vision of her swollen with his child nearly brought tears to his eyes. She simply had no idea how much he'd fallen in love with her, but he planned on telling her tonight. The waiter approached the table, setting their appetizers in front of them.

"Leo, I…" Laryssa began. The love in her heart felt as if it was going to burst if she didn't tell him how she felt. She needed to say the words.

"You look very sexy tonight," Léopold said, changing the subject. "I love when you wear skirts, do you know that?"

The dominant tone of Léopold's voice sent chills up Laryssa's spine. She licked her lips and gave him a small smile.

"Well, I do enjoy making you happy." Laryssa felt his hand on her leg underneath the table and she jumped in her seat. The heat of his palm sent desire singing through her body. Knowing he'd sense it immediately, she picked up her fork and stabbed a piece of lettuce in an effort to act normally.

"So very glad to hear that, because I thought this would be the perfect place to continue our lessons." Léopold let his hand drift to her knee.

"Lessons?" she croaked. "What lessons?"

"Perhaps I've used the wrong word. Experimentation. Oui." His devious grin told her she was in trouble.

"Experimentation? With what?" Beyond her enjoyment of being restrained, they'd discussed how she'd enjoyed being spanked in front of Dimitri. *Oh God, not that. Not here.* Before she could protest, she felt him nudge her knees open, the cool air wafting up her dress. Looking around at the other patrons, she straightened her back as he began to tug up the hem.

"Um, Leo. What are you doing, darling?" She laughed as his fingers trailed up her inner thigh. Looking around the restaurant, she hoped no one could see what he was doing. Even though the white tablecloth obscured the view, Laryssa couldn't stop the rush of heat that filled her cheeks.

"Saying hello."

"Um, hello to you, too. You do realize we're in a restaurant...a very busy restaurant?" she whispered.

"Oui, I'm acutely aware of our location. You know, I've been thinking about that day on the dock." *The spanking.* She projected her arousal at him and his cock jerked in response. He grinned and gave her a knowing look. Léopold couldn't wait to test her limits. "I see you do remember."

"Yes, I remember clearly. It was..." *Embarrassing. Erotic. Hot.* "interesting."

"So I thought, why not experiment further?" Caressing her soft skin, he edged her panties with his fingers. He could feel the heat emanating from between her legs and sought to tease her mercilessly.

"But Leo," she began, but was unable to finish as he slipped his forefinger underneath the flimsy fabric. He brushed through her slick lips and pressed a single finger up into her. She closed her eyes and grabbed onto the cloth napkin. Trying not to let anyone know what he was doing, she opened her lids and sighed. "Please."

"Shhh...you wouldn't want everyone to hear you now, would you?" He laughed "You're wet, mon amour. So nice."

"Leo," she breathed as he pumped into her core, circling his thumb over her clit. Biting her lip, she shot him a sideways glance. *Is he crazy? Someone's going to know. We're going to get thrown out of the café.* As if he could read her exact thoughts, he upped the ante.

"Don't worry your head about what's going to happen next. I got you a gift." He gave a broad smile and winked. Withdrawing his hand from her underwear, he swiftly reached into his pocket and retrieved the pint-sized silicone horseshoe-shaped device he'd bought her. He easily concealed the toy, which was no more than two inches long. When his hand fell back to her lap, she'd closed her legs. "Open, pet. Or would you prefer a spanking?"

Laryssa shook her head back and forth, completely shocked that he was pressing her with this game. Overwhelmed with her own lust, she vacillated between doing as he said and running away from the table. Dear God, the man tested her. It was frightening and exhilarating, but all the while, he had a way of tapping into her darkest thoughts.

"What'll it be?" The side of his lip curled upward, but his tone told her he was completely serious.

Laryssa took a deep breath and blew it out. Her heart skipped a beat as she complied with his instruction. She resisted the urge to leap off her seat as the smooth outer layer of the toy brushed over her pussy. As he slipped the tiny vibrator inside her, she rocked from side to side on her bottom, causing the overlapping design to brush her clitoris. From her swollen nub to the thin stretch of nerves inside her, she was tantalized every time she shifted in her chair. With no area left untouched, she swore she'd come by the end of her appetizer.

"Leo…Oh my God. What is that?" She watched intently as he withdrew his hand from underneath the table, licked his fingers and then proceeded to drink from his wine glass.

"Hmm…you are much tastier than any culinary delicacy." He picked up his fork and began to eat his salad. His eyes caught hers and she frowned. "Just a bit of fun. Sweet torture for both of us, I expect. You're not eating. Come on now, don't waste your dinner."

"Are you kidding?" she responded, trying to keep her voice down.

"Do I ever?" He continued eating with a glint of amusement in his eye.

By the time their entrees arrived, Laryssa was nearly undone. As she scooped a shrimp out of her étouffée, the device pulsed inside her and she muffled a squeak. Her eyes landed on Léopold who grinned.

"What are you doing?" she asked, keeping her voice steady. The vibration ripped over her clitoris, deep into her pussy, causing her to drop her utensil. She gripped the edge of the table as desire rolled through her. She studied Léopold. "How are you doing that?"

"Not a witch, I'm afraid. A man must keep his secrets. Now remember, dear Laryssa, don't make too much noise. You'll have an audience."

"You're evil." A spasm of pleasure rolled through her again, and she coughed, trying to disguise the loud moan that threatened to escape her lips. Deciding fair play was in order, she picked up a breadstick and seductively slid it into her mouth, never taking her eyes off of Léopold's.

"I prefer to think of it as doing you a favor…expanding your horizons and such." Léopold's cock hardened to steel at the sight of her trembling with need. The scent of her arousal saturated his nostrils. He didn't think he could get any harder until the little temptress plunged the rod into her mouth. Sucking his breath, he adjusted his erection. At this rate, he'd be the one coming at the table. "The food's delicious, no?"

"Leo," she groaned.

The vibrations increased in intensity, bringing her closer to orgasm. The room turned hotter and hotter as the assault on her pussy continued. Reaching for the buttons on her shirt, she undid one. She grabbed at his pant leg and dug her fingernails into his thigh. Stifling her panting breaths, she tried to figure out how he was operating the device. With one hand on his fork and the other on the table, the mystery only continued. Her eyes quickly roamed the room, terrified that someone would hear her, discover the tremors racking her body.

"Come for me, pet. Come in front of all these people," he encouraged, loving how uninhibited she was. While it was true he'd instigated their exhibitionistic play, she'd embraced it with passion. As her orgasm began, he offered her his hand. The only thing that would have made the moment any better was if he'd been inside of her himself.

"I...I...Leo...Oh my God...I'm..."

"Shhhh....just let go."

As her release slammed into her, she crushed Léopold's hand and dropped her head. Small high-pitched grunts escaped as she let the climax shudder through her body. Sweat beaded on her forehead, and she closed her eyes. As the convulsions began to cease, she panted for breath.

"You are the most stunning woman I've ever met in my life," Léopold praised.

"Home. Now," she gritted out, unable to control her thoughts.

"But you haven't finished..." he laughed.

"Oh, I finished. We're leaving. Now," she demanded forcefully, pushing out of her seat with the palms of her hands on the table. Brushing her damp hair out of her face, she strode across the room, aware that Léopold was following in her wake.

Léopold threw money on the table, and hurried after his wanton naiad. *Absolutely spectacular,* he mused. He'd never met, nor would he ever meet again, a woman like her. He hurried in front of her, opening up the door so she could pass through it.

Laryssa, blazing in desire, couldn't get home fast enough to make love to Leo. Striding through the courtyard, she hardly noticed anyone around her. The only thing that mattered was getting out of the restaurant. As she brushed by the maître d', who attempted to flag down Léopold, she caught sight of Dimitri at the bar, grinning like the cat who hadn't just eaten the canary but its whole nest. *Fuck. What is he doing here?* Certain it had something to do with Léopold, she spun and saw the broad smile on his face.

"Hey cher," Dimitri said, letting his eyes roam over her.

"What are you..?" she began but was interrupted.

"You have something of mine?" Léopold asked his friend.

"Why yes I do," Dimitri drawled, continuing to smile at Laryssa.

"Merci beaucoup, mon ami," Léopold said, opening the palm of his hand.

"Any time, bro," Dimitri laughed.

Laryssa's eyes widened as Dimitri dropped a quarter-sized remote control into Léopold's palm. *Dimitri had been controlling the toy?* Too aroused to be angry, she feigned indignation.

"You…" she stammered and pointed to Dimitri. "I cannot believe you let him talk you into this. Bad, bad, bad wolf."

"And you," she pinned her eyes on Léopold who looked sexier than ever. With utter dominance, she approached and grabbed him by the tie, forcefully yanking him toward her, "are a very naughty vampire….one who deserves his own little punishment. You had best get me home…I believe you owe me."

"You heard your woman," Dimitri laughed. "Time's a-wastin'"

"That it is," Léopold responded. Without giving Laryssa warning, he scooped her up into his arms and shoved through the front door with the back of his shoulder.

Giggling, Laryssa kicked her feet and pressed her face against his white dress shirt. As Léopold kissed the top of her head, she began to undo his buttons, gliding her hands underneath the crisp fabric, caressing his chest. Within ninety seconds, he'd rounded the corner of the block and was frantically punching his finger at the security pad.

With a light buzz, the door clicked open and he captured her lips with his. Using his foot to slam it shut behind him, he stumbled into the foyer with her in his arms. He heard buttons sprinkle all over the floor like little discs doing a tap dance and realized she'd split his shirt wide open. A bite on his shoulder sent a jolt to his cock.

Laryssa couldn't get enough of him. Aggressively, she tore at his clothes, biting and licking at his skin. Her feet landed shakily on the floor, and she ripped his shirt all the way off of him. Lifting her arms so he could bare her, she moaned at the loss of contact. She was hardly aware that he'd undone her bra until it slipped to the floor. Reaching for him, Laryssa speared her fingers up into his hair, clutching at his head.

His lips found hers again. In frenzy, they passionately kissed, his tongue sweeping up against hers. Seeking, questing, he stroked her mouth with a hungry urgency. Laryssa savagely returned his kiss, fiercely claiming him for her own. Immersed in each other, their bond flourished, escalating their intimacy.

Léopold's erection pressed into her belly as he backed her into the living room. He gently pushed her onto the floor, and she moaned into his mouth. She kicked off her shoes, reaching her hands down to his pants, and unbuckled them. Laryssa freed his iron-hard cock and stroked it, gliding her thumb over its glistening head. With her other hand, she gently massaged his tightened balls until he groaned in pleasure.

Léopold couldn't wait another second to be inside her. He shoved up her skirt, tearing off her panties with his claws. Reaching between her legs, he cupped her mound. He'd considered removing the u-shaped vibrator, but decided to leave it in place. Fingering the top of her folds, he depressed a barely visible button, activating the sultry vibrations. Laryssa moaned in response, guiding his shaft toward her entrance.

"Leo, the toy…" she spoke into his mouth. The engorged head of his arousal pressed against her entrance and she fell back onto the floor, widening her thighs.

"Oui," Léopold guided his swollen flesh into her wet pussy. The slick surface buzzed against his erection as he drove into her.

"Too much… yes, Leo," she breathed.

"You're taking me, all of me. Ah yeah, that's it." He plunged in slowly, allowing her to stretch as he rocked inward.

From his root to his tip, her quivering pussy and the slow trembling of the device stimulated him, sending shockwaves throughout his body. He wouldn't last very long inside her this first time, he knew, but he planned on making love to her all night long. *Goddess, I love this woman.* As his pelvis settled into hers, he leaned onto a forearm. With his other hand, he cupped her breast. Caressing her ripe flesh, he took to her rosy peak, teasing her nipple with his teeth.

"Leo, oh God. Fucking yes." Laryssa saw stars as the pressure on her clit resonated deep into her core. Writhing up into him, she whimpered under the glorious sensation.

"Look at me, mon amour," he grunted, staving off his own orgasm. When she refused to comply, he took her chin in his hand. He smiled as her eyes slowly met his.

"Leo, I…I…" *love you.* Her heart felt as if it would shatter. No one had ever broken her down into such a basic state, holding her life in his hands. He'd infiltrated every fiber of her being, wrecking her for anyone else. And her soul rejoiced that he had.

"Can you feel me?" *I love you.*

She nodded, panting as he slowly rotated his hips against hers.

"You are my blood and flesh…my reason for living, my sweet naiad."

"Leo."

"I love you, Laryssa. You've stolen my heart. Forever. You and I. Hear my words…feel my words." He closed his eyes, funneling the swirling vortex of love he'd held back.

The emotion in Laryssa's chest bubbled over at his words. *I love you.* Her eyes began to tear, but he gave her no time to adjust. A wave of his memories, thoughts and feelings crashed over her, reverberating down from her head to her toes. She felt his pain as if it was her own. *The death of his children and wife. The loneliness he'd hidden throughout the centuries. And finally, the tremendous love and respect he held for her.* And then she heard the words again as if he was speaking them aloud to her; *I love you. My love, my life.*

"I love you, too. You mean everything to me. I love you so, so, much..." her words trailed off as he began to thrust deeply inside her.

Even though Léopold had heard her project the words in her mind many times, he'd never acknowledged them. But now, as the words spilled from her lips, he sought to claim her. He'd never be able to show or tell her how much she meant to him. Like his own personal savior, she'd torn apart his shallow existence, giving him a new life.

With each surge of his hips, Laryssa arched up to meet him. Looking within the deep abyss of his eyes, she opened her soul to him. Nothing short of his possession of her would satisfy her desire. The craving gripped at her chest. Reaching upward, she brushed her hair to the side, submitting, offering him her neck.

At the sight of her surrender, Léopold's fangs descended. Her pussy contracted around his cock, tightening like a vise as her climax teetered over the edge. The sound of flesh meeting flesh filled the room, as he pounded his shaft into her warm center. He felt the barrage of her emotions, ones filled with sheer contentment, filter through him. Soaring over the edge, Léopold lost control. Like a cobra, he struck, his sharp teeth piercing through her milky skin. Her exquisite blood flowed down his throat, weaving itself into his cells.

A sharp prick to Laryssa's neck was quickly replaced with the exhilarating ecstasy that only Léopold could deliver. She cried his name, embracing the furious climax. Wrapping her thighs around his waist, she snared him to her pelvis, undulating up into their simultaneous release. Together they moved in rhythm as their orgasms tore through them at the same time.

Laryssa's cries subsided once Léopold retracted his bite. Shivers ran down her spine as he licked the sensitive skin that ran from behind her ear down between her breasts. She felt him remove both himself and the toy from between her legs as his lips latched onto one of her tender nipples. The delightful sensation brought a smile to her face and she giggled softly.

"No laughing in bed, woman," he growled, giving her a nip.

"Ah...hey, no more biting," she teased. "I need to recover."

Léopold crawled up to her so that he could meet her eyes. Filled with love and dedication, he gently kissed her. Their tongues fluttered softly with each other's.

"I love you," he asserted once more. Rolling onto his back, he brought her with him.

"I love you too," she whispered. "You do know I plan on getting you back for what you did today."

"I'm looking forward to it." Léopold kissed her head and closed his eyes.

In a thousand years, he'd sought to suppress every emotion and experience that would lead him toward a relationship. Yet it was that very connection he'd avoided that now brought peace and tranquility into his life. As he held his mate in his arms, he smiled. It may have taken him centuries, but he'd finally achieved the nirvana he'd sought. His life, once latent with obscurity and death, had been transposed into one of tenderness and love. With Laryssa at his side, nothing would ever be the same.

-~⚙· *Epilogue* ·⚙~-

As the waves rolled in, Dimitri considered his decision to take a vacation by himself. With Logan and Wynter busily adjusting to their new family situation and Léopold and Laryssa ensconced in their bond, he had needed to take a break from New Orleans. Since Jake had promised to fill in on his role of beta, he'd left town, content that he'd wrapped up loose ends.

As he looked up at the spectacular panorama of the night sky, he marveled in the expanse of the universe. While it was altogether stunning, it caused him to pause, wondering how he'd gone all these years with no real purpose. His role as beta had been important to the pack, no doubt. But aside from assisting Logan, he wondered what else was out there and if maybe, in his absence, they'd never miss his presence.

A nagging itch plagued Dimitri as he sat on the wide expanse of beach, looking out over the Pacific ocean. Ever since he'd returned from Rylion's pit, he couldn't shake the feeling something had gone awry. As he'd risen from hell with the baby in his arms, he could've sworn something had latched onto his wolf. He'd felt Ilsbeth's eyes on him, but she'd denied anything was wrong when he'd questioned her. He hadn't expected that Léopold would have noticed anything wrong with him, but his Alpha felt every emotion that ran through his veins. Yet when Dimitri had withdrawn, Logan hadn't said a word. He should have mentioned it to him, he thought. But every time he'd gone to approach Logan, the house was lit up with the coos and giggles of their princess.

Even though he'd tried to shake it off, Dimitri felt dirty. Tainted. Bringing his personal angst into their warm and loving home wasn't something he would do. No, running had been the only option. San Diego wasn't the furthest he could travel on his bike, but it sure as hell was the place with the nicest weather.

He'd known better than to go into another pack's territory without giving fair warning, but he'd lost focus. When the moon rose, he planned to seek out the Alpha. But until then, he planned to sit his ass on the beach. Maybe he'd learn how to surf. Maybe he'd drive up Pacific Coast Highway. Maybe he'd stop by La La Land, get himself a new tattoo. It didn't really matter as long as he felt his skin tingling as if it was crawling with lice. Whatever it took, he had to get his shit together again.

Dimitri had lived a hundred and fifty years on the bayou and aside from Jackson Hole and New York City, he hadn't left his Cajun roots...until this week. Trying to shake off his guilt for leaving the pack, he took off his shirt, and laid his bare skin on the sand. Praying that his suspicion wasn't true, he dug his toes into the sand and breathed in the sea air. Since he'd left seven days ago, he hadn't gone wolf. He was lying to himself, he knew. Something…something insidious…evil had touched him. His wolf had gone silent, and he was terrified to test his suspicions.

Tonight, though, he'd face his fears. He'd run in the desert, maybe kill a meal by himself. As one with his brothers in the Acadian wolves, he'd never once considered going off as a lone wolf. But the voice that he'd picked up in hell told him to run from New Orleans, to flee. And flee he had. He stared up at the stars, hoping his silent meditation would rouse his inner wolf, the fighter that had gotten him through life. In his mind, he called the warrior to the surface and for the first time in his life, no howl of existence responded. He clutched at his chest with his hand as panic set in, and he choked to catch his breath.

Even though his wolf went silent, his preternatural hearing picked up the patter of paws along the shore. A yip in the distance alerted him to the danger. Leaping to his feet, his eyes honed in on a dozen pairs of eyes. As they attacked, their teeth sinking into his flesh, he cried out for his wolf, who as if in a coma, lay sleeping in his mind. Sounds of his own screams reverberated as he was dragged to the ground. Kicking and punching, he tried in vain to fight off his attackers. A final blow to his neck, took him into the sand. As the blood drained from his mortal body, he screamed out to his wolf to wake.

DIMITRI

~⚬ Chapter One ⚬~

Dimitri yanked on the restraints, his wrists firmly secured above his head. The sweet scent of a woman danced through his mind and he swore he felt the warmth of a smooth hand on his thigh. A moan alerted him to the fact that he wasn't alone, and his cock hardened in response. If it weren't for the caustic pain tearing through his muscles, he'd have thought he was having a wet dream. But as he attempted to open his eyes, memories of his last thoughts slammed into him.

Teeth. Claws. Blood. Submission. As his chest heaved for breath, his hands curled into the bed and saliva dripped from his mouth as he recalled being attacked on the beach. A pack of feral wolves had torn into him. Helplessly, he'd fought them, unable to shift. At some point the slashing agony of the attack had ceased; the smooth sound of a woman's voice curled around him in comfort as he surrendered to unconsciousness.

"Shh…you're okay. Stay still."

Not his Alpha's command, yet Dimitri's mind quieted. His dried, cracked lips parted. But before he had a chance to utter a word, the seal between where her skin met his began to heat. His eyes flew open and rolled back into his head as tendrils of healing seeped into his skin. Instinctively, he thrashed against the bindings. His hands fisted the leather, and he shook the bed's metal frame until it rattled uncontrollably. As the tingling spread throughout his body, overwhelming relief from the pain swept through him and he gasped. By the time it was over, tears ran down his face. Not only had the crushing misery disappeared; for the first time in weeks, his wolf howled in celebration.

"My wolf," he cried. "You healed me? How? What are you?"

"You should be okay once you shift…for a few days, anyway," the female responded breathlessly, her lips accidentally brushing his chest. "Can't promise you any longer. You need to see a witch. A shaman may be able to help."

"But how did you know? My wolf…" Dimitri's words trailed off as his vision slowly came into focus. He glanced down to the silky raven hair that brushed over his abdomen.

"Your wolf…he recovers."

"Jesus Christ, the pack. They tried to kill me. How did I get here?"

"You've got an awful lot of questions for an almost dead man," she responded.

"What can I say? Near death does that to a guy. Last thing I remember, those dogs were takin' a bite outta my neck. As much as I wish I had nine lives, I ain't no cat, if you noticed."

"Oh I noticed." She laughed, concealing her face. "Seems to me, you should be doing a little more thanking and a little less asking."

"Now don't take it the wrong way, cher. It's not that I don't appreciate ya healin' me with whatever voodoo you do, but you've gotta see this from my perspective." He gave a small chuckle as his wrists tugged the straps taut. He glanced at his makeshift handcuffs, noticing she'd used belts to restrain him. "So ya want to tell me why I'm tied to the bed? Believe me, I'm down with the kink as much as the next wolf. But call me crazy, this doesn't really seem on the up and up."

"Sorry, lover boy, but I did it for my own safety. You were a bit wild when I brought you here. You know what they say when a dog gets hit by a car…it can bite out of fear and pain."

"Hey now, no need for name calling. There's no dog here. You got yourself a wolf, darlin'."

"I know what you are. Doesn't matter. I take my life pretty seriously. I admit I'm not in the business of tying up men, but I can assure you that I trussed you up for self-preservation purposes only."

Dimitri felt the lilt of her smile curl against his skin and silently cursed as his dick twitched in response. He laughed inwardly at his predicament, as he jerked at his bindings. Sure, he was tied up good. On the up side, he'd survived the attack and had woken up with a beautiful woman next to him. Not the optimal situation, but it could be worse. He was alive and damn, if it didn't turn him on to feel the top of her thigh brush against his own. 'Bondage anytime anywhere' just might become his new motto. He knew it was wrong to be thinking about sex, given the seriousness of the situation, but hey, when in Rome…

"You never did explain how a lil' bit of a thing like yourself took out a wolf pack." Dimitri left the statement open, hoping for an explanation. As much as he wanted to demand answers, he was tired and enjoyed the warmth of her next to him. He was horny, no doubt. But moreover, he needed comfort.

"No I didn't," she hedged.

"Seriously, I need to know. Why rescue me? How did we get in this shitty hotel room?"

"I'm a healer." Gillian pushed upward, releasing herself from the warm embrace she'd provided to Dimitri. She sat on the edge of the bed, her face toward the door and looked to her palms. "I usually use just my hands."

Dimitri resisted the urge to beg his savior to come back to bed. As the covers fell away, he caught sight of her white cami, which had ridden up, exposing a small tattoo written in Chinese. Before he had a chance to read it, she tugged down the fabric, concealing the ink. Her black thong trailed down into the cleft of her perfect heart-shaped ass.

He closed his eyes for a split second, knowing full well he shouldn't try to flirt with the sexy stranger who'd rescued him. But his wolf, seeking mischief, howled in amusement. Curiosity got the best of him. He lifted his head, straining to see her face, which was hidden beneath a stream of silky hair. A small growl of frustration escaped his lips. He wished he could touch her, but fuck it all, his hands were bound.

"Listen, cher. I'm feeling better now. Promise I won't bite. How's about you loosen up these belts?" he suggested, eyeing his bindings.

Her pink lips parted in a devious grin as she climbed up him, straddling his torso. It was then that he finally caught sight of the gorgeous female holding him hostage.

"Tell me how you did it. How'd you save my ass from that pack?" he asked, distracted by her scent. One of her hands pressed firmly next to his face, and he instinctively turned his nose toward her skin and sniffed. Underneath the clean cucumber smell of the soap, he detected the presence of shifter blood. "Are you a wolf?"

"No," she responded as she checked to make sure his hands were still well secured to the bed and that the strap wasn't cutting off his circulation. She leaned over and unbuckled his ankles. Still bound, he wasn't going anywhere. "I'm just the person who healed you. Nothing special about me."

"Excuse my French, but I call bullshit. You've got to be something special. No man or woman interferes with a pack attack and walks away unscathed." Dimitri sensed her distrust. Despite the untruth that slipped from her lips, she wasn't successful at looking him in the eye while she said it.

"Let's just say I've got a few tricks in my bag. I got lucky and managed to get you away from those assholes. All you need to know is that I'm a healer and that it worked."

As she attempted to retreat, Dimitri rattled the bedframe, attempting to free himself. "Why? Please. I need to know why you saved me. Why you're half naked in bed with me. Don't get me wrong, what you did…you look…" *Beautiful.* "Nice." *Real smooth D*, he thought to himself.

Gillian focused in on his rugged masculine face. His deep brown eyes met her own. "I use my hands to heal. Your injuries…you almost didn't make it," she sighed. "I don't heal people very often."

"But you did a helluva job here." He glanced to his torso as she moved to peel a large bloodied bandage off his neck. Her fingers trailed over the newly scarred skin.

"Don't take this the wrong way." She gave him a broad smile and lifted herself off him. "As cute as you are, I don't jump into bed with strangers. Well, maybe I did for you, but that doesn't include sex. It was just necessary to heal you. I had to use all of me. Skin to skin."

Skin to skin, huh? Dimitri laughed as he watched her leap off the bed. Oh yeah, he could think of quite a few things he'd like to do with this little minx, skin to skin. He bit his tongue as she continued.

"I've only done it one other time. All you need to know is that on the beach I healed you enough to stop the bleeding. Then, I paid a few guys to help me move you here. You know, a no questions asked kind of thing," she explained, and began to rummage through her canvas backpack.

"So you think I'm cute," Dimitri teased.

Gillian stopped cold, her jaw dropping. She turned her head to him and glared, before returning to her task.

"Doesn't matter what I think of you." She blew out a regretful breath and yanked out a pair of jeans. "You're not the only one who's got trouble. I've gotta go."

"Hold up there, girly. You did notice you didn't untie me all the way. I suppose I could break this freakin' metal if I yanked hard enough…"

"Just cool your jets, wolf. I called your friends. They'll be here soon enough, and they can untie you. You know… so you can shift." She slipped on her pants, zippered up, and turned around to face him. "I healed you, but that doesn't mean you can go ballistic over there trying to get out of the damn bed. You need to shift. But not while I'm here."

Dimitri licked his lips. His gaze fell to her perfect little nipples, which were standing at attention. His eyes darted up to hers, and he laughed, aware she'd seen his actions. He thought it interesting that she pretended not to notice him. Instead, she retrieved a black leather motorcycle boot from under the bed and hastily shoved her foot into it. Even though his Alpha was the shopper in the pack, he recognized the expensive camera equipment she had stowed on the dresser. They may have been holed up in a shithole of a motel, but this girl had assets. He suspected that she might be a photographer and wondered what kind of trouble was chasing her.

"Why don't you explain to me exactly why I can't shift in front of you? Afraid of the big bad wolf? I'm not lookin' to eat you."

"No offense, but you don't scare me. I do recall it was me saving your ass."

"I've got a fine one."

"Yes, yes you do." She laughed, shaking her head. "But did it occur to you that maybe it is you who should be afraid of me?"

"Never crossed my mind, cher. Come on now, let me go. I promise to be a good boy…shift and shift back. I can't imagine they allow pets in this," he looked around the seedy hotel room, "flea shack."

"No, I don't imagine they do. Just please don't…"

"Dimitri…Dimitri LeBlanc. Rolls right off the tongue." He gave her a broad smile, attempting to throw her off her game.

"Dimitri, I just can't be around another wolf. Please, I swear your friends will be here soon," she said nervously. She plucked a black tank top out of her bag and slipped it over her head.

"You're telling me you're not a wolf?" he began.

"Yep." She offered no information.

"But you saved me from a pack of wolves."

"Yeah, I guess you could say that."

"And you're not going to tell me how you did it or what pack you've been hangin' out with?"

"Um…" She turned to him, smiled, and shook her head. "Nope."

"And you think that just because you saved me, you get to call the shots."

"Well, let's see. I'm here. And you," she laughed and yanked on her other boot, "you're indisposed…at least until someone comes for you. Not much you can do about it, huh?"

Dimitri had had enough of her games. The rush of the challenge surged through his body, and his wolf pressed him to take her, to show his majestic presence. He jerked his right arm and tore open the metal clasps of the belts. Quickly releasing his other hand, he leapt off the bed, wearing nothing but his boxers. As quick as lightning, he backed her against the wall, his hands on either side of her head.

His beast unleashed, Dimitri lowered his face, sniffing his prey. The wolf had gone feral, too long kept hidden away in a dungeon of despair. It trusted no one. As he took in the exquisite scent of the female, he drew closer, yet still didn't touch her body.

"What are you doing?" she breathed against Dimitri. Her palms reached up slowly until they were laid flat on his chest. Gillian didn't want to stop him; she secretly wished to feel him one more time, to soak in the power of his wolf.

"Your blood," Dimitri growled. "You're shifter. But how does one woman take on an entire pack? I sense no wolf…you are something… something special."

"I…I…I'm not wolf," she protested breathlessly.

"You smell heavenly," he breathed. Dimitri reined in his wolf, exhilarated that he'd found the animal within. Taking a deep breath, he slowly raised his head, and stared deep into her amber eyes. A small rectangular section of brown bled up into her irises. Captivated, he drew closer still.

"Your eyes," he whispered.

"I know." Flustered, she broke eye contact and looked to the floor.

"No." Dimitri gently caressed her chin until her gaze once again met his. "Don't hide from me. Let me see your eyes."

"Heterochromia, um, that's the technical term. I was born with…"

"They're beautiful. Like a cat." He smiled, pondering her origins.

"Yes," she agreed, unable to stop the burn that grew in her gut.

"Very pretty eyes. Unique. Tell me your name," he asked. Unable to resist, he brushed his cheek against hers.

"Gillian…Gilly. My name's Gilly," she confessed. A shiver ran through her body as his soft beard brushed her lip.

"Thank you, Gilly." He smiled, retreating. "I'm grateful you saved me."

"Well, yes, but you'd better let me go. As I told you, I've gotta get out of here. They're after me," she said nervously.

"Let me help you, repay you for your kindness," he told her. *Now, just what kind of trouble are you in? Tell me why you saved me. How do you know the wolves that attacked me?* Yes, he wanted to help her but this interesting woman was hiding something. His wolf would not rest until he knew everything. It had been his experience that neither humans nor immortals did good deeds with no reward in mind. Whether to relieve their own conscience or get compensation, there was always a reason. "At least let me see you home. If you called someone from my pack, they'll help us."

"No, the people after me are going to track us eventually. They'll know your scent. I'm sorry, but it isn't safe. Your wolf is weakened. What you need to do is find a witch to help you. I don't know where you live, but you need to go home...alone. We can't stay together. You can catch a flight out. The airport's only about twenty minutes from here. I'll divert them...I'm going by land," she rambled.

"Darlin', I'm the beta of Acadian wolves. You don't need to worry about me."

Is she serious? Does she really think I'm going to up and leave her when she has someone chasing her? Dimitri registered the look of disbelief that crossed her face in response to his previous statement, and grinned.

"Let me clarify that statement. Now that you've healed my wolf...I can hold my own."

"Acadian wolves? New Orleans?" she gasped, trying to break free of the cage he'd built with his arms.

"You'd like to test me?" His eyes fell to her mouth, watching her tongue tease over her bottom lip. *Kiss her,* his wolf demanded. *Fuck no,* he replied. Reason won out and he quickly averted his gaze. Unfortunately, it fell from her lips to her bosom.

"No, please," she whispered. Gillian followed his line of vision and parted her lips in expectation. "You have to listen to me. This is no joke."

"Come now, cher. Let me help you. Don't fight this. Besides, from the looks of things," he glanced down to his naked chest, and then met her eyes with a wicked smile, "you've had your sweet hands all over me. Cleaned me up real nice. Warmed me in your arms. It's almost like we're already dating."

"We're not dating. I...I..." Gillian stammered.

"Say yes." Dimitri leaned forward until his breath warmed her lips, and he fought the temptation. Unfortunately weakness took over and he moved to her ear, his tongue darting out to the hollow behind it. His cock hardened, and he pressed a kiss to her skin.

A knock at the door startled them both. Dimitri briefly turned his head toward the noise.

I've lost my mind, Gillian thought. *Goddammit.* The only reason she'd saved the wolf was out of guilt. The pack had been after her that night, not him. They'd chased her down after she'd escaped. When they'd attacked the stranger, she'd shifted, protecting him from certain death. A healer by nature, she couldn't tolerate the deliberate infliction of torture on another being. At the time, she'd thought the man on the beach was a human, but by the time she'd gotten him back to the room, her beast had recognized his.

Gillian had used every ounce of her power to heal his wolf. With her skin against his, her hands had explored every hard ridge of his abdomen as she gave of herself. She'd indulged, letting her fingertips trace his tattoos while he'd slept. The man was undeniably hot, and she suspected he could be the kind of man who'd make her want to give into a mating.

Gillian had known her whole life that mating wasn't in the cards for someone like her. Steadfast in her decision, she refused to sacrifice her own beast for a man. The secrets she kept inside were what had almost gotten her killed when the Alpha of Anzober wolves, Chaz Baldwin, discovered what she could do for him.

She should have known coming to San Diego on a too-good-to-be-true photo shoot was a bad idea. She'd been working in New York City, making a bare bones living as a photographer when she'd been contacted by an agent who was willing to pay her top dollar for a high-end magazine spread. When she'd arrived in the desert to check out the location, she'd been confronted with the cold reality that Chaz had deliberately drawn her into his web.

He'd taken her captive to his beachfront home, all the while promising not to hurt her. Chaz had pressed the issue of a mating, knowing that it was impossible. After three days of living in the Alpha's gilded cage and a brutal assault, she'd summoned the courage to shift and tore apart her guards. But as she took off down the beach, she hadn't considered the collateral damage she'd leave in the wake of her escape. *Dimitri.*

She hadn't known his full name until he'd told her in bed. When she'd taken his cell phone and called the first three numbers, the men on the other line weren't forthcoming about his identity, threatening retribution if their friend wasn't found alive when they arrived. With the knock on the door, she was reminded that not only did she have to fear Chaz; the gorgeous but deadly beta could attack if he shifted. His friends, who'd made it clear to her that he not be harmed, were now on the other side of the paper-thin door. Would they try to kill her? Would they return her to Chaz? What if they'd found out about her background? No, she couldn't let that happen.

Gillian waited until Dimitri took his hand off the wall. As he turned toward the door, she reached into her backpack and picked up the gun she'd stolen from the pack house.

"Who's there?" Dimitri yelled.

"Open the fuck up, D," Jake replied from the hallway. The door flew open and he caught the sight of Dimitri smiling, wearing only his underwear. A woman stood near the dresser, aiming a firearm at him.

"Hey, bro. Thanks for coming." Dimitri gave him a quick hug. As much as he enjoyed getting to know his prickly but lovely female rescuer, the sight of Jake came as a relief.

"Good to see you, too. What the hell happened to you?" Jake grimaced, taking sight of the fresh scars marking Dimitri's chest and throat.

"It's okay, really. I just have to shift." Dimitri downplayed his injuries. "I almost forgot, this is Gilly…"

"You mean the hot chick pointing the gun at us?"

"Gun?" Dimitri's eyes widened. Surprised that she'd pulled a weapon, he held up his hands in a defensive posture and slowly approached her. "What've ya got there, cher? You can put that down. This is Jake. He won't hurt you. He's a good friend of mine. Acadian Wolves."

"Jake." Gillian tilted her head and then nodded at the handsome man who'd come to save his beta. "Nice to meet you. Now that we have all of the pleasantries out of the way, it's time for me to leave."

"But I just got here," Jake protested.

"Sorry, but I've gotta run. As I explained to your beta here, I've got some nasty folks after me. Same ones who attacked him, as a matter of fact. The good news is, that if you get your asses on a plane and out of here, I'm pretty sure that'll be the end of your troubles. The bad news is that they are going to find me soon. They've got my scent and his. My plan is to high-tail it out of here to Vegas. I'll lead them away from you. This is my mess, not yours."

"It may be your mess but I told you that we're not leaving you," Dimitri said, his voice serious.

"That's where we're going to have to agree to disagree. You need to shift and heal. If you go up against the pack, who knows what will happen? The evil you carry is only temporarily suppressed by my magic. It won't last and I won't have your death on my hands…I can't do that to you." Gillian fought the emotion that welled up in her chest. The truth was that she was scared shitless to go it alone, but the beta wouldn't be strong enough in his current condition to survive another wolf attack.

"What the fuck is wrong with your wolf?" Jake exclaimed. He'd been suspicious that something had been off with his friend.

"Goddammit." Dimitri turned and pounded the wall with his fist out of frustration.

"How long, D?"

"A couple of weeks. I don't know. Too fucking long."

"Your girl here says it's evil. Now the only place I know you could've picked up something like that is that hell-infested demon pit you jumped in with Leo."

"I don't want to talk about it." Three weeks before, Dimitri had followed his friend Léopold into a netherworld to help him save his girlfriend and ever since, he'd had difficulty shifting.

"Well, you should've fucking told me."

"I didn't know how bad it was. That night on the beach…I couldn't shift," Dimitri confessed. He raked his fingers through his hair and glanced over to Gilly, who was hoisting her bag onto her shoulders.

Jake blew out a deep breath and his lips formed a tight line. Things were going to be all fucked up to the tenth degree if his beta couldn't shift. It was kind of a requirement that if you were a member of a pack, you actually could shift. He had to know for certain how badly his friend was still affected by whatever the hell had attacked him.

"Shift."

"What?" Dimitri asked, incredulous at the demand.

"Just hold it right there!" Gillian yelled. No fucking way did she want to be in the room when two wolves fought or shifted. Her beast would be called to the surface, and she'd have little control to stop it.

"What's the issue?" Jake began to approach her but quickly stopped as she raised the weapon again.

"No shifting until I'm gone. And lucky for you, I'm outta here."

"Gilly, please. You can't fight an entire wolf pack on your own. I'm not letting you go," Dimitri said.

"See, that's the thing. I'm not asking for permission. Follow me and I'll shoot you in the leg. I know you can shift but are you willing to chance it?" Gillian kept her eyes trained on both men, moving slowly to the entrance. She wrapped her fingers around the doorknob and twisted it open. "Yeah, I didn't think so. Okay, then, well, be safe. Go home to New Orleans. Find a witch and have a Bloody Mary for me. Just remember that this is my problem, not yours."

Neither wolf moved to stop her as she gave them a wink, slamming the door shut. Jesus Christ almighty, she prayed that she was doing the right thing as she ran toward the rental car. Fear coursed through her, but she continued on, clicking the car locks open on the Audi she'd had delivered.

Gillian swallowed the hard lump in her throat and threw her bag into the car. There was nothing in the world she would have liked more than to go with Dimitri to the airport and hop a plane to the east coast. But her paranoia was stronger than her desire to get to know the handsome beta. Aware that she was putting her own life at risk in order to divert attention away from him, she sucked a breath and told herself it was for his own good. It was her fault he'd been attacked. It was her who Chaz sought. It wasn't fair to Dimitri or his friend to let them help her. At the end of the day, she could die in peace if she got caught. Putting Dimitri in danger again was simply not an option.

Chapter Two

Dimitri insisted on following Gillian. If she thought she'd dismiss him, she had another think coming. *Nice try, cher. You will not escape so easily.* After she'd slammed the door to the hotel room, he'd quickly shifted to heal his remaining injuries. It wasn't long before he and Jake had taken off after her in their car.

Loathe as he was to admit it, whatever had latched onto his soul was still there. Like a dark shadow, it lingered. Part of him knew he needed to get back to New Orleans as soon as possible to see Ilsbeth, the one witch he knew who could help him. But given the brief interaction he'd had with his Florence Nightingale, that'd have to go on the back burner. For once his brain and his dick were in perfect agreement; get the girl.

"Tell me again why we're following some mystery chick? One who I'm pretty sure was responsible for helping get your face torn off," Jake commented, hoping Dimitri would catch his eye roll.

"Her name's Gilly. And because the lady was nice enough to save my ass and now I plan to save hers."

"You wanting her ass is one thing we probably can agree on. Why? Well, that's a whole other question."

"It's nice. That should be reason enough."

"I bet she exercises a lot. Squats would do it."

"She was in the room with you for all of two minutes and you took reconnaissance on her ass?"

"Special ops, bro. I've got eyes in the back of my head," Jake joked.

"Then you must have also noticed that she needs our help."

"Whatever you say. It's just that with your wolf on the fritz, don't ya think we oughtta get back to NOLA? Listen, I know you and the witch had a bit of a fallin' out, but damn; it's your wolf. This is some serious shit. When Logan finds out what happened…"

"Logan doesn't need to know right now." Dimitri knew he should tell his Alpha, but Logan hadn't even noticed that his wolf had gone silent. Both he and his mate had been over the moon, doting over their newly adopted daughter. Dimitri didn't want to worry him any more than necessary. He'd tell them when he got back to New Orleans. As he figured it, he'd catch up to Gillian and convince her to fly back to Louisiana with him. When they got to the city, he'd ask Logan to call the asshole Alpha from California and smooth things over. Since their packs didn't abut boundaries, no territory disputes would arise.

"You must've knocked your head in when you were attacked. You really think our Alpha doesn't know what happened? You do know your girl called every number on your damn cell, right? Said she wasn't going to chance having someone forget she called."

"Fuck," Dimitri swore, blowing out a breath. "Give me your phone."

"Finally, you see reason." Jake dug his cell out of the console and tossed it to Dimitri.

"Yeah, yeah." Dimitri began tapping at the screen.

"You aren't calling Logan, are you?" Jake slammed a palm down on the steering wheel.

"Hell, no. If I tell him what's happenin', he's gonna leave his mate and babe and come runnin' out here. He's been through enough. They've both been through enough."

"What about Léopold?"

"What the hell? How many people did she call?"

"I told ya. She called your contacts."

"All of them?" Dimitri exclaimed, stroking his goatee. It looked more like a full grown beard, since he hadn't shaved in a week.

"How the hell am I supposed to know? I can tell ya that she called Logan, Léopold and me. It's possible she called a few of your *special* friends," Jake drawled, knowing that it would irk Dimitri.

"Fuck me."

"Yeah, well, Logan sent me. You're lucky that he and Leo are up to their eyeballs in love or Logan'd be out here in a pack war. And Leo? Hell, he'd probably be ripping out hearts and sucking wolves dry…including your little shifter girl. Speaking of which…what kind of shifter is she? I couldn't get close enough to tell by her scent…"

"I don't know," Dimitri said flatly, unwilling to share that she'd been nearly naked, skin to skin against him but he still hadn't been able to tell what she was.

"You sure she's not wolf?"

"Nope. Not a wolf. Why do they make these buttons so fucking small?" Dimitri swore, continuing to toy with the cell phone. "I don't get why an Alpha wants to mess with another shifter?"

"Why, indeed?" Jake glanced over to his friend. "And how the hell are we supposed to find her? She's been gone for a while now. As good as I am, and oh, I am good, there's no way in hell we're gonna track her from the wind flyin' by on a highway."

"No, but we will find her using a tracking app." Dimitri smiled and waved the device in the air.

"Clever wolf. I just assumed she trashed your phone afterward."

"She likes me." Dimitri waggled his eyebrows and chuckled. "She's still got my phone. Just couldn't give up a piece of the big D."

"Yeah, yeah. Where's she headed?"

"Sin city. She's on I-15. Looks like she's stopped for gas. It's only about five hours to Vegas from here."

"What's the deal with this woman? Do you think she was in on it? Logan put a call in to the local Alpha. He denies that he approved the attack. Claims they were rogues."

"No. The girl's on the run. As for the Alpha, I'm not buyin' his story. It had to be his wolves."

"I get that you didn't check in with him right away, but the odds of them finding and attacking a non-aggressive stranger are pretty low. It doesn't sync."

"They were after her, not me. I was just a casualty." Dimitri shook his head. He knew that he should get his ass back on a plane to New Orleans, but there was something about Gilly. The need to protect her, to repay her was overwhelming. Like a compulsion; he hadn't given a second thought to chasing her. If she'd been wolf, he might have been worried that she could be his mate. But since she wasn't wolf, there was no way that she was. Maybe she didn't want to reveal her nature, but once he found her, he planned on getting the truth. "She's a shifter. Whatever she is, it must be badass. 'Cause Jake, I'm tellin' ya, bro, I was messed up bad. I called for my wolf…" His words trailed off into silence.

"I've never heard of such a thing happening. Whatever was in that pit…we've gotta get you to Ilsbeth. Maybe we shouldn't worry about Gilly. I know you think she's something special, but for all you know, she shifts into a skunk."

"Fuck you," Dimitri snorted. "There's no way. I've had her sweet little body wrapped around mine. My girl's probably a fox….sly and smooth."

"Or a bear."

"Hey, don't hate on the bear. A bear? Well, she'd probably be wild in bed. Uninhibited."

"Not many people survive bear attacks."

"Oh, I'd survive and love every minute of it. I like it a little rough. Besides, it doesn't matter. Whatever she is, my wolf likes her. She saved him, and he wants to return the favor."

"Yeah, your wolf wants to do something with her, all right. Somehow I don't think it involves just savin' her."

"Yes, he does." Dimitri laughed. "And why not? He deserves a little fun."

"Seriously? She just held a gun on us. Do I need to answer that question?"

"No, and it doesn't matter, cause it's gonna be cool when I do find out what she is. I know I'm gonna like it."

"Maybe you need to take it easy."

"I'm fine now," Dimitri said, not sure if he was trying to convince himself or Jake.

"Just sayin', D. You just recovered from a beat down. We don't know when or if your wolf is going to go on the fritz or whatever else the hell could happen. I know you are, uh…" Jake tried real hard to select his words carefully. Near-death experiences had a way of giving one a new perspective on life, yet Dimitri seemed as courageous and impulsive as ever, "…compromised. Dying has a way of doing that to you. Let's face it; we're used to being immortal. But with your wolf gone, you and I both know that you were nothing more than human."

Dimitri tried to shake off Jake's comments, meeting his observations with a quiet contemplation. He'd known it was serious. He was damn lucky Gillian had done whatever magic she had to heal him.

"It's not like I don't know you're right. I mean, going to the airport and flyin' home would be the rational thing to do. But Gilly, she saved my life. Yeah, I don't know her. I guess I don't owe her a damn thing. But the way she left…she's in danger. She may look tough, but she's not. I'm telling you, I watched her, the way she moved. Did you hear how she talked? She strikes me as more of a city girl. She's scared, hiding something. I don't know why…I just can't walk away and wash my hands of her."

"You wouldn't know if something happened to her or not. You don't even know if that's her real name, for that matter," Jake replied.

"We're friends, right?" Dimitri asked.

"Seriously?"

"Oh yeah, I'm going there."

"Yeah, we're friends," Jake sighed.

"If you don't want to go with me, you don't have to, but this is something I have to do. Once I make sure Gilly gets safely to wherever she calls home, then we'll fly straight to the witch. It's the least I can do. If it weren't for her, I'd be dead."

"If it weren't for her, your biggest worry would be which bikini-clad Cali girl to hit on."

"Can't deny the possibility." Dimitri gave him a broad smile, knowing that was exactly what he'd planned on doing. "But she needs me. And I owe her. So are you in or are you out?"

"Bellagio or Hard Rock?"

"Venetion?" Dimitri countered, relieved that Jake had agreed in his non-conventional way.

"Four Seasons?" Jake suggested.

"The Four Seasons it is. Viva Las Vegas, baby." Dimitri glanced down to his phone. Her car had begun moving. "We'd better speed it up if we're gonna catch our girl."

Gillian felt feverish as her anxiety took hold. She only wished it was the fucking desert heat. No, she knew exactly why she was drenched in sweat, and it had everything to do with the Alpha who had kept her captive. Coming out to California was one of the single biggest mistakes she'd ever made in her life. She should have known that it was too good to be true. When she'd gotten the email from the agent explaining that they'd seen her work and wanted her, a mid-list photographer, to shoot an A-list actor in front of an Anza-Borrego metal sculpture, she should've verified the job.

As the sun melded into the horizon in her rearview mirror, she cursed. She should have driven directly to the airport. But the guilt in her chest bubbled like hot lava. The only reason the beta had been attacked was because they'd been after her.

She suspected that Dimitri would have been able to fend off Chaz's pack had his wolf not been impaired. As she'd lain in bed healing him, allowing her mind to explore his energy, she'd felt the spirit of a warrior wolf, a man whose pure sexuality threatened to shake her resolve to remain single. If he'd only been mortal, she could have remained in control. Yet as soon as he'd awoken to her touch, she'd nearly caved.

It had been so long since she'd been with a man, let alone a wolf. In order to remain true to her species, she'd sworn herself to celibacy when it came to wolves. She simply couldn't risk meeting her mate. If she did, she'd be forced to give up the only beast she'd ever known, with no guarantee that she'd remain immortal. *Weak. Defenseless.* She refused to succumb to the consequences of a mating.

She sighed. It wasn't fair; a girl needed release every now and then. And her current strategy just wasn't cutting it. Although humans were a poor substitute for what she craved, Gillian had implemented a 'mortal men only' dating rule. That was how she'd survived her teenage years, passing as human, dating boys, then later colleagues she'd met at work.

Yet her nature drew the wolves to her like moths to a flame. She'd hidden the secrets of her heritage to the best of her ability, but it hadn't been good enough. The Alpha of Anzober wolves had discovered her secret. How, she wasn't sure. All she knew was that he'd made it clear he intended to force their mating. A forced mating wasn't natural, although it'd been rumored that it could be done by an Alpha.

She rubbed the back of her neck where he'd bitten her. Tears pricked her eyes as the memory of his attack played in her mind. He'd ordered his men to restrain her with silver. They'd tied her face down to his bed and stripped her shirt off in preparation for his mark. He insisted that he'd never take her sexually against her will as he ground his erection into her bottom, pressing her into the bed. Her poisoned restraints kept her from shifting as he dug his claws into her shoulders, sinking his fangs into her neck. As his foul-smelling breath drifted into her nostrils and the pain faded, she shook uncontrollably against the satin sheets, expecting him to mount her.

She'd bitten her lip bloody, refusing the satisfaction of letting them see her cry as he hoisted himself off of her, declaring that he'd marked her. His goons made the mistake of misinterpreting her silence as acquiescence and they'd released her bindings. As soon as they'd left the room, she'd called on her beast, killing all three wolves as she fled.

Gillian had to get back to New York. Her brother was the only one who could get her out of this mess. Her fingers grazed the spot where Chaz had bitten her and she thanked the Goddess that he'd failed to mark her. He was not her mate. And as long as she got her ass back to the Big Apple, she'd be safe from the predator who'd lured her all the way to California.

After a quick stop for fuel, she double checked the address of the Las Vegas airport in her GPS app. Even though she'd bought an extra-large coffee to stay awake, the truth was that her nerves had her lit up like a Christmas tree. There was no way she'd fall asleep; her mind was running races. The hot beverage was for comfort only. Even though it tasted like sludge, the bitter fluid reminded her of home. As she looked out onto the dark highway, it was as if a cold claw clutched her chest, reminding her of the danger she faced. *Fucking desert*. Of all the trips to make in the middle of the night alone, driving to Nevada wasn't up there with the world's safest sightseeing trips.

She considered that she might have been able to make the trek as a shifter had she known where she was going. But since this was her first trip to the golden coast, she had no idea in hell how to get there. Given her limitations, this was a time to rely on technology. She glanced quickly to the red dot on her cell phone that was moving slowly down the green line toward the border.

A light flashed in the distance. What the hell was that? Lightning? A desert storm? *I thought it wasn't supposed to rain in California. Get a grip, girl, there's no way he can find you out here.* Gillian reached over to turn up the radio. *Hotel California* wailed through the speakers, and she quickly flipped it over to *Fuckin' Perfect* by Pink. *Yeah, that about sums things up nicely.*

Gillian took a sip of her lukewarm coffee and grimaced as it coated her tongue. Shoving the paper cup into its holder and glancing into her side mirror, she noticed the rare sight of headlights approaching in the distance. As her eyes flashed back to the road, she caught a glint of metal fifty feet ahead on the highway. Two seconds too late, her foot slammed on the brake. Her car hit the shiny silver spike strip. Gripping the steering wheel, she lost her fight for control. As the car slid across the dry road, she screamed. A cold hiss was all she heard before the car rolled over into the dusty desert.

The airbag inflated, knocking her unconscious for several minutes. The creak of the car door alerted her to their presence. In a haze, she barely felt the blade against her belly as they cut her free and her body tumbled onto the ceiling of the car. Unable to move, she groaned as someone tugged on her legs, her face scraping the jagged broken window as they dragged her limp body out onto the cold ground.

The shock of the scent of her own blood drove her into consciousness. Roused, her head bobbed up as meaty hands jolted her upright. Her feet scraped a trench through the gritty sand as the strangers dragged her into the night. The sight of her headlights became pinpricks as they drew her further into the darkness.

Gillian heard Chaz's voice and her blood turned to ice. *How the hell did he find me?* She'd suspected they would have found the motel room where she'd stayed overnight. But she couldn't piece together how they'd found her on the run. She plotted to shrug off her captors, intending to shift, but when she attempted to yank her arm free, she was swiftly rewarded with a silver chain around her neck. The metal immediately poisoned her blood, stifling any chance of a transformation.

"Get off me," she cried, her voice barely audible.

A cold laugh echoed ahead of her.

"Gilly, Gilly, Gilly. My dangerous but lovely mate. You've been a bad girl," Chaz taunted.

He nodded to the two thugs who'd taken Gillian, instructing them to drop her. He smiled coldly as she grunted in pain, her palms stretched out onto the dirt. She attempted to push up onto her feet but fell back onto her hands and knees. Chaz rounded behind her, leaned over and gripped her hair, yanking her up into a kneeling position.

"Ah, yes. Now this is how I shall like to see my queen. On her knees. Submissive. With my cock in her mouth." He laughed, and dragged his hand along her chin. "But not right now. No, no, no. Penance must be done. You killed my wolves. Pity, but you must receive your punishment."

Gillian spat blood up at him and he shoved her toward the earth, wiping the saliva away with the back of his hand. He reached to her collar and wrapped the chain around her neck once more, ensuring her compliance. As he gripped her leather jacket and peeled it off her arms, Gillian fought the fear that wrapped around her mind. The sound of fabric tearing spiked her anxiety, but she refused to give him the satisfaction of her tears. She watched helplessly as he threw her tattered shirt aside. Wearing only a bra, her skin was exposed to the cold air, and she shivered in response. Gooseflesh rippled across her skin.

This man is incapable of mating me. No matter what pain he plans to inflict, I will not become his. Her beast would never allow it. Any submission he gained would not satisfy her nature. Rationally, she knew the truth of the situation, yet she also was cognizant that he could easily kill her in her disabled state. His voice jarred her back into the moment.

"My wolves…they will bear witness to my mark." He lifted her hair, inspecting his work. Shocked and aggravated with what he saw, he slapped the back of her head with his palm. "What the fuck, bitch? What did you do?"

"I told you," she coughed. She shook her head, the sting of his slap still fresh on her skull. "You cannot mate with my kind. You cannot force a mating."

"Like hell I can't," he growled, his canines descended. Clothed, Chaz mounted her from behind, slamming her face into the dust. "Guess I'll just have to bite you a little harder this time."

Gillian screamed in terror as his teeth sliced into her shoulder. Even though she knew that his mark would be gone the next time she shifted, disgust and loathing roared to the surface.

"No, no, no," she repeated. Tears began to fall and she cursed the silver that restrained her far more than any creature could. Heaving breaths rocked her lungs and she flailed, trying unsuccessfully to get away from him.

Gillian's blood gushed fresh from her wounds as Chaz retracted his teeth. The Alpha licked his lips, smirking with satisfaction. He pushed to his feet, releasing a frightening howl into the night. The four men who'd helped him abduct her joined in chorus, celebrating.

"Your taste was made for me," he continued, reaching to accept a whip from his colleague. "I could fuck you right now in front of everyone, but unlike you, I'm capable of restraint."

"Fuck you," she cried, once again on her knees. Her defiant eyes met his, refusing to submit in any way, shape or form. The crack of the whip didn't shake her resolve. As far as she was concerned, he could shove his demand for her submission down his throat. The only way she'd submit was if she was cold, dead and six feet under.

"Don't worry." He laughed, cracking the popper, enjoying the thunderous sound it made throughout the valley. "I plan to fuck you nice and hard. But first things first. You must be punished for your indiscretions. I want you to remember your place. You're nothing more than a wild animal, one who must be tamed by the lash of my whip. I plan to teach your beast the discipline she needs. I assure you that your beating will hurt you far more than it will me."

Dimitri had grown worried the second the flashing dot on his GPS had gone still. Viewing the satellite image, he immediately knew that she couldn't have stopped to refuel. As far into the desert as she was, there wasn't a gas station within thirty miles of her location.

"Jesus Christ," Dimitri exclaimed, as the wreckage came into view.

The Audi rested upturned thirty feet from the asphalt. Its interior remained dimly lit, and the driver's door hung wide open. Jake slammed on the brakes, and Dimitri hit the ground running toward her car. His gut told him that she was gone but he still wasn't prepared for the shock of seeing the empty cabin. Her camera lay smashed against the windshield. Reaching inside, he snatched her open backpack off the floor and threw it to Jake, whose lips were pressed tightly together.

"They fucking took her," Dimitri raged.

"We'll find her," Jake said.

"Turn off the car lights," Dimitri ordered, fumbling for the headlight controls inside the wreck.

Jake ran over to his vehicle and hit the switch. Except for the light of the stars, the desert was blanketed in darkness.

"Now we look and listen." Both wolves could see in the dark, but the absence of light accentuated the illumination that danced several miles into the desert. "There, south. They're out there. She's out there."

Jake set his eyes on their target, awaiting his beta's orders. Dimitri took a deep breath, sniffing, and was relieved when he smelled her in the wind.

"She's bleeding." The coppery tang of her scent angered him.

"Goin' wolf?" Jake asked.

"Yeah." Dimitri began to strip.

"Either way, it'll be tough to keep under the radar."

"I love a challenge." He shrugged off his pants, readying to shift.

"Never known you to back down."

"You get Gilly. The fuckers who took her are mine," Dimitri ordered, suspecting that her abductors were the same people who'd attacked him.

"You sure?" The concern about his beta's wolf was left unspoken.

"Mine," Dimitri growled. Shifting, he took off into the brush.

Gillian swore she scented Dimitri and thought she was losing it. No, it must've been a hallucination brought on by the fear. She steeled her mind, preparing to embrace the cut of the whip. She felt the vibrations in the dirt before the crack of the tail reverberated into the night. Chaz was drawing out the torture, forcing her to wait for the punishment.

"I think ten lashes will do nicely," the Alpha declared.

He drew his hand upward. His sight aimed toward Gillian's bare flesh, pleased that she was shaking. With the flick of his wrist, he prepared to implement what he believed was not only justice, but the means to her submission. But as the braided cord flew backwards, not even a hiss was heard.

"Sorry pal, clowns aren't allowed to handle the big boy equipment at the circus." Dimitri smirked as he snatched the braided cord mid-air, thoroughly enjoying the shock and surprise that crossed the Alpha's face.

With a jerk, Dimitri yanked him to the ground. As Chaz fell, the beta pounced. Sitting atop his waist, Dimitri pressed him onto his back. Chaz fought for control and attempted to dislodge his attacker so he could shift. But before he could do so, Dimitri deftly coiled the leather around his neck until only a short length remained on either side. Holding tight to the hilt and the tail, Dimitri tightened the noose, forcing the Alpha to gasp for air. He pushed up onto his feet, dragging Chaz upward, leaving his feet kicking up dust.

"Do you know who I am?" the Alpha spat.

"Don't know. Don't care."

"Chaz Baldwin. Alpha of Anzober wolves."

"Yeah, still don't care. Call off your wolves," Dimitri ordered.

Jake lunged at the wolf who stood watch over Gillian, tearing at his throat. Before he knew it, he was surrounded by two other wolves, and braced himself for the pack's wrath.

"Back off or your Alpha dies tonight," Dimitri commanded, his voice bellowing at the wolves.

Dimitri hid the rage that surfaced as he caught sight of Gillian on her knees, bared in front of the others. He observed the blood streaking down her back, and his heart clenched. The fucker had bitten her. It made no sense. Had she been wolf, he'd suspect the Alpha had tried to force a mating, to mark her. But she wasn't wolf, so that only left torture.

"Get the silver off her. You do it." He nodded to one of the wolves who immediately submitted to his order. He didn't want Jake touching the poison. They were already outnumbered as it was.

"You fucking piece of shit. Look real close…your wolves do my bidding," Dimitri taunted. Chaz revived and struggled to free himself, and Dimitri kneed him in the back, stilling his actions.

You'll be lucky if I let you live when this is all over."

"Need to shift," Gillian whispered as the chain fell to the ground. She raised her head and saw the dominant beta forcing Chaz to submit. Her eyes met his and her beast came to life. *Dimitri*. He'd come for her.

Jake heard her request and gave Dimitri an inquisitive look, as if to ask for permission to take off her clothes. They both knew she had to shift but there was no way in hell, with the way his beta had gone feral, overpowering another Alpha, that Jake would attempt to touch a woman who Dimitri perceived as his.

"Do it." Dimitri's gaze fell to Gillian, whose eyes were glazed with tears.

He watched as his friend peeled off her clothes and even though he was altogether comfortable with nudity, possessiveness stabbed at his chest. He didn't want anyone else looking at her right now but him. He took a deep breath and shook off the disturbing emotion.

Dimitri and Jake had been too focused on Gillian when a wolf attacked Jake from behind. Jake fell to the ground and spotted the silver chain that had been around the female. His finger extended, scooping up the metal. The smell of his burnt flesh wafted into the night but he didn't let it deter him from his task. Within seconds, he'd tied it to the wolf's forearm, rendering him back to his mortal form. Dimitri never once let go of the Alpha as he watched Jake with confidence, knowing he'd subdue the lesser wolf.

A roar cut into the melee, alerting everyone of the new danger that had arrived. Dimitri nearly dropped his prey as his eyes focused on Gillian. *Spectacular.* It was the first word that popped into his mind as he watched the white tiger leap onto a second wolf and tear its throat open. Blood sprayed into the air, and the great feline shook her head in delight.

"What. The. Fuck?" Jake transformed back to his mortal form, slowly backing away from the enormous animal. A smile broke across his face when he realized it was Gillian. "You win, D. She's not a bear."

"Told you she'd be awesome."

Dimitri contemplated what to do with the Alpha, who'd gone still in the presence of Gillian's beast. The ramifications of killing the Alpha weren't worth the price. Dimitri knew that if he ended Chaz's life, he'd have to take over his pack. While he had the strength and heart of an Alpha, his loyalty belonged to Acadian wolves. As he considered his dilemma, he looked to Gillian and decided there was no rule against giving him to her. *I love loopholes.* He smiled, throwing the bound Alpha at her feet.

Dimitri watched with pride as the slender cat eyed her nemesis, stalking toward him, emitting a low menacing growl. Within seconds, Chaz unraveled the whip and transformed into his wolf. He curled his lips upward, and assumed a defensive posture. Gillian's dark eyes fixed on his neck. A thunderous roar exploded from her muzzle as she attempted to pounce on the Alpha. Faltering, she missed her target, grazing his hindquarters with her paws. Chaz yelped in response. He seized the opportunity to escape, sprinting off into the night.

It was clear to Dimitri from the wolves' hasty retreat that Chaz knew he'd never survive a fight with a tiger. The magnificent feline could have easily caught the wolf had the fight been fair. But apparently, she was still reeling from being poisoned. After nearly a one hundred yard chase, she came to a stop, glaring at her prey.

Jake approached Dimitri, the two men still nude. "What's wrong with her?"

"She's sick," the beta observed, rubbing dirt from his eyes. *Shit.* He'd wanted so badly to kill the Alpha but consequences were a bitch. He'd made a calculated decision to let him live. It was the right choice, he knew. But his wolf thirsted for blood.

"The silver," Jake agreed. He looked to Gillian who'd circled around, slowly padding toward them. "You didn't kill him."

"Nope." Dimitri's lips tightened.

"The fucking asshole was about to whip her."

"He's sadistic," he replied, growing annoyed with the topic.

"That must've taken some great restraint…not to end it."

"You know it fucking did, but number one, I have no desire to lead that asshole's wolves. Two, I love my own pack. And three, well, we both know Logan'd have my nuts in a sack if I'd killed him. Things are just getting settled down at home. The last damn thing he needs is to lose his beta and have to deal with the shit people will give him about my mistake, which was thinking I could have two fucking minutes in the sand without declaring my presence to a pack."

Dimitri blew out a breath, realizing that he'd just taken a well-deserved rant. He caught sight of Gillian staring at him in the distance. She'd gone still, her gaze upon him like a thick fog. He'd raised his voice and she'd heard. *Goddammit.* She'd been attacked and was traumatized. He knew better than to yell, especially after he'd just gotten finished demonstrating his dominance over the man who'd tortured her. Was she expecting him to do the same?

He needed to try to get her to shift, to get her back to the car. Despite their short-term victory, it was the middle of the night and dangerous to remain in the desert. For all he knew, they could return any second with a high-powered rifle and take out all of them.

Dimitri eyed Jake and gestured to the ground. In order to make himself less imposing, he knelt on one knee. Jake followed and they both faced off with the tiger.

"Gilly, it's okay now. I won't hurt you," he said, his voice soft. The great cat growled in response and he tried again to earn her trust.

"Jake won't hurt you either." He glanced to Jake and gave her a small smile. "Darlin', as much as I love seeing your beautiful kitty cat, we've gotta get moving. You wanna shift? We'll go to the car, drive to the airport. All three of us. I'm goin' to make sure you get home safe. I promise."

The majestic beast took a few steps toward him and bared her teeth. A hiss tore through the air.

"Okay, okay. No shifting." Dimitri held up his palms, letting her know he wasn't going to fight her. Frustrated, he couldn't fully communicate with Gillian, but he was certain she understood him. "Look, Gilly. We've got to go. They could come back any minute now…with weapons."

He didn't want to scare her but it was the stark reality of the situation. She turned her head as if she was looking for the enemy.

"That's right, baby. You don't need to be afraid of me. You know that. I know you saw what I did to the Alpha, but I'd never hurt you…ever."

Gillian stalked toward him a few more steps, and he sighed in relief. He was getting through to her.

"Come to me, Gilly," he gently instructed, extending his hand. "You know my scent. You healed me, touched my skin. You're safe."

Dimitri held his breath as she approached, pressing her head upward into his hand.

"Aw yes, darlin'. You're so soft. So gorgeous. I know," he whispered. "The silver is hurtin' you. It'll be okay in a few hours. If you want to stay how you are for a while, that's fine, just fine."

As he lifted his head, he looked over to Jake whose jaw was wide open in disbelief. Dimitri gave a small chuckle, unashamed of his interaction with his kitten. *Fuck, since when is she my kitten?* He knew it was ridiculous to feel this kind of connection to another shifter, but there was something about her. But in the heat of the moment, he wasn't going to try to overanalyze it. In the past seventy-two hours, both she and he had been attacked. She'd saved him. He'd saved her. Maybe it was a hero complex but he didn't care what the hell Jake thought.

"She's not going to hurt you, man," Dimitri said with a grin.

"Okay, whatever you say. You did just see her tear through that wolf's throat, right? It's not like the fight was even close."

"I saw it, and *you* were awesome," he cooed, rubbing her ears.

"Oooookay. Well, I'm a wolf. And she's, uh, a little scary."

"Did you hear that, Gilly, girl? Badass Jake is actually afraid of something. I want to remember this moment." He stopped to laugh and look at Jake, who huffed, not at all amused. "So, you need to go easy, okay, kitten. Jake and I are going to shift and the three of us are goin' to run back to the car. We won't be able to communicate when I'm wolf, so just follow us back. Your sense of direction might be a little off…it's just the poison."

Dimitri waited on Jake to go first, concerned how Gillian would react to him. As his friend took off toward the car, he let his hand fall from her mane. He recalled how she'd embraced him in her human form, her soft tendrils caressing his skin. Letting the pleasurable memory drift, he focused on their task.

"Time to go, cher," Dimitri said, as he called on his wolf. With the transformation complete, he and Gillian ran together toward safety.

⟶⟨❀⟩· *Chapter Three* ·⟨❀⟩⟵

Gillian contemplated her fate, staring into Dimitri's dark eyes. If she'd let arousal rule her thoughts, she'd have capitulated long ago. From the second she'd laid her bare skin against his, she'd known Dimitri was powerful. But the sight of him nearly killing Chaz confirmed her suspicions about his abilities. The image of the beta almost killing her captor, an Alpha, was seared in her mind. Why he'd let him live, she wasn't sure. Instead, Dimitri had thrown the flailing wolf at her feet, as if he'd bestowed on her a precious treasure. As much as she appreciated the gesture, he'd overestimated her ability to catch prey, her body sickened from the silver.

When he'd called for her, she considered running away. But her beast recognized his actions as one of an Alpha, and she found herself respecting, fearing and desiring him all at once. The way he'd easily restrained and commanded Chaz demonstrated to her that she should be wary of him. It was true that she was lethal in her own right, but it was in that moment she knew that Dimitri could do her far more harm than she could ever inflict on him.

How Chaz had discovered her in the first place, she wasn't sure. Even though her mom had isolated her and had gone as far as to change her name after her father's death, Gillian's birth was well known. Given Chaz's influential status, he would have access to detectives who must have unearthed her identity. The existence of her breed, while rare, was known in the feline community. The secrets surrounding her kind, however, were kept closely guarded. The undesired destiny that could befall her was not one that she advertised. Her mother had warned her of what would happen should she meet a wolf who was her mate, a wolf that would be so devastatingly compelling that her beast would gladly submit to him. This man would destroy her nature, transforming her into a weaker being. No longer would her tiger surface. Generations of women before her had suffered the same fate. If Gillian found her mate, she was destined to lose herself, possibly losing her immortality altogether.

Unfortunately, it wasn't easy for her race. Other than immediate family, the great cats wandered life as loners, never congregating like prides or packs. Even if she was lucky enough to find another tiger, they'd be reluctant to breed with a hybrid, to continue the impurity of her line.

Gillian's mother, hopelessly in love, had relinquished her status, mating with an Alpha. As a result of doing so, she was left mortal, unable to ever shift again. After her mate died in an attack, she'd left his pack, relocating them to Washington. It was there in the open space of the mountains where

Gillian had learned how to shift into her cat. Strong and swift, she had grown up secure, knowing that she could protect herself from virtually anything.

Upon graduation, she'd moved to New York City to attend NYU. It was in the rich cultured city where she'd learned photography. From a distance her mom had encouraged her hobby, which soon grew into a profitable business. At twenty-eight years old, she wasn't in the top echelon yet. But her career was advancing and she'd slowly started picking up editorial shoots here and there.

Gillian couldn't risk being around wolves, accidentally finding her mate. There was no such thing as fate, only determination, at least that was what she told herself. She loved being a tiger, and wolves represented her death. If she happened to find a tiger, she'd consider it. But since the odds of that happening were slim to none, dating humans was the only safe option. She'd never met a man who'd broken her resolve, someone who'd light every one of her nerves on fire just by breathing the same air…until Dimitri.

Gillian was drawn out of her reverie as the beta patted the car seat. He talked to her as if he were speaking to a lover, his voice sweet and gentle. She hated it…mostly because it was working. She was scared. But it was his witty repartee that made her want to know him more. When he'd saved her, demonstrating his commanding nature, one that would match hers, the man had been magnificent. He'd been incredibly dominant, yet promised not to hurt her. She told herself not to trust him, because if she did, it would only give her an excuse to be near him, to breathe in his scent like she'd done in bed….his delicious, intoxicating scent.

She looked to his nervous friend. He feigned nonchalance, but nude, he defensively flexed his hands, poised to shift. *Does he seriously think I'm going to eat him?* Well, had she gone truly feral, she might have, she supposed. Sure, she'd killed the wolf, but he'd participated in her torture, allowing his Alpha to attack her again. They'd held her captive, intent on breaking her beast's spirit. But Jake, he, too, was a man of honor, one who'd risked his own life to save hers.

Dimitri smiled at her as if he'd read her thoughts and the battle shield around her heart cracked. Slowly she crept toward him, gingerly taking a place on the seat. The simple act of allowing him to touch her fur had been submission in itself. *What if he has the capability to steal my beast away, to mark me?* She could feel her feline nature rebel at her concern, yearning to take him. No, she couldn't allow that to happen.

Gillian fought a yawn. So tired…if she could just nap for a bit, heal her own body, she'd thank them and say goodbye, thwarting the developing lust that grew in her belly. As a hybrid wolf, there was always a chance that he'd be the one. The one for whom she'd make the ultimate sacrifice. As she fell asleep in his lap, she gave him her trust.

Dimitri took a deep breath and nodded. Fuck it all, he was about to let a two hundred pound cat get into the back seat with him. *I must be an idiot. No, just horny*, his brain answered. Jake gave her a wide berth, not wanting to get too close, but Gillian still hadn't gotten into the car. It occurred to Dimitri that perhaps he wasn't the only one having second thoughts. Summoning up the courage, he decided a few encouraging words were in order.

"Now I know it looks like a tight fit, but you know you want to cuddle up with me. You're a very tired kitty. Come on, now. Let's go. Poor Jake is going to get cold out there. Just look at him." Dimitri cocked his head and smiled at his friend, who'd hesitated to get dressed. He suspected that Jake didn't want his clothes to restrict him, not until he was sure that Gillian wasn't going to attack. As long as he was naked, he could easily shift back to defend himself if necessary.

Unlike Jake, Dimitri had yanked on a pair of pants. There was no way in hell he was about to get into closed quarters with a clawed tiger, leaving his dangly bits swinging in the wind.

"Remember your first time?" Yeah, it all came back to sex for him. Maybe she wouldn't get the analogy but it was the best he could do, given the circumstances. "Is this the first time you've shifted with wolves? I bet it is, cher. Well this is our first time, too. Jake's a little nervous over there. We're all a little nervous. I'm tellin' you that you can trust me, trust us. Come sit with me, come rest. You can stay tiger as long as you need to," he reassured, patting the seat.

"She can't go on a plane like that…" Jake started to say, when Dimitri held up his hand to shush him.

"Gilly just needs a little time. She needs to be with me, don't ya, darlin'?" he coaxed sweetly. His breath caught as she pushed a fat paw onto the leather seat, and he was relieved that she hadn't extended her nails. With the grace of a ballerina, she quietly ascended into the interior and settled down next to him. The crushing weight of her forearms on his thighs was yet another reminder of her power. But as she relaxed her muscled body against his chest, the pressure became more comfortable. Both his hands moved to stroke her fur. "That's a girl. Just rest. I've got ya."

"Your girlfriend is a cat," Jake stated with a blunt tone.

"She's not my girlfriend, but if she was my girlfriend," Dimitri looked to the giant tigress in his lap, who gently snored, "it wouldn't matter what she was. She's brave. And funny. And she smells nice."

"What's, up, Pussycat....ooooooh," Jake broke out in his best Tom Jones impression.

"You're hilarious."

"And I thought Logan was bad enough bringing one home from the pound. You topped him, all right. You slept with one, and not in the cuddle-me-kitty kind of way."

"Hold up. Sure, she was on top of me...I'll give you that. But we didn't have sex. The bottom line is this; no matter how much I'd like to get to know her," he shook his head, wishing they'd met under different circumstances, "she's not pack. Therefore she's not my mate."

"That hasn't stopped you before. You just fucked a vampire, for Christ's sakes."

"Yeah, well, Lacey is a lovely little memory. But she knew the score. One night or two....nothing but play. There's been no play with this one. Oh no, she tied me up. Not that I mind a little bondage, but shit, she just left me there." Dimitri stroked his hand over her fur and sighed. "Gilly, here, is on the run and not just from that Alpha back there. She's got a thing about wolves."

"She's got a thing all right...a bad thing."

"Yep. She's spooked."

"As well she should be. You saw what they did to her."

"He marked her," Dimitri said softly, disgusted at the thought of another wolf piercing her creamy white skin. "It makes no sense."

"Probably just a dominance thing. The guy doesn't strike me as mentally stable, shall we say."

"Ya got that right. Hell, he was gonna fucking whip her. Something's missing, though. He knew she wasn't wolf. The question is, did he know she was a tiger? And if he did, why is he trying to keep her? Why mark her as his own in front of others?"

"Look, you and I were just guessing what she might be. Maybe they guessed right...or knew exactly what she was."

"This doesn't make any sense. I know we've gotta get home, but before we leave, I intend to get answers. Kitty, here, has some explainin' to do." Dimitri gingerly reached into Gillian's backpack, which Jake had thrown onto the car floor. He fumbled inside, finding his phone. "I'm texting Logan. I'll give him the deets when we get back, but for now, I want him to send the jet. It'll take a while but who knows how long she's gonna stay cat."

"Coach sucks anyway."

"No first class on the way out here? Poor baby," Dimitri teased.

"It was brutal."

"My ass doesn't fit in those tiny seats anyway. Even first class feels like a tin can," he laughed. "Truth is that we can't risk goin' commercial. Chaz could have someone try to stop her, or board the flight. I want a pilot I know and trust to get us home safely."

Dimitri tapped at the glass clumsily with one hand and kept his other on Gillian's back. It made it difficult for him to type, his large thumbs tripping the autocorrect. After several minutes of messaging with Logan and a few curse words later, he'd made the arrangements to have the private plane meet them tomorrow.

"Let's hit the hotel tonight. Logan's getting things in motion but it'll take time."

"You think Chaz's reach stretches to Nevada?"

"I don't think so, but a guy like that doesn't strike me as someone who follows the rules. Just to be safe, Logan was calling the Vegas Alpha to let them know we'd be in the territory. We'll get some rest and then get the hell out of there."

"What about her?" Jake asked.

"What about her? She's…I don't know. She's gotta go home." Dimitri glanced out the darkened window. His stomach clenched in what he blamed on hunger, but part of him knew it was his wolf pining for Gillian. He rubbed the scruff on his face, his lips tight with concern. "I wish we could take her home but I don't think that's such a good…"

The weight on his legs lightened considerably, and he lost his words, watching Gillian transform into a beautiful woman. *Shit, now I really am going to have a hard time with this.* Part of him had hoped she'd stay tiger. Then he wouldn't have an excuse to pursue her, but his mind warred against it. He told himself that he needed to talk to her so he could get answers, but in reality, he just needed her. Naked and against him.

"A good, what?" Jake asked. His eyes flashed to the rearview mirror; he could no longer see the white cat. "She shifted? Let me see."

"Eyes on the road, bro," Dimitri said. He glanced to his own hand, which rested on her belly. Her back was pressed flush against his abs, her long mane feathered over her shoulders and breasts. He took note of a dusky pink tip that strained through the dark waterfall and his cock jerked in response. *Not now*, he thought. "Throw me my bag."

Jake laughed and launched the duffle over the seat. Dimitri caught it mid-air with one hand. He bent over, careful not to crush her, and tugged a button-down shirt out of the bag. Gingerly, he draped it over her bare skin, so she was covered. Looping his forefinger through the edge of her hair, he brushed it back, revealing her full lips. She smiled as if she were going to wake up and then mewled, reaching her fingers between his thighs. Dimitri sucked a deep breath as her thumb brushed over his burgeoning erection. As she settled once again, he closed his eyes, praying for self-restraint.

Fucking hell. Why does she have to be so goddamned beautiful? And a tiger? Really? I barely survived being killed and the universe doesn't owe me one? Guess not.

He blew out a breath and caught Jake's gaze in the mirror, who gave him a knowing laugh before setting his sight back to the highway. Dimitri knew right then that he'd better get Gillian back to New York as soon as possible, because if not, he was pretty sure the next time he caught sight of her sweet nipple, it would be nestled between his lips.

❦ *Chapter Four* ❦

Gillian watched the numbers light up as they ascended in the elevator, and considered her attire. She'd bitten her lip, attempting to pretend it was completely acceptable to stand in bare feet, dressed only in a man's dress shirt in the lobby of the five star hotel. As they'd passed by the concierge, she smiled demurely. *What happens in Vegas stays in Vegas.* She was fairly sure it wasn't the strangest thing he'd ever seen.

She took a deep breath, taking note of the large pair of feet on either side of hers. Afraid to make eye contact, she mentally shrugged and stared ahead, reflecting on how she'd gotten herself into this situation.

When she'd woken up naked in Dimitri's lap, she hadn't said a word. She could hardly believe that she'd fallen asleep for hours with her head snuggled against his warm thighs. The only saving grace had been that she hadn't buried her face in his crotch. Thankfully, she'd slept in the opposite direction, allowing her to hide her reddened face. In the darkness, she'd pushed up, sliding her arms into the shirt and buttoning it. She scooted over to the opposite door, stealing a glimpse at the striking beta. Stealth wasn't her strong suit, she noted, as he pinned his eyes on hers. Her breath caught, feeling as if he could see into her heart, knowing her deepest thoughts. A warm smile bloomed on his face, breaking their heated interaction.

Silence lingered and she knew then that she was on borrowed time. He'd want an explanation. Reason told her to be afraid, very afraid of going up alone into a hotel room with two wolves. But instinct won over. This man would not hurt her. He'd saved her life. She'd give him what he wanted and then some. But in the morning, she'd be back to her life and home in New York.

Dimitri exchanged glances with Jake. Gillian had been unusually quiet in the car. He had to admit that she was well composed, considering her attack and the fact that she was barely dressed. As he glanced down to her toned legs, all he could really think about was touching her again, feeling her skin against his.

The elevator bell sounded and they came to a smooth halt. He reached and took her hand, happily surprised when she laced her fingers through his. Easily finding the room, Jake opened the door and led them into the richly decorated suite.

"Through here." Dimitri guided her into a bedroom.

Quietly, he shut the door behind them for privacy. Releasing Gillian's hand, he went to the bar and grabbed them a couple of bottles of water. He unscrewed the tops and handed one to her. She took it without meeting his eyes, and he suspected she needed time to collect her thoughts. A shame that wasn't going to happen.

"You're a tiger," he began. Dimitri strode to the windows and opened the drapes, exposing the spectacular sea of lights twinkling upon the strip.

"Um, yeah," Gillian replied, tracing her finger along the rim. Tears threatened to fall as her emotions rose to the surface. She'd almost died. She shook her head; shame washed over her. "Thank you. If you hadn't come for me…"

"I don't get it, Gilly. It's like I'm looking at a puzzle but a few of the pieces are missing. Tell me," he walked over to the bed until he stood towering above her, "why does an Alpha, one who is a wolf, want to mark a tiger? Why are you so important to him? I want the truth and I want it now."

She sniffled, and lifted her gaze to meet his. "He wants me to be his. I shouldn't have ever come here. I've gotta get back to New York."

"I can help you. Tomorrow I'll take you wherever you came from as long as I know you'll be safe. But I need the truth if I'm going to be able to do that."

"You don't understand. I'm not what you think I am."

"You're a shifter. I knew that from the second I opened my eyes. A tiger? Well, yeah, I didn't expect that, but you were amazing."

"I don't know how he knew about me…Chaz. Tigers, we're not like you. We're loners."

"I'm sorry, but you're losing me here. He's a wolf. You're a tiger. What am I missing?"

"I'm not all tiger," she coughed. It was the first time she'd ever said the words out loud to anyone in her life. "My father…he was a wolf. An Alpha."

Dimitri's blood pressure spiked as she spoke. A hybrid. A tiger-wolf hybrid. And her father was an Alpha. A million questions spun through his brain. He took a deep breath, attempting to stay calm. The last thing she needed was for him to lose his shit, scaring her further.

"So he was going to mark you?"

"It's the second time he's tried," she admitted softly. Gillian reached her hands back into her hair, twisting it up into a ponytail, revealing the area where she'd been bitten. "But it doesn't work that way. See? The magic. It's a curse really. My mother called it a destiny, but it's not."

Dimitri couldn't help himself. In an instant, he was on the bed beside her, the pads of his fingers smoothing over where the bite mark had been. Nothing but smooth skin remained. He wasn't sure why but relief that she remained unmarked coursed through him and he winced.

"Why does he think he can mark you?"

"He was trying to force me to mate with him," she divulged.

"But a wolf can only mate with another wolf. A human hybrid? Yes. But any other shifter combo; it's a no go."

"True…for most. But not for me."

"Cher, I don't think you know what you're…" Dimitri began, but didn't want to insult her. She'd been through a lot. The trauma must've confused her. Shifters could mate only with those of their own kind. That fact gave him great comfort, considering he wasn't looking for one. He'd already watched Logan's boat sink. No way was he going down that road.

"The only way it could work is for me to submit. I'd die before that happened," Gillian continued, ignoring his comment. She couldn't help the tears that had begun to fall. Her nerves had been like steel throughout the duration of her abduction. Dimitri offered her soul respite from the danger, a safe place to be herself.

"Come here, darlin'. It's okay. He's never gonna get you again." He hoped. Dimitri hadn't heard the entire story yet and suspected part two of whatever nugget she was hiding was not going to be good.

"I'm sorry. I don't even know you." She pressed her palms to his bare chest, and lifted her eyes to meet his.

"We know each other just fine." Dimitri smiled, trying to lighten the mood.

She raised a questioning eyebrow at him.

"Okay, maybe I don't know your favorite color yet."

"You don't know anything about me," she smiled.

"Not true. I know you have a tattoo on your back. And we've already cuddled in bed," he joked. "Hell, you've even tied me up. I'll admit that I've never been with a woman who's tied me up on a first date but I'm not knockin' it."

"It wasn't a date," she laughed.

"I do feel somewhat slighted. You tied me up and I didn't even get kissed."

Gillian's gaze fell to his lips and her stomach did a nervous flip. She fluttered her lids, and forced herself to look away. Her heart began to race as he wiped a remnant tear from her cheek with the pad of his thumb.

"Our second date wasn't too much fun either. I got in a fight and ended up in the backseat with a stray cat," he teased, his fingers playing with her hair.

"You weren't afraid of me."

"No, but let's say I had a healthy respect for you. My mamma didn't raise a fool. I've seen a lot of things, cher. But seeing a full grown Bengal tiger up close and personal is pretty impressive."

"So you like my kitty?" she asked.

"Oh I like her all right, but I like who's in front of me more." Dimitri smiled, enjoying her flirtatious banter. His hand fell to her bare thigh, and he consciously warred to keep it from sliding up under her shirt.

"I guess I owe you that kiss, then. I mean, it is our second date, after all," she said.

Dimitri gave her a broad smile, briefly contemplating the temptation.

Naked girl. Hotel room. Don't do it. But the devil on his other shoulder disagreed. After all, he just saved the girl. *What harm could one little kiss do?*

Slowly, he leaned in. His gaze fell to her lips and quickly darted upward, connecting with her soul. Just one small kiss to let her know he liked her was all he needed; one to make sure she wouldn't doubt that he wanted to see her again after they sorted out all their issues. He smiled slightly as he caught her eyes, inwardly nervous that his action would change his life.

As his lips took hers, he groaned in delight. The little minx who'd saved him tasted more delicious than he could have imagined. As he pulled her against him, he stiffened in arousal. She climbed atop, straddling him with her knees. His hands speared upward into the back of her hair. Sliding his fingers through her silken mane, he fisted her locks, drawing her closer to him still. The sweep of Gillian's tongue against his, her soft lips against his own, drove him out of control with desire. When she placed her hands on his chest, and drew her finger over his nipple, his cock hardened to rock. As she began to grind her bared center onto his denim-covered hardness, he ripped his lips from hers, panting.

Dimitri rested his forehead against hers, his thoughts racing. He was going to fucking lose it. This woman was aggressive and sweet like honey. The craziest part about the situation was that she was right; he didn't really know her. They'd both nearly died in the past few days. It had to be the stress of the situation that was causing his reaction to her. The chemistry was undeniably explosive. If he kissed her a second time, he'd be balls deep in sixty seconds. *Deep breath. Deep breath.*

"Cher," he breathed. "Before we do something we'll both regret, I'm going to put you down. Okay?"

"Okay," she nodded, still trying to catch her breath. She removed her hands from his chest and carefully slid off his lap, back onto the bed.

"Okay," he repeated. The sexual fog lingered in his brain. He groaned loudly as he righted himself and stood. Despite the granite bulge in his jeans, he managed to hobble over to the door. "So, yeah, thanks for the kiss. Great date."

"The best. Um, well, thank you." She giggled, wrapping her arms around her waist. She crossed her legs, remembering they were open and that she wasn't wearing panties.

Dimitri looked away as one leg went over the next. *Fuck, she's going to kill me*, he thought. He curled his fingers around the doorknob, and turned it.

"I'm goin' to let you use the shower in here. I'll, uh, go use Jake's…that way we won't….you know, get in anymore trouble. I'm goin' to order us up some room service. Come on out when you're done."

"Okay," she managed, her face red with embarrassment.

"Guess I'll go get ready for date number three. You in?" Dimitri brushed his fingers over the sensitive nipple that she'd fingered only seconds earlier, and winked.

He didn't bother staying to watch her reaction to his invitation. As soon as he shut the door behind him, he blew out a breath as if he'd been holding it all night. *Fuckin'-A.* If he didn't get back to New Orleans in the next twenty-four hours, he'd be dating a tiger *for real.* With his wolf impaired, he risked losing the ability to shift. No, he'd get Ilsbeth to do whatever magick she had to do to fix this mess. He swore to stay stronger than the little feline in the room next door who already had him purring.

Holy Fuck. Gillian pressed her face into her palms as the door clicked shut. *What the hell am I doing?* She'd just climbed Dimitri like she was scaling Mount Everest. Her tiger paced, encouraging her to go after him. Gillian had never spent this much time around wolves. Being around Dimitri and Jake rocked her equilibrium. Her beast didn't see them as a threat, leaving her mind open to the possibilities. She'd spent so much time avoiding pack members, hating what they represented - the loss of her tiger - that she'd never given much thought to what it would feel like if she liked them, or worse, desired one.

She closed her eyes, imagining her tongue tracing Dimitri's tattoos from the curves of his shoulder to his neck. Still damp between her legs from their kiss, the thought of licking him took her breath away. Gillian knew she had to get back to her brother, beg for his help. But Dimitri was a pleasant unforeseen wrinkle in her plans.

As she pushed off the bed and trod into the bathroom, she sighed. *What am I thinking? I want to date a wolf? Just no.* The trip to California must've done something to her brain, because that was a rule she'd never break. It was a choice. Preserving her tiger took priority over looking for love in the eyes of a wolf.

As Gillian stepped under the hot spray, she considered what she'd do once she reached New York. Several months ago, she'd been approached by a sophisticated gentleman at a photo shoot for a new coffee club in Manhattan. He'd introduced himself as the New York Alpha, Jax Chandler, owner of the chic magazine, ZANE, who'd paid for the images. Jax and his beta, Nick Sterling, had expressed interest in seeing her portfolio with the intent of hiring her. Gillian had been thrilled with the prospect of being offered a staff position. When she called her mother and mentioned his name, she'd confessed to Gillian that she had a half-brother, who also lived in the city. An Alpha...Jax Chandler.

Gillian, concerned that he'd force her into his pack, cut off contact with Jax, giving him no explanation. If he found out that they were family, he wouldn't relent. He'd want her to mate with one of his wolves, let her tiger die. It had crushed her to alienate her only brother. Growing up with just her mother had been a lonely existence. She'd spent many days dreaming she had a sibling, someone close who'd be family. Giving up her nature in order to gain family, however, was simply not an option.

Thanks to Chaz, Jax now represented survival. Chaz had told her repeatedly that he'd never give up on finding her, stealing her gift. Jax was the only one she could trust to protect her.

Dimitri had his own battles to fight. He didn't need to fight hers. While he'd surprised her in the desert with his insurmountable strength, it wasn't fair to ask him to help her. They both knew that at any moment, his wolf could falter. And what if he died because of her? She couldn't allow him to sacrifice himself for her. She'd never let that happen.

She stepped out of the shower, catching sight of her swollen lips in the mirror. His kiss. *The* kiss. She'd felt her tiger calm in his arms, and it terrified her. The more she talked to him, the more she felt herself entangled in his web. He was charming with a flair for humor that brought a smile to her face. Dominating and sexy, his powerful presence told her that he'd take her in ways she'd never known. The thought of him driving deep inside her core made her ache with need.

She cursed, rolling her eyes. Here she was in a hotel room with two shifters, knowing full well they'd scent her arousal the second she opened the door. She had to get her shit together, or at least try not to throw herself at Dimitri...again. *For the love of the Goddess, stop thinking about sex.* Her libido was in overdrive, making her feel as if she was a hot-air balloon about to take off into the wild blue yonder.

Gillian toweled her hair dry and pulled on a white cotton spa robe. She tightened the belt around her waist and pulled the collar tight, as if it would keep her grounded. Slipping on the matching terry slippers, she shuffled over to the door. Closing her eyes, she took a deep breath. Wrapping her hand around the knob, she opened it, praying she could resist the delicious beta in the next room.

Nothing had prepared Gillian for the heavenly scent of steak teasing her nose. Her stomach grumbled and she laughed, catching Dimitri's hungry gaze, one that she suspected had nothing to do with the food. She noticed how Jake tensed his grip on his fork as if he was expecting a wild animal to leap at him. She laughed, finding it comical that such a strong wolf would be afraid of her.

"Hey, darlin'. Why don't ya come sit down here?" Dimitri pulled out a chair for her and eyed Jake. "Relax, man. She's just this itty bitty thing of a woman. She's not going to hurt you."

"Shut it," Jake grumbled, not fond of being on the end of the ribbing. "Maybe I'm just allergic to cats."

"It's okay, really. I know that some people aren't used to seeing me," Gillian said softly, placing a soft hand on his forearm.

"You were really cool looking, I'll give you that. It was a clean kill if I've ever seen one." He gave her a sideways grin, beginning to feel more at ease.

"She's one badass kitty cat, that's for damn sure," Dimitri added proudly.

"I'll take that as a compliment." She paused and picked up her fork. "I just want to thank you both again. I know I kind of asked you not to follow me, but I'm really glad you did. I'd be dead if you hadn't."

"Well, to be technically correct about it, you held a gun on us, but okay, we'll go with asked," Dimitri laughed.

"Threatened to shoot us," Jake interjected.

"I know and I'm sorry." She cut up her steak while continuing to speak. "It's just that you saw Chaz. They're crazy. I knew they'd follow me and I didn't want you to get hurt. It was already my fault that..."

"Bygones, cher," Dimitri assured her. "Tomorrow's a new day."

"Speaking of tomorrow, the plane should be here around twelve. We'll fly to New York and then we'll be back home, hopefully later tomorrow night." Jake picked up his glass of wine and took a deep sip.

"I've gotta call Ilsbeth," Dimitri said, his voice growing serious.

"I'm sure she's got some spell that'll help you," Jake offered.

"What's wrong with you?" Gillian asked quietly, almost regretting her choice of words. She'd felt a touch of the evil on his wolf. She'd healed him but knew it was only temporary.

"Nothing's wrong with me...nothin' date number three won't fix, anyway," Dimitri joked.

"No, there's something. Your wolf...there's something in you..."

"I don't know," Dimitri said, cutting her off. "I helped a friend with a bit of otherworldly business. Seems I've picked up some kind of traveler, for lack of a better term. I couldn't shift that night on the beach. I'd had trouble before that, though. I thought that by getting away on vacay...maybe I'd get my mojo back. Didn't work out so well...except for you."

"Whatever it is, the witch better send it the fuck back because this not shifting bullshit isn't going to go over too well in a pack. I hate to break it to you, D, but it's not like you can go on being beta if you can't shift."

Silence fell as Jake laid the cards on the table.

"Now's not the time or place to discuss this," Dimitri growled.

"Just sayin'....maybe we should go to New Orleans first."

"We've gotta get Gilly home and then we can go home."

"I can get a ticket at the airport and fly by myself," she suggested. Gillian didn't want to see the two friends fight. She could get back to New York just as easily on a commercial flight. She had to see Jax as soon as possible. As painful and awkward as she expected it to be, she had to talk to him in person.

"No," both wolves said at the same time.

"Why not? Nothing's going to happen to me on a plane." She bit down on another piece of the rare meat.

"We have no idea who's going to be on that plane or who's going to be waiting for you when you get off. Not happening," Dimitri said flatly.

"After what I just saw back in that desert…just no," Jake agreed.

"Jake's right. I've been around a long time, and I'm tellin' ya that what that Alpha did…he was going to beat you…with a bull whip. And it wasn't some kink fest out there…no, he meant to torture you."

"So you'd submit?" Jake asked, attempting to conceal the utter disgust on his face.

"Yeah, that and he wanted to punish me for killing his wolves. But it was self-defense. When he'd captured me…" Her voice faltered and she lowered her eyes.

"I'm not sure what's so important about you. Sorry, don't take that the wrong way. It's just that it doesn't make much sense…a pack of wolves goin' after a tiger." Jake paused. "Hell, I guess it doesn't matter. You traveling alone back to New York isn't an option. But D can't travel alone either. No way am I leaving him after what just happened."

"Okay," she said calmly and took another bite of her meal.

Gillian sat quietly listening to the two wolves plan, all the while plotting how she could catch a flight. She reasoned she could use her cell phone to call the airline. In the morning, she'd skip out of the hotel, catch a cab to the airport and be in New York by the afternoon.

As much as Gillian wanted to go with them to New Orleans, she didn't want Dimitri sacrificing any more time helping her. She hated lying to him, but if he didn't seek a witch soon, his wolf would falter to the evil within. Gillian finished eating and looked up, to see both wolves staring at her. They'd stopped talking.

"What?" she asked innocently. Gillian pushed away from the table and stood up, smoothing down her robe. "I'm tired."

"Go ahead, I'll be there in a minute," Dimitri urged.

"What do you mean?" she replied in surprise. *Does he think he's sleeping with me?* A grin crossed his face, and she knew that was exactly what he meant. A date.

"I'll be there in a minute," he repeated, his gaze smoldering.

Gillian took a deep breath, heat rippling over her skin. Whatever they'd started earlier with the kiss was far from over, and damn, if she didn't want to take it further. After everything she'd been through, the thought of being within Dimitri's arms comforted her. She caught a glint of amusement in Jake's eyes and knew that no matter how much he wanted Dimitri home, he also found their emerging relationship entertaining.

"Gilly," Dimitri called as she reached the door.

"Yeah?" She swallowed. Her tiger paced, aware of the sexual anticipation that edged her mind.

"Don't fall asleep without me. I'm bringing you dessert," Dimitri commented with a grin.

"Dessert," she stammered. What was he trying to do to her?

"You know, something sweet before bed. Mama always told me a little sugar washes out the bitter taste of a bad day. I thought you could use some."

"Yeah, okay," she answered, caught off-kilter by his provocative comment. *Oh my God, this man is making me lose every last brain cell. Kinda hard to think when all that's in your head is sex.* He was teasing her, enjoying making her blush in front of Jake. Before she could stop the words, she heard herself flirting in return. "Well, I guess I shouldn't argue with your mama. Hope whatever you bring me has some whipped cream on top."

Gillian held her breath as she entered the bedroom. The door closed, and she rested the back of her head against it, taking a deep cleansing breath. *Holy shit.* This was exactly why she shouldn't be around wolves. Dimitri excited her, but the thought of being with a wolf, making love to him, was beyond her comprehension. She had to fight off her desire to touch him. *I should make him sleep on the couch.* Yes, that would save her from the temptation of entertaining the carnal fantasies that danced in her mind.

Better yet, I should tell him to sleep in Jake's room. Immediately, she pictured the two hot men together in bed and sucked a breath. The image of her wedged between them flashed in her mind. Her pussy tightened and she swore, admonishing herself for indulging the idea for even one second. How long had it been since she'd had sex? Too damn long. Her lack of male contact had to be what was driving her wild thoughts. *Get with the program, girl. No wolves. No Dimitri. No sex.*

Gillian spied her bag that was sitting on the floor. She needed to get home and work things out with Jax. As she picked up her cell phone and looked up the airline, she knew Dimitri would be pissed. But she'd rather him be angry as a healthy wolf, than risk his very being just for her.

~⚜· *Chapter Five* ·⚜~

Dimitri cracked open the door, cupping chocolate mousse in one hand as he entered the bedroom. He spotted Gillian's robe, which was lying across the guest chair, and wondered if she'd gone to take another shower. But as he glanced to the bed, Gillian pushed upward to sit, bunching the covers over what he believed to be her naked body.

"What do you have?" Her eyes went wide, spying the decadent confection.

"Ah, cher, if there's one thing you can count on with me, it's that I'm true to my word. Dessert in bed is something we all should experience," he said, climbing onto the comforter. The mattress dipped as he walked across the surface on his knees until he was at her side. He laughed, attempting to balance himself and the delicacy he'd brought.

"You're funny, you know that?" she grinned.

"I'm determined." With surprising grace, he settled next to her. He crossed his legs and gave her a sexy smile.

"I thought you were a beta, not an Alpha," she observed. Despite his status, everything about him screamed dominance. She wondered if he was even capable of submitting.

"I'm beta of Acadian wolves, but then again, you already know that." Dimitri dipped the spoon into the creamy mixture and held it up to her lips. "Eat."

She parted her lips at his demand. Her eyes met his as he slid the mousse into her mouth. She moaned in delight as the rich cocoa coated her tongue. Closing her eyes, she savored the taste and then quickly opened them, realizing the way she must have looked. He'd practically just given her a food orgasm in under ten seconds. *Clever, clever wolf.*

"You distract me," she admitted.

"You like?"

"What's not to like?" Her eyes fell to his mouth and she swiftly looked away. She nervously plowed her fingers through her hair. "You could have killed Chaz...but you didn't."

"And?" He took a bite and licked his lips.

"You could have been Alpha," she stated, accepting another spoonful.

"I'm good right where I'm at in New Orleans. Cali is nice, but it isn't home."

"Don't all wolves want to be Alpha?"

"No. Sometimes being Alpha chooses us, but it's not something we always choose. My Alpha, Logan, didn't want to be Alpha...but that's a story for another day."

"But out there in the desert tonight, it was clear to me that you were the smartest, the strongest…"

"You're goin' to make me blush," he teased, shaking his head. It wasn't that he didn't know what he was capable of; he knew all right. So did every wolf in Acadian wolves. "Let's just leave it at this, shall we? I wasn't about to kill Chaz so I could run his pack. I don't want to leave home. I've got my own Alpha and pack."

"Do you submit?" she asked softly. The question seemed innocent enough when she'd thought it yet the air was laced with sexual tension. Her lips curled in amusement.

"The question is, 'do you?'" he replied in turn. "Open."

"Never," she promptly answered, yet her lips widened at his demand.

Dimitri laughed, watching her obey his command. He supposed tigers didn't submit, but things were not always as they seemed.

"What?" she asked. The tip of her tongue traced over her bottom lip. "What's so funny? Do I have chocolate on my face?"

"So you never submit?"

"Of course not. I mean, it's not like I don't take directions when I'm working but I'm not a doormat."

"What about in other ways?"

"What other ways? Wait…are we talking about, you know?" Gillian blushed.

"What do you think we're talking about? Last bite…here you go. Open." Dimitri smiled as she listened to him once again. Perhaps she was incapable of seeing what she was doing. "To answer your original question, I will submit, but only to my Alpha. I do it for the pack. It benefits all of us. We are more powerful collectively than we could ever be on our own."

"Well, I guess that makes sense, but I'm not in a pack. Tigers don't do packs."

"But wolves do."

"Yeah, but I'm not…"

"You're hybrid. Somewhere inside you, your wolf lies in wait."

"No. No, she doesn't," she said flatly. Gillian felt her pulse race at the thought of turning wolf. "I'm a tiger."

Dimitri considered Gillian's denial of her wolf. Maybe she was right. He'd never met a tiger hybrid. It was rare. He'd seen her shift, and she was one hundred percent feline, yet his gut told him there was more. Something about the way she'd already submitted without intending to do so.

"Well, my little kitten, you know what you are. But the lesson for you is that often the strongest submit for reward. Within a pack and in other areas of life as well." *I'd like you to submit to me*, he thought. *Hell, yes…on your hands and knees, with me driving into you from behind.* The fleeting thought was all it took to stiffen his dick.

Noticing a smudge, he reached out, cupping her chin. He dragged his thumb across her bottom lip, catching the chocolate. When she wrapped her fingers around his wrist, Dimitri hesitated, wondering if she would stop him. Instead of resisting, she pressed her cheek into his hand and closed her eyes. Her lips took his thumb into her mouth, licking its tip.

The temptation was too great, Dimitri knew. He'd be taking advantage if he made love to her. His stomach churned, aware that with any other female, he'd bed her and leave her without a second thought. Wolves were sexual creatures, yet Gillian wasn't truly lupine. It wasn't fair to her to let her think that they could have some kind of a long-distance relationship. Exercising what he didn't know existed in control, Dimitri gently pulled his hand away.

Gillian's heavy lids opened, her chest heaving slightly from the exchange. The delicious taste of his skin lingered in her mouth. *Where is he going?* She clung to the sheet as he pushed off the bed. She opened her mouth to speak but held back the words that faltered on her tongue. Never before had she felt so drawn to a man. And for the first time in her life, she didn't care what kind of shifter he was, nor did she care if all she felt was pure lust and nothing more. All that mattered was that this beta called to her heart, causing her breath to catch. The nervous butterflies in her stomach weren't just dancing; these babies were moving full tilt into a heated Paso Doble.

"Where're you going?" Gillian breathed. She blinked her eyes, disbelieving that he'd left her alone.

"I'm just gonna sleep over here for a while, let you get some rest. You've had a tough day," Dimitri mumbled, gesturing to the couch. He set the bowl on the night table.

"Okay," she said softly, disappointed that he hadn't continued.

She settled back down into the mattress, bringing the fluffy white cotton down comforter up to her chin. The weight of the blanket did little to ameliorate the tingling that singed her skin. But she felt as if it somehow hid her true feelings, the desire to make love to the wolf. A deep breath centered her thoughts. It was short lived as she took sight of Dimitri stripping off his pants.

His curved glutes flexed in the dim light. Even though she'd seen him nearly nude when she'd dragged him into bed after he'd been injured, sex had been the furthest thing on her mind. But now? Lust was paramount, coursing through her veins. It was so wrong…so very, very wrong.

She knew she'd be breaking her rules. But it was only one teensy weensy night, she reasoned. Her tiger couldn't possibly have time to decide if she wished to submit, to give herself over to a wolf. In the morning, she'd be off on a plane, never seeing him again. Jax would provide her with protection, and she'd go back to her safe but otherwise uneventful life.

By the time her eyes switched over to night vision, Dimitri had yanked a spare blanket off the shelf, shielding his yummy man-bits, and she threw her head back onto the pillow in a huff. *Seriously?* It was as if someone had just laid him out on a platter and handcuffed her wrists. Even then, she supposed she'd happily use her tongue. Her fists pounded the bed in frustration.

"Can you throw me a…" He was about to say, 'pillow' when a large white mass launched across the room at him. Catching it with one hand, he smirked. *My little kitten has her own case of blue balls?* Satisfaction that he wasn't the only suffering party made his painful erection slightly more tolerable.

Dimitri curled his legs, attempting to jam his six-foot-five body onto the cramped sofa. *How the hell am I supposed to sleep like this all night?* He caught the glint of amusement in her eyes as he struggled to make himself fit into the small space. *Just punishment*, he supposed.

"Comfortable?" she asked through the darkness.

"Yeah. All good," he lied.

"Wow, you do look so relaxed." She grinned.

Dimitri tugged at the blanket, which looked like it belonged in a toddler crib. He blew out a breath and closed his eyes, willing his dick into submission. *Shit, shit, shit.*

"Something wrong?" she asked, the smile evident in the lilt of her question.

"Tell me a bedtime story." Dimitri stared up at the ceiling. *Do not look at her. Resist.*

"A bedtime story?"

"Yeah, come on."

"Once upon a time there was a very lonely girl. She wanted so badly to find love, but she was afraid."

"What was she afraid of?"

"Shh…my story."

"Okay, okay."

"She was afraid of losing herself, her independence. You see she was convinced that if she met the wrong person, she'd never be the same." Gillian stared at Dimitri, who appeared to be avoiding eye contact. "So she built herself a safe world. A bubble."

"Bubbles aren't very sturdy structures. I guess she wasn't an engineer."

"No." Gillian laughed. "No, she wasn't. But the bubble worked for her. It was very comfortable."

"Doesn't sound too exciting."

"It wasn't."

Dimitri listened intently as she spoke. Why would she live a cloistered existence? Why was she so afraid of wolves when she was part wolf?

"But one day, she met someone who made her question what she was doing, even though she'd just met him."

"Did she start living?"

"I'm afraid the story doesn't have an ending. As it stands now, the girl leaves the boy. She's deciding what she should do."

"Wait a second," he said gruffly. "I wanted you to tell me a story."

"I told you one," she said.

"I like happily-ever-afters. Change the ending." He wasn't talking about make believe.

"Yeah, I like happy endings too, but that doesn't mean we always get one," she teased, referring to how he'd ended their romantic interlude.

"Touché. But for the record, I would've been glad to oblige. Being a gentleman isn't easy. I'm hanging by a thread here, darlin'," he replied. Little kitten was still upset that he'd removed himself, he thought. For all the talk about avoiding wolves, it appeared she was interested after all.

"Dimitri?" Gillian wasn't sure why, but she wondered if he was dating anyone. Of course he was dating someone…probably lots of someones, she reasoned.

"Yeah."

"You promise to go see a witch?" She changed the subject, trying to distract herself from the fact that in the course of twenty-four hours she was wavering on her rule not to date wolves.

"Why do you ask?"

"No reason. I just want to see you well."

"Are you saying you care about me?"

"Maybe." She paused. "I felt him, your wolf. I haven't healed many shifters."

"I don't think I want to hear about you being with other shifters if you healed them the way you healed me," Dimitri said seriously. It bothered him to think that she'd been intimate with anyone else yet he knew that she had to have been with other men.

"I've only done it a few times growing up as a teen…easy things like cuts. The truth is that it's really not a super useful skill. Shifters can heal on their own, but hybrids have more difficulty."

"And what you did to me?"

"You were my first. What I meant to say was that you're my first wolf." She bit her lip, recalling how he was attacked. The bleeding wouldn't stop. "I've never gone full contact before. I usually use just my hands. But with you, it wouldn't work. That's why I needed to get you into bed."

"So it wasn't my handsome face that made you take my clothes off? You wound me," he teased.

"No. And if I was going to pick a reason to get you naked, it'd be something else," she laughed.

"Ah…you do like the wolf."

"Maybe," she hedged, shifting in bed.

"You ever been to the Big Easy?" he asked innocently.

"No." Was he inviting her? She shouldn't encourage him no matter how much she yearned to get to know him better. If he were a tiger, hell, any other kind of shifter, he'd be safe.

"Hmm? Is that a 'no', but I'd love to come visit you? Or a 'no' as in hell, no?"

"It's complicated."

"Because I'm a wolf?" Dimitri rolled his eyes, hoping she couldn't see him. Someone had daddy issues. Her father was an Alpha. He didn't understand what her problem was with being around wolves.

"I told you, it's…"

"I heard ya. Just trying to figure this out…Your father's a wolf."

"My father's not alive."

"I'm sorry to hear about your dad. But still, he was a wolf. It's your heritage. Yet you don't want to be around wolves."

"My tiger…it's important she stays away from wolves. That's all I'm gonna say."

"Date number four," Dimitri drawled, noting her evasive answer. If she thought this was the end of the conversation, she was sorely mistaken.

"What?"

"I said, date number four, that's how long I'll give you to come clean about your wolf hang up."

"I don't have a hang up."

"If we're gonna date, you can't lie to me, cher. You've got a free pass for tonight. After that, all bets are off."

"But there's not going to be a date number four," she said, shaking her head.

"See now, that's where you're wrong. There will be another date. And it'll be a proper date. Dinner. Dancing."

"Are you sure you're not an Alpha? Because you're awful bossy."

"You say bossy, I say persuasive."

"You're relentless."

"Ah, perhaps, but I always get what I want." *And I want you.*

"I'm not sure that we should see each other again. My tiger…"

"Date number four. I expect answers before we make love."

"So we've gone straight from a date to sex?"

"Not yet…but I will have you, darlin'," he promised. His cock thickened as he said the words.

Dimitri hoped they'd continue their flirtatious banter, but she'd gone quiet at his statement. He'd purposefully riled her, sensing that she was reconsidering her decision not to be with him. It was only a matter of time before they made love, and the thought made his blood thick with desire.

Sleeping on the sofa might just kill him before the night was through. How stupid could he have been to suggest it? He was regretting his chivalrous gesture. Shifting once again, he pounded the pillow, attempting to get comfortable. Taking his painful erection into his hand, he slowly stroked it in an attempt to assuage the pulsing need.

Gillian squeezed her eyes shut, tucking the covers against her chest. Did Dimitri seriously tell her that they were going to make love? He simply had no idea how impossible that would be. *Consequences,* her mother's voice played in her mind. Her tiger purred, refusing the logical argument. She wanted to cuddle against the delicious beta. Gillian bit her lip and stared up at the ceiling as she wavered. It would be impossible for her to sleep, knowing that Dimitri lay sleeping two feet away from her. Rationalizing her next move, she told herself that it would be best for both of them, a temporary comfort to get them through the night.

"Dimitri," she whispered.

"Hmm?"

"Come to bed with me."

"I'm not sure that's such a good idea," he growled, his wolf urging him to go.

"You're never going to get any sleep on that tiny sofa," she warned. Scooting over a few inches, she threw open the cover, revealing not only the inviting sheets but her bare thigh.

Dimitri caught sight of her silky skin and groaned.

"I promise to behave," she told him, unsure if she could really keep her hands to herself.

No longer able to keep away from her, Dimitri shoved off the cushions and slipped into the bed. He curled onto his side to face her, their foreheads touching. He deliberately bent at his waist so that his hardened shaft wouldn't accidentally poke her. If he made any kind of contact, it'd be even more difficult not to take her right then.

"Ah, thank you. I can actually feel my legs," he groaned.

"Better?" she asked.

"Better," he confirmed.

Locked in a gaze, Dimitri smiled at Gillian.

"When I get done with the witch, I'm coming to see you," he told her.

Gillian closed her eyes and took a deep breath, but didn't respond.

"Tell me yes."

"To what?" she breathed.

"Date number four. Telling me your secrets."

"I can't…"

"You can," Dimitri countered.

"I…I…" Gillian stammered, mesmerized by his eyes, his voice.

"One date. A real date." Dimitri slid his hand out from under his pillow and cupped her cheek.

"But I live in New York…it's not like we can date," she protested. With her mouth mere inches from his, her heart thumped a hard beat in her chest.

"Say yes," he whispered.

Dimitri knew he shouldn't kiss her, but he was too far gone. Capturing her lips, he gave in to his wolf's inner desire. His tongue swirled against hers and before he knew it, he'd pulled her flush against him. The tip of his cock brushed her stomach and he contemplated how easy it'd be to slide home into her tight heat. The kiss deepened, and he tore his mouth away. Quickly stopping, he flipped her around so that her back was against his abdomen.

One hand reached around her waist, grazing up over her breasts until it was around her neck. He licked her shoulder, biting as he moved toward her ear. His right hand rested on her abdomen, slowly teasing its way downward. Like a predator, he held his prey tightly within his arms, effectively immobilizing her.

"Dimitri," she breathed, brushing her backside against him, seeking his rock-hard shaft.

"Say yes," Dimitri spoke softly into her ear; his hand slid to her mound. As she wiggled her hips in an effort to get him to touch her, he gently bit down onto her lobe as if to warn her. "Say it."

"You weaken me."

"Tell me, kitten. Say it." His fingers flitted lightly between her legs.

"Yes," Gillian cried.

"Yes," Dimitri repeated, gliding his forefinger though her wet lips. He lingered for only a second, pressing a thick digit into her pussy. His hips rocked into her ass as he did so. "Our date is going to be spectacular. How 'bout a little preview?"

"Dimitri…my tiger…"

"Your tiger wants this. And so does my wolf." Dimitri yearned to make love to her, but for tonight, he'd only give her pleasure. Soon enough, he'd have her with no boundaries or secrets.

He plunged two fingers inside of her channel, pumping her slowly. As she began to move her hips in rhythm to his thrusts, he noted the hum of energy over his own skin as if she were magically infusing him with her power. His cock slipped between her legs, and he groaned. Loosening his hold about her neck, he slipped his thumb into her mouth. She sucked and swirled her tongue around it.

"Ah," she managed. "Please."

"Oh darlin', you don't even know how hard I'm gonna fuck you one day. But tonight…" He withdrew from her core, taking her clitoris between his fingers, pinching slightly. She gyrated her hips into his hand, and he applied pressure to her nub, circling it. "You're gonna come so hard you'll see stars."

"Oh Goddess, yes. Harder," she demanded, biting the thumb she'd been sucking.

Increasing the pressure, he circled her taut pearl. His cock pumped between her thighs. He grunted as the urge to come mounted.

"Fuck me, yes, like that. Oh…please. I'm coming." Reaching behind her, Gillian clutched his neck, bringing him closer to her throat. *Mark me*, her tiger roared. Her eyes flew open at the demand. Had it not been for the magic of Dimitri flowing through her veins, she'd have stopped the pleasure right then and there.

"Fuck," he cursed. His orgasm was too far gone to hold back. Plunging three fingers inside her, he sought to drive her over the edge.

Gillian splintered as her climax rolled through her. Breathlessly, she repeated Dimitri's name as she felt the hot spurt of his seed between her legs. He'd come on her skin and she fought the urge to reach for it, to taste and touch it. Like an animal, she'd gone feral in her own lust.

The knowledge that she'd physically solidified her connection with a wolf rocked her. In her soul, she knew things would never be the same. She'd never get enough of Dimitri. She'd let him make love to her, mark her. What they'd done wasn't merely fooling around. This man would make her submit, and she feared she'd gladly do it. Sucking a breath, it was of no use to stifle the tears that began to flow.

Goddess, how she wanted to hide all the conflicting emotions that churned inside her. Never had she let a man restrain her, touch her until she came so hard she thought she'd need resuscitation. Her beast wanted this man to claim her. It terrified and thrilled her, yet reason would win out, she knew. In the morning, she'd leave him, go to New York. Maybe if she put distance between them, the craving for his touch would subside. He'd be better off without her, able to travel directly to the witch to heal himself. By the time he'd rolled her on her side to face him, she'd recommitted to the heart-wrenching decision to leave first thing in the morning.

"Hey, cher. Did I hurt you?" Dimitri asked. He thumbed away a tear from her cheek.

"No, baby," she whispered, cuddling up to lay her head on his chest. Her thigh draped across his. "What you did…we just did…it felt so good. I wish we could stay like this forever." And she meant it, even though she knew they could never be.

"Shhh…get some sleep. We'll talk in the morning," he said, with a kiss to her head.

"In the morning," she repeated. *I'll be gone.*

·❦· *Chapter Six* ·❦·

"Where the hell is she?" Dimitri asked, flinging open the door of his bedroom. He took sight of Jake, who was busy making out with a pair of long legs that ended in fuck-me shoes.

Dimitri huffed, ignoring the hand that silenced him. Tearing into Jake's room, he found no sign of Gillian and returned to the living area. He coughed in an effort to get Jake to remove his tongue from the blonde's mouth long enough that he could get an answer. When Jake finally released the girl, he shot him a glare.

"What the fuck, Jake?"

"What? Oh, sorry. Jenny, meet Dimitri," he offered with a slick smile.

"Hi-ya," his perky date greeted Dimitri. She gave him the once over from his wet hair down to his toes, settling her eyes on the small towel wrapped around his waist. "Didn't know you had a friend? If I didn't have to get to work, a threesome might've been fun."

"Yeah, not happening," Dimitri barked, irritated that Gillian was missing.

"He's a grumpy one, huh?" she asked with a giggle as Jake kissed her neck.

"Somethin' like that. He's got a tiger in his panties. Sorry, babe, but I gotta help my friend out."

She raised an eyebrow at him.

"No, not like that. He's, uh, looking for a girl."

"Well, I got a friend if you wanna meet at six."

"Sorry, we're outta here today. Maybe next time I'm in Vegas."

"Or I'm in NOLA?"

"You bet," Jake promised, opening the door.

"Thanks for last night, sweetie. See ya round. And you too, big guy," she added with a wave, stopping to whisper in Jake's ear. "Maybe next time. I love tattoos."

"Yeah, maybe," he lied, knowing that Dimitri was out of sorts.

Dimitri paced while Jake said his goodbyes. Where the hell had she gone? When he'd left to go take a shower, she'd been sleeping soundly in bed. She'd given no warning that she was getting ready to fly the coop. Rubbing his scruffy beard, he blew out a breath.

The familiar cadence of his cell phone sounded. Running back into his bedroom, he picked it up off the bed stand and read the message: *Thanks for last night. Sorry to kiss & run. Gotta get back home. Go see the witch.*

Dimitri threw the phone down on the bed and tore off his towel. *Fuck. Fuck. Fuck. She did not just leave me without saying goodbye. Yeah, that's exactly what just happened.* Rummaging through a dresser drawer, he pulled out the same pants and shirt he'd worn the day before, and sniffed. They smelled like blood and wolf…Chaz. He shook his head in disgust.

"Here," Jake said, tossing him a new pair of jeans.

"Where the hell were you?" Dimitri growled, snatching them. He shrugged into the stiff denim, wincing as the rough material nicked his dick.

"Thank you so much, Jake, for getting me new clothes. I feel so much better not stinking like the Alpha pig that I almost killed last night," Jake taunted.

"Fuck you," Dimitri said as a t-shirt hit him in the head. He shot his friend a nasty grimace before slipping the garment over his head. Dimitri glanced down to the slogan printed boldly across his chest in bright gold letters. He shook his head.

"For real?"

"Elvis has Left the Building!" Jake joked, reading it aloud. "The king's the bomb, bro."

"Where the fuck were you? How did you not hear Gilly leave?"

"Uh, for the same reason you didn't."

"I was in the shower."

"Yeah, my guess is that you were strokin' off a case of blue balls in there. I, on the other hand, was making love to my sweet lil' Jenny."

"Showgirl?"

"Too cliché. Travel agent. We met at home. We were busy, making up for lost time and all that."

"I am a goddamned idiot. I should've known she would take off. Come on, if we hurry we can catch up to her." Dimitri grabbed his cell off the bed and pecked at the phone number from where she'd sent the text.

"What are you doing?"

"What does it look like I'm doing? I'm calling her. It's not safe out here. Who the hell knows if New York is safe?" The call went to voicemail and he ended the connection. Sending her a quick text back, he told her to wait at the airport for him.

"Listen, D," Jake began, plowing his fingers over his cropped hair. "I know you're sweet on the tiger but you've got to let her go."

"We're going. Now," Dimitri ordered, sliding his feet into the pair of Vans that Jake had provided. He strode out toward the exit.

"I'm just saying that we can try to catch up with her, but if we don't find her," he paused, trying to keep up with Dimitri as he opened the door and started toward the elevator, "I think she's right. You need to go see Ilsbeth. You're vulnerable."

Dimitri grabbed Jake, shoving him up against the wall. Quickly, he realized his transgression and released him.

"I'm not vulnerable," he denied. *I'm compromised. I'm a liability.* Dimitri's jaw ticked in anger as he mulled over the situation.

"I know this can't be easy, but ya know, Gilly left because she wants you to go home. She healed you and knows that whatever piece of shit evil took your wolf from you the first time could happen again. And then what good are you to her?"

"Let's just see if we can catch up with her." A ding resonated, alerting them the lift had arrived. They entered and Dimitri stabbed at the lobby button with his finger.

"She'll be okay. You saw what she did last night."

"Yeah, I saw, all right. I saw her tied up like an animal for a whipping. If we hadn't gotten there in time, they would have..." *Raped her. Killed her...she'd never submit.* "...hurt her."

"But we did get there, and now she's skipping town to where she'll be safe. She's lived in New York for a while. New Yorkers are tough."

"Badass," Dimitri added, hoping their speculation was true.

"Yeah, that's right. She's tough. Nothing happened to her while she lived there. The danger's here. Chaz would have to have a death wish to go to New York City. You and I both know that Jax wouldn't take kindly to strangers in his town, causin' a ruckus."

"Maybe." Jax Chandler, the New York Alpha, was an arrogant prick who wouldn't have allowed a rogue wolf anywhere near his territory, let alone another Alpha who was looking to attack a shifter.

Still, it rubbed Dimitri the wrong way that Gillian was on her own. He was angrier at himself that he couldn't guarantee that he wouldn't end up mortal, unable to protect his woman. He quickly corrected his runaway thought. *His woman?* Yeah, right. Dimitri didn't keep women like belongings. It was more like he entertained the ladies, no ties, no promises.

His rule may have gotten him in trouble a few times. A certain witch in New Orleans came to mind. But for the most part, women respected his honesty and he respected them. One hundred and twenty years of dating, and he hadn't tired of the revolving door of beautiful ladies who'd warmed his bed. So why did it bother him so much that one gorgeous kitty cat went stray?

They reached the car and his phone buzzed. Another text: *Don't try to come to the gate, baby. Won't pass security w/out a tix. Go see the witch.*

Dimitri huffed, irritated that she'd called him a term of endearment while telling him what to do. *Baby? Baby, my ass.* The girl had a lot of freakin' nerve. Not only did she just leave him holding his dick in his hands, but she'd bossed him no less than twice in the course of the day. Clever little kitty knew how to sneak out and then found bravery behind her texts. If she thought this was the end of things, she was dead wrong. When he saw her next, he planned to spank her ass pink. For the first time in the day, a smile broke across his face.

No matter how cheery she'd tried to sound in her texts to Dimitri, Gillian was scared shitless. She was certain that Chaz would be hot on her trail. On the way home from the airport, she'd considered calling her mom, but knew if she spoke to her that she'd spill every detail about what had happened in California. Instead, she'd sent her a short text, letting her know that she was okay and that she'd returned to New York. Gillian hated lying to her mom, but didn't have the heart to worry her.

Carbon dioxide gushed out of a passing pickup truck, and Gillian choked on the fumes. Her taxi swerved to the curb, and she tossed the driver a twenty. She yanked her hoodie down over her head, and ducked out of the cab, then slid into the shadows of an alley and waited. She wiped the city grit from her eyes, observing the steady flow of pedestrians. Her gut told her to be cautious. Her salary didn't afford her a doorman. She knew that just about any good-looking guy could talk her neighbor, Mrs. Beasley, into letting him into the building. A nice smile and a smooth story was the key to the kingdom.

Deciding a disguise was in order, she lowered her head and hoofed it two blocks to the corner store. As loathe as she was to do it, she needed to change her looks. She sighed, vacillating between her choices. Blonde or redhead? Blondes may have more fun, but something about red hair appealed to her. She pondered her options for only a second, taking care to be cognizant of her surroundings.

Gillian grabbed a box of the strawberry hue, praying she'd chosen wisely. The only other time she'd dyed her dark brunette hair was in high school, and she ended up looking like Ronald McDonald. Instead of fretting, she'd proudly worn it until the roots had grown out. Her mother had fits over the two-toned tresses that graced her graduation pictures. The memory caused her to chuckle in spite of the danger that could be lurking back on the streets.

In haste, Gillian swiped her credit card, and made quick work of getting back to her building. Trekking toward her apartment, she got the distinct feeling someone was watching her. Her stomach clenched, and she glanced over her shoulder and back again to the passing crowd. A young mother hurriedly bustled her children down the sidewalk. An older woman fussed over her toy poodle, who apparently was having trouble doing his business. Gillian jumped as a teenager bumped into her, obviously not looking where he was going as he tapped at his phone. The strangers appeared innocuous, but her instincts remained on high alert. Crossing past the threshold of the entrance, she panted a small breath, relieved that the lobby appeared empty. Tapping in the security code, she prayed she'd make it safely to her home.

Gillian could have won a medal for the world's fastest dresser, because she'd gotten in and out of her apartment in less than thirty minutes. In the time it took to go from brunette to red, she was on her way to see the Alpha. Unsure of how to best approach Jax, she hadn't called him, deciding it would be best to go see him in person. Within seconds of entering the building and asking for her brother, she'd been ushered into the elevator. Glancing up into the small orb on the ceiling, she got the distinct feeling she was being watched. Her eyes fell to the bellman, whose fake snobbish accent told her he thought she was some kind of bottom feeder, who didn't belong in his lobby, let alone in the penthouse. She twirled a strand of her newly dyed hair, and glanced down to her royal-blue toenail polish. She supposed that in her rush to pack, she hadn't taken great care tending to her appearance, but she was merely grateful to have made it safely across town.

Gillian tried not to think about the melancholy that had washed over her when she'd opened her apartment door. She was relieved that there hadn't been a thug waiting for her inside, but the sight of her portfolio on her kitchen table brought tears to her eyes. Although she'd been lucky enough not to lose her wallet and cell phone during her ordeal in the desert, her new camera was lost and that was going to cost her money she didn't have. Replacing it would have to wait, though. Right now, her first priority was securing protection. Security from a family member who didn't even know she existed.

Gillian's heart raced in tandem with the overhead flashing numbers that ticked away. Her stomach lurched as the lift came to a stop. Within seconds, she'd face the Alpha who had the potential to save her. This was either going to go really well, or she'd be out on her ass. Would Jax help her? Would he accept her as his sister? If he did, would he force her to live with him…as wolf? She took a deep breath and tried to halt the tornado of questions that whirled in her mind. A gruff demand brought her out of her contemplation.

"You're here," he grumbled, nodding toward the opening doors.

"What?" she asked, taking a second to steel her nerves.

"I said, 'you're here'. Mr. Chandler is waiting," the bellman announced, extending his arm to usher her forward.

Putting a foot over the grate, she stepped onto the shiny Spanish marble. The enormous modern glass chandelier that hung from the cathedral ceiling captivated her, and she nearly tripped as her shoe slid over the smooth floor.

"Easy, Gilly," she heard Jax say. The rumble of his voice caused her to startle.

"J…Jax." Surprised to hear his voice, she turned her head toward the large sunken living area. The commanding Alpha stood tall behind his beta, Nick, who was sitting on the sofa, stroking a small white wolf who lay in his lap.

Although she knew that wolves thought little of clothing, the sight of them only wearing jeans took her off guard. Both men, with their tan sculptured bodies, looked as if they belonged in the magazine they ran. Gillian's eyes met Jax's and she studied his face, recalling how their eyes were the same shade of gold. Even though she'd rehearsed her speech well, no words left her lips and tears pricked at her eyes.

"Here, kitty, kitty," he taunted, giving her a wry smile.

He knows. "Jax...I...need your help," she managed.

"Come sit. We need to have a chat," he told her, walking around the large red leather sofa. Looking toward Nick, he nodded. "In private."

Gillian slowly moved toward her brother but abruptly stopped as the animal on the couch shifted into a naked woman. Intrigued by the transformation, she watched as Nick kissed her before letting her off his lap. She gave Gillian a sideways glare before traipsing down the hallway.

Stunned at the display, Gillian forgot what she was doing. Being a tiger, she wasn't used to the open sexuality that wolves exhibited. She, too, stripped bare before shifting into her beast, but unlike the wolves, she ran alone. Taking a quick breath, she composed herself and returned her gaze to Jax, who gestured for her to take a seat. Her heavy backpack remained on her shoulders as she sat in the far corner of the couch.

Nick scooted across the sofa until his thigh brushed hers. He sniffed and smiled, and she flinched in response. Yet when he reached over to help remove the straps of her bag from her shoulders, she relaxed enough to allow him to take it. The close proximity of the other wolf brought forth an odd familiarity, making her think once again of Dimitri. She closed her eyes, forcing herself to concentrate. Now was not the time for lust or pipedreams.

"She smells of a wolf," Nick noted, brushing his fingers through her red locks. "And chemicals."

"Well, she is a wolf, isn't that right, sister?" Jax asked, his expression impassive.

"I'm...I'm a tiger. But you know that, don't you, brother?" Sweat beaded on her brow as her anxiety rose, but she refused to show fear.

"A sister?" Nick clapped his hands and laughed. "Now this is an interesting development."

"Indeed, it is," Jax replied.

"How did you know? I didn't say anything..." Gillian stopped speaking and shook her head, feeling both inexperienced and vulnerable. Dammit, she'd been foolish to think she could hide from an Alpha.

"This morning, I got a call from Logan Reynaud."

Gillian stared back at Jax, putting the pieces together. *Logan Reynaud?* She recalled her conversations with Dimitri. He'd mentioned the first name of his Alpha: Logan. Dimitri must have called his Alpha. He'd gone back to New Orleans, all right, but not before making sure she was protected by Jax.

"Dimitri," she whispered. "But how did you know about me...my tiger...about us?"

"Ah well, after you blew me off a few months ago, it got me to thinking.

Why would a starving photographer refuse to speak to someone who was offering her the job of a lifetime? So I did a more in-depth background check. Your mother, Mirabel, I knew her many years ago. When my father died…"

"She was devastated…couldn't live here anymore. I don't have any memories of my father…our father…or you."

"It isn't surprising you don't remember. When Alpha died, Father, you were a toddler. I knew you existed, but when Mirabel asked me to leave her alone, I did. I understood that you were a tiger and the dangers that would be presented to you should you grow up around pack. What I didn't expect was that Mirabel would change your name to one I didn't easily recognize. I knew you as Kaitlen. But here you are…Gillian Michel."

"Gillian…it's my middle name. My last is a family name on my mother's side. She wanted to protect me. I didn't even know you existed until we met a few months ago. You have to understand, I've gone to great lengths not to be around wolves. When I told Mom about you, the opportunity, that's when she told me…that I had a half-brother in New York."

"You stopped calling. Wouldn't return my calls. You do know that doesn't go over too well with an Alpha, don't you? Did you really think you could get away with that?"

She gave him a small grin, sensing he was teasing her. She'd thought it difficult, but not impossible.

"It's part of the reason I went to California. It seemed like such a great job, but…" She sighed. "I guess if you talked to, um, Dimitri's Alpha, then you know why I'm here."

"We'll get to that in a minute. Let's be frank, shall we? I know why you don't want to be around wolves. Mirabel, she couldn't shift. She gave up everything for my father. Yet in the end, the gifts she gave him were wasted. He died fighting for all of us during that attack."

"I'm sorry." She'd never known her father but sympathized with his loss.

"I killed his murderer," Jax stated without emotion. "I lost everything. My father. My stepmother. I know what it feels like to mourn. I would never have done anything to compromise your ability to shift."

"I'm relieved that you understand why I can't be around your pack. I do. But I need your protection. If you could just talk to Chaz or do whatever Alphas do…please," she pleaded.

"Jax, I don't mean to interrupt, but when I said she smelled like a wolf, I wasn't referring to her," Nick explained further.

"Well, that's not at all possible. I'm a tiger and you both know that, not that I let people go around sniffing me like a dog. No offense," she added, upset that she could have been so careless as to compare a wolf to a domestic animal. *Shit. This is so not going well.* "I'm sorry. It's just that I'm afraid. Dimitri almost killed Chaz. I should have done it…I wanted to do it, but the silver…it made me sick."

"Did you just say that Dimitri almost killed the Alpha?" Jax exclaimed.

"Yeah, he could have easily killed him but he released him."

"Isn't that interesting?"

"I don't think he wants to be Alpha. I don't know Dimitri that well, but he seems loyal to his pack."

"Well, I wouldn't say that," Nick laughed. He got up and crossed the room. Slipping behind the wet bar, he rummaged underneath it. "Something to drink? Soda? Water?"

"Beta, be clear with your thoughts. Do you think our sister lies about her relationship with the Acadian wolf?"

"His scent is all over her," Nick confirmed. He pulled out three tumblers and set them on the counter. "Maybe we need something stronger. Wine or whiskey?"

Jax's eyes flew to Gillian, who wished she could cower behind the furniture. Her face grew hot, as she wondered how they could smell him on her. She'd taken a shower, but apparently that wasn't nearly enough to hide the intimacy of their night together.

"It's five o'clock somewhere," Jax quipped, rubbing his chin. "Wine. Bring the bottle."

"I'm not sure what you think went on between Dimitri and me but I'm telling you that nothing happened. Not that I need to report who I sleep with to you." Gillian looked over to Nick. "Wine. Best idea of the day."

"I'm your big brother, kitty cat." Jax smiled and raised an eyebrow at her.

"Very funny. Thank you," Gillian said. She gladly accepted the filled glass that Nick handed her. Taking a sip, she thanked the Goddess for grapes.

"You do know what happens if you mate with a wolf?"

"Mate," Gillian choked, spitting out her drink. "Who said anything about mating?"

"You carry his scent. That means you've been intimate," Jax noted.

"Oh my God, do you wolves have no secrets?"

"This is our nature. Besides, a simple review of the facts would tell me you care about him. You saved him from certain death. He reciprocated. You left without him. Now that I don't quite understand, but and this is a big but, he specifically had Logan call me to tell me everything and to request protection on his behalf. It's a very unusual circumstance for an Alpha, one in a state hundreds of miles away, to call another Alpha to ask for protection for an individual who is not even in his pack. He is now indebted to me, you realize? Of course, I owed him one, but nonetheless, this is a sacrifice on his part."

Gillian sat silent. She hadn't needed him to summarize the past seventy-two hours for her to tell him that she cared about Dimitri. But as she sat quietly, her beast purred at the thought of seeing him again, yearning to have him inside her, his mouth and hands taking whatever he wanted. One night would never be enough.

"Are you listening?" Jax asked.

"Yes, sorry, I just was thinking."

"Good, I want you to think, because Mirabel lost her ability to shift when she mated with my father. I'll admit, I don't know the details. Perhaps she denied her wolf and that is why. But nevertheless, there was a sacrifice. Her tiger died."

"Don't you think I know that?" Gillian responded, frustrated with her predicament. She missed Dimitri, and despite her otherwise good judgment, she knew she'd end up in his arms again.

"This thing with Chaz...you're in deep, lil' sis. What exactly made you think you could travel to Cali, into another wolf's territory, without notifying him?" He changed the subject.

"It was supposed to be a job. Technically, I'm wolf, I know that. But Jax, I'm a tiger. You haven't seen me yet...but believe me, Chaz sure as hell did."

"What did he do to you?" Jax asked softly, knowing that she'd been attacked.

"You don't want to know," she said, unconsciously rubbing her shoulder where he'd bitten her.

"We're family, Gilly. We may have been alone before, but no longer. What did he do?" he continued.

"He wants to mate with me. He tried to mark me," Gillian admitted. She glanced up to Nick, who left the room, and she swore she heard him growl. "It didn't take, though. If you know how it works, then you know I've got to choose who I mate with. He knew I was tiger but he underestimated my abilities. I shifted, killed his wolves and escaped. But he tracked me down...that's how he found Dimitri."

"Ah yes, that part of this story is quite interesting. One minute he can't shift, the next he overpowers an Alpha."

"That night on the beach...I healed him."

"Yes, I do recall Mirabel had that ability as well."

"It's not a big deal really. As I told Dimitri, not many shifters actually need help recovering from an injury. But he did...and it worked," she recalled.

"And the desert? What did they do to you?" Jax pressed.

"Stripped me." Gillian lowered her eyes. It wasn't her fault, she knew. Yet she was embarrassed that she'd been caught, tortured. "He was going to beat me...make me submit."

"Sister, I'm very sorry for your ordeal. Good and evil exists in all beings. I swear to you from now on, you'll be protected. As always, I have a plan. But first things first....Nick," Jax called into the open foyer.

The hairs on Gillian's arms stood up, waiting on the beta. A painful grunt tore into the air, and she sprang to her feet to view the source. Two large men, shackled in the arms of guards, stumbled into the foyer. She recognized them as two of the wolves who'd attacked her in the desert. Her chest pounded, adrenaline flooding her veins. *What are they doing here?*

A caustic mixture of fear and hate seized her. The assailant who'd dragged her from her car was tall, with the musculature of a body builder. His eyes locked on hers as he exuded venomous hostility. She could tell he wanted nothing more than to kill her, but despite his huge size, Jax's wolves easily held him in place. His partner, who was of smaller stature, was badly beaten; a red welt formed around his eye and blood dripped from his lower lip. Tears pricked at her eyes as she realized he was the same person who'd stripped off her clothes.

"You're safe, Gilly. Breathe," she heard Jax tell her. He placed his hand on her shoulder.

"Jax...what's happening?" Gillian asked, looking at her abductors and back to her brother. "Where did they come from?"

"I picked them up a block from my place. They knew you'd come to me for protection. Probably hoped they could nab you again before you got here."

"But how would they know I'd come to you? Oh my God, I knew I felt like I was being watched. I think they may have been at my apartment," she rambled. Unable to control her anger, Gillian's tiger roared to attack, smelling blood in the air. The desire for vengeance grew strong. Certain she could kill them, Gillian kicked off her shoes, readying to shift.

"No need, sister," Jax cajoled, stroking her arm gently. "You're under my protection now."

"But Jax...they won't stop. Let me kill them," she protested.

"The need for revenge is sweet only in the moment. One must consider the big picture. These mongrels are but insignificant links in the pack chain of command. Nick," Jax called to his beta, nodding for him to come take his place by his sister.

Gillian rooted her bare feet onto the cool tiles. She fisted her hands tightly, fingernails digging into her palms. *Stay calm. Stay calm. Stay calm.*

Nick obeyed, flanking Gillian. He gave her an understanding smile and reached for her hand. He loosened her balled fist until she allowed him to put his fingers in hers.

"What we must do is address the source...the cause of your difficulties. The root of the problem, if you will." Jax strode over to the tall, muscular wolf and pinned him with a cold stare. "This man, he attacked you? Was going to allow the Alpha to beat you?"

"Yes. He took me." She nervously licked her lips, itching to shift. She'd never asked for permission to do so, but it was as if her tiger knew her brother was Alpha, acquiescing to his request to stay human. "He dragged me from the car...by my hands and hair. Held me down."

"You attacked my sister?" Jax growled at the wolf.

"Fuck, yeah. She killed our wolves...she deserves to die. If my Alpha didn't want to mate the bitch, I'd kill her now," he challenged, glaring at him eye to eye.

"Now that is rude," Jax said, glancing at the other prisoner, who lowered his eyes in submission. "You see, there's an order in a pack. And guests, I'm afraid they're not excused from rules."

Gillian jumped as the large wolf ripped his arms away from his guards and lunged at Jax's throat. Nick put his arm around her shoulders, keeping her from going toward her brother. She screamed, watching as Jax punched his entire fist into the chest of the wolf. As he retracted his bloodied arm, a beating heart pumped in his grip. A loud thump reverberated throughout the home as the dead man hit the marble.

Even though Gillian had killed as tiger, she'd never seen such a violent act. She closed her eyes, willing the vomit rising in her throat to retreat. Within seconds, she'd composed herself, nausea replaced with relief. She wasn't normally an aggressive person, but she was glad that her attacker could no longer harm anyone.

Jax approached the smaller wolf, who'd urinated at the sight of his friend's death. Opening his palm, Jax rolled his wrist and the crimson organ fell to the floor with a splat.

"Don't worry, friend," Jax assured him, tilting his head. As if he'd tacked a fly to an insect board, the Alpha observed his work. "You'll live. And you're going to go back to California with a message for your Alpha. Are you listening?"

"Yyyyyesssss," he stuttered.

"My sister, Gillian Michel, is off limits. Tell your Alpha that not only does he not have my permission to pursue a mating," Jax paused, well aware that the bomb he was about to drop would shock his sister. He wished he didn't have to take such extreme measures, but considering what they'd done to her in the desert, the California Alpha wouldn't be deterred easily. He blew out a breath and continued, "My sister is going to be mated. To the beta. I will be announcing it tomorrow night but now you can save me the trouble."

"What?" Gillian gasped. *Did he just say I'm going to mate his beta?* She glanced at Nick who wore a huge grin as if he'd won a giant stuffed panda at the fair.

"Gillian is to be mated. She has chosen. So you see, she is no longer available. Do you understand?"

The wolf turned his head away, refusing to answer.

"You will tell your Alpha! Do you understand?" Jax yelled, shoving him up against the wall.

"Yes," he cried.

"Get him outta here," Jax ordered. "And clean up this mess. You two...my office, now."

"What just happened?" she asked. Jax silenced her with a hand and pointed down the hallway.

Gillian shook her head, trying to wrap her mind around what her brother had said. Did he seriously think she would choose to get mated just to keep an Alpha from kidnapping her? *He's out of his damn wolf mind if he thinks that's happening*, she thought.

As Nick pulled her into Jax's office, she wished she had stayed with Dimitri. She'd never really needed anyone besides her mom before, but her feelings toward her beta hadn't faded like she'd expected. She knew it was irrational, but she had to see him again. When this was all over, she swore to herself that she was getting on the next plane to New Orleans.

"I apologize for killing that wolf," Jax began, but Gillian interrupted him.

"I would have killed him myself, but still…the way you killed him." She stopped herself from chastising him. He was an Alpha. He could do whatever he wanted, she knew. She held her palms up in the air, surrendering, and then raked her fingers through her hair, forgetting that she'd shortened her locks. "No judging. I will not judge you, okay. But Jax, I'm not mating with Nick."

"Tomorrow, I'm going to announce that you're to be mated to the beta. We'll do it at one of the magazine events. The press will be there," he replied, unfazed by her reaction. Snatching a decanter off his desk, he poured himself a shot of whiskey and downed it. Refilling his own, and two other glasses, he fell back into his leather chair and slid the tumblers toward her and Nick. "Sit."

Gillian was too tired to argue and did as he asked. Reaching for the liquor, she gladly took a healthy swig as if she were a pirate.

"No," she coughed, the amber liquid burning her esophagus. While she was unable to speak, Jax was quick to contradict her.

"Yes. Even the announcement probably won't keep this asshole from coming for you. I'm thinking that the best we can hope for is that he'll come to New York, and I'll kill him here. Worst case, he kidnaps you back. This is serious shit, Gilly. He wants your gift."

"But I can't mate…"

"Of course, I know you can't mate with Nick. We're just going to lead him to think you're with him," Jax explained.

"If we're lucky, he might give up," Nick offered.

"You think so?" Gillian asked.

"I don't know Chaz very well, so it's hard to say. It won't hurt that I killed his wolf. He'll know he's in danger if he comes here or sends anyone to get you," Jax speculated. "But for now, this is the best plan I've got to keep you safe. I know you're not going to like this but you'll need to stay here with me. I'll keep the pack members out of the house."

"But my work…"

"Congratulations. You're officially employed at ZANE. Staff photographer. I was getting ready to offer you a job before you stopped calling anyway. When you go on shoots, I'll send protection. If you don't want wolves, I'll get other security."

"Jax, I can never repay you for your help," she whispered, staring into the bottom of her glass.

"Repay me? Why would you ever even think that? You're my sister. We're family, G."

"G?" she laughed.

"Hey, I owe you a few silly nicknames. Lost time and all that." Jax shoved himself up from his seat, and approached Gillian. He took the glass from her hands and pulled her up into an embrace. "When and if you decide you want to mate for real, I'll be there for you. But until then, I'll keep you safe, okay? You're family...the only family I have."

"Family," she agreed, grateful for her big brother.

Gillian hugged Jax, still apprehensive about their plan. With her budding feelings for Dimitri, she wasn't sure she could pull off a lie. Her beta would never understand that she was just pretending. She was sure that she'd have to at least touch Nick tomorrow night and there was a good possibility he'd kiss her. Her tiger paced, distressed by the idea of another man's hands on her skin. Gillian yearned for Dimitri, the only wolf she desired. The craving burning in her chest reminded her that she was growing precariously close to breaking every rule she'd ever known.

⤛❦· *Chapter Seven* ·❦⤜

Dimitri lay nude on the cold slab of concrete, staring up at the stars. Two dozen chanting witches circled him, and he pondered why the sight of the naked women hadn't even caused so much as a twitch of his dick. He should be focusing on healing his wolf, he knew, but it bothered him that he wasn't feeling the slightest bit aroused during the skyclad ceremony. He was a red-blooded wolf, after all. Suspecting the tigress was the cause of his erectile dysfunction, he planned on calling her as soon as Ilsbeth set him loose.

With Gillian's scent ingrained in his mind, he couldn't shake off the attraction he felt for her. He'd been so pissed off that she had slipped out of the hotel room and hopped a plane to New York City, that he'd called Logan on their flight home. Caring less whether she wanted to be around wolves or not, Dimitri knew that Jax Chandler would see to her safety. Dimitri had asked his Alpha to call in the favor for him directly, so there'd be no misinterpretation of the request. He'd come clean with Logan, telling him every detail of the trip, including their romantic tryst the night before. Like brothers, they kept no secrets.

After he'd hung up, he'd nodded to Jake, pretending as if he'd washed his hands of Gillian and the west coast danger they'd faced. Lying to himself wasn't his usual style. Dimitri was honest and straightforward in all aspects of his life. But at no time had a woman gotten under his skin the way Gillian had. Still, it made no sense to him, as he really didn't know her.

True, they'd saved each other's lives. He knew well enough that tough battles had a tendency to forge deep friendships within pack. But this was something more, something causing his wolf to howl in distress, knowing she was on her own without him. At no time had his wolf cared one way or another who he'd bedded. The scary part was that he hadn't even made love to her yet. Oh, but he planned to one day, hard and all night long. Maybe that was his problem, he mused. If he could just have sex with her, then he'd get it out of his system, move on and come back and ask for another 'healing ceremony' from the witches.

A smile crossed his face as he heard the words of Marvin Gaye run through his mind. *Sexual healing?* He was pretty sure Ilsbeth, the sexy head witch, would be happy to give it to him. Sure they'd had somewhat of a disagreement when he'd refused to see her exclusively, but she'd still agreed to try to heal him. When they'd had their falling out, he'd given her a tuft of his wolf hair, hoping to mend their friendship. In return, she'd given him the cold shoulder a few weeks ago. Today, however, when he'd shown up on her doorstep, begging for help, she'd welcomed him with open arms.

As he glanced to his right, she gave him a small smile, wearing nothing but her birthday suit. He sucked a breath as she approached, wishing that for one second he could put Gillian out of his mind. *Naked women everywhere but not a drop to drink. What was the saying? Not women, it's water,* he laughed to himself. Regardless, he should have been hard as a rock by now. Several witches approached him and began to brush anointing oil over his skin. Ilsbeth, at his head, reached forward, her taut nipples grazing his face as she leaned to smear the earthy-scented mixture from his temples to his abdomen, clear down to the crease of his groin, where his torso met his legs.

Her fleshy nubs rubbed across his open lips. Panic seized him as the realization hit that he hadn't even needed to resist the temptation to suck the pink tips he'd once coveted. His limp cock hung heavy on his leg, despite the fingers that massaged tincture into his inner thighs. *Holy hell. No fucking way.* Like lightning striking down a tree, he knew instantly his promiscuous bachelor days had been decimated.

Something was terribly wrong. Dimitri screwed his eyes tight, attempting to concentrate on finding a solution to the quagmire. *Could Gillian be my mate? How could this happen? Tiger wolf hybrids don't mate wolves, do they?* Goddess almighty, this was exactly why Gillian didn't want to be around wolves. She'd been afraid something like this could happen to her. He wasn't sure why she wanted to avoid being mated but he sure as hell knew why he did. Dimitri had never tired of his endless nights with blondes, redheads and brunettes. His lovely rainbow of ladies had all just come to a screeching halt, the epiphany hitting him as a bevy of beauties pranced around him in their glory. Some might call it poetic justice while others might call it fucking bad luck.

Maybe he was wrong about Gillian being his mate. Maybe he was just experiencing some sort of performance anxiety. Stage fright. He wished he could laugh this one off, but his stress wasn't eased at all by the sound of Ilsbeth's voice calling him.

"Dimitri," Ilsbeth said softly, running her fingers through his hair.

"What?" he asked, blinking his eyes open.

"You okay?"

Dimitri wiped his hand across his mouth and noticed everyone was gone. Only Ilsbeth remained. The empty garden courtyard smelled of the fragrant sweet bay magnolias and wisteria. The white and purple petals reflected the moonlight like a mirror. Crickets serenaded them as silence fell. Warm spring nights often led to romance on the bayou, and Dimitri hoped that whatever conclusions he had about having a mate weren't true.

"Where is everyone?" he asked.

"We're done. They're going home. How do you feel? Can you stand up?" Ilsbeth stroked his cheek. "Let me help you."

Was she seriously talking to him like he was an injured animal? Didn't she realize he was the kind of wolf who others feared, one who could be Alpha any damn day of the week if he wished? Bristling with angst from his revelation, he knew he was redirecting his anger at her, when the real problem was his mate. *Mate?* He shook his head and shoved up off the table.

"I'm good."

"You sure?"

"Yeah, thanks."

"We need to talk, Dimitri." Ilsbeth gracefully glided around the altar. She reached for his knees. When he didn't flinch, she pushed his legs open further, sliding her body between his thighs.

"Hey there, cher," Dimitri laughed.

He wasn't sure if he was uncomfortable or not that she'd pressed her belly against his softened cock. As her arms laced around his neck, he settled his hands on her hips. The look in her eyes was recognizable as the lust they'd once shared and he found himself unable to hold her gaze. He wrapped a finger around a lock of her platinum blonde hair and tugged, lifting his eyes with a small smile.

"Whatcha want to talk about. How bad is it?" he asked.

"I shouldn't have let you leave for San Diego," she admitted. "I feel like this is my fault."

"You knew?"

"Something just felt wrong when you came out of that hell hole, but you know, I couldn't be sure. I was so mad at you...I just, I didn't take time to find out."

"It's not your fault, darlin'. You didn't do this. Now stop beating around the bush. What's the prognosis?" Dimitri knew that whatever Gillian had done to heal him had only been temporary. By the time he'd landed in New Orleans, he could feel his ability to shift starting to slip again.

"It's not gone, Dimitri. What we did tonight, it'll only keep the evil at bay for so long. Maybe a week. Maybe less."

"What the hell is it?"

"It's not possession, if that's what you're worried about. It's more like a parasite, eating away at you...your wolf. I need a stronger spell to get rid of it entirely, but I don't..."

"You don't know if you can do it?"

Ilsbeth nodded. Surprising Dimitri, she pressed herself into his arms and laid her head on his shoulder.

"You can do this. You're the most powerful witch I know."

"I have something you can take...a tonic of sorts. I made it earlier today, using your own hair, the sample you gave me before this happened to you."

"Okay, so I'll drink it or rub it, whatever you want me to do with it until you find a spell that works."

"It may take a while. Maybe you should stay here with me," she suggested. Lifting her head, she pressed her cheek against his. "I can be there in case the tonic stops working...to help you."

"Now you know that's not a good idea. I've got to be with Logan," he hedged. Dimitri considered that he could make love to Ilsbeth if he wanted to have her. Even though she was bare in his arms, he felt no hint of desire.

"I want to help you," Ilsbeth breathed, moving her lips to touch his. Desperation laced her voice as her eyes met his. "I may not be able to cure you tonight but I can keep this from killing your wolf…I promise."

"I need to find a way to end this…permanently," he said. There was a time when he couldn't get enough of Ilsbeth, but she wanted too much. And now with her in his arms again, all he could think about was the woman he'd only known for two days, *Gillian*.

"Please Dimitri. Just think about this…us…we could be good together."

Before he could stop her, Ilsbeth pressed her lips against his. He thought that he should force himself to kiss her, to prove his theory wrong. But as he tasted her, both his mind and wolf revolted, solidifying what he'd suspected. He'd always known that Ilsbeth wasn't his mate. She'd been a friend and lover but nothing more. And what they'd shared, once upon a time, was truly over. He pushed her away, shaking his head.

"What? Why are you stopping?" she asked, breathlessly. As she attempted to fall into his embrace, he held her at bay.

"I can't do this…you and I, it's over. I'm sorry. I'm so damn sorry. I shouldn't have let you…I've gotta go. Just give me whatever mojo juice you've concocted and I'll be on my way. Where are my clothes?" Dimitri pushed up to stand on the grass, and gently pried her fingers off his arm. *Goddess, how I've fucked this up*. He felt terrible for letting her kiss him, for leading her on, unsure whether he even had or not.

"Where are you going?" she said, her voice laden with anger.

"Look, Ilsbeth. Whatever we had a few months ago was great while we had it, but it's over. You and I both know it's not going to work out. You know that despite your snarky remarks a few weeks ago, I still care about you. I just can't," he gestured back and forth with his hand, to her and to his chest, "I can't do this…have a relationship. There are things going on with me. Things you don't know." *Like that I've got a mate.* "I need your help, but I'm not going to sleep with you and go and make things worse between us."

Dimitri crossed the courtyard, locating his clothes on a hammock. He picked up his jeans and shoved his legs into them.

"Fine. Have it your way. But when you can't shift again, and you need help immediately, don't be surprised when I can't get to you right away. I do have a life, you do know that? I'm not going to come running, just because you snap your fingers. If you stay with me, then I'd be around you more, maybe could work with you to fix this thing that's eating you from the inside out."

"I can't live with you." Dimitri slung his head through the t-shirt and continued dressing.

"Who is she?" Ilsbeth said, grabbing her robe off a nearby chair.

"What?" Dimitri pretended not to hear her as he slid his shoes onto his feet.

"Who is she? The shifter who healed you? You never did tell me. It's an unusual ability to heal others," she commented with a flip of her hair.

"Okay, well, number one, I never told you the shifter was a woman, but yes she is. And number two, you don't need to know who she is because she's not from around here."

"Really? Nothing special?" she asked.

"Ilsbeth, how about we not do this, okay? You and I...we're friends. Some day when you need something, and you know you will, you have in the past, and you will in the future. When it happens, I'll help you. But right now, I need your help, okay? I need you to find the spell."

"You're lying." Ilsbeth stomped out of the garden and returned just as quickly. Holding out her hand, she opened her palm, revealing a small flask.

"What do I do with it?" Dimitri took it from her.

"Well, if you'd stay, we'd have time to discuss this further..."

"Done talkin', cher. Let's have it."

"A couple of teaspoons a day. If you feel like you're losing touch with your wolf, call me. In the meantime, I'll put some calls in to a few people who owe me favors. That should last you a few days, but you'll have to come back."

"Ilsbeth..." He wanted to hug her goodbye. She'd helped him and he appreciated it but touching her again would send the wrong message. He shoved the flask in his pocket. "Thanks for what you did tonight. I wish things were different, but you wouldn't be happy dating me."

"Don't tell me what makes me happy or what doesn't. This isn't over," she warned.

"Thanks again," he said, making no move toward her. She crossed her arms and grimaced, and he took his cue to leave.

Dimitri followed the long outdoor path around the garden to get to his car, not wanting to go through her home. He figured that he'd best get out of dodge before she either hexed him or attempted to seduce him again. Ilsbeth, one of the most powerful witches on the east coast, was not one to be trifled with.

Dimitri had known Ilsbeth for over sixty years, and they'd weathered many a storm together, but he never trusted a jealous woman, let alone a jealous witch. Green with envy could get you turned into green mold if you rubbed her the wrong way. The only reason he was getting off without harm was because she cared for him. He'd pissed her off well and good tonight, and he knew she suspected that he fancied another woman. No matter what she thought, he wasn't going to tell her anything about Gillian, not until he knew the truth about whether or not she was his mate.

In the face of not knowing for sure, he wasn't going to admit his suspicion to anyone yet. Logan would know instantly if he had a mate, as would most of his friends. It would be hard to conceal. He needed to go to her tomorrow, confirm what he suspected to be true.

Unlike how Logan had hidden the knowledge from his mate, Gillian would be the very first person he told. Dimitri wasn't even sure she'd accept it. She'd already run once. He wouldn't be surprised if the little hell cat tried to go on the lam again. *Fool me once, shame on you. Fool me twice, shame on me,* he thought. He planned on teaching his feisty tigress a lesson or two on submission. He smiled inwardly, knowing he'd fully enjoy the challenge.

As he reached his car, his phone buzzed in his pocket. Reading the text from Jax, he gave a small chuckle. *Ready or not, Kitty, here I come.*

~⚜ *Chapter Eight* ⚜~

Gillian's feet hurt. She shifted again in the painful heels she'd chosen to wear and cursed the personal shopper that Jax had assigned to dress her for the evening. She smoothed down the black strapless couture gown, thankful for the thigh-high slit, which allowed movement in the otherwise skin-tight material. Given her impaired mobility, she felt unusually vulnerable.

She wrapped her hands around the brass handrail, and glanced down to the theater patrons who were busily taking their seats. Even though felines weren't typically afraid of heights, she tightened her grip, revealing that the human side of her feared the very thing her beast craved. But she knew it wasn't just the distance from the floor causing her stomach to tie in knots.

Gillian had thought of a million different ways to tell Dimitri that Jax would be announcing her mating to his beta. Jax had explained that this evening's event was for the magazine, which employed both humans and supernaturals. Although mortals and wolves were well integrated in society, mating was a term used only by the shifter realm. Marriage, on the other hand, would be seen as more socially acceptable to the humans in attendance. Jax had warned her that their engagement would be presented as well, so that all understood his intention.

She'd attempted to reach Dimitri, but he hadn't returned her calls or texts. Waiting alone for Nick to join her, her heart ached. Gillian wiped a small tear from her eye, the disappointment more than she expected. Goddess, she felt so stupid. She'd only known Dimitri for a couple of days, and she'd allowed herself to form an attachment. What had she expected? That he'd come for her like he'd said? That he'd decide to date her after she'd insisted that she wouldn't be with a wolf?

Maybe he'd already found out from his Alpha about her supposed mating with Nick. She shook her head at the thought. It wasn't even a real mating for Christ's sakes, but still, it was being publicly declared. Nick told her he planned to kiss her, insisting that it would be best to make it more believable, and foolishly she'd agreed. ZANE was planning on doing a feature on them, and they needed to make it look real. She could just imagine Dimitri seeing a picture of her kissing someone else, a wolf no less. If she needed a nail driven into the coffin of her fantasy of seeing Dimitri again, an image of her locking lips with Nick would be the hammer.

She heard footsteps behind her, and assumed Nick had finally come up to join them. Earlier, he'd accompanied Gillian to her seat. He'd left momentarily to check with the guards, explaining that although none of Chaz's wolves had been spotted, they expected he'd send in humans to report back to him. Lilac scented perfume alerted her that she'd been wrong about who'd entered, and she turned to the source.

"What are you doing here?" Gillian asked. The woman who she'd seen curled on Nick's lap sidled up next to her. She wasn't sure of the relationship between her, Jax and his beta, but sensed hostility from the second the woman had shifted, back in his apartment.

"I'm Star," she announced, affording herself the view below. Never making eye contact, she presented herself with an air of entitlement.

"I'm Gillian."

"I know who you are. Jax's half-breed sister."

"Excuse me?" Gillian's eyes flared in anger.

"Listen, I don't know what's going on with you and Nick, but he's mine, do you hear me? And your brother shares my bed as well. So whatever you've done to get me kicked out of their place, you better fix it or let's just say you might become uncomfortable with your new home." Star flicked her candy-red fingernails, admiring her manicure.

"Are you threatening me?"

"What do you think?"

"I think you're dumb as shit if you think you can threaten a tiger. And must have a death wish doing it where my brother can hear you." Gillian released a small growl but tamped down her cat's urge to shift. *A tasty wolf would be very satisfying right now.* She took a deep calming breath, and her eyes flew to Nick who stood in the doorway.

"Nick darling," Star sang, her demeanor sweet as taffy. She sashayed over to him, her see-through dress tugging at its seams.

Gillian turned her head away from both of them, willing her feral eyes back to their golden hue. She didn't want Nick seeing her lose control, but she knew he'd heard every word she said. Grateful he'd come along, she used the opportunity to compose herself. Patience was a commodity she was running short of, and Jax would be less than pleased if she ate one of his wolves at his elegant event.

She heard Nick dismiss Star, and went to ask him when Jax was supposed to speak. All the attendees had been seated and the lights began to dim, signaling the performance was about to begin. But when she turned around, he was gone. The curtains to the entrance of the booth had been drawn. As she was about to leave to find him, the theater darkened and a single spotlight shone on Jax who stood smiling on stage.

With his typical charismatic and voguish style, he adjusted his tie and waved to several ladies in the front row, who swooned in response. For the first time in her life, Gillian felt sentimental, wishing she'd known her father. Had he been like Jax? Larger than life, lethal with a casual flash of his smile?

He began to speak and she quickly sat in her red velvet chair. Her heart started to beat faster, and she opened her purse to check her cell phone for the twentieth time today. No calls. No text. With no time to wallow in her disappointment, she heard Jax call her name.

"I'd like to welcome everyone to ZANE's celebration of the arts. As you know, ZANE is dedicated to many charitable causes, and all proceeds from tonight's performance and silent auction will go directly to our local chapter of Community Hospice and Service Pets International. This organization primarily helps to house and train animals for local hospices and has recently started to train service animals to work with autistic children and adults. I appreciate your support tonight and also the generous time and donations by the Lyceum Philharmonic who plan a Broadway-themed performance. Please give them a hand for their dedication."

Jax gestured to the director, who came out from behind the curtain only briefly to acknowledge his contribution.

"Before we get started, I'd like to take a minute to indulge in a personal announcement. Many of you in the audience work for or with ZANE, so this will directly affect you. Recently, I've connected with my sister, who happens to be a terrific photographer. She's going to be joining the ZANE team, and promises to bring a fresh eye to future spreads. Please say hello to Gillian Michel. Stand, Gilly," he told her.

Gillian's legs shook as she pushed out of the chair. A light blinded her as she waved, plastering a smile on her face. She thought she'd be sick, embarrassed that she was deliberately about to lie to hundreds of people, that the lie would sever any chance she'd be able to see Dimitri again. She steadied herself by holding onto the railing, and waited for Jax to continue. Nervously, she stole a peek over her shoulder. *Where is Nick?*

"There's my baby sis. And I have wonderful news that I'd like to share, as it appears I'm going to be expanding my family further." The faces of a few of the females in the audience went pale and Jax laughed. "This news directly affects my sister, ladies. No worries…our date is still on for later," he joked.

Gillian waited for him to drop the bomb, and forced herself to open her eyes that she hadn't realized she'd closed. Like watching a scary movie, she couldn't take the suspense and had looked away. Everything about the moment felt incredibly wrong. She contemplated sneaking off to the airport, hopping a plane to some remote island where no one would ever find her. But running wasn't really her style. Even though she'd left Dimitri in Vegas, she'd done it to protect him. Hearing Jax's laughter reminded her that any minute now, her mating to Nick would be announced…that was if Nick actually showed up.

"So as I was saying, my family's about to grow. I'm thrilled to announce her intended mating to someone I'd be proud to call my brother." His declaration was met with several whistles from shifters in the audience. "In other words, she's getting engaged."

The patrons broke out in loud applause and Gillian thought the smile frozen on her face would get stuck. Her dry teeth glued to her lips, the muscles in her cheeks began to hurt.

"Before we get started, I'd like to introduce her mate, her fiancé, Dimitri LeBlanc. Everyone please put your hands together, and wish them a long life together," he told them with a broad smile, and gestured upward to her opera box.

Gillian's knees buckled as she heard Jax tell everyone in attendance that Dimitri was her mate. *Dimitri?* No, she must have heard him wrong. Where was Nick? Bewilderment rushed through her as a large familiar hand wrapped around her waist.

"Congratulations, darlin'," Dimitri whispered in her ear. His hard arousal left no room for interpretation. She gasped at his greeting, and he continued. "What do you say? Shall we put on a show?"

Gillian's heart stopped, hearing his voice. How could it be? What was he doing here? Shocked, her eyes widened as she turned her head to see Dimitri standing next to her. Towering over her small frame, he gave her a dashing smile, turning her legs into jello. Her gorgeous beta, dressed in a tux, casually slid a hand down her back. The well-fitted suit did little to hide his extraordinarily well-built physique, and the sight of him took her breath away. Her mouth gaped open; she was at a loss for words.

"I'll take that as a yes. I do enjoy an audience."

Gillian melted into Dimitri's arms as his mouth captured hers. Her tongue swept against his and she purred in pure joy. She moaned as Dimitri broke his kiss, yet she remained happily within his embrace. Overjoyed to see him, she slid her hands underneath his jacket, relishing his hard muscular body against hers. The taste of him remained on her lips, and she clung to him tightly, remorseful that she'd left him in Vegas. She heard him give a small chuckle and opened her eyes. Remembering that there were a couple of hundred people watching them, Gillian cleared her throat and caught sight of Jax, his eyes pinned on their display. All the while, she never let go of her beta.

"Well, folks, uh, now that we've had our first performance of the night, let the real show begin. I give you the Lyceum Philharmonic," Jax introduced and walked off the stage.

❧ *Chapter Nine* ❧

Dimitri didn't need more than one kiss to confirm that Gillian was his mate. Goddess, the woman looked stunning in her gown, but all he could think about was peeling it off of her. When Jax had called him with his plan, he hadn't been convinced it was the best course of action. He wanted to see Gillian again and had planned on coming to see her already, but to tell the world he'd found a mate? That pushed him straight out of his comfort zone, not to mention he wasn't sure how Gillian would react to the news.

Just the scent of her had turned his shaft harder than concrete. By the time he'd touched her, it took every ounce of restraint not to make love to her with the lights on. The touch of her hands burned through the thin fabric of his dress shirt and as the lights dimmed, he knew self-control was a lost cause.

The music roared to life and Dimitri guided them to their chairs in the private booth. His hand found her thigh and he gently squeezed.

"Did you just purr?" he whispered.

"Maybe," Gillian laughed.

"You missed me, didn't you?"

"I plead the fifth."

"Something tells me I'm going to enjoy being your mate." He waggled his eyebrows at her.

"I, um, did Jax tell you about…"

"Ah, yes, our great hoax. I'm here, aren't I?" *And it's no hoax, cher. You're my mate.*

Dimitri knew it'd only be a matter of days before the urge to mark her would surface. Fortunately for them both, she'd have to make a conscious choice to accept him, otherwise their mating would never happen. He was torn about this dilemma. On the one hand, he wasn't terribly thrilled about giving up his fun-loving bachelor days. On the other, Gillian drew him like no other woman; the attraction was unbearable. The fact that he'd flown up to New York City to engage in a public fake mating was proof of that.

"I'm surprised Jax called you. My brother…"

"Whoa, step back a second…you have a brother?"

"Jax."

"What about Jax? He's the Alpha of the New York pack. I had Logan call him, to protect you. Then Jax texted me last night."

"Yes, Jax." She looked out into the theater for Jax. He caught her gaze, nodded and gave her a knowing smile. She leaned back into her seat, realizing that Dimitri hadn't known about her family ties. "Dimitri…you do know that Jax is my brother?"

"Now that is an interesting development," he quipped.

When Jax had contacted Dimitri directly, asking him to assist with Gillian's protection, he'd suspected that the Alpha knew she'd met her mate. Even if she'd taken a shower, it was likely his scent was all over her skin. He'd have known they'd been intimate, that their relationship involved more than saving each other's lives. But Jax was her brother? That was a surprise. Nonetheless, it wouldn't deter him in the least from pursuing her.

"I take it you didn't know," she said softly.

"You guessed correctly, but it doesn't matter. Jax asked me to be here, and I already had the flight plan in before he called."

"You were coming...to see me?"

"Hell, yeah. Date number four. Although I'm afraid I won't be able to find out your secrets while we're here."

"No? Why not?" She smiled.

"Because making love to you is the only thing on my mind, cher."

"Here?" she whispered, her eyes widened.

"Here and now," he confirmed.

"But there're people down there...shifters...Jax. He'll know."

"And the problem is?" His fingers began to bunch up the fabric of her dress.

"Someone could hear us...scent us."

"You know what I love about these booths? They're nice and private. The folks across from us can barely see us...and so what if they do? This wall here in front of us, it's very handy." He tapped his palm on the rail.

Dimitri stood and lifted her chair, sliding it into the shadows. A deafening crescendo filled the air as the orchestra finished their first piece. As it ended, the theater went dark and Dimitri knelt before her. He gripped the hem of her dress and slid it upward, exposing her legs. Pressing his forehead against her knees, he heard himself groan in delight.

"Open," he ordered, his fingers pressing between her legs.

Dimitri caught the look of surprise in her eyes, but she obeyed, her thighs falling outward. His hands drifted over her smooth skin until he reached the edge of her lace panties. With his forefingers, he traced the rim down to her core, finding her drenched with arousal. Slipping under the fabric, he glided his fingertips over her mound until he was at her hips. Slowly, he dragged her thong down, until it hooked over her heels and he shoved it into his suit pocket.

"You're beautiful," he said, pressing his nose into her sex. "And mine."

Using only his tongue, he licked open her pussy, dragging the tip over her clit. With his thumbs, he separated her folds so that he could have better access to his prize. He laved around her swollen nub, never directly making contact. As her hips began to undulate in response, he hummed against her flesh.

Removing a hand, he sucked two of his fingers, and swiftly plunged them deep into her hot channel. In tandem with the music, he licked at her clitoris, curling his fingers against the thin strip of nerves inside of her. Her fingernails dug into his shoulders. He glanced up to her face, and caught her staring at him, lost in ecstasy. There was no one in the room as far as either of them was concerned.

Taking her swollen bead into his lips, he gently sucked and tugged. Gillian moaned as her pussy tightened around his fingers. Adding a third finger, he plunged in and out of her, until he felt her shake in release. Her juices flooded into his mouth as she clutched the back of his head, pressing his face to her clit.

Wrenching himself away from her, he stood, took her hand and led her to the back corner of the darkened room. In a theater full of shifters, they'd be heard, but in the recesses of the alcove, they wouldn't be seen. Roughly spinning her around, he unbuckled his pants and took out his rock-hard arousal. Gillian braced her hands against the wall, panting with desire. Dimitri stroked his dick, seed leaking from its tip.

"I'm going to fuck you, Gilly. You want this?" Dimitri prayed she'd say yes, but he wouldn't go forward if she didn't agree.

"Yes, please....don't stop," Gillian found herself begging. Her head spinning with lust, she needed him inside her.

Dimitri wrapped his hand around her waist, bending her ass toward him. Finding her wet opening, he guided his cock to her entrance and plunged into her in one smooth stroke. Her hot lubricated core immediately tightened around him almost making him come.

"Jesus, darlin'. You feel so good. Don't move…just hold it a sec." Dimitri felt as if he was a virgin, afraid he'd explode inside of her right away. He took a deep breath, regaining control, and began to slowly move, gradually increasing his pace.

"Dimitri…yes," Gillian breathed.

"You've been a very bad kitty, leaving me in Las Vegas." Dimitri pounded into her, sweat forming on his brow. "I'm looking forward to punishing you for taking off on me."

"Oh God, Dimitri. What? I'm sorry," she said, gasping.

"Goddess, you're incredible. So tight. And your pussy…" He reached to cup her mound, sliding his middle finger through her lips. Using the tip, he flicked at her clitoris.

"Ah yes, there. Don't stop…yes…yes."

Dimitri bent his knees, pumping up into her, harder and harder. His left hand pulled down the front of her dress, exposing her breasts. Gentle wasn't on the menu as he cupped her soft flesh, pinching her hardened nipple. She cried out, and reached to cover his hand, encouraging him to continue.

"Shhh, baby. You want everyone to hear?"

"You started this," she bit back at him, pressing her bottom into his thrusts.

"That I did, my little wild cat. How about we finish it together?" With his thumb, he applied pressure to her hooded pearl, circling and caressing.

"Dimitri...Dimitri...yes," she began to scream, despite his warning to quiet her moans.

He laughed, moving his hand from her breast to cover her mouth. But as he got near her lips, she bit him, sucking his fingers into her mouth and swirling her tongue around them as if she was giving him head. Between her pussy and mouth, he lost it, thrusting, heaving up into her. She contracted around his cock and his orgasm slammed into him.

Gillian wasn't sure whether it was the taste of him or his touch to her clit, but her senses crashed into overdrive. Her climax spread from her toes to the top of her head. She shook with ecstasy, incognizant of space and time. All that mattered was Dimitri. Her tiger begged her to submit, to let this man make her his. Only a thread of sanity remained, allowing her to refuse the beast.

As the last of the tremors left her body, Dimitri withdrew himself from her. Strong arms turned her around, taking her lips once again. This time, however, his searing kiss was gentle and all too intimate. As their lips lost contact and he carefully guided them to the floor, she rested her head on his chest.

Gillian couldn't believe she'd just made love with Dimitri. It was all supposed to be a great deception, one to lead her to safety. Yet within his loving embrace, she knew this was much more than just a passing one night stand. She craved him, mesmerized by his charming personality and dominant demeanor.

"You okay?" he asked, still catching his breath.

"More than okay. You?" she replied, not at all convinced that what she was saying was true. Sexually, she was spectacular. Emotionally, not so much. Stunned with the knowledge that she was officially addicted to a southern beta, she attempted to hide her obsession, praying it was just a chemical reaction.

Dimitri kept her comfortably wrapped in his arms, but released her hand to look at his own. Finding a perfect set of teeth marks indented into his skin, he laughed. And he'd thought he'd been too rough with her?

"Damn girl, you bit me!"

"Let me see." She took his palm and examined the damage. Kissing it, she spoke softly into his hand. "I'm so sorry I left marks on you. Are you bleeding?"

As soon as the words left her lips, she went still. *Marks. I marked him.* Not in the true sense of the word that a shifter would consider for mating, but she'd taken a step toward it.

"It's nothin'," Dimitri lied. His tiger had bitten him. In her defense, he'd put his fingers in her mouth, but the implications were that she'd considered claiming him. Despite the innocent nip, he suspected she had no idea she was his mate.

They lay quiet for several minutes, allowing the lull of contemplation to set into their minds. Rodgers and Hammerstein floated through the air and Dimitri closed his eyes, enjoying the feel of his mate against his chest. As *Some Enchanted Evening* came to a close, he sighed, deciding it was time to find out the truth.

"Why don't you want to be around wolves?"

"I can't."

"You just did."

"You're the first shifter I've ever been with," she admitted quietly.

"No other wolf? Not even a tiger?"

"Nope." She shook her head, still keeping her cheek close to his shirt.

"We're goin' to be spendin' a lot of time together."

"I suppose we are. This plan of Jax's. I'm not sure it's going to work."

"We've gotta smoke em' out. Chaz is a bad guy. If he hadn't sent those thugs here to find you, this would be a different conversation. I've been around a long time, and it's rare that someone's got the balls to send his pack onto another Alpha's territory. This guy, there's something not right with him. You're not safe."

"I'm glad you came."

"I told you we were going on another date. And as I recall, you said yes."

"I was under duress."

"Since when is coming considered duress?" he asked, his hand stroking over her stomach. Shit, he'd just made love to her and his cock was stirring once again.

"That was amazing."

"Now or then?"

"Both," she laughed. "I've never been able to just let go. I really am sorry that I bit you."

"We're just getting started, cher. I assure you. We're goin' to be doin' all kinds of things."

"I wish I could say I wasn't looking forward to it, but I am." She kissed his chest.

"That's the spirit," he cheered. Dimitri reached up and untied his bow tie, unbuttoning the first few buttons of his shirt. "You're avoiding my question."

"I know. Too many ears here in the theater."

"Fair enough, but you owe me, understood?"

"Yes." She smiled, aware that she wanted to tell him, not because he was asking, but because she wanted a solution to her problem. The beta had been relentless, and now, she feared she couldn't go back to the lonely life she'd once led. In the course of a week, her entire perspective on life had shifted.

It was no use to lie. They'd be pretending to be mates. Gillian had no idea what that really meant. But the warning of her mother's words rang in her ears. *Mate a wolf, your tiger will die.*

❧ *Chapter Ten* ❧

Gillian raised her head, gazing into Dimitri's eyes. When the music stopped, the curtains to their booth flew open. Jax, the devastatingly handsome Nordic wolf, leered down on the lovers, who smiled up at him in amusement.

"I said pretend to be her mate. At any point, did you hear me say, 'Come up to New York and fuck my sister in public...during one of my company events?' Did I say that? I really don't recall saying that." Jax scrubbed his fingers over his tightly cropped hair. He moved to the balcony, overlooking the patrons who were shuffling into the lobby for the intermission.

"Sorry." Dimitri laughed. He knew that they should have been slightly less conspicuous but the draw of his mate had been too much to resist.

"Sorry? Really? That's all you've got?" He turned to Gillian, who scrambled up to her feet, adjusting her dress. "And you? What's your excuse, little sister? Seriously, every shifter in the room could hear you."

"Um, well, yeah, sorry about that. But technically this is your fault. I mean, what did you expect? You asked Dimitri to come here...to pretend to be my mate." Gillian reasoned that her comeback sounded solid, inexperienced in dealing with her Alpha brother.

"This isn't funny, Gilly," he growled.

Dimitri put himself between Jax and his sister, hiding his grin.

"It's cool, man. Look, the only ones who could have possibly heard us were shifters. You just announced us as mates. You know full well that any shifters wouldn't think twice about us puttin' a little rhythm into a musical number. No harm, no foul."

"You don't know what harm you can do to my sister..."

"Jax." Gillian shot her brother a glare in warning. It was her place to tell Dimitri her secret, not his.

Jax sighed, reconsidering his words. "I asked you up here because it was obvious to me that you already had a relationship with my sister. That, and that you can protect her. Don't make me regret it."

"I swear it on my life, but I'd like to remind you that even though I saved her, she saved me. She's badass when she goes cat."

"I'm sorry, it's just that some of the folks in my pack aren't too crazy about having a tiger stay with the Alpha. They don't trust her. I haven't seen hide nor hair of Chaz's pack and..." Jax paused. Retrieving his cell phone from his inner jacket pocket, he swiped at it with the pad of his finger. "Goddammit."

"What's up?" Dimitri asked. The hard crease in the Alpha's forehead told him something bad was going down. He'd seen that look too many times from Logan, and he knew the shit was about to hit the fan.

"Drive-by shooting in front of my building."

"Not good."

"But this is the city…I know you live uptown, but still…" Gillian argued.

"Something's off. I can't explain this to you, sis, but I just know. It's part of the reason I asked Dimitri to come for you."

"But you killed that wolf yesterday."

"Yes, but the fact that they were able to get in the city unnoticed…it's not safe for you here. I need to stay and sort things out as best I can, and then I'll come for you."

"It could be internal," Dimitri theorized. Someone within Jax's own pack may have known about Chaz's wolves, allowed them to get close to his home.

"I'd like to think it's too early to speculate. As much as I trust you to take care of Gilly, you're not from our pack. So this discussion's done."

"No worries. I hear ya." Dimitri knew that Jax would keep his cards close to the vest. No matter how cordial he'd been so far, Jax was an Alpha for a reason. Dimitri had almost killed one Alpha on the west coast, the last thing he needed was to challenge Jax.

"What are you trying to say?" Dimitri heard Gillian ask. He felt a tinge of sympathy for her. She hadn't grown up around pack, and was clearly having trouble seeing the picture that Jax was drawing.

"You're leaving. Now," Jax said, putting his phone away.

"What do you mean I'm leaving? I just got here. You said I had a job with ZANE. I've gotta work. You can't just cart me around." Her voice grew louder.

"Gilly, it's going to be okay," Dimitri began. He got that she felt out of control. The past week had been hell for her and she sought some peace in the storm. But Dimitri knew that yelling at an Alpha was a bad idea even if she wasn't a wolf. "We're mates. It'd be expected that you'd travel with me, and I with you. You ever been to Mardi Gras?" Dimitri gave Jax a knowing look, hoping he'd throw him a bone.

"That's right, Gilly. We can do a spread for the magazine on Mardi Gras. Maybe a 'past meets future' feature. Talk to locals, get some photos. Help readers who don't live there get a feel for what it's like."

"That's a great idea. There's so much history. We can check out the parades. I know you'll enjoy it."

"Chaz is going to come for me there, you know."

"Yes, he is. And we'll be ready. Believe me, he won't be able to hide in the shadows like he's doin' here. We can always go straight to the bayou if we think the city's not an option. We'll call Logan from the plane, set up a plan of action."

"Nick and I will be down as soon as we clean things up here. I swear it."

Gillian silently resigned herself to the fact that she'd be leaving New York. Wrapping her arms around herself, she nodded in agreement.

Dimitri took off his jacket and draped it over her shoulders. He locked eyes with Jax as he put his arm around her. Understanding passed between them; the Alpha knew she was his mate. Logan would know, too. Dimitri, himself, wasn't comfortable with the idea, but it didn't matter. Gillian could easily choose to reject his wolf, his mark and their mating. Chaz had attempted to mark her, and not even a scar remained. Why would he be any different? They'd made love, but he didn't trust that she wouldn't leave him. She'd been upfront, telling him that she didn't want to be with a wolf. It still hadn't made sense to him, because he'd never heard of a wolf mating with a tiger, not even a hybrid.

Everything about her was different. Too different. She was a loner, never relying on others for hunting, friendship. Even if every issue resolved itself, there was the huge elephant in the room; his pack. Would his pack accept another shifter into their lives?

Gillian tensed as they pulled onto the tarmac and the deafening engine of the Learjet roared to life. She carefully navigated the steps up into the cabin, the warmth of Dimitri on her back reminding her that she wasn't alone. Trying to appear nonchalant, she slid into a cream-colored leather chair. Gillian wasn't used to this kind of luxury. Flying coach, jammed in the middle seat, last row was more her style.

Dimitri gave her a warm smile, and it was as if someone had wrapped her in a protective cocoon. From the second she'd met him, it felt as if she'd fallen down the rabbit hole. Surreal, it had gone against everything she'd ever known. But as she watched him take off his coat and roll up the sleeves of his white dress shirt, she couldn't help but think about being in his arms again. For the first time in her life, she considered what her life would be like without her feline spirit. Could she wake up in the morning with the knowledge that she couldn't shift? Even if she managed to transition to wolf, how would she feel being forced to submit within pack? Would Dimitri only want to mate her so he'd receive the gift she'd sacrifice to be with him?

She gazed out the tiny oval window at the flickering runway lights trailing off into the distance and shoved the thoughts to the back of her mind. She needed to focus, to attempt to shake the lust from her mind and think clearly. Chaz had somehow learned of her gifts. What if Dimitri had found out too? What wolf wouldn't want to have both the power of a tiger and wolf? Dimitri'd told her that he didn't want to be Alpha, but she didn't know him well enough to trust that he really meant it. All she knew for certain was that he didn't want to leave New Orleans, his Acadian wolf pack. Observing him interact with his own Alpha would provide further insight to his intentions.

A familiar voice captured her attention and her eyes caught Jake's.

Casually dressed, in jeans and button down shirt, he was as handsome as she'd remembered. *Are all wolves this freakin' hot? No wonder my mom told me to stay away from packs.* She tried to hide the smile that crossed her face, and he laughed. Her stomach rolled, and she prayed he didn't read minds.

"Hey, Gil," he greeted. "Ya ready for a little fun in the Big Easy?"

"Fun? Yeah, if that's what you'd call being on the run from a maniacal jackass." She grinned and nodded. "Something tells me you're a glass half full kind of a guy."

"You bet. Besides, you two seem no worse for wear. Dimitri's in a good mood, that's for sure."

"He either wants to go on another date with me or he really likes cats," she laughed, knowing he scented Dimitri on her once again.

"I suspect it's a bit of both."

"I was just joking. It's more like he and Jax decided I was going on a trip."

"I wasn't. Logan's got a cat. Mojo. Dimitri is constantly talking to it like a baby. Kissing it. Embarrassing really. You'd think the damn thing was the Alpha, the way it does whatever it wants."

"Ah…that's the thing about us cats, we don't take orders very well."

"Is that so?" he chuckled. "I can't wait to see how that works out for the both of you."

Dimitri came out from the cockpit, and caught the tail end of their conversation.

"Don't you worry about Gilly, bro. She'll do just fine. Although I do owe her for leaving me in Vegas," he commented, casting Gillian a devious glance.

"You wouldn't have gone to see the witch if I had let you come with me to New York," she began.

"And that's your first mistake, kitten. It was all good in Vegas." Even though he felt like shit by the time he'd gotten to Ilsbeth, he wouldn't admit it to her. "I know you like your independence, but there's no foolin' around at home with my pack. I give the orders and you listen."

Gillian resisted the urge to roll her eyes…exactly why she didn't want to be with wolves.

"Cat got your tongue?" Jake teased. "I don't think she's gonna submit easily, my friend."

"Submit? Who said anything about me submitting? I'm going on a plane ride to take pictures of Mardi Gras. Technically, I'm working. While you all are begging for doggie treats, I'll be happily on my own, snapping pics of the city," she taunted. Unsure of why she goaded the two men, Gillian cautiously chose her words, aware there was a line she should not cross.

"You've got your hands full, beta," Jake responded. He laughed out loud, holding his hand to his abdomen.

"It'll be my pleasure when you do submit," Dimitri promised, coming up behind her chair. He knelt behind her, wrapping a strong arm around her chest. His fingers lingered on her collarbone as he whispered into her ear loud enough for Jake to hear. "And when you do, I'll make sure Jake's there to watch. After all, you seemed to take quite nicely to it earlier tonight. I'm thinking you liked having a little audience."

Gillian's eyes met Jake's and her nipples hardened at Dimitri's statement. *Damn it all.* Blood rushed to her cheeks, and she fought the urge to moan as his lips pressed to her neck. Her head lolled back onto his shoulder. Closing her eyes, she reveled in the sensation of his tongue behind her ear, causing her to break out in gooseflesh. She sighed, her pussy aching in arousal. Surprised, cold abandonment washed over her when Dimitri stood and walked away.

"What?" she said, blinking her eyes in disbelief. *Wait. Where is he going?*

"Sorry, cher. Gotta sit down. We're taking off. Better buckle up," Dimitri said with a wink. He enjoyed playing with Gillian, gauging her willingness to submit.

"Things were taking off, all right. Just came to a screeching halt." She caught the sly grin on his face, and realized he was teasing her.

"You're evil," she said, feigning anger with him. Jake shook his head and laughed. She'd completely forgotten that he'd been there, watching them. "Both of you."

Gillian crossed her legs and squeezed them tightly together. Her tiger roared, letting her know that she yearned for the beta. Gillian's lips tightened in a fine line. *No, no, no. No submission. No mating. No giving up my nature.* She could feel Dimitri's eyes burning through the back of her head as she stared out the window. The plane lifted off and soon there was nothing but blackness.

Dimitri's dick was as hard as a lead pipe. Hours ago, they'd been intimate, and he couldn't wait to be inside his mate again. Glancing at Jake, it wasn't lost on Dimitri how his friend looked at Gillian. He resisted telling Jake to put his eyes back into his head, as they roamed her body. Her fiery spirit and quick wit would be enough for any man to find her attractive, but tonight, she looked incredibly sexy, her toned thigh peeking through the slit. Dimitri wasn't the jealous type, having shared women with both Logan and Jake. Yet the wolf in him wouldn't allow it until she'd allowed him to mark her as his, to begin the mating process.

Needing to talk with her alone, Dimitri gestured with his hand, in an effort to get Jake to leave. His friend shrugged in response and made his way out of the main cabin. Dimitri knew that Jake was probably thinking he just wanted to join the mile high club. While that option was fully on the table, he and Gillian first needed to clear the air about why she was so resistant to dating him. The knowledge that she was his mate was a secret that he couldn't keep for much longer.

"Gilly," he called to her with a smile. His kitten had been aroused by his words, suggesting the terms of her submission. He suspected that she was intrigued by it, the idea of Jake watching. Interesting that she'd conceal her desires, yet he looked forward to testing her limits.

"Yes," she responded, her face still flushed.

"Let's go lay down. The seatbelt sign is off and Jake's gone up to talk with the pilot," he said, pushing out of his chair.

Dimitri held out his hand, smiling as she put hers in his. He led them to a sofa that had a long chaise. He released her briefly, so he could reach up to retrieve a pillow from out of the overhead compartment. Throwing it onto the couch, he sat down, bringing her with him.

"Lie back," he directed. Pleased that she did what he asked, he took her feet into his hands and slipped off her shoes.

"Not sure how you women walk around in these," he commented, massaging her instep. Gillian moaned, and he laughed.

"Oh my God, that feels so good," she sighed, laying her head back.

"So tell me, what's the deal with not wanting to be around wolves? I know you didn't want to tell me before at the theater, but now, it's just you and me."

"You want the truth?" Gillian's eyes flashed open.

"No, I want you to lie to me. Of course I want the truth. No more coy excuses. The plan ole truth will suffice," Dimitri told her.

"Seeing that we made love, I suppose I owe you as much. But for the record, I wasn't trying to lie to you. It's more like I was protecting myself." She tried to pull her foot away from him, but Dimitri held her tight.

"No running. Spill."

"I told you before that a wolf can't mark me," she explained. Even though his touch calmed her animal spirit, she'd never told anyone else and her voice began to tremble. "If I choose a mate, and I must be the one to make the decision, then it will happen. I'm a rare breed of tiger. Maljavan. That's why I can mate a wolf. Most shifters can't mate outside their breed. Even hybrids can't, not unless they're human."

"No doubt, you're strong enough to take on most wolves, individually anyhow, but I still don't get why you don't want to date a wolf."

"Because...if I mate..." her voice faltered.

"Hey, it's okay. You can tell me," he cajoled. Dimitri released her foot, slid next to her and adjusted her body so that she lay on his chest.

"My tiger...she'll die," Gillian managed. It was the first time she'd said the words out loud.

"I'll admit, I've never heard of a tiger, or any other shifter for that matter, mating with a wolf, but shifters don't just die."

"Mine will." Gillian lifted her head and turned to look in his eyes. "She'll die. My mother mated with my dad. The Alpha. Afterwards, she never shifted again."

"She's mortal? I thought you said your mom was alive?"

"She's alive. She hasn't aged but she doesn't shift. Not ever. Jax said he thinks she may have turned wolf when she mated, but denied her beast."

"What do you think?"

"Remember when I healed you?"

"Yeah?" Dimitri pulled her closer.

"Your wolf. It was weak." Gillian slid her fingers underneath his unbuttoned shirt, touching his abdomen. "I can sense him. I haven't done it very often but I knew. My mom, I've hugged her, touched her hand. I feel nothing. It's as if she's human."

"But how do you know what you're saying is true? Is there anyone else you can ask in your family?"

"I told you, we're a solitary species. I don't even know my grandparents. From the small amount of research I've done, it seems that if I mate with a wolf, it's unlikely my tiger would survive. There's a small chance that my wolf, which I highly doubt even exists, would show herself."

"So you avoid wolves because you don't want to meet your mate?"

"I can't risk it."

Dimitri sighed, disappointed that she couldn't feel what he felt. He knew she was his mate. She hadn't a clue. Worse, if she chose him, she might not be able to ever shift again. Yet he suspected there was more to the story.

"It still doesn't make sense why Chaz is after you. What does he get out of it if you're no longer a tiger?"

"I don't know what he knows," she lied. She didn't want to tell him that whoever she mated with would receive the gifts of her tiger. He'd run faster, have the claws of a feline, would possibly even be able to shift into a cat.

"You're sure about that?" Dimitri pressed, sensing she was hiding the truth.

"I don't really know. Maybe he just wants to say he killed a tiger. It doesn't matter because the only way I'll mate is if I choose it. I'm very much like a human that way."

"So if you met a wolf, your mate...you wouldn't consider it?"

"Do you remember what it felt like not to be able to shift?"

"Hell yeah, it was terrible..." Could he ask her to give up her cat just so he could be with his mate?

"What if I couldn't shift? Would you choose a mate who'd never be able to run with you? Someone who was practically human?"

"I'd choose the person I'm supposed to be with. Sorry, darlin' but I believe in fate. I also believe in mates. You can call it chemistry, if it makes you feel better. But with wolves, we know when we find a mate...it's meant to be. The more ya fight it, the worse it gets. The desire to mark, to mate her will become intolerable. The wolf must be satisfied. There are some things in life you can control and some you can't."

"What if you couldn't shift? You felt what it was like on the beach that night, not to be able to shift. What if you were like that, vulnerable, forever?"

Dimitri grew quiet as she spoke his worst fear. Ilsbeth still hadn't found a cure. The tonic in his duffle bag was only temporary. He hadn't told a soul about his prognosis, not even Logan.

"You saw the witch?" When Dimitri shrugged in response, Gillian withdrew her hand from his shirt and pushed up to see his expression. "What? You saw her, right? I can feel your wolf now. What aren't you telling me?"

"I saw her," Dimitri said with a small grin.

"So? What happened? Did she do a spell?"

"Yeah." Guilt churned in his belly as the memory of the naked witches played in his mind. He shouldn't have let Ilsbeth so close. When she'd kissed him, he'd gone cold. Now that he'd made love with Gillian, the knowledge that he'd touched the witch made him sick.

"It worked?" Gillian brushed her fingers over his jaw.

"Yes." Dimitri justified his answer by telling himself that his wolf was alive…for now. He questioned what to do with his mate. Not only could he lose his ability to shift, asking her to mate with him could cause her to lose hers as well.

"Is there something wrong?" she asked.

"No, cher. Just thinkin' is all," he answered. Dimitri yearned to tell her that she was his mate, but now that he knew why she'd avoided wolves, he doubted his original plan. His avoidance couldn't continue forever, he knew. The more he was around her, the greater the attraction would grow. His wolf would demand that he mark her, mate her.

"If you're worried about me being around your pack, finding a mate, I'll just stay away from the other wolves. Jax will come for me soon." She hoped. "We could always just stay in bed for the next five days. I'm sure that'll keep me safe."

"Now what makes you think that? How do you know that I'm not your mate?" he laughed.

"Well, I don't know. I mean, I'm not a wolf, but wouldn't I know something like that? I always just figured that some kind of wolf ESP would kick in if I were around wolves…that I'd just know."

"And then?" *Goddess, she really doesn't know.*

"Well, I'd have to stay as far away as possible. That's always been my plan." She slid her hand lower, past his belly button and wrapped her leg over his.

"Someday, you may find that doesn't work so well," he advised. Soon, he'd be forced to tell her. The closer he allowed himself to get to her, the worse it would be when they had to part ways. As much as his wolf wanted this woman, he couldn't be the one to kill her tiger.

"I never thought I'd date a wolf," she reflected, her fingers grazing his beltline.

"You admit we're dating?" Dimitri's cock thickened as her fingers played with the trail of hair below his abdomen.

"I don't know what's really going on. I just know that tonight when you showed up, I was so relieved."

"Not a fan of Nick?"

"Nick's fine. He's nice," she said and took a deep breath. "But there's something about you. I just...I don't know what it is. Tonight...what you did to me, what we did. I've never felt that way before."

"There's something about you, too, cher."

"I've never done anything like that in public...never even thought about it. It was crazy."

"I'm looking forward to teaching you all kinds of things."

"But Dimitri...we can't keep doing this. It's dangerous."

"How so?"

"I don't want to get hurt."

"I'd never hurt you...ever." His voice grew serious.

"But what if you find your mate?"

"What about it?" *You are my mate, little one*, he thought to himself.

"I'm not the kind of girl who plays around a lot. Between the wolves and not finding a tiger, I've only been with humans. They've never been enough," she admitted.

"Too tame?" he guessed.

"Yeah, it's just, like tonight...when we made love...God, I felt wild. I've never felt like that before."

"So what's the problem?"

"You could find your mate. I've heard that wolves don't commit to anyone else. Don't get me wrong, I mean, we just met, but I'm not a 'friends with benefits' kind of girl."

"What makes you think I wouldn't commit to a woman?"

"Because that's how wolves are."

"That's how a lot of people are, not just wolves," he countered.

"True, but humans are different. Hybrids are different. They aren't sitting around waiting to find a mate. Seriously, have you ever dated someone for a long time, committed to them, knowing they weren't your mate?" she asked.

"Well, no, but that doesn't apply here."

"What would happen if you committed to a girl and then your mate came along?" Gillian pinned him on the spot, getting to the crux of her argument.

"The attraction to one's mate cannot be denied. There've been many women I've cared about. I'm not a callous man. But with my mate, it's chemistry. Nature, fate at its finest. No matter who I'm seeing...who I've seen in the past, they will all pale in comparison to her." Dimitri dug his fingers into her hair, loosening the pins. "I won't be able to resist her. I may have been a single man, but she'll change my life."

"And that's why we can't continue. What if you find her? Even if you weren't looking…"

"I haven't been looking…it'll be destiny."

"Exactly. You won't mean to hurt my feelings, but you will. You won't have a choice."

"I told you once…I'll tell you a million times, darlin', I'll never hurt you. It's not meant to be." Dimitri wished he could tell her she was his mate, but now that he knew the truth about what their mating would do to her, he needed to think about what to do. As he twirled his finger into her hair, he wondered if maybe Ilsbeth could help them. She'd be pissed as hell, but even the witch couldn't deny his preordained future.

"Why do I want to believe you? I really do, you know. But we both know that if you meet your mate, I'll be but a distant memory."

"You need to trust me."

"I'm learning to trust you. But even you can't control what the universe has in store for you. So this is why we can't keep doing what we just did…it's only going to make it harder."

"Do you know how beautiful you are?"

"No. Are you changing the subject?" she giggled.

"I can't seem to keep my hands off you," he admitted, rubbing her neck.

"Staying away from you…it won't be easy," she breathed.

"Impossible," he agreed. Letting his fingers drift down her chest, he lightly stroked her skin. "We'll be careful…we shouldn't stop."

"What you said to me earlier…about submitting. Why'd you say that?"

"Your submission?" He'd meant it at the time, telling her he'd do it in front of Jake. Now, however, that he knew what he could do to her beast, he had second thoughts about moving forward.

"I've never submitted to anyone."

"Maybe you haven't found the right person."

"You mean, the right wolf?"

"No, I mean person. Someone you trust. Someone who you feel so comfortable with that you will allow your true nature to surface. That person…you'd want to be wild and uninhibited without judgment."

"I don't know. Giving myself to someone, unconditionally trusting them?"

"Yes, exactly that…like tonight in the booth. It's not something you have to plan, it can just happen."

"I lost myself…I was so happy to see you."

"What do you want?" he breathed as her hand skimmed under his waistband. "Gilly, do you know what you're doing to me?"

"I want you…now," Gillian found herself saying, unsure of why she couldn't control her own feelings for Dimitri. Her hips began to undulate against his leg and her fingers traveled through the springy hair above his shaft. "Just one more time."

"One more time," he repeated. As she turned her head to look in his eyes, he kissed her gently, licking and nipping.

"Dimitri," she moaned, her tongue sweeping against his. Gillian's hand reached down past his dick, teasing the crease where his groin met his thigh.

"Aw, fuck. Take my cock," he growled. She ran the tip of her fingers over his skin, toying with him, and he ordered her again. "Now, Gilly."

Gillian did as he told her, fisting him, and he hissed. Fuck if it didn't turn him on even more to watch her obey his demand. He could tell she was inexperienced and the fact she'd opened to him the way she'd done told him it was in her nature to experiment. Thankful that destiny had given him a curious mate, he swore he had to find a way to keep her.

"That's it...just like that...ah, yeah," he encouraged as she gently pumped him.

"You're so hard," she whispered, sliding the tip of her forefinger over his wet slit. Using the moisture, she gripped him, stroking his length.

He slid his hand down her chest, tugging the fabric down until she was exposed. Cupping her soft breast, he pressed his lips into her hair. The hard length of him throbbed, needing release. Considering his words, he decided to push her limits.

"Unbuckle my pants," he told her. "Get up on your knees."

"But Jake could..."

"Yes," he responded, knowing that Jake might return. She'd grown aroused earlier when he'd suggested she liked being watched. She lifted her head and her eyes met his. "Do as I say, Gilly."

Gillian's gaze locked on his as she pushed upward, straddling his legs. Her hands reached for the front of her dress to cover herself.

"Leave it. I want to see you," he said, the back of his knuckles brushing over her nipples. They stood at attention in response. "Look how hot you are."

"I...I...what if someone sees me?" she replied, her head turning to the cockpit and back to Dimitri.

"Doesn't matter. Leave it down. You're beautiful."

Gillian's pussy dampened at his demand. On a visceral level she hadn't known existed, she wanted this, to please him, to explore her sexuality with Dimitri. Despite her desire, her face turned red as she acquiesced. The fabric of her dress bunched up around her hips as she leaned forward and began to unbuckle his belt. Slowly she freed his cock from his pants, taking it back into her hands.

"Now suck me," he told her.

With her eyes on his, Gillian bent over, her lips parted as she guided him into her mouth. The salty taste of his essence hit her tongue and her tiger came to life with hunger. She licked his broad head, enjoying the power she felt, knowing she could bring him pleasure. Cold air hit her core as her bottom lifted into the air, reminding her that Dimitri had taken her panties earlier. The ache between her legs grew painful and she tilted her hips, attempting to relieve the pressure.

A sound behind her alerted her that they were no longer alone, and she saw Jake out of the corner of her eye. He looked as if he'd eat her alive. Gillian knew that wolves were a sexually open breed, but she'd never been exposed to their ways. For but a second, she considered her dark fantasy of what it would be like to have both men at once. Even though she found Jake attractive, it was Dimitri she craved. Her eyes fell back to her wolf and his eyes locked on hers. He gave her a wicked smile as if he knew what she'd been thinking. Their connection drove her desire, and her attention went to his thick flesh. Lost in her own lust, she took him into her mouth again.

Gillian had never had sex in front of another man, let alone a wolf. It should have felt wrong but it only made her pussy throb in excitement. She glanced to see where Jake had gone but he was nowhere in sight. Confused by her slight disappointment that he wasn't watching, she shook off the guilt that she'd even had the thought. If she stayed with Dimitri, he'd push her boundaries further than anyone she'd ever dated. This had to be the last time they made love. She had to cut her addiction to him before she needed an intervention to leave. Tonight she'd have him, though. Like eating a gallon of ice cream the day before a diet, she indulged, bingeing on all that was Dimitri.

Releasing his shaft, she climbed up his torso. Positioning her entrance above his cock, she flattened her hands beside his head. She reached between her legs and swiped his hard sex through her wet folds, stimulating her clitoris. Throwing her head back, she hissed, flicking his plump head against her tight opening.

"Ah yes, fuck me. Now," Dimitri demanded. He tilted his hips upward, his erection probing at her wetness.

Gillian grunted as she impaled herself on him. His broad cock stretched her channel, and she lowered herself all the way down until her clit brushed against his bristly hair. Slowly, she began to grind her pelvis against his, her taut nub engorged in arousal. Leaning forward, she darted her tongue against his chest, tracing the lines of his tattoos, until she reached his nipple. Taking the hard tip between her teeth, she tugged until Dimitri released a groan.

She lifted her hips, so that he slid out of her, then with a hard drop, she descended, pressing him deep inside. Her orgasm built as Dimitri increased the pace. His fingers dug into her hips and she moaned against his chest. Her pussy quivered as her climax rolled through her.

Dimitri took her soft breast into his hand as Gillian contracted around his cock. Plunging himself into her over and over, he bent his head forward, guiding her rosy nipple into his mouth. The pulsations around his cock caused him to buck uncontrollably. With a primal cry, he stiffened in release, his seed erupting deep inside her.

Gillian collapsed in ecstasy atop him and they both panted, attempting to catch their breath. Dimitri reached to flip the back of her dress over her bare bottom. But before he did so, he slapped her ass. She squeaked, but didn't move an inch. Seconds passed, and he wondered why she'd gone still. Dimitri pushed the hair away from her face, and tilted his head to observe a small grin on her face. Her eyes closed, she'd fallen asleep. He lay his head back onto the sofa and dreamed of a long life with his mate. The only way he'd be able to have her was if he could find a way to save her, to ease her transition through the mating. But before he did that, he'd have to find a way to save himself.

⟶⟨ Chapter Eleven ⟩⟵

Dimitri stared at the spread of pain perdu, grits, and creole cream cheese with berries and sugar. Wearing only an apron around his hips, he took a quick swig of his freshly squeezed Satsuma juice before cracking an egg. The timer buzzed and he nearly burned his fingers, forgetting to don an oven mitt.

"Goddammit," he swore.

For the past two days, Gillian had stayed in his home, and he was crawling the walls. True to her word, she'd insisted that making love on the plane had to be their final tryst. As such, he'd situated her in his guest room. Like a teenager with his first girly magazine, he'd spent a good portion of the time since then holed up in the bathroom, jerking off in a cold shower. And she'd been just as guilty, secluding herself in her bedroom. It wasn't as if he couldn't hear her soft moans as she touched herself. The scent of her arousal filtered throughout the house, driving him insane with desire.

The morning after they'd arrived, a delivery containing a camera and computer equipment arrived, courtesy of Jax. Gillian had used it as an excuse to ignore him, but today, he'd told her they'd go to see one of his favorite Krewes' parades.

If he didn't get out of the house soon, he was going to fuck her senseless or lose his mind. His sanity was stretched far. Not hearing from Ilsbeth only added stress to the situation. He'd texted her a dozen times, but she hadn't called him back. He needed a damn cure for his wolf. When he'd made love to Gillian, something about their lovemaking had energized his spirit. But two days later, without his skin on hers, he could feel his ability to shift waning. Earlier he'd taken a double dose of the tonic, and he still wasn't feeling well.

Out of desperation, he'd begun cooking. While he usually found the culinary arts a calming hobby, he was far gone. He'd already cooked enough breakfast to feed the entire pack and he'd just started on the grillades. Hearing a rap on his door, Dimitri called out to Jake.

"Come in," he said, rummaging in the drawers for a meat mallet.

"Holy fuck, bro. What in the hell?" Jake's eyes widened at the sight of all the food and his friend wearing next to nothing.

"Help yourself," Dimitri said. He turned away, postponing the inevitable conversation that he'd delayed since the flight.

"Listen, D. I don't know what the fuck is going on with you but I haven't seen you cook this much food since Marcel died. Not that I don't appreciate a good meal, but damn." Jake sat at the kitchen counter, took a plate and snatched a biscuit off of the tray Dimitri held in his hands. "Ah…so good. You make the best muffins. God rest my mamma's soul, these are the best I've ever had. Butter?"

"Honey?"

"Yeah, now stop with the shit. When are ya gonna spill it? Don't think I didn't notice you weren't sharin' on the plane." Jake raised his eyebrows at Dimitri and smiled. "That's right, beta. You wanna tell me or should I say it? No, I take that back. I'm not making it that easy for you."

"It's complicated." Dimitri lifted the last pastry off the pan and dropped it into the bread basket.

"It always is, friend." He picked up the honey bear and squeezed it onto his plate. "The question is…is it your wolf or your tiger?"

Dimitri picked up a dishtowel and wiped his hands. "Try both."

"What's the good news?"

"What the fuck do you mean, what's the good news? I'm not sure there is any right now. Keep your voice down," he shushed, glancing behind him. "She's in the shower, but she's goin' to be out soon, and I don't want her to hear us."

"You do know I'm a wolf and not a psychic, right?" Jake smeared the sticky sweet mixture onto the flaky bread and took another bite.

"Let's start with my wolf."

Jake chewed. His mouth stuffed with food, he gestured with his hand for Dimitri to continue.

"Ilsbeth didn't cure me. Whatever the hell hooked itself onto me is eatin' at my wolf like a fifty-foot tapeworm."

"Hey," Jake protested. "Easy there…I'm eating."

"She said it's like a parasite. Not like a possession or anything like that. But it's bad. She's lookin' for a spell, but she hasn't returned my calls."

Dimitri took a stool and pulled it to the other side of the kitchen bar. He sat down and reached for a plate.

"But Gillian did something to you in San Diego? She healed you. Can't she keep doing that?"

"Well, yeah. But again, it's complicated."

"Logan's going to know. You're his beta, for Christ's sake."

"Know what?"

"D, you may not mind lying to yourself, but come on."

"Not lying…just hungry." Dimitri took a big scoop of grits and shoveled it into his mouth, with a smile.

"The plane. I saw Gilly with your cock…"

Dimitri held his fingers to his lips and then pointed down to the hallway, which led to the bedrooms.

Jake shook his head and continued. "I saw her. She saw me. You saw me. And neither of you minded. But and this is a big but for you, because I'll give her the benefit of the doubt, you didn't even so much as ask me to watch, let alone join you. Now, I may not know Gillian that well but I know you. You, me and a hot chick on a long plane ride, and you ignore me? Well, that speaks volumes. And do you know what that says?"

"What?"

"Really? You're going to make me say it?"

Dimitri grinned.

"Okay, fine. Have it your way." Jake snatched another biscuit. "My point is that you like her. A lot. Too much. And you were possessive, a trait that's not necessarily a bad thing but highly unusual for you."

"She's my mate," Dimitri whispered. "Don't make me say it again, 'cause I told you it's complicated."

"Not possible. She's a tiger," Jake replied. "Hybrids can't mate either. You must be confused. Maybe what you feel has to do with what's got your wolf. No way she's your mate."

"Keep it down, will ya?"

"Hey, mum's the word. But I'm still not buying it."

"I know. It makes no sense. She said that something about her breed gives her the ability to mate with a wolf. But the mating isn't a given. She can deny any mate she finds. It's why Chaz's mark doesn't stay on her."

"That's a neat trick," Jake quipped.

"Yeah, I could almost deal with that one. When I'm with her, it's just like we're combustible…she's so hot," he reflected. "The other thing is that my wolf seems to shake off this thing that's killin' him, or at least, I can't feel it when I'm with her, skin to skin."

"So why aren't you with her?"

"Catch number two. Long story short, if she takes a mate, she says it'll kill her tiger."

Jake gave him a look of confusion.

"Apparently, when her mom mated a wolf, she lost her ability to shift."

"Having a wolf for a mate is a death sentence? No wonder she avoids wolves."

"Thanks so much for puttin' it out there like that, but yeah, if we mate, she makes it sound like she'll never shift into a cat again. She's hybrid. Maybe she'd shift into a wolf? Who the hell knows? Like I said, complicated." Dimitri sighed. "And to top it all off, she doesn't recognize me as her mate. Not a clue. Nor does she know that my wolf isn't healed."

"Still waiting on good news," Jake joked.

"It gets better…wait for it…and then there's Ilsbeth," Dimitri continued, pushing up out of his chair. He reached for a bowl of eggs and began to whisk. "She wants me to move in with her."

"You gotta be shittin' me."

"I wish. The ceremony she did involved a bunch of naked witches and one very horny Ilsbeth telling me her spell didn't work and that I should be with her at all times in case something happened."

"Hell, no."

"She kissed me."

"The witch still has the hots for you?" Jake laughed.

"I told her it wasn't going to work," Dimitri continued. "And now that I've found my mate...well, you know that's not going to go over well. Ilsbeth's already a tad cranky."

"Goddess, that woman is beautiful," Jake began, "but so is a samurai sword. Both can kill you or slice your dick off. Knowing Ilsbeth, she'd go straight for your big head."

"And this thing with Gilly...shit, she's so fucking amazing. I want her so bad...fightin' the chemistry is like trying to paddle up the Mississippi with a toothpick."

"I can see that's goin' real well for ya." Jake glanced to the dishes spread all over the kitchen.

"We aren't even sleepin' in the same room, let alone in the same bed. Not only does she not want to be around pack, because she's afraid she'll meet her mate, she doesn't want to date me because she's afraid I'm gonna meet my mate, and leave her. It's all sorts of fucked up."

"Isn't that a kick in the nuts?"

"Worse. My balls are bluer than the sky on a spring day."

"You have to tell her."

"What am I'm goin' to tell her? That I'm her mate and that I want to mark her? That I want to take away her ability to shift? Kill her tiger? No fucking way, man. I can't do that to her," Dimitri insisted.

"Are you sure that she'll die? I mean, maybe something else happened to her mom," Jake suggested.

"I don't know. Honestly, I never heard of a hybrid shifter that wasn't part human mating with a wolf. It's impossible. So this thing about her spirit dying...I just don't know."

"Logan's mate went wolf."

"She was human. And besides, and don't take this the wrong way, I love my wolf, but she's a tiger. You saw her. She was magnificent."

"Badass."

"Yeah, she was," Dimitri said, recalling the way she'd gracefully run over to the car. "I can't do that to my mate...kill her beast. I've got to either let her go or find a way to save her."

"Ilsbeth."

"Maybe. I'm not going to be able to go on for much longer. I've got to be with her. This roommate shit isn't cuttin' it."

"What was your first clue?" Jake asked, a smartass grin crossing his face.

"What? Cooking soothes me."

"Don't take this the wrong way, but it's kind of funny to see you inked and muscled out, wearing pretty much nothin' but an oven mitt. It's a new look for you."

"It is what it is." Dimitri heard Gillian turn the doorknob and again held his fingers to his lips, shushing Jake. "Not a fucking word."

"You have to tell her."

"Just please. Not now."

"Logan's going to freak out the second he sees you. This thing with your wolf…you're the beta."

"I think I know my role in this pack. My wolf is…"

"What's wrong with your wolf?" Gillian asked. Surprised, her eyes went as large as saucers as she saw all the food. "You made this?"

"I like to cook," he said without explanation. "Have a seat."

"Expecting company?" She smiled. A rosy tinge spread across her cheeks as her gaze traveled from his ripped abdomen up to his eyes. Desire ran hot through her body, and she glanced away. Reaching for a glass of juice, she held it to her forehead before taking a drink.

"No, I just, uh…it's a hobby." Dimitri fought the erection that threatened to give his 'Kiss the Cook' apron new meaning.

"We're going to see a parade, right?" Gillian had heard their muffled voices and suspected something was off, but seeing Dimitri half-naked distracted her thoughts. Resisting him was turning into an impossible feat.

Locking herself in a bedroom had been the only way she'd been able to keep her hands to herself. Confused by her out of control libido, she'd immersed herself in the company information that Jax had sent with her camera equipment. Nick had emailed her first assignment, and she was actually looking forward to shooting today.

"Yeah, it'll be fun," Dimitri said.

"Okay," she responded.

"It's Saturday, so that means everyone's going to be out…humans and supes. I've got a few pack members who will travel with us, keeping an eye out for trouble. So far, there's been no sign of Chaz in the city, but we can't be too careful." It wasn't that wolves couldn't handle the issues, but shifting out in the open wasn't accepted. They needed to blend…go get the pictures and come home. The only reason Dimitri was even considering taking her out was because he couldn't take another second of being locked in the house, caged with no hope of release.

"Don't forget. Tonight's the Loups and Sorcières Ball." Jake stood and took his plate over to the sink.

"Ilsbeth better damn well be there," Dimitri blurted out, then quickly regretted he'd mentioned her in front of Gillian. He blew out a breath. Sooner or later she'd find out about the witch.

"What's Loups and Sorcières? Who's Ilsbeth?" Gillian asked. Intuition warned her that her wolf hadn't told her everything, but she kept her own secret held close.

"It's a Mardi Gras event we hold every year with the witches," Jake explained. "Mostly wolves and witches, but he invited a vamp."

"Leo's a friend," Dimitri said, pouring the scrambled yolks into a hot pan.

"He got you into this mess," Jake noted.

"Sorry, I don't follow." Gillian looked to Jake and then Dimitri.

"Léopold Devereoux. Vampire. His woman got herself involved with a demon, and my beta, here, jumped into a hell pit to save her and Logan's kid."

"Your wolf got injured," she commented.

"Yeah, my wolf." Dimitri kept his back to them, not wanting to share his pained expression. Fuck, he needed to get this situation fixed yesterday. Between not being able to make love to his mate, walking around with a hard-on twenty-four-seven and his wolf fading fast, he had to find resolution. But instead of going over to the coven to break down the damn door, he was going to a freakin' parade.

"But who's Ils…"

"Ilsbeth's the witch I saw. She was helping me."

"Why do you need to see her? I thought everything was okay."

"I need to ask her about something else." It wasn't entirely a lie, he reasoned. Aside from asking Logan and Léopold for help, Ilsbeth was the only other person he could think of who would know anything about mating tigers, how to save her ability to shift. He cringed, afraid that once she found out he was lying, she'd throw his ass to the curb. Unlike his wolf, who'd already rolled over in submission to the idea of mating, she had to choose him.

"Gilly's already the talk of the pack," Jake noted with a grin.

"What do you mean?" Gillian's stomach dropped.

"He means that you're my mate. Or did you forget?" Dimitri flipped the omelet, added a sprinkle of cheese and onions. He turned off the gas and set it aside.

"I, um, I didn't forget." Gillian's eyes widened. When he'd said mate, it had taken her off guard; she'd forgotten that they were supposed to be pretending to be mated.

"You should see your face," Jake laughed. "D, I think she forgot."

Dimitri came up behind Gillian, who sat on the bar stool. It had been the perfect excuse to touch her again. His arms coiled around her waist, resting underneath her breasts. Nuzzling her hair aside, he pressed his lips to her neck. The fragrance of her coconut-scented shampoo drifted into his nose, but it was her natural essence that registered with his wolf. His cock jerked to attention, grazing against her back.

"Mate," he growled. "We must be convincing. No more hiding in bedrooms."

"I…I…" Gillian lost her speech with Dimitri so close. Her tiger had gone wild, lusting after the wolf who she had been working carefully to avoid.

"That's right, cher. You feel it too, don't ya? Don't deny it," he told her. Dimitri darted his tongue against her skin, yearning for a taste of his mate.

Barely cognizant of Jake walking out the door, he ran a hand down the top of her thigh.

"Dimitri…I…what's happening?" she breathed. Excited and bewildered with her reaction to him, Gillian rested the back of her head against his chest. It should have felt wrong to be with a wolf, to desire someone so badly that she'd give anything to be with him. Rebuking her own feelings for the past two days had done nothing to quell the emotion blossoming in her chest. She was changing, transforming just by being in his presence and she wasn't sure if she could go back.

"Today, you're my mate. Tonight, you're my mate. That's what's happening, darlin'," Dimitri said. Forever she'd be his mate…if he could find a way to keep her.

"Okay," she found herself saying. *Okay? Did I just agree to be his mate?* No, this was role playing, a farce to keep her safe…wasn't it?

"See, that's right. You know me…can feel me…your mate."

"Dimitri, please. We can't…"

"Oh we can and we will, cher, but first we gotta go take some pictures."

"What?"

"Laissez les bons temps rouler!" Dimitri released her, untying his apron.

"Where're you going?" Gillian asked, stunned by the surging electricity running through her veins. As he walked away, her mouth gaped open at the sight of his spectacular bare ass.

"To get dressed. Work before play. And believe me, we've got lots of play to do. So we'd better get busy." It wasn't lost on Dimitri that Gillian had just about chosen him, and she didn't even know that they were mates. Damn if he was giving up the woman who fate had bestowed upon him.

Even though she had a press pass, the enormous crowd kept shifting, rhythmically jostling the spectators like shells being tossed about in the sand by breaking waves. Bracing her arms, she steadied her camera and focused the lens. A series of clicks fired as she captured the brightly colored float. Beads flew through the air like streams of plastic rain. Snap. Snap. Snap.

Gillian felt Dimitri's hands on her waist, his chest at her back. Lowering her arms, a broad smile crossed her face. Even though she was working, it felt like a date. They'd toured the French Quarter so she could take shots of the elaborate purple and gold Mardi Gras decorations that adorned the buildings. Despite the enormous breakfast he'd cooked, he insisted on taking her out to his favorite open-air café. They'd sat at a window table, talking for hours. She'd told him about growing up in Seattle, her life in New York. He'd told her stories of life on the bayou, how he'd come into being a beta within the pack, about his close relationship with Logan and Jake. They'd laughed and people-watched, drinking Bloody Marys and eating oysters and crawfish.

During their adventure, she'd felt woefully underdressed for the celebration in the streets. They'd ducked into a gift shop and she came out wearing a frilly red tutu and a matching mini-hat that clipped into her hair. On the way to the parade route, they'd stopped to listen to street performers, dancing in the streets. Infected by the spirit, Dimitri had taken her in his arms, twirling her as if they were in a ballroom. With a dip, he'd kissed her in front of an applauding crowd.

As another parade commenced, a teddy bear flew by her head, reminding her that she was supposed to be paying attention. Dimitri reached a long arm up into the air, easily catching it. Bright blue beads flew toward her and she extended a hand. With a snap, she caught the slippery chain and screamed in excitement. Laughing like a child opening a gift, she turned to Dimitri, whose warm eyes locked on hers.

Gillian's smile waned as the moment turned to heat. She lifted the beads as high as her hands would go until Dimitri bent over to receive them. At the same time, he turned over the stuffed toy, and gave it to her. She smiled, their lips inches apart, and she prayed he'd kiss her. When he leaned in, only brushing his cheek against hers in a hug, she exhaled, her heart pounding hard in her chest.

Music blared as the marching bands passed for what seemed like several minutes, but she'd gone limp, uncaring of everything and everyone around her. For the moment, the world had stopped. Gillian had lost count of the dates, and knew for certain that she didn't want just one more date. No, she wanted a lifetime.

The gut-wrenching knowledge of their dilemma tore at her heart. In her entire life, she'd never considered abandoning her great cat. Being with Dimitri was confusing everything she thought she knew. His warm lips pressed softly to her hair and she squeezed her eyes tight, hoping she wouldn't cry. From sadness or happiness, she couldn't tell. With the emotion brimming over, she breathed deeply. Clearing her head of all negative thoughts, she simply allowed herself to become immersed in the joy of being with her wolf.

~⚙· *Chapter Twelve* ⚙~

After taking a long shower, Gillian unsuccessfully attempted to put thoughts of Dimitri out of her mind. Fixing her hair, which was beginning to sprout dark brown roots, she imagined dating him for real. Going to the movies. Listening to music in the park. Debating whether they'd be having Chinese or Italian for dinner, knowing all the while she'd choose Cajun delicacies any day of the week.

As they rode in the limo on their way over to the party, she glanced up to Dimitri, who watched her with amusement. He was so easygoing, yet dominant in every single thing he did. Today had been one of the best days in her life. After spending so much time with him, her tiger was ready to roll over like a submissive lap dog waiting for her next treat. When he'd talked about running in the bayou, she envied him, wishing she could have just a taste of what he'd felt. Being free and open. Having others to rely on. All things that had eluded her.

While she'd never admit it, Gillian was beginning to suspect her own wolf existed. Although she'd never felt her, it had to be the reason why she'd fallen so easily under his spell. The call to date a wolf, her wolf, Dimitri, had taken hold.

"You can do this," she heard Dimitri say, as a gentle squeeze on her knee drew her out of her contemplation.

"I don't know. I've never been around so many wolves before…Chaz…well, even he didn't introduce me to his entire pack. How many people are going to be there again?" Gillian asked, fidgeting with the hem of her skirt.

"A hundred, give or take. But there's only one wolf you need to be concerned with." Dimitri eyed the private driver who'd picked them up to take them to the ball. With a flick of a button, he raised the privacy partition.

"Oh God. A hundred?"

"Are you all right?" he asked.

"I'll be okay," she lied.

"It's just a little party."

"Jake said the pack knew about us. Did you tell everyone? That I'm your mate?" She made air quotes with her fingers.

"Yes and no," he replied with a chuckle.

"This isn't going to be good, is it?" she smiled.

"It's kinda like this. Sometimes news is better going through the grapevine. No need to announce it on the PA system."

"A rumor?" she asked.

"Somethin' like that." He smiled.

"What did you do?"

"Miss Edmee. I kind of mentioned it to her. That's as good as tellin' everyone."

"Okay, but we agreed? No big proclamations, right? Just a party."

"Just a party." He brought the back of her hand to his lips and kissed it. "But you're going to meet Logan."

"The Alpha?" Gillian's voiced boomed throughout the cabin of the car.

"Now don't you tell me you're even a little bit afraid of an Alpha. Your brother's an Alpha."

"But he's not...I don't know...he's not scary. Chaz...now that's scary," she said. Her hand began to shake as she remembered her ordeal.

"He's not here," he reassured.

"He will be," she countered.

"Logan's a good man. He knows about us. I didn't have a lot of time to talk to him on the phone but he knows about our plan."

"Our lie."

"That we're tellin' people that we're going to mate. He knows exactly what Jax told everyone. And when I see him tonight, he'll know everything." Dimitri despised pretending. When he saw Logan, he planned on coming clean with all the details, including his wolf and his mate.

"Do you tell him everything you do?"

"Yeah, he's my Alpha. No secrets. We share everything," he disclosed.

"Everything?" she laughed.

"Everything," he confirmed, recalling the night of passion he'd shared with Logan and his mate.

Gillian opened her mouth and promptly shut it, contemplating whether or not to delve further into his statement. She'd heard that wolves sometimes would share sexual partners among themselves. Her understanding of it, however, was limited to stories told by humans, who only knew secondhand.

"It was once," Dimitri said, filling in the pieces of the puzzle. He'd just about had his fill of lies. He refused to pretend that he was anything but what he was. There was no shame in what he'd done with Logan and Wynter. She'd suffered terribly during her transition. Sexually heightened, they'd asked for his help and he'd been glad to oblige. "Logan and Wynter."

"You were with your Alpha's mate? Had sex with her?" Gillian attempted to hide her shock.

"Yes, but I wasn't alone. I was there to help Logan and Wynter get through her transition. She was hybrid and had just learned to become a wolf. Wynter almost died soon after. A vampire...he'd nearly drained her."

"Léopold?"

"No, no, no. I mean, don't get me wrong. Leo's a lethal son-of-a bitch, but he's my boy."

"You're close?"

"Yeah, we're tight. He'll be at the party, too."

"Does he know…about us?"

"No, but he will in about an hour or so."

"Are you sure we're doing the right thing? Lying about our relationship? Maybe Chaz would have come anyway."

"It would have taken too long. We need him to come to us. He's going to want to stop our mating."

"We should have killed him in California." It felt strange to openly acknowledge that they were luring him to his death. But Chaz gave her no option. Kill or be killed.

"Perhaps, but my place is here with my wolves. Had you been well, you would have done it yourself. Chaz had a chance to let this all go but when he sent his guys to New York, he signed his own death warrant. Aside from me wanting to kill him, Jax and Logan will mete out justice."

Gillian knew what he said to be true. Jax had already killed in front of her. The brutality had been shocking, yet there was no other acceptable solution. Pack law dictated the outcome.

Dimitri took her hand in his, and his burning touch reminded her of the spectacular day they'd spent together. She brought her fingers to her lips, recalling the feel, the taste of him. A shiver rolled over her as she thought of how they'd made love on the plane, the incredible ecstasy he'd brought to her world. Restraint was a skill she had practiced ever since she'd first learned to shift. Yet staying away from Dimitri had been nothing short of exhausting.

She'd been willing to dismiss the sex as nothing more than a physical attraction. However, hours of talking and laughing had led to a deep burning need, one that she'd have difficulty denying tonight.

She glanced down to her dress that fit like a glove. Dimitri had taken care of every last detail, down to her strappy heels. At one time in her life a hot pair of shoes would have been enough to make her day, but now, the only thing that mattered was the wolf consuming her thoughts.

"Thank you." She smiled.

"For what?"

"Today. The parade. Everything."

"Ah, darlin'. No need to thank me, and for the record, I haven't nearly finished showing you everything." He winked. "You just wait."

Gillian laughed softly, but was certain that he meant what he said. Like a knife, his words sliced through her reservations. Would she sacrifice her tiger in order to experience love? It terrified her. It thrilled her. Gillian had no idea what it felt like to know that someone was her mate, but if she could choose anyone, it'd be the wolf holding her hand.

Gillian took a deep breath, counting to ten. Like an actress, she plastered a smile on her face, attempting to regulate her breathing so that no one would detect her consternation. Never in her life had she been around so many wolves. She scanned the ballroom, observing the crowd engaged in lively conversation, dancing and drinking as if they hadn't a care in the world. Both males and females wore masks, dressed up for the lavish affair.

Allowing Dimitri to lead her through the mass of celebrating partygoers, she glided across the floor. She nodded to Jake, who was already dancing with a pretty blonde. People passed and greeted her as if they'd known her all her life. It was as if she'd stepped into an alternate universe. They all looked human in their dresses, suits and ties. But it was an illusion. The hum of magic and nature buzzed in the air along with the zydeco waltz.

Gillian held tight to Dimitri's hand as an imposing gentleman approached. Though he was not as tall as Dimitri, Gillian immediately registered the power emanating from him. *Wolf. Alpha.* Instinctively, she lowered her eyes. The shock of her submission startled her as it was the first time she'd felt compelled to honor an Alpha.

"Hey man, how are you?" Dimitri greeted him, intrigued by Gillian's gaze.

"D, I'm glad you're back. Introduce me," Logan told him.

"Gilly, this is Logan, our fearless leader. Alpha, meet Gilly."

"Nice to meet you, Gilly. Can I get you a drink?" he asked, signaling to a server. Flutes of champagne were swiftly brought over on a silver tray. Handing her a glass, he gave Dimitri a knowing grin.

"Thank you. Nice to meet you," Gillian managed. She tried to remember how nervous she'd been meeting some of the most famous subjects that she'd photographed. Holding tight to a thread of calm, she smiled up at him.

"It's I who should be thanking you. I hear you saved my beta."

"He saved me right back. We're even." She glanced at Dimitri and back to Logan. "Thanks for helping me. I'm sorry I've brought danger to your pack."

"Don't give it another thought. I'm looking forward to some payback for what they did to D."

Gillian was about to tell him how incredible Dimitri had been when he saved her, but was interrupted by a pretty woman who'd wrapped her arms around the Alpha's waist. He laughed, bringing his lips to hers. Dimitri smiled at Gillian in understanding; this was Logan's mate. Logan laughed, and broke the kiss with her, and Gillian swore she saw him blush.

"Dimitri," Wynter squealed. Breaking free of her Alpha's arms, she gave Dimitri a quick hug and kiss. Within seconds, she was back in Logan's embrace.

"Hi there. I'm Wynter," Wynter said, reaching for Gillian's hand. "Nice to meet you."

"Hello," Gillian replied, returning her greeting with caution. This was the woman who'd made love to Dimitri. Intellectually, Gillian knew Wynter was mated, yet the idea of Dimitri deep inside another turned her stomach.

"Sorry I'm late. I was busy with our baby girl. This is the first time we've left her with a sitter."

"A baby?" Gillian asked.

"Ava. We just adopted her. I'm afraid we won't be staying all night."

"How old is she?"

"Four months," Logan answered. "Sweetheart, do you mind if I get a minute with D? Just need to catch up on a few things."

"Sure thing, baby," Wynter agreed, giving him a kiss. She smiled at Gillian. "Gilly, would you mind going to the ladies' room with me? I was in such a rush to get out of the house that I didn't have a chance to check my dress. I think I might have a spot of formula on it."

"Sure," Gillian agreed. She gave Dimitri a nod, leery of wandering off on her own in a room full of shifters.

"Don't worry. I'll keep her safe," Wynter told Dimitri with a wink. "Promise not to steal her for too long."

Wynter launched into a story about her daughter, and Gillian forced herself to let go of her jealousy, deciding that whatever had happened was truly in the past. As their conversation progressed, she wondered if the Alpha had told his mate the truth about the sham they were perpetrating. Or like everyone else at the party, was Wynter under the impression that she really was Dimitri's mate? Gillian knew it would only be a matter of time before they all found out she was a fake. If they got close enough, they'd know she wasn't a wolf. She couldn't imagine the animosity they'd feel knowing they had been lied to, and guilt gnawed at her.

With talk of babies, Gillian unconsciously held her hand to her belly and thought of how she'd like to have children of her own someday. Most days, she put it to the back of her mind. Her career had allowed her to do so. Mating itself seemed like wishful thinking. To be pregnant with a child of the man she loved seemed like an impossibility of extraordinary proportions.

"I know that you're pretending to be mates to draw out Chaz, but you're telling me that she's your mate, as in for real?" the Alpha asked, amused with his friend's misery. It wasn't that he didn't love him like a brother, but karma was a bitch. Dimitri had made fun of him, enjoying every last drip of angst Logan went through when he'd found his mate, so turnabout was fair play.

"You betcha," Dimitri said, taking a sip of his whisky. He watched Gillian across the room. Dressed in a slinky red number, she threw her head back, giggling at something Wynter had said. Her amber eyes flickered behind her delicate black metal mask. "Look at her."

"She's sexy, isn't she?" Logan answered.

"My mate, not yours."

"Ah yes, she's beautiful as well. But what are you going to do with a cat? I think it's ironic you had a laugh riot over me adopting a kitten and now you're gonna mate with one." Logan laughed and slapped Dimitri on his shoulder.

Dimitri waved to his friend, Léopold Devereoux, who crossed the room.

"Here comes trouble," Logan commented.

"Bonne soirée, mes amis," Léopold greeted them.

"How's it going? Where's your better half?" Dimitri asked.

"Mon amour is on her way over from Kade's house," he said, referring to Kade Issacson, who led the New Orleans vampires. Léopold was his sire, and unfortunately, Kade's fiancée, Sydney, had been turned vampire, in a tragic accident involving a demon. "Sydney isn't doing so well, I'm afraid. Laryssa feels responsible. The girls have been taking turns, visiting."

"Sydney's seeing visitors? That's progress," Dimitri noted.

"Perhaps. But she's not speaking to anyone. Laryssa goes anyway. Sits with her. Reads to her. I'm not sure she's going to survive the transition. Of course, I haven't mentioned it to Kade. There's no stronger medicine than hope."

"Sorry to hear that, Leo."

"Not to change the subject, but did you tell him?" Logan asked.

"No, I did not." Dimitri glared at his Alpha, who was delighting in his predicament entirely too much.

"Our beta here's got himself a problem."

"He does?" Léopold mused, trying to read Dimitri's face.

"Part of being an Alpha is knowin' when to ask an expert. Leo's older than both of us tenfold. Perhaps he's got a solution for your problem," Logan suggested.

Léopold studied his friend, noting how Dimitri kept his eyes on an attractive redhead at the bar. Listening to his pulse race when she stole a glance at him, he smiled.

"Now this is interesting…a mate for our beta."

"How do you do that? It's creepy, ya know," Dimitri remarked to Léopold. "My Alpha's been 'round me since I've been a babe. But you…what's your secret?"

"And look at her eyes…well, now, that is surprising. A lion? Leopard, maybe?" he asked.

"Tiger," Logan corrected.

"Yep," Dimitri sighed. "She's my mate. But we've got issues."

"Does she even know?" Léopold asked.

"What do you think?"

"I've heard of this happening before. A hybrid, I assume. Her tiger's a rare breed. Maljavan would be my guess."

"Are you making this shit up?" Logan asked with a chuckle.

"Her eyes. Like a cat's. It's a trait of her species. She can mate with a wolf, but she could lose her ability to shift. Like Sydney's transition to vampire, her cat may not survive. May I ask, she's hybrid, but her mother, was she full tiger or hybrid as well?"

"I'm pretty sure that her mother was hybrid. Her father was an Alpha," Dimitri replied.

"Here comes the punch line," Logan warned, waiting on Léopold's reaction to the next tidbit of information.

"Her brother is Jax Chandler." Dimitri took a deep draw of the amber liquid in his glass and exhaled. "Gilly said her mom lost the ability to shift after she mated. But Jax thinks she denied her wolf and that's why she can't shift. I haven't met her, so I'm not sure."

"Jax's father's been dead for a while. Jax and I became friends when he took over several years ago. But he never mentioned a sister," Léopold commented.

"Family secrets run deep, I guess. After what went down in San Diego, she went to him for help."

"Any news on Chaz Baldwin?" Léopold inquired.

"He's not in NOLA," Logan replied.

"Yet. It's just a matter of time," Dimitri said.

"If you mate with her, he can't have her," Léopold told him.

"If is the optimal word in that sentence. And even if I manage that, he's still comin' for her. What I don't get is why he wants her so badly. Why would an Alpha force a mating on someone who wasn't all wolf?"

"It's rumored that she'll give a gift to the one who mates her," Léopold speculated.

"What?"

"A gift," he repeated. "Not sure what it is, but it appears it's worth killing for. Jax's father probably knew. Therefore Jax knows. And your pretty little pussy cat, mais oui, she definitely knows."

"She didn't say anything," Dimitri grumbled.

"Secrets, secrets…we all have them. Do not judge her harshly, my friend. She's vulnerable," Léopold said, touching his shoulder. A shiver ran through him, and he grimaced.

"There's got to be a way to mate without killing her cat…I can't do that to her."

"Perhaps. Jax is a wise leader. It's very likely that if she's half wolf, her wolf will emerge. If she can go to wolf, then maybe she can also call on her cat. I imagine the transition is similar to Sydney's in that you have to want it to happen. The mind is a powerful influence. You both know this."

"I guess that gives me something to work with." Dimitri's lips tightened as he caught sight of a man watching Gillian.

"Now that we have that settled, let's discuss what in the hell's wrong with you. Does he know?" Léopold pinned his eyes on Dimitri, his tone growing serious.

Perpetrating deceit bored a hole in Dimitri's chest. It was time to share the truth.

"I won't ask how you knew…it's only been a few days since I saw the witch." Dimitri took a deep breath and blew it out. "My wolf. Something's still got a hold of me. Ilsbeth gave me this tonic. But it's not enough. Strange part is that when I've been with Gilly, I felt a little better. You know she healed me."

"She does have gifts," Léopold observed.

"For real. I was near death on that beach. My wolf wouldn't surface," he recalled. "But the witch. She wants me to move in with her."

"What the fuck?" Logan blurted out.

"Yeah, that's about it. I told her no, of course, but she kissed me. And ya know, she was already pissed that I wouldn't date her anymore. She's still holding a grudge. Not sure how the news of my mating's goin' to fly."

"I imagine she'll continue to be put out, but she won't hurt you," Léopold assured him.

"I'm not so sure about that. You and I both know she's one scary bitch. Gorgeous, but scary."

"That she is, mon ami, but she will find a way to fix you."

"Leo's right, D. Ilsbeth knows full well she's not your mate. She may be bitter but she's not stupid. If she wants the symbiotic relationship between the vamps, wolves and witches to continue, she's gotta get over it. It's the only way. In the meantime, I suggest you talk with your woman about you know…your mating status," Logan suggested with a wicked grin.

"Really? Hello, Logan. Pot meet kettle. I recall you marking your mate without even telling her. How soon we forget," Dimitri snorted.

"Oh, I don't forget. It was a little difficult." Logan smiled. "But hey, it all worked out just fine."

"Okay, must be nice rewriting history."

"Ah, I do enjoy a spirited debate," Léopold chuckled. "But in the interest of time, because my sweet Laryssa's going to be here soon, let's just all agree that you'll tell her. I understand you don't want to kill her tiger, but I'm going to side with Jax on this one. If she wants to shift after the mating, she'll do it as a wolf. It's hard to tell from this distance but she seems made of strong stock. You must engage in preparation to make it happen."

"Jesus, Leo, you make it sound so clinical. Holy shit, this sucks," Dimitri huffed.

"Life has not promised us easy, only love."

"I love it when he goes all philosophical on us," Logan commented.

"He's almost as old as Socrates," Dimitri joked.

"Hardly. You're off by a thousand years," Léopold sniffed, grabbing a flute off a passing waiter's tray. "Speaking of ancient, I do believe the witch has arrived."

All eyes turned to the petite woman whose customarily blonde hair had been dyed turquoise. Her stunning appearance captured the attention of everyone in the room, her emerald-green velvet dress trailing several feet behind her. Smiling as if she were the queen of New Orleans, her face drew tight as she caught sight of Dimitri.

Gillian found the Alpha's mate, Wynter, welcoming, introducing her to members of the pack. But she felt disingenuous pretending that she belonged to Dimitri. Sooner or later, they'd suspect the truth. Animals were not easily deceived. Yet as she met one wolf after the other, she grew certain about her feelings for the beta. She might not be his true mate, but she wanted to be.

She blinked over to Dimitri who smiled at her. He talked with his friends, while he protectively watched her from a distance. She smoothed down the fabric of her dress, taking in the sight of her stylish wolf. He wore black dress pants, his white dress shirt unbuttoned so that she could see a hint of the tattoos on his chest. His black leather mask did little to hide the fire in his eyes.

Wynter left Gillian's side to address another pack member when a stranger sidled up to her at the bar. She hardly noticed him as all eyes fell to an attractive woman entering the ballroom, who appeared to glide across the floor, her hair tied up in intricate braids. Her silver mask sparkled underneath the black light, illuminating her ice-blue eyes.

Amazement turned to jealousy as Gillian watched Dimitri turn his focus to the beautiful woman. Her tiger hissed as he embraced the blue-haired beauty. Dimitri took her by the hand, leading her to a secluded corner of the room. Gillian's eyes flared in anger, her heart pounding blood through her veins. Did he have a mate? Was everything he'd told her, the way he'd made her feel, all a lie? Was it all part of their hoax? Rage coursed through her. She went to cross the room to confront him, when the stranger spoke to her.

"You're new here," he commented. "Can I get you a drink?"

"Yeah," she responded mindlessly, unable to take her eyes off of Dimitri.

"My name's Alex. I'm visiting my friend, Seth, for Mardi Gras. I live in Chicago," he explained, extending his hand.

Gillian smiled, attempting to be polite.

"You wanna dance?" he asked.

"You're human?" she asked, her thoughts distracted.

"Yeah, pretty crazy, right? The Alpha said it was okay, since I was in town on business. Seth and I go way back. You a wolf, too?"

"Yes." Who Seth was she had no idea and wasn't about to ask. Gillian found it difficult to concentrate on his questions.

"You wanna dance?" he asked again.

What Gillian really wanted was to forget, to run away. The woman stroked her hand over Dimitri's forearm, and Gillian thought she'd be sick. She'd never been a jealous person before, but she could hardly contain the green-eyed monster that threatened to throttle the woman touching her man.

"Um, what did you say?" she asked.

"Let's dance," he said, taking her hand.

Gillian glared at Dimitri, but he didn't even notice as Alex led her out onto the dance floor. He was preoccupied, infatuated with another woman, someone who was possibly his mate. She glanced at the human, reasoning that he couldn't hurt her. Dimitri didn't seem to even care. It was just one dance.

But as the stranger wrapped his hand around her waist to lead her in a waltz, she felt nauseous and attempted to pull away. Alex held tight, yanking her flush against his arousal and her head grew dizzy at his touch. Before she knew what was happening, he'd spun her around, making her lose sight of her wolf. The stranger's hand fell to her bottom and her tiger roared, warning the stranger to free her. She lost control, and her claws emerged.

"You're looking well," Ilsbeth noted, the corners of her lips curled upward.

"Ilsbeth, cut the crap. Have you found a cure?" Dimitri said, taking her by the hand, leading her into a corner. He restrained the anger that had bubbled to the surface soon after she'd purposefully hugged him as if they were still dating.

"Did you finally realize that you need to come stay with me?" Ilsbeth tilted her head. She darted her tongue out of her mouth, seductively dragging its tip along the rim of her martini glass, and smiled.

"Jesus Christ, witch. Not tonight, okay? Did you find it or not?"

"Something's different about you," she observed. Ilsbeth reached for his arm, gliding her thin fingers over his inner wrist until she reached the crook of his elbow.

"Ilsbeth. Please." Dimitri cringed as the words came out as if he was begging.

"What is it? You feel different, too. Your energy is running hot," she noted.

"No, don't," he snapped at her. Across the room, Gillian glared at him, her rage emanating like a laser at having another woman touch her mate. "I'm here with someone."

"Who?" Ilsbeth asked. She retreated somewhat but still kept her hand on his skin. As a server passed, she set her glass on the tray. Taking his hands, she closed her eyes, concentrating on his aura.

"Ilsbeth, I'm sorry. I told you this would happen. This is why I couldn't commit to you," Dimitri answered.

Ilsbeth slowly opened her eyes. Her lips compressed into a fine line as awareness of the situation took hold.

"I've found her."

"No," she whispered, withdrawing her hands.

"You knew this was my fate," Dimitri stated, shaking his head. He hadn't meant to hurt her, but he'd grown tired of asking for forgiveness for something that was beyond his control. It had been months since they'd stopped seeing each other, and he was done apologizing.

"Yes, I did." Ilsbeth took a deep breath. "But that didn't mean I wanted it to happen."

Dimitri smiled but then his face dropped as he saw Gillian talking to a stranger at the bar. Jerking his attention back to the witch, he sought to speak his piece.

"I need your help. This thing with my wolf. Do you have any news?"

"A sorcerer from Miami is arriving tomorrow. He's quite powerful and has promised to engage convocation with our coven. It is at that time I expect an answer. I apologize that it has taken even this long. My offer to stay at my house remains."

"I appreciate that but I can't…" Dimitri's words trailed off as he watched his mate take the hand of another man. He growled as she was swept up into an embrace not his own.

Ilsbeth followed Dimitri's line of vision until she saw the woman who had stolen his heart.

"This is the female who commands your soul?"

"Yes," he spat out.

"She goes with another…interesting."

"She's hybrid…she doesn't know."

"How do you expect this to work?" Ilsbeth honed in on Gillian's eyes, which met hers. "A tiger?"

"Yes."

"The mating is uncertain."

"You're wrong," he vowed. "I've never been more certain of anything in my entire life."

Dimitri's canines dropped as he sensed Gillian's fear and in response, he tore across the dance floor. The scent of human blood permeated the room. The sound of Gillian slapping the man's face rang in his ears.

"What the hell? This fuckin' bitch just scratched me!" the stranger screamed.

Dimitri roared, shoving him across the room into the wall. Gillian, stunned and embarrassed, retracted her claws and fisted her hands. Logan ran over to Dimitri, prying his hands off the man's neck. He held his beta around the chest, while Jake and Léopold dragged the bleeding man out the door.

"It was just a matter of time," Logan quipped, patting his friend on the back. "Take a break, D. Let's get back to the party. Leo will take care of him. Can I let you go now?"

Dimitri nodded, panting as his Alpha released him. Feral, he turned to Gillian, who'd begun to retreat from the dance floor. The room went quiet as his eyes pinned on hers. Stalking his prey, he advanced on Gillian, who shook her head, wiping the blood on her dress.

"It's a lie," she said under her breath, recalling how she'd seen him with another woman. Her voice shook in anger. "I'm not your..."

"You're my mate," he asserted, loud enough so that everyone in the room could hear him.

"But you...you...and her." Gillian's eyes darted to the nearest exit.

"Acadian wolves," Dimitri called to his pack. It'd never be enough for the rumor to spread on its own. No, his wolf demanded a public claiming of his mate. He'd lay it on the line. She may ultimately reject him, but he'd be damned if he'd go one more second lying to her. "This female, she's mine. We'll be mated soon."

Gillian stared at Dimitri as if he'd lost his mind. She'd expected they'd stick to their original plan of letting the news of their mating slowly permeate the pack through the grapevine. A public announcement was over the top. Neither one of them would ever recover from the lie.

"What are you saying?" she croaked as Dimitri took her in his arms.

"You. Are. My. Mate. And as proud as I am that you just tore into that asshole with your claws, no other male puts his hands on you until we're mated," he warned. "Understood?"

"This can't be," she whispered into his ear. The scent of him calmed her, despite the fact that she'd been angry. Every last man and woman watched them intently as if they were on a stage, putting on a play.

"Oh, it be, cher. Choose me or not, you're mine."

Shocked, Gillian blinked. Her heart raced at his declaration. The animal inside of her rejoiced in quiet celebration. Oh Goddess, how had she missed the fact that Dimitri was hers? She hadn't wanted to acknowledge that the desire she'd been feeling could be true. *Choose me or not.* Gillian didn't want to admit it to Dimitri but she'd already made the choice. Her great cat would sacrifice anything to have the wolf who laid claim to her.

Panic set in and she began to hyperventilate. She sucked air, unable to breathe. Her eyes teared, gasping for air.

"Gilly." She heard him call her name, but the circle of black began to close in on her.

"Gilly," he growled, his tone firmer, commanding her.

"I...I can't breathe," she mouthed.

"Feel me, breathe with me...now." Dimitri unbuttoned his shirt and slid her hands underneath the fabric.

"Dimitri..."

"Breathe, Gilly. In and out. Do it with me. You're going to be just fine, kitten," he told her, his voice calm and steady.

"No, I can't..."

"Yes you can. In and out...concentrate on my voice, the feel of my skin on yours." He plowed his fingers into her hair and locked his eyes on hers. "See? You're okay now. This is real and happening. We're mates. You'll be okay. That's it."

Gillian focused on Dimitri, obeying his command. So wrong to submit, yet it felt natural. As her breathing returned to normal, the heat between them combusted.

Dimitri is my mate. Her eyes fell to his lips and within seconds, he'd captured her mouth, drawing her into his embrace. Digging her fingers into his skin, she moaned into his mouth, wild with desire. With the realization that they were still on the dance floor, she nodded as he tore his lips away from hers and followed him blindly as he led her outside.

By the time they'd reached the open courtyard, she was on fire with lust for her mate. She moaned as he took her again, his tongue plunging into her mouth. Returning his savage kiss, she clutched at him, giving in to the passion she'd held back for the past two days. Stumbling back against the trellis, she gasped as he hiked up her thigh and wrapped it around his waist.

"I'm sorry," she breathed. "I shouldn't have gone with him..."

"Stop talking," he ordered, pressing his lips to her collarbone.

"But we're at...ah," she moaned as he tugged at the front of her dress, exposing her breast. Her ripe peak hit the cool night air, puckering in arousal.

"I'm claiming you tonight. I will have you...now," he stated. His mouth latched onto her firm nipple, and he twirled his tongue over it, sucking and nipping at her flesh.

"Oh God, yes..." Gillian couldn't believe she was agreeing to making love, without regard to over a hundred people who partied inside the hall.

As Dimitri shuffled backwards toward the brick wall, he swore. *Goddamn it, I should have done this earlier where there was a bed.* They didn't seem to have a good track record when it came to actually making love in one. No, public displays of affection were more their style.

Laving at her breast, he cupped her ass, driving his rock-hard erection up into her belly. Dimitri bunched the fabric of her skirt and hooked a claw under her panties. The shredded panty fell to the ground and he reached between them, unbuckling his pants. Gillian tore open his shirt, scratching and biting at his chest. His pants dropped around his ankles, and she threw her hands around his neck. Hoisting herself upward, she wrapped both her legs around his waist. Dimitri stroked his hard arousal once, before driving himself up into her hot core.

His canines descended, and he dragged his teeth from the hollow behind her ear down to her chest. Using the only semblance of control he could summon, he turned his head so that he didn't risk nicking her with his teeth. Resolved, he'd already decided that when he marked her as his, she'd submit to him, welcoming his bite. Tonight, claiming her within the shroud of honesty, his mind and animal would be satisfied with the knowledge she was his.

Gillian screamed with each pump of his hips. She breathed into his kiss, biting at his lips. She was barely aware that her own fangs had dropped, her tiger celebrating in a ravenous frenzy. She tilted her pelvis, building a pulsing rhythm against her clitoris.

"Harder, yes, fuck me," she groaned into his mouth.

"You're mine. Do you hear me, Gilly?" Dimitri plunged his cock into her, accentuating every word he said.

"Yes, yes…please. Oh God, yes," she cried.

"Mate. Say it," he commanded, thrusting. His orgasm threatened, but he held back. He needed to hear her *own* their relationship.

"Please." Gillian bit her own lip as her tight channel quivered around him. "I'm coming."

"Not yet. Say it, cher. I swear to God, I'll stop right now," he warned. "You know it to be true."

"I don't know how…"

"Mate."

"Yes, oh my God. You're my mate," she cried out, her forehead falling against his chest. At her admission, a spasm of ecstasy rippled through her.

"Yes, Gilly, yes," he grunted, his fiery release pulsing deep inside his mate. Holding her tightly, he nuzzled into her shoulder. A small chuckle broke from his lips.

"What's so funny?" she asked, slipping gently down off his softening erection.

"Easy, darlin'. You're going to break something if you move too fast," he warned with a smile.

"Come on, what's so funny?"

"I've got a feeling I'm going to need to see a doctor tomorrow on account of my ass being pressed against these bricks."

"I feel like a teenager." She laughed.

"You did *this* as a teenager?"

"Um, no…but the feeling…like I can't get enough of you. God, I can't believe we just had sex out here."

"No worries. Besides, no one saw us," he assured her. *They all probably heard us.*

Dimitri was unconcerned about public sex. That was commonplace in some of the clubs he'd frequented. Even in the wild, on a full moon, wolves were known to make love outdoors, with little regard for others. But Dimitri was worried at how feral he'd become. Never in his life had he lost control like he'd just done. It was the way he'd taken her on the dance floor, forcing her to admit the feelings she had for him, that gave him pause.

"We've got to talk, Dimitri," she began.

Dimitri sighed, knowing this discussion would need to be held. He settled her onto her feet, and yanked up his pants. After zippering up, he took her back into his arms, uncomfortable with the loss of her warmth, and spoke into her hair.

"Listen, Gil. I'm not sure how this is going to work out, and you're right, we need to talk. But tonight, seeing you with that jerk, and shit, even before that...I'm not the kind of guy who lies to anyone, let alone his mate. I'm sorry I even waited this long to tell you."

"Yesterday and last night were the hardest hours of my life. I was just worried...that my feelings for you were getting too strong. I don't want to get hurt. That woman..."

"Ilsbeth. We'll talk about her tomorrow," he promised. Dimitri had been with many women over the past century, but explaining his complicated relationship with the witch to his mate wasn't a conversation he was looking to have tonight.

As Gillian lay her head against his chest, his heart grew heavy with awareness of the consequences of mating. Even though he'd just publicly announced her as his, she remained unmarked. No choice had been made yet, but it would be soon. If Gillian chose him as her mate, her tiger would die.

~❧ Chapter Thirteen ❧~

Dimitri ushered Gillian into the limo, thankful that Logan and Jake had kept their mouths shut about what had happened at the ball. Despite the missing buttons on his shirt and the tear in the backside of his pants, they'd walked back into the party as if they hadn't just had hot animal sex during the fancy event. Not that a soul in attendance had expected a quiet night anyhow. With Mardi Gras in full swing, everyone tended to be a little more rambunctious. Making love in the courtyard had added a pleasurable amount of crazy to the evening, Dimitri thought. Even Léopold had simply laughed, aware that his friend had taken his mate right there against the wall. Dimitri supposed had he cared what people thought, he'd be apologetic, perhaps embarrassed. But as Gillian gave him a sexy smile on their way out, nothing but desire for her played in his mind. Even the reality of their problems wasn't enough to deter him from enjoying her.

As he settled her against his chest, he considered his trip to the west coast had been one of the worst and best vacations he'd ever taken. Almost getting killed was a snag he hadn't expected. But finding his mate was turning out to be one of his most exciting adventures to date. He knew soon enough, he'd have to settle back down, working for Logan in security in his investment firm and assisting with pack matters.

The only regret he supposed he had was losing one of his favorite bikes. He'd reconditioned the thirty-year-old Harley, and wished it hadn't been trashed on some California beach. But like every other material possession he'd acquired over the years, he'd never gotten too attached. Things could be replaced. Although wolves rarely died, he'd watched as human friends had submitted to the aging process. On their deathbeds, they never wished for more trinkets.

Gillian's caress to his arm brought him out of his reverie. He noticed that she'd gone quiet and grew concerned.

"You okay?" Dimitri asked her.

"Yeah, I'm just thinking about things."

"Things, huh? Like what?"

"Like where we're going? Wondering why you still need to talk to the witch?"

"We're taking a trip outside the city…to my home. Jake's goin' to round up your things and bring them to us, so don't worry about your pictures," Dimitri answered, purposefully avoiding her second question.

"Okay, thanks. I'm not worried, though. I already reviewed some of them…shot Jax an email with a few I thought we might be able to use for the spread."

"Whatever's going to happen with Chaz is going to happen soon. I just prefer to be on the bayou for a few days. Get some fresh air. The full moon's in two nights."

"And the witch?" she pressed.

Responding with silence, Dimitri kissed the top of her head, hoping she'd relent.

"What aren't you telling me? I don't know what it is, but you're starting to worry me. I'm not asking you to explain what's going on between you and her, I'm asking about you." Gillian pushed out of his arms and placed her palms on his shoulder. When he didn't answer her, she slid both her hands under the collar of his shirt, touching his skin. Concentrating on finding his wolf, her eyes flashed open. "Something's off."

Dimitri reached for her hands, taking them in his own. He took a deep breath and glanced out the window.

"Your wolf." Her voice trembled as fear replaced her calm demeanor.

"I didn't want to say anything. It's just that whatever latched onto me, it's not gone. Ilsbeth…she gave me something…but it's temporary."

"A demon?"

"No, some kind of parasite. My take is that it's energy…evil energy. Ilsbeth isn't sayin'."

"What do you mean, it's temporary? Like it's going to go away?"

"No…more like I could lose my ability to shift again. And if that happens…well, you can see how that might be a problem for me. You think Logan would mind if I followed them around in an ATV when the pack goes for a run?" Dimitri tried to play down the serious nature of the issue. If he could no longer shift, he couldn't be beta. He wondered if they'd even let him stay in Acadian wolves.

"I'm so sorry."

"Hey now, this is my problem, not yours. You weren't the fool who jumped in the hell pit."

"You did it to save the baby. For your friend. That makes you a hero." Gillian briefly placed her lips on his, and continued. "We're going to fix this. Together. If that witch can't help you, we'll find another one. I'll ask Jax. I promise you…this is not the end."

"We're a fine pair, aren't we? I'm losin' my wolf. And by mating, your tiger…" Dimitri shook his head, disgusted. Usually optimistic, talking about the situation drove home the reality of their perplexing conundrum. "The witch is bringin' in a sorcerer from Miami tomorrow. As for you, kitty cat, no one says you gotta mate with me."

Gillian paused at his words. *Doesn't he want to mate with me?*

"That's true, wolf. But maybe you're changing my mind about things. And it's my decision to make."

"Don't get me wrong, Gilly. Tonight in that courtyard…I couldn't get enough of you. If this feelin' is half of what happens when we mate, it's goin' to be incredible. My wolf may be distant at times, but he…I…the desire to mark you…I'm not going to be able to hold off much longer."

Gillian gave a silly smile at his declaration. It wasn't rational, she knew. But after being with him all day, getting to know him, she wanted more of a commitment. Seeing him with Ilsbeth drove her to stake her claim on him. Her beast sought to brand him as her own, and despite it being the death of her, the hunger grew with each passing minute.

"What's funny?" Dimitri asked, unable to discern how she felt.

"Nothing…It's just that I've spent my entire life avoiding wolves. And now…"

"Now?" he asked, sweeping his fingers into her hair. Her pink lips parted in anticipation of his kiss.

"Now," she breathed. So close, she could feel the heat of him at her mouth. "All I can think about is staying around wolves."

"Wolves?" he challenged, gently tilting her head, exposing her neck.

"One wolf," she corrected with a sigh.

"Hmm?"

"My wolf," she cried as he nipped at her neck.

"Are you ready to belong to this wolf?" Dimitri traced the tip of his tongue along her bottom lip.

"Ahhh…Dimitri," she moaned. She tried to kiss him, but he held her firmly by her hair, controlling her every movement. Her pussy flooded in arousal with his command. In another place and time, submission wasn't a word in her vocabulary. But in his arms, she'd give him whatever he wanted and then some.

"What's that, kitten? I'm afraid I can't hear you?"

"Please…"

"I do enjoy hearing you beg, darlin' but I want an answer." Dimitri licked at the corner of her mouth, amused when she tried to kiss him. His wolf wouldn't tolerate any more games.

"Yes," she breathed. Her eyelids fluttered open, her eyes locked on his. Fate was stronger than fear. She yearned to belong to him, and his mark on her skin would begin the journey.

"Yes." He smiled, pleased with her response.

His lips crushed against hers, drinking in her essence. Her breasts pressed against his chest, and she clawed at his back. The electricity seared the air, their connection exploding into fireworks. Desperately, they kissed and caressed, lost in each other. It was as if nothing but the two of them existed. Nothing mattered but the realization that they'd chosen each other.

Gillian barely noticed when the car came to a stop. She'd reached to unbutton his shirt, but firm hands prevented her from doing so. Dimitri reluctantly tore his lips away from hers. Panting, he reached for the door handle and exited, helping her out of the car.

"In the house," he told her.

As she went to exit the car, Dimitri effortlessly lifted her into his arms. Gillian giggled, amazed at his strength. She had no idea where she was and didn't care. Tearing at his shirt, she exposed his chest, pressing her lips to his skin.

Barely cognizant of her surroundings, she caught sight of the illuminated herringbone stone walkway. Fireflies lit up the foggy night sky against a backdrop of draping Spanish moss. The scent of the bayou permeated the air while an orchestra of insects played in the distance.

By the time they'd reached the front door, she'd only slightly composed herself, impatiently waiting for Dimitri to unlock it. A few seconds seemed like a lifetime as he punched in the security code. The heavy cedar wood door creaked open, and she wiggled in his arms.

"No time for a tour," Dimitri managed as he carried her up the staircase. His mouth found hers and he fell back against the entryway, kicking off his shoes. He laughed as she reached for his pants.

"Faster," she demanded. The heat between her legs grew unbearable. Yearning to touch him, she attempted to unbuckle his belt with one hand.

"Now that's not very submissive of you, mate. You know I'm lookin' forward to it," Dimitri teased. Oh she'd submit, all right. And he hadn't forgotten about his promise to have Jake watch. But tonight, it'd only be him and her, together.

"I need you," she cried, grazing his nipple with her teeth. Unable to loosen his pants, she slid her hand underneath the waistband and wrapped her fingers around his rigid shaft.

"Damn, girl, now that's gonna leave marks. You're asking for a spanking," Dimitri grunted as she stroked him.

By the time he made it to his bedroom, he was sweating in anticipation. Her lips on his skin. Her hands on his dick. It was too much and not enough all at once.

Gently, he helped her steady on her feet. As the realization hit them that they were about to go forward with their relationship, committing in a way that could not be undone, they paused, gazing in each other's eyes. Dimitri stood statuesque above her, his dark eyes trained on hers. His white dress shirt hung wide open, his bronze chest reflecting the light from the moon and stars. The sexual tension escalated as they stood inches from each other, no longer touching.

Dimitri reached for her waist and found the zipper to her dress. He tugged, until he reached her hip. Hooking his thumbs over her spaghetti straps, he pulled downward until the fabric lay pooled at her feet. Gillian stood smiling in only her black lace bra and matching heels. She wore no panties, thanks to their earlier antics in the courtyard. With care, Gillian glided her palms over his ripped abdomen. When she reached his broad shoulders, she dragged his sleeves off his arms, undressing him. As the shirt hit the floor, she gave him a seductive smile, reaching behind her and unsnapping her bra.

Not giving him a chance to touch her, Gillian braced her hands on his hips. Carefully she descended, softly kissing his belly as she lowered herself onto her knees. Dimitri sucked an audible breath as Gillian unbuttoned his pants, freeing his hardened arousal. She slid her fingers over his muscular buttocks, jostling his trousers until they fell down, joining her dress at his feet. Pressing her cheek against his tight corded thigh, she moaned, her hot breath causing his shaft to jerk in response.

Gillian teased his skin, lightly skimming her fingertips over the backs of his calves, never losing contact until she'd cupped his firm buttocks. Eyeing his straining erection, she darted her tongue outward and laved its broad crown. She licked at its slit, moaning in satisfaction as his salty taste amped her desire. Parting her lips, she took him all the way into her warm mouth and sucked hard. Gillian twirled her tongue against his silken steel, plunging up and down, from his tip to the root of him. She gently dug her fingernails into his ass, pulling him closer toward her so that she could swallow him more deeply.

Dimitri bit his lip as the sweet torture continued. Unable to take her lips around him for another second, he growled. There was no way he was coming in her mouth. She'd had her fun and now he'd have his.

"Cher, up," he commanded. Raking his fingers through her hair with one hand, he fisted it and tilted her head backwards, lifting her chin. Her mouth released him with a soft pop.

Gillian smiled and licked her lips as he slowly guided her upward and onto the bed. She tried to hoist herself further back onto the mattress, when she heard him tell her to lie back.

"Put your hands above your head…that's it…flat against the headboard. Soon enough I'll have you tied to my bed, but tonight, I want to test your self-control." Dimitri smiled as she complied, doing what he'd asked.

He knelt on the bed, his hands opening her thighs so he could get a better view. "Goddess, look at how beautiful you are." Leaning forward, he blew softly on her mound, intending to pay her back for what she'd just done to him. Tracing his thumbs over her swollen labia, he gently spread her.

"You're so soft. Your pussy smells of my scent and yours," Dimitri whispered. He flattened his tongue over her swollen clit, smiling as he felt her shiver underneath his touch. He pressed his lips to her folds, her juices flowing into his mouth. The delicious taste of her made his wolf howl, reminding him of his ultimate goal.

"Dimitri, oh my God, please," she pleaded, her body on fire with need.

Gillian sighed in pleasure as his fingers stroked deep inside her core, teasing her sensitive band of flesh. Dimitri flicked the tip of his tongue over her clitoris, and her body arched off the bed. She screamed, his mouth at her sex setting a thousand synapses firing. Her climax slammed into her. She thrashed and clawed her nails against the bed frame, losing control.

As she fought for breath, Dimitri hoisted her legs over his shoulders.

With her eyes locked on his, she gasped as he gripped her thighs, sheathing himself completely. She thought he'd rip her in half, her pussy quivering around his enormous cock. He paused only for a second for her to adjust to the size of him, grunting as he began to move.

"Yes…ah, God," Gillian said mindlessly, lost in the feel of him within her. She fought the desire to reach for him, her palms flattened against the wood.

"Fuck, yes…you feel so goddamned good," he growled.

Her breasts, heavy with arousal, jostled in tandem with each of his thrusts. She contracted around him, her breath coming in punctuated grunts.

"I've got to come…please," she begged, so close to her release.

"That's right, cher. Say it," he encouraged. Dropping his hand between her legs, his thumb found her hooded flesh.

"More…Dimitri, I can't…please right there…" Gillian whimpered as Dimitri flicked over her clitoris, putting pressure on the sensitive nub. Uncontrollable spasms ripped through her once again. With no time to recover, she felt him pull out, flipping her onto her stomach.

"Hands and knees," he ordered, nudging her thighs apart with his knee.

"Don't stop. I need you in me."

"Now," he demanded.

Gillian scrambled into position, her own canines dropping in response and she hissed. It wasn't exactly submission, but for tonight, it would have to suffice.

"Ah, my sweet kitten. You've a lot to learn." He laughed, slapping her ass. She squealed and then moaned as he rubbed his palm over the heated skin. "You like that, don't you, darlin'?"

"Stop playing with me." She avoided answering. He responded by spanking her other cheek. "Ah, yes, I like it…fucking yes…now please, I can't wait."

"No matter what you want…" he glided his open palm down her back. When he reached her bottom, he trailed his thumb down her crevice, stopping to circle her tight puckered flesh, "no matter how dark you imagine the desire, you will tell me the truth."

"Yes," she acquiesced, unable to deny the urge to press back into his hand. She'd never explored anal play, but her body ablaze, she craved to experience everything.

"Don't you worry…we're gonna do everything…I'm gonna take you every way possible…including here," he promised, probing her with his thumb. Dimitri took his throbbing dick in his hand, sliding it over her entrance, moistening it with her juices. She heaved a breath, impatiently pushing back into him. But he held her still, slowly pressing into her anus. "We're gonna make love soon enough, cher. Feel me in you."

"Ah…it's so tight," she whispered, her head lolling forward.

"Relax now…here we go," he warned. Guiding his hot flesh into hers, he slowly entered until he was fully seated, his digit all the way into her ass. "That's it...give in to me, Gilly."

"Yes...please," Gillian breathed. The overwhelming sensation rippled through her body.

Dimitri began a slow pace, in and out, making love to her, but soon the craving to mark his mate overrode everything else. He withdrew his finger, cupping both sides of her bottom. Using her for leverage, he increased the pace, moving deep within her. In rhythmic fashion, he pounded in and out of her. Gillian rocked back into his thrusts, the sounds of flesh meeting flesh sounding throughout the night.

In a frenzy, Dimitri leaned over, his weight forcing them both onto their stomachs. She tightly gripped the sheets as he surged into her from behind. Wrapping her hair around his hand, he guided her head to the side, exposing the tendons of her neck.

"Do it," she cried. In the midst of their fervor, clarity struck and she willingly sought his bite. She was tired of being afraid of what she'd lose, and focused on everything that she could gain. *A partner. A life. A family. Perhaps even love.* The stakes were high. A risk to be certain, yet she refused to cower from fate.

Dimitri's wolf went wild at her call. His fangs descended. Pumping hard into her heat, he struck, clamping down on her creamy flesh. She cried out, and he held her still, careful not to puncture or tear Gillian's skin. With a final thrust, he came hard, flooding into her. Shuddering, he let the remaining tremors claim him.

Releasing his jaw, Dimitri licked over where he'd bitten. She moaned and he lifted off her torso. He lay on his back, bringing her with him, resting her onto his chest. Embracing her, he kissed the top of her head and sighed.

While he'd initially been consumed by the lust and urge to mark his mate, he now reflected on what was in his heart, which felt tight with emotion. It wasn't just that he mourned the eventual loss of her tiger, although the thought weighed heavily upon him. For the first time in one hundred and twenty years, he'd developed strong feelings for a woman, one he wouldn't give up without a fight to the death.

⤚❧· *Chapter Fourteen* ·❧⤙

Gillian awoke, the sun shining through the window panes. She moved to reach for Dimitri, her hand fondling the sheets. She realized he was gone, but in surprise, her fingertips touched a fragrant object that lay on his pillow. Her vision came into focus and she gazed upon the beautiful bouquet of irises. Each flower was unique with its silky purple and gold petals. She brought them to her nose, taking a deep sniff, and a broad smile broke across her face.

Holding them to her chest, she looked up at the cathedral ceiling, remembering how they'd made love the night before…twice. But it was recalling his bite that generated her deep sigh. Without even looking, she knew it was there. In the limo and then again in the house, she'd given him approval, given herself permission to accept his mark.

Her stomach growled and she marveled that she was more concerned about eating than the fact that she may soon not be able to shift. It wouldn't be decided until they'd mated, but what they'd done last night was the first step. She tried to conjure up a thread of regret. After all, she'd spent so much time trying to avoid the very thing she'd just thoroughly enjoyed. Yet nothing came to her. The excitement of seeing him again was the only thought spinning through her mind.

The sound of a piano startled her, and she jumped to her feet. Altogether nude, she found her way into the bathroom and spied a note on the mirror: *Robe is on the door and toothbrush is in the drawer. Come downstairs when you're ready, my lovely mate.* And he'd drawn a heart…a big ass freakin' heart. No one had ever written her a note. She laughed, thinking that her dominant wolf was a romantic; the more she knew about him, the more fate was convincing her that it knew what it was doing.

Gillian turned her back toward the mirror, and lifted her hair. As she'd suspected, a light pink pattern had appeared on her shoulder where he'd bitten her. Like a fine tattoo, its intricate design colored her skin. Exhilaration mixed with trepidation filled her heart. She could hardly believe she'd chosen Dimitri, that he was hers.

She considered that after it was all said and done, neither of them might be able to shift. Despite it all, the happiness in her chest refused to be thwarted. Though she'd detected his injured wolf when they'd made love, she hadn't thought about the consequences of her actions or the taint on his beast. Her only focus had been on the strong man holding her in his arms. She knew that today serious conversations needed to be had. As she traced the contours of the lines on her skin, pride in his mark superseded every other emotion.

After freshening up, using the bathroom, she tied the robe around her waist. Making her way to Dimitri, she heard classical music. It grew louder and more intense, and she found it interesting that he liked the genre. She'd expected him to listen to zydeco or rock n' roll, with his bad boy good looks, but this was a surprise, reminding her that she still didn't know him very well.

Quietly, she padded down the hallway, taking note of the colorful modern paintings on the wall. Holding tight to the banister, she descended into a bright, airy great room. She smiled at the sight of Dimitri sitting at a grand piano. Shirtless, the corded muscles of his back curved down into his shorts. Even though she was certain he'd heard her enter the room, he continued to play. His body rocked in rhythm, his fingers moving up and down the keys with the fluidity and ease of a concert pianist.

She came up behind him, placing her palms on his shoulders. His muscles tensed as he continued, lost in the piece. Energy flowed through him to her hands, and it was as if he were creating power via his connection to his instrument. As his fingers came to a rest, she pressed her lips to his back.

"That was beautiful," she said.

Dimitri quickly reached around to his mate. Before she knew what had happened, he'd lifted her off her feet and had her cradled in his lap.

"Good morning...or good afternoon, should I say?" Dimitri kissed her shoulder with small pecks until he reached the sensitive area behind her ear.

"You play the piano?" She giggled from the sensation.

"Hmm...yes but I'm more interested in playing with you," he replied. Tugging on her loosely tied belt, he slipped his hand over her skin, laying it on her belly.

"You were amazing." She smiled.

"Why thank you, cher. You were quite the little minx yourself. You ready to go for round two or is that round three? The courtyard counts, right?"

"Stop it." She slapped him softly on the chest.

"What? Is my count off?" Smiling ear to ear, he cupped her breast.

"Is sex all you think of?" she asked.

"That's a loaded question that I refuse to answer. Besides, your nipples don't lie." He gently pinched her pebbled peak. "I'm not the only one thinking of sex."

"Maybe, but that's only because of you. Now come on. Tell me about this." She gestured to the keys.

"This," he leaned forward and took her rosy tip into his mouth, sucking until she moaned, "this is soft and delicious."

She rolled her eyes and laughed. Crossing her legs together, she tried to thwart the ache that throbbed between them.

"I smell you, darlin' and it ain't the bacon that has my mouth waterin'." Dimitri pressed his face into the hollow between her breasts and kissed her skin.

"The....the piano," she stuttered, attempting to focus.

"You are tenacious."

"I am. Please, tell me."

"Mama insisted I learn how to play. 'The classics', she'd say. So the classics I'd play. Bach. Chopin. Beethoven. Once I shifted, well, I took up the squeezebox. Mama wasn't crazy 'bout it but she got used to it. Bought my first les tit noirs after the turn of the century…1910, it was. I've got a small band I play with sometimes. But at the end of the day, I always return to the eighty-eight."

"It's beautiful," she remarked, stroking her fingers over the ivories.

"Oui, ma chérie."

"French?"

"Ah, we're a bit French here, all right, but I'm afraid I've been hangin' out with Leo too much."

"And your parents?"

"Are in Philadelphia. Mama and Papa joined Tristan after he became Alpha up there. They come down from time to time."

"And how do you think they're going to respond to having their son mate with a tiger?"

"After a century, cher, they're happy to see me mate with anyone who makes me happy. Ya'll don't know how fast a rumor spreads 'round here. I'm sure the entire city of brotherly love was ablaze with the news after my announcement last night. I already got a call from my mama this mornin' wanting to know everything about you. I promised we'd come up there next month."

Gillian laughed. "I can't wait to meet them."

"How do you think your mama's gonna react to you matin' with a wolf?" Dimitri asked.

"Not fair. She can't shift. Not to mention that my father was an Alpha who's no longer alive." She averted her gaze and sighed. Raising her eyes to meet his, she continued. "Truth?"

"Truth."

"She's not going to be too happy. She didn't exactly encourage me to get to know Jax, and he was my own brother. I love my mom dearly, but I'm thinking it may be best we break it to her after we mate. You know the saying about asking for forgiveness? Let's go with that plan."

"Are you upset with your mom? About Jax?"

"I don't blame my mom for not wanting me to see my brother. At the time, I was the one who made the decision to cut off contact. She had me so scared about what could happen. She's worried I won't be able to shift. But at the same time, I want to be with you. No one's going to stop me from doing what I need to do."

"All that Alpha in ya…oh my." He laughed.

"What?" she asked with a grin.

"Submitting's not gonna be easy." He shook his head.

"Are we back talking about sex again?"

"Let's just put it this way." Dimitri paused, considering how she'd get along with everyone. She'd have to fall into the natural cadence of life within a pack. "When we mate, I think you're gonna still shift, but you may be wolf. Even if you're not wolf, you're gonna have to learn how to integrate into the pack. In the end, all wolves must learn to submit, to have discipline. We do it to ensure order. Order keeps peace. Peace keeps us safe, well organized."

"Last night with you was great and all. But I'm not that experienced with submission in any part of my life. I'm feline. I don't think I can do it," she confessed.

"Last night was beautiful." He winked and took her hands in his. "You need to look at it this way, cher. Submission is about trust. In bed. In life. Take Logan for example. I trust him to do what's best for us. Now that doesn't mean I don't advise him or disagree at times. But when push comes to shove, his word goes. I support him in the same way the rest of the pack submits to me."

"I guess it's hard for me to understand. It's not like I don't know that my DNA has wolf in it. Technically, I was born into a pack. But my life with my mom...we were isolated. It's not just about having anyone to submit to. It's so much more. I've never had anyone, period. No one to trust. No one to rely on. Sure I have friends, but the kind of thing you're talking about...it's not the same."

"Which is why we'll go slow with the pack. You felt it with Logan, though...the power. I saw it on your face when you met him. Humans can't feel it, they just have a sense that he's dominant. Leo, on the other hand, he acknowledges Logan's power but damn if that old ass vamp isn't putting out some serious high volt wattage of his own. What you felt with Logan is the natural order calling you."

"I felt it...he was strong, but I wasn't afraid."

"It isn't about being afraid. It's about trust, respect and knowing without a doubt that he's in charge. That he'll keep you safe."

"And you?"

"Look, Gilly, I'm not going to sit here and tell you that you not submitting is an option. I think you know that being in the pack...it's a team...a family. My family. And I hope someday yours, too," he said, brushing her hair from her eyes.

"And what if we can't shift? What if we mate and I lose my ability? What if we can't get rid of this thing...whatever it is inside you?"

"We'll face it together, that's what. But I'm a fighter. You don't get to be in my position without battlin' it out every now and then."

Gillian didn't want to know what he meant by that. She wasn't sure she could handle watching him in a challenge.

"We'll get through this," he reassured her. "Besides, I have a feelin' you're going to come through stronger than ever."

"Why hasn't the witch healed you? Last night…when we were together, I could feel it…that evil. But when I concentrate, letting my energy out, I know I can heal you. Why can't we just do that? I'll be there for you…every single day if that's what it takes."

"I wish." Dimitri kissed her forehead and took a deep breath. He hadn't wanted to admit that his wolf had grown weaker. Their recent interludes had done little to help. "Ilsbeth needs to purge this. It can't be done without magic."

"But maybe I can…" Gillian knew of her gifts. She wasn't certain that like her father, he'd be given them when they mated. Her mother had told her stories about how her father had shifted into a tiger. Like a childhood fairytale, she found it difficult to believe. She'd never seen it with her own eyes and didn't want to raise his hopes. But in the back of her mind, it remained a last resort.

"Ilsbeth is bringing in a sorcerer. We'll have to go to them…see what he recommends. She thought he'd have to meet me in person for it to work."

"What's the deal with you and her?" Gillian hated asking but she'd seen how close they'd been, the beautiful woman's hands on her wolf.

"She's a friend."

"No…she's more," she challenged.

"It's not what you think."

"I saw it in her eyes last night. Are you dating?" Gillian held her breath, waiting on his answer.

"She's a friend," he sighed. "Was she more than a friend at one time? Yes. But I'd always told her that we couldn't be more. I'm not goin' to lie to you. I've lived a long time, and I'm not exactly celibate."

"Okay," she said, pensively balling up her hands. The admission punched her in the gut. She knew she shouldn't be jealous. Of course he'd dated, but hearing him say the words pained her.

"Every wolf knows that he or she is going to meet their mate. And when it happens, the chemistry…the call of it…it can't be ignored. It's not fair to lead another person to think that they can be your partner, your spouse or whatever, when you know at any moment you could be walking down the street and bam, it's over. I told her…" Dimitri went quiet, scrubbing his hand over his brow, uncomfortable with the conversation. He didn't want to hurt Gillian but if she was going to meet Ilsbeth, there was no knowing what the witch would tell her. "I told her that we couldn't date. She's been around a long time, too. It's not as if she didn't know. She, uh, isn't my biggest fan right now."

"That's not what it looked like last night," Gillian responded.

"She doesn't know what she wants. Believe me, Ilsbeth is all about Ilsbeth," he mused.

"Are you sure she's the right witch? Maybe she's not helping you on purpose."

"I don't think so. Don't get me wrong, she was pissed at me big time, but she didn't even know about you until last night."

"She didn't know when she did the spell?"

"No…she didn't." *But she asked me to move in with her and tried to kiss me.* Guilt tore at him but disclosing those facts didn't seem in either of their best interests. Ilsbeth knew he had a mate and that was all that mattered.

"We're meeting her tonight?"

"Yeah. So, uh, what about you? No boyfriends?" He smiled, changing the focus.

"Me? Not really. I dated humans. I've only met a few tigers, none were my mates. Avoided wolves."

"Not anymore."

"And look where that got me." She shook her head, lifting her eyes to his. Her lips couldn't help but curl upward despite the unpleasant conversation they'd just had about the witch.

"On my lap, that's where." He laughed. "And the problem is?"

"Are you always so…I don't know…funny? Optimistic?" she asked.

"Is there any way else to be? I may be immortal but I'm not wastin' this life in misery or fear."

"Hence driving your motorcycle cross-country? Single-handedly almost killing an Alpha? Jumping into hell pits with dangerous vampires? What else do you do for fun?"

"Tiger taming…it may be the scariest gig I've taken on."

"Tiger taming, huh?" She laughed, rolling her eyes. "I didn't realize you worked for a circus."

"Oh, no, no. I don't believe in caging animals, darlin'. Wild animals should be free," he proposed, spreading open her robe.

"No ringmaster?"

"I may be a master but only in the bedroom. No circus here."

"I'm impressed with your bravery," she said, tracing a small circle on his chest, "but if you're in the tiger taming business, what makes you think you'll come out unscathed? Tigers are deadly, you know…ferocious."

"Indeed."

"You may get scratched…we like it rough."

"Aw cher, I plan on earnin' a few scratch marks along the way, but my cat, she's going to be purrin' like a kitten when I'm done with her."

"You may get bitten, then what?"

"A few bites never hurt anybody." He glided his hand down her forearm, teasing her inner wrist. "I can take care of myself."

"So you plan on using a whip?"

"Only if she likes it. But you've gotta be gentle when taming tigers…coercing them only makes them more aggressive." Without warning Dimitri lifted her up onto the piano, her bottom hitting the keys. The ping of the notes sang into the air. "Careful, calculated attention…now that's what trains a tiger. You must get close to her…earn her trust."

"Sounds dangerous," she gasped as his palms glided up her inner thighs. Off balance, she held onto the rim of the fall board.

"Lethal," he agreed. Locking his eyes on hers, he skimmed his hands over her knees until they fell wide, exposing her sex.

"You're very confident." The heat grew between them as Dimitri's sensuous mouth approached her abdomen.

"I can be commanding when I need to…my tiger knows she can trust me to take care of her," he said. Pressing his lips to the soft skin below her breasts, Dimitri smiled.

"Yes," she breathed. Her pussy ached as it brushed against his chest. She began to pant as he placed small kisses on her skin, dipping underneath her belly button but never going any further.

Dimitri lay his cheek flat against her stomach, letting her cradle his head with her hands. His fingers glided beneath her robe, caressing the small of her back

"Have I successfully demonstrated my technique?" he asked softly.

"You scare me," Gillian admitted, her lips brushing the top of his head. Dimitri's erotic touch seared her senses, eliciting arousal through every cell of her body. But it was his flirtatious banter, laced with a hint of truth, that had touched her heart. The more she got to know him, the man behind the wolf, the more she realized she'd never be the same. It wasn't just about her not shifting; it was about caring for someone so much that she could barely breathe. She was falling for him.

"You terrify me," he replied, hiding his expression from her.

"This thing between us…it feels so…"

"Yes it does."

"How do you know what I was going to say?" She laughed.

"I care about you, Gilly," he said, not quite answering her question. "I'm not a fool. I know there's this physical thing that draws us together. Whatever that magic is that give us our mates."

"Chemistry."

"I never thought I'd find someone…it's been a long time."

"I haven't lived as long as you, but I know what it feels like to be alone." Gillian rubbed her cheek into his hair.

"No more." Dimitri lifted his head to look deep within her eyes.

"No more." Gillian's heart raced. It wasn't as if they'd declared their love for each other, but the intimacy around their fears and optimism allowed them to share the vulnerable nature of their feelings. A new beginning for them both.

As Dimitri leaned forward, Gillian took his face into her hands, cupping his cheeks. His eyes fell to her lips and then caught her gaze again. Slowly, he leaned into her embrace until his mouth claimed hers. Gently his tongue slipped between her trembling lips. Gillian's fingers tunneled up into his wavy brown hair. Fisting his locks, she hungrily kissed him back.

Gillian's hands fell to Dimitri's waistband, tugging down his shorts, freeing his erection. Her smooth pussy grazed his belly, and she struggled to get leverage, to alleviate the ache. Dimitri sensed her need and bent his knees so that his hardness pressed against her entrance. Using a hand to guide himself, he eased himself into her, inch by inch, gingerly joining their bodies as one. Never breaking contact, Dimitri built a slow rhythm.

Gillian absorbed the way he moved inside her and moaned in pleasure. It was only a matter of time before her beast submitted completely, marking him in return. By doing so, she'd fully accept her fate. Like an all-consuming force of nature, Dimitri destroyed every last preconception she'd held about wolves mating. His intoxicating presence in her life had become a delicious necessity.

"Always," she spoke into his lips as he surged within her, unsure of whether she was talking to him or herself.

"Goddess, yes. You're everything," he breathed. The physical attraction was banging hard, he knew. But the more time they spent together, the more he emotionally committed to Gillian and he started to believe that it'd be possible for him to find love.

The piano keys chimed as he delved deeper into her core, rocking into her body. Her staccato breath told him she was close, and he could no longer hold back the release they both sought. With slow, forceful thrusts, he stimulated her clitoris with his pelvis, throwing them both over the edge of ecstasy.

Gillian screamed against his lips as Dimitri heaved against her, matching his intensity. Merged together, she contracted, shaking as the rush of her orgasm tore through her body. Holding on for dear life, she wrapped her legs around Dimitri's waist, encouraging him to go deeper.

Dimitri felt her inner muscles fist around him, and he no longer fought his impending climax. With a grunt, he came, pouring himself into her. He kissed her again, wishing he could say all the words that lay hidden in his heart. She'd slay him, he knew. Yet the taste of her was like lifeblood, pulsating into him with explosive passion.

Desperate to own their feelings...for each other...for their future, they succumbed to the delicate intimacy that had begun to weave itself into their hearts. As their kiss slowed, they continued to seek each other, not wanting the moment to end. Eventually, their lips stilled, their breath softening. Gillian and Dimitri drew closer, cheek to cheek, eyes closed, lost in the surreal sensation. An intense state of intimacy existed, one neither of them had ever experienced. Danger would come. It lurked outside like an evil cloak waiting to suffocate them. But for the moment they relaxed into their newfound relationship; never again would they be alone.

‑◆· *Chapter Fifteen* ·◆‑

Gillian sat at the black metal table, tracing her fingers over the small diamond grate. Her face was frozen with anger, glaring at the witch sitting across from her. After making love and eating breakfast, she'd had a leisurely shower and then taken some photos of the bayou abutting Dimitri's home. The slow-moving stream teemed with wildlife and she'd snapped some amazing shots of an egret in flight. A snake swam across the surface of the water and she squealed but still managed to capture its image.

Her relaxation came to crash when Dimitri told her that it was time to go see Ilsbeth. No matter how many times she told herself that the witch was going to help Dimitri, her intuition told her otherwise. As soon as they entered the tiny bricked courtyard of the private café, her stomach knotted in consternation.

There was something about Ilsbeth that bothered her. While she'd been cordial, shaking Gillian's hand, introducing her to the handsome sorcerer she'd brought to help Dimitri, the petite angelic-looking woman gave her the chills. It wasn't lost on her how the witch had kissed Dimitri's cheeks, lingering seconds longer than necessary. Gillian tried to shake off the feeling that something was wrong. She tried to blame it on their impending mating; her cat would resent any female touching her mate. It was natural to distrust others, especially a woman who'd been in Dimitri's bed. Despite the nagging concerns, Gillian sucked a breath, resolving that she'd give her the benefit of the doubt. Her first priority was Dimitri and she didn't want to do anything to jeopardize their chances of finding a spell, a cure for his affliction.

The waitress set their drinks on the table and Gillian nodded, giving thanks. She immediately picked up her diet cola, wishing she'd ordered rum to go in it. Having restraint she hadn't known she possessed, she forced herself to calmly listen to the discussion as if the woman sitting across from her hadn't fucked her mate a half dozen times. She glanced to Dimitri, who had his eyes pinned on Ilsbeth and the sorcerer. Jake sat on her left side and when she turned to him, he gave her a sympathetic smile. Logan, the Alpha, sat next to Dimitri, but she could tell he planned on letting his beta handle the situation. The tension was so thick she thought it'd wilt the ferns hanging from the balconies.

"Marcus has told me of a spell that can reverse the taint on your soul," Ilsbeth began.

"Reverse? Don't you mean remove?" Dimitri asked.

Gillian resisted the urge to reach for him. The tone of his voice, low and dominant, called both to her need to comfort and the desire to submit. She coiled her fingers around her tall glass, ensuring she'd keep her hands to herself. There was no room for mistakes. She refused to allow her impulsivity to distract him.

"Remove, reverse. Whatever," Ilsbeth repeated. "It's not as if this happens every day. I've lived almost as long as you have and I've never met one shifter who's lost his wolf. Marcus, on the other hand, has experienced it."

"In the 1960s, I worked a case," Marcus said.

"He offers his services to hire for humans," Ilsbeth interrupted with a note of disdain.

"Yes, Ilsbeth is correct," he agreed, visibly annoyed with her assessment. "Supernaturals aren't the only ones worthy to receive our gifts. But I digress...in the case I'd worked, the shifter had become involved with a human, one who'd suffered from possession. As you can imagine, the Church was involved. After the cleansing, the man, let's call him John for the sake of our discussion. Within weeks of the exorcism, John was unable to shift."

"Were you able to use a spell to resolve the issue?" Dimitri asked.

"Yes, we were, but it was a nasty demon who'd metaphysically leapt from one soul to another. I understand from Ilsbeth that your entity is more parasitic in nature. Given that it's non-intelligent, technically, it should be easier to oust."

"Surely it has an instinct to survive?" Dimitri challenged.

"Like any parasite, it's deriving benefit without a true symbiotic relationship. Unlike the demon, which seeks to kill its host, it seeks only to exist without motivation. If it kills its host, that would result in its own demise."

"But it is killing my wolf. I mean, the stuff Ilsbeth's given me has helped. Between that and Gillian..." Dimitri looked to her, as if to ask for her permission to tell them what she'd done to help him. Her ability to heal was a gift, one she hadn't shared with many people.

"No, it's okay," Gillian said. She saw no harm in divulging this information. In contrast to Ilsbeth's secretive disposition, Marcus seemed open and willing to share his experiences. Gillian steeled her nerves, looking to both Dimitri and Logan. "I, um, I can heal people sometimes. Only shifters...at least that's how it's worked so far. It's not like I really get to test it all that often. It's not super-powerful or anything, but I was able to pull back his wolf. You know, in California when Dimitri couldn't shift. When we're together..."

Dimitri reached for her hand, taking it in his and kissed it. "When we are together, skin to skin, I can feel her positive vibes. But it's not working as much. Whatever this is, it's getting stronger."

"Interesting...your abilities." Marcus paused. "It makes perfect sense, though. Even just a week ago, the parasite, it was newer, a larva if you will.

But now that it's grown, it's larger, stronger, not as easily subdued by your efforts."

"If it kills my wolf, then it will die?"

"Well, yes. It feeds off your magic…the inherent energy that feeds your wolf, causing you to shift. But I'm afraid if it comes to that, you cannot go back."

"But you can fix it?" Logan interjected.

"The spell we used…for John, it was successful. Ilsbeth and I have discussed the necessary arrangements, and it can be done. But you'll need to acquire the blood. It must be given to you freely, of course."

"Of course," Dimitri said sarcastically. He'd already given Ilsbeth hair from his wolf, gifting it to her in an attempt to make amends for their argument. Clearly that hadn't worked.

"Blood?" Gillian couldn't help but gasp at the suggestion.

"Vampire blood," Ilsbeth stated coolly.

"That's easy enough…I'll ask Leo," Dimitri told her.

"It must be a female," Ilsbeth added. "Tell me, do you know any lady vamps willing to give you their blood?"

Dimitri returned her icy stare. Her comment made him suspect she'd been stalking him.

"Leo's introduced me to some vamps. I'll ask him to help me."

"I'm sure he has," Ilsbeth retorted.

"Is there something you want to say, witch? 'Cause if there is, out with it. I don't have time for games."

"Nothing…just saying that Léopold gets around. I'm sure the two of you have had your adventures."

"In which case, it would be no business of yours," Dimitri replied.

"I'm not sure what you're getting at but I can assure you that all I care about is the spell. Even though we no longer are seeing each other," Ilsbeth looked to Gillian, "that doesn't mean I don't care. We shall do the spell when you get the blood."

"Is there anything else I need to know? Any other freaky-ass ingredients you need?"

"Dimitri, I don't know you that well," Marcus began. He took a deep breath and sighed. "I'm going to be straight with you."

"Please do."

"With these kinds of things…"

"The leech on my wolf?"

"Yes, well, that's one way of putting it. You don't have much time. If this thing is successful, it'll kill your wolf within the week," Marcus surmised.

"The end game?" Dimitri asked.

"You won't be able to shift. Ever again." Marcus spoke with an eerie calmness.

"I'd be mortal," Dimitri stated. He breathed deeply, letting his anger settle like volcanic ash smothering a mountain. It was important his Alpha realize the severity of the situation. He'd no longer be pack. Like other humans, he'd age, die. His life as a wolf would end.

It wasn't as if Gillian hadn't considered what could happen to Dimitri. It was no different than what she was facing by agreeing to mate him. But it was the exchange between Dimitri and Ilsbeth that captured her attention, noting that his cool demeanor had been replaced with controlled irritation. While he may have dated the witch, her words had drawn his ire. Provoking Dimitri, she supposed, took a lot of effort, yet Ilsbeth deliberately had pressed him. Gillian wasn't sure why her question had the effect that it did, but her intuition told her it all had to do with their previous relationship. As she quietly mulled over what Ilsbeth had said, Gillian imagined it might have to do with another woman.

Dimitri tugged at her hand, alerting her that it was time to leave. She pushed out of her chair, wondering about where they were going to find a vampire. Gillian supposed she should have been afraid, but after being captured by wolves, twice, all she cared about was getting the blood. Too bad it had to be given willingly, she thought. Otherwise, she'd happily hold someone down to get a tiny sample.

When she thought about not being able to shift again, she knew she'd be crushed. But Dimitri had so much more to lose…his beast, his place within the pack, his family.

As they left the restaurant, Gillian turned her head to catch one more glimpse of the witch. Her eyes locked on Ilsbeth's, and it felt as if the witch was reaching into her chest. A chill blew over her arms, causing gooseflesh to rise. Gillian recoiled from her gaze, bringing Dimitri's arm around her shoulders. In her gut, she knew that the witch sought her harm. Maybe she had everyone else in the room fooled, but Gillian knew otherwise. Witches kept hocus pocus in their bag of tricks, but tigers took no prisoners. If Ilsbeth wanted to start something, she could bring it, because Dimitri was hers.

❧ Chapter Sixteen ❧

I'm not afraid of vampires. Gillian repeated the phrase as she walked into the dangerous club, Mordez. She dug deep, searching for the courage that she knew existed in her inner kitty. Yet as she took in her surroundings, she reasoned that she was close to being more like the cowardly lion. As she ran through the excuses in her mind for her lack of courage, her reaction seemed perfectly reasonable. In order for her to shift, she'd have to waste precious seconds stripping off her dress. Vamps on the other hand, had the advantage of speed and were always ready to go, their fangs protruding like nails from their gums.

Dimitri had warned her on the way over to the bar to stay close. From the way he spoke, he wasn't exceptionally fond of the establishment, even if Léopold was a close friend. They had entered via a back entrance, a tunnel through a labyrinth of underground hallways. Gillian held onto the back of Dimitri's shirt as he and Léopold parted their way through the crowd. Blinding strobe lights flashed as the band raged toward the back of the room. The low bass pounded loudly, the vibrations filtering throughout the arena. Hard driving heavy metal music blasted them as they reached their final destination.

Some patrons wore gothic clothing and some dressed as if they'd gone to a New York City night club. Many had a dazed, sexual look in their eyes, dancing, drinking, feeding and fucking. It was a chaotic contained free-for-all.

A pale human female writhed on the copper bar. Her breasts exposed and skirt hiked up to her hips, she moaned in ecstasy as two males fed from her. One was latched on at her neck, pinching her nipples; the other suckled from her inner thigh. The threesome appeared oblivious to the crowd that had gathered to watch. Uninterested parties hailed the bartender as if the spectacle was nothing more than a common occurrence.

Gillian contemplated Dimitri's demeanor. On the way back from meeting with Ilsbeth, he'd been uncharacteristically quiet. No jokes or sexual innuendos. He'd been all business, calling Léopold and discussing whether or not they'd bring her with them. Gillian had insisted she come to help get the vampire blood. With Dimitri's wolf weakened, she couldn't bear to leave her mate alone, unprotected.

Although she hadn't told them, she had every intention of shifting if danger presented itself. A wolf or vampire, she was not. But her tiger would battle to the death to protect Dimitri. Regardless of her fear, fight or flight response invoked, she'd fight to the death.

Through the din, Gillian heard Dimitri say something to Léopold, pointing to a raised section of tables. Flowing sheets of white satin hung from the ceiling, bunching onto the floor, effectively separating the area into individual alcoves. Black lights shone onto the white leather sofas and chairs, creating the illusion of privacy within VIP seating.

Jake extended his hand, ushering her onto a loveseat. Dimitri sat next to her while Léopold and Jake took captain chairs across from them. A waitress dressed in a black leather corset and matching panties approached, setting down drinks they hadn't ordered. Léopold laughed and picked up the glass, nodding to her with a cool, knowing smile.

Confused, Gillian glanced to Dimitri, who had already brought the amber liquid to his lips. Although she'd never seen him so serious and determined, she found this new side to him captivating. Exuding sex appeal and power, Dimitri appeared to be unaware of all the females taking note of his arrival. Casually dressed, he wore loose jeans and an untucked white shirt with rolled up sleeves. A smile crossed her face as he caught her ogling, and she laughed. The respite from the dark mood was welcome, yet short lived.

Two women approached and Gillian noted that Dimitri's expression had turned to stone. A striking woman glided toward them, her presence bringing a new level of electricity to the air. Refined, she looked as if she belonged in the eighteen hundreds, her gothic velvet gown trailing behind her. Her blood-red lips accentuated her creamy-white skin and her dark brown hair was coiffed into an updo. Looking as if she'd stepped off the cover page of a romance novel, she smiled and nodded at each person in their party. A second woman, wearing a hot-pink spandex bodysuit, followed.

Nervous, Gillian took a sip of her drink and coughed as it burned her throat. She looked down to her floral mini-sundress and thought she should have worn a different outfit. On second thought, her platform shoes showed off the lean contours of her legs and were easy to shuck in case she needed to shift. She owned a corset and as much as she enjoyed the way it looked, it took considerable time to get it laced up correctly. When she'd worn it, she'd been locked in tight, making shifting difficult.

"Why hello, boys," the beautiful woman greeted them.

"Lady Charlotte. Bonsoir," Léopold replied, standing. "Thank you for meeting with us,"

"How's your lovely nymph?" she asked.

"Naiad. She's doing very well," he answered.

"Dimitri, so good to see you." She extended her delicate fingers toward him.

"Lady Char. Thanks for having us. You look, um," he paused, reaching to shake her hand. "Mysterious, very chic. That dress is one of a kind."

"Why thank you. I take it your Alpha is well."

"Logan's doing great, thanks."

"Jake, long time no see," she remarked.

"Hello," he replied.

"Ah, Dimitri, you've brought a friend." Lady Charlotte set her vision on Gillian. "So pretty. And young."

Gillian concentrated, forcing herself to breathe slowly, controlling her heartbeat that threatened to race, revealing her trepidation. As the vampiress leaned forward, Gillian took her hand. She'd expected a simple exchange but Lady Charlotte held tight, taking the opportunity to hug her, sniffing her hair.

"Fascinating," she laughed, releasing Gillian. She placed her palm on Dimitri's arm. "Where did you find her?"

"We found each other." Glancing at Gillian, who appeared exceedingly calm, he sought to make it clear that she belonged to him. The excitement on Lady Charlotte's face indicated that Gillian had piqued her interest. "Gilly, this is Lady Charlotte. She owns this fine establishment. A good friend of Leo's. Lady Charlotte, this is Gilly. She's my mate."

"Your mate. Now how can that be? What you propose is unheard of. She's a shifter, but not a wolf." Lady Charlotte sniffed again in Gillian's direction. "And she smells so good. Do tell, my lovely, what are you?"

"I'm a tiger, but I'm also part wolf." Gillian looked to Dimitri, whose face registered surprise. Publicly acknowledging her lupine heritage hadn't been planned, but as the words left her lips, she felt relief.

"Hybrid tigers don't breed with wolves, so what is this magic?"

"It's my breed."

Lady Charlotte rounded behind Gillian, lifting her ponytail. Gillian restrained her protest yet her claws extended at the intrusion. She took a deep breath and played it cool, waiting to act. She was in a room full of vampires and it would be risky attacking the owner.

"Easy, pet." Lady Charlotte dropped her locks and eyed Dimitri with curiosity. "You've marked her. I don't think in all my years I've seen such a thing."

"We're here about me, not her," Dimitri said, taking Gillian's hand. "Let's sit."

"My friend needs a favor, one that I'd gladly give him but I need you to do this for both him and me," Léopold told her.

"Out with it," Lady Charlotte said, her voice terse. She smoothed her dress and sat down.

"I need vampire blood," Dimitri replied. "From a woman."

Lady Charlotte gave an insincere laugh, shaking her head. "Léopold, darling, why on earth do you think I'd ever give my blood to a wolf?"

"Because I'm asking nicely. One hand rubs the other." Léopold's icy smile was but a warning. His fingers curled into the arms of the seat.

"It seems as if I'm the one who's been doing all the work lately," Lady Charlotte complained. She glanced at Dimitri and blew out a loud breath, displaying her annoyance.

"I'm not asking you twice. You will assist us," Léopold challenged.

"What is he to you anyway? He's handsome, I'll give you that. Lacey raved about his sexual prowess. But to you? What difference does it make if he dies tonight?"

Léopold sprung from his seat. Before Lady Charlotte had a chance to respond, he stood behind her; his hand delicately squeezed her throat, not quite choking her.

"This beta is my brother; that is all you need to know. Now will you help him? It must be given freely," he told her, his finger stroking the hollow of her neck.

"No need to explain," she said sweetly. Placing her hand over Léopold's, she attempted to pry his fingers loose, but his grip held firm. "Yes, okay, yes."

Léopold released Lady Charlotte and nodded at Dimitri, who smiled, admiring his friend. The ancient vampire emanated power, and had displayed his lethal nature on more than one occasion. Both humans and supernaturals were foolish to cross him.

"Oui, I'm pleased that we understand each other," Léopold commented blithely.

"Oh fine, already. But it won't be me….Lacey, there." She pointed to the female in the cotton-candy-colored outfit. "She'll do it."

Léopold raised a questioning eyebrow at Lady Charlotte.

"What? You can't possibly expect me to give *my* blood to a wolf. You do what you want," she began. A look of disgust crossed her face. "That's right, I know about you saving the Alpha's mate. And now with this 'brother' nonsense. Your prerogative, I suppose, but I for one am not in the business of donating my body to dogs. This isn't an animal shelter I'm running."

"Lacey is acceptable, no?" Léopold looked to Dimitri, who nodded in response.

"The witch said as long as it's given freely, it'll work."

"Now wait a damn minute," Lacey interrupted. The pink stretchy fabric strained to cover her breasts as she rose to meet Léopold's gaze. "If Charlotte needs me to do this, I'll do it. But I think it's only fair that I get something in return."

"If it's money you want, no problem," Dimitri said. A silent understanding passed between him and Léopold.

"I want a dance…maybe even a taste of that hot wolf blood you have pumping through those muscles of yours."

"No," both Dimitri and Gillian said at the same time. Gillian stared at Lacey, challenging her to lay one undead finger on him.

"What? Is it wrong to want something for my trouble?"

"Lacey, I don't think that's a good idea. Gillian's my mate."

"So what? She's already marked up like a chalkboard. Have you marked him back?" she challenged.

"No," Gillian bit out, hostility in her voice.

"Well, that's your own fault. You snooze you lose, pussy."

"No. Just no." Gillian stood up, looking to Jake, Léopold and Dimitri.

"Well then, I just may not feel in a giving mood tonight. Charlotte said I had to give you my blood, but she didn't say when."

Furious, Gillian's canines descended and out of embarrassment, she covered her mouth with her hands. Emotion swirled inside her like a hurricane, and she tried to compose herself. She'd never shifted in front of strangers; it seemed bad form to do so out of jealousy. Turning her head, she took a deep breath, her teeth returning to normal. Dimitri rose to look at her but she held up a hand, indicating she was okay.

"Jesus Christ, Charlotte. Are you really going to let her get away with this?" Dimitri yelled.

"I'm hardly responsible for Lacey's small demand. Seems quite reasonable given your history. You didn't mind letting her taste you the last time you were here. In fact, I recall you did all sorts of things. Perhaps you'll be more careful where you decide to wag your tail in the future."

Gillian's head swung toward Dimitri, her eyes wide. He'd slept with Lacey too? She told herself it shouldn't matter. He had been single and dating; he'd lived a long time. He'd been with many women. But still, the knowledge of his indiscretions cut deep.

"Léopold?" Dimitri looked to his friend for assistance.

"Sorry, mon ami. You know that our blood is a gift. It would be no effort to force her, but that defeats your need."

"It must be given freely," Gillian repeated. Thoughts of Dimitri with Ilsbeth and Lacey forced her to bite her lip, hoping the pain would distract her from her anger. Her eyes narrowed on the blonde vampire who fluffed her hair with a snide smile.

"Gillian, no," Dimitri started to say.

"It's all right. Desperation comes in all forms. Apparently, she hasn't gotten over you either," Gillian noted. "She's right. You aren't marked. Although, judging by the women I've met today, I clearly misjudged things."

"You know it was before you...we hadn't met." Dimitri sought to assuage her anguish over the situation but it was of no use.

The air thickened as reticence set in, Lacey's demand bringing them to a crossroads. Jake shrugged at Dimitri and began silently counting the tin tiles on the ceiling. Léopold laughed, aware that his friend had his dick caught in a trap. For all the chaff Dimitri had given him over the past weeks, he found it slightly amusing.

"We're all grownups," Gillian stated, breaking the silence. Her lungs felt as if they were collapsing as she spoke. She fingered the pleats of her dress, her brow knitted in anger. Gillian took a deep breath, telling herself that it was time to put on her big girl panties and suck it up. Regardless of what happened between her and Dimitri, she wasn't about to put his wolf further in danger.

"Please, Gilly. Let's go talk in private," Dimitri pleaded. He reached for her but she drew back her hands, wrapping her arms around her waist.

"No. We don't have time to waste. Let's get to it." Gillian's lips pursed. Her fury bubbled at the surface but she contained it. "One dance."

"See there, that wasn't terribly difficult," Lacey drawled. She held out her palm to Dimitri; her other hand rested on her cocked hip.

Dimitri turned to Gillian, taking her in his arms. She feigned resistance, but soon gave into him as he cupped her cheek.

"This means nothing, okay?" He brought her close and whispered in her ear. "Remember today at the piano...I meant every word I said. Forever."

Gillian's heart melted as she lifted her gaze to meet his. She nodded, tears brimming in her eyes. Unable to respond, her words choked in her throat. He leaned in to capture her lips, and she accepted his searing kiss, running her hands up his back. Barely aware of their audience, she sought to possess him, reminding him that he belonged to her. As they reluctantly parted, Gillian and Dimitri rested their foreheads against each other's, their eyes locked in understanding.

"Jake," Dimitri called, still focused on Gillian. "Take Gilly. Do not let her out of your sight. I'll be gone two minutes." He turned to Lacey. "I'll get the blood and we're out of here. Leo, keep watch, would ya?"

"Oui," Léopold said. He glanced at Lady Charlotte. "We have business to discuss. I'm not going anywhere."

"Let's go," Dimitri commanded, reaching for Lacey's hand. She laughed and gave Gillian a triumphant smile as they headed to the dance floor.

"You wanna dance? I promise not to step on your toes," Jake joked.

"Okay," Gillian replied, her voice shaky. She gave him a small grin, but never took her eyes off her mate. As Dimitri took Lacey into his arms, Gillian thought she'd be sick.

"Hey, you know he's only doing this for the blood, right? She's nothing." Jake took Gillian's hand.

"I gave him permission, didn't I? I'm not as fragile as I look," Gillian commented.

Jake laughed and placed his hand around her waist, taking her palm with the other. "Oh believe me, sugar, I've seen you in action. Fragile isn't exactly the word I'd use to describe you."

"Thanks...I think." She relaxed into the sway of the music, stealing glances at Dimitri, who wore a pained expression.

"It's a compliment. I like a woman who can take care of herself." He spun her around as a sultry song began to play. "You're good for Dimitri."

"How so?"

"He's been lonely. I think after Logan and Leo, he realized he's been by himself a long time. Take that trip to California, for example. Sometimes we all need to take a little walkabout...get our thoughts together."

"Didn't exactly turn out how he planned."

"No, it turned out better." Jake smiled and drew her closer.

"How so? He almost died."

"Yeah, there's that. But there's times when…well, death is always there, even when you're immortal. Life's a calculated risk. You weigh the danger. When possible, avoid things that might kill you. It's rare but even wolves die…vamps too. Bottom line is that Dimitri didn't die out in San Diego. He found you."

"And you?"

"And me what?"

"Do you feel alone?" Gillian looked up at Jake. Muscular and clean cut, he looked as if he belonged on a professional baseball team.

"I'm content," he whispered in her ear.

"I've always been alone," she confessed. "But Dimitri…he makes me feel…"

"He's your mate. He'll make you feel things you never thought possible."

"Yes. But more than that, he makes me want to be with others…to find my wolf. Being tiger is everything to me…was everything."

"And now?"

"I don't know. None of it seems to matter. I just want to be free of Chaz. I want Dimitri to be well…so we can be together."

"And if you lose your tiger? Become wolf?"

"I'd mourn her, but I'm in a different head space than I was a week ago. I can't go on fighting Alphas who want me for my gift. It's futile, especially when I've found Dimitri." Gillian bit her tongue. She'd said too much. She hadn't even told Dimitri about how the mating would affect him and here she was blabbing her secret to Jake.

"Your gift?"

"It's nothing," she lied.

"Nothing, huh?" he questioned, not believing a word she said.

Gillian leaned her head against Jake's chest. Regretting her words, she said nothing more as she glared at the woman who touched her mate. Sharp fangs descended from the vampire's ruby-red lips, poising to strike Dimitri's shoulder. As the vampire tore open Dimitri's shirt, Gillian's tiger attempted to shift.

This is the most fucked up shit I've gotten myself in in a while, Dimitri thought to himself. Sure, he'd had sex with Lacey. *One goddamned fucking time.* He didn't have a mate when he'd done it. As a matter of fact, he'd been going through a dry spell and had only been at Mordez to help Léopold. It was that night he'd met Lacey. One drink led to a dance and one dance led to a hot quickie on the corner of the dance floor. It had meant nothing to him or her.

Women, he mused. His entire life he'd been clear with every single woman he'd ever been with that he couldn't commit. He'd refused to date them exclusively, because inevitably it led to feelings. Feelings led to bruised hearts and worse, damaged egos. He'd never been in love, not even once in over a hundred years. He'd been careful to mostly have sex with only wolves, because at least they knew the score. Each and every wolf knew that the universe had selected a special person just for them. Most females from his pack understood and reciprocated his philosophy on dating. They knew that it was just a matter of time, give or take a century or two, before they met their mate. Committing to someone else led to disaster.

He'd told the witch. He'd told the vampire. Decades of having sex and it was never an issue…until now. Why fate had to go and kick him in the balls, he didn't know. He was true-blue honest, easygoing, would give a stranger the shirt off his back. But today had been one of the worst days ever. Sure it'd started off well enough. Making love to Gillian had been a dream. But the day had taken a nosedive, first with Ilsbeth, and now with Lacey.

Seeing the crushing look of disappointment in Gillian's eyes had nearly killed him. He'd never meant to hurt her. But nor would he lie. The past was the past. Gillian was his future; one that would be built on trust, not deceit. If Lacey wanted a dance to inflict some kind of sick punishment on him, he'd let her have one dance, but she wouldn't have his blood.

When he got home, he planned on explaining everything to Gillian. If the cards hadn't been stacked against him with the whole 'tiger hybrid' snafu, they sure as hell were now that she knew he'd slept with both the witch and vampire. He was acutely aware that no matter his desire to mate, Gillian had to choose him…choose their mating. He'd grovel if he had to, but he'd damn well get things straightened out.

The sickening sweet scent of vanilla drifted into his nostrils, causing him to cough. Disgusted, he continued to move to the music, Lacey's fingernails digging into his pecs. He glanced to Gillian whose blank expression told him she'd had enough. It made him sick that he was the cause of her pain. Although he'd imagined the pleasure of sharing his mate with another, watching Jake take Gillian in his arms in order to calm her crushed his heart.

He heard Lacey say something to him, and in his peripheral vision, the gleam of white pointy fangs flashed. Snatching her arm out of thin air, he held her still.

"What the hell do you think you're doing?" he yelled, astonished that she'd try to bite him.

"I told you that I wanted a taste. You didn't say anything, ergo, you said yes. Seriously, Dimitri. Are you so stuck on that hybrid that you don't want to have sex? I can't even get a little bite? It's fucking ridiculous," Lacey ranted. 'Even if you managed to mark her, that kind of mating is unheard of…a wolf and a tiger. How long have you even known her?"

"Are you crazy? She's my mate. I get you're a vamp, but don't play dumb.

You see she's marked, and you asked to touch me. I told you flat out when we first met that I couldn't commit. I'm a wolf. Not a human. Not a witch. Not a vampire. I'm a goddamned wolf. You know what that means. But you still play games?" Dimitri saw Jake holding Gillian back; she'd tried to come for him, no doubt. Her eyes were a fierce shade of gold, her claws extended. Screaming, she attempted to yank free of Jake's restraint.

"I was just having fun is all. You wolves are so sensitive. What is it? Maybe you haven't gotten your kibbles tonight. Hungry?" she taunted.

"We're done. You hear me?" he told her, his voice booming over the music. "Go get the blood now. I expect it in a container. No funny business either. Make it clean. Make it quick. If not, you'll have to answer to Leo. As much as I'd love to discipline your ass, I expect leaving it to your kind would be the best punishment I could think of. Yeah, I think Leo would have a lot of fun with you. Wanna try me?" Dimitri jerked free of her hands, enjoying the spasm of terror that twisted her face. "That's right, noob. Leo loves dishin' out a little killin' every now and then. You saw how he grabbed Lady Char around her chicken neck. Imagine what he'd do to you."

"You are making a mistake," she warned.

"Yeah, yeah. The only fucking mistake was being with you. Now scamper off. A little more blood, a little less talkin'," he demanded.

"Fine. You can freely have my blood but trust me, I'm the least of your problems."

Lacey turned on her heel and headed for the back of the club. Immediately, he went to Gillian who growled as he approached.

"Gilly, I'm so sorry, cher," he began, just as she cut him off from speaking.

"Don't cher, me. No." Gillian pried Jake's fingers off her arms and rubbed her wrists.

"I told her that she couldn't…" Dimitri attempted to explain.

"Did you get it? Did you get the blood?"

"She's gettin' it now. Please, I can explain. She's a vampire…this is how they are."

"Just no. I don't want to hear it now. I've got to get out of here. The bathroom. Where's the bathroom?" she asked, scanning the room.

"I'll come with you," he offered.

"No. Just get the damn blood," she told him, confused, hurt. "Jake. He can go with me."

Dimitri's jaw tightened at the slight. He understood her anger. It tasted bitter but was justified. Swearing he'd fix this, he nodded at Jake to go ahead.

Dimitri, disgusted with the evening's events, shook his head. He watched as Jake ushered her off the dance floor through the crowd. Gillian, who was of a smaller stature, was swallowed up into the horde of people. He glanced up to Léopold who caught his gaze, but was soon distracted by Lacey, who impatiently tapped on his shoulder.

"What?" he growled. "Where is it?"

"Here," she said, slamming a vial of blood into his hand.

"Thanks." He took a deep breath. His mama had taught him manners, but he was finding it difficult to appear grateful after the antics she'd pulled. "Listen, I'm sorry, but you knew the deal. I'd never try to hurt you on purpose."

"Yeah, yeah. I'm a vampire. I don't have feelings." Lacey flipped her hair and crossed her arms across her chest.

"Tell yourself whatever you need to, but that's bullshit in my book. Look at Leo. You just haven't found that special person yet. It's just not me."

"Tigers don't mate with wolves."

"I already explained it. It's rare but she's my mate. You've gotta let it go."

"I'm not the one who has to let it go. I feel sorry for you," she said cryptically. Cupping her breasts, she adjusted them, making her cleavage more visible.

"Okay, well, thanks again." He turned to leave, giving a small wave with the vial in his hand.

"Just remember, I'm always here, wolf," she laughed. "If you ever wanna go vamp, look me up."

Dimitri shook his head, stroking his beard. His instincts told him that Lacey had more to tell him, but he'd had enough of her antics and wanted to get Gillian home. Eyeing the crimson gift, he slid the glass tube into his back pocket. He nodded to Léopold, who appeared deep in conversation with Lady Charlotte. He pointed in the direction of the restrooms, and set off to find Gillian.

By the time he'd made his way across the dance floor, he spotted Jake leaning against the wall, looking at his cell phone. Dimitri's eyes caught his as he approached.

"How bad is it?" Dimitri inquired, knowing full well that Gillian was beyond pissed about his past sexual transgressions.

"She's been crying," Jake responded.

"I'd better go in there," Dimitri told him, waiting for him to move out of the way.

"It's died down. She'll be okay. She just needs time."

"You clear the bathroom?"

"What? You think I'm an amateur? Give me some credit, bro," Jake said, patting his jacket, indicating he'd brought a concealed weapon with him.

"Noticed you enjoying your dance," Dimitri commented with a smile. He'd hoped that Gillian would get along with his closest friends. Eventually she'd get to know everyone in the pack a little better. All they knew so far was that she was his mate and that they'd gone at it hard in the courtyard. The thought brought a smile to his face.

"What's not to enjoy? She's a sweet little thing. I give her credit hanging in there. This place…it's not for the faint of heart."

"True dat. This place is hard core. I can remember my first time, coming here with Logan, watching Leo do his thing right out there in the bar."

"No one can ever accuse Léopold of being understated. Although considering you just fucked your mate at the ball, well, glass houses and all that. Just sayin'," he joked.

"Yeah, what happened…it's not like a full moon where everyone's just gettin' their freak on whenever and wherever. This mate thing…it's driving my wolf, making me a little crazy. Now that she's accepted my mark, it's taken the edge off a little. You notice I didn't go berserk when you had your hands all over her?"

"I noticed," Jake smiled. "I do like her, by the way."

"I like her, too," Dimitri responded. *I like her way too much. Falling for her is more like it.*

"I'm sure you've been 'liking' her a lot lately." Jake waggled his eyebrows at Dimitri.

"All night and all day long, my friend. Say, I get she was mad at me but what do you suppose is taking her so long?" The hair on Dimitri's neck stood up as soon as he asked. A high-pitched scream, belonging to his mate, tore through his gut.

Gillian sat on the closed toilet seat, her face in her palms. *I can't do this. I just want to go back to New York.* She regretted the way she'd lost her cool. Yet her emotions felt out of control. One minute she was a lust-filled vixen, the next, she was ready to stake a vampire. She closed her eyes, trying to get in touch with her beast. A flicker of recognition registered, but her connection was weakened.

Unable to take the stress of losing her tiger, and wondering if her mate was capable of being faithful, the tears began to fall. Dimitri had given her no reason to doubt his fidelity but she couldn't help but wonder why the witch and vampire were so attached. They treated their impending mating with as much respect as a bag of soggy diapers.

She wiped her eyes with the back of her hands, taking a deep breath. Trying to put things in perspective, she told herself that she was just over reacting. She'd never seen a vampire try to bite someone before. Perhaps the shock of seeing fangs was the factor that had thrown her into a fit of rage. But that wasn't enough to explain the sheer jealousy that had coursed through her. Her tiger needed to mark her mate, she knew.

As she concentrated on breathing, deeply inhaling and exhaling, she heard a distant noise…a howl. Gillian jumped to her feet, her heart racing. Again it sounded, and she realized the noise was coming from inside her. *What the hell? No freakin' way. Do I have a wolf inside me?*

Gillian grabbed a wad of tissue off the roll, blowing her nose. Panicked, she fumbled with the lock. She had to tell Dimitri what she'd heard. Before she had a chance to open the stall door, a creaking sound caught her attention. Confused, she wondered if Jake was coming into the ladies' room. He'd insisted on not letting anyone in with her while she was in there, telling her that she wasn't safe. She hadn't argued and waited until he'd cleared the area.

"Jake? Dimitri?" she called, slowly sneaking a peek through a crack.

"Sorry, doll. No boys, only girls."

"How did you get in here?" Shocked, Gillian flung the stall open, and stared at Lacey, who admired her own reflection in the mirror, carefully checking her hair.

"Ah…it's a secret. But that's what girls do…we tell secrets." She reached into a sparkly heart-shaped purse and took out a small tube. Popping off the top and twisting it upward, she applied the lipstick to her already heavily made-up lips. "I've got a couple of secrets for you. You'll keep it just between us, right?"

"Are you crazy?" Gillian carefully navigated to the sink furthest away from the vampire and turned on the spigot, washing her hands. "If you're referring to the fact that you dated Dimitri, I got that."

"Fucked, sweetie. We fucked. He let me bite him, too. And we did it all out in public. He's a wild one, all right. But then again, most people who come here are."

"Why are you telling me this?" Gillian thought she'd be sick as Lacey told her details about her relationship with her mate. She couldn't erase his past but she sure as hell didn't need to relive Dimitri's greatest hits.

"Because your mating may not take, you know?"

"Not that it's any of your business, but it's already taking. Hence, his mark." Gillian dried her hands and sighed. "You know, I haven't been around very many vampires, but I always imagined they'd be a bit brighter than you."

"No need to be nasty." Lacey used a fingernail to wipe a stray smudge of red from her mouth. "Personally, I enjoy a fine wolf. He's wrong, though. It's not as though I'm expecting any sort of commitment. I've been recently turned and am very much enjoying the height of my sexual prowess. But the witch…well, she wasn't quite as happy. Wolves mate. No matter what you do, there's no way around that…unless you find a way to make someone a wolf no longer. Tricky business I suppose, but who says it can't be done? Dimitri is in a bit of a pinch, isn't he?"

Gillian closed her eyes briefly and blew out a breath, taking in Lacey's enigmatic rant. *Is she seriously telling me what I think she's telling me? Is Ilsbeth responsible for Dimitri losing his wolf?*

"What are you trying to say?" Gillian asked.

"It's rumored that they'd broken up months before the incident with the demon, that she demanded more of a relationship. Just saying that it's awfully convenient that the witch was in the vicinity right around the same time Dimitri starting having trouble shifting. If he'd lost his wolf completely, even sooner, he wouldn't have been able to detect you as his mate, now would he?"

"Why do you care anyway? I still don't get why you're telling me this." Gillian moved toward the door. Pity for the pathetic vampire rolled in her belly. Despite Lacey's words to the contrary, she must have crushed hard over her one night with Dimitri.

"My other secret is even better. Are you ready for it?" Lacey asked, taking a small key from her purse. She located a raised fleur-de-lis on the wall, and slid it open, revealing a keyhole.

"You've really lost it, haven't you? I'm done here. If you have anything else to say, sorry, I'm not interested. Go tell Léopold. I'm sure he can help you with whatever your issue is. Insecurity? Jealousy?"

"You're wrong. I could care less what bitch that mutt chooses to mate with. I do take pleasure in watching him squirm, however. But money? That I could use. Lady Charlotte hardly pays me enough to stay in this damn job but every now and then I run into someone who makes it worth my while."

Gillian set her hand on the locked door, reaching for the small chain that Jake had told her to lock. As if she'd submerged her fingers in ice water, they clumsily picked at the small metal hook. Gillian swore, watching Lacey turn the key, aware that whatever she was about to reveal was dangerous. A secret panel along the side wall of the restroom slowly slid open as Gillian yanked at the chain. Her heart seized in her chest as she caught sight of a man and a wolf. Chaz's wolves had come for her.

"No hard feelings, doll. Money's money," Lacey sang as she slipped into the clandestine compartment, leaving Gillian alone with her attackers.

"You," Gillian gasped, recognizing one of the men who'd been at Chaz's home. The upside down cross tattoo on his forearm led to a hunting knife clutched in his left hand. In the other, his gloved fist held silver cuffs. A bulky fellow, he walked with a slight limp. But if she remembered correctly, it hadn't kept him from holding her down for Chaz when he'd bitten deep into her flesh.

"Alpha's gonna be happy we caught you," the menacing grey wolf who flanked him replied with a growl. "We got lucky. Stopped in here to ask around and lookie, lookie. Who knew vamps were so easy to bribe? You'd think you'd want to lay low, but no, here ya are, out partying."

"You'll never get away with this," Gillian began. She kicked off her shoes and tore off her dress as fast as she could.

"Should be an easy grab. Whadya think, Rex?" The animal offered no response as he plodded toward her. "You go ahead and strip down, bitch. Once we silver ya, you ain't gonna shift again. Maybe we'll give you a go in the car."

The wolf snarled.

"I didn't say we'd fuck her. No, the Alpha wants that pussy all to himself. But ya still got a mouth. I'll teach you how to open wide on the way over to the airport," he taunted. Flicking open the cuffs, he approached. "Look at those lips on ya. Bet you like a big dick. You're gonna have one real soon."

Gillian didn't stop to remark on his crude comments. Hoping that Jake had his ear pressed to the door, she screamed at the top of her lungs, right as she shifted into her tiger. The transformation was rough, painful like she'd never known. A hot slice tore through every cell. It'd never been such agony to shift, but she kept telling herself that she was changing, her great cat dying, her wolf emerging. If she didn't concentrate, she'd die. She'd cry later. *It's normal,* she told herself. *I'll get through this.*

Transformed, she lunged at the thug, her powerful jaws ripping at the man's arm. His whiskey-soaked blood gushed into her mouth as her head thrashed from side to side. If it weren't for the adrenaline pumping, she'd have noticed the razor-sharp wolf canines carving into her hide. It didn't deter her. Anger at Chaz and his pack fueled her attack. She registered the horrified cry of the man as she crushed through his bones, ripping his forearm from its socket.

As she spat out the appendage, she turned to the wolf, that had lodged its teeth deep into the back of her neck. Her own blood spurted from her wounds, distracting her from her initial attacker. She whimpered as he slapped a silver cuff around her right paw; the excruciating burn flashed through her body. Her naked human form slammed into the floor with a thud, her head splitting open on the red-stained tiles. The wolf continued to shred her throat, growling and scratching as he did so. The last thing she heard was gunshots, before darkness claimed her.

Dimitri shoved at the door, breaking the metal chain off its hinges. The stench of sweat and blood smacked at his senses as he plowed forward into the bathroom. He cried out as he caught sight of the armless man, pinning Gillian to the floor. As she lay face down naked, a feral wolf locked his jaws deep into her flesh and had begun shaking his head furiously.

Enraged, Dimitri stripped off his shirt, calling his wolf, yet only a whimper registered in his mind. He cursed, realizing that once again, he was losing the ability to shift.

"Gun," he called to Jake, who'd begun taking off his jacket.

Jake tossed the weapon to Dimitri, and commenced shifting.

"Get the fuck off of her," Dimitri ordered, taking care to aim so that he wouldn't hit Gillian.

"Piss off, buddy," the stranger replied with a grunt. Ignoring Dimitri, he began to try to undress so he could shift and heal. He pushed up so that he sat on Gillian's legs.

Dimitri had had enough. He fired off a pop and the bullet traveled straight through the asshole's head. Dimitri winced as blood sprayed against the walls. Eyes wide open, the man fell dead against the pedestal sink.

Jake had leapt upon the grey wolf, but it refused to release Gillian from its bite. Without hesitation, Dimitri advanced toward it. Pressing the muzzle into its fur, he pulled the trigger. With a whimper, the wolf stumbled backwards, a breathy rattle coming from its throat. As it shifted, a blonde male, who looked to be in his mid-twenties, came into sight.

"Get him," Dimitri called to Jake as he knelt down next to Gillian. She lay motionless, despite no longer being mauled about by the wolf. The smell of burnt flesh drew him to the cuff on her ankle. Dimitri tugged at the locked silver, singeing his fingers. "Fuck."

Figuring that one of them had brought the keys, Dimitri crawled to the large man, who still wore clothes. He dug through his jeans, locating the metal chain that was jammed deep into his pocket. Dimitri pinched it with his fingers, quickly yanking it free of the fabric. Wasting no time, he unlocked the shackle from her leg.

"Gilly, can you hear me?" he cried to her.

When she didn't respond, Dimitri gently rolled her over onto her back, supporting her head in his lap. Although she was breathing, he immediately noticed the two-inch gash on her forehead as well as her bloodied swollen eyes. He curled her up against his chest, hoping she'd regain consciousness. The wounds on her neck had already begun to heal, but he knew the poisonous metal had injured her tiger, making it more difficult to shift.

Dimitri took a deep breath and fought back the rage that threatened to overtake reason. He glanced across the room, at the detached arm that lay in a puddle of blood. She'd defended herself. What he couldn't figure out was how they'd gotten into the room. However, as he lifted Gillian into his arms, he took note of the open secret panel.

"Gilly. Please, Goddess," he said, brushing the hair from her eyes. "Jake, leave that fucker. Give me your shirt."

"Here you go." Jake threw it to him and then leaned over to scoop up the weapon that his beta had tossed aside. He toed at the guy who was laid out cold. "I gotta make sure this douchebag isn't going anywhere. He's going to be out for a while. Lucky he's not dead with the plug you pumped into him. Looks like it went straight through. How the hell did they get in here?"

"There." Dimitri nodded to the open door. "They didn't just get in here on their own. Someone did this on purpose."

"Jesus, is she okay? Why isn't she shifting?" Jake asked. Using his jacket, he snatched the handcuffs up off the floor. "Goddamned silver."

Dimitri only heard half of what Jake was telling him as he held his mate. Gillian coughed; her mouth twitched but no words came. Her eyelids slowly opened, and he breathed in relief.

"Darlin', say something," he pleaded. His lips mere inches from hers, he cradled her head, stroking her hair.

"Dimitri," she whispered.

"You're safe now. I'm sorry. I'm so damned sorry." Dimitri looked to Jake. "Grab my phone. Text Leo. I want him here now."

"I think the whole bar probably knows," Jake commented, looking up to the crowd that had gathered around the door. Léopold pushed through with Lady Charlotte following close behind.

"What the hell happened here?" Lady Charlotte began but Léopold unceremoniously cut her off.

"Tais toi." Léopold held up his hand, shushing her. She crossed her arms and rolled her eyes in response, but didn't make a move to disobey his command. "Wolves, no? But how did they get in?"

"I'd cleared the restroom. But apparently vamp lady has secret doors...doors that I'm sure only she knows about," Jake stated, his eyes pinned on Lady Charlotte.

"You did this? You attacked Dimitri's mate?" Léopold accused, gripping her arm.

"Of course not. Why would I do anything like this? I keep these exits...passages for emergencies. Look at me, you know I'm not lying."

"Shut the fuck up," Dimitri yelled.

"I'm sorry," Gillian managed, her voice barely audible.

"Gilly, you're gonna be okay. Do you want to shift?"

"Can't...I feel so weak."

"It's the silver."

"The wolves...where are they?"

"Don't worry about them. I'll tell you when we get home." Gillian attempted to push out of his arms but he held her tight. "Wait a second, cher. Leo, find out what happened...how these wolves got in here without us knowing. If that bitch over there doesn't know about it, go down the chain, starting with Lacey. As much as I'd like to personally kill whoever did this, I've gotta get Gilly home. Can you get these assholes out of here? Give us some privacy?"

"Oui." Léopold gave Lady Charlotte a hard stare and released her, gesturing for her to go. "You heard him. Get rid of your customers. Now!"

Lady Charlotte scurried into the hallway and began ordering everyone out of the area, funneling them onto the dance floor.

"Call Logan. We've got to secure that fucker over there. Keep him for his Alpha. I'll ask Leo to clean up the rest. Can you shut that door?" Dimitri ordered.

"Ya'll broke it off the frame. I'll just," Jake picked up the heavy wooden door and leaned it against the doorjamb, "there you go. No one can see in. Let's get her to shift so we can get her the hell out of here."

"Thanks, man. And thanks for back there...I couldn't...aw, fuck. You know." Dimitri shook his head, reliving how it felt to call on his wolf. The deafening silence was like a knife to his chest.

"We'll fix this," Jake said. He put his hand on Dimitri's shoulder and then turned away to the sink and began to wash the blood off his hands.

"Hey, Gilly. You ready?" Gillian had fallen back asleep. He gently kissed her forehead and her lashes fluttered.

"Yes," she whispered.

"That's a girl. You go ahead and shift right here. I've got ya. Just remember not to claw me up. Go easy, okay?" he joked.

Dimitri smiled as she transformed. Elated that his injured mate had gone to her great cat, he stroked her fur. She roared and licked his face, letting him know she was healed. The magic of shifting never ceased to amaze him, even after having done it himself all these years. The spectacular sight of her tiger caused him to experience both pride and regret, concerned that she'd never be able to shift after their mating. No matter how many times he told himself that she'd be just as happy as wolf, his conscience warned him not to do it.

-❧· *Chapter Seventeen* ·❧-

The smell of lavender bubble bath filled the air, and Dimitri took a deep breath into his lungs, praying it would calm the tension. He sighed, his heart heavy, as he massaged the shampoo into Gillian's hair. As he sat behind her on the stool, he noticed that her thick dark hair was finally starting to shine through, the cheap dye fading away. Contemplating the night's events, he knew they needed to have a serious conversation about their future.

During the car ride home, Gillian had been quiet. Except for a squeeze of his hand, she'd been essentially despondent. In the bathroom at Mordez, she'd eventually shifted back to her human form. While physically she'd been healed, he immediately knew her emotional wounds had not.

Dimitri had wrapped her in Jake's coat and carried her out to his car where they'd met Logan. After filling him in on what had happened, the Alpha went to help Jake with the lone wolf who was still alive. By the time he and Gillian had arrived back to his house, Dimitri had received a text from Léopold about who'd led the wolves to Gillian. It came as no surprise that Léopold had needed very little interrogation time to affirm the identity of the individual. Apparently the wolves had paid Lacey a considerable amount of money to get access to Gillian. Léopold mentioned that she'd accused Ilsbeth of wrongdoing but that he hadn't given her a chance to explain. Dimitri hadn't asked what he'd done with her, the punishment he'd given. He knew the vampire wouldn't think twice about killing a traitor. Incredulous, Dimitri didn't feel an ounce of pity for her as she had to have known the wolves were planning on torturing his mate.

Dimitri glanced at the gun Jake had given him. It sat on the sink counter, a cold reminder of his affliction. With his wolf unable to respond, he didn't trust himself to be able to protect Gillian. Dimitri had asked Jake to stay overnight and expected him to return as soon as he was finished at the club.

The only saving grace, he thought, was that they'd safely arrived at his home without incident. His sanctuary, it was large and contemporary. The enormous bathroom and shower area, consisting entirely of glass walls, could be viewed through the master bedroom. An oversized tub sat centerpiece. While he rarely used it, he'd personally helped design the layout. The open area reflected his soul, no walls, no pretenses. What you saw was what you got.

"Dimitri." Gillian's soft voice broke his rumination.

"Lift your head up a sec," he told her, turning on the water. He removed the hand-held faucet and sprayed away the lather. "All done, relax back."

"About tonight," she began, pressing the heels of her hands to her forehead.

"You defended yourself." Dimitri wrung the water out of her hair, rolled up a towel and set it behind her head.

"They're not going to stop."

"That's the idea. They'll come to us and we'll take care of Chaz."

"You mean we're going to kill him," she said flatly.

"Yes. I'm not gonna lie about how things are. He'll either give up and go home, which I doubt. Or he'll come here and die on our land."

"Lacey. She told me they paid her."

"So I heard. You know, I'm friends with Leo, but vampires in general…I don't trust them."

"You slept with her."

"Yeah, I did." Her words burned deep, but he knew she had to get this off her chest.

"The thing is, in that bathroom, I talked to her. Lacey doesn't want you or care about you. She reminded me a little of my mom's cat. She'd find a mouse and she'd just kind of bat it around. She wouldn't kill them. She just played with them for entertainment. Lacey is the same way. Tonight, she took perverse pleasure in causing you pain…for fun. What she did to me…that was about money."

"It doesn't matter why she did it. Sometime before she was turned, she learned right and wrong."

"She wasn't attached to you. She understood that you'd find a mate."

"It was just a fling. It meant nothing. I thought that she got that. Vampires usually get it and so do wolves. Single wolves don't make it a habit to fall for someone they've had sex with because they know there's always a chance of finding their mate. There's something innate that tells us it's okay to fool around and we don't get attached. It's just how it is."

"Ilsbeth didn't get the memo," Gillian said quietly. She submerged deeper into the soapy water.

"She's a witch. She knew the deal from the very beginning. I tried to make it up to her, but she's pissed." Dimitri sunk his hands onto Gillian's shoulders, massaging them. "I'm just sorry that you have to be privy to all this nonsense. You know you can feel the difference?"

"What do you mean?"

"I'm not the first person you've dated. Had sex with. This is different. And it's not just the mating, Gil." He paused, pressing his lips to her wet hair. "The heat, the passion we have is off the charts. But it's not just sex, cher. It's everything about us. The way I feel about you." Dimitri cringed at how inarticulate he sounded, but his words eluded him.

"I care about you…too much," she admitted, reaching up to his hands. "I get that you dated other people, but what's going on inside me; it's like I'm feeling everything tenfold. I'm not a jealous person, I swear. But tonight I could have killed Lacey when she went to bite you. And Ilsbeth? She's just a bitch."

Dimitri laughed softly. "Yeah, that's about it. But she's a powerful bitch. So I'm trying to play nice."

"Did you ever think that maybe she isn't?"

"What do you mean?"

"Just something Lacey said."

"You can't really trust her, ya know. Tonight. Case in point."

"I know." Gillian turned around onto her knees, facing Dimitri. She pushed out of the water, her breasts dripping, and balanced herself with her hands on the side of the tub. "But maybe you shouldn't trust the witch. Maybe she had something to do with you losing your wolf."

"No, I know where I picked up this crazy bit of evil. I was there, remember."

"But Ilsbeth was too. She had reason for you to lose your wolf. Witches can be with mortals, right?"

"Yeah, but…"

"What happens when you lose your beast? You'll essentially be human. Maybe you'll continue not to age, but you'll still be vulnerable like a human. No shifting. No pack. No mate."

Dimitri's blood pumped hard as Gillian formulated the accusation that had grown from the seed Lacey had planted. He shook his head, and wiped his hands on his towel. Here he had a beautiful wet and naked woman in his room but they were discussing evil that had no bounds. He swore to himself that before the night was through, they'd be back to making love instead of talking about his exes.

"Just listen," she persisted. "If you weren't wolf, then you wouldn't need to mate. She could be with you…there'd be nothing stopping you from being with her."

"Except for the fact that I don't love her. I wasn't even close to falling in love with her, so there's no way that would happen," he argued. He laughed as he spoke, amused at how Gillian didn't know how much he liked her. "I want to be with you, Gilly. Not because you're my mate, either. I mean, sure, that's what brought us together. But you're brave. And you don't give up. I want to be with you…just you."

A smile broke across Gillian's face at his confession.

"I want to mate with you now," she declared. "I don't want to wait."

"I don't know if that's such a good idea," Dimitri found himself saying. He'd kill to mate with her, but that was exactly the problem; her tiger would die.

"Why would you say that? No, forget it, I know why. Is this about me?" Gillian splashed hot water over her chest, trying to warm herself.

"Of course it's about you," he snapped, torn about what to do. He didn't want to hurt her any more than he already had.

"Tonight I heard a howl…" She looked down into the bath, then slowly lifted her gaze, aware that she'd dropped a bomb. "I heard…I think it was my wolf."

"You what?" His voice grew louder. He shoved out of his chair, and began to pace, plowing his fingers through his hair. "This is crazy. We haven't mated yet. There's no way…we must've done something…what about your cat? I saw what you did to that guy tonight. A wolf couldn't do that by itself. And when you shifted, you were a cat. I saw your tiger with my own two eyes."

"I don't know what's happening, but I know what I heard. Before Lacey came into the bathroom I was all by myself."

"You know what this means?" he huffed, concerned about her feline.

"I'm changing. I can already feel it."

"Because I marked you, goddammit," he said, flooded with guilt.

"I let you. I wanted it as much as you did," she insisted, fingering the area where he'd bitten her. "It's done. And there's something else…something I haven't told you."

"What?" he asked, scrubbing his face. Goddess, what hadn't she told him? When she didn't answer, he approached the bath and sat down in front of her, resisting the urge to take her in his arms.

"I should have told you…I just didn't want you to want me because of it. Chaz, he knows. It's what he wants. It's why he won't give up." Her voice cracked.

"I don't know what you're about to tell me but we'll deal with it. What is it?"

"My mother told me…Jax thinks that…"

"Fucking Jax knows this secret and you haven't told me? Honesty, it's all I ask," he yelled. Dimitri could forgive many things, but lying wasn't one of them.

"Just, please let me finish. I don't even know if it's true. It's like this urban legend about our breed. But Jax thinks it's true. He knew my father, so maybe he saw it firsthand."

"What?" His patience grew thin.

"Supposedly when I mate, the person I mate with…"

"Me. I'm the person you're going to mate with, Gilly. You're mine," he asserted.

"You…you'll take on attributes of my tiger. I lose my cat, but somehow you get them…like gifts. You'll be stronger. Your teeth, your claws, they can change. You'd still be a wolf, but you'd gain her strength."

"You've got to be kidding me?" Léopold had mentioned that she might have gifts but he'd always thought whatever it was had to do with her healing abilities.

"I'm not joking. I lose my ability to shift to tiger. Well, we don't even know if that's true but I can feel her fading already. My mate, on the other hand…you, you'll be able to call on her."

No longer able to restrain himself, Dimitri took her by the arms, gently pulling her upward, until they were inches apart, face to face. "Why, Gilly?

Why after all this time did you keep this a secret?"

"I'm sorry. I know I should have told you but…"

"It didn't make any sense why Chaz was after you. He's doing all of this just so he can steal your power?"

"Yes," she nodded.

"Did your father do this to your mother? Did he hurt her?"

"No, no. She loved him. She always made sure I knew how much he was loved…how much he loved me. They knew when they mated that this could happen."

"You haven't answered my question, though. Why didn't you tell me about your gifts? Did you think I'd steal from you?" He felt her shiver, and pressed her to his chest.

"No. Yes. No, it's not like that. I'm just afraid. I didn't want you to want me so you could be Alpha." She tried to pull away but he held her still.

"We need to get one thing straight, darlin'. I chose not to kill Chaz that night. I don't want to leave to be Alpha of someone else's pack. I don't want to be Alpha of my pack either. If I wanted to challenge Logan to be Alpha, I could do it any damn day of the week. But I don't. Dealin' with the weight of the pack is something that Logan took on when Marcel died and he's got a load of responsibility on those shoulders. Our pack has had enough upheaval in the past twelve months. What I did choose was my position as his beta, supporting Logan, because I love him. It's where I'm most needed in our pack." Dimitri took a deep breath. He couldn't believe she'd hidden the truth from him, thinking he'd want her gifts. His Alpha knew what he was capable of when it came to a battle of strength, but when Logan agreed to lead the pack, Dimitri had made a deliberate decision to support his friend. "Gillian, do you think so little of me that I'd be just like Chaz? That I'd take a mate just so I'd be able to sprout tiger fangs? Seriously?"

"You don't understand. I had to be sure…after what happened with Chaz. I didn't know you."

"I'm not like Chaz. And you know it."

"I just…I just wanted to be loved by someone. Not because I can give them something. Or because of who I am. I hate this mating thing…I just want to be able to choose on my own who I love. I don't want some stupid fate thing to take over my life. I want you…I want you to choose me for me," she cried. "Is it so much to ask? Don't answer because there is no other way for us."

"Gillian, I can't change our circumstances. We are who we are."

"In here." She pounded her chest with her palm. "This is what should matter. I needed to know that you liked me for me, not because I can give you something."

"Goddess, you know I care about you. Why do you think I'm worried about mating you? I don't want to hurt you. To know that I'll be the reason you'll lose your ability to shift…I just don't know if I can do that to you. It's not fair to you." He cupped her face, his thumb tracing her bottom lip.

"All I know is that I can't lose you," she responded. "If we mate, there's still a chance I can give you my gift. This thing with Ilsbeth. What if she did this to you on purpose?"

"What does any of this have to do with Ilsbeth?"

"Because maybe she has no intention of really healing you. Think about this. If she's so powerful and all knowing, why did she have to bring in someone else to help her? Maybe she's just waiting this thing out…waiting for your wolf to die. If there's no wolf, then she certainly doesn't have to worry about you finding or at this point, keeping your mate. Once your wolf is dead, there's no reason to mate with me."

"Listen, I'll be the first one to admit that Ilsbeth was pissed at me, but I don't think that she'd go that far."

"Really? What makes you think she wouldn't? She's not just a little bit upset with you. I saw the way she was looking at you…the way she touched you and no matter what you say, she still wants you. I may not know witches very well but I know when a woman is jealous."

Dimitri sighed, thinking it had been one hell of a night. As much as he loathed to admit it, Gillian's theory had merit. A pit of disgust curled in his stomach as he realized that Ilsbeth could have done this to him on purpose. The night he'd come out of hell, having saved Logan's daughter, Ilsbeth had given him a look of pity. At least that's what he'd thought at the time. Maybe it was guilt for what she'd done? Anger boiled inside him as he gave the situation new perspective.

"Even so, the sorcerer seemed legit. I've got to give his spell a try. There aren't many options left on the table."

"What if…" Gillian paused. "What if we mate tonight? My gifts…they could destroy this thing inside you…maybe forever."

"No. No way. You're grasping at straws. This thing with my wolf. You tried healing me before and it only worked temporarily. I'm not doing that to you."

"I am not grasping at straws. Am I desperate? You're damn straight I am. I'm not going to sit back and wait for the witch who did this to you to save you," she cried, pushing out of his arms. "No, just let me go. You don't believe me. You don't believe I can do this."

"Believe what? That you want to kill yourself to save me?"

"I'm doing this to save us. Us!"

Dimitri shook his head and blew out a breath.

"I healed you once," Gillian pressed. "My ability to heal is still there, maybe not as strong as before, but when we mate, my gift, it may be enough."

"No." Dimitri couldn't allow her to sacrifice herself for him.

"Please, Dimitri. Just hear me out. Maybe when it's all said and done, I'll never be able to shift as cat again, but my wolf, she's there. I just know it…she's in here." Tears streamed down her face and she swiped at them, turning her head away. "You have to let me do this for you. I need you in my life. There's not much time left. Tonight you couldn't shift. Soon there won't be a wolf to even save."

"Please don't cry, Gil," he pleaded.

"I'm losing my tiger already. You're losing your wolf. We can save each other. And I'm not crying," she said with a small smile.

"Okay, tough girl. So those aren't tears, huh?"

"No," she lied, beginning to laugh. She wasn't sure if it was out of frustration, grief or the fact that she was sitting naked in a tub arguing with her handsome beta, who looked like he was about to go feral at her suggestion.

"I don't like lying," he replied, unfolding a large black towel.

"I'm not lying," she stated with a grin.

"I think you might be. You've done many things today to get yourself in trouble. You goin' for broke?"

"Not crying. You see any tears here?" She lay back into the tub, intentionally keeping her erect nipples at the surface so he could see them. "I'm merely trying to get you to see things from my perspective."

"What are you doing, cher?"

"Nothing, what do you think I'm doing?" She gave him a seductive smile.

Dimitri wanted to argue that she was wrong, that they shouldn't mate, but he craved the woman before him. The Goddess had given him a fighter, to be sure. In the past week, she'd killed and maimed, protecting herself from the enemy. Her spirit never faltered despite the fact the war was far from over. The more he thought about it the more he thought she was right about Ilsbeth. *Could she heal him by mating?* In lieu of hard evidence one way or another, he wasn't convinced either way.

Regardless of whether or not it was true, his wolf would demand their mating sooner or later. With her naked and flirting, he was definitely leaning toward sooner. The only real way to deny their mating would be for him to leave, to physically separate himself from her. Doing so was as impossible as asking him to fly to the moon on the wings of an eagle. It just wasn't happening.

Her amber eyes flashed, bringing him back to the crux of the situation. *Mate or not to mate?* The only thing he knew for certain was that he'd make mad love to the woman in his bathtub tonight and wait until tomorrow before deciding on their mating. It would tear him to shreds if she chose not to mate with him in the morning, but he wanted to give her time to make sure that she wasn't overreacting to the earlier trauma. Her choice had to be made with a clear head and heart.

Dimitri's cock jerked as his mate turned up the heat, cupping her breasts, teasing him. He laughed, guessing that she was attempting to use her feminine wiles to get her way. *Yeah, doesn't matter. Kinda likin' it.* Dimitri kept his eyes locked on his mate, as she played with herself. The sexy lil' vixen didn't realize the fire she was starting.

Dimitri glanced over to his cell phone, attempting to check out the time. He knew Jake would be home any minute, and they didn't have much time to make love without an audience. He hesitated, wiping his hands on the towel, but as she pinched her nipples into hard points, Dimitri lost control.

Gillian sensed the exact moment that Dimitri had shifted his position on their mating. A sense of victory and relief filled her chest. She knew it was crazy to fall for someone after only knowing them for a week, but the entire concept of mating wasn't based on reason. Destiny drove two souls to merge hearts, not logic.

Love wasn't supposed to make sense, she supposed. Love just was. She smiled as the thought popped into her head. *Falling in love?* She couldn't even say what she felt was love, mostly because she never had really been in love. But what she did know was that she'd sacrifice everything for Dimitri, her wolf, her heart, her life.

She'd purposefully taunted him with her white lie, telling him that she hadn't been crying. It had hurt that he hadn't jumped at the opportunity to mate with her, but she could see the conflict in his eyes, having believed she'd never shift again. And she, too, had believed the same until earlier when she'd heard the wolf. Like an owl in the woods at night, it had sounded its unique call. The realization that she'd transform again gave her hope that she could survive mating and save Dimitri all at once.

Gillian watched intently as Dimitri silently contemplated her words. Filled with a longing for him, she touched herself, hoping she could seduce him into making love. She craved his hands on her body. Intimacy with her mate would wash away the evil of the day, refreshing all that was well with her life.

As he turned to her, she'd begun to fondle her creamy flesh, pinching her tender peaks. The hunger on his face sent a jolt of lust to her sex. She squeezed her thighs, in response to the ache that built between her legs. With her eyes pinned on his, she deliberately let her left hand slide down her stomach into the bubbly water.

Like a cobra, he struck, tearing off his shirt and jumping into the tub, still wearing his pants. She gasped as he straddled her with his legs, water sloshing onto the floor. Her hands went from her own skin to his. Dimitri raked his hands into her hair, stealing her mouth in a hard, possessive kiss. His tongue forcefully slid through her lips, exhaustively exploring every inch of her warmth. She fought for breath, surrendering to his savage kiss, his hands fisted in her hair.

"Fuck, Gilly," he groaned. "Look what you do to me."

He grabbed her wrist, setting her hand onto his steel-hard cock. She clutched at the wet denim, earning a hard groan from Dimitri. Breaking free from his lips, she sought to taste him, biting and licking at his muscular chest. Reaching his nipple, she nipped him until he cried out at the sensation.

"Oh no, kitten. I'm having none of that," he told her, tugging her head away. His eyes were wild with desire; his lips turned upward in a devious smile. "Tonight, you're submitting."

"What makes you think that?" she challenged with a giggle, her hair still held tight in his grip. At the sight of his wet slippery abs, her lips parted. She tilted her pelvis upward, grinding her mound against his erection.

"Bad kitty," he scolded playfully.

Before she could return his banter, he wrapped his hands around her waist, and stood up straight in the tub. In one smooth movement, he threw her over his shoulder with ease, her legs dangling over his chest. Water splattered all over the floor as he stepped out of the bath.

"What are you doing?" she screamed, laughing at the same time. "You're making a mess."

"My mess, my house, my woman," he responded.

"But…"

"I think it's 'bout time for that lesson in submission. What do you think, Jake?"

"What? Jake's here?" Gillian strained to see as Dimitri twisted his body, giving her a view of Jake, who was standing in the doorway. She gasped in embarrassment, but oddly, the idea of him watching made her hot with arousal. On the plane, he'd seen her suck Dimitri's cock and she'd secretly fantasized about Dimitri's earlier warning that he'd be there again.

"I was going to ask how Gillian was doing but I guess all's well that ends well. Hey, Gilly."

"Hi," she giggled, giving him a wave. "Would you please tell this caveman of a beta to put me down?"

"Wouldn't dream of it, sugar. I expect this is going to be fun. Wish I could participate, but I got a feeling you two got something going on that needs settling."

"My mate's been askin' for a lesson in submission. And during our lil' talk, she bit me. That's twice now."

"That doesn't sound very submissive to me," Jake laughed.

"And I do recall me promising her that when she submitted you'd be here to watch, so feel free to take a shower. You do want him to watch, don't you, Gilly?" he asked, smoothing his hand over her bottom. "You seemed to like it when we were flying."

"I never said that…" Gillian silently cursed, wondering how Dimitri knew she was turned on by the idea of it.

A hard slap hit her bottom and she screamed out loud. The hot sensation caused her to wiggle against him, needing to alleviate the pressure between her legs. Her pussy ached with need, and she dug her fingernails into his back, trying to get him to move to the bedroom.

"I'm thinking maybe after we mate, she may even want to play with both of us," Dimitri suggested. "Do you want Jake to touch you, Gilly? Do you want to play with the big wolves?"

"I can't talk like this," she protested. *Yes, I want to play all right.* She was falling in love with Dimitri and sought to explore her sexuality within the safe confines of their mating.

"Yes you can. No more lying." Dimitri slapped her cheek once more. "Tell me, do you want Jake to touch you?"

"Please…Dimitri." She dug her face into his back, but her smile gave away her desire.

"I'll take that as a yes, darlin'." He smiled to Jake, who in response reached to stroke Gillian's smooth globe, eliciting a small hiss from her. "See Jake, she does like that."

"Your mate is so soft."

"She is. Ah, look at how you respond, Gil. Does it feel good to have both of us touch you?"

Jake ran his fingers down the crevice of her bottom, brushing over her rosebud, his fingers lightly grazing the wetness of her core. Gillian squirmed, her hips pressing back into his touch.

"Yes, Dimitri, please…" she gasped. If he didn't make love to her within the next two minutes, she'd rip out her hair. The man was infuriating and hot, so very, very hot.

"You're suffering aren't you, my lovely mate? We'll leave Jake now. Time for our lesson."

"Shower." Jake pointed to the clear blocked-off stall. Since the bathroom was made entirely of glass, he could easily see them on the bed and they could view him.

Gillian kicked her legs as Dimitri strode into the bedroom. She laughed as she attempted to bat his ass through his wet jeans and promptly earned herself another swat on her wet bare bottom.

Dimitri bent, carefully depositing her on the bed. Gillian went to scurry across it when he latched onto her legs.

"Sweet, Gilly. I'm not joking about your submission tonight. You're going to be wolf soon."

"Yes," she breathed. As she lay belly down onto the white cotton down comforter, she relaxed into his hold.

"You're mine, do you accept this?"

"Yes."

"Do you trust me?"

"Yes."

"Put your hands to your sides. No arguing, understand?"

When she didn't respond, he swiftly spanked her twice. He cupped her reddened cheek, and slid a finger into her slick pussy.

"Ow," she cried and then moaned in pleasure as he entered her.

"Now that I have your attention, I'll ask you again. Do you understand?"

"Yes," she breathed. His low voice sent a delicious chill down her spine. At his command, she stopped trying to get away and lowered her arms.

"That's a girl. Now, I'm going to move you sideways here, because I want you to be able to see Jake watching you."

"Why would you want that?"

"I want to be able to share with you what it's like to submit, to be with other wolves. I also know that you seem to be interested in this sexually. Does it turn you on to know that someone could watch you?"

"I don't know. I guess so. It seems wrong, but I know wolves do it."

"Lots of people do it, not just wolves. And there's nothing wrong with it as long as it's consensual. Do you want Jake to watch us fuck? If you want him to leave, I'll tell him right now."

"Yes." Gillian groaned at her admission. She dug her face into the blanket, having a hard time believing the words that spilled from her mouth. Deep within her, she wanted this, to know that she was being possessed by Dimitri with Jake watching. But it was more than that; she wanted to see Jake's reaction, watch him touch himself. As if Dimitri read her mind, he probed further.

"You want to see him, too, don't you?"

"Yes."

"Look at him. Someday we can play with Jake, too. Do you want that?"

"Maybe," she hedged, still embarrassed by her own desires. "He's attractive...but he's not you."

"Whatever we do, I'll always take care of you. You come first in everything I do. We're wolves...what you feel for me, what I feel for you...we'll always have that connection. Just you and I. But playin'? If we choose to do that, it's our decision, but you'll always be mine and I'll be the same with you."

"I won't share you with another woman," she admitted.

"That's fine, because you're the only woman for me. When and if we play with Jake, we'll decide together to do it. Okay?"

"Okay," she agreed.

"Tonight I just want you to enjoy watching and being watched."

"Yes," Gillian breathed. Her pulse began to race as she glanced over to the shower, and Jake's eyes fell on hers.

"Now back to our lesson," Dimitri laughed.

"Please, I'm so hot. I can't take it..."

Dimitri tugged on her legs so that they fell over the sides of the bed, her bottom completely exposed to him. He reached over into his drawer and took out a few small items, placing them on the bed. Unscrewing a small blue bottle, he poured the cinnamon-scented oil into his palms.

Gillian slowly turned her head, the side of her face pressed into the mattress. She lifted her eyelids, taking in the sight of Jake. Stark naked, the water sluiced down the sinewy muscles of his back and over his chiseled buttocks. It was as if she was watching a movie, but she knew it was real. If she wanted, if Dimitri let her, she could walk over and touch him.

Dimitri's warm hands massaging her back diverted her attention, the spicy scent filling the room. Her body lit on fire with desire as he worked his magic fingers into her neck, slowly moving down her back, carefully working out the knots. She watched with interest as Jake washed his hair, his eyes closed, the bubbles rolling off his lithe body. He turned in her direction and she caught sight of his erection jutting outward.

Dimitri's palms reached her bottom, continuing to caress. Using his knees, he parted her legs until they were wide open to him. She looked back and saw him unbuttoning his jeans, finally shucking them off onto the floor.

"Tell me about this?" he asked, tracing a finger over her tattoo. "What's it mean?"

"Strength within. It's how I first felt when I shifted, like there was something inside me. But then I started to realize it wasn't my tiger who gave me that. I needed strength no matter what."

"You're the strongest woman I've ever met."

"Hmm? I feel like the horniest when I'm around you," she giggled.

"You're definitely the sexiest. Goddess, I love your ass. And this," Dimitri cupped her cheeks, dragging his thumbs down the crevice until he reached her puckered flesh. "I'm gonna have this, too, darlin'."

"Hmm," she replied, calmed from his massage. Gillian had never known nirvana, but expected that this was it. Relaxation and arousal swirled into one delicious reaction.

"But first we've gotta get you ready for me. We can't rush these things. I know you've had my fingers in you before, but I have something new we're going to play with tonight...besides Jake, that is." Dimitri caught Jake's eyes and reached for a small pink bulbous object. "I've got a little toy here for you, Gil."

"Toy?" Her eyes flew open in surprise.

"That's right, darlin'. Open your legs for me. A little more now." He waited as she spread herself wider, and dribbled the lube onto her bottom. He coated the soft rubber and pressed its tip into her anus. "I'm gonna go slowly."

"What? Ah..." Gillian tensed as Dimitri worked it into her.

"That's it, cher. Just relax." He continued, gently stretching her.

"I don't know if...oh my God." The foreign sensation caused her to release a small moan. Gillian had begun to gyrate against the mattress, seeking relief. His hands on her bottom stilled her movement.

"You okay?"

"I feel so...I don't know...Is it wrong that this feels so good?" she breathed.

Gillian, at a loss for words, glanced to Jake who soaped his body. Unable to do anything but enjoy the moment, she immersed herself into the delightful fullness that overtook her body as Dimitri adjusted the toy into her.

"Just imagine when I'm inside you. It's all the way in now."

Gently, he rolled her onto her back and she smiled up at him. He leaned over and pressed his lips to hers, briefly sweeping his tongue into her mouth. Gillian moaned in protest as he retreated. Her disappointment was short-lived as his hands fell to her breasts, and he circled his forefinger around her aroused tips.

"Hmm, you're so beautiful. I can't get enough of you." Dimitri smiled down at her lovingly. He abandoned her nipples, gliding his hands toward her belly.

Gillian's head rolled to the side and she caught sight of Jake watching them through the steamed glass. With his forehead resting on his arm, he stroked the lather over the length of his erection.

"Look at what you do to Jake," Dimitri said.

Gillian laughed and glanced up at Dimitri, who gave her a hungry stare.

"And this," Dimitri held her hips, trailing his thumbs over her bare mound. Working them into her slick folds, he spread her wide open. "Your pussy is...oh yeah." He flicked the pad of his thumb over her glistening nub, "so wet," then plunged his thick middle finger up into her, "tight...ah, yes."

"Dimitri," she cried, her hips pushing upward so that his finger went as far as possible into her. She went to move to reach for him but he placed a palm on her belly.

"Stay," he ordered, his voice laced with a sexy tone that surrounded her in its demand. "Play with your breasts. I want to see you touch yourself."

She shook her head no, but found herself reaching to her chest. She quivered as the pads of his fingers glided over the ridges inside her core. The sensation intensified in her bottom as her climax built.

"That's it. Goddess, you're so fucking gorgeous. This, darlin', this is the start of your submission. And it's beautiful." Dimitri added another finger, using his thumb on her clit. "Look at Jake. He's going to come with you."

Gillian threw her head back, quivering on the edge of orgasm. Dimitri began to pump into her faster, sliding into her at the same rhythm that his friend touched himself. The smell of sex teased her nostrils, and her heart pounded at the sight of her mate. His piercing eyes bore through her, emanating dominance.

"This is real between us. It's not just the mating," he assured her, curling his fingertip inside her hot channel, teasing out her orgasm. "This...is magic."

"I'm going to come," she cried, continuing to tease her breasts. Pinching herself, she surrendered to the devastating climax. As if electricity stung her body, she convulsed, her back arching off the bed. A loud grunt sounded, and she caught the sight of Jake's tightened abs crunched over as his milky essence sprayed against the glass. He looked up, catching Gillian's gaze as he turned to grab his towel to leave.

Dimitri withdrew his fingers, dragging her cream across her taut belly.

Gliding his hand over her breasts, he cupped her face, his wet thumb plunging into her mouth. She tasted herself, closing her eyes.

"Up here," she heard him call.

Her eyelids fluttered open, and she focused every ounce of her attention on him. Unable to speak with her lips wrapped around his finger, she simply waited, her heart pounding in anticipation. Dimitri stroked his glistening cock, brushing its plump head over her clit. She moaned in response.

"I'm going to fuck you, kitten, so fucking hard, you'll never forget where you belong. You want this?" His strong fingers curled around his dick, tapping her clit.

"Yes," she managed, his fingers still in her lips.

"Fuck, yeah," he grunted, guiding his shaft into her.

"Ahhh," she responded. As his hand moved from her lips down her body, she cried out, his thick sex stretching her.

"Yes," he repeated.

"Fuck me, yes," she gritted out, her hands fisting the blankets.

Dimitri lifted her hips off the bed, and increased the pace. Their flesh met, sounding throughout the room, and the thought of how Jake watched them flitted through her mind, heightening her arousal. As he slammed into her, all her focus returned to the magnificent male worshipping her body with his erotic dance. Her core clamped down around him as the tingles of desire built again.

"Ah Goddess, yeah…like that," he growled.

"Harder, fuck me harder," she demanded. The urge to grab him grew but she resisted. Her hands fisted the fabric so tightly she swore it would tear.

Dimitri quickly adjusted his position, pinning her to the bed. Capturing her wrists, he held her arms above her head. The weight of him pressed down onto her, and she gasped at the intimacy. Restrained, she widened her legs, accepting his hard pounding thrusts.

Awestruck by his commanding presence, Gillian had never felt more erotic or powerful. As if she'd been caged for a thousand years, Dimitri released her from her own sexual confines. She jutted her full breasts against his sweat-covered chest, their bodies sliding together. She greedily took every inch of him inside her as he pounded himself into her pussy.

"Please, Dimitri, please," she begged. Again, she teetered on release, but only he could give her what she needed. She gladly accepted her position, certain her mate would bring her to orgasm.

"Submit, Gil," he ordered. He coiled one hand around both her wrists, freeing a hand to tend to her breast. With a primal heat, he plunged in and out of her wetness.

"Please, don't stop, please….don't stop, don't stop," she repeated as he rocked against her sensitive hooded nub. Baring her neck to him, she let him guide her into release, giving into him the only way she knew how. Heaving for breath, her body shook, the frenzy of orgasmic pulses rolling through her.

As her climax continued, her tiger roared, demanding her due. *My mate.* Giving herself over to her beast, her canines extended. In a flash, she bit deep into his flesh, breaking his skin. Blood rushed down her throat, and she succumbed to the mating.

"Holy fuck! Gilly, no," Dimitri yelled, his orgasm rupturing throughout his body.

Immediately, he registered her intent. *Mate.* Unstoppable and deliberate, his wolf surfaced, breaking through the shackles of the evil eating away at him. Although he'd never intended to complete the mating, his instinctual response was quick and unfettered as he struck her neck with his fangs. Her essence flowed into him, nourishing his craving for the only one who could save his soul.

Gillian shattered, never having experienced the blood of the lupine. *Dimitri.* Like the shards of a broken mirror clattering onto stone, every presupposition she'd had about who she was and what she'd expected from love was destroyed. She'd told herself that love was something that needed to grow over time. The lie crashed around her. Love was a commitment, devotion to each other. Embracing trust and submission to their fate was all she needed to move forward.

A tear escaped her eye as she reached for her tiger who only purred, disappearing into the darkness. Her lifelong friend perished without protest. In the distance, a triumphant howl sounded, its song comforting her. Unfamiliar, the melody of its cry revitalized her, confirming her decision to mate.

Her palms traveled over Dimitri's skin, seeking his wolf, exploring to make sure he was healed. Allowing the heat of him to penetrate her pores, she sought answers. In the silence of their reflection, she recorded the strength beneath his flesh. His wolf ran free, no longer encumbered by the parasite. Gillian supposed she should be crushed by the loss of her cat, yet joy for Dimitri resided deep in her chest. She felt vindicated by her actions; she'd rescued her great wolf.

"Gillian. Goddess, what have we done?" Dimitri cried, the stupor of climax subsiding.

"Hmm?" Gillian asked.

He rolled off her, lifting her onto his chest. Pushing himself up to lie on a pillow, he cradled her tiny form.

"You bit me…"

"It's done. You're whole," she whispered, confident that she'd done the right thing. Her body fell limp against his and she pressed her lips to his chest. "You're mine."

"No, Gilly. I shouldn't have…We should have waited." He cuddled her closer. "I'm sorry. Your cat…"

"I'm better than I've ever been in my life. You have no idea how I feel about you, do you?" she posed. "You're well now. It's all that matters."

"But…"

"I'm going to be just fine. As sure as I know you are my mate, I will shift again. Stop worrying," she told him. The warmth of her love for her beta blossomed in her heart and mind. There was no explanation that would satisfy a scientific mind for how she felt. She was done trying to plan every detail of her life. Destiny had led her to Dimitri, and she'd surrendered to fate, accepting her new life with her wolf.

Dimitri wrapped his leg around hers, creating a protective cocoon. The wolf inside of him rejoiced. The second she'd bitten him, the spell of his imprisonment had broken, releasing the evil back into wherever it had come from. He fought the emotion that rose in his chest. There was no way he'd ever be able to repay his mate's selflessness. She'd stolen the decision away from him, piercing his skin, initiating the mating. In doing so, she'd alleviated the guilt he'd forever carry if he'd done so himself.

A surge of power pumped through his body; the recognition of his century-old strength emerging once again. Dimitri blinked through suppressed tears and gazed up through the skylight to the stars. A month ago he couldn't have fantasized a more perfect existence. The loving, self-sacrificing female wrapped around him had become his world, and he prayed he'd be able to keep her safe.

The full moon beckoned. A second chance at meting out justice was upon him.

·❧· *Chapter Eighteen* ·❧·

Dimitri stirred, the beams of the late morning sunshine warming his face. Gillian writhed against his heated skin. The slickness between her legs painted his hip, alerting him that she was awake. His eyes flew open as her soft hand wrapped around his already hardened cock. Her hand traveled up and over his abdomen.

"Gilly," he hissed.

"Shhh," she hushed. With the pad of her thumb, she swiped at the wet slit of his arousal.

"Aw fuck," he said, jutting his hips in tandem with her slow strokes. "What are you doin' to me?"

"No talking," she commanded, asserting her dominance.

In all his life he'd never been submissive, yet in the delicate balance between sleeping and waking, the desire to surrender to her demand reigned. Tendrils of her hair teased his chest as she peppered kisses on the smooth skin beneath his arm, down his side and onto his hip. Her lips continued their sensuous journey to the muscular cut V above his groin.

Dimitri heard her exhale softly, her warm breath along the sensitive ridge of his dick. Clutching his shaft with one hand, she lightly raked her nails down his abdomen. Dimitri sucked a breath as the hot moistness of her mouth surrounded him. Arching his back, he lifted his pelvis as she held him firmly by the root and swallowed his entire sex. Her head bobbed up and down, branding him with her lips. Her fingers moved to his tight sac, gently caressing. As her mouth descended, tantalizing him with her tongue, her other hand moved to his ass, where she teased the stretch of skin between his testicles and anus.

"Ah, Gilly," he growled as the dark sensation tempted him.

Her fingers traveled further, circling sensitive puckered flesh. Dimitri cried out in aching desire as the tip of her finger probed him. His balls drew tight, pressure mounting from within. Dimitri swore, realizing he was seconds away from coming in her mouth. He reached for her shoulders, dragging her up his body. She moaned in protest, but he silenced her with a deep, passionate kiss. Their heated connection broke their power exchange. Guiding her upward, he forced her to straddle his chest. He directed her legs so that her knees were on either side of his head.

"Come here," Dimitri growled, shifting her hips, yanking her closer to his lips. "Goddess, I love the smell of you. You know I like to cook, but there's nothing like having my mate for breakfast."

With a smile, he gazed between her legs. He took to her glistening pussy like a fine meal, dragging the tip of his tongue through her lips. She hovered above him, accepting each lash with pleasure. He gripped her ass, pulling her flush to his mouth. Sucking and lapping at her core, he tasted arousal and sex upon her.

With one flattened palm against the wall, she writhed against his face. As he plunged his tongue up into her core, she screamed in orgasm. Taking her swollen clit between his lips, he milked every spasm from her before releasing her hips.

"Dimitri," she panted, recovering from her climax.

"Gilly," he breathed. He slid her down his body and sheathed himself inside her ready center. "You...are..."

"I...I..." Gillian tried to speak, but her words were lost in his kiss.

"Feel how much you mean to me...can you feel it?" he asked, thrusting up into her.

"Yes," she affirmed. Leaning upward, she wrapped her fingers around his wrists, caging his head with her arms.

Passion claimed them as Dimitri allowed Gillian to sink down on him. Resisting the instinct to dominate, he celebrated the way she'd taken control. He marveled as she threw her head back, her breasts arching toward him, yet still out of the reach of his mouth.

"Fuck yes," he grunted as she rose up, slamming herself down onto him.

The threads of his restraint shattered, and he grabbed onto her hips. She ground her pelvis into his as he made short, deep strokes up into her. As the explosive orgasm rocked into him, he called out her name. She released a cry of pleasure, ecstasy flowing through her.

Dimitri fought for breath, bringing her into his embrace. He felt as if he'd run a marathon, his heart thumping in his chest. Physically and emotionally, he was overwhelmed by Gillian. *Life is incredible*, he thought. *No, my mate is incredible.* Feelings he'd never experienced surfaced. It was more than just possession; he needed her in his life, protecting and loving her. *Am I in love?* As much as he tried not to believe it was true, in the recesses of his mind, the thought spun, bringing him to a new level of happiness.

"I love this," Gillian smiled.

Realizing she'd almost told Dimitri that she loved him, Gillian wrapped her arms around his neck, burying her face in his chest. *Oh Goddess, I'm falling in love with my wolf.* No matter how insane it was to develop feelings so quickly for someone, the damage had been done. Every time they made love, exchanged a laugh, another piece of her had been destroyed, only to be reborn and renewed as his mate and lover.

Dimitri clicked out of his email, his thoughts drifting to Gillian. Like an earthquake, she'd shaken his very existence. He laughed to himself, recalling how he'd mercilessly teased his Alpha when he'd found his mate. Only now did he comprehend the wonderment of mating. An incredible rush of happiness welled in his chest, the strength of her blood renewing his wolf and his soul.

He knew he should regret how they'd mated, her forcing his hand, but he couldn't summon any. Still, though, he remained amazed at Gillian's gift. Even this morning, she'd continued to give to him and appeared at peace with her decision. She'd told him that she was no longer able to feel her tiger, but that the wolf within her paced. How she'd merge with his pack was still in question. She may have been willing to submit sexually, but doing so within a group dynamic remained to be seen. Her beast had been independent and dominant, and he wasn't convinced that anything had changed.

Jake entered the kitchen, jarring him from his thoughts. He gave a wave and picked up his coffee, taking a draw of the black chicory.

"Afternoon." He glanced to catch the time on the wall; it was nearly one o'clock.

"Hey." Jake moved to the coffee pot and rummaged through the cabinet, searching for a mug. As he poured himself a cup, he looked around the kitchen. "What's up? Cooking spree over?"

"You know I only do that when I'm thinking."

"Upset is more like it."

"All is well with the world, my friend." Dimitri smiled, his eyes lighting up over the rim of his coffee. He set it down and gestured to the food on the table. "Sit. Brunch. Eggs. Bacon. Yogurt. Granola. Fruit."

"What the hell? I was hoping for flapjacks and biscuits."

"No way, bro. Eatin' healthy. I gotta maintain my girlish figure," Dimitri joked, touching his hand to his belly. "Keepin' it tight for my woman."

"Yeah, right. As if you don't work out every freakin' day anyway. What is up with you?" Confused, Jake had expected them to deal with the fallout from the drama of last night's killing in Mordez.

"I'm great. No, scratch that. I am phenomenal." Dimitri laughed and slapped his friend on the shoulder.

Jake shook his head.

"You wanna know why I'm in such a good mood?"

"This have anything to do with Gilly?"

"Close. This wolf here," Dimitri set his cup on the counter and held his arms wide open, "is officially mated and lovin' it."

"You're fucking kidding me, right?" Jake asked, astonished at his beta's declaration. "I was there for most of the, uh, show last night and you're telling me I missed this?"

"Nope. Not kidding. And yep. Ya missed it." Dimitri laughed, exhilarated with his news. "It's done."

"Don't you think that's a little quick? I mean, you just met her less than a week ago. Don't get me wrong, Gilly's great and I've heard that mating thing is hard to fight. But I thought the marking would give you some time. Do you love her?"

"Number one. Yeah, it's fast. Number two. Don't care. Too late now. Number three. I'm not an idiot. Of course I was goin' to wait to mate with her. But there were extenuating circumstances." Dimitri avoided the last question. *Do I love her? Goddess, help me.*

"Extenuating circumstances, huh?" Jake shook his head in disbelief. He reached for a piece of bacon and popped it in his mouth. "What in the fuck could cause you to go and mate her when you couldn't even shift last night? Obviously your wolf had enough in him to drop fangs, but shit, you've got issues. You should call the witch."

"Don't need her."

"Have you lost it? All that sex knock your brain around?"

"Maybe you need a demonstration." Dimitri stripped off his shorts, and made his way around to the open area of the family room.

"Not sure what demo you got going on but seeing you nekkid has been done. I'll give you last night. That was freakin' awesome, but bro, we're alone. Everything ya got there," Jake gestured to his groin, "seen it."

"I'm not talking about sex," Dimitri said. "I'm talking wolf."

Calling the power within, he allowed the seamless transformation to commence. The spectacular brown wolf barked and growled. He stalked up to his friend, who wore an expression of amazement. Jake reached out to Dimitri, running his hands through his fur as if to confirm what he was seeing was really happening.

Easily shifting back into human form, Dimitri crouched at Jake's feet. The thrill of the metamorphosis left him energized, optimistic and looking forward to the full moon.

"But last night? You couldn't…"

"Gillian," Dimitri stated, his voice serious. "She did this."

"What?"

"Her breed. It's why Chaz was…is after her. Her mate would inherit her gift. The spirit of her beast. The mating healed me. She healed me."

"I don't understand how…"

"She lost her tiger. It's gone." Dimitri raked his hands through his hair and reached for his shorts. He put them on and waited on Jake's reply.

"She can't shift anymore? No way. She was beautiful. Her cat…just no."

"This is why she always stayed away from wolves. She knew she'd find her mate. I wanted to wait, but last night…" Dimitri paused, recalling how she'd bitten him. "We'd discussed it and agreed to wait until the morning to make a decision. But then she bit me. Really bit me….hard. Not a mark. She broke skin. It's not like I had a choice. Once she drank from me, I was done for. Game over." Dimitri picked a bowl off the table and spooned in the yogurt. "I wish I could feel guilty. I know we should have waited, but my wolf wanted her so damn bad. I can't even blame it on him. It's me. She's mine. I want her in my life."

"You're in love with her," Jake laughed.

"I cannot confirm or deny those allegations," Dimitri said with a sly grin. He could hardly believe it himself that he was falling for one female. The idea of him being with one woman for the rest of his life had been a foreign concept, but this morning, he couldn't see himself with anyone else.

"So that's how it's gonna be? Okay." Jake shot him a sideways glance and picked up an apple out of a basket on the table. "You got it bad."

"Maybe I do. Again, that falls into the category of 'don't care'. She's mine and no one's taking her away from me now."

"Again...what about her shifting? What's the deal?"

"Don't know yet. She said she can feel her wolf. Heard her last night when she was at the club. Gillian seemed okay with everything this morning."

"I don't know how. Think about it. You've been an animal your entire life. And poof. It's gone."

"I hear ya. Even after she told me her theory about being able to heal me with the mating, I didn't want to do it. But what's done is done. There's nothing we can do but wait and see." Dimitri didn't mention to Jake that he might have super kitty powers. But his wolf was healthy and robust, as if nothing had ever happened.

"So is she going to try to shift? Before the run tonight?"

"I'd like to see her try. Let's give her some space, when she gets down here, okay? I want her to eat and relax before we start shifting. 'K?"

"You got it."

Dimitri nodded to the steps, alerting Jake that Gillian was coming downstairs. She may have already heard part of their conversation, but he'd been serious. Gillian needed both sustenance and rest if she was going to try to shift and run with the pack. Knowing how she'd battled the wolf in the bathroom the previous evening, he was certain she'd be ready for revenge. Taking a deep breath, he steeled himself for the conversation.

Gillian adjusted the straps on her bikini. An odd sense of calm had settled over her mind. It was as if their mating had infused a shot of happy juice into her veins. Showering, she'd thought of her tiger, still unable to feel her. But the wolf inside paced, growing stronger. There was no doubt in her mind that she could shift. She'd been tempted to transform right there in Dimitri's bathroom, but thought better of it, considering she should have the support of others as she did so.

She dragged the brush through her hair, securing it into a ponytail. As she turned to go downstairs, she smiled, seeing Dimitri's mark on her shoulder.

Feeling light as a feather, she bounded out of the room. Giddy like a schoolgirl, she couldn't believe they'd mated.

Never wanting Dimitri to feel guilt for their actions, she'd taken the decision away from him. Knowing that his wolf had been fully restored, her heart was full of pride and what she knew was the seeds of love. Hearing voices coming from the kitchen, she smiled.

"Hey there," she called, her bare feet padding across the smooth wooden floor. She fell into Dimitri's embrace, giving him a quick kiss.

"You trying to get me back in bed, woman?"

"What?" she laughed

"That bathing suit is killin' me. You're gonna give me heart failure."

"You're the one who gave it to me." She shoved at his muscular arms, ones that never moved from her waist. "I need sun. I'm tired of lying in bed."

"I can give you something to do in bed if you want," he countered.

"Is that right?" She smiled. "Guess I better eat something to keep up my strength."

"Hey there." Jake waved hello and opened the refrigerator, looking for orange juice.

Gillian gave Dimitri a devious grin and broke free of his arms. Slowly approaching Jake, she glanced back to Dimitri right before she swatted Jake's bottom. He jumped, nearly banging his head on the inside of the fridge.

"Hey, now. What's that for?" he asked, smiling.

"That's for not coming to my rescue last night." She pointed a finger at him.

"What can I say? I know better than to interfere when my beta's trying to teach his mate how to submit. Although I must say, D, I don't think you trained her very well. She just spanked me."

Dimitri raised his eyebrows, shrugged and laughed.

"And this," Gillian wrapped her arms around Jake, hugging him, "is for saving me last night."

"Now this is more like it. Oh yeah." Jake returned her embrace, watching the look of amusement on his friend's face.

"And this," she stood on her tip toes and kissed his cheek gently, "is for last night. Turns out, that after you refused to help me, I got lucky...really, really lucky."

"Aw baby, I'm the one who should be thanking you and D."

She reached behind him, grabbing a bottle of water, then pulled away from his arms. Unscrewing the bottle, she gave him a flirtatious wink before taking a drink.

"She's somethin'," Jake said, still surprised. He held his fingers to his lips, and looked to Dimitri, who seemed to enjoy the way his mate had thrown his friend off kilter.

"Yes, she is." Dimitri drew Gillian into his arms. They exchanged a brief embrace, and he guided her to the table. Standing, she began to pour herself cereal.

"I've gotta make a call to Logan, let him know what happened last night," Dimitri announced.

"Last night?" Wide eyed, Gillian looked at Jake and then Dimitri.

"Not everything, cher," he assured her. "I want to let him know I'm healed, find out what dickhead told him."

"Dickhead?" she questioned.

"The wolf from last night. Logan has him held up in a cell. They're coming soon."

Gillian silently nodded in response.

"Can you two play nicely while I'm gone?" Dimitri asked.

"Hey, I'm not the one who's slapping asses this morning. Look to your girl over there." Jake grinned at Gillian.

"What? His ass was just there…waiting for me. Besides, it's true. He didn't save me. All's fair."

"Also, I forgot. Jax texted me earlier. I sent him my address, so he should be here any minute," Dimitri mentioned as he walked out of the room.

"Do you have any sunscreen?" Gillian asked.

"What?" Dimitri turned, giving her a questioning look.

"You know. Sunscreen. I want to lay out for a bit."

"You don't get sunburned. You know that, right? You're a shifter."

"Yes, but I don't want to dry out my skin." Gillian smiled, giving a side glance to Jake. "Besides, Jake, here, owes me. I think a nice back rub will suffice."

Dimitri laughed in response. "No sunscreen, but the lotion's underneath the sink. And before you make any wise cracks, wolf, I like to keep my skin soft, too, okay? No judging. I'll be back in a bit," he told her.

He thought to tell her he loved her as he left, as if he wouldn't see her for eons. The words caught in his mouth; he was aware that it was completely irrational. Yet as he walked down the hallway, looking over at his mate, her smile melted his heart and he was certain he'd fallen in love.

~⚜· *Chapter Nineteen* ⚜~

Gillian stretched her hands above her head, reveling in the sunshine. The deck provided a spectacular view of the bayou, and Gillian began to understand why this place was so special to Dimitri. The day he'd refused to kill Chaz, unwilling to take over his pack, had confused her up until now. Most wolves aspired to be Alpha, no matter the circumstance. But Dimitri showed steadfast loyalty to both his Alpha and pack.

The quiet hum of crickets serenaded her as she spread a towel on the chaise. She smiled at Jake who joined her, wearing only his shorts. Barefoot, he trod across the cedar planks. Silence settled, each unsure of what to discuss. Gillian, unable to handle the quiet contemplation, broke the reticence.

"So…about last night. I meant what I said."

"Thank you," he responded.

"For what?" she asked.

"Dimitri."

"He told you?"

"About your mating? Yeah, he told me. You okay?"

"Me? I'm fine."

"But your cat? If it were me…"

"I think I can shift… we'll see. I just can't feel my tiger. She's gone," she replied.

"Last night in the bar. When we saw you on the floor…the way you'd attacked that asshole. Dimitri's lucky to have you for a mate," Jake began, reaching for the bottle she'd set on the outdoor table, unable to look her in the eye. "Anyway, just wanted you to know I'm grateful. D is a tough son-of-a-bitch, but this thing with his wolf…he would have lost his family, our pack. You changed all that."

"He's my mate. I can't explain it more than that."

Gillian avoided Jake's question, realizing she really didn't have answers. All she had were feelings, the kind of feelings that wouldn't be shaken no matter what happened in the future. None of it made sense, except for the fact that it felt right. After years of hiding from wolves, their mating had turned her world on its side.

Crawling onto the chair, she lay on her stomach. She took a deep breath and blew it out as her muscles began to relax. She blinked, her eyes focusing through the slit of gate surrounding the deck. In the distance, small lilts of waves rolled through the water, the tide receding. Warm strong hands settled on her back.

Jake remained quiet as he caressed the balm onto her skin. Gillian recalled how, on Dimitri's instruction, she had thoroughly enjoyed watching Jake in the shower. Although she thought him good-looking, she'd never been with two men at once and had never dared to imagine a scenario where she'd engage her fantasy. Yet Dimitri continued to push her sexual limits all the while making her feel as if she was the only woman in the world. She supposed it was the wolves, their openness that was rubbing off on her as she began to look forward to the possibilities and what Dimitri would teach her next. Closing her eyes, she fantasized, imagining her hands touching them both. As her body began to heat up in more ways than one, she smiled.

"What are you thinking about?" Jake asked, his hands moving down the back of her thighs.

"Um, just thinking about how good the sun feels," she lied. His hands were like sweet goodness all over. He moved to the soles of her feet and she released a loud moan.

"The sun, huh?" he laughed.

"Oh my God. Do. Not. Stop," she groaned.

"Hey now, what's goin' on out there?" Dimitri called from an open window, holding his cell to his chest. "No gettin' fresh with my mate, wolf. Lotion on her back. Nothing more."

"You're getting us in trouble," Jake teased.

"Hmm…it feels good, though." She laughed. Gillian gave a squeak as Jake smacked her butt, and lay next to her on a twin chaise.

"Better?" he asked, pushing on his sunglasses.

"Yes, thanks. Very nice. I was great before the rub, but now I feel awesome. I almost started purring," she said. *No I didn't. Never again will I purr.* A hint of sadness tinged her heart as she thought the words, reminded that she'd never be feline again.

The doorbell and commotion in the house caused her to lift her head. Hearing male voices, she assumed someone from Dimitri's pack had come to see him. She took a deep breath, focusing on the sounds of birds chirping.

"Hey, baby sis," Jax called from the kitchen.

Gillian startled at the sound of her brother's voice. "Jax. We're outside."

She jumped off of her chaise to greet him. Even though they'd recently established their familial connection, her heart filled with happiness as she caught sight of her brother strolling out onto the deck. His blonde hair reflected like an angel's in the sunlight. He was dressed casually, wearing a t-shirt and shorts, but there was no mistaking his commanding presence. Nick walked behind him, giving her a wave.

Jax opened his arms to Gillian and she fell into his comforting embrace. Her protector, she owed him her life.

"Jax, I'm so glad to see you. Is it weird to tell you that I missed you? I know we're just getting to know each other, but you feel like family," she admitted.

"We are family. You're not alone anymore," he assured her.

"Thanks." She kissed his cheek and broke their hug.

"What about me? Hello? Chopped liver over here?" Nick gave her a wide smile, holding out his arms.

"He just wants to hold a hot chick in a bikini," Jax commented. "Be careful with my sister."

"Hi, Nick. Sorry." Wrapping her hands around his neck, she gave him a quick hug. "Thank you for coming down. And thank you for not being my mate."

"Oh my Goddess," he exclaimed. Nick leaned in and sniffed her. "You didn't?"

"Didn't what?" she asked.

"Jax. Really? You're not going to say anything?" he asked.

"He's her mate. Always has been. Question is, what's happened that has my beta in a tizzy?" Jax gave her a scrutinizing look.

Gillian bit her lip and looked to Jake, who gave her a smile before he headed inside. She mouthed 'chicken' at him as he left. She guessed he didn't want to be around for the fallout; a serious conversation with one badass New York Alpha. She looked to the ground and wrung her hands.

"It's done," she said softly.

"What's done?"

"We, um, we completed the mating last night. Now I know that you might not understand, but," she began. Cringing slightly, she made eye contact with her brother. "He's a good man. An even better wolf. He needed me."

"Come here," Jax said. Gillian slowly padded over and was surprised when Jax brought her into his arms again. "Tell me what happened. I know he's your mate, but why so soon? It's your gift, isn't it?"

"Yes. He's been ill. I don't know if he told you or not. That witch. She did something to him. And wolves will never stop trying to get me. I just decided he was worth saving. I need him in my life."

"Did he know about your gift?" Jax growled protectively.

"No. If he'd wanted to be Alpha, he could have done that when he had Chaz the first time. Last night, the vampire…what she said. It just made sense. The witch was never going to cure him. She wanted him," Gillian explained. "And that was just too damn bad because there was no way I was letting her kill my wolf. He's mine."

Jax laughed. "Possessive already?"

"Yeah, I am. Dimitri's wolf was dying. I told him that I thought I could heal him. But he didn't want to so I…you know, I bit him."

"You started the mating? Without his permission?"

"Well, technically if you put it that way, I guess that is what I did, but I prefer to look at it as me taking the initiative."

"You are your Alpha's sister," Nick interjected. "Dimitri's going to have fun with you."

"It's done. And it worked. But my tiger…"

"She's gone?"

"Yes, I think so. But Jax," she whispered. "There's a wolf in me. I can feel her. I heard her last night, even before we mated. I want to shift. I've just been waiting."

"What for, girl? Come on now. Show us what ya got!" Nick said excitedly as if he'd been given a new toy.

Jax kissed her forehead and she fought the urge to cry. She wasn't sure how he'd react, but he was understanding, caring; everything she needed her sibling to be. He cupped her cheek in his hand and smiled down at her.

"Congratulations, sister. I'm so happy you're a wolf. I would've never forced this on you. I want you to know that. And even though I have a pack, you're blood." He turned to Nick and nodded. "You and Nick are my family. And he's right. Let's see what you've got. I want to see you shift."

"Really?" Gillian asked. Excitement lit through her as she realized she was going to do it. She thought to wait for Dimitri but then she decided it would be a wonderful surprise for him to see that she was all right, that she could, indeed, shift.

"Yes, let's do it. You go first and we'll run with you a bit." Both Jax and Nick began to undress in preparation.

"Okay, but not too far. I want to surprise Dimitri," she told them. Stripping out of her bathing suit without a care, she bounded onto the lawn.

She smiled at Jax and Nick, letting her magic flow from inside. As if she were transforming into a cat, the mystical power took over and within seconds, she stood as a four-footed wolf. Feeling lighter, she stumbled, rolling onto her side. She whined, unable to find her balance. Determined to get comfortable in her new form, she tried again, her paws gripping the grass. She forced herself upward, thrilled when she finally stabilized her footing. Instinctively, she went to roar, but nothing emerged. Frustrated, she cringed and cowered toward the ground.

A large black wolf approached, flanking her. He barked, as if to teach her. She sniffed, recognizing him as Jax. A smaller light grey wolf howled in response and ran around them in circles. Gillian would have been comfortable to stay nuzzled against her brother, disappointed in her diminutive stature. A firm paw on her side urged her to vocalize.

Raising her head, she began a low growl, which grew louder until it resonated throughout the yard. With a final effort, a loud bark resounded and she celebrated by running around, chasing Nick. Gillian realized the strength, speed and agility of her feline hadn't faltered, yet she'd suspected her ability to leap was stilted. Nevertheless, it didn't thwart her excitement that she still could shift.

She and Nick circled the Alpha in play, taunting him with a nip. After two rounds of their antics, Jax sprang after her, forcing her to roll to the ground. With his forepaw over her belly, she cried, unable to move. Gillian didn't do submission well, she knew. The feeling of helplessness in her new form was unacceptable. Struggling to get out from underneath him, she growled and gnawed at her brother. Without hurting her, Jax held firm, attempting to teach his sister a lesson.

A loud blur from her side barreled into Jax, freeing her. She bounded to her feet as the two wolves tussled in the turf. Realizing that Dimitri had come to her, she ran to them. A sense of fear washed over her, seeing them fight, and she crouched, yipping loudly for them to stop. Both wolves slowly disengaged, turning to stare at Gillian.

Transforming back, Gillian sat naked on the lawn, her feet curled under her. Grateful that she'd been able to run as wolf, tears of joy streamed down her face. Unlike her mother, who'd lost her abilities, she retained the magic of a shifter.

Both Jax and Dimitri altered back to their human selves, giving each other a hard stare. But their interaction was short lived as Dimitri broke their gaze, setting his attention on his mate. He closed in on Gillian, falling to his knees before her. He took her face in his hands, his own emotion brimmed from his lashes. Guilt. Pride. Amazement.

"Gilly. You did it!" he cried. "Why didn't you wait for me? I could've helped you."

"I...I wanted to surprise you," she stammered.

"You're stubborn, you know that?" He took her into his arms, pressing her against his chest, kissing her hair. "I heard you, I knew it was you. When I saw Jax on top of you, I wanted to kill him."

"I'm okay, baby. Really. He was just playing."

"No, no. He wasn't playing. He was trying to teach you, but I'm afraid those Alpha genes are goin' to make it tough for you."

Gillian laughed into his kisses. His lips pressed to her forehead, onto her eyelids and cheeks, until he finally reached her mouth. She reached into his hair, pulling him to her, kissing him back. But as she heard voices surround them, she smiled. With her head against his, they gazed into each other's eyes one last second, pretending they didn't have an audience.

"Ah, to be young and in love," Nick mused, yanking on his shorts.

"He'll deny it," Jake said from the deck.

"I pity the beta. She's not one to be tamed," Jax noted with a grin, almost as if he enjoyed it.

"Hey, I may be wolf now, but this girl's tiger, through and through. Don't worry, I'll learn to get along in a pack."

"There's no challenging the Alpha, Gilly," Jax huffed. "Or your beta for that matter."

"I wasn't challenging anybody. I was simply trying to get out from underneath you big hunk of a wolf. "

"Good luck with her," Jax warned.

"There's nothing wrong with her. She's just spirited, is all," Dimitri praised her, helping her to her feet.

"He's got it bad," Nick jested.

"Oh he does," Jake agreed.

"Ya'll are jealous," Dimitri shot back.

"Don't pay those boys any mind, baby. There's only one man I'm submitting to, and it's not them." She winked.

"Seriously, folks. I just got off the phone with Logan. The guy we picked up last night said Chaz brought in half his pack, thinkin' he's going to get his due. He wouldn't say where they're holed up, but we think they're waitin' on the full moon to make their move." Dimitri hated changing the subject, but they were in for an attack this evening.

"Gillian's not going," Jax stated.

Gillian opened her mouth to protest but Dimitri interrupted before she had a chance to speak.

"Gilly, I know you want to come, but Jax might be right. I think maybe you should go with some of the younger pack members. They're goin' into Baton Rouge. There's a secure gated wildlife sanctuary up that way. It's far enough away from where we run, where they'll be safe from Chaz. Wynter's taking Ava out of the city...we've got a few of the males going, too, for extra protection just in case. The full moon's tonight and you're gonna want to shift. You'd be safer there."

"Why would you want me to go there when I can help here?" she asked. Confusion washed over her face. *No fucking way*, she thought. *I'm going to help kill that asshole who tortured me and who's trying to wreck my life.* "No, wait. Don't tell me. It doesn't matter. I'm going with you. You just saw it. I can shift. I'm not staying back."

"I know you're strong, cher. But you're new at this. Jax and Nick, they'll come with us. Chaz doesn't have a chance with all of us here. You, on the other hand, are a new wolf. You could get hurt." Dimitri tugged on his shorts, and reached to hand Gillian her bathing suit.

"No, Dimitri." Gillian grabbed her things and stormed over to the deck. "I'm the one who was captured and tortured by that maniac. Now that he can't have me or my gifts, he's going to want to punish me for killing his friends. I'm not going to sit here and let people I don't know go out there and fight for me. Not without me by their sides. No way."

"Look, you did great just now. Don't get me wrong, you're a fighter, but you've never run with a pack," Jax reminded her.

"So what? I'll stay with the pack. Of everyone talking right now, I'm the one who, as shifter, has killed the most wolves from his pack. I may not be a tiger any longer but I'm still strong."

Dimitri sighed and put his hands on his hips, shaking his head.

"I can do this. Believe in me. It's not right to let you all go out there and put your lives on the line while I'm safe. Please, Dimitri. Please, I swear I'll stay with the pack. I'll do whatever you tell me to do," she begged.

"She goes," Dimitri snapped. "I've seen this woman here, and she's tough. And she's right. She's not a damsel in distress. She's defended herself before. We just need to keep her tight in the pack."

"Okay, okay. As much as I hate to say it, she knows the adversary better than we do. The way she just fought me back there," Jax smirked, "she's going to be as good as any male out there. I don't know whether it's the tiger in her or what but she's really strong."

"Thank you," she said softly, her head hanging low.

Dimitri wrapped a strong arm around her shoulders, and she melted into him. He'd stood up for her, believed in her. And her brother, who she once hadn't trusted, now trusted her as well.

Gillian contemplated her decision, knowing she could die. Yet she refused to allow fear to blur her judgment. She was determined to get Chaz out of her life, once and for all, even if she had to kill him herself.

Chapter Twenty

"Logan and Jax are taking the lead tonight," Dimitri informed the small group who waited outside his home. The full moon rising shone brightly onto the bayou, its reflection glistening off the small waves. "Gilly, you'll stay with Nick and me. Since I'm not running with Logan, Jake's gonna be running with the pack."

"You don't need to stay with me," Gillian began.

"No, darlin', that's where you're wrong. Ya'll know I love Logan, and my place would normally be at his side. But not tonight."

"But…"

"No argument, Gilly," he growled. "Logan and I have discussed this. You have no say in this decision. You stay with your mate, tonight. I know you can hold your own, but it's my responsibility to help you learn how to run within the pack and protect you if necessary."

Gillian startled at his dominant command. She refused to lower her gaze despite her wolf cowering in her mind's eye. The last time he'd said similar words they'd been in the bedroom, submission in a different form. Yet tonight, it'd be in a pack. Gillian wished it would come naturally to her, yet acquiescing felt artificial. She recalled her conversation with Dimitri. *Submission is about trust.* No matter how independent she'd been with regards to her tiger, she trusted Dimitri.

"Okay," she managed. Gillian's heart squeezed as a small smile formed on his lips and his face softened. She saw relief in his eyes. He wanted her to be safe tonight.

Dimitri brushed the back of his knuckles against her cheek, and turned to Jake.

"You ready?"

"You bet. Hey, where's Leo?" Jake asked.

"Let's just say I've got him on standby. This is a wolf dispute. Logan's not going to want him involved unless things go south," Dimitri explained. "Wynter's taking Ava out of town. We don't want to risk them trying to attack our homes. Given the extremes this guy went to to force a mating, who knows what he'll try?"

"Ah, the putrid smell of desperation," Nick commented.

"Yeah, I think maybe he thought he'd come here just for you, but when he finds out you've already been mated, he's going to go off. Hell, he brought his pack here," Dimitri offered. "He has his jet at the airport. Some of them flew commercial. I've never seen anything like it."

"Who even does that?" Nick said.

"Someone who wants power they don't have," Jax said.

"Well, we don't always get what we want. My gift is gone." Gillian looked to Dimitri, her gaze steeled in determination. "He's going to regret coming here."

A large wolf approached, giving a commanding bark. Several dozen wolves followed.

Gillian's nerves jittered as she set her eyes on the pack. As a tiger, she'd been unaffected by any shifters she happened to pass in the middle of the night. But as wolf, the hum of their energy was palpable. Like an orchestra, they played as one, each individual wolf playing their own part for the greater good.

"Stay with me," Dimitri said, stripping off his jeans.

"I will," she promised.

"Whatever goes down, do not go it alone. Don't leave the pack. If something happens to me, stay with Nick. You sure you still want to run?"

Gillian nodded as he embraced her, kissing her in front of the entire pack. His lips destroyed any remaining wisps of trepidation. As he released her, she wished she could tell him that she loved him. Her heart overflowed with emotion and she fought to keep it at bay, knowing it was not the time to disclose her feelings.

The magic of the moment broke as Dimitri released her hand and shifted. She followed his lead, transforming and padding alongside him. They broke into an easy lope, yet the tension remained high. Amazed at how natural it felt to be in a pack as wolf, she took a deep sniff. Even this early in her journey, she was able to identify pack members by their singular recognizable scent.

After an hour of traveling through the soft brush, they stopped to drink from the bayou. She observed how the other wolves kept watch over each other, aware of the gators that lingered, waiting on their next meal. Heat lightning flashed in the distance and she glanced to the stars. The moon still shone brightly, but a dark line in the sky warned of an impending storm. Thunder cracked, and she instinctively huddled into Dimitri. She felt his muzzle underneath her own, and gave him a quick lick, letting him know she was all right.

A chorus of barking commenced and through the din, she heard the sound of shots being fired. The pack split up, groups of three to five wolves dispersing into the brush. Dimitri growled, warning her to stay against a tree. Out of the corner of her eye, she spied a human atop the hill. Sparks lit up the darkness as the bullets sprayed into the forest. Her stomach lurched as a glint of light illuminated Chaz's face.

The sickening cry of wolves being attacked trumpeted into the night. Aware that her pack mates might have been injured, her adrenaline pumped. Instinct enticed her to go on the offensive, but both Nick and her mate warned her back, keeping her nestled between them. A blood-curdling whine tore through her as bullets whizzed by their heads. Dimitri barked in command and took off toward a thicker patch of trees. With Nick behind her, she followed him.

By the time they'd reached safety, she noticed Nick had gone missing. Dimitri shifted back, holding his fingers to his lips.

"Stay here," he whispered to her. Mouthing the word, 'silver', he pointed to Jax, who lay bloodied against the dirt, having been hit in the leg. He pointed up the hill to Logan. A hundred yards away, their Alpha fought Chaz. Both had transformed to wolf, the gleam of their fangs intermittent as the clouds moved in, blocking the moonlight. A second wolf attacked, latching itself to Logan's hind quarters. Dimitri sniffed into the air, hoping to scent Nick or Jake but he couldn't locate them. With Jax injured and Nick and Jake missing, Logan was alone.

Gillian shook her head no, realizing he was going to go to his Alpha. It was his role, she knew, but she was terrified. The smell of blood hung heavy in the air, and Gillian's urge to fight back began to supersede her desire to submit to his wish to stay put.

"I'm serious. Do not follow," Dimitri told her. "Just stay here under the brush where I can see you. Logan's getting torn up over there. I fucking hate leaving you but he's in trouble. Where the hell are Nick and Jake?"

She whined in response and swiveled her head, looking for Nick, who was supposed to be behind her. Unable to see him or Jake, she scratched at Dimitri's arm, growling in distress. Something was wrong, very, very wrong.

"Right here, behind this tree. Stay put," Dimitri repeated, shifting back to his wolf.

As he took off toward Logan, a torrential downpour commenced. Gillian heard a small cry, one made from a familiar human voice. She hesitated. Dimitri would be pissed if she left her position, but with the hard rain she was no longer visible to him. An agonizing moan resonated through the patter of water drops, and she took off in search of its owner.

Sheets of rain cut through the night, and within minutes the ground was saturated. Several howling wolves called into the clatter nearly stopping her dead in her tracks. She'd never expected that as pack, she'd instinctively feel and know their pain, their fear. But it was a small gurgle that caught her attention. Turning toward the noise, she slid into the deep mud, her claws clutching at the dirt. Scenting the air was difficult due to the potent ozone, but as she stumbled forth, her heart caught.

Barely visible in the mist, she caught sight of Nick clutching at his throat. Shifting back to human, the cold driving pellets rocketed into her skin. Her vision came into focus and she stifled a scream. Stark white, he looked grey, almost as if he was glowing. His eyes bulged, a hard rattle came from his chest and she threw her hands over his. Gillian applied pressure in an attempt to stem the hemorrhage. Blood spurted through her fingers and she cried out helplessly for Jax.

"Jax, please." Her slippery hands shook as she attempted to close his wound. "No, Nick, please Goddess, no. You need to shift."

"Jax," he croaked. "Love him. Sorry."

"You tell him yourself. Please Nick. Please, I need you to fight." Gillian gently laid her body next to his, hoping that she'd be able to warm him, to heal him. Her tears mixed with the deluge falling from the sky as she tried to summon the power that had belonged to her cat. With her face on his chest, she heard his heartbeat slow, and the realization he was going to die hit her. "No, Nick. We need you. Jax needs you."

Gillian searched deep within her psyche for her healing powers. Weak, her energy flickered like a defective light bulb. Her concentration faltered upon hearing a hiss escape his lips. As Nick's final breath ceased, his limp arms fell open, his spirit ascending to the Goddess. Gillian fought the hysteria that seized her at the realization he'd stopped breathing. Sobbing, she caressed his cheek, refusing to believe he was dead. Growls in the distance reminded her of the imminent danger, but she refused to leave him behind.

A branch broke, alerting her, and she sensed the Alpha. *Jax.* When he reached Nick, he gave a mournful howl and promptly turned to his human form.

"Nick." Jax fell to his knees, raking both his hands through his wet hair.

"I'm sorry. I'm so sorry. He's gone. I tried to heal him but it was too late." Gillian backed away from Nick, placing a final kiss to his brow.

"Nick," Jax repeated. Sitting in the muddy grass, he gently cradled his friend in his arms. Burying his head into Nick's hair, he sobbed, crushed by his loss.

Gillian put her arms around her brother, and he clutched at her, seeking comfort. Five more shots rang out into the night, startling both Jax and Gillian. She searched the darkness and caught sight of Logan falling to the ground. Dimitri ran across through the woods toward Chaz, who'd begun firing again. Her beta ducked and weaved, lurching onto his enemy's back. Chaz, shifting to wolf, went feral, his eyes glowing red. The crunching of teeth against bone reverberated in the wind.

A surge of hatred coursed through Gillian, and her beast growled in response. The barrage of rain falling wasn't enough to drown out the sound of the small roar in her chest, and she rejoiced at the realization that somewhere within her the great cat lived. Tearing across the woods, Gillian let her power flow. While she was still a wolf, her claws and fangs extended further and sharper, like she'd known as a tiger. With unleashed fury, she lurched at Chaz's back and swiped her talons at him, tunneling his flank wide open.

The split second reprieve was all Dimitri needed as he lunged for the Alpha's throat. His teeth sunk deep into Chaz's fur. The beta thrashed, gnarling, until he'd ripped out his opponent's trachea, tearing at the tendons.

Blood sprayed as Chaz hit the earth and Dimitri howled in victory.

Killing Chaz would have been cause for celebration if it hadn't been for the burning hole in Dimitri's gut. The grief from his mate flowed through him. He transformed, Gillian smashing into his embrace. Her tears warmed his wet skin. Taking her by her shoulders, he gently pushed her away so he could look at her. She gasped, crying and shaking her head.

"What is it?" he asked, his eyebrows drawn tight in concern.

"Nick, it's Nick," she cried.

"No."

"He was behind us. I don't know what happened."

"Fuck," Dimitri grunted. Something else ate at him. He'd seen Logan lope off, having been hit by a bullet. He scanned the woods, searching for his Alpha and Jake. "Jake. Logan. Where are they?"

"I don't know. I didn't see…"

"Logan! Jake!" Dimitri called, his voice bellowing across the bayou.

He began to run on foot, sniffing into the air. Within seconds, he'd managed to find Jake lying up against a Cyprus tree. Dimitri closed his eyes, willing himself to remain calm. A hole the size of his fist had blasted through his friend, blood painted over the large man.

"Jake, can you hear me?" Dimitri knelt, taking Jake into his arms. Unconscious, Jake didn't move. Like a ragdoll, his arms fell open, his head rolling side to side as Dimitri lifted him.

"Logan's coming." Fresh tears came as Gillian took Jake's hand in hers.

"Logan…Oh Goddess. Logan, please. He's not doing so well." Dimitri's voice wavered as he pushed the hair out of Jake's eyes.

"He's gotta shift," Logan said.

"He's been out before. Remember that time with Leo. Just tell him to shift. Command him."

"Shit, I can't believe this. Nick is dead. Now Jake," Logan lamented.

"Jake isn't fucking dead. Come on, Logan. We need to do this," Dimitri told him. The only words Dimitri wanted to hear were that Jake was going to live. It had to work.

Logan took a deep breath and exhaled, nodding in agreement. As the pack began to gather, Dimitri gingerly set Jake in Logan's arms. As he backed away, his mate came up behind him, circling his waist with her hands. She lay her cheek to his back, sniffling.

Logan whispered to Jake, and Dimitri closed his eyes, putting his hands over Gillian's. He'd been given so much in his life, blessed in many ways. He silently prayed, hoping the Goddess would spare Jake's life. But when Jake didn't regain consciousness, his heart broke, the grief pouring like a river into his chest.

❧ *Chapter Twenty-One* ❧

"I know you were close to him, D," Logan said, putting his hand on Dimitri's shoulder. "I care about him too."

"I *am* close to him. As in present tense. Jesus Christ, Logan. He's not dead yet." Dimitri pushed away from his Alpha. He carefully sat on the bed next to Jake and took his friend's hand into his own.

Recalling the evening's events, he sighed. With nearly a dozen Anzober wolves dead, including Chaz, most of the Acadian wolves had stayed to help move the bodies. Dimitri had called Léopold to assist Jax with Nick's remains. The vampire had known the New York Alpha for years. As much as Dimitri had wanted Léopold to stay, Jax was despondent and Gillian hadn't wanted him to go alone to his jet.

Dimitri had carried Jake the long trek home on foot. When they'd arrived, he'd taken him to the first available bed, which was in the downstairs guest room. In the open brush and again at the house, Logan had failed to elicit a response from Jake despite repeated commands for him to shift. The fist-sized hole in his chest no longer bled, yet the wound hadn't healed. With Jake's heartbeat irregular, they all believed it was only a matter of time before he died.

"Where the hell is Léopold?" Dimitri asked Logan.

"I'll go call him again. They probably aren't even at the airport yet," his Alpha responded.

Gillian exited the bathroom, a towel wrapped around her. Intent on cleaning Jake, she'd brought warm washcloths to his bedside. Seeing the Alpha, her eyes lowered submissively to the floor. As she padded over to Jake, Logan approached her, cupping her cheek.

"It's okay, Gilly. You'll get used to having an Alpha."

"Sorry, I just…I'm not used to being wolf." She lifted her chin, looking into his eyes.

"My mate. She wasn't always wolf either. I promise it'll get easier."

"The shifting was easy, but being with the pack. It felt…"

"Overwhelming?"

"Yeah. I'm used to being on my own. My cat," she looked to Dimitri, "she's independent. Tonight, I don't know. I can't feel her when I'm here, but when I attacked, I felt feline. I felt it in my claws. You saw what I did to Chaz."

"You're strong…stronger than most wolves." Logan wasn't sure what to say about her transformation. They'd all seen the damage she'd inflicted on the Alpha's back. The gash had been much deeper than most wolves were capable of doing with their paws alone. "We'll work it out. I'm here for you if you need help."

"Thanks." Gillian gave Logan a small smile, still unsure of how it would be to have to answer to an Alpha.

As she approached Dimitri, he turned and wrapped his arms around her waist, resting his head against her belly. She dropped the wet cloths next to him and cradled his head in her hands.

"I'm so sorry," she said, her voice quiet.

Dimitri didn't respond as anger and grief seized him. He held onto the hope that Léopold could use his ability to materialize back to his home and would agree to turn Jake. However, Dimitri knew that Léopold didn't give his gift freely. The only wolf he'd ever saved had been Wynter. Logan had told him that Wynter had lingering side effects from being given so much blood. Even if he could get Léopold to agree, he was unsure of Jake's feelings about being saved by a vampire.

A kiss to his hair brought his thoughts back to his mate. Her presence calmed him, and he held her tightly. His safe harbor, he thanked the Goddess she'd initiated their mating.

"Baby, why don't you go clean up?" Gillian gave him a squeeze. "I feel better now that I took a shower. I'll stay right here with Jake. I'm going to clean all this blood off him. You're covered too."

They'd been coated in dirt and body fluids from their battle. Dimitri had insisted Gillian go take a shower when they'd returned. Between Nick, Chaz and Jake, she'd been covered in blood. He looked at his own hands, the dried caked grit stuck to his palms.

"Go on. If there are any changes, I swear I'll come to you," she promised.

"She's right, D. You're wearing Chaz's scent," Logan informed him.

Dimitri gave him a hard stare.

"Yeah, yeah. I know. Me too." Logan rubbed at his forearms.

"I'll take the guest shower," Dimitri told her. "You sure you'll be okay alone with Jake? If there's any change at all, come get me."

"I swear it." Gillian took his place on the bed and began to gently clean Jake's face.

"Here's your phone." Logan pressed open the door and tossed him his cell. "I'm sorry D, but I've gotta check on how the wolves are making out with moving the bodies. I also have to make sure that Wynn and the others are okay. I'll come back and check on Jake in a bit, see if I can get him to rouse. His wound doesn't look as bad as it did earlier. He may just need time," Logan offered.

"I'm gonna call Léopold again," Dimitri said.

"You know, Leo might not want to…" Logan began.

"I know. I know. I'm calling him anyway." Dimitri turned his focus onto his phone, leaving the room.

Gillian watched as Dimitri slowly went into the bathroom. His sadness emanated through her. She shook her head, aggravated that she was helpless to alleviate his suffering. Alone with Jake, she focused on cleaning his skin, hoping he'd miraculously wake. Inch by inch, she worked, carefully navigating around the puncture in his chest.

When she heard the spray of the shower, she finished washing away the last bits of dirt from his body and tossed the dirty linens aside. She hadn't wanted to give Dimitri or Logan false hope, but she'd set her mind on trying to heal Jake. Prior to mating, she would have easily been able to call her powers, but in the woods with Nick, her healing ability had waned. Given that there weren't many viable options, she had to attempt it.

Peeling away her towel, she knelt onto the bed, and gently lay on Jake. She closed her eyes, trying to picture her cat, to conjure the magic. A small smile formed on her lips as the first tingle rippled over her. Her hopes were dashed when she was unable to maintain the energy she needed for healing to ensue.

"What's going on?" Gillian heard Dimitri ask. She cursed, aware that she'd been caught.

"I just…I want to…" she hesitated.

"Want to what? Wait, are you fixin' to heal him like you did with me?"

"I know it's stupid, but I had to try. When we ran tonight, I tried to save Nick. I felt a flicker of something, but it wasn't enough," she explained.

"But you felt something?" Dimitri approached her.

"Yeah, I could feel a little bit of my cat. And just now, again, just the smallest…I don't know. I know it sounds crazy. I'm just thinking maybe…if you got my gift, we could heal him together." Gillian pressed up to look at Dimitri, her forearm on the bed. "Do you feel my cat? Anything at all?"

"When we mated, you got rid of that thing inside me, but I really don't feel very cat-like. I'm still just me. You saw me tonight. I'm wolf." He paused, unconvinced it would work. "Listen, cher, I'm desperate too, but maybe we should just wait for Leo. I've seen what he can do."

"As much as I'd love your friend Léopold to show up right now, he's not here. I know you want him to help but we don't know if he will. And Jake? Would he want that? I don't know about you, but I'm not sure I'd want all that vampire blood in me anyway."

"I'm not going to let him just die on me."

"Then, please. Let's just try," she said, her voice cracking. Her heart broke for him. Although they hadn't said it out loud, they both felt responsible for what had happened.

"I don't know about this." Dimitri raked his fingers through his wet hair.

"Please." Gillian looked to Jake and back to her mate.

"Okay, okay, we'll try it. What do you want me to do?" Dimitri asked, resigned.

"Get underneath him, maybe if we're on both sides of him, it'll be enough."

"Don't get your hopes up. I'm telling ya. Since we've mated, I haven't felt special mojo, not like what you did to me."

"We've got nothing to lose. He's dying. I can hear his heartbeat slowing. Please, he needs us close. Just take my hands."

Dimitri tore off his towel with a growl. Naked, he slid into bed, lifting Jake so that his back was on his chest. Gilly reached for her mate. Their bodies tangled into one, she took a deep breath, concentrating, and began to direct them.

"Just feel me, baby. You know that special energy we have when we shift?" she asked.

"Yeah?"

"It's kind of like that, but restrain it. Don't let it go that far. Don't shift. When I healed you, I let my energy flow. You need to focus it...focus on directing it into Jake."

"But I don't think..." he began.

"Don't think. Just close your eyes. Feel me. Listen to my voice. Feel your magic. Search for my cat...look for her. You're my mate. She's in you now."

"I..." Dimitri's voice trailed off as he concentrated. As wolf, he'd never had to think about shifting. Being wolf was as natural as breathing.

"That's it. I'm going to start, but my energy is weak." Gillian began to purr, forcing the sound from her throat. It wasn't organic. As if she were a human mimicking an animal, she allowed the noise to grow louder. Slowly, the hum built, bombarding every cell in her body.

"Oh my God. I feel it," Dimitri cried out. "It feels...it feels like...electricity."

"Help me," she told him. "Find my cat."

In his mind's eye, Dimitri saw his wolf. He stood stoic, waiting. Soon the small sizzles going through him became rhythmic jolts. A loud roar sounded, the tiger coming forth. Shocked by the sight of her, Dimitri gasped for air. He'd never seen anything like it. The resplendent animal came forth, driving through pounding pulses of magic.

As if Jake's pain were his own, he sucked a deep breath, the slicing hot agony of the silver fragments dissolving into his flesh. Darkness began to close in, both animals fading into obscurity. He attempted to speak, but his throat closed, his lips moving without words.

Jake stirred above him, and he heard Gillian's voice.

"Jake, Dimitri, you okay?" she asked. Dimitri's eyes fluttered open, with a surreal awareness that told him his friend had survived.

He felt the weight of Jake lighten on his chest as he slid out from between them. Gillian's soft breasts pressed into his chest, the scent of her shampoo teasing his senses. Her silky palm glided against his cheek.

"Dimitri? Can you hear me? Please, say something," she pleaded.

"Gil, did you see it?" he asked, still shocked by what he'd seen.

"Did you see my cat, baby?"

"You're beautiful, do you know that?" Dimitri smiled as she came into focus.

Gillian released a sigh of relief, and they both laughed.

"If I'd known all it would take was getting shot to get into bed with you both, I'd have done it sooner," Jake joked, shifting up onto his side.

"Jake, oh my God. How do you feel?" Gillian exclaimed. She threw her arms around his neck and kissed his cheek, her lips lingering next to his.

"Now this is what I'm talking about," Jake teased, his eyes meeting Dimitri's.

"Jesus Christ, Jake. You scared the shit out of us. Are you for real? Let me see you," Dimitri insisted.

Gillian kissed him once more before sitting back on her heels. Both she and Dimitri watched as Jake ran his palms down his chest and patted his abs.

"Not sure what you did, but I'm good as new."

"You need to be thankin' Gillian, here. She's the one who suggested we try to…"

"My cat's inside him." Gillian diverted her eyes to her hands, which she held tight. Although she'd willingly given up her ability to shift as a feline, a sense of melancholy filled her chest. She'd been unable to heal Jake on her own.

"No fucking way. You're a cat?"

"Way." Dimitri sensed Gillian's change of mood, and brushed his knuckles under her chin.

"We got lucky. I just wish I'd been able to heal him like I'd done with you," she said softly.

"Hey, cher. You did this. We're a team now, you and I. And us, with the pack. There's no going it alone." Dimitri took her hands and brought her to him. Gillian fell into his embrace, exhausted from their night.

"Gilly, look at me," Jake said. His eyes moved from Dimitri and locked on hers. He reached for her, his fingers trailing over her shoulder, down her arm. "We're all connected. Tonight you must have felt the pack?"

She nodded, grateful for the commitment to Acadian wolves, for helping her and Dimitri kill Chaz. Without reserve, they'd accepted her during their run.

"I feel you. What you did for me. Even though I was unconscious, I knew you were there. When you were healing me, it was you and Dimitri. I felt both of you."

"But I wasn't able to do it by myself."

"Exactly."

"This may have been an unconventional mating, but it's done. We're one now." Dimitri took her hand.

"Never alone," Jake added.

"Thank you." Gillian glanced at Jake then Dimitri. "Both of you."

Their heated gaze smoldered, her eyes never leaving his. She reasoned that it may have been the mating or the run driving her heightened libido and emotions. After learning to grow comfortable within her own skin, there was no way she'd ever leave. Together, they'd taken her gift and saved Jake. Dimitri had come into her life like a hurricane, sweeping her off her feet, changing her perspective.

She parted her lips, her eyes focused on him. But before she had a chance to speak, Dimitri wrapped his fingers around the nape of her neck and captured her lips. Aware that Jake had left the bed, she thought for a second to end their embrace, but Dimitri's fingers speared into her hair, demanding her attention. As he deepened the kiss, she slid her palms up his chest, her fingertips teasing his flat nipples. He growled at the intrusion, flipping her onto her back. She squeaked as she fell back onto the bed, his legs straddling hers.

Frantically, she nipped at his lips. His energy poured into her, and the realization hit her that she was finally free, as was he. Free to love, to live, to begin their future together. A surge of passion coursed through her, her wolf seeking his. His hardened cock lay heavy on her thigh, and the touch of him sent desire to her core.

Aching for him, she strained to bow her pelvis into his, seeking the relief she needed. He wrapped a hand into her hair. Their lips forced apart as he tilted her head, exposing her neck. She bared herself to him, relaxed into her submission.

"Yes, that's it, my little wolf. Don't move," he told her, sucking her earlobe.

She gasped, her nipples grazing his chest. His warm wet tongue traced a small circle behind her ear, slowly making its way down to her chest. A clean fragrance mixed with his masculine scent, brushed by her nose as he buried his face into her cleavage. Gillian moaned as he licked, circling her areola.

"I love the smell of you, the taste of your skin." His lips claimed a rosy peak, and she gasped as the delicious pain sent quivers of desire straight to her core. Wetness dripped onto her inner thighs. Once again, she lifted her hips, attempting to get him to enter her, but it was of no use, as he held her down firmly with his torso.

"I love your breasts." His moist tongue traced a path around her areola.

As he made love to her nipple with his mouth, she cried out in pleasure. All Gillian could think about was how she yearned to have him inside her. Moreover, she wished she could tell him how she was falling in love with him, but she held back, not wanting to scare him with her feelings. Even though they were mated, it seemed too soon to say the words that would reveal her heart. A firm pinch to her taut tip, brought her out of her contemplation and her eyes flew open to meet his.

"Your arousal….it's intoxicating." Dimitri smiled. He grazed his nose in between her fleshy mounds and sniffed.

Gillian's face flushed, her nails digging into his shoulders.

"How far would you go to experiment, cher?"

"Hmm?"

"You're safe with me always."

"Yes, I know."

"The last time we played with your submission I saw the way you watched Jake."

Gillian turned her head in embarrassment, the thrill of watching Jake stroke himself still fresh in her mind.

"No hiding." He cupped her chin.

"But it's not right…everything that just happened."

"Everything that happened is exactly why we should be together. We did something special tonight. All of us."

"But how I feel…I shouldn't feel like this." Her desire for the secret fantasy blurred with shame.

"We're wolves, Gilly. That means we're sexual. Being turned on by watching or being watched is natural. I'll share you tonight, but I won't lie," Dimitri reached between her legs and clutched her mound, "this may be the only time I ever do. You're mine."

Gillian's breath hitched at his commanding tone. His thumb slid through her wet folds, teasing her swollen nub.

"You felt the pack tonight…your libido heightened. It's a full moon, time to be wild." Dimitri closed his eyes and howled.

"Jake's nice, but Dimitri, he'll never be you. No one will ever be you."

"Do you trust me?"

"Yes," she whispered, her voice quivering. Excitement rippled through her veins, the anticipation of making love to both men.

"I'll be in control tonight, not him, not you, understood?" Dimitri growled, his thumb swiping up and down her slit.

Dimitri didn't wait for her response as he kissed her, driving a long finger deep inside her hot sheath. Gillian panted into his mouth, their tongues sweeping against each other's. As he began to pump into her, she writhed underneath him, unaware that Jake had come into the room. A knock jarred their attention. She gasped as Dimitri tore his lips from hers. His finger still deep inside her, he gave her a sexy smile before turning to Jake, who stood with a wet towel slung around his hips.

"Hey, sorry, D, but I just wanted to let you know that I'm going to go home now. You mind if I borrow some jeans? I want to take my bike home."

Gillian's heart raced; her insatiable hunger left her starving. Dimitri caught her gaze as if to warn her of his intentions.

"Come join us."

"Stay," she heard herself say. Gillian caught Dimitri's smile as she extended a hand forward.

"Are ya'll sure? I swear I'm okay. You don't need to babysit me." Jake inhaled deeply, taking notice of Gillian's flushed skin, her full breasts. His cock jerked, shifting the white terry cloth.

Gillian nodded, grunting as Dimitri plunged into her again with his hand. Her eyes locked on Jake's as he sat on the bed.

"Look how beautiful my mate is." Dimitri sat up, resting back on his heels. He backed up, so that he could part her thighs further. With her legs spread wide open, she lay exposed to them.

"Ahh." Gillian's eyes darted to Jake's, her hips moving up to accept Dimitri inside her.

"Gilly's special, all right," Jake agreed, allowing her to take his hand.

"Yes she is. She's inexperienced in our ways, but she's very aroused and all wolf."

"Please Dimitri," she cried. With their eyes upon her flesh, her desire spiked. The pad of his finger curled inside her core, causing her to quiver.

"Not yet, my sweet lil' mate." He glanced at Jake. "We're going to take care of you tonight."

"Gilly?" Jake asked, his hand slowly sliding up her arm.

"Yes," Gillian breathed, giving him permission. Her body lit on fire as Dimitri sank two fingers into her and Jake's palm glided over her silky skin. Gently he caressed her, playing with her breasts.

"She's so soft," Jake whispered. He lay next to her on his side, letting his hands roam over her.

"It feels so..." Gillian lost her words as she gyrated rhythmically to Dimitri's sensual probing.

"Touch him, cher," Dimitri directed.

With her eyes on Dimitri, she slipped her hand underneath Jake's towel, wrapping her palm around his swollen shaft. He groaned as she swiped her thumb over his weeping head. Jake tore the loin cloth away so he was bare and Gillian broke eye contact to watch her small hand stroke up and down Jake's cock.

"That's it. See how good that feels. So natural," Dimitri coaxed.

"I've never...I've never done anything like this," she began.

"It's all good. Let your wolf guide you. Remember what you told me, don't think. Just feel." Dimitri withdrew his fingers from her, and she moaned in displeasure.

"Don't stop," she demanded.

"We're just getting started," he assured her. Taking his dick into his hand, he pressed the length of him through her lips, coating himself in her cream.

"I don't think your mate has learned submission very well," Jake noted, giving her tip a hard pinch.

"Hey." The sting on her nipple sent a jolt to her pussy. She sighed heavily.

"I think you're right. Maybe she needs something to keep her busy?" Her beta suggested in warning.

Gillian's eyes widened, both excited and worried about what Dimitri had in mind.

"Suck his cock, Gil," Dimitri told her.

With her eyes on Dimitri's, she leaned toward Jake. She hesitated, waiting for approval from her mate.

"Go ahead. That's it, darlin'. I want to see you take him all the way into your mouth."

Gillian smiled, closed her eyes and then blinked them open, nodding in acceptance. Craving both men, she tugged gently on Jake, as he brought his hips nearer to her. The clean scent of Jake's shower was thick in the air as she brushed his broad head over her lips.

"Oh, Goddess," Jake groaned. His hand fell into Gillian's mane, stroking her locks as she took him inside her mouth.

"You're so fucking hot, Gilly." Dimitri continued to coat himself in her wetness, teasing her clitoris but not yet entering her.

Gillian moaned in response, jutting her hips upward. Sucking Jake hard, she gasped as Dimitri drove himself into her. Simultaneously and with her eyes on her beta, she relaxed, taking Jake far down her throat. Like a lollipop, she licked his shaft, grunting every now and then as Dimitri thrust deep inside her. She embraced her loss of control as Dimitri held her hips, slowly pumping in and out of her.

"Yes, so good," Dimitri said.

"Aw, fuck," Jake groaned.

"Yes, that's it. Take all of me." Dimitri slowed his pace, plunging into her until he was balls deep.

"Oh shit," Jake said, Gillian sucking him hard. His hand glided down her abdomen until he reached her slick mound. "Your pussy is so..."

"Fucking tight," Dimitri finished.

Gillian released Jake from her mouth, continuing to cup him with her hand. As Jake applied pressure to her clitoris, she almost flew off the bed.

"Yes, don't stop, yes," Gillian screamed.

"That's it, Gilly. Come for us."

"Ah, I..." Gillian's body lit on fire with passion. The words escaped her.

"I think she likes that. How 'bout a little harder," Gillian heard Dimitri say. With her core full and fingers on her clit, she saw stars, her climax slamming into her. She shook uncontrollably, both men giving her no quarter.

With her breath ragged, she barely had time to recover as Dimitri quickly flipped her onto her stomach. She rested her hands on Jake, who'd helped move her into place. He seated himself in front of her, waiting on Dimitri.

"Up onto your knees, cher. Relax your head there onto Jake," Dimitri guided.

She rested her head on Jake's thigh, and took his cock into her hands. She caught sight of his smile right before she slipped him into her lips. The sound of Jake's head thumping against the headboard in pleasure made her giggle, but she managed to stay on task.

A cool gel dripped onto her bottom taking her off guard, but as Dimitri's fingers warmed the slippery fluid over her back hole, she registered his intent. She moaned as his fingers pressed into her pussy, but it was his thumb probing her puckered flesh that caused her to tense.

"I'm going to fuck this sweet little ass of yours, tonight." Dimitri gently worked his way into her rosebud.

"Dimitri…it's so, ah, tight." Gillian withdrew Jake from her mouth.

"Relax, now, cher. I've got you. You're okay. Just let me ready you."

"That's it, Gil," Jake praised her as she took a deep breath, rubbing her breasts against his thigh.

Gillian could feel the flood of wetness flow between her legs as Dimitri withdrew, then guided two fingers into her ass. Instinctively, she wiggled her bottom, trying to get him to go deeper.

"We're both going to make love to you. You ready, darlin'?" Dimitri asked with a smile, amused at how much she was enjoying his touch.

"Ahhh…yes." Her body relaxed into the dark sensation. Gillian moaned in pleasure, rocking back into his hand.

"I'm going to need you to let Jake go, so I can move you up a little."

"Dimitri," she cried. Gillian's orgasm began to build, the flickers of electricity running from her chest down to her clit. She wished she didn't like the feel of his fingers inside her but the more he stretched her, the more she wanted him.

"I know you want to come, cher, but let's get you in position," he directed.

Doing as he'd asked, Gillian let Jake slip from her mouth, and pressed up onto her palms. Letting Dimitri guide her hips, she crawled up so that she straddled Jake's hips. She met Jake's gaze and her lips parted as he leaned forward to touch his lips to hers. It was a soft kiss; more than friendly, yet it didn't have the passion that she only shared with her mate. She wasn't in love with Jake, but she cared about him. His gentle caress of her cheek told her that he reciprocated, understood the nature of their sexual encounter. Neither she nor he was in control, yet they both embraced their close relationship.

The cold gel dripped onto her bottom once again, jarring her back into the moment. So close to coming, she ached between her legs. The tip of Jake's cock grazed her clit and she shivered. Gillian attempted to move her hips toward him, but Dimitri held them firmly in place.

"You ready, Gil?" Gillian heard Dimitri ask. She panted in anticipation, waiting for him to direct her.

"Yes," she breathed, just about coming undone as Jake took her breasts into his hands. "Please…I can't wait. Now…do it now."

"She is a demanding lil' thing," Jake noted with a sultry smile. He rolled her firm nipples with his forefingers and thumbs.

"You really aren't getting the concept of submitting are ya, darlin'?"

Dimitri resisted the urge to spank her and instead removed his fingers.

"Please, no don't go. I need you. I can't…I'm so close." Gillian seriously thought she'd lose it. He was teasing her she knew, but her orgasm was so close. She began to claw at the sheets.

"Easy now, Gilly. I'm not goin' anywhere. I'm going to go slowly. Hold still for me." Dimitri took a deep breath and guided himself into her tight ring of muscle.

"Oh my God. Yes," she cried.

"That's a girl. Breathe and push back onto me," Dimitri instructed.

A flash of pain registered and then ceased as Dimitri pressed the head of his cock into her bottom. She gasped as he pushed in further, trying to follow his directions. Breathing deeply, she panted. Her entire body felt as if she'd combust with desire. She attempted to move, but it was useless, as Dimitri held her firmly around the hips. Jake lovingly ran his fingers over her shoulders as she took all of Dimitri inside her.

"That's it. Relax. Don't try to force it, Gil. Just a little bit more of me." Dimitri released a loud breath, fully seated inside her. "I'm in all the way."

"Oh God, please…I need you to fuck me now," she demanded, feral with lust. She bit her lip out of frustration.

"I know, just let me go slowly." Dimitri gently slid out and back into her, getting her used to the sensation. "You're so goddamned tight. I'm not going to…"

"It feels so good…please don't stop," she pleaded.

"Now Jake's going to join us, you ready, Gil?"

Gillian nodded, her eyes on Jake's. He brushed his cock over her clitoris a few times and she groaned in ecstasy. Within seconds, she felt him separate her folds, pressing himself into her.

"Oh yeah," Jake grunted.

"You okay, darlin'?" Dimitri asked, wrapping a strong arm around her waist.

Gillian, so desperately full and aroused, nodded. Dimitri pushed her limits, bringing her to levels of ecstasy she'd thought she'd never understand. It was as if they were no longer individual people, their souls and bodies united as one. She loved him even more for allowing her to explore her fantasy, expanding her world.

She closed her eyes, utterly engrossed in the sensation of being pleasured by two men. As they began to plunge in and out of her, she gave herself over to her dark fantasy. Her mate commanded their experience, his love for her evident in each stroke. Dimitri's hand glided upward to support her chest, claiming her as his as he bit down into her shoulder.

She cried out, allowing him to bring her torso upward slightly so that she was seated on Jake. With each strong thrust, she ached with a pulsing need. As if Dimitri had read her mind, he found her clit, squeezing it between his fingers, driving her over the edge.

Gillian's orgasm slammed into her, rocking her entire being. Screaming Dimitri's name over and over again, she panted for breath, her release rolling from her belly to her limbs. Jake's muscles tightened underneath her as he pounded up into her, coming hard. She heard Dimitri grunt, his cock thrusting into her.

"Oh Goddess, I can't hold it." Dimitri lost control as her contractions rippled through her core, stimulating his cock through the thin membrane. Spilling his seed deep inside her, he stiffened against her. "Fuck, yes."

As the last waves of her release ceased, tears of pleasure came to her eyes. She closed them, immersing herself in the surreal afterglow. Her skin continued to tingle as exhaustion claimed her. Dimitri's lips pressed to her shoulder as he carefully removed himself. She felt Jake gently slide out from underneath her and she cuddled into the comforter, barely aware of the warm washcloth between her legs. As her mate cleaned her, she moaned, satisfied and relaxed. She felt Dimitri pull the covers over her, his abdomen warming her back as he spooned her, encircling her within his strong arms. His soft lips met her hair. Within the safety of his embrace, she fell asleep.

Dimitri took another draw of her ambrosial scent into his nostrils, amazed that the Goddess had given him such a brave and sensual mate. From her reaction to watching Jake in the shower, he'd known that their time with him would be special. But now that they'd experimented, the possessiveness of his wolf growled, warning him not to share her again.

He glanced at Jake, who'd wrapped a towel around his waist and had lain back onto the bed on his side, watching them. Dimitri's heart had nearly broken, seeing his friend near death. Guilt for what had happened to Jake racked his thoughts. Like the Alpha, as beta, he was responsible for protecting those in his pack.

"You almost died tonight," Dimitri murmured over Gillian's head, catching Jake's attention. He played with her hair as she slept soundly.

"Yeah, I guess I did. This immortality talk is crap. Oh we can live a long time, but every one of us has a weakness, including those vamps," Jake mused.

"True. You headed back home?"

"Yep. Chaz is dead, I assume?"

"As a doornail." Dimitri's expression flattened, growing solemn. "So is Nick."

"Nick is dead? Goddammit." Jake shook his head and blew out a breath. "I didn't know him that well but he seemed like a good guy. Is Jax okay?"

"Don't know. Léopold went with him. Losing a beta...you know it's gonna affect his whole pack. Let's just hope Jax is strong enough to survive this, because Gilly just found her brother, and she seemed like she was growin' kind of attached to him."

Only once in his lifetime had Dimitri watched an Alpha lose his beta. He'd been a boy at the time. When the Alpha had gone missing, his mama had told him that he'd gone to find himself. But he'd known, even at that young age, that their Alpha had killed himself. Like the connection between him and Logan, the Alpha and his beta were as bonded to each other as he was to Gillian.

"You think he'll make it?"

"Don't know. I'll ask Leo tomorrow. Right now, all I wanna do is go to sleep."

"I'm goin' to go, give you guys some privacy." Jake pushed up to sit on the bed. He paused, glancing to Gillian and then to Dimitri. "Tonight…I needed this more than you did. You and Gilly, you know I love you, right? I don't mean to get mushy and shit, but I've never been so close to the other side…never in my whole life."

"We all needed this tonight. Seeing you like that…"

"Hey, I'm good now." Jake smiled. "Gilly's really special. I'm glad you found your mate."

"Someday you will too."

"Maybe. But for the record, I'm not lookin'. I guess it's in destiny's hands."

"Yeah, well, destiny handed you your ass tonight."

"Yes, she did, my friend."

"Speaking of destiny, I see food in your future." Dimitri's tone changed, reflecting his usual jovial attitude. "That's right, bro. Tomorrow, you'd better get over here and make us breakfast. I'm getting tired of cooking and I have a feeling my mate's going to be keeping me mighty busy for a while."

"Ya'll know I don't cook. Take out, okay? Beignets?"

"You bet," Dimitri replied, pulling the covers up further onto his chest. "Hey, can you do me a favor before you go?

"Sure, what do you need?"

"Can you text Leo and Logan? Make sure they know you're okay. And lock the house on your way out, 'K?"

"Done and done." Jake gave a wave on the way out the door.

Dimitri heard the sound of his footsteps patter up the stairs to his bedroom, presumably so he could borrow clothes and get dressed. Within minutes, he heard his boots pounding downstairs, ending with the creak of the door opening and shutting.

He lifted his head, elated to see the small smile on Gillian's lips. His heart crushed with an emotion that he hadn't experienced in his whole life. Not only had Gillian courageously fought with the pack, she'd given her cat to him, saving his wolf. Their sexual compatibility was icing on the cake as far as he was concerned, but the fresh memory of being inside her caused his cock to twitch. He silently laughed to himself, thinking that he might be spending the next couple of years locked in a bedroom.

As he lay his head back down, he pressed his lips into her hair, softly whispering the words that were true to his heart. "I love you, Gilly."

~⊛· *Chapter Twenty-Two* ·⊛~

Gillian stirred, smiling as her eyes fluttered open. She glanced back to Dimitri, who, although lost in sleep, kept his arms firmly secured about her waist. Pressure in her lower belly had caused her to wake. As much as she loathed leaving the warmth and safety of her mate, the call of nature was greater. Carefully, she peeled Dimitri's fingers away, gently kissing his cheek before she got out of bed.

After using the bathroom, she plunged her arms into the sleeves of a spare robe that hung on the back of the door. She tied the sash, and brought the lapels to her nose, deeply inhaling Dimitri's masculine scent. With a satisfied smile, she quietly padded out of the guest room and into the kitchen.

She reached for the refrigerator door, opening it. Rummaging around, she found a pitcher of filtered water and grabbed a clean coffee mug out of the dish rack. As she went to pour, she heard a high-pitched cry. The recognizable sound of a kitten in distress pierced her chest.

Setting down the cup, she approached the sliding glass doors. She called Dimitri's name, hoping he'd hear her. Her fingertips curled over the metal pull, her thumb flicking the lock open. She called to Dimitri once again, concerned that a stray animal had been hurt. The hairs on the back of her neck stood up, her intuition warning her of danger. Whatever had attacked the young cat was still out in the yard. A loud cry sounded again, sending her into action. As she flung the glass open with the force of ten men, her protective instinct overrode self-preservation. It was as if the remaining tendrils of her cat called on her to save the young feline.

She tore out onto the deck and the screeching continued. Letting her nocturnal vision come into focus, she scanned the yard. She quietly advanced but saw nothing. Dimitri's footsteps sounded in the house, when the sharp slicing pain of claws stabbed into her neck, causing her to freeze in place. A bony hand dangled a kitten, barely twelve weeks old, in front of her face. Gillian's heart caught as it dropped to the ground, safely landing on its feet and scurrying underneath the crawlspace.

Gillian went to scream but as the talon pierced her skin, it restricted air flow to her windpipe. She gasped for breath. Her eyes widened in panic. Unable to see her attacker, her gaze darted from side to side. Heart racing, she lost her concentration; her ability to shift failed her. Terror seized her body, blood flowing from her neck. Gillian swiveled her head, which drove the slicing barbs further into her flesh. She caught sight of Lady Charlotte behind her, her fangs dripping with saliva.

"Get the hell off of my mate," Dimitri growled, barreling through the exit.

"Dimitri." Gillian's lips moved but only a gurgle of his name escaped her lips.

"Don't move, wolf," the vampiress hissed.

"You're going to die tonight," he calmly stated.

Dimitri calculated his next move, observing that the vampire had gone stark raving mad. Her usually coiffed upswept hair had mushroomed, tendrils sprouting all over like overgrown weeds. Her lips were cracked and reddened, making Dimitri wonder if she'd already killed someone. Her blood-stained shirt and pants hung loose on her scrawny frame.

"This is all your fault. You needed vampire blood...came to me for help. He killed her," she spat.

Gillian's arms gripped at Charlotte's wrists, attempting to dislodge her hold. But her iron-clad grip wouldn't budge. The more Gillian struggled, the deeper the vampire's nails curled into her throat.

"Killed who?" Dimitri asked. Deliberately, he stalked toward her.

"Lacey. Léopold did it. He killed her. And for what? Because she'd taken money from a wolf?"

"No, because she signed Gilly's death warrant. Rules are rules, vamp. You've got to either have a death wish or be fucking stupid to mess with Leo. You know it. I know it. And Lacey knew it. She gambled and lost."

"Shut up! You don't know what you're talking about!" Lady Charlotte screamed.

"Nope, I think Leo got this one right," Dimitri mused, giving her a cool smile. "I wonder how long it took for him to kill her. A minute? No, no, no. Not my boy. He strikes as fast as a cottonmouth on a hot summer day. Those fangs probably sucked her dry in seconds."

"I said, shut it, wolf." Lady Charlotte extracted a silver dagger from her back pocket and tore open Gillian's robe. "I'll gut her right now, I swear it."

"Or maybe he just cut off her head. Nah, Leo's not much for weapons, I suppose," Dimitri pondered, edging closer to her. "Ya know he told me he can make it hurt, real bad. I bet that's what he did."

Gillian tried to shift, extending her claws. Lady Charlotte swiftly responded by jabbing the knife into Gillian's abdomen.

"Nice try," she jeered. "No shifting for you."

The razor-sharp weapon lacerated Gillian's creamy skin, crimson droplets spilling down her torso. Her throat constricted; she coughed, her breathing growing ragged. As a fingernail pressed through to her trachea, a drowning sensation commenced, Gillian's lungs filling with blood. Eyes bulging, she hoped the bond she shared with Dimitri would somehow allow her to silently communicate with him. But he wasn't looking at her. She couldn't understand why his gaze was firmly pinned on the vampire.

"You know, I thought you were kind of smart when I first met ya, bein' that Leo went to you for help and all. But all I see now is a pathetic excuse of a corpse, refusing to take responsibility for her own mess." Dimitri's eyes flared at the sight of his mate's injury. He carefully strategized his attack. If he moved too quickly, he knew Lady Charlotte would flay her open like a fish. Gillian's ability to shift had faltered, she couldn't fight back.

"Lacey was my lover. Before you say anything, always know that it was me who let her fuck you. Me! I did that. I gave to her, cared for her. She was mine. And now because of this piece of shit cat here," Charlotte shook Gillian until her body went listless, her legs barely holding her upright. Acidic tears rained down Charlotte's cheeks, hate spewing from her mouth. "She's gone. Léopold showed no mercy that night in the club. He killed her, and now I'm going to kill your mate. If you'd never set foot in my club, none of this would have ever happened. An eye for an eye. I want justice."

"This isn't Gillian's fault. Ilsbeth is the one who…"

"Ilsbeth," she scoffed. "You're a fool, you know that. She's the one who set the dominos in motion. If I'd known at the time, I'd never have agreed to give you the blood."

"What are you talking about?"

"She's always wanted what she couldn't have. I should've known how far that bitch would go."

"I broke off with her months ago. Maybe she didn't like it but she's always known that I'd find my mate."

"She's clever, I'll give her that. Making it so you couldn't shift. Trying to kill off your wolf. She put on a good show. You bought it hook, line and sinker. The sorcerer…that was a nice touch."

"You're lying," he growled.

"Truth hurts, doesn't it? Had to torture it out of her. But as you can see, I have a penchant for the fine art of persuasion."

"Fuck," Dimitri cursed. Even though Gillian had tried to convince him, he'd held out hope that Ilsbeth hadn't been responsible for his affliction.

"Don't fret now. Ilsbeth got hers."

"What did you do? Where's Ilsbeth?"

"I ruined her life the way she's ruined mine. Don't worry, she's still alive. Death is too good for her," she sniffed. "Let's just put it this way, she won't be casting any more spells for a while…if ever. It will be as if she never existed."

"You'll never get away from Leo." Dimitri's eyes narrowed on her, his voice emotionless. He moved a few more feet closer, his body preparing to shift.

"I'll leave town. I'll leave the country. None of you can touch me."

Gillian's vision blurred as her spirit faltered. Their argument was but static in her ears, her mind no longer able to process their words. She reached within her mind's eye and saw her wolf struggling to appear. The soft roar of her tiger echoed in her mind yet she couldn't see her anywhere. Her eyes fluttered open and she caught Dimitri's gaze but for a moment. Her heart broke for him, the life draining from her body. She loved him heart, body and soul. If she was going to die, she was going to tell him before she left this earth.

"Dimitri, please," she begged, her voice barely audible. Tears sprang from her eyes, her fingers too weak to hold onto the vampire's forearms. As her lips moved to say the words, no sound could be heard.

"I love you," she mouthed, her eyes rolling back into her head. A blanket of unconsciousness fell over her as she began to convulse.

Dimitri had managed to distract Lady Charlotte long enough to close the distance, yet it hadn't been enough. Gillian's confession spurred his wolf into a feral state. Dimitri lost the restrained control he'd demonstrated, determined to kill Charlotte. Transforming seamlessly, his wolf launched itself at the vampire, shoving them all down into the dewy yard.

Lady Charlotte threw Gillian aside, launching her barbed fist into his flank. Like a missile, it cleaved through him. The intense pain drove him into darkness, but the beasts inside him fought through the haze, both the wolf and the tiger coming together as one. As they merged, he felt as if he'd been hit by lightning. The sizzle of their interaction cracked a loud thunderous explosion into the night.

Calling on the tiger, he shifted fully into the great cat, his massive paws tearing up the turf. Enraged, he barely registered the slice of her knife into his hindquarters. As Charlotte sank her fangs deep into his shoulder, he repelled her with a tremendous shake of his muscular body, smashing her into the ground. She raised the blade to slay him and he swiftly evaded her knife, his sharp claws tearing across her throat. Blood sprayed into his thick fur, and he roared in victory as Charlotte's head rolled from her body, quickly turning to ash.

As he shifted back, the unimaginable reality slammed into him that he'd somehow become feline, driven by his need to protect his mate. But the fleeting thought disappeared as he saw Gillian lying unconscious on the ground. The cicadas sang in anguish, as if they were aware that she'd been critically injured. Dimitri scooped her up into his arms, pressing the wound together with his fingers.

"Gillian, please," he cried. Spent, and uncertain if he could heal her like they'd done with Jake, he commanded her. "Listen, Gilly. You have to shift. Can you hear me? This is your mate. Gillian!"

Gillian moaned, aware of him calling her name. No longer in pain, the endorphins rushed through her body, causing her to feel as if she was floating up to the sky.

"Goddammit, Gillian. You will shift. Do you hear me?"

"No, no...I'm flying...I'm leaving," she murmured, her face pale.

"No, Gilly. Stay with me. You're a wolf. Now, shift," he demanded, his eyes brimming with tears. He could tell that she was lost in some sort of haze, unaware of her situation.

The sound of Dimitri yelling startled Gillian back into reality. She clutched at the wound in her belly. Panting, she began to beg. "Oh my God. Please stop the pain. I'm going to die. Please stop it…"

"Yes, you're in pain. That means you're fighting. You have to do as I say. You will listen. Submit to me now. Do you hear me? I am your beta. And you will obey."

"Oh God…I don't know…help me." Gillian began to scream as she flittered in and out of consciousness.

"Obey and shift," he ordered, his voice dominant. No longer could he afford to treat her with kid gloves, he had to appeal to her wolf's sense of the pack.

"Shift," she repeated.

"Shift now!" he yelled at her.

Dimitri breathed a sigh of relief as the magic that was the wolves circulated around them, and within seconds, his little black wolf was lying before him, whole and healed. He plowed his fingers into her hair, kissing her fur. He'd seen Logan command his wolves to shift a million times, but never had he done it himself. Having killed the Alpha, Dimitri was certain that his Alpha tendencies had graduated; no longer would he be able to keep them secret within his own pack. Yet the desire to remain in the bayou with his Acadian wolves would far outweigh the need to dominate Logan or to lead his own pack.

"Jesus, Gilly, you scared the shit out of me," he told her, patting her on her rear. "You need to learn submission."

She barked at him, nearly nipping his fingers and began to run circles around him. Dimitri fell back on the heels of his hands, shaking his head at her.

"You," he pointed to her as she growled and wagged her tail, "are in so much trouble it's not even funny. There's no bitin' your beta, cher. Not unless you want a punishment which I have a feelin' you're itchin' to get."

Gillian whined, pressing her paws to the ground and bowed her head. She rolled over onto her back and whimpered, then shifted back into her human form. Dimitri leaned forward, easily scooping her up into his arms, embracing his mate.

"I love you," she whispered, her lips to his chest.

"Goddess, I love you, too," he replied, kissing the top of her head. "I love you so damn much. I never thought I'd fall in…"

"Love?"

"Yeah that."

"Yeah that," she laughed. "Me either."

For a long minute, they both sat silent, contemplating their confessions. They touched and caressed each other's skin as if they hadn't seen each other in years.

Gillian paused, and looked around the yard in surprise, unaware of what had happened to Charlotte. The last thing she remembered was hitting the ground.

"What did you do with the vampire?" she asked, her eyebrows drawn in concern.

"About that. It's a funny story." Dimitri paused. He wasn't sure how to tell anyone, let alone Gillian, that he'd shifted into a tiger. He hardly believed it himself. It was as if he needed video evidence to confirm his actions. It was so entirely unbelievable, he needed a day or two to come to terms with the cat inside him.

"I'm afraid to know. No, wait. Is she gone?"

"She's gone." Dimitri pulled her closely against his chest, hiding his expression of amusement.

"Dead?"

"Yeah."

"Even better," Gillian replied, relieved that they were safe from retaliation.

"But you, my little wolf, are in trouble for trying to bite me. You know, Leo's taught me a few tricks...he loves spankings." Dimitri smiled, coiling his hands around her wrists, giving her a fair warning.

"Spankings, huh? Something tells me I'm going to enjoy it," she said with a coy grin. "Maybe I should bite you more often."

Gillian gasped as Dimitri swiftly flipped her onto her back, pinning her to the ground. His hands held hers to the sides of her head, and he let the pressure of his hips immobilize her. He may have been in love with her but she would soon learn that he wasn't joking; she'd surrender her control to him. Her wolf would demand it, regardless of what the cat had taught her, and he'd enjoy every second of the struggle.

"Now," he whispered into her ear. "This is much better."

"Hey," she giggled. Her cheek brushed the cool grass. "Don't I get a break? I was just attacked by a vampire."

"You seemed pretty healthy to me a few minutes ago. You've got some sharp fangs, cher," he growled, sucking her earlobe with his lips. Taking it between his teeth, he tugged until she moaned.

"No fair," she cried.

"This isn't about fair," he laughed. "This is about you and me. And you're about to find out why I'm the beta of this pack."

As Dimitri took her lips, he felt her body go limp, submitting to his will. Twice during the full moon, he'd almost lost someone he loved. But the exhilaration of having her back in his arms, the knowledge that she could shift, washed away any lingering concerns. When he'd entered his home with her in his arms, he'd never been happier in his entire life. Their home, their future, their love. A new life with his little wolf.

⟿⟡ *Chapter Twenty-Three* ⟡⟾

The wind whipped Gillian's raven locks around her helmet. The warmth of Dimitri heated her palms as she fingered the ridges of his abs. She laughed as he slapped her wandering hands that had traveled underneath his t-shirt. He'd insisted she keep her arms wrapped around his waist, but her caress to his bared skin had proven to be far too distracting. The soft blindfold around her eyes kept her in darkness.

After two weeks without Dimitri, Gillian was ravenous for him. Not being able to spend days and nights with her mate had been a necessary evil. She'd gone to New York City with her brother while Dimitri had traveled to San Diego. As much as Gillian had wanted Dimitri to come with her to Nick's funeral, Jake had needed his help to settle the Anzober wolves.

Initially, Jax had been reticent, but eventually he'd broken down, confiding in Gillian, accepting her comfort. She'd held him as he cried, and did her best to console him. Despite his grief, he'd continued commanding his subordinates, conducting business as usual and planning future issues of ZANE.

During the days leading up to the burial, she and Jax spent hours talking, catching up on childhoods lost. They'd pored through old photographs. For the first time in her life, she'd gotten a glimpse inside the world that had eluded her. His mother, a Nordic wolf, had been a beautiful woman. Sadly, she was killed during a territorial dispute shortly after Jax had been born, and he had few memories of her. The Alpha, their father, had been strikingly handsome, also with blonde hair, yet he looked more rugged than her brother. She could see why her mother had fallen in love with him. Not only was he good-looking, Gillian learned he had been steadfastly loyal, a great warrior in his time. He'd been an Alpha through and through. His blood ran thick in her veins and she suspected her difficulty submitting came naturally.

Gillian had chipped away at the anguish that consumed Jax. She'd felt hopeful, thankful that she had a brother. He too, had expressed his happiness that they were no longer alone. But the day of the funeral, Jax fell back into his dark depression. Since Nick had been well loved by wolves and humans alike, they'd held a public memorial service in Central Park. Afterwards, they'd traveled to the Fingers Lakes region to hold the private burial on pack lands.

Later in the evening, on a damp night during the new moon, they placed Nick into the trenched earth. Gillian and Jax had shoveled the dirt onto the deceased body. An audience of wolves stood watching, the earthy aroma fresh in the air. Sweat and tears misted their bodies, grime staining their skin.

With their bare hands, they attended to his gravesite until they'd patted the mound tight.

After a long run with his pack, they'd traveled by limo in silence back to the city. It was as if a switch had gone off; Jax had withdrawn from both her and his pack. On her insistence, he'd flown with her back to Louisiana. She'd lied, telling him she'd felt uncomfortable flying alone, urging him to come with her. The reality was that she thought he could use a change of scenery.

But once they'd arrived in the city, he'd arranged for Dimitri to meet them at the airport, explaining that he planned on traveling, needing to find peace. Gillian knew that despite her concerns, Jax had to deal with his grief in his own way. Having no mate or children, her brother had spent years confiding in and caring for his beta. It was as if he'd lost a mate, and she was worried that he wouldn't recover. As he hugged her goodbye, he whispered in her ear, promising that he'd be okay.

Sadness filled her heart, watching Jax reboard his plane. But as she turned to leave and saw her mate, Gillian's libido roared to life, her emotions instantly transforming into lust. Dimitri casually leaned on his motorcycle, waiting for her arrival. She ran to him, stopping short of his embrace. The sight of her beta took her breath away. Altogether sexy and confident, his wicked smile made her want to tear off her panties and beg him to fuck her right there on the tarmac. But in his typical dominance, he'd controlled the situation, first by kissing her senseless, then promptly blindfolding her before she had a chance to speak. He straddled her on his bike, running his strong hands up her inner thighs. She gasped, her nipples hardening in response. Her vision, cloaked in blackness, heightened the sensation. Even though she was well aware they were still at the airport, it was as if they were the only two people in the world.

As they rode, Gillian had no idea of their destination. She relished the feel of his ripped torso against her palms, inhaling his distinctive scent. With her head pressed to his leather jacket, she lost track of time. She couldn't say for how long they traveled, her stiff peaks denting into the hard expanse of his back. The vibrations from the seat reverberated in a sensual tempo against her groin. By the time they'd arrived at their final destination, she'd nearly come undone. She hadn't anticipated that their traveling arrangements were only the beginning of the delicious torture her mate had planned.

As he helped her onto the ground, the salty mist hit her face. Licking her lips, she tasted the briny air. She'd never heard of a beach near New Orleans, yet she swore she heard waves.

"Where are we?" She laughed as he gently pulled the helmet off of her head. His fingertips trailed along the nape of her neck.

"It's a surprise," he promised.

Gillian could almost visualize his devious grin behind the lilt of his southern accent.

"Can I remove this…" She reached for the blindfold, and immediately received a jolting slap on her bottom. Through her jeans, it felt more like pressure as opposed to pain, but the message was received.

"No peeking. You'd think spending so much time with your Alpha brother would've taught you a few things," he whispered in her ear, his chest to her back. "You don't listen very well. I'm afraid we are going to need to have multiple lessons…ones involving just you and me."

Gillian giggled, her arousal spiked. Every cell of her body awakened to his touch.

"Not funny, cher. Feel what you did to me on this trip." He set his hands on her hips, tugging her backward. He took her hand, leading it behind her back and pressed it onto his enormous erection. "I said, no touching my skin. You almost caused me to wreck."

"It's been two weeks. It's not fair to expect me to keep my hands off you," she protested with a broad smile.

Dimitri brushed his lips to the sensitive area behind her ear. A firm palm traveled from her belly, rising slowly between her breasts and over her chest until his hand was wrapped around her neck. His other fell between her legs, cupping her denim-covered mound. "Goddess, I missed you…every square inch of you."

"I missed you too…so much." Gillian released a moan, her body falling limp against the strength of her mate. After her long visit with Jax, always being careful not to offend other wolves within his pack, she'd grown exhausted of wearing a mask of serenity. She didn't want to think, she just wanted to feel and exist within Dimitri's arms. Nothing else mattered. Letting go of her inhibitions was impossible except when in the care of her mate.

"It's very difficult being apart, our wolves, our souls needing each other," he growled, grinding his hard arousal into her bottom. "But tonight, we're alone. Just you and I…all night long."

"Please," she cried. Her palms pressed backwards, digging her nails into his muscular thighs.

"I love hearing you ask, cher. So nice." His soft lips peppered kisses along her neck.

Gillian sighed with anticipation, as his tongue danced over her skin. The rush of desire ached between her legs, her body tensing.

As quickly as his hands left her body, they returned, lifting and cradling her against him. She heard his feet moving upon the ground, but didn't ask where they were going. She didn't care. Wherever he took her, she'd follow. He'd give her what she required; the trust and love for her mate was steadfast and complete.

A door creaked open, alerting Gillian that he'd entered a room. Yet, she got the distinctive feeling she was still outside. The roar of the ocean breaking against the shore confirmed her suspicion that he'd brought her to a beach. Unable to hear another soul, she assumed they were alone but couldn't be certain. He set her on her feet, kissing her once again, leaving her breathless as he tore his lips from hers. Before she had a chance to say a word, he spoke.

"And now that we're finally alone, I need to properly prepare you," he drawled.

"Prepare me for what? Dimitri!" Gillian gasped his name, the fabric of her t-shirt rolling up over her head. With a snap of her bra, she was exposed. The instinct to cover herself was overruled by the cuff of fingers around her wrists. Unable to see, she groaned, as warm lips suckled her nipple.

"Ah, yeah, that is what I've been cravin'…sweet." Dimitri licked circles around one areola then paid attention to the other. "Delicious like warm peaches. 'Cept no sharin'. All for me."

His bare chest brushed hers as he released her. The cool sea air blowing against her wet tips caused them to further swell into tight peaks. Before she had time to speculate exactly where he'd taken her, or if anyone could see them, she heard her zipper opening. Seconds later, she stood devoid of clothing.

"You're so beautiful, Gil."

"Baby, you have no idea how much I want you."

"I think I do, because I've been needin' you just as bad. Do you know I like surprises?"

"Surprises, huh?"

"I've got a big one for you, but first," Dimitri kissed her, slipping his fingers through her glistening folds.

Gillian melted as he kissed her, moaning into his mouth as he plunged two digits deep inside her. Her core tightened around him in response. She'd been on the precipice of coming for the past hour and knew she'd fall hard and fast.

"That's it, cher," he encouraged, briefly tearing his lips from hers. His forehead pressed to hers, and he sighed. "Fuck, I love watching you come."

His thumb strummed her clit. With her body already on fire, she shook, letting the orgasm she'd held at bay roll through her.

"I…I…oh God." Gillian attempted to articulate her pleasure, but the convulsions of her climax seized her, making it impossible for her to speak. The love for her beta had taken everything she'd ever known and made it seem insignificant. Her heart felt as if it would burst.

"You okay?" he asked.

"I'm more than okay. Great. But I need you. Please don't make me wait."

Shaken, she smiled, still unable to see. Having relied on him for balance, she felt abandoned as his hands left her skin.

"Patience, little wolf. Stay there," Dimitri ordered, releasing her waist. He stepped back, admiring her gorgeous body and smiled as she brought her hands to her eyes, toying with the fabric. He inwardly laughed, knowing how difficult it was for her to take orders. Although she tried, submission was sometimes a struggle, and he expected it was something she might never fully learn, given her feline and Alpha ancestry. "Do not touch that blindfold."

Dimitri had waited weeks to tell Gillian about his ability to shift to cat. It had been extraordinarily difficult to leave his mate to go to San Diego, never disclosing how he'd killed Lady Charlotte. Before telling her, though, he had to be certain that what had happened was real. He'd reluctantly agreed that she should go with her brother to New York. After what had happened to Nick, she was Jax's only blood. Watching the interaction between them caused his chest to ache, knowing that she'd been raised in isolation by her mother, and now her brother had become compromised. She and Jax needed each other, but Dimitri knew the Alpha had a long road ahead of him.

In truth, Dimitri would never have taken her to the West Coast, not after what had happened to her there. With the trauma fresh in her mind, it was best she healed her wounds away from California. The long trip had been arduous at best. The pack had been disjointed, many families losing members, ones who'd come to Louisiana under Chaz's orders. Dimitri was grateful that Logan hadn't insisted that he take over as Alpha, instead assigning Jake to the temporary position. Neither Dimitri nor Jake wanted to move so far away from Acadian wolves. With their pack in disarray, Jake would lead them for only a few months, eventually allowing the natural order of selection to determine their new Alpha.

As Dimitri watched Gillian stand on the deck naked, a satisfied smile crossed her face. He stepped away toward the bed and stripped. He'd practiced his transformation many times, since it had happened the night of Lady Charlotte's attack. As he reflected on that night, he recalled her chilling words. Ilsbeth hadn't been heard from or seen since, but after what she'd done to him, he hadn't gone looking. The only person he'd shown or told about the tiger had been Logan. Thankfully, his Alpha had merely laughed, finding it monumentally amusing that not only had he been mated but now he shifted to both wolf and cat.

"Gillian," he called, summoning his transformation.

"Yes, sir," she teased.

"Take off your blindfold." The magic flowed through him. Passing over his wolf, he announced his arrival with a thunderous roar.

"Oh. My. God. No way. I mean yes," Gillian stammered.

Amazed, she stared in disbelief, unable to move her feet. Her magnificent beta had taken on a feline form. She took a deep breath, slowly walking toward the bed. Tears came to her eyes as she set her palms onto his gold and black striped fur. Even though she hadn't been able to shift back to her cat yet, she, too, felt her inside and was convinced that someday soon, she'd have both animals within her reach. But the spectacular sight of Dimitri lying on the bed was surreal.

Dimitri gave a final growl, shifting back to his human form. As he did so, he rolled her onto her back.

"I wasn't sure how to tell you," he said, his lips brushing her sternum. Excitement and relief tore through him as he saw the delight on her face. He buried his head between her breasts.

"You... I've never seen a male...I mean, a male tiger...an animal like you. You were just...beautiful."

"Hmm....I like the sound of that. So I'm your first, huh?"

She laughed in response, plowing her fingers into his hair. The weight of his body against hers pressed her into the soft mattress.

"A virgin. Yep, I've got myself a virgin," he teased.

"Not exactly a virgin, but yes, you're still my first. My first in so many ways," she replied, continuing to smile.

"I love you." He stilled, his voice growing serious.

"I love you, too. I never thought I'd find anyone. And now..."

"Now, you've got yourself a tiger by the tail?"

"A little pussy cat?" she joked.

"Speaking of pussy," he laughed, pushing up onto his hands. Dimitri loved teasing her, making love with her. He wasn't sure whether it was her quick wit or her stark independence that drove him mad with hunger for her, but with her warm and ready underneath him, he didn't care. They had a lifetime and more to discover all the reasons they loved each other.

"I think I'm going to like this part." Gillian grinned, her golden eyes flickering with arousal.

"You and me both, cher." Dimitri took her lips with urgency, sucking and pressing his tongue into her mouth.

Giving her no time to rest, he guided his thick cock to her entrance, sliding into her with one strong thrust. Her tight channel fisted him, yet accommodated him as if she were a custom glove. She moaned in pleasure as he passionately kissed her. Never taking his lips off hers, he reached for her legs, wrapping them around his waist. His hand found her full breast, the hard length of him pounding into her. Rough and wild, he laughed as she nipped at his lip, nearly drawing blood. Feral, they made love, letting all inhibitions go.

"Dimitri," she screamed as he thrust into her, the bed springs creaking.

"I love you," he responded with a grunt. "Do you hear me, Gil?"

"Yes. Yes, I love you, too. Dimitri, please, oh God, yes, that's it...please," she begged. Her head thrashed from side to side as she came undone, their passion unleashed. Gillian lost herself in her release.

Dimitri dug his fingers into her bottom, guiding her hips back and forth as he slammed into her. He held his breath, as his own orgasm exploded.

The starburst of their simultaneous climax pulsated through them, leaving them in a state of delicious exhaustion. They lay motionless, immersed in the love they felt for each other.

Dimitri sighed, brushing the hair from Gillian's face. When she smiled up at him it was as if she'd reached into his chest, holding his heart in her hands. Everything he was and would be was hers. His tiny mate owned his heart, even if she didn't know it. Gillian had been the gift he'd never expected, one he'd treasure all his immortal days. He cuddled her into his chest, his lips to her forehead. Lovers and soul mates, they lay watching the sunset, looking forward to endless days and nights, together forever.

~❦· *Epilogue* ❦~

Jax gritted his teeth, the corrosive scotch burning over his tongue. From the circular balcony of his private VIP lounge, he watched the twenty-somethings move as a mass, undulating on the dance floor. The pounding bass and flashing lights charged the jam-packed New York City dance club.

The bar had been a regular haunt of his and Nick's. From their eagle's nest, they would observe the fine-looking women, often poaching one or two for their own entertainment. Other times, they'd simply play chess, discussing business and their plans for the weekend. *Never again.*

Seventy-two years as best friends. Twenty-seven of those as Alpha and beta. The bitter taste of grief and rage boiled inside Jax. What had gone down in New Orleans should have been nothing more than picking a flea off a dog. They'd gotten sloppy. He'd gotten sloppy. Guilt for not watching Nick and underestimating the Anzober Alpha's strategy ate at him.

He downed another shot and slammed the glass onto the stainless steel table, reflecting on his current state of affairs. He'd always known Gillian had existed, but he'd purposely left her alone. He supposed his stepmother had good reasons for leaving the pack. Between the loss of her husband and the loss of her tiger, she'd gone to great lengths to put distance between herself and New York City. He could have easily located his sister with one call, yet seeing the devastation Mirabel had suffered when his father died, knowing she'd never shift, he couldn't bring himself to inflict that kind of pain onto his own sibling. A firm believer in fate, he was of the mindset that if it was meant to be, they'd find each other.

Jax thought it ironic that as the Goddess took one loved one from his life, she gave another, Gillian. Reminiscing about his father had been solacing, never having discussed his life and death with another person, let alone a family member. Even though he and Nick had been inseparable, the topic of his father had been off limits. The only thing to have been said about him was that Jax had loved him and that he was a great warrior. The detailed memories of his father teaching him to hunt, singing to him as a boy had been lost, buried deep, until his long talks with Gillian brought them to the surface. Having never known her father, she'd laughed and cried while listening to his childhood stories.

He'd wanted to stay with Gillian in New Orleans. However, his pack needed him to act as Alpha, to guide them through their loss. Their collective mourning resonated throughout every cell of his body. He had to settle his own mind for the sake of his wolves, as his torrent of grief was crushing them all. Coming back to New York City was unavoidable. The magazine wouldn't run itself; his conglomerate was in desperate need of attention. As chief operating officer, Nick had taken care of day-to-day operations, and Jax loathed having to take action to find his replacement. That task would be easy compared to selecting a new beta, something he could not even begin to comprehend doing.

Leaving Gillian had been paramount to ensure her happiness. Newly mated, she and Dimitri required time alone, without her needy big brother in the wings. It killed him to leave her just as they were starting to connect, but as Alpha, he never questioned the validity of his decision.

Jax sighed, glancing at the beautiful women who pranced like peacocks around the bar. On any given night, he and Nick may have easily indulged, either alone or sharing a female. While they may have played the game, always honest about their status as non-mated wolves, Jax had at one time suspected his mate existed.

Kat Livingston, sister to the Lyceum wolves Alpha, had crossed his path one icy Christmas evening. She'd arrived at his private event with a mutual friend. Immediately, he'd taken notice of the mysterious striking woman, hearing her intoxicating laugh across the room. Introducing himself, he'd taken her hand in greeting. For a long moment, they'd stood silent, their eyes locked as the electric current seared their palms. The scent of her drove his wolf to howl for the one he'd thought was his mate. With haste, she'd broken the connection. She gave him a small smile and explained that she had to leave to get back home for the holidays. Nick interrupted but for a moment and when he'd turned back to see if he could get her contact information, she'd already left.

She'd gone to Philadelphia, implying to her brothers that he'd attempted to force a mating. Nothing could have been further from the truth. While he may have called Kat and her brothers, he never once sent his wolves after her. Disgusted with her antics and lies, Jax let it be, eventually making peace with Tristan.

Jax Chandler didn't chase women. Quite the opposite, women chased him. Powerful and charismatic, the Alpha had no intentions of further pursuing the cagey female he'd met that snowy eve. He chalked up his wolf's interest in her to a rare miscommunication and never gave it another thought.

As he poured his third glass, however, he wondered if maybe he'd been wrong to give up so easily. He sighed, thinking he must be losing his mind. The strain of his depression from losing Nick weighed heavily on his heart as he contemplated stepping down as Alpha. He fantasized about going off into the wilderness of Canada, becoming a lone wolf. It would be a struggle to get out of bed every morning, let alone continue to act as if everything was business as usual. By the end of the week, he'd make his decision. Above all else, he'd do what was in the best interest of the pack, even if that meant disappearing into obscurity.

As he brought the rim of his glass to his lips, he heard a scream from below. Often the elicitor of this response both in and out of the bedroom, he was attuned to the difference between sounds caused by delight, ecstasy or pain. This one was induced by terror.

Even though it wasn't his responsibility to intervene, he set down his drink, honing in on the source of the ear-piercing sound. A crowd had gathered in the center of the floor. A woman, he presumed, had fallen to the ground, not necessarily unusual for a dance club. Her black-leather bondage heels were attached to long shapely legs.

His friend and owner of the club, Finn, peeled back the layer of spectators, allowing Jax to identify the owner of the gorgeous pins. *Kat?* Heart racing, he jumped to his feet, frantically tapping at the elevator door that led from his suite down to the main area. After what seemed like centuries, it slid open and he descended.

Jax raked his fingers through his hair, second guessing what he'd thought to be true. It made no sense that Kat would return to New York City. *Why would she come here again after telling her brothers that I was trying to force a mating? If she wanted to see me, why wouldn't she follow protocol, letting me know she'd arrived?*

The heavy metal doors slid open and he yelled over to Finn, attempting to catch his attention. His commanding presence registered with nearly every soul in attendance, the crowd parting as he stalked toward the injured female. The music ceased and the house lights shone brightly, illuminating the floor as if it were daylight. An eerie sense of calm followed, soft chatter resounding throughout the club.

Jax pulled out his phone and tapped in 911. Taking sight of Finn holding the woman in his arms, he intervened.

"What happened to this female?" Jax asked, his booming voice reverberating over the hushed whispers of the patrons.

"I don't know. She's out cold. Must've slipped."

Jax knelt, carefully cradling her head.

"Get these people out of here," Jax ordered.

Finn quickly ushered people toward the door, emptying the area.

Jax studied the female's face, recalling the contours of Kat's profile. While the woman appeared familiar, her hair was blond. Her scent registered neither human nor wolf. Although she looked similar to the woman he'd met long ago, he wasn't a hundred percent certain she was who he'd thought she was. His concern lifted as she began to awaken, her eyes fluttering open.

"Kat, sweetheart. Are you okay?" he asked softly.

His caring tone of voice surprised him, but his expression remained impassive, as he was well aware that other pack members were watching. Her blue eyes caught his, a look of confusion on her face.

"Who's Kat?" she responded. Clutching at her belly, she moaned. "Help me."

"I've got you," Jax told her. Perplexed, he shook his head. It was unusual for his first instincts to be wrong.

Whether it was due to the death of Nick or finding Gillian, Jax Chandler didn't know, but he considered that for the first time in his long life, he'd been thrown off his game. Never one to second guess his decisions, he committed as the emergency workers arrived. As they strapped the beautiful stranger to the gurney, he rose to his feet. With a nod to Finn, he proceeded to follow them.

"I'm going with her," Jax declared.

"Sorry sir, only family." The paramedic, a human and unaware of his status, attempted to hold him back with an arm.

"She's my wife." As the lie slipped from his lips, he saw Finn's jaw drop. He glared at his friend in warning not to reveal his identity. Regardless of whether or not she was Kat, his wolf urged him to go with her.

"Jax," Finn called. "You need me to go with?"

"No, I've got this," Jax said, his voice wavering.

Even though his gut told him not to go alone, he couldn't bring himself to ask for help. While he was close to Finn, it felt wrong to have him go as if he was replacing Nick. No, it was Nick's place to travel with the Alpha, to be at his side.

He paused, catching Finn's concerned gaze and stepped into the ambulance, taking a seat next to the fragile-looking woman who lay motionless on the stretcher. The doors slammed shut, the emergency vehicle's sirens blaring into the night as it sped off toward the hospital. Jax was startled as her fingers reached for his. He glanced to their joined hands, hoping he'd done the right thing.

"Don't leave me," she whispered, her eyes closed.

"I'm not going anywhere," he promised.

"No, Jax. You aren't," she responded.

As the blade sliced into his thigh, he hissed in pain. Shock and confusion played across his face. The woman on the gurney flickered in his vision like a hologram. As the poison pumped through his heart, he succumbed, wishing he'd never come back to New York City.

LOST EMBRACE

–֎· *Chapter One* ·֎–

The demon gored its claw into her belly, boring through her organs. She fell to the ground, and the thump of her skull cracking on the pavement reverberated in her ears. The black tunnel closed in as the beast spat into her wound, its acidic saliva burning her flesh. Clutching the cavernous gash, her bloodstained hands slipped from her skin as the life drained out of her.

Never wanting to be vampire, her love of her humanity had superseded all else. Despite having been guaranteed immortality by her vampire lover, she learned that such promises were relative to the manner of death. Though age and disease would not come for her, the demon's talons would prove to be fatal. Unlike everything she'd been told about death, her life didn't flash before her eyes. Only *he* was omnipresent in her thoughts. With her last breath, she called for him to save her. *Kade*. She'd always been a fighter until her final moment when hope was lost. As light turned to darkness, she accepted the inevitable. Giving in to death's embrace, she smiled, knowing that she'd loved, was loved.

Sydney braced for the seizure, her body tensing, readying for the barrage of spasms it would endure. It had been a month since she'd been attacked. She'd been protecting an innocent child from the monstrous demon who sought to claim her. As a police officer, it wasn't the first time she'd been in danger. But that day, she'd been no match for the evil beast who impaled her with his fist. As death reached for her soul, her fiancé, Kade Issacson, had saved her from its finality. Turned her without consent.

Sydney loved Kade more than life itself, but they'd always had an understanding; she'd remain human. She'd agreed to drink miniscule amounts of his blood, allowing her the benefits of immortality. As Kade's singular source of sustenance, she'd always known that if she were to be turned, he wouldn't be able to feed from her. Having been transformed into a vampire, no longer could she serve that role in his life. In the blink of an eye, her life had been destroyed, promises crushed.

The first round of chills racked her body, and she bit her lip raw. She curled into the corner of the room, the hardwood floor grounding her. She'd watched through the window as the donor approached the house. A healthy pink tinge on the woman's cheeks told her she'd rushed to her appointment. Even though Sydney knew Kade wouldn't partake of the stranger's blood, it didn't matter. Jealousy clutched at her gut. He'd feed eventually…sometime, somewhere, from someone else…but never from her. He'd need a human, and human she was not.

A tear rolled down her cheek as her muscles relaxed. She and Kade had barely spoken over the past month. She knew he loved her, had done what he thought needed to be done. Yet being turned had rocked her world, shattering the delicate life they'd built together.

Weak, she had been unable to feed without causing the donors excruciating pain. It was as if her fangs were intoxicated with the demon itself. Screaming herself awake had become the only relief from her nightmares of the beast. She'd convinced herself that Rylion had infected her with his saliva. Now her own fluids had brought terror to anyone she'd touched.

When Kade brought donors to her, Sydney would wait for him to sink his teeth into their wrist. She'd be forced to watch the woman shake with desire caused by her lover. At one time, his bite was meant only for her. On this dark night, however, another stranger would quiver at his touch.

A knock sounded before the doorknob creaked. Sydney shoved herself to her feet, and found a chair. Wiping the tears from her face, she took a deep breath, trying to find the courage to proceed. She struggled with thoughts of suicide, yet today the fight to survive prevailed. Reluctantly she'd accept the nourishment.

"Sydney, are you ready for us?" she heard Kade ask. The door edged open an inch.

"Yes," she whispered.

Her eyes met Kade's as he walked into her bedroom. A rush of excitement filled her belly as he came into view. His blond hair had grown long, its shaggy edges brushing his collar. Sydney found his permanent five o'clock shadow every bit as sexy as his usual clean-shaven face. She wished she could hate him, leave him, but the deep burning love in her heart never ceased. It tore her apart to know she'd never be what he needed.

"Love, it's okay," he said, his warm voice attempting to calm her.

A petite blonde followed behind him. She knelt before Sydney and presented her arm in silence. Sydney glanced at her for only a second before meeting Kade's gaze. She fought the moisture that brimmed in her eyes.

"We'll do this quickly," Kade promised.

"It's okay," she lied.

"Hey." Kade cradled her face with his palms, his thumbs gently brushing the tears away. "I love you. We're going to figure this out. I promise you."

When he told her he loved her, it broke her heart. Sydney's gaze fell to the floor, unable to look at him. His warm lips grazed over hers, and she swallowed the soft cry that bubbled inside her throat. As his hands fell from her skin, she gazed out the window. She wished she could pretend to be blind to his actions. She refused to watch his fangs descend, but the sigh of the donor's arousal rang in her ears. Sydney thought she'd die another death, her chest heavy with emotion. By the time the blood hit her lips, she'd made a decision. She knew he wouldn't agree, but it was of little consequence. One way or another, it was time to regain control of her life.

←❀· *Chapter Two* ❀→

Kade snatched a bottle of scotch off the bar and fell back into his leather chair. He recalled the debacle of a feeding that had just played out with Sydney. He'd bitten into the strange woman, her blood like paint thinner on his tongue. In turn, Sydney had barely been able to choke down more than a few drops, and still wasn't nourished.

Kade cursed the fucking demon that had stolen Sydney's spirit. As she'd lain dying on the sidewalk, he hadn't thought twice about turning her. He'd known the consequences, but like a doctor performing an amputation, he'd chosen to cut off the limb to save a life. In the process, he'd killed the human within the woman he loved.

He'd known it would be difficult for Sydney to accept her new lifestyle. But he'd anticipated that in time she'd grow to understand that it was a matter of existence. He'd explained several times that the sexual feelings induced by their bite was necessary, a survival mechanism for the vampire race.

Footsteps in the hallway thwarted his racing thoughts and alerted him to the fact that he wasn't alone. His best friend, Luca Macquarie, stood watching him, his arm braced on the doorjamb. He'd known Luca would come, sensing his discontent.

"Scotch?" Kade poured a drink and slid a tumbler across his desk.

"Is that a question or an order?" Luca approached and took a seat.

"I'm running out of time." He held up his glass to the light, studying the amber legs trailing down the sides.

"We've got nothing but time, my friend."

"Not her."

"Did she feed?"

"What do you think?" Kade locked his tired eyes on Luca's.

"Is that a no?"

"She ate…barely. She's unable to control her bite."

"Still causing pain?"

"Tried it two days ago."

"And?"

"Let's just say I had to bite the donor a second time just to take the edge off her screaming. Needless to say, she won't be back."

"Can't you just continue as is? You bite the donor then she feeds?"

"Let me ask you this." Kade took a deep draw of the liquor, his lips drawn tight. "How would Samantha feel if you bit another woman? Another man for that matter? Had to rely on someone else for food?"

"She'd hate it. Look, I see your point, but you're running out of options here." Luca rimmed the edge of his drink with his forefinger. "What's the great one say?"

Kade gave a small smirk, realizing Luca was referring to Léopold, the ancient vampire who'd turned him.

"Léopold believes it's psychological but won't rule out the possibility that the demon somehow mutated her. If that's true, she'll never be able to feed on her own...not bite easily, anyway. The human will struggle. Every time would be torture. She could end up killing them."

"Okay, well, let's assume the former, shall we? Have you tried male donors? It could give her an incentive...you know...make things more pleasurable for her."

"Yes," Kade bit out. The male had been every bit of a disaster as the woman.

"I take that it didn't go well."

"That would be correct. Not to mention that I know for damn sure you wouldn't want your woman's mouth on another man." Kade plowed his fingers through his hair. "I don't know...it's not that I'm opposed to her eating from a man per se, but it was just all wrong. I didn't know the donor. She didn't know him either. Learning how to control the pleasure without it turning sexual is an acquired skill."

"You let me bite her," Luca noted, averting his gaze.

"*She* let you feed from her. Once. To save your ass. And if you recall correctly, I told you that I wouldn't share her again," Kade replied.

"Yes, I do, but now you may have to do the same to save her."

"I'm not sure what you're implying."

"Let her feed from someone she knows. Samantha is pregnant so that's out but perhaps one of the wolves..."

"Maybe. I'd have to ask the Alpha."

"Think about it...their blood is strong. The Alpha's mate, Wynter, she would be a good choice. She's a woman. And she and Sydney are friends. The Alpha owes you this anyway. Sydney ended up in this predicament saving her and their child."

"Wolves aren't our usual food source."

"Who then? Does she have any other human friends who are willing?" Luca asked.

"She hasn't been down here very long. She doesn't know many people," Kade hedged. "I've got to do something, though. I'm losing her."

"You're not losing her."

"I am. I can see the desperation in her eyes. Some days," Kade pinched the bridge of his nose, "she's not fighting. That day I saved her, I think she was ready to die. I mean, despite everything I could give her, her job had certain dangers. Dying...she knew it was a possibility. She always told me that she wanted to stay human. She was my mortal, and now...things are changed. We must rely on others for blood. She can't handle me feeding from another woman. And fuck, I can't blame her. I don't want to see her bringing someone else pleasure."

"Remember that night in the club?" Luca asked, the corner of his mouth upturned.

"What?"

"Sangre Dulce. We were working the Asgear case."

"Yeah, what of it?"

"You know I love Sam, so don't take this the wrong way. But that night on the dance floor…Sydney and I…when we danced. I know you watched."

"So?"

"So? You damn well know she was pleasuring me. Well, maybe she wasn't doing it entirely on purpose, but still. Dancing like that. And then you joined us for a little sandwich action. I was harder than a fucking rock out there. You knew." He laughed. "Not only did you know, you liked it."

Kade shook his head, unwilling to admit it. Seeing his best friend and Sydney enjoy each other had been a turn on, no doubt. But he'd always controlled the situation and he hadn't bonded to her yet.

"Don't tell me you didn't like it, because you did. And the three of us together, when I was injured? You both came to me in bed. Granted you knew I needed her blood, but still. When I bit her, she touched me. You would never have let it happen if there wasn't a small part of you that was open to it."

"It doesn't matter, Luca. Even if I did enjoy it, which I'm not saying, it was you. Sydney and I are both close to you. There's no one who fits that bill."

"What about Jake? He was with her when this demon shit all went down. Sydney knows him. He's wolf. His blood may help her transition more quickly."

"It's not happening," Kade said, but the idea lingered in his mind. While it was true that Jake had come to Sydney's aid, she didn't know him that well. As loath as he was to admit it, maybe he should ask the Alpha if Wynter was willing to help. Sydney and Wynter had cared for the child together, and since the attack, she'd come to visit her. His cell phone rang, breaking his contemplation. He slid his thumb across its glass and answered it.

"Kade," he responded.

"Detective Anthony Salucci."

"Anthony." Kade had expected he'd call sooner or later. Sydney's former partner still lived in Philadelphia. Prior to the accident, they'd kept in touch quite often. Lately, however, unless someone came to the house to visit her, she avoided speaking to anyone.

"What's going on down there? Syd isn't picking up my calls. I texted her and nothin'."

"Detective," Kade paused and glanced at Luca, "I'm very sorry to tell you…"

"What happened? No, don't tell me. She's not…"

"No…she's not dead," Kade replied, and took a deep breath. "There was an incident."

"Was she shot? Is she in the hospital?"

"No but…she was attacked."

"Goddammit, Kade. Why the hell didn't you call me? I would have come down there."

"There hasn't been time. And besides, she's recovering." Kade stalled and changed the subject. "I'm sorry but she isn't taking calls right now. I'd be happy to give her a message."

"Listen, I wanted to tell her first, but this concerns both of you now." He sighed. "There's been an escape."

"A what?"

"An escape. From prison."

"And you thought to call Sydney because?" Kade asked.

"The guy who escaped is dangerous. He's had a hard on for Syd ever since he laid eyes on her."

"You think he's coming down here?"

"*They're* coming for her."

"They're?" Kade's jaw tightened. As if she didn't have enough problems, some two bit criminal planned on attacking Sydney? He'd have laughed at the ridiculousness of the situation if it weren't for her seriously impaired state.

"Yeah, this guy. He's got connections. We busted him three years ago, and he's been tied to over twenty murders," Anthony told him.

"If he thinks he's coming to New Orleans to get Sydney, he's going to have to get through me first." Kade's eyes met Luca's.

"All the same to you, I'm flying down there. He's my responsibility and so is Sydney."

"She's not your partner anymore."

"She's my friend. You may be marryin' her but she'll always be my responsibility in my mind. I don't know what the hell happened to her and I can see you're not planning on tellin' me. Doesn't matter. I'll be there tomorrow and we'll work it out."

"You're welcome to stay with us, but you need to know something." Kade paused, concerned about how Sydney would react to seeing Anthony. "Listen, please don't take this personally, but Sydney may not be up for visitors. I think once she sees you, she'll be okay. But just in case she's not, I feel like I need to warn you."

"Then I'll visit with you. The best shot we've got to keep her safe is to work together. I want this guy and I plan on bringin' him back."

"Whoever even attempts to lay a hand on my mate will be going home in a coffin."

"I hear ya, but all the same, I'm coming to help."

"All right. We'll talk about it tomorrow." Kade clicked off his phone and slammed it onto his desk. "When it rains, it pours."

"I take it from your conversation the detective expects trouble. He worries too much." Luca took a sip of his drink and continued. "It's like you just told him; if anyone goes after Sydney, they won't be successful. They're mere humans. Criminals who've already been caught once. How bright can they be?"

"We should be cautious nonetheless. Sydney's condition is precarious at best." Kade picked up the bottle and poured another drink. "I'm worried about her. I know my girl. Something's cooking in that head of hers. She's going to strike out soon."

"Perhaps. It's to be expected, though. Even for a mortal, she was a fighter. She's proven herself to be a fine asset."

"An asset, huh? You do have a way with words. How I missed your candor." Despite never being fond of humans, his friend had grown attached to Sydney.

"Miss Willows has always been stronger than most. Most humans are so very weak…a shame really."

"They serve a purpose. You and I both know it." Kade gave a small laugh, slightly amused with Luca's condescending attitude.

"So what to do with the human who is no longer human? You must learn to share donors. It can be quite pleasurable." A small smile crossed his face.

"She doesn't want a donor, that's the problem."

"Perhaps try a donor who'd agree to have you drain them artificially? They exist."

"No, it's a temporary fix. Not acceptable."

"But in the short term…"

"You and I both know she needs to learn how to feed on her own. I don't think it's the demon changing her. I've never heard of that happening. I tend to agree with Léopold. She's got some kind of block going on. I'll consider your idea about Wynter, though. I think knowing the person could make a difference. It's worth a try anyway."

"Did I hear the detective say he's coming for a visit?" Luca raised an eyebrow at him.

"Yeah." Kade stared into his glass, swirling the liquid and contemplating the bait his friend had laid on the table. Given the agony Sydney had caused her donors, he doubted she'd ever agree to feed from Anthony. He'd bet his life the detective would let her, however.

Sydney had confessed to him that, at one time, she'd considered dating Anthony, but never did so for fear of losing the respect of her peers. Kade had never been jealous of Sydney's friendship with her partner, because he knew with certainty that no one else was her mate.

As Kade downed the last of his drink, he heard the squeal of wheels in the driveway. His eyes met Luca's, anger flaring. As he'd suspected, she'd snapped; Sydney had left.

～❀ *Chapter Three* ❀～

Sydney had given it considerable thought. She couldn't go one more day depending on Kade for her survival. Her life had become miserable. There was no reasonable explanation for why she couldn't feed. If the demon had truly spawned her dilemma, then she was the only one who could regain control of the dismal situation. It had become a sickening ritual, watching Kade bite another woman, then dribbling the blood into her mouth as if she were a baby bird. A few tablespoons of blood hadn't been enough to fully heal her from the attack. She'd rather die than be forever reliant on the demeaning process that had barely kept her alive.

Sydney stood in front of the mirror gathering the courage to do what needed to be done. She finger combed her curly blonde hair, observing the dark circles that rounded her eyes. With shaky hands, she applied concealer to her pale skin. Tears wouldn't come, though her heart felt as if it had been shattered in a thousand pieces. She'd cried so hard in the past two hours that dehydration had set in, her mouth dried due to her stinted saliva.

Running her palm over the jagged scar on her abdomen, she closed her eyes. She resisted the temptation to stare at it one more time. The obsession to heal faster had done nothing but throw her further into a depression. Earlier in the week, she'd overheard Kade telling Luca that she should have been further along in her transformation. Her skin should have been flawless, yet everything about her was flawed.

Sydney reached for a t-shirt and tugged it over her head. She slipped into a prairie skirt, and stole a glance at the woman she didn't recognize. The tight fabric constricted her torso, showing her ribs. The weight loss only reminded her of how weak she was. She needed to drink more in order to recover.

Sydney rummaged through her purse, looking for her keys. As she did so, she was reminded that she no longer had a badge or gun. Her superiors had told her she'd been placed on sick leave but she knew it was just a matter of time before they fired her. Only humans worked on the police force. Supernaturals worked for P-CAP: Paranormal City Alternative Police, an organization she'd grown to tolerate but hadn't quite accepted. When she'd lived in Philadelphia, she and Anthony had worked with them on occasion on cases where human and supernatural crimes crossed paths.

As a police officer, she'd never gone out without a weapon. She thought it ironic that as a vampire she should be stronger than any human, yet she was the most vulnerable she'd ever been in her life. She closed her bag, resigned to the fact that she'd have to go without protection. At this point, it mattered little. The only thing she needed where she was going was cash.

As she made her way to the car, sneaking by Kade, she knew what she had to do, and the only way she could do it was alone.

Sydney took a deep breath as she stepped onto the sidewalk. Gas lamps flickered overhead, their flames dancing to the bass that bled out into the street. The shuttered doors had been held back by brass hooks and eyes attached to the brick outer wall. Laughter spilled from a young couple exiting through the blue satin drapes that hung in the vestibule. A black wooden sign carved with gold calligraphy greeted patrons with a single word, *Embo.*

It wasn't as if Sydney hadn't been to clubs that catered to humans and supernaturals, places that allowed them to share blood and sex. Both Philadelphia and New Orleans hosted establishments that fostered the symbiotic relationship. But Embo was special. It was the only place she knew that had been restricted to vampires and humans only. No other supernaturals were allowed entrance. Of greater interest to Sydney was the purist nature of the feeding arrangements. Every human who stepped foot inside had unequivocally given their consent as a donor. And every vampire knew it. More importantly for Sydney, it was the only place in New Orleans where they provided the kind of food she sought.

Sydney grasped the curtain and pulled it aside. Her heart pounded against her ribs, the scent of incense in the air. A tall man dressed in a black suit fiddled with a reservation list, busily checking off names. She steeled her nerves as the maître d turned his attention to her.

"Good evening, detective," he said from behind a podium, not making a move to unchain the red velvet rope that stood in her way.

"No detective here. You see a badge?" Sydney opened her arms wide.

"Really, Miss Willows, then please tell me why you're here," he asked, a snobbish tone to his voice.

"The same reason everyone else comes here." Sydney resisted the urge to punch the arrogant ass as he rolled his eyes.

"This is no place for someone like you. Unless you have official police business, I suggest you return to your car. I'd be happy to have someone escort you."

"I just want a drink. Nothing more, nothing less."

"No offense, but I'm aware you're bonded to Mister Issacson. All of New Orleans is aware, as a matter of fact. There's no way your fiancé would allow you to come here by yourself. Besides, all humans who come to our club are donors. You and I both know that you cannot be a donor to another vampire. Anyone who looks at you is as good as dead."

"Do you want me to call him? I'm sure he'd love to know who denied me entrance." As she spoke, she deliberately took slow breaths. Her mind swirled in chaos, but he'd never be privy to the conflict inside.

"I don't think that…"

"Sir, take a look at me," Sydney demanded. She didn't have time to mince words. Despite her efforts to avoid Kade, she knew when she'd taken the car, he'd hear her leave. She suspected he'd activate the stolen vehicle tracking and quickly learn of her location. "I said, 'look at me.' Do I look well? Better yet, do I smell human to you? I know you can smell me…just do it."

Sydney rooted her feet into the ground as he leaned toward her, coming within inches of her face. She fisted her hands tightly, readying to strike if he came any closer. Her nails dug into her skin, reminding her that even though she was now immortal, she could still very much feel pain.

"Vampire," he whispered, reaching for the brass clip on the end of the rope. "I'm very sorry, Miss Willows. I was not aware Mister Issacson had turned you. Please forgive me."

"Forgiven," was all Sydney could manage as a rush of breath hissed from her lips.

"Perhaps I should call your fiancé. This really is no place for a lady."

"As you so eloquently pointed out earlier, I'm a cop…was a cop. I think I can handle it." Sydney's eyes fell to the barrier and then met his. She wouldn't be intimidated from entering, dissuaded from her task.

"As you wish," he replied, ushering her into the foyer. "If I can get you anything at all, please let me know."

"Thank you but I'll be fine," she insisted.

Sydney never looked back as she moved toward her destination. The small foyer led to an arched hallway. Pinpricks of light poured from the unusual lighting fixtures, making it look as if the ceiling were made from stars. She pushed through a waterfall of bamboo beads, finally arriving in the main room of the club.

A fusion of Caribbean and new age décor surrounded her as she made her way toward the bar. Palm tree leaves appeared to sway, reflecting the soft flicker of tea lights. Traditional jazz music filtered throughout the airy space; a live band played in the far corner while patrons danced. In her peripheral vision, she caught sight of a tall brunette pinning a muscular man against the cream-colored wall. His torn shirt lay on the floor, a stream of bright red blood trailed down the side of his abs while he shook in a delirious state of bliss.

Sydney approached the bartender. He slid bottles of beer toward a group of twenty-somethings who nervously played with their hair extensions and chatted incessantly. Observing their behavior, she suspected it was their first time donating. A month ago, Sydney would have intervened, possibly used her police authority to escort them out of the club. Tonight, she felt nothing for the neophyte humans who sought the thrill of vampires. They'd committed, now they'd have to learn to deal with the consequences of their decisions. Whether they embraced or despised the experience, it was of no concern to Sydney. Like a speck of sand, they were insignificant in the grand scheme of things. People lived. People died. And some, like the immortal predators in the room, simply survived.

Sydney eyed the crimson tubes connected to large oak vats, disappointed that she simply couldn't drink it like water from a spigot. While the imported, aged blood was a delicacy, it wouldn't suffice to provide the nutritional needs of a vampire, especially a newly-turned one such as herself.

She caught the eyes of the attractive barkeep, who smiled at her. Shirtless, his loose white linen cargo pants hung precariously low on his hips. A flimsy drawstring, tied casually, swayed as he worked. Sydney noted there wasn't an ounce of fat on his artificially tanned chest. As he drew closer, she forced the corners of her lips into a friendly grin, and readied herself for the conversation that led her one step closer to her goal.

"Hello there, blondie. What can I getcha tonight?" His grey eyes twinkled as he spoke, and Sydney resisted the urge to ask him if he was vampire. "Drink? Donor? Sex? All of the above?"

"Donor only. No contact." Sydney wasn't sure what they called it; she only knew what she'd seen when she'd been in the club months ago. Working a case, they'd searched the bar for a suspect. That was when she'd discovered the special draining rooms, one for donors who sold their blood, but refused to be bitten. At the time, it struck her as perhaps a fetish. Clinical as it was, apparently the desire to drink from a glass appealed to some in their community. Likewise, squeamish humans who sought monetary compensation for their bodily fluids, had found a niche in the underground ecosystem.

"No contact, huh? You must be referring to our siphon specialty. It's extra, you know?"

"Cost isn't an issue." Sydney retrieved the cash from her wallet and slid ten one hundred dollar bills across the bar. She glanced over her shoulder, making sure she hadn't been followed.

"It's five hundred. This is too much." He counted out the bills and offered her back the extra money.

"Keep it for my tab," she told him. "How long will it be? I, um, I'm kind of in a rush."

"We usually have a wait, but," he picked up his iPad and began pecking at a scheduling app, "we can squeeze you in with number eleven. She just got in. Hold a second."

Sydney struggled to conceal the relief that overcame her. It wasn't ideal by any stretch of the imagination, but siphoning could be her salvation. As she waited for him to finish the arrangements, she scented the tinge of the iron delicacy in the air. *Hungry, so hungry.* Her hands shook and she steadied them onto her purse.

"This is Elia." He pointed to a petite woman who hurriedly strode across the dance floor. Her crushed black velvet dress reflected specks of silver under the black lights. "She'll escort you to your donor."

"Thank you," Sydney replied.

"No problem. Hey, listen, my name's Gil. If you're looking for some fun afterward, I'll be here for a few more hours." He winked.

"Um, thanks but I don't think…" She didn't bother finishing as she gave him a small wave.

Her guide gave her a nod and gestured toward the back of the room. Without speaking a word, Sydney obediently followed her. They weaved their way through the crowd of dancers, and her stomach clenched in anxiety and starvation. As they pushed through a set of swinging Cypress doors, the din of the club ceased. The calm-inducing spa-like atmosphere was a stark contrast to the actions transpiring behind the walls. As they made their way down the quiet hallway, she noted the sequentially numbered rooms. Elia abruptly stopped at eleven, and with a gentle knock, opened the door.

"Hello," a perky woman greeted them from inside. Lying comfortably on a dark leather chaise, she rested a paperback on her lap.

"Um, hi," Sydney answered. She looked to Elia, who continued to ignore her. "I'm not sure where you'd like me."

"She won't speak to you."

"Excuse me, what?"

"Elia is our technician for today but not present."

"But she kind of is present….she's right there." Sydney glanced to the woman who had begun to arrange the sterile dressings and tubing.

"Is this your first time?"

"Yes, sorry."

"I'm Mya," she said, offering her hand.

"I'm Sydney." She shook the woman's warm hand and quickly released it. Feeling disoriented, a wave of dizziness threatened to topple her.

"Hey, you okay? Here, sit next to me." Mya pointed to a soft cushioned chair.

"Thank you." Sydney quickly sat, placing her bag on the ground. She found comfort that the donor appeared entirely content, but Sydney still felt out of place.

"Siphoning really isn't as bad as they make it sound." Mya glanced toward Elia and then back to Sydney. "This experience is for you. I merely provide your food. And Elia, she's not present as in she's deliberately silent and will leave immediately after your blood is prepared."

"Why?" A part of Sydney just wanted to feed, but curiosity got the better of her. The human part had to know why they'd pretend as if someone wasn't even in the room.

"Not all humans and vampires publicly feed or have sex. Many of the vampires who seek the siphon option prefer the privacy we offer. While the intimacy of the feeding is removed, we can artificially provide the one-on-

one interaction. When a vampire feeds from a human, they go unassisted. Therefore, it is just you and I. Elia is merely an instrument to our interaction. Therefore, she isn't *present*. She's not allowed to speak, because this is our experience. Your experience."

"I see," Sydney said. Admittedly, she'd never asked Kade about the rooms she'd seen here or why vampires would need blood this way. All she'd ever known was the bond that had existed between them.

"I know siphoning is a novelty for some vampires, but I do have some regulars. I mean, not all vampires want or need to…you know, make humans feel. They just want to eat, plain and simple."

"You mean sex?"

"Well, yes." Mya fingered the single braid that brushed her waist then raised her gaze to meet Sydney's. "It's none of my business why clients come to me but I suspect it's the same reason why a human wouldn't want to seek pleasure from another person when they've already committed to someone else. Even single people don't always want sex. And what are vampires really?"

"What do you mean?"

"Deep down, somewhere inside, they are human. Okay, well, I've met a few who really are no longer in any way human. But most have a tiny part of them that remembers."

"Why do you do this?" *Human,* Sydney thought. It hadn't been that long since she'd been turned. She swore she'd never become a monster, forgetting who she'd been, but she knew the truth. Her response at the bar demonstrated that she'd already changed.

"I know what a bite can do to someone," she replied, shaking her head. "I mean, I know how it feels. The intense emotions…the incredible sex. I simply can't risk becoming attached to anyone. It happens all the time."

"With donors?"

"I'm not supposed to talk about it. But it happens. I don't mind donating my blood. The money's good. This works for me. When I fall for someone, supernatural or human, I want to know them first."

"I understand." Sydney remembered the first time she'd made love to Kade, allowing him to infect her with his intoxicating bite. But she'd been attracted to him long before that amazing night. She'd never doubted the honesty of her feelings.

"If you don't mind me asking, why are you here today?" Mya rolled up her sleeve, allowing Elia to prepare her skin. Although she was speaking to Sydney, she paid close attention as the alcohol was applied.

"I, um, I can't feed." As the needle pricked Mya's arm, Sydney involuntarily dropped her fangs. Tears brimmed in her eyes.

"Hey, no worries. It's all good."

Sydney shook her head and looked away.

"I'm not sure what's going on with you but really, you're going to be okay soon. Look…see…the blood is coming. You're just hungry. There's no need to be ashamed."

Sydney's eyes fell to the end of the tube where the blood flowed into a tall champagne glass. Mesmerized by the sight of the dripping sanguine fluid, her eyes darted to Mya who gave her a comforting smile. Within minutes, Elia clamped the flow and offered the drink to Sydney. As she reached for it, Sydney once again looked to Mya as if seeking her permission.

"Please, take it," she insisted.

Sydney brought it to her nose and sniffed. The ambrosial scent caused her to salivate. Her animalistic response couldn't be stifled. With no emotional tie to the source, she freely drank the warm delicious sustenance. Unlike the sexual pleasure she'd experienced tasting of Kade, she likened it to eating a batch of freshly baked cookies. Perhaps it didn't offer an earth-shattering orgasm, but it was entirely comforting and provided satisfaction that could only be obtained from food.

When she reached the bottom of the glass, her eyes flew open. Electrified by the nourishment, her body tingled from head to toe. She shoved the glass onto a counter, barely noticing that Elia had left the room. Yanking her shirt upward, she ran her fingers over her belly. The scar had disappeared. Energy spiraled throughout her cells, and a broad smile spread across her face.

"It's gone, tell me it's gone," she shouted at Mya who laughed in response.

"What's gone? I don't see anything."

"Thank you. Oh my God, you saved me." Sydney rushed to Mya, taking her in her arms. Her laugher turned to tears and back to laughter.

"It's okay, now," Mya told her.

"I'm sorry. I know you don't know but I couldn't eat and now this…you…everything has changed. I feel so…so great. No, wait," she released Mya and took out a mirror from her purse, inspecting her newly rejuvenated skin. Pink-tinged cheeks and bright eyes stared back at her. "I'm fine. I feel so good. So strong."

"Well of course, you're a vampire." Mya sat up and steadied herself onto her feet.

"I didn't ask for this," Sydney confessed. She offered Mya a glass of juice that had been prepared earlier by Elia.

"Not everyone does," Mya replied, her expression somber. "I'm no vampire expert, but it's my take that most don't. But hey, look at humans. No one asks for what we're given either. Life can suck. We do what we have to to survive. And you, my friend, are doing just that…surviving."

"It's going to be okay…for both of us." Sydney wasn't sure what had happened to Mya but whatever it was, she suspected it had been horrific. She'd recognized the trauma, having seen it on many a victim.

"Yes." Mya offered a small smile.

"I don't want to be too forward, but is it okay for me to see you again?"

"Yes. I'm new so I'm only here once a week or so, so make sure you schedule at the front desk." She paused. "Listen, I'm not supposed to do this. I seem to be breaking rules left and right today, but here…"

Mya took a pen out of her bag and scribbled a number onto a napkin. Carefully folding it, she handed it to Sydney.

"My cell number."

"Are you sure? I don't want to get you in trouble."

"If you were a dude, there'd be no way. Even some of the supposed ladies in here are pretty aggressive. So I don't usually do this." She sighed, as if contemplating her decision to share her personal information. "No one deserves whatever happened to you. I mean, you need to eat, right? If for some reason I can't get here, you can always go see one of the other siphon donors. Twenty-four seven, Embo is open. But if you need someone…"

"Thank you," Sydney replied softly.

As she went to hug Mya, she heard Kade's voice bellow through the walls. He'd found her.

Chapter Four

"I've gotta go," Sydney said, grabbing her purse.

"Are you in danger?" Mya asked.

"No, I'm fine. I'll see you next week. Thanks." Sydney opened and shut the door, not wanting Kade to see where she'd been.

She ran down the hallway, grateful that he hadn't found her yet. As Sydney flew through the doors, she caught sight of Kade coming into the bar. She settled her back against a wall, and tried to gather her thoughts, so she could articulate the miracle of what had happened. In her peripheral vision, she caught sight of a familiar woman who approached from the dance floor. Sydney turned her attention to the human, studying her face, and soon realized that Kade had brought her to their house. At the time, she'd been in a daze, but memories of the buxom beauty flashed before her eyes; Kade trying to get Sydney to bite her. Unable to accept that she'd been turned, Sydney had refused. Her heart raced as she recalled the meeting. Unwilling to cause a scene, Sydney felt helpless to move as the donor cornered her.

"Can I help you?" The natural phrase of a police officer rolled off her tongue. She'd always trusted her instincts as a human, but as a vampire, all her senses were amplified exponentially. Confusion swept her mind.

"You know me, right?" the woman asked, her hands on her hips.

"You were at our home," Sydney responded. Her eyes darted to Kade who was deep in conversation with the bartender. He'd sensed her, she was sure of it.

"Yeah, that's right. I'm Gemma." She twirled a strand of her hair and gave Sydney a wide grin. "I didn't think you'd remember. You were kind of out of it."

"Yeah, I was sick."

"So, um, I don't mean to be so forward but you aren't married yet. And I noticed that Kade seems really unhappy. He used to be so…"

"My mate's feelings are none of your concern," Sydney said flatly. "Wait. What do you mean by 'he used to be'…used to be what?"

"Oh," she exclaimed innocently. "He didn't tell you? That's just like a man, isn't it? What I meant was that he used to feed from me. You know…before he met you. It's not the first time I've been to his house."

"What did you say?" Sydney felt her pulse race as her anger spiked.

"Before you met him, he fed from me. That's why he brought me to you. We know each other."

"He's a vampire. Of course he had to eat." Sydney's eyes narrowed on the blonde's fingers as she toyed with the ribbons on her pink corset. Her

447

tight black pencil skirt accentuated her ample curves. It was at that moment Sydney wondered how far Kade had gone with the human who clearly sought to provoke her.

"We kind of had a thing. I just thought with you being turned and all...I wasn't sure if you and he were still seeing each other." Gemma shifted on her feet and glanced over to Kade. She cupped her breasts, as if she were serving them up on a plate. "The last time I was at his house..."

"Our house." The rage within Sydney bubbled to the surface. This woman was an enemy, threatening her relationship with Kade. When she'd been human, she might have restrained her response. But now, her primal instinct was to protect, kill if necessary.

"I'm just sayin', it's not like you can feed him anymore. From what I heard, you can barely feed yourself." She laughed. "Honestly, if you can't take care of yourself, you should let him go. I really think you should..."

How does this insignificant twit know that I can't eat? Did Kade tell her? Does he really only want to be with a human, someone who can cater to all his needs? Doubt swirled within Sydney and as if a switch had flicked inside her, she lost control. Seizing Gemma by the neck, she slammed her face first into the wall. Instead of releasing her, Sydney held her tightly in place, coming up behind her. With her breasts tight against the woman's back, she yanked the hair out of the way, exposing the tight cords of her neck.

"Don't fucking move, bitch," Sydney hissed. Her fangs descended, rage filtering throughout her mind.

"I didn't mean to..." Gemma began.

"Shut the fuck up. You want me to feed, huh?"

"But he's not your..."

"Tell you what; you can have him when you pry him out of my cold dead hands." Sydney, poised to strike, caught Kade's gaze as she continued. "And about that feeding. How about I take you for a test drive?"

As Kade's hands landed on her shoulders, Sydney sank her fangs into Gemma's shoulder, slicing through her muscles. Before she had a chance to suck her blood, Kade extracted her off the human.

"No," Sydney yelled, aware that Gemma had fallen to the floor. "She's mine."

"Let her go, Sydney," Kade commanded. "It's alright. She's nothing."

"Leave me alone." Wild with anger, she flailed, attempting to free herself. The desire to kill consumed her.

"Okay, guess we're going to do this the hard way," Kade quipped as he slipped in front of her and hoisted her over his shoulder.

"Put me down! What the hell do you think you're doing?" Sydney clawed at his suit, barely cognizant of Kade climbing the stairs. *How many donors has he fucked? Brought to his house?*

"Almost there," Kade told her as they reached the landing.

"Just stop, Kade. Put me down," she pleaded.

Removed from the situation, the reality of what she'd done hit her. Sydney had never been one to take shit but she'd always kept calm, made decisions based on facts. Since she'd been turned, her every action tied itself to an emotion, rational or not. She sucked a breath, aware that she'd just bitten someone, intending to inflict suffering. If she'd been truthful with herself, she would have admitted that she'd flirted with the idea of killing the human. And she knew that she'd have done it without remorse.

As her feet hit the floor, she took in her surroundings. Kade had brought them up to a private terrace, which overlooked the club.

"Out," Kade yelled at two young women who were staring at them from a corner settee. Without argument, they scurried down the steps.

"You have no right to come in here and treat me like that." Sydney pushed the hair out of her eyes, scanning the balcony to make sure that they were alone.

"Wrong. I have every right to keep you from killing someone. You were out of control," he countered.

"Damn right I was out of control. That woman…that donor…you brought her to our house," she choked. Pacing, she raked her fingers through her curly locks. "I can't do this, Kade. You know I love you but I can't watch you with other women. You can't expect me to let you bring your lovers into our home."

"I'm not sleeping with her. I'd never do that to you."

"She told me you slept with her."

"I'd never lie to you," he asserted, deliberately lowering the volume of his voice. "I may have been intimate with her, but it was long before we met. She's always been a reliable donor and that's why I had her come to the house. I haven't touched her since we met. I swear it."

"But you did touch her…a few weeks ago…after you turned me…"

"That day, I brought her for you only. I'm only going to say it one more time. I did not touch her," he insisted.

"Why would you ever bring her to our house?"

"I just told you why. I used her in the past. I know it was wrong but you have to put yourself in my position. I was upset and had to do something. Jesus, you almost died. I needed someone reliable to help. I don't like to just grab people off the street." Kade sighed.

"How many donors have you fucked?" Sydney put her face in her hands and blew out a breath. She lifted her gaze to meet his.

"That's not fair. We both have pasts." Kade paused. "Sydney, I'm really sorry. I know I shouldn't have brought her, but I was desperate to help you. I made a mistake."

"I can't do this."

"It doesn't have to be this way. If we can find a way for you to feed from a human, we can enjoy this together. Any woman or man is nothing more than food."

"But I can't, can I? Look at what's happened to me. I didn't ask for this."

"I am looking at you," he said softly. He approached her slowly and cupped her face, tracing his thumb over her bottom lip. "You're as beautiful as the day we first met. I can see that you ate. Tell me what happened. Please tell me you didn't kill anyone."

"I knew about this place...I'd been here on a case," Sydney stammered. She shouldn't feel guilty for coming here alone, yet shame overwhelmed her. Closing her eyes, she took a deep breath and then raised her gaze to meet Kade's. "I went to a siphon room. I'm sorry but I just had to do this. And it worked...I feel..."

"I can see you feel good again. But I don't understand why you ran. You have a bad habit of doing that, you know? No more running, Syd. Jesus. Come here," Kade ordered. He embraced his fiancée, a comforting hand massaged the nape of her neck. "We're going to figure this out. But you have to trust me."

"This is my fault. I did this." Within his arms, she relaxed. Confused, she held no answers. "Something's wrong with me. I can't ask you to give up the way you've lived for over two hundred years just for me. It's not fair to you."

"This isn't about fair, love. This is about us. You're the only woman in the world for me."

"But those women..."

"Shh." He kissed her hair. "They're nothing. There's never been anyone but you."

"I love you so much. I want this to work. Please." Sydney wasn't sure what she was even asking. With her life in a blur, she couldn't remember the last time they'd made love, that she'd felt like a woman, desired.

She glided her palms up his chest as he backed her against the wrought iron railing. She wiped the back of her hand across her cheeks. Crying had never been her style, but her emotions spun wild.

"This will work. There is nothing that can ever come between us. Not this," his fangs descended, his lips pressed to her neck, "not this." Dragging his thumb across her lips, he teased them open. He ran his fingers over Sydney's teeth, and her own incisors dropped in response. "Your blood will be the only blood I ever want. Your lips...you, love."

As his mouth descended on hers, Sydney's heart raced. Allowing him to take control, she surrendered to his will. The taste of her mate spiked her arousal, and she was reminded how Kade could erase all worries from her mind. Coming alive with fire, she desperately kissed him in return. When he tore his lips from hers, she protested with a whimper.

"Turn around," Kade demanded, placing her palms onto the cool metal. He wrapped his arm around her waist. "These people...the vampires, the donors, they know nothing of our lives. Anyone who says otherwise is a liar."

"Kade," she breathed. Her bottom brushed against his rock hard erection.

"Nothing else matters. But you," he growled. He gathered up her skirt until he found the front of her thigh.

"Please, I…I missed you so much." Her line of vision drifted to the floor where onlookers had stopped to watch from below.

"From the moment we met, I knew you were mine. Nothing about your transition has changed that." Kade concealed his hand underneath the fabric, working his fingers into her panties. Cupping between her legs, he whispered in her ear. "Your pussy yearns for me, doesn't it, Sydney? Your master has been gone too long."

"I…I…" At a loss for words, she resisted the urge to run. The heat between her legs intensified, confirming what she'd always known. She belonged to him…her heart, her mind, her body. Despite her independence and bravado, the comfort of being cared for, loved, superseded any notion that she could survive as an island.

"I know what it's like to be so consumed with someone that you can't breathe without them. I may not have been the one starving this past month, but I've struggled to survive without you." He bit down on her earlobe as he slid a finger into her slick folds. Teasing her clitoris, he refused to give her a chance to retreat. "Goddess, I fucking missed you."

"Kade …they can see us," she breathed.

"That's exactly the point, love. I want them to see us. To see the pleasure I bring you." He plunged deep inside her pussy, withdrew and added two more. "Fuck, yes. You're so wet for me."

"I can't do this here…oh shit," she cried. It had been so long since he'd touched her. The ripples of excitement speared through her and she fought the orgasm she knew would come all too soon.

"Never again will you hide from me. Everything we do we do together. Feeding. Fucking. All of it. Do you understand me?" When she didn't respond, he removed his hand and lightly smacked her mound.

"No, don't stop." He was angry that she'd fed on her own. She'd known what his reaction would be but had convinced herself he'd understand. Yet here he stood, teaching his lesson in front of an audience. She was helpless to argue as the ache between her legs grew.

"No running. Ever. Tell me you understand." His palm, that had rested on her belly, glided up her chest until he held her throat in his hands. Taking her chin, he turned her head so that his lips brushed hers. "Say it, Sydney."

"Kade," she breathed.

"Say it."

"I'm sorry…I knew. I needed to do this on my own. But I won't ever share you. I love you too damn much." She grasped his thigh, digging her nails into his leg.

"This pleasure, my soon-to-be wife," Kade pumped his fingers back into her wet core, "will only ever be yours."

"Ah, yes. Harder," she cried. Her head lolled back on his shoulder and she clutched his leg.

"And your blood…this pleasure is only ever for you," he said, his fangs slicing into her neck.

The familiar delicious sting of his teeth at her flesh sent her into a state of ecstasy. His bite was a validation of her role within his life. *Desired. Accepted. Loved.* She shook, the climax rolling through her. As his tongue laved over the wounds, she twisted around in his arms.

"Let's go home, love. I think we've made our point," he laughed.

"I'm not so sure about that. You started something, and I think we oughta finish it." No longer encumbered with concern that the humans doubted his commitment to her, Sydney pressed her palms to his chest, guiding him against the wall.

Kade thanked the goddess that he'd found Sydney when he had. He was aware that she knew he'd be able to track her. She'd been in the club long enough on her own that she could have gotten in serious trouble. Glowing, Sydney had been nourished. Even as she kicked and fought him on the way up the steps, he marveled at her strength. His happiness was countered with guilt for not suggesting siphoning from the minute she'd been turned. He knew damn well the method existed, that certain vampires preferred the complete lack of interaction it provided. But it was a course of last resort. Old school norms led him to teach her otherwise. She'd be extraordinarily vulnerable if she didn't learn how to obtain food on her own, to bite without pain.

Although Kade was relieved that Sydney had finally fed, Gemma was a complication he hadn't expected. At one time, she'd been a trusted food source. Irresponsibly, he'd fucked her on one occasion, but it'd meant nothing…to him. She'd played it down when he'd asked her to help with Sydney. He should have known that Gemma still had feelings for him. Bringing her home had been a lapse in judgment, one that could have cost him dearly. In Sydney's feral state, she surely would have killed Gemma.

Claiming his mate publicly had been the only way to convince her and everyone else at the club that she, despite being vampire, belonged to him. The rasp of his zipper coming down drew his attention back to Sydney, who clearly sought to continue the demonstration.

"What are you doing, baby?" Kade asked with a smile. He laughed as she pushed him over to the wall.

"What do you think I'm doing?" She lifted her shirt and cupped her breasts. Teasing her nipples into fine points, she licked her lips. The fabric fell and she grinned, slipping her hand into his trousers.

"You sure about this, love? It's not something you usually do in public…aw, fuck," he cried, as she took his dick in her hands.

"Yep…pretty sure," she responded with a giggle. Stroking the glistening come off the tip of his crown, she pumped him in her hand. "I want you now. No waiting."

"Not out here." Kade spied a door in the corner of the alcove. A storage closet, he hoped. Without bothering to remove her grip, he guided her toward it. They shuffled toward their destination, kissing as they went. Reaching for the door handle, he opened it and they laughed, realizing how desperate they were. She'd been ill for over a month. Like a shaken bottle of soda, they both were ready to explode.

"In here," Kade ordered. With his pants wide open, he dragged her into the small space and slammed the door shut behind them.

"Off," Sydney growled, dropping to her knees.

"Jesus Christ, woman…" His head fell backward onto a shelf, and he cursed as she tore down his boxers, unleashing his erection into her hands. She took his cock between her lips, and the momentary pain was soon replaced by ecstasy. He'd forgotten how amazing her hot mouth was, her talented tongue darting over the seam on his head.

"This cock belongs to me, do you hear me, Kade?" She gave him a wicked smile.

"Goddess, don't stop." He caught the gleam of desire in her eyes flickering red in the darkness.

"My cock." Laving upward with her tongue, she bit down gently as if putting him in a vise. "Every last inch of it."

"Fuck yeah," he agreed. Wrapping his hands into her hair, he guided himself through her lips.

Sydney stabbed her fingernails into his ass as he fucked her mouth. Kade's orgasm rose to the surface and he tilted her head backward, her face wet with saliva.

"Come here," he demanded.

Complying, Sydney shoved herself to her feet. She kicked off her shoes, and shimmied out of her panties. He slid his hands under her skirt, cupping her ass, and heaved her upward. She wrapped her ankles around his waist, her legs scraping the wall.

"Fuck me," she cried, dragging her incisors along his neck.

"Demanding lil' thing, aren't you?" He spun around, kicking a bucket in the process. Laughing, he reached for his shaft, still holding her to him.

"I need this. Need you in me…now. I don't care who hears."

"You better hold on, Syd. This is gonna be a rough ride." Kade readied his cock, lubricating himself in her wetness. He grunted as he buried himself in her.

"Holy shit. Oh my God," she breathed.

"Fuck, your pussy is so tight." He withdrew and slammed into her again.

He felt a metal object digging into the back of his skull but pleasure outweighed the pain. He momentarily lost his concentration, and his grip slipped. "The shelves."

"The what?" Sydney asked, her hands wrapped around his neck.

"Brace yourself," he warned. His lips captured hers, his tongue invading her warm mouth.

Kade heard the ping of items scatter all over the floor as Sydney wildly reached for the shelf behind him. A mop fell over, barely missing his head. He'd have laughed had she not constricted around his cock, driving him to near climax. He felt as if he was a virgin again, unable to hold back.

"Harder," she cried into their kiss, desperation in her voice. She clutched at the ledge, clawing her nails into the wood. "So close. That's it."

"I want to hear it."

"What?" She bit at his lips, locked in his gaze.

"I want this entire fucking place to hear you come." He thrust into her hard, causing her teeth to scrape his lips.

"Oh God, yes. Just a little more…oh shit." Sydney sucked at his lip, lapping the blood of her mate into her mouth.

"Can't hold it….Sydney…fuck, yes," Kade grunted. His balls drew tight, the pressure exploding inside him. Her pussy fisted him in rhythmic pulses, taking him from pure pleasure to unbridled release. His fangs descended, plunging into the soft flesh of her neck. Resisting the urge to take deep gulps of her essence, he controlled the impulse, gently suckling her skin and laving it with his tongue.

"I'm sorry. I'm so sorry." Tears flowed as she convulsed with him, her orgasm rolling through her.

"You didn't deserve what happened to you that day. None of this is your fault."

"I should never have left Logan's house. The demon…I knew there was something wrong. I fucked up."

"No, no, no. It's going to be all right. I promise you." He pressed his lips to her neck, her cheek, her hair, cradling his mate.

"Don't lie to me. Please. I couldn't take it."

"I have a plan. I always have a plan, my sweet Syd."

"God, I love you."

"I love you too. I swear to you on my life we will fix this." As Kade gently removed himself from inside her, he held her against him in the darkness, unable to let go.

❧ *Chapter Five* ❧

Kade lay watching Sydney sleep. It had been the first night in over a month they'd slept together all night in the same bed. While he'd never left her side after her attack, she'd been unconscious for weeks. After she awoke, she'd spent most nights pacing or crying, with no semblance of peace.

His conversation with Luca weighed heavily on his mind. As happy as he was that Sydney was temporarily sated, it was just a matter of time before she needed to feed again. She'd told him of Mya, and her desire to keep using her. But his concern remained that she'd never be fully independent.

Making love to her several times throughout the night, it wasn't lost on him that she'd never bit him. Her desire to had been palpable but he knew she resisted, afraid she'd hurt him, too. They couldn't go on forever like this.

His thoughts drifted to Anthony's impending arrival. Within hours he'd be at the house, and Kade still hadn't told Sydney about the prison break. With everything she'd been through, he didn't want to worry her. But the discussion was inevitable. As soon as she found out what had happened, he knew she'd want to help Anthony with the investigation. He'd argue that she was vulnerable, and she'd counter that she'd been healed, and was ready to go back to work. It would be nearly impossible to stop her.

But that was why he'd fallen in love with her. She'd always been strong, a protector of humanity. Given her challenging recovery, he feared she wasn't ready. Unable to feed properly, she'd soon become a danger to others if she was unable to control her impulses. She'd have killed Gemma if he hadn't stopped her. He anticipated she'd need several months to adjust to her transition. Having the discipline to restrain the urge to retaliate when faced with confrontation was a skill she'd hone under his wing. Letting her loose on the streets with her former partner could lead to disastrous consequences.

His primary concern kept circling back to her ability to feed on demand, especially if she became injured; something she'd be hard pressed to do if she was relying on a donor to surgically drain the blood from their vein. If what Léopold had suspected was true, that she'd developed a psychological block, they had to break the cycle. Kade reasoned that inducing pleasure during feeding would build her confidence and allow her to live a normal life as a vampire. He considered Luca's suggestion that Anthony could be the one to help. Only once had he shared Sydney and they'd both done it to save Luca from dying.

Kade leaned over, and pressed his lips to her cheek. She stirred for only a moment before continuing her healing slumber. He slipped out of the bed and went to the bathroom. As he stared at himself in the mirror, he contemplated the hard decision he'd have to make.

"Hello, Anthony," Kade said. The bitter pill he planned to swallow rested on his tongue. He wasn't sure how to broach the subject, but the idea was set in his mind. "You can put your bag over there."

"Hey man, how's it goin'?" Anthony replied. He shook Kade's hand and set his carry-on luggage next to the door. "Where's Syd?"

"Yeah, about that. She's still sleeping. Come into the kitchen and I'll get you some coffee." Kade gestured toward the hallway, talking as he went. "I really need to talk to you about what happened…she isn't herself."

"I need to see her," Anthony pressed.

"I've been thinking about this ever since you told me. When you tell her about the prison escape, you do know she's going to want to go after him? She's not feeling well, but that won't stop her. But she shouldn't. It's just not wise given her condition. How did this guy get out anyway?"

"How did he get out? Your guess is as good as mine. Can you believe they're still trying to figure out how the hell this happened?"

"Go ahead, have a seat." Kade turned on the coffee machine, and rummaged through the cabinet for mugs. He pointed to a chair at the kitchen bar. "Tell me more about him."

"Thanks, it was a helluva flight. Someone behind me lost his cookies on the landing. I hate flyin'." Anthony rubbed his eyes and shook his head. "The name of the perp is Pat Scurlock. He's a real piece of work. We caught him holdin' a woman in a dungeon as a sex slave."

"What else?" Kade suspected there had to be more to the story.

"The vic we found in his house was alive. But the others…" Tony accepted a cup from Kade.

"Others?"

"Yeah, thirty-three others to be specific. They were dead. Found 'em all buried on his property."

"How exactly does something like that go unnoticed in the city?"

"He lived with his mother. We tracked him to a secondary location in the boonies. The property was under an alias name. Hundreds of acres with plenty of woods gives a serial killer a nice playground."

"So he goes it alone?"

"That's what we thought at first. But we found unknown secondary DNA on the bodies. Soon it was up to five."

"Accomplices?"

"Yes. His mother for one. She's behind bars. The rest have gone underground. All were into the occult in some form or another."

"What exactly were they into?"

"The women dealt mostly in psychic hotline sort of shit. They were busted a few times on shoplifting charges before all this went down with Scurlock. We're not likin' them for the actual killings, though. Most of the cases were brute strength; strangulation, beatings, things like that. More than a few had died of exsanguination. Two of them were decapitated. We're thinkin' they killed them and the women helped dispose of the bodies."

"If you caught this, uh, Pat, what about the other guy?"

"We got him on tape at a couple of local vampire clubs, but he's still out there, too. No offense, man, but you know that some of your, uh, vamp friends aren't exactly riding on the right side of the road. We've had some bad shit goin' on up in Philly, you know that?"

"Indeed," Kade agreed. Alexandra, a vicious vampire in Philadelphia, had a reputation for torture.

"I'm just sayin'. Things at home aren't as under control as they are down here. It's pretty ironic considering this is New Orleans, huh?" he laughed. "Anyhow, let's just say ole Patty has contacts in the supernatural community. We suspect he may have been involved in human trafficking."

"How's that?"

"Takin' victims, selling them to well-off vamps who need blood. There's been rumors of blood slaves, not kept individually, but in some kind of caged community."

"Jesus Christ, Anthony. Do they have evidence?" Long ago, it had been commonplace for vampires to capture and enslave humans. Sex, blood, it was stolen from the innocents against their will. But in the past century, their community had evolved and it was no longer acceptable or legal.

"Honestly, we've got nothin' except the one victim we rescued from Pat's house. But she was delirious at the time and once she started her recovery, she clammed up. Blah, blah, blah, patient doctor confidentiality…not ready to talk…and now it's just a rumor."

"So why Sydney? Why does he want my fiancée?" Kade leaned against the granite countertop and crossed his arms.

"Because he's a fucking psycho. Because she was the one to take him down. My girl put a," Anthony paused at his words and corrected them, acknowledging Kade, "*our girl*…she plugged him in the shoulder, then handcuffed the fucker until the paramedics showed up. Testified against him."

"That would do it."

"He was kinda pissed. But then again they all are. The difference is that Patty started threatenin' her from jail. Phone calls at first. Once he lost those privileges, he managed to send her a few presents using connections."

"I'm afraid to ask."

"At first it was letters. When that didn't get a rise out of her, and you know Syd, it's gonna take a lot, our buddy sent her a tongue."

"What the...?"

"Yeah, a tongue. And it wasn't the kind you eat either." Anthony sighed and took a drink. "It was identified as belonging to a woman. It'd been preserved, pickled if you can believe that shit. Never identified who it came from."

"When did this go down?"

"A few months before you met her. He was convicted about a year ago."

"So you're concerned he's got contacts down here? Supernaturals?" Kade stroked the scruff on his face, and mulled over what he'd been told. Despite Anthony's comments to the contrary, an evil undercurrent was alive and well in his city. His consistent and dominant rule was the only barrier between calm and chaos.

"Yeah, this guy has a real hard on for Syd." He coughed. "Uh, pardon my French. It's just he's gunnin' for her and we've gotta find him first. A good offense is the best defense with this guy."

"I'd better get Luca over here. We'll put some feelers out. If he shows up anywhere, he's as good as dead."

"Hey now, Kade. My virgin ears didn't hear that. Law enforcement, remember? As much as I wanna see some of these assholes take a dirt nap, I don't get to go around killin' humans, and neither do you."

"No worries, friend." Kade put his hand on the detective's shoulder and let the heat of Anthony's body seep into it. Even though Anthony wore a shirt, Kade could detect his pulse. Thoughts of blood twisted through his mind, and he imagined, but for a second, the intimate encounter they'd have should he agree to let them feed from him. Kade struggled to concentrate on the topic and crossed the room, staring out the window.

"You okay?" Anthony paused. "Ya wanna tell me what's going on with Sydney? You never did tell me why she was sick....what happened?"

"There was an accident," Kade began. He reflected on the day he'd found her lying on the bloodstained pavement calling his name. "Anthony, I know you don't have a lot of experience with the supernatural. There was a time when Sydney didn't either." *No, I brought her into this world.*

"You'd be surprised what I know. Is she okay?"

"She was attacked...by a demon."

"What? Wait. Where were you?" Anthony stood, plowing his fingers through his thick dark hair.

"Before you even ask, yes, I fucking blame myself. But you know Sydney, and it wasn't as if she was alone. She was at Logan Reynaud's house. The Alpha of Acadian Wolves. It doesn't matter because what's done is done."

"What the hell's that supposed to mean?" Tony asked, his voice growing louder.

"She almost died..."

"But you said she's here, so what is it? Just tell me. Maybe I can help her."

"You can help her but I assure you it's not at all what you think." Kade faced Anthony, his jaw tight with angst. He flattened his hands on the cool stone counter and pinned his eyes on Anthony's. "I had to turn her. She's a vampire."

"No…no, this can't be happening…"

"It already happened. The transition…it didn't go well. She's not coping. She's having problems feeding."

"When did this go down?" he asked.

"About a month ago. You have to understand, she didn't want me to tell anyone." Although after last night's spectacle, the entire community would be aware of his fiancée's newfound state. "Well, more people probably know now but the point is that she wasn't doing well. She can't feed."

"Yeah, I just heard you say that, but what the hell is that supposed to mean? I don't know much about vamps but if she's still alive and obviously still tellin' people what to do, then she must be…you know…uh, drinking blood," Anthony choked out, shaking his head in disbelief.

"Keep your voice down," Kade instructed. He heard Sydney's footsteps in the hallway above him. "The drinking isn't the problem. She's having trouble biting."

"Is there something wrong with her teeth? I mean her fangs? Jesus, I can't even believe I just said that. How can she be a vampire? You should have found some other way to save her."

"Don't you think I would have? There was no other way." Kade slammed his fist down onto the granite.

"I'm sorry, it's just that Sydney…look, I know she loves you but it's not like she's exactly crazy about all this supernatural shit. She told me she didn't want to be turned, you know? This may be TMI, but we talked about a lot of things. She told me about your arrangement…you bite her, she drinks your blood and stays human. She never wanted to be anything other than what she was."

"I know. Believe me, I'm so fucking sorry…you have no idea. And now she can't bite. Technically, she can, but she can't do it in a way that doesn't hurt the donor."

"Donor? Don't you mean human?"

"Same difference to Sydney. Our bite, it gives pleasure for a reason. It's an evolved survival strategy for our species."

"Nice," Anthony replied sarcastically.

"I won't apologize for our way."

"I'm sorry, man. It's just that this is all hard to take. I can't imagine what she's going through."

"Léopold thinks it's some kind of block. She loved it when I used to do it to her so it doesn't make sense."

"Exactly, Kade. She loves it when *you* do it, but not her. It's what she wanted when she was human, and now? Now, she's not, is she?"

"Just so you know, I've never heard of this happening," Kade continued.

"Sure, some people are repulsed by blood at first, but once they feed, that moral concern disappears. Last night was the first time she fed successfully."

"I'm confused. I thought you just said..."

"She used a siphon donor. The blood is removed manually...drained into a glass."

Anthony grimaced, unable to conceal his disgust.

"It worked," Kade told him. "But unless she can do it the old-fashioned way, she'll be vulnerable, unable to feed herself should the need arise. Siphon donors aren't always available. Besides, when it comes to donors, most want the full experience, if you know what I mean."

"If most people are actually asking to be bitten, it must feel pretty damn good," he laughed.

"Yeah, it doesn't suck," Kade joked. "Well, I guess it does but still, we make it as pleasant as possible."

"So, uh, what's the plan?" Anthony took a sip of his lukewarm coffee.

"I'll be frank. Until yesterday, there was no plan. I don't want to pressure you. What I'm about to propose...you asked how you can help." Kade paused, seeking the words that eluded him.

"Of course."

"It's just that Luca and I think that maybe if she fed from someone she knows..."

An amused smile crossed Anthony's face as soon as Kade spoke, but he remained silent.

"You're close to Sydney. If I wasn't totally secure in our relationship, I wouldn't suggest this, but..."

"You want me to let her bite me?"

"Yes, I do."

"I'll do it," Anthony responded without hesitation.

"You may want to take some time to make this decision."

"What's a little pin prick, huh?"

"I suppose you could say that." Kade smiled, pleased that he'd agreed quickly. But full disclosure was in order. "I think this may work, but you must understand. There are consequences."

"Like what?"

"First of all, this experiment could fail. The donors she's bitten...it wasn't pretty. In terms of pain level, it could feel like someone is pulling out your tooth." Kade raised an eyebrow at him. "Without Novocain."

"Hey, I'd take a bullet for that woman. I've been stabbed at least once. I think I can tough it out."

"Second, there's, uh, feelings. You know, like sexual ones. If we do this, it'll be intimate. We must make it as pleasurable as we can for her. Whatever she wants...whatever she needs." Kade could hardly believe he was agreeing to this, but desperation ran deep.

"Hold on now, are you saying that she," he pointed to the hallway, "and me," he placed his palm on his chest, "we'd be...together? No, no, no...you'd never..."

"It wouldn't just be the two of you." Kade laid it on the table, waiting for what he was proposing to take hold in Anthony's mind.

"You mean the three of us?" Wide-eyed, Anthony laughed as Kade nodded. "Well, shit...of all the things I thought were going to happen today, I did not expect to be propositioned by a vampire. For a ménage at that. Okay then."

"This isn't a trivial decision for me. Sydney trusts you. You're here. Most of all, you are willing. If this could work to trip whatever block she has, I know we'd both be grateful." Kade hoped he wouldn't change his mind. The more he talked with Anthony, the more certain he was that this would work.

"I'm in." Anthony stood up and nodded.

"You sure?"

"Yep, I'll do it."

"You need to know that Sydney...she doesn't know." Kade had heard Sydney's footsteps on the stairway and was hoping to finish before she reached the kitchen, but he'd run out of time.

"She doesn't know what?" Sydney asked. Spying Anthony in the corner, she squealed. "Tony! Oh my God. What are you doing here?"

She jumped into his arms and he spun her around. Kade smiled, observing the interaction. Maybe Anthony was exactly what she needed.

"How's my Philly girl? I missed you." Anthony hugged her, locking eyes with Kade. He kissed the top of her hair as if testing what Kade had told him.

"I missed you so much," she cried.

"Yeah, yeah, don't answer my calls. No texts. I think you forgot me," he goaded.

"Stop it." She pouted. Leaning back from his embrace, she slapped his arm. "I'd never forget you. Not ever."

"I don't know. I hear you've been kinda busy."

"He told you, didn't he?" Her face went flat, her eyes darting to Kade.

"Why don't you guys go into the family room and catch up," he suggested.

"Don't you think we should do this together?" Anthony asked, surprise in his eyes.

"I think old friends need privacy. You okay with that, love?" Kade crossed the room, settling a palm on each of their shoulders.

Sydney responded, reaching for him. He leaned down, gently pressing his lips to hers. Uninhibited by Anthony's presence, they deepened the kiss. She swept her tongue between his lips. Passion stirred inside, and he lifted his lids to meet Anthony's gaze. He wanted him to have a small taste of what to expect. Regretfully, he did have business to attend to, and thought it important for Sydney and Anthony to have time alone.

Kade retreated, giving her, then Anthony a smile.

"Go talk with the detective. I'll join you in a bit."

"You invited him here?" she asked.

"Yes and no. He called me," he replied truthfully. "You weren't answering your phone."

"But you knew he was coming?" she pressed.

"I did, but this is much better as a surprise, don't you think?"

She eyed him suspiciously in silence and Kade knew she suspected something was awry. She'd know that Anthony would not visit without a reason, and Kade trusted him to tell her why he'd come to New Orleans.

"You heard him, Syd. Lead the way," Anthony interjected, his eyes meeting Kade's in understanding.

"I'm sorry, Tony. I didn't mean to be rude. This way," she said.

Kade watched with interest as she fell into her partner's trusted embrace and they traveled out of the kitchen. He prayed what they were about to do would cure her. But at the moment, more pressing issues required his attention. The human who planned Sydney harm was on the loose. Retrieving his phone, he texted Luca.

⊸🙚· *Chapter Six* ·🙚⊹

Sydney's heart melted. For years, Tony had been her rock. Partners, they'd faced the best and worst of situations, surviving in the face of death itself. Next to Kade, he was the strongest man she'd known. *Loyal. Courageous.* Like coming home, she'd fallen into his arms. Emotion bubbled in her chest anticipating their conversation. He'd understood her desire to remain human more than anyone else.

"I'm sorry, I, um, I didn't return your texts." She moved to cross the room, but he held firm to her hand.

"No, Syd. Stay and talk. It's me," he pleaded.

"Tony, I can't…Kade told you everything?" Sydney turned her face away, unable to stomach the shame inside her. "I'm sorry, I should have been the one to tell you. I just couldn't do it."

"You should have told me, because you know what?" He reached to cup her cheek, forcing her to meet his gaze. "It doesn't matter what you are. You're my friend. My partner."

"Not anymore," she said, a sad reflection in her voice.

"Come here." Anthony led her to the couch. As they sat, he didn't release her. "Of all the people on God's green earth, I know you hate this. Remember when we first met that vamp you're marryin'?"

Sydney's eyes lightened and she gave him a small smile. She'd known he'd give her a pep talk. She considered that perhaps that was the reason she hadn't called him. She didn't want to feel good again. She deserved to suffer, given her mistake. She'd left the Alpha's compound, too confident she'd be able to protect them from the demon.

"You used to hate vampires. And maybe for good reason most of the time, but look at Kade. Luca. Even the wolves. You know I hang with Tristan now. He's one of the good guys."

"It's my fault. I thought I could handle it. Stupid. Stupid. Stupid." Sydney placed her palm on top of Tony's hands. She stared at her fingers, recounting what had happened. "I really don't remember that much. I went outside. This guy came at me. He looked suspicious but he was human at first. I fired my gun and then I was drifting away. I was alone."

"It's okay, Syd."

"Kade told me I was out of it for a few weeks. I couldn't even remember what they'd done to keep me alive." She sighed and gave Anthony a small smile. The light through the atrium doors flickered, and she took note how it deepened the color of his amber eyes. "When he told me what he did, I couldn't accept it. I was so angry at him for doing this. I should have died that day."

"He couldn't let you go."

"I know that, I really do. It's just at the time, I was so upset. And then the feeding…it's been a disaster. It wasn't the blood per se. I mean, you'd think I'd be disgusted drinking blood but I'm not. But hurting someone, that's not something I do to innocent people. The donor was screaming. It was awful. I just can't do that to someone. I *won't* do it."

"We're gonna work through this. There's nothin' we haven't faced. This is just one more thing. I promise you I'm going to be there for you," he assured her.

"There's nothing you can do. There's nothing anyone can do," she replied, her eyes brimming with tears. "I'm sorry I didn't call. I didn't want you to see me like this."

"This is exactly why I need to be here for you. Come here," he told her. Bringing her into his arms, he cradled her against his chest and stroked her hair.

"I missed you so much." Sydney laid her cheek against his soft cotton shirt and breathed in his masculine scent. Relief that he'd come flowed through her and she let herself revel in his comfort.

Anthony kissed Sydney's hair, refusing to let go. He couldn't believe what had become of her. Though he feigned a calm demeanor, his pulse raced in anger. How could this have happened? He wanted to blame Kade, but deep down, he knew that criminals walked the cities in all forms. The reality was that she could have been similarly injured on the force. Not everyone came out the end of a bullet the same way they were before they'd been shot. But it didn't matter; he'd made up his mind before she or Kade had a chance to ask. There was no way he'd leave New Orleans until she was healed.

His heart ached as she spoke, her words laced with despair. It didn't surprise him that she'd chosen not to tell him. His girl had pride as big as the city of brotherly love. All that she'd known had been destroyed, her life as she knew it gone.

Kade's request for assistance in helping her feed had been unexpected. Just the thought of Sydney at his neck caused his cock to twitch. He silently admonished himself for his response and tried to shake off the guilt. *I should be ashamed, for Chrissakes. What kind of a sick fuck gets off on his partner's problems?* He knew it was because he'd always been attracted to Sydney. They'd even kissed once, but she'd quickly shut down. She'd worked hard in the force and didn't want to jeopardize her reputation by dating him. He'd respected her choice and learned to accept their platonic relationship.

On the day she met Kade, he let go of the final piece of hope he hadn't known he'd possessed. At no point, however, had he felt bitter. He knew that being physically attracted to her and loving her as a friend didn't mean he was in love with her.

Sydney stirred in his arms and his thoughts moved to the escaped prisoner. He needed to tell her about Pat. No matter her own turmoil, she'd want to go after him. But in her vulnerable state, he thought she should stay within the safety of her home and allow Kade's security to protect her. Easier said than done, he knew.

"Sydney," he said, pulling out of their embrace. The aroma of her lily-scented hair teased his nostrils and he struggled to focus.

"Thank you for coming, Tony. Having you here...it just makes it a little better," she sniffled.

"I need to be honest with you. I came for another reason. I already told Kade and I probably should wait for him..."

"What is it?"

Anthony looked back toward the hallway for Kade.

"Just tell me already," she pressed.

"It's about Pat Scurlock." Tony hesitated, gauging Sydney's reaction.

"What? Please tell me that fucker's gotten a little poetic justice." Sydney wiped the back of her hands across her cheeks. Her shoulders straightened as she pushed away from Anthony.

"He's out." Like ripping off a bandaid, he thought it best just to do it quickly. He reached for Sydney's hand but wasn't fast enough as she jumped to her feet.

"What do you mean, he's out?" Sydney exclaimed. "How does a serial killer get out? Please tell me there wasn't some kind of legal loophole."

"Yes and no. He was granted a psych eval. His lawyer had him moved to a separate facility," he began. "They're still looking into it. Doesn't matter at this point, 'cause he's out. We're gonna protect you."

"Protect me?" She laughed. "No, no, no. It's the other way around. Somebody better protect him because this time he's not going back to prison," she promised. Holding up a palm, she silenced his attempt to interrupt. "This is the last straw. Just no."

"Maybe we should get Kade. We need to strategize what's gonna happen next. He says you're not feeling well."

"I'm fine," she insisted. "I'm not sitting at home while that psychopath comes after me. That's why you're here, isn't it, Tony? You and I both know what he's planning. He's coming after me. And he's got the contacts to do it."

"Okay, yeah. But Syd, I still think you oughta stay here and let Kade protect you. What I mean to say is that you look great." He stammered over his words. "Aw shit...it's just with you not being able to eat right."

"I've got options. I fed last night."

"Yeah, but Kade said that might not work in the long term."

"Goddammit, I'm so sick of this." She walked away from Anthony and stared out the atrium doors. With a heavy sigh, she continued. "Look, I know what I did isn't the perfect solution, but it worked. Besides, there isn't any other way. I'm stuck. I can't bite donors without hurting them."

"Maybe you just need a little help. I can help," he suggested, his hand on his chest.

"If you really could, I swear I'd let you, but so far, nothing has changed. I can't feed like Kade does. I have to just learn how to live like this. There is no other choice."

Anthony knew better than to argue with her. If Kade was right, she'd crash sooner or later. And when her world came crumbling apart, he planned on being there for her and Kade.

~⚜· *Chapter Seven* ·⚜~

Kade estimated that Sydney would only make it through a few more hours before needing more blood. Unless a vampire was mated to a human, the reality was that one couldn't survive an immortal life relying on one donor. He knew Sydney had acquired Mya's contact information, convinced she'd forever feed from her. But siphoning was a temporary solution to a complex problem. A vampire couldn't function independently if they relied on others to prepare the blood.

Kade was certain he'd made the right decision by asking Anthony to help Sydney. He'd sensed Anthony's arousal as soon as he'd presented the idea. Her partner had happily agreed, confirming what Kade had always suspected; Anthony desired Sydney. Still unsure of how to broach the topic with Sydney, he considered that it might be best to wait until she showed signs of hunger. At that point, she might be more willing to accept his proposal.

One thing had become clear since his conversation with Anthony; locating and killing Pat Scurlock was a priority. While vampire activities were generally under his tight control, a small element of unrest always existed. Kade had contacted P-CAP, making them aware of the escape and potential supernatural involvement. When he'd spoken with Logan, the Alpha had assured him that his pack would alert him if they heard of any suspicious activity going down on the streets.

A knock at the door interrupted his thoughts. He shoved out of his chair, making his way toward the foyer. He opened the front door, and Luca's stern expression met his. Dominique, who'd become Luca's security assistant, followed. While she'd never intentionally hurt an innocent human, she'd proven herself deadly on many occasions. Kade shook his head when he caught sight of her skin-tight black catsuit and over-the-knee boots. Her red hair had been twisted up high on her head into a ponytail. If there ever had been a vampire who reveled in her race, it was her.

"Come in." Kade gestured for them to enter.

"You talk to Logan?" Luca began.

"Yes. They're going to keep a strong presence in the city," Kade replied.

"How is Sydney doing?" Dominique asked.

"She's doing better today." Kade hesitated. "She fed last night."

"Siphon donor." She sniffed with contempt. "It's weak."

"I'm with her on that one," Luca added.

"Yes, I know," Kade agreed. "But I've got a plan for that. I've given some thought to what we discussed.

"You mean...a friend?"

"Anthony's here."

"The detective? From Philadelphia?" Dominique asked.

"Yeah. Her partner," Kade confirmed.

"So she's agreed?" Luca questioned with a cocked eyebrow.

"She doesn't know yet. We'll discuss it later."

"I think you might want to tell her sooner than later," Luca suggested.

"Can someone clue me in as to what you're talking about?" Dominique whined. "Why are we just standing here anyway? Let's get this show on the road. I'm looking forward to staking out that Matt guy."

"Pat," Kade corrected.

"Matt. Pat. Whatever," she sighed and flicked her nails. "So, where's Sydney?"

"Sydney's in the living room with the detective. We don't know where we're going, let alone who's going. I called you over to talk to Anthony and strategize."

It wasn't as if Kade hadn't given it thought. On the contrary, he knew exactly what he planned to do. If he had to visit every blood club in the damn city, he would. The last thing he needed was this asshole criminal stirring up trouble. All it took was one vampire with delusions of grandeur to cause an uprising. His cell buzzed and he swiped his thumb across the glass. He read the text, and blew out a breath.

"There's been an attack at Embo," he said.

"What happened?" Luca asked.

"I don't know. The text is from Gil Martin."

"The bartender?"

"Yeah. Looks like a couple of vampires are dead. P-CAP is on the scene."

"Well, shit."

"It's time to roll. I'm gonna go tell Anthony. Get the car," Kade ordered.

·⊷ Chapter Eight ⊶·

Kade took in the scene at Embo. Blinding house lights illuminated the blood-sprayed walls. Bar stools and chairs strewn about the floor indicated signs of a struggle. From what he could tell, there weren't many witnesses alive to question. The only employee he recognized was Gil Martin, who stood behind the bar pouring himself a shot of tequila.

Despite his best efforts to convince Sydney to stay at home with Dominique, she'd insisted she'd be safer with him. It wasn't as if he hadn't expected her refusal, but he gave her points for persuasion. She and Anthony stayed close as they checked out the debris, never leaving his sight. He kicked through a pile of ash and assumed that a vampire had been staked. His gaze caught Gil's and the bartender nodded in silent understanding.

"Who did this?" Kade asked.

"There were four of them. All wearing masks."

"Ski masks?"

"No, man. I'm talkin' full head coverings. Devils and animals."

"Okay," Kade breathed. "Well, this is New Orleans. They could have gotten them just about anywhere."

"Not sure if this matters, and you know I already told P-CAP, but the masks...they weren't the cheap ones. They were leather. The kind some of the more expensive stores sell."

"Or they could have bought them on the internet."

"Yeah, I don't know. It all went down fast. I would have called you sooner but you know how P-CAP is."

"What time did this happen?"

"It was about six or seven this morning." Gil slammed the liquor down his throat, coughed and scrubbed his hand over his hair. "I was getting ready to turn things over to the dayshift. Counting tips. Not many people are here at that time."

"Who was?"

"They killed Sean. You know, he works the front. The band had already gone. There were just a few other vamps still here. Both are dead. You're walkin' in 'em."

"Donors?"

"Yeah, they seemed more interested in them."

"What're you talking about?"

"They wanted names. Wanted to know who was here, like they were lookin' for someone. I gave them the inventory list."

"Where's the list?"

"I don't know. It's on an iPad. We keep track of everything that way. I gave it to one of them and that was the last I saw of it. Hey, when the bullets started flying, I lost interest."

"Syd, Anthony. We're looking for an iPad," Kade called out. "Let's get back to the donors. How many were still here?"

"I don't know. I think maybe six or seven. A few dove back here with me. P-CAP took them down to the station." Gil looked over to a pool of blood underneath one of the tables and wiped his hand across his mouth. "Two are dead. One they took out on a stretcher. Not sure if she'll make it."

"Anyone else?"

"Yeah, man." He paused, tightening his grip on the bottle. "Gemma."

"What about her?" Kade was surprised she'd stayed after Sydney's attack, but he also knew how much she got off on vampires.

"They took her. She was alive, though." He shook his head and put the rim of the bottle to his lips, not bothering to pour it in a glass this time. "She was screaming. It all happened so fast."

"How do you know it was Gemma if you were back here?"

"I've worked here a long time. You know she's a screamer." He blew out a breath. "Shit, I know that's wrong to say at a time like now, but it's true. I heard her scream, and peeked over the bar for all of about two seconds before a slug whizzed by my head. I saw them dragging her out of here. For the record, I did shoot back. I keep a handgun back here but it was no match for what they were packin'. Fuck, this has been a night."

"So you think the perps were vamps?"

"Only one. The way he took out the others…he had to be a vampire. The other three seemed human."

"You sure?"

"I've been working here for five years, boss. I'm tellin' ya, I know the difference. Mask or no mask."

"This it?" Anthony interrupted. He held up a black leather case and opened it.

"Yeah," Gil responded. "We've got an app that tracks the appointments. It's what was up when I gave it to zebra guy."

"It's busted," Anthony said.

"Let me see." Kade took the iPad from Anthony, observing a web of cracks across its glass. He pressed a button and it flared with light. "Still working."

"Well, that's something."

"You keep personal information on employees?" Kade asked. His eyes darted to Sydney, whose shocked expression told him she already knew what he was about to say.

"Yeah, we've got personnel files but we keep addresses and phone numbers stored in there so we can call in staff when we need to…go pick them up if they need a ride. Stuff like that."

"They were looking for her." Kade flipped the tablet toward Sydney, so she could view it. Mya Everhart's address and appointment information flashed across the screen.

"He went after her because of me," Sydney whispered. "Shit. How could he have known?"

"Someone told him," Kade said, his eyes meeting Gil's. After their performance on the balcony, it hadn't been a secret that both he and Sydney had been at the club.

"Hey, I don't know who you're talking about but whoever it is, ya'll know I wouldn't tell anyone anything. Look at the donor list if you're looking for a suspect. Humans don't all get the privacy rule. Just sayin'," Gil said.

"We've got to go to Mya." Sydney tugged on Kade's arm.

"I think we should get you home," Kade suggested.

"This is my fault. I came here. I used Mya. There's no way I'm not going to check on her."

"Look at me," Kade said, taking her hands in his. Her cheeks remained flush with color and she appeared healthy.

"I'm fine. I swear it."

"The second you feel the slightest twinge of hunger, we're going home. Understood?"

"Yes, I promise."

"Let's go," Kade reluctantly agreed.

As they left Embo, he pulled Luca aside and asked him to go ahead with Dominique to Mya's apartment and make sure it was clear. He caught Anthony's look of concern as the detective ushered Sydney into the car. Someone had alerted Pat that Sydney had been at Embo. It was likely the informant was alive and well, assisting Pat, and looking to lure Sydney into a trap with Mya.

It wasn't as if Sydney hadn't been to a crime scene before, but this was personal. Mya was missing because of her. She studied the décor and took note of the perfectly straightened books that sat on a dusted bookshelf. A small trail of destruction led from the foyer into the bedroom, everything in its path strewn onto the floor. She spied an overturned picture frame on the carpet and bent over to retrieve it. Sydney ran her finger over the edge of the cold metal frame and picked away the broken glass. Underneath, Mya kissed a fluffy white lap dog, a pink diamond collar around its neck. Every detail about the apartment told a story of an innocent young woman, one who appeared to be in college. Her psychology book lay open on a small kitchen table, and Sydney wondered how the fresh-faced coed had found herself employment as a siphon donor.

Kade waved to her, gesturing to the bedroom. She entered, scenting the blood, but concealed her reaction to the scene. A torn shirt lay on the floor. A set of bra and panties were tied around one of the poles of the white four-poster bed. Dark brown bloodstains were splattered across the pink sheets.

"Are you sure you wanna stay?" Luca asked Sydney. When she nodded, he leaned over and sniffed the linens. "There's semen. It's fresh. It's possible she was raped."

"It would be in line with Pat's M.O.," Anthony interjected.

"Yeah, it is." Sydney turned her head, sickened by the sight. She made her way into the tiny bathroom and what she saw took her breath away.

"Wait a minute, Syd," Luca said. "I didn't have a chance to tell you…"

"Kade." Sydney's heart caught in her chest as she saw the folded note taped to the mirror. Kade went to reach for it but she blocked his hand. "No, he left this for me."

Her hands shook as she tugged at the smooth paper, careful not to tear it. *Pat Scurlock. He attacked Mya because of me.* Carefully, she opened it, a gasp choking in her throat as she read it. *You took my girls. Now I'm taking yours.*

"He's not going to get to you," Kade assured her.

"He's going to kill her," Sydney whispered. Dizzy, she gripped the sink.

"Syd. You know him. He never kills right away," Anthony said

"No, he'll play with her, torture her. I don't get it, though. Who is the vampire helping him? What could Pat possibly have that he'd be worth causing this kind of trouble in New Orleans? Maybe he's not from here."

"It could be a 'she'," Luca commented.

"A woman?" Sydney asked with surprise.

"They had on masks. But who knows? It all went down fast and Gil didn't see much from behind the bar."

"Gil never mentioned he scented or suspected it was a woman," she countered.

"It's unlikely but still possible," Luca continued.

"I guess."

"Back to your other question; why does a vampire involve himself with miscreants?" Luca took the note from Sydney's hands and studied it.

"Power would be the obvious answer, but if there was one strong enough to challenge me, why would he wait for the help of a human? It makes no sense," Kade said.

The conversation faded as Sydney spied the red spray on the flowered shower curtain. Bile rose in her stomach and she fought the pangs of hunger that arose out of nowhere. She closed her eyes briefly, and attempted to gather strength. Something was happening to her. The rush of Mya's blood waned. She'd need to feed, find another donor. Yet curiosity drove her as she put one foot in front of the other. Her fingers curled into the nylon fabric. As she pulled it across, a thick trail of caked blood clung to the textured fiberglass tub. A tunnel of black engulfed her vision as she pointed to her name, which was written across the white tiles.

Chapter Nine

Kade gently laid Sydney onto the crisp cotton sheets. After she'd fainted, he'd gathered her into his arms, cursing himself for not seeing the signs. He'd dismissed her shaky hands, but knew she'd never show fear. Before her accident, the threat in the shower wouldn't have caused her to falter. While she'd been temporarily nourished, it wasn't nearly enough for a new vampire to thrive. As if she was a newborn, she'd need frequent feedings.

When he'd left Mya's apartment, he'd instructed Luca to wait for Xavier, so they could turn it over for clues. Despite his orders, Kade suspected they wouldn't find anything else. Pat Scurlock meant to toy with Sydney. Like a cat batting around a mouse, he'd play with her first, making his kill all the more sweet. Delighting in a sick sense of torture, Pat sought to instill both fear and guilt.

Kade had asked Anthony to help him transfer Sydney back to the house. He played the scenario in his head, the act scrolling through his brain. A mixture of excitement and apprehension arrested his thoughts, and he prayed Sydney would accept the inevitable.

After they'd arrived home, he'd given her a bath. Cleaning the stench of the evening away, he'd washed Mya's blood from her skin. He'd dressed her in a warm robe and brought the covers up over her hips. Brushing a stray hair from Sydney's eyes, he studied her face and considered how much he loved her. Sharing her with Anthony would be the ultimate act of devotion, yet he was fully prepared to see it through. He wasn't sure why he thought it would work, but instincts told him that she'd never allow herself to hurt her friend.

Kade turned his head toward the door, where Anthony stood silently watching. Wearing only a pair of pajama pants, he stood bare-chested. Kade gave him a small smile and waved him into the room. As the detective made his way toward the bed, Kade leaned to kiss Sydney's forehead. Her eyes flickered open in response. She stared up into his eyes wearing a look of confusion.

"Hey there, how're you feeling, love?"

"I, um…" Sydney's eyes darted from Kade to Anthony, who stood next to the bed. "How did I get here?"

"You had a little spell is all."

"I passed out, didn't I?" She groaned.

"Not unexpected, I'm afraid. I should have watched you more carefully," he apologized.

"This isn't your fault."

"I should have known you were about to get sick."

"How would you...?"

Kade cocked an eyebrow at her and smiled.

"Hmm...you know everything, huh?" Sydney moved to sit up, but fell back onto the pillow in exhaustion.

"Just relax, now."

"Back in the bathroom, I don't know what happened. I remember feeling dizzy, hungry. I need blood again, don't I?" she asked.

"I may omit details every now and then," he gave a small laugh, looked up to Anthony and back to her, "but I'll never lie to you. You need to eat."

"Where am I going to get blood? Mya's gone." She sighed and closed her eyes. "I can't do this, Kade. I can't bring one more donor into our house. I can't do it. There's something wrong with me. I'm a terrible vampire."

"No you're not. You're just a little fang challenged." He smiled down at her, gently sliding the back of his hand over her cheek.

"I'm the worst." Her gaze moved to Anthony, who leaned against the wall, his arms crossed. Her eyes lit up and she reached for him. "Tony. What are you doing all the way over there? Come here."

"You scared me, there. How's your head?" he asked.

"My head?" Sydney smoothed her hand over her hair. When she found the knot, she grimaced. "Shit. I thought being a vampire was supposed to give me some kind of super healing power?"

"You need to feed," Kade told her.

"But I did."

"More often. At least every day for a few weeks. It won't always be this way, but you haven't been well." Kade brushed his lips to her forehead.

"I can't believe he took Mya," she began. "If we hadn't made a scene...we did this."

"Stop it, Syd." Anthony's eyes met Kade's. He moved to sit on the bed, bringing his legs next to hers. He shoved up onto his side, resting his head on his hand. Bringing her hand to his chest, he continued. "You know Pat better than anyone. The women he takes. The ones he tortures. He's been after you for months. But not once did you flinch. Not once did you cave to the phone calls or the letters. And I'm not going to let you now. We," he glanced to Kade, "aren't going to let you be a victim. If you were feeling better, you'd kick both our asses."

"How am I supposed to fight like this?" she replied.

"I want to help you." Anthony kissed the back of her hand, refusing to let her go. His eyes met Kade's.

"What do you mean, *help* me?"

"Anthony's going to be your donor," Kade said, his voice calm and caring. He knew she'd protest at first but he wouldn't take no for an answer.

"No." Sydney tried unsuccessfully to sit. She grunted and fell backwards once again.

"Yes," Anthony insisted. "Listen, Kade's been talking to Léopold about what's causing this to happen to you, and I know you know this already, but he thinks you need a friend to help you get through this thing. It's just like anything else in life. You have an accident and you're afraid to get in the car and drive. Fall off a horse and you're supposed to get back on."

"I was never on the horse."

"Okay, bad analogy but the principle is the same. Until Kade, you'd steered clear of the supes. I know you love Kade and you've become friends with some of his friends, but for a long time, all you saw was the bad side of vampires."

"And humans," she added.

"All the donors we've had to date have been strangers. And normally that's fine," Kade explained. He'd thought discussing his proposal would be the easiest path to get her to acquiesce, but he was starting to rethink his strategy.

"I can't control it. It's not like I haven't tried," she told them, shaking her head.

"I know, but we need to try again…you'd never hurt Anthony. Please. Let him do this for you, Sydney. Let him do this for us. Once you learn how, you'll be free."

"I don't know. This seems wrong. What if I can't control the rest?"

The rest? The devil is, indeed, in the details. Kade knew what she was thinking. It was perfectly normal to arouse and be aroused when feeding, but the act itself could be restrained. One learned discipline through experience, but first she must learn the basics.

"I'll do that for you." Kade took her hand in his. Like mirrored souls, he and Anthony flanked her.

"I don't know…are you sure about this?" Her eyes darted from Kade to Anthony. "Tony, if this works…I need to know you'll be okay afterward. I don't want to use you."

"I'll be fine. It's not like it's a secret that I find you attractive. But we both know that we aren't meant to be together…not that way."

"You know I love you, Tony, but I'm *in love* with Kade." She gave him a small smile.

"I get it, Syd. It's okay. I want to do this for you."

"I don't know if this will work," she hedged.

"This will work, love. All you need to do is trust me." Kade pressed his lips to hers, indulging in the warmth of his mate.

"I don't know," she whispered into his kiss.

"Trust us to take care of you." Kade spoke into her mouth.

"Yes," she agreed softly. Her face flushed as she caught Anthony watching her.

Reluctantly, Kade broke away and slowly turned her to Anthony, who brought his palm to her cheek. "I want you to taste him…scent him. Know your prey."

Sydney's mind warred against what she yearned for, Anthony's vital essence flowing beneath his skin. As she took his wrist to her lips, she shivered with desire. An ache grew between her legs, arousal flowing through her veins. She fought the burn in her gums, concerned about the pain she'd cause Anthony. Her eyes flew open to Kade, who stroked his hand over her hair. Unsure, she shook her head in refusal, yet she never let go of Anthony's arm.

"What's wrong, love?"

"I...I don't want to hurt him." Sydney's eyes fell on Anthony, whose erection pressed into her hip.

"We'll do this together," Kade promised. He leaned forward and brushed his lips over her forehead. "All of us."

Her chest constricted with emotion as Kade's fingers trailed down her collarbone. She relaxed into his touch, his strong hand massaging her shoulder. Their eyes locked, and her anticipation heightened as she felt a tug on the belt of her robe. He opened the fabric and the cool air teased her nipples. Exposed, she arched her back as he thrummed the pad of his thumb over one of her taut tips. Moaning softly in arousal, her mouth grazed over Anthony's arm.

"That's it. Let go," Kade told her. His eyes caught Anthony's and he nodded.

"You sure?" Anthony hesitated.

"Tony," she began. In tandem with her arousal, the urge to bite him grew stronger. She took his hand and rested it on her bare stomach. "Please. I'm scared but I want this."

"Syd," Anthony breathed. He tore his arm from her grasp and slid it around the back of her neck.

As his lips met hers, she opened to him. His tongue swept into her mouth and she whimpered in pleasure. Unlike Kade's possessive kiss, his was soft and gentle. His succulent taste flared every nerve in her body, and she wrapped a leg around his waist. Allowing Kade to undress her, she breathed into Anthony's lips as her mate's bare chest grazed her back. Kade's strong hand cupped her breast, his cock prodding her bottom.

"This is what you need," she heard him tell her, his fangs scraping her shoulder.

"Kade, I...ah," she cried. Her eyes focused on Anthony's; his cheek brushed into her cleavage, his soft lips grazing over the swell of her breast. The unmistakable feel of Kade's fingers slipping into her wet folds left her pleading for more. "God, yes."

"That's right, feel me inside you. Let your senses take over. Scent Anthony's blood. Can you feel his pulse? Take what he offers. He wants you to have it."

"But what if I…"

"You won't hurt him. It's okay. He's agreed to this. You can do it. Give him the pleasure he seeks," Kade commanded.

Granted permission to enjoy the experience, Sydney smiled. She slid her hand into the front of Anthony's pajama pants and gripped his cock, swiping the glistening wetness over his slit. A rush of dominance surged through her as she heard his groan of pleasure. His head lolled back onto the pillow, exposing the cords of his neck as she lapped his skin.

"That's it, love," Kade encouraged.

Sydney's hips gyrated against the heel of Kade's hand, his fingers plunging deep inside her. His thumb grazed her clitoris and her breath caught. Drenched in arousal, the walls of her tight channel contracted as he fucked her. Anthony took her nipple between his lips and sucked hard. The seductive pain rolled through her and she cried out, her fangs distending. She fisted Anthony, rhythmically stroking his cock.

She growled as Kade lifted her hips toward him, his fingers still deep inside her pussy. He pushed her legs open with his knees and began to tease her opening with the crown of his dick. She protested as he withdrew his fingers and spread the wetness of her core through her folds. He applied pressure to her clit with his thumb, and Sydney responded, tilting her ass toward him.

"Fuck me," she pleaded. Her mouth dropped to Anthony's neck. The scent of his delicious blood called to her and she flicked her tongue at his shoulder. Her razor-sharp teeth scraped his skin, drawing a thin white line across his flesh.

"Ah yeah," Anthony grunted as she cupped his balls.

Jolted by the sound of Anthony's voice, Sydney froze.

"What's wrong?" He sighed, leaning his forehead onto her shoulder. "Why are you stopping?"

"I hurt you," she whispered, jarred from the moment.

"I'm fine. I want this. You won't hurt me…you'd never hurt me."

"Give me your arm," Kade told him.

Anthony gave him a look of confusion, but complied. He released Sydney's breast and reached his arm around the back of her neck within inches of Kade's lips.

"We'll do this together, love. You with me?" he asked, his eyes meeting Anthony's.

"Fuck, yeah. Syd, ya got me hangin' by a thread here," Anthony moaned.

Fear had strangled Sydney for far too long. Releasing her anxieties, she bared her fangs, allowing herself the freedom to take what he offered. She nicked his lip, a drop of his blood coating her tongue. Wild with arousal, she grunted as Kade slammed his cock into her pussy.

"Yes, yes, oh God, I want you, Tony," she rambled as she fisted and stroked him hard.

"Faster," he ordered, thrusting his shaft into her palm.

"Now," Kade instructed.

The sight of his sharp teeth inches from Anthony's forearm drove her into frenzy. Lost in her desire, she followed Kade's lead as they both sank their fangs deep into Anthony's flesh. As he thrashed in pleasure, his sweet blood flowed freely down her throat. Her mind open, she focused on driving him into a state of unbridled euphoria.

"Holy fuck, yeah...I should have...this feels...don't stop," Anthony cried.

Blood ran down his neck and over her lips, and Sydney drank her fill, lapping her tongue at his wounds. Her own orgasm built as Kade plunged into her from behind, his fingers pinching her swollen nub.

"Harder," Anthony yelled.

Sydney caressed his sac while pumping him faster and faster. He screamed in climax, his seed spilling into her hands. As Kade released his arm, she removed her mouth from Anthony's neck.

"Get up," Kade demanded. "Hands and knees."

Sydney obeyed without argument. After Kade had shared her with Anthony, he'd dominate every square inch of her body. Out of the corner of her eye, she smiled as she spied Anthony lying on his back, still reeling from his orgasm. The glow on his face exuded satisfaction and his eyes caught hers right before she felt Kade thrust into her from behind. His fingers dug into her hips, and she concentrated on balancing herself. Eagerly awaiting his next move, she wriggled her hips and was reprimanded with a hard slap on her bottom.

"Do I have your attention now?" He laughed.

"Sorry," she giggled. Elated that she'd fed from Anthony, she allowed herself to relax into submission. No matter what he'd ask, she'd give it to Kade.

"You're magnificent, my little vamp," he praised. "Look what you did to our poor detective. He can barely move."

"No pain," she grunted. Flesh meeting flesh resounded throughout the room as he pounded into her. The smell of sex permeated her nose and her core clamped down around Kade's cock.

"No pain. Only pleasure. You did that."

"I did that..." Her words trailed off as he slammed into her again.

"We did that. You and I." He dug his fingers into her hair, fisting it.

The sting of her hair being pulled reminded her that she was as alive as before she'd been turned. Kade, her husband-to-be, master of her body's pleasure, had done what he'd promised. She'd survived and he'd never leave her unprotected.

With her head tilted back, she was able to catch a hint of Anthony's smile as he enjoyed the show. Deferring to Kade, she surrendered to her own desire to be watched.

"Yes," she breathed, unable to speak the words that eluded her.

"You're mine, Sydney. From that very first day we met." He reached underneath and cupped her breast, pinching her nipple between his fingers. "You are everything to me."

"Always." She was overcome with emotion; tears brimmed through her lashes as her climax teetered on the precipice of its explosion.

"Whatever you need, I will always give it to you."

"Please…I can't wait, harder," she pleaded.

Kade plunged into her, over and over, increasing the pace. Her pussy convulsed around him as he stroked the strip of nerves inside her core with the tip of his cock. The first wave of her climax tore through her and she screamed his name at the top of her lungs. The sound of his grunting drove her to widen her stance, welcoming every hard thrust he gave. As he came, she fell onto her stomach and he rolled her onto her side, while still quietly pumping into her.

"I love you," he told her, grazing his lips against her hair.

"I love you so much. What you did for me…I'm sorry about everything. I should have trusted you."

"Shh, my sweet little vampire. You're going to be all right. It's all going to be all right."

Kade pulled a sheet over her, shielding her nude body from Anthony's view and Sydney suspected he hadn't planned to share her any further than he had. What he'd done was only to ensure that she be able to learn to feed, to give and receive pleasure within the safety of his presence.

Anthony tied his pajama pants and shoved himself out of bed. As he went to walk away, their eyes locked and she mouthed the words, 'thank you'. He gave her a wink and left her and Kade alone. What had happened between the three of them had forever changed her life; she'd now be able to control the sensations caused by her bite, giving her independence.

As darkness fell, Sydney reveled within the warmth of Kade's loving embrace. In the morning they'd face a killer, but in the heat of the night, they'd celebrate their love. No longer drifting apart, their passion and devotion to each other had withstood the impossible. Tomorrow, healed, they'd go after Pat Scurlock and Sydney swore to herself that this time when she found him, he wasn't going to be leaving New Orleans alive.

~❧ *Chapter Ten* ❧~

Kade kissed the nape of Sydney's neck, his arousal prodding her back. She moaned but didn't yet wake, and he recalled the events of the prior evening. The erotic exchange with Anthony had been an extraordinary success. Surprisingly, Kade hadn't felt jealousy as his fiancée pleasured another man. She'd shown restraint by going no further than touching Anthony, demonstrating the ability to control both her hunger and desire.

Thoughts of the killer infiltrated his mind. He had to identify the vampire who was aiding and abetting the escapee. It made no sense that a supernatural would allow a human to lead any kind of activity, let alone one of a criminal nature. He'd ordered Luca to take an account of every vampire in the city. With over two hundred in the surrounding parishes, it wouldn't take long to rule out the innocents, narrowing the others down to a short list. Whoever it was obviously hadn't been in the town very long. A bigger question was how they had a connection to Pat Scurlock.

Sydney stirred, and Kade spooned her, wrapping his arm around her waist. Despite the danger they faced, he wished he could stay like this forever. Within seconds his phone buzzed and he glanced to the bed stand, noting Luca's text. Without releasing his mate, he reached and touched a forefinger to its glass. He cursed as he read the message: *Problem at Sangre Dulce.*

Kade shook his head and rolled away from Sydney. With no time to waste, he headed toward the bathroom. He'd let her sleep for a few more minutes before their hunt continued.

The odor of smoke hung thick in the air as Sydney carefully navigated through the charred remnants of what used to be Sangre Dulce. It had been months since she'd been there. At one time, it housed a mixed venue for kink lovers, both humans and supernaturals alike. Unfortunately, it'd also been the scene where a former psychopath mage, Asgear, had chosen to target his victims. The dark club tended to attract both good and evil, experienced and neophytes, all congregating for the purpose of pleasure and pain.

She was focusing on looking for clues, when she caught sight of Kade in a heated discussion with Anthony. Her stomach fluttered as she recalled her evening with both men. She could have taken it further, she knew. The desire to make love to Anthony had been strong. She and Kade had talked about the experience in detail on the way over in the car. She'd been afraid to admit her feelings, but he'd assured her she'd done well. Sexual arousal was an illusion, one that could be controlled. She suspected she'd want to drink from Anthony again, but knew she'd never fall in love with anyone but Kade. He was her universe and reason for living, every breath she took was a dedication to their love.

The sound of her foot breaking through a piece of soggy wood drew her focus back to the scene. *Why did Pat Scurlock burn down Sangre Dulce?* Kidnapping and torture were the hallmarks of his crimes, not arson. Pat had always resorted to all too common ways of selecting his victims, such as trolling mall parking lots for women who shopped alone. She considered that maybe he was trying to kill a vampire. Torching the building would certainly have done the trick. But according to the firemen, Sangre Dulce was closed when the fire started; no human bodies had been found. Sydney kicked at the soot beneath her feet. Ash was ash. If a vampire had been killed, the fragments stuck to her boots could be the disintegrated remains of vampire. No one would ever know.

"Maybe you and Anthony should go get some coffee," Kade suggested, startling her.

"I know you're worried and I love you for it, but seriously, I'm okay," she assured him.

"You let me know if you get hungry. No more dizzy spells. I've got donors on call." He glanced at Anthony, who approached. "The detective is still here for you, too."

"Thanks." She smiled and reached for his hand. "I'm doing well. I think last night…"

"Hey," Anthony said, a warm smile crossing his face.

"Hey, yourself," Sydney said. "I was just telling my fiancé here that I feel great. About last night…I know I already thanked you, but it meant everything to me…to us. I'm feeling like a new woman."

"It was pretty hot, huh?" Anthony teased. "Who knew getting bitten could be so much fun?"

"Don't get used to it, my friend," Kade warned with a wink to Sydney. "On second thought, Sydney may need some practice."

"Now, now, boys. We did have fun, but it may have been a one-time kind of thing."

Both men feigned saddened expressions and she laughed. "Okay, maybe a couple more times, but I can't keep Tony in New Orleans forever."

"I won't lie. It was pretty awesome. You think Philly's got any hot vamp women?"

"I'm sure Tristan could hook you up in his club," Sydney replied.

"Tristan is the only one I'd trust with our detective's safety." Kade's face dropped as he spoke.

"What's wrong?" Sydney asked.

"Everyone quiet!" Kade yelled. "Shh…"

"What is it?" Anthony whispered.

"Shh." Kade held up a hand, silencing them.

Not a sound but the whoosh of passing cars could be heard in the room. In the distance, a baby cried.

"I thought I heard footsteps…something." He shook his head in confusion and waved Luca over. "I want you to stay here with Anthony."

"But Kade…" Sydney began.

"No arguments, love. If there're any surprises in the back rooms, Luca and I will ferret them out."

"Both P-CAP and the firemen have been through this building. It should be safe." As much as she tried to rationalize what she was saying, the same instinct that had always kept her alive told her something was off.

"Safe or not, I agree with Kade. You'd better stay with me," Anthony insisted.

"I know, it's just that I don't want him going alone."

"I'm going with him, darlin'. I promise we'll be back in a few minutes." Luca rested his palm on her shoulder.

There was a time she and Luca had fought like cats and dogs. But their relationship had evolved into one of respect and friendship. They lived on the same property and Sydney had become close with his fiancée, Samantha, a witch, who was expecting.

"Okay, but both of you better be careful. You've got a baby on the way, big man. No messing around, you hear me? Call us if something happens," she told him.

"Whatever the noise was I don't hear it now," Kade lied. He leaned in and pressed his lips to hers. "I promise we'll just have a quick look."

"Be careful."

"I'll be right back." Kade's eyes met Anthony's. "Detective?"

"We'll kick around in here, check out what's left of the bar and kitchen."

Kade nodded and took off through the rubble. Luca shoved away debris that blocked the entrance and they disappeared into the darkness. Sydney bit her lip, wrapping her arms around her waist. Never in her life had she considered herself 'needy'. She wasn't sure if it was their bond strengthening, perhaps caused by Kade turning her, but without him near, her stomach churned in worry. Resisting the urge to cry, she took a deep breath and allowed Anthony to take her into his arms. *Bawling at a crime scene is not an option*, she thought. *Get your shit together.*

Within minutes, she'd calmed her emotions, cognizant that with her transition, she had to learn how to better control her primal impulsivity. Ready to resume her work, she broke out of Anthony's arms and pointed to the bar. In silence they picked through the remnants. She found herself looking back toward the hallway where Kade and Luca had gone. No matter the reassuring silence, she teemed with restless worry. Scurlock's motives for burning the club to the ground may have been nebulous, but Sydney was certain he'd been the one who had done it.

Anthony called for her to go into the kitchen and she nodded. Her cell phone buzzed and she retrieved it from her pocket. By the time she'd finished reading the text from Mya's number, the color had drained from her face. *495809 Mattise Lane 9pm* The hair on the back of her neck stood up as Luca's voice reverberated throughout the musky air. Without giving it a second thought, she sprinted through the pitch black hallway toward the back of the club. Suspecting something had happened to Kade, she ignored Anthony's calls for her to return.

Kade speculated that Sydney's senses were becoming more sensitive, but she hadn't yet developed them enough to hear the soft crunch of the embers in the alleyway. Both he and Luca had heard footsteps, but as they made their way down the hallway, they were met with dead silence. Kade reasoned that it could have been looters, but his instincts told him that danger lurked in the darkened sex rooms. As they moved further into the labyrinth, it became apparent that the fire hadn't progressed past the bar and seating area. He ran his finger along the soot-covered wall, its smooth texture sticking to his skin. The plastered structure remained firm as he rapped it with his knuckles.

Luca passed to his right and he nodded, acknowledging his departure into a larger room. Several feet up he spotted a door to a private alcove. The claustrophobic area housed just enough room for two lovers to engage in what surely would be an intense encounter. Approximately five by five feet, there was little room to wield a whip. While many of the spaces encouraged exhibitionism and voyeurism, this tiny closet did not allow for observation.

Kade wrapped his fingers around the cool brass doorknob and turned it. A loud click gave way to silence. He glanced over his shoulder, checking behind him. Confident no one was following, he placed a foot through its entrance. Scanning the room, he saw no other doors. A cool breeze grazed his face, and he caught sight of a small piece of cardboard fluttering in the wind. His attention was drawn upward to a large hole in the ceiling. The heart-shaped paper had been wound around a metal ring which was attached to the concrete wall. With both caution and curiosity, Kade approached. He took it between his fingers, noticing that unlike everything else in his surroundings, it was dry as a bone. He flipped it over, and saw the message: *She's dead.*

By the time he heard the door slam shut, the heavy silver chain had fallen onto him. He swatted at it, the stench of scorched skin permeating the room. It fell away to the floor but his reprieve was brief. Kade grunted as a wooden dart pierced deep into his thigh.

"Luca!" He yanked the splintered projectile from his flesh.

A hidden door slid open and a blinding stream of light speared into his eyes. As the first human came at him, he swung, landing a solid punch to his face. A second chain wrapped around his neck, and he struggled to free himself. He fell to his knees, clawing at the interwoven rings. His head smashed against pavement as they dragged him into the van. A tunnel of darkness closed in, and his final thoughts were of Sydney.

~⊱ *Chapter Eleven* ⊱~

"Where's Kade?" Sydney cried. Luca blocked her from entering the room where Kade had disappeared, and she pounded on his chest. "You fucking said you'd keep him safe."

"We'll find him," Luca told her.

"What happened? Where is he?" She pushed around Luca and stumbled into what remained of the room. She caught sight of the large breach in the ceiling and wall. She ran into the alleyway, and looked up and down the street.

"We got a number on the car," Anthony offered, coming up behind her.

"You didn't answer me." She confronted Luca. "How could you let this happen?"

"I was in the other room. There was no one back here. I swear it," he explained, raking his fingers through his hair. "When I heard him yell, I ran down the hallway and he was gone. You know we're like humans during the day. I can't chase down a car."

"Are you fucking serious?" she growled. He attempted to reach for her and she broke free of his hold. "Don't touch me. That is it. I'm done with this bullshit. Look at this." She held up her phone, showing him the text.

"What?"

"The time and address. Tonight. He wants me to come alone." She laughed. "I'm going all right. By the time I'm done with him, he'll wish he'd stayed in that shithole prison."

"Syd," Anthony began.

"No. Don't say anything, Tony. He's fucking dead. This," she hissed, allowing her fangs to drop. She gestured to her mouth and then to Luca who'd also exposed his teeth, "is who I am now. I'm not human anymore. I may have lived by human rules before, but those days are gone."

"But…"

"She's right," Luca interjected.

"Last night you saw the best of me, but deep inside there's a monster that's going to be let loose. Every single human and vampire involved with taking Kade is going to die. You can either help or leave, but you will not stop me."

"Sydney, you know I'll always have your back…it's just…" Anthony stammered.

"Tony. Please just stop. Are you with me? 'Cause I know for damn sure Luca's coming."

"Fuck yeah," Luca agreed.

"This asshole thinks that I'm weak…that I can't feed because he's got

Mya. He thinks that because he took Kade, he owns me. But he's so fucking wrong," she growled. "He's mine."

Sydney took a long draw of blood from Anthony's wrist while he lay back on the sofa. She'd been so concerned that she'd lose control that she insisted that Luca and Samantha stay with her in the room. After fainting in Mya's apartment, she was determined to feed more often and stay strong. Concentrating, she'd focused like Kade had taught her. Reaching within her mind, she focused on knowing he was her friend, that she'd never hurt him. She cut off all sexual thoughts, but still ensured it was pleasurable for Anthony.

As she released Anthony's arm, she felt a small comforting hand on her shoulder and glanced up at Samantha. The red-haired witch was full with child, and they expected she'd go into labor within the month.

"You did nicely," she said softly.

"Thanks, Sam. You okay?" Sydney asked Anthony. Relief poured through her as his eyes flickered open and he gave her a grin.

"Yeah, I'm good."

"Thank God," she sighed.

"Not as good as last night, but with the big man out…"

"Don't even joke about it."

"We're going to find him."

"I know, but right now, I can't think of anything else but getting Kade home safe."

"He's a strong vampire." Samantha sat down next to Sydney and took her hand. "And you're strong too. I can see it in your aura. Everything has changed. You and Luca can do this."

"Hey, what about me? I'm startin' to feel a little underappreciated here." Anthony inspected his forearm and rubbed his fingers over the newly formed skin.

"You're human. You must be careful," Samantha noted.

"The humans never understand how truly weak they are," Luca added, brushing his hand over Samantha's hair. "It'd be comical if it weren't so pathetic."

"Hey," Samantha scolded, glaring at the father of her child. "Not nice."

"But true," he countered.

"Still not nice. You're going to have to learn some manners when our daughter is born."

"I'll teach her how to fight off the vampires who seek to court her."

"She'll be able to fight them off herself with magic. Now, don't distract me." Her eyes darted over to Anthony, who looked amused by their exchange. "Even though Anthony is human, he can still help. But he must be extra cautious. Remember, dear, I was able to defend myself."

"But you were a witch when you did that. When you were mortal...darlin', you know that didn't turn out so well."

"True, but Sydney was the one who saved me," Samantha countered. "And she was human when she did it. Now she's like you. And more determined than ever."

"Thanks for sticking up for me, ma'am, but I'm going no matter what these vamps say. I may not be all badass like Luca the Drac, but I'm a sharp shooter. I'm good with a stake too, if I must say. Been trainin' at home."

"You're not serious." Sydney shook her head.

"Like a heart attack. I just need a glass of juice and I'm gonna be ready to go here."

"Do you feel okay?" Sydney asked again, her voice soft with concern. She placed her palm to his cheek. "Did I take too much? I'm really sorry. I thought I only took a little bit..."

"I'm fine. It's like blood bank day at the station. Although I could use a cookie. Maybe a kiss to make it feel better." He waggled his eyebrows at her and she slapped his arm.

"Stop trying to distract me. If anything happens to you tonight, I'll never forgive myself."

"Ah, as much as I detest humans, I must give credence to the detective's courage," Luca said, giving Samantha a smile.

"He's going." Sydney blew out a breath and shook her head. "Dominique and Xavier stay home with Samantha."

"I don't need them," Samantha protested. "I'm well able to take care of myself."

"No arguments, darlin'. You and our baby are my world right now. Whoever did this will suspect I'm going with Sydney. They'll know you're alone."

"Sam, I know how it is to feel a little..." Sydney searched for another word besides helpless. It wasn't that Samantha didn't have powers, but they couldn't put her in jeopardy. She already had difficulty walking the distance between their homes. "...vulnerable. I know you got magic, girl, but with the baby? No...just no."

"Hell no," Luca added.

Samantha looked to Anthony, who shrugged.

"Sorry. Gotta agree with the two of them on this one. This is getting ugly and the last thing we need to do is put your baby in danger."

"What about Logan? He could go with you," Samantha suggested.

"That's a good idea. I'll give him a call on the way over. As wolf, it's likely they'll go undetected," Sydney agreed. She glanced at the address on her phone once more time and flashed it at Luca. "This is in St. Tammany Parish?"

Luca checked the screen. "Yeah. Not too far out of the city."

"As soon as the sun falls, we're outta here." Sydney shoved out of her chair, twisting her hair up into a knot. She dug a rubber band out of her jeans and made quick work of tying it up into a bun. "Weapons?"

"Yes, weapons," Luca repeated. "If there's one thing I have, it's those."

"I thought vamps didn't need guns," Anthony jibed.

"Just because I don't need them doesn't mean I don't like them." The corner of Luca's lip curled upward.

Sydney ignored their banter. Her thoughts drifted to Kade and her chest tightened. She knew Pat sought to punish her in the worst possible way, to inflict immeasurable pain by taking the one she loved. She closed her eyes, taking a deep cleansing breath in an attempt to focus on her task. Whatever went down tonight, she'd kill Pat Scurlock. The beast inside her would seek its revenge and she'd allow it its due. A night of reckoning would come, as her true nature was revealed.

The gravel beneath the tires spit up onto the car, cracking the windshield. The sound of the splintering glass should have startled Sydney, but she remained focused. From the satellite image, they determined that the secluded home was set deep into the forest. The lush landscaping had been well kept, indicating the property wasn't abandoned. It belonged to one D. Tessa Saulnier.

Luca had scoured the security records, and no person of that name was a registered vampire, nor had Logan heard of her. They assumed the individual was human, but neither Sydney nor Anthony could find any connection between the prior murders, Pat Scurlock and the home. They'd considered the possibility that perhaps there was a relationship between Scurlock and Saulnier. Yet with no evidence to prove it, they surmised it was more likely that Pat had broken into the home while Ms. Saulnier was on vacation. Repeated attempts to call the phone number on record were ignored, as were the several texts Sydney had sent to Mya.

Sydney choked on the dust streaming into her open car window. She glanced at Luca, who quietly nodded, then set his eyes back on the road. The click of Anthony's Sig Sauer told her he'd begun checking his weapon. It was a nervous habit she'd watched him do many a time when they worked together. Sliding the clip out and working the action, he made sure the weapon was loaded. Oddly, she found the sound of snapping metal comforting. They'd started this case together, arresting a murderer, and tonight she planned to end it.

"Here," Luca said, pointing to an entrance that sat fifty feet up the road.

He pulled the car over into the grass, got out and slid into the back seat with Anthony. Sydney jumped over the console and sat in the driver's seat. The large SUV's tinted windows blocked the view from outside, so only the faint outline of a driver could be seen inside the vehicle.

"We do this like we planned," Sydney told them. "I go in first. I'm who they want. Tony, you go around back with Luca. Get Kade before you come for me. If Mya's still alive..."

"Doubtful," Anthony stated. "It's been more than twenty-four hours. There's a good chance he's killed her by now."

"I have to agree with the detective."

"Like I said, Kade's the priority. Once you get him freed, come help me. If by some miracle Mya's still alive, we'll try to get her out."

"I'm not thrilled about this plan." Luca shook his head and placed his palm on her shoulder. "If something happens to you, Kade's going to kill me."

"Luca," Sydney began. She caught the flicker of his eyes in the rearview mirror. "We already went through this. I'll be the first to admit it; this half-baked plan of ours sucks, but we don't have any options. If they see you or if you try to go in after me, they're going to kill him. Knowing Scurlock, he's got him in the basement cuffed and silvered, with someone waiting on standby to stake him."

"He'll try to do Kade before he does her," Anthony noted. "He's keepin' him alive. He wants her to watch when he kills him. It's all part of the high ...getting off while his vics cry and plead. He's got a hard on for torture, I'm tellin' ya, man."

"As soon as I'm in the house and the door shuts, you go round to the back. If for some reason they rush us, we go balls out with fire power and hope to hell that we make it. But that is like plan Z as far as I'm concerned. I'm not gonna park too close to the house. I'll run up to the door to keep the focus on me. Hopefully, they won't try to search the car. If they try to, I'll make a scene, and they'll take me inside faster."

"This is some fucked up shit, Syd. We don't even have backup," Anthony said.

"Logan will be around," Sydney reminded him.

"If things go south in the first two minutes, they'll join the party. But they won't get involved right away," Luca cautioned. "If we can handle this on our own, that's best. The last thing we need is to be responsible for one of the Alpha's wolves getting hurt, or worse, dying on us."

"Remember, take the path around to the back door. It used to be his M.O. to chain up his vics in the basement but we don't know what we've got going on here. This is Louisiana, so if there's no basement, he could be in the garage. He doesn't like to make a mess in the main living areas. When we caught the son-of-a-bitch, you would have thought he had a maid, it was so clean in there." Sydney patted Luca's hand and then turned the keys in the ignition. She kept the lights off and put the car in gear. "He's not going to kill me right away. This asshole wants retribution. But he'll want to torture me first. If I can keep him talking long enough for you to get Kade, then we have a chance. You need to find him."

"We'll get him, Syd," Anthony assured her.

"Once we get Kade, we're taking everyone out," Luca told him.

"Scurlock is mine," Sydney reminded them, her voice cold and even.

"Anthony, if we run into any trouble, let me handle it," Luca ordered. "No heroics, you hear me?"

"Jesus, you vampires are bossy. I think I can handle it. We're the ones who got Scurlock the first time."

"Well, he's out now, so as far as I'm concerned humans created this shit show. What I say goes."

"Hey, chill. Save that testosterone. In a few minutes, you'll be able to kick as much ass as you want," she promised.

The conversation died as they approached their destination. She turned into the entrance, noting the huge decorative pillars that loomed on the corners of the property. Ominous gargoyles sat atop their stone perches, warning visitors of the impending danger that awaited them. She slowly navigated the winding herringboned driveway which was lined with Southern magnolia trees. In the distance a light flickered on the porch of the restored colonial revival mansion. Modernized, its exterior appeared freshly painted, its elaborate landscaping illuminated with spotlights. Two Mercedes sedans sat parked in the circle. Instead of driving through the carport, she opted to turn the car around so it was facing the street.

"You guys ready to rock and roll?" Sydney whispered. "'Cause I've got dinner waiting and this one's going down screaming."

She didn't bother waiting for a response as she exited. The front door flew open, and two large men wearing suits came toward her. Their leather masks, while distracting, did little to intimidate her. Showing no fear, she didn't resist as a pair of meaty hands dug into her forearm and hauled her into the house. As she stumbled into the foyer, the stench of cigarettes wafted into her nostrils, and she remembered that Pat was a chain smoker.

Sydney took note of the condition of the home's interior as her captors guided her into a large living room. From its impeccable cherry hardwood floors, to its ornate crown moldings, to the oriental carpets, the luxurious décor had gone unmarred. In the corner, a thick plastic tarp was spread across the floor. Mya's lifeless form lay wedged in the corner, blood splattered around her in speckled flecks. Blindfolded, her wrists tied with a belt, she'd been dressed in a black satin corset. Sydney caught sight of red panties that peeked through a long white tutu. A heavy black leather collar coiled around her neck. Several puncture wounds lined her pale shoulder and Sydney inwardly cringed, knowing she'd been violated. Despite the deadly silence, Sydney breathed in relief as she heard the shallow thump of Mya's heartbeat.

"Mya." Sydney wrenched her arm away from the guard and ran to Mya, her preternatural strength no match for the humans.

She reached for the weapon in her holster and fired off two shots. The bullets whizzed through the air, cleanly piercing through the leather that covered their foreheads. A trace of recognition that she'd just killed two criminals without thought as to whether or not they had a weapon on them flittered through her mind, but the animal inside her would seek a justice of its own. No longer encumbered by human law, she'd seek retribution without guilt.

"It's okay," Sydney assured Mya as she removed the bindings from her wrists. She studied the leather choker, looking for its buckle. As she ran her fingers around the back of Mya's neck, she discovered the small metal studs and rectangular battery. She stifled her disgust and removed the electrocution device, revealing angry flesh burns. "Oh my God, what the hell…"

"No," Mya moaned, to Sydney's relief.

"Hey, Mya. It's Sydney. Remember me from the club?" she asked.

Sydney heard footsteps behind her and went to turn but was too late. The nightmare she'd put away behind bars stood in the vestibule pointing his gun at them. Out of the corner of her eye, she caught the glare of the red laser dot on Mya's forehead.

"Long time no see, detective," he sneered.

"What do you want?" Sydney asked, already knowing full well he wanted her. She prayed Luca and Anthony had found Kade, but until they arrived, she'd have to hold her own.

"I've been waiting for so long, it almost feels like Christmas," he chuckled.

Sydney observed his appearance, noting that he'd lost weight. While still tall in stature, his gangly legs swam in his jeans, his thin tattooed arms poking through a muscle shirt. He looked as if he were a scarecrow, broomsticks for arms with not nearly enough straw stuffed into his middle. She knew better than to mistake his scrawny build for weakness. It was his mind, not his body that his victims feared.

Her heart began to race, anticipating the violence to come. The battle. His imminent death. She'd come to him as judge, jury and executioner and was prepared to carry out the sentence. But it would not come without cost.

"You shouldn't have come to New Orleans." She glanced to the gun in her hand.

"Drop it, detective." He swirled the red dot on Mya's skin, reminding her of his true hostage. "You can probably shoot me. You might even kill me, but I'll definitely kill her. Do you really want to be responsible for ending an innocent life?"

Sydney knew he'd murder Mya in a New York minute. She was certain he was waiting to parade a shackled Kade in front of her, his grand finale of torture. What she didn't know was if there were more victims in the house.

She wished her supernatural senses would kick in so she could hear what was happening in the other parts of the house, but so far, her ears were almost as human as the murderer standing in front of her.

She slowly backed away from Mya. Pat would have to make a choice, her or the girl.

"No, no, no, detective," he chided. "Gun on the ground. Now."

Sydney forced a cold smile onto her face and gently laid the weapon down on the woolen carpet. Adrenaline pumped as she considered her next move. He took a step toward her, and she launched herself at Scurlock. As she tackled him to the floor, he fired off a shot. The slug whizzed by Mya's head, shattering a Tiffany lamp. Sydney ignored the exploding shards of colored glass and wrestled Pat onto his back. She pinned his wrists to the ground, and he spat at her face. The slimy sputum dripped down her temple, and she coughed at the foul-scented nicotine.

"Get off me, bitch!"

"You're dead," Sydney hissed. Her fangs lengthened as she tasted victory.

As she reared her head to bite him, a loud pop fired into the air, and the heat of a bullet sliced into her thigh. Although it pierced her flesh clean through, the silver metal poisoned her system and she was unable to hold onto her prey. Tears streamed down her face, as her back hit the wooden planks. Through the haze of the moisture, the outline of a woman came into view...*Mya*.

"I'm sorry," Mya mumbled. As if she were drugged, her words came out jumbled.

"Why?" Sydney wiped her face with the back of her hand, refusing to give in to the excruciating pain.

"I can't...he's always loved me...mother...mother needs him." The gun tumbled from Mya's hands and Pat shoved to his feet and grabbed her by the back of her neck.

"About time, you dumb bitch. She almost killed me. At least you didn't kill her." He dragged Mya over to the tarp and threw her to the floor.

Confused, Sydney tried to process what was happening. He'd abused Mya, yet she'd saved him. As she pushed up onto her elbows, Sydney heard the click of heels in the hallway. Tearing off her jacket, she wrapped it around her thigh in an attempt to stem the flow of blood pouring out from her wound. The tapping grew closer, and she sensed a vampire was near.

She crawled toward the wall and clutched at it, using it as leverage. But as she hoisted herself upward, she lost her footing and slipped in her own blood. She shoved onto her hands and knees, clawed at the chair rail and fought to right herself against the wall. Pat's maniacal laughter echoed in her ears. She knew he'd let her rally, to prolong her suffering. He'd allowed his victims to heal, even if it took weeks, so that he could torment them over and over.

Heaving for breath, she stared into his seething eyes as he fell back onto the sofa and chuckled. Pat waved the gun, his arms spread wide across the back of the couch. He broke eye contact, and Sydney turned to see who'd caught his attention. Her heart dropped as the vampire entered the room, holding the victim by the back of her hair. Sydney released a cry she hadn't known she possessed as her eyes locked on Samantha's. With her mouth duct taped shut, she was unable to speak, and the tears in her eyes told Sydney that she was unable to use her magic.

"How could you do this?" Sydney exclaimed.

She moved to rescue Samantha, but the pain was too much. As her leg became numb, she shifted all her weight to one foot in an effort to stand.

"Hello, Sydney. We've been expecting you," the vampire told her.

"Kade's going to kill you." Sydney sucked a breath, summoning every last ounce of energy that remained.

The vampire merely laughed, throwing the pregnant prisoner to the ground. Sydney fell reaching to catch Samantha. The shock of her leg hitting the floor shot a stabbing pain throughout her entire body. She grasped at the carpet, dragging herself over to her friend. When Sydney reached Samantha, she took her into her arms, and glared at her attacker. *Dominique.*

⊷❦ *Chapter Twelve* ❦⊷

"I told you not to make a mess." Dominique glared at Pat.

"I swear I'll clean it up. It's her fault. Look what she made me do," he complained.

"You're a disgrace."

"No, stop saying that," he whined.

"Look what you did. All this blood wasted..."

"Let me kill her...she deserves to die. She put me away. She *ruined* my life."

"How can you do this?" Sydney interrupted their conversation.

"Shut up, bitch." He pointed the gun at her.

"There's still the matter of Issacson." Dominique smoothed a stray hair from her face and brushed a tiny speck of lint off her crisp white sleeve.

"I don't care anymore. I just want her dead."

"You never did master torture the way I taught you. Such a disappointment you are." Dominique glanced at Sydney, and gave a strong kick to her injured leg. Ignoring her cries, she approached Mya. "And her, she's never been anything. No matter how hard I've tried, she's failed me."

"If you'd just make us vampires, we wouldn't have to do this..."

"Silence, you idiot. The only reason I brought you down here...*allowed* you to come here into my home was to take her out." She pointed at Sydney. "And you haven't even done that right. Now look what you made me do."

"How could you do this?" Sydney couldn't fathom why Dominique would attack her. "I know we haven't always been friends but this isn't you."

"You don't even know who I am," she snapped.

"Why don't you tell me then, because Kade's going to be here soon and I'll tell you what, he's going to kill you... and him." She looked over to Pat.

"He's not going anywhere."

"Luca's going to find him and they'll be coming for you."

"Yeah well, not anymore. Once he sees that I've got his precious cargo on board, he'll leave Kade with me." Dominique spun and snatched a tissue out of her small purse. She knelt down and began to scour a tiny smudge of blood, which soon blended into a pink blob on the cream-colored carpet. "I can't believe you ruined my rug. It's an antique."

"I didn't mean to do it...accidents happen." Pat scrubbed the barrel of the gun against his chin.

"Must I do everything myself?" Dominique leaned over and grabbed Samantha by her arms, yanking her up to her feet.

"Mother," Pat declared, pushing off the sofa. "This is your responsibility."

Dominique is Pat Scurlock's mother? What the ever loving fuck? If she is his mother, *then who is ...?* Sydney's eyes fell onto Mya, who'd fallen back into a drug-induced haze. Unresponsive, she lay passed out in the corner. Dominique laughed, and Sydney's attention was drawn back to the vampire who dangled Samantha like a rag doll. Shocked, she studied the red-haired vampire, who looked identical to her friend. *No, no, no. Dominique would not do this.*

Sydney focused on Pat as he crossed the room and approached the one he'd called Mother. Sydney began to feel dizzy; she'd lost too much blood. Her heart started to race. If she didn't feed soon, she'd pass out like she'd done in Mya's apartment. Her mind went fuzzy. As if she'd entered an alternative universe, she observed Pat take Dominique's free hand. He began to kiss it, not like a son, but as a lover. Sydney fought the bile that rose in her stomach. By the time his lips met Dominique's, Sydney's vision had begun to blur. She prayed to God that Kade and Luca would arrive soon. She wouldn't last much longer.

Kade's voice bellowed through the robin's-egg-blue steel cellar doors. Anthony secured his gun with both hands, keeping it upright. His heart pounded against his ribs in anticipation. Luca held his fingers to his lips and reached for the handle. Anthony had never been one to cower away from a dangerous situation, but he was well aware that he was no match for the supernatural forces that lay in wait. But having made a connection with Kade, he'd known he'd give his own life to save him.

The creaking storm door flew open, and within seconds he and Luca had broken down the oak door which stood as the home's last defense. As he stepped into the darkness, he choked on the stench of urine. Reaching for his small flashlight, he flicked it on and caught sight of Luca wrestling a vampire into the far corner of the basement. He swiveled to the right and spied a woman lying motionless on a stained futon. Her blouse had been torn open, her neck littered with small bites. Her eyes bulged, blindly staring into the rafters. Certain she was dead, he moved to Kade, who groaned his name.

"It's okay, man." Anthony stifled his reaction as he shone the light onto his friend. Tethered by silver to sewer pipes, Kade's pale skin had been marred with cigarette burns.

"Get me out of here," Kade pleaded; his voice, usually strong, wavered.

"How many are there?"

"Maybe four or five. I'm not sure."

"I got ya."

"Tony...there's a guard. Where's Luca?" Kade coughed, his chin lolling forward onto his chest.

"I'm good," Luca yelled from across the room. The clatter of wood breaking sounded in the corner.

"Is he smiling?" Kade joked.

"You know he loves a good ass kicking." Anthony couldn't believe Kade was making light of the situation, given his condition. He gingerly tried to remove the silver chains, but they'd been wound in knots, a padlock securing them in place. "You couldn't get tied up by something a little easier? Cuffs I could do. Rope even. But a fucking padlock? Jesus Christ."

"Stop complaining."

"Yeah, yeah, gotcha." Anthony laughed. He pushed up onto his feet, searching for a tool to open the lock. It wasn't lost on him that Kade had called him Tony. As long as he'd known him, Kade had maintained a formal disposition, one that set him apart from vampires and mortals alike. Anthony suspected that his vulnerability had altered his usual reserved demeanor, but he decided not to call attention to it. A loud grunt sounded from the corner, and he flashed the light over to Luca, who'd taken a right hook to his cheek. "You need some help over there?"

"Hell, no. We're just having a little fun." Luca dug his foot into the guy's chest, and sent him flying across the room. "Now would you stop jerkin' off over there and get Kade loose?"

"Goddamned fucking vampires." Anthony shoved boxes to the side, looking for something he could use as a tool. He picked up what he thought was a screwdriver but it was made out of plastic. Hurling it across the room, he spied what he needed in a cobwebbed corner. "The only reason I'm here is because Sydney was once human. A very nice human."

"We were all human once. Luca's right. Stop fucking around and get this off me," Kade goaded.

"Ungrateful motherfuck…" Anthony wrapped his hands around an axe and hauled it out of the debris. It lodged in the boxes, and he continued to yank it toward him until he broke it free.

"No need for name calling." Luca smashed an antique crib headboard over his knee, and broke a jagged shard off into his fist.

"Scurlock is human," Kade reminded him.

"Glass houses." Luca lunged at the vampire.

"Pot meet kettle." Kade spat up blood and a sickening gurgle came forth from his throat. His eyes fluttered shut.

"Fuck, no. Now, you listen to me, Kade. You're not going to die on me, man." Anthony rushed to Kade's side, tapping the side of his cheek with the palm of his hand. Pulling out the silver, he extended it far enough so he could break it off without snaring one of Kade's arms. He lifted the sharp instrument into the air and swung down hard. The metal sparked as the chain split open, and Kade's head slammed against the concrete floor. "Not on my watch."

"Shit." Anthony threw the axe onto the floor. Out of the corner of his eye he saw Luca staking the vampire. "About fucking time."

"What?" Luca asked breathlessly, his lips curled in victory.

"Help me. There's somethin' wrong with him." Anthony slid his hands under Kade's arms and dragged him into the middle of the room. He sat on the concrete, pulling his injured friend onto his lap. Cradling him, he shined the flashlight onto his skin and checked his pulse.

"He's gonna be fine," Luca assured Anthony. He knelt down and thumbed open one of Kade's eyelids. "He's gotta eat, though."

"I got this." Anthony rolled up a sleeve. "Check on the girl over there. I think she's dead."

"Aw, shit." .

"You know her?"

"Name's Gemma. Used to be a donor. She's gone."

"This isn't working." Anthony held his arm to Kade's mouth but he didn't move to feed.

"You aren't doing it right." Luca stood and towered above him. "Open his lips with your fingers. Put your skin right on his tongue. He's alive. He'll get the hint."

"I swear to God, I'm never hangin' out with the two of you again." Anthony reluctantly did as Luca told him. Recalling his reaction to Sydney's bite, he attempted to remain calm. He wasn't sure which would be worse, the sting or the ecstasy. He'd never been attracted to a man before but with Kade and Sydney, lines became blurred.

"You do realize Sydney's up there? Hurry up with it."

"Fuck off." Anthony sucked a breath as Kade's tongue traced a warm path along his wrist. His body jerked; fangs sliced into his skin. "Oh shit, oh shit, oh shit…ahh."

"Buck up. You humans are such weaklings," Luca chastised with disdain.

"This is so wrong." The rush of pleasure overcame Anthony as Kade suctioned his blood. Masculine hands grabbed his forearm, tightening the seal on his flesh. His cock jerked in response and his eyes rolled up into his head. "Is it over yet? I can't do this. Come on, Kade. Are we good, man?"

"We're good," Kade breathed, licking at the wound.

"Hold on a second. Jesus," Anthony said, his semi-hard dick pressing at his zipper.

"Shake it off. Let's get moving." Kade jumped to his feet, energized by his feeding.

"Yeah, I'll get right to that." Anthony gingerly pushed to his feet and adjusted himself.

"I think your donor liked it," Luca noted.

"I'm not his fucking donor." Anthony pulled his shirt down over the bulge in his pants.

"Of course he liked it. They all like it when I do it." Kade smiled at Anthony and clapped his hand on his shoulder, then shoved him toward Luca.

"You guys are assholes, you know that, right?" Anthony retrieved his gun from its holster.

"We love you too." Kade moved to the stairs. "Now where the hell is my woman?"

"How do you know we let her come with us?" Anthony asked.

"I know my mate. There is no 'letting' Sydney do anything. I knew she'd come for me. It was just a matter of when." Kade ran up to her, his feet barely touching the steps.

Chapter Thirteen

A gunshot sounded and Kade tore through the house. As he rounded into the living room, confusion crossed his face. Dominique smiled coldly back at him, her arm wrapped around Samantha's neck. He held his hands up to halt Anthony from coming any further, but it didn't stop Luca from bursting past him.

"Don't move another step," Dominique sneered, her fangs inches from Samantha's neck. "I always enjoyed the taste of a pregnant woman. There's nothing like the innocence of the unborn."

"Get the fuck off her," Luca yelled.

"Dom. What's going on here?" Kade regarded her face. The woman before him looked like Dominique but the fine lines around her lips appeared deeper, as if she was a long time smoker.

His eyes fell to Sydney, who stared blankly back at him. Her sallow complexion indicated significant blood loss, and his anger spiked at the sight. A flicker of recognition flared in her eyes, and he suspected she was purposely feigning despondence.

"My son has a bone to pick with your fiancée...her bones," she laughed, tightening her grip on Samantha's neck. "And this witch? Pity she can't chant her mumbo jumbo with her mouth taped shut."

"Let her go," Luca demanded, taking a step toward her.

"Get back," she hissed. "This is between Patty and his detective. If you leave right now, I may let her go." She licked Samantha's neck clear up to her cheek and temple. "Or not." She gave a wicked smile and lapped at the skin. "I've forgotten how delicious witches can be. Mmm...I can taste the infant in her belly."

"No!" Pat waved his gun in the air. "Kade stays here. I want to play. You never let me play, mother."

"Only when you've earned it," she chided. "Look what you've done to my house. A punishment is in order."

"No!" He stomped his foot like a petulant child.

"All of you leave now, and the witch stays alive," she explained calmly.

"I'm not leaving you." Luca's eyes locked on Samantha's. She violently shook her head. Smothered garbled words came from underneath her gag.

"See? The little woman agrees with me," Dominique told him.

"I don't know who you are or what you did with Dominique, but you aren't her." Kade's fangs descended and he caught sight of Sydney reaching for her gun that had been tossed underneath the sofa.

"Clever, clever boy. Doesn't matter much what I am now, does it? I hold

499

the cards." With ease, her fangs pierced Samantha's creamy white flesh. Instantly, she retracted them, laughing as blood ran down her face. Samantha began to heave, the adhesive gag restricting her breathing.

"Stop, you're hurting her. Take me," Luca pleaded, inching closer.

"Tsk, tsk, tsk…you've always been a killjoy, Macquarie." She licked her lips and glanced at Pat and then to Sydney. "Kill her now. I'm bored."

"But mother…"

"No arguing," she spat at him. "No one better move to stop him or the witch dies too."

Pat slowly turned to Sydney, who raised her gaze to meet his. With his gun trained on her, he reached for her collar. Kade had seen her sneak her weapon behind her back, but he couldn't be sure that she had enough strength to use it. Sydney gave her attacker a bitter smile, her sharp teeth beckoning him. As he hauled her to her feet, she spun around and aimed at Dominique. Firing off a shot, she clipped her shoulder.

"No!" Pat backhanded Sydney across the face in response.

The sight of his mate being attacked sent Kade into a rage that was only slightly tempered when Sydney stood firm. Instead of faltering, she rebounded from the blow to her cheek and laughed at Pat's surprised expression. She lunged at him, pinning him onto his back. Kade made a move toward Pat, but Mya leapt to her feet, a knife in her hand. Her attempt to thwart him was interrupted as Anthony fired his weapon, his bullet slicing into her thigh. By the time Kade had reached Sydney, she had Pat's face wedged against the floor with her hand. Like a rabid dog, she'd gone feral, with her fangs poised to kill. Kade watched with pride as she took her prize, tearing her teeth into his flesh.

Maniacal laughter emanated from Dominique, and he caught sight of her dragging Samantha across the room. Holding Luca's gaze, she lodged her fangs in Samantha's shoulder. Luca charged and jammed his fingers up into Dominique's lips, trying to pry her jaw open, but like a vise, she tightened her bite. Kade slipped behind Dominique and dug his claws deep into her neck. She thrashed but didn't relent as his fingers strummed at her carotid. Extending his nail further, he sliced at it, sawing away the tendons that held it in place.

Blood streamed from the wound as she fought death. Kade closed his eyes, relieved when life drained from her body. She slumped in his arms, finally releasing Samantha into Luca's waiting embrace. Kade stumbled back onto the ground, carefully placing Dominique's limp form on the carpet. Drenched in her blood, he fought the regret that he hadn't helped her, stopped her from evolving into a debauched nightmare. Despite her identical appearance to Dominique, he still doubted that the life he had taken was that of his friend. Conflicted, his instincts warred with what appeared to be the reality of the situation.

Kade gazed over to Sydney, who wore a sympathetic expression. Pat lay dead and mangled beside her. Physically, she'd healed herself, stealing his essence. Shoving off the ground, Kade went to her, carefully scooping her up into his arms. As her tears began to flow, he crushed her to his chest. The familiar scent of his mate calmed his beast, his fangs rescinding.

"It's okay, love," he whispered.

"He's dead."

"It's over." Kade's heart broke for her, aware that she was still far too human to go unaffected by her actions.

"I killed him…I knew I would but I feel…" she stammered.

"You did what you had to do. You knew this world…my world, it wasn't your own. But now, it is." A surge of guilt for changing her into a vampire rushed fresh through his mind. "I wish things were different."

"No, don't…don't apologize. Whatever just happened, I'd do it again. You're the only thing that matters to me…nothing else." As the shock wore off, she pushed away from Kade and scanned the room for Samantha. Her friend shook and cried within Luca's arms, but was still alive. Although Samantha was a witch and had the capability to heal herself, she'd been badly attacked. "Oh my God. Is she okay? The baby?"

"They'll both be all right, but I've gotta get her out of here," Luca responded.

"Thank God," she breathed in relief. "Where's Tony?"

In the melee, he'd gone missing, but Kade heard his voice coming from the hallway. He glanced over and caught him talking to Mya, who was laid out on the hardwood floor. Her eyelashes blinked but she wasn't verbally responding

"He's okay. He's right there," Kade growled.

"Mya… I don't understand what happened. I just don't know…"

"Don't know what?"

"How they're all linked together. Scurlock said Dominique was his mother. That makes no sense. And Mya…they knew her somehow. She shot me…protecting *him*. I don't get it. He tortured her. Why would she protect him? My God, you should see her neck." Sydney shook her head in confusion. She moved to go to Anthony but Kade wrapped his fingers around her wrists.

"Leave them. Tony can handle it." Kade intentionally held her back. While Sydney appeared to be calm, he was concerned she'd kill again.

"We can't just leave him."

"We'll text P-CAP. Look, Tony's cuffing her right now. She's not going anywhere."

"But we need to know why she did this."

"Soon enough, love. Right now, what we need to do is get home."

"And Dom…why would she do this? That woman…she looks like Dominique but it's crazy. Is that really her? Something is off here. I don't get it." Sydney rubbed her eyes with the back of her hand.

"We'll talk about it later." Kade still hadn't come to terms with the fact that he'd killed Dominique. It was out of character for her to commit such a heinous crime. Something about the way she talked, the slight changes to her skin was contrary to what he'd known for decades. He wondered if his mind was playing tricks on him, but like Sydney, he still had trouble believing it had been her.

"I know what you're thinking.... how else could she have gotten to Samantha? We need to talk to her and find out what happened," Sydney continued.

"Not now."

Sydney nodded in agreement, acquiescing to his suggestion. Kade stood and lifted her into his arms. On any other night, he'd stay and investigate, searching for a resolution to the unresolved questions that remained. Whatever answers they sought could wait until morning. Tomorrow was a new day, and the only thing he needed was to have his mate, to be lying in bed with her, in her, to claim her again.

Chapter Fourteen

The hot spray pelted her skin and she dipped her head forward. The wretched remains of death washed away down the drain with any remnants of regret she'd harbored. Reborn as vampire, she'd now live by Kade's law. Her decision made, she'd never return to the police force. She wasn't sure what she'd do moving forward, but she was certain her immortal life with Kade promised opportunities beyond her wildest comprehension.

Her thoughts turned to Samantha, who on the way home swore up and down that the red-haired vampire wasn't Dominique. As soon as they'd returned home, Samantha had been checked by the doctor, and neither she nor her baby had been seriously harmed.

Sydney had always known that as a vampire, Kade couldn't father a child. It was only through Samantha's magic that she and Luca had conceived. Recalling the demon's attack, Sydney held her hand to her belly, grieving for the child she'd only recently discovered she'd wanted. It was a bitter pill to swallow, knowing that she was physically incapable of bringing life into this world.

"You're thinking too hard, love," she heard Kade say as he rounded the glass enclosure, coming up behind her.

"I suppose I am," she replied.

"You upset about tonight?" he asked.

She moaned and laid the back of her head against his shoulder. His cock prodded her back, causing her to smile. Even when her mood had soured, Kade could lift her spirits.

"Hmm…no answer?" He kissed her temple.

"Just thinking," she hedged.

"About tonight?"

"Samantha and her baby. Ava, too."

"The Alpha's child? Were you thinking about the demon?" He paused. "The night you were attacked?"

"Maybe. No. I don't know…just about babies, period." Sydney held her breath as Kade's silence hung in the air.

"Wait." Kade spun her around in his arms. He took her chin into his hands and guided it upward until her eyes met his. "We haven't talked about this very often. I always assumed…"

Sydney gave him a small smile. She found it amusing that he was searching for words to articulate what he suspected.

"No…you never wanted any…Are you trying to tell me…?"

"I don't know…just forget it," she lied. Attempting to look away, her effort was thwarted as his hold grew tighter.

"Look at me, Sydney."

She did as he said, her heart pounding in her chest. *Is he angry with me? I should never have brought it up.*

"Do you want a child?" Kade asked softly. He released his tight grip, sliding his fingers upward to caress her cheek.

Sydney pressed her face into his palm, accepting his comfort. She nodded, closing her eyes. It broke her heart to come to this realization at a time in her life when it was no longer a possibility. Tears brimmed, and she lifted her lids, meeting his gaze.

"Don't cry…it's okay."

"But I shouldn't want this…it's not fair to you."

"Hey now, just because I never said I wanted a child with you didn't mean that I didn't want one. The only thing that's mattered is being with you." His lips grazed her forehead. "I've been alone for what seems like forever. And when you came along…Goddess, I just couldn't have been more shocked. You breathed life back into me."

"But…"

"Let me finish. When you said you didn't want kids, it was a relief to me only because I knew I couldn't give them to you, but never because I wouldn't want you to carry my child. If you'd told me you wanted a baby when we'd first met, I wouldn't have pursued you. I wouldn't steal your right to have children from you."

"I didn't want kids. It's just being around Ava and seeing Samantha all these months. I can't explain it." Flustered by her own feelings, she struggled to express why she'd changed her mind.

"Six months ago, you were a young woman who had options. People grow, Sydney. Not all people know they want children. Sometimes we change, our priorities change."

"I feel like I should have known. But I'm a different person now."

"It's natural to want more. I want more. I regret we waited to get married and I want to do it…as in yesterday."

She laughed and slid her palms up his chest.

"I'm not joking. Who knew this was going to happen this week? Some asshole comes back and tries to murder you. I could've died too. I'm not saying it's going to happen again, I'm just saying we've got to live life as if we were human…as if this day could be our last. We're not terribly immortal when staked. No matter how much we'd like to predict the future, that isn't one of our abilities."

"I wish."

"Yeah, me, too. So that's why I want to get married this week. No waiting."

"Okay." Kade never ceased to amaze her with his decisiveness. Even if she wanted to, she couldn't deny him.

"And after that, we can figure out this baby thing."

"But we can't..."

"We couldn't have kids when you were a human, but maybe there's something we can do. Look at Samantha and Luca...they're pregnant."

"But she's a witch."

"True. But even vampires hold a little magic. Sam might be able to help us. We can ask Léopold too. Just because I haven't heard of it ever happening, doesn't mean it doesn't exist. I'm old, but not nearly as old as him. He'll help. And if they can't help us, there're people...you know, agencies who can help us."

"Adoption?"

"Of sorts. Not human of course, but there are all kinds of beings around us, love. And not everyone is ready or wants to be a parent. It's an option."

"Are you serious?" Sydney asked. Her heart felt as if it'd burst from the hope he'd given her.

"Completely."

"I love you so much," she cried, squeezing him tight.

"I love you, too." He raked his fingers up into the wet strands of her hair, bringing her lips to meet his. "No more tears. We got this."

"Yes..."

Breathless, she welcomed his tongue as it swept against her own. Her nipples stabbed into his muscular chest as he commanded her body. Strong hands gripped her thigh, wrapping it around his waist. The cool tiles against her back contrasted with the explosive heat that grew between their slick bodies. Delirious from his kiss, she rocked her aching pussy against his leg. She bit at his lips, and reached for his rigid shaft, her fingers teasing its crown. Before she had a chance to stroke him, he'd dropped to his knees, nudging her open with his firm shoulder.

"Wider." Kade's fingers flittered over her hipbone.

Obeying, she stepped aside, giving him full access. Her heart raced as his eyes flickered to red before focusing on his task. The first lash of his tongue to her clit startled her and she reached for his head to steady herself.

"Don't move," he ordered, his warm breath teasing her pussy.

The dominating tone of his voice spiked her arousal and she whimpered as he sucked her sensitive nub into his mouth. His fingernails scraped her bottom, crushing her mound to his face. He feasted upon her, and she shuddered as his fingertip teased her entrance.

"Kade," she breathed.

"Tonight," he swiped at her clit with his flat tongue, "we begin anew."

"Yes, that's it." Her hips tilted forward, her body trembling as he plunged two fingers inside her. She rose onto the balls of her feet, the rush of orgasm shaking her to her core.

"Hmm." He hummed at her lips, flicking her swollen pearl and sucking it into his mouth.

"Ah yeah...like that. Oh, fuck, don't stop. Yes, yes," she screamed. Heaving for breath, her body fell limp as the waves of climax rolled through her.

Giving her no time to recoup, he spun her around and bent her at the waist so her ass was exposed to him. She trembled in anticipation. More than needing to be possessed, she sought to lose herself in the ecstasy of all that was her mate.

She groaned aloud as he buried himself inside her from behind, filling her to the hilt. With her palms flat on the misty wall, she braced herself for each forceful thrust, the sound of his flesh slamming against hers. The sweet prick of his fangs at her shoulder held her in place, reminding her to be ever mindful of the moment. His warm lips on her skin, the scent of him in the air while wrapped in his strength overwhelmed her.

"So hard...yes!" She gave a cry of pleasure as he fucked her with unrestrained fervor.

"Ah yeah. Jesus, you feel good."

"Don't. Ever. Stop."

"This is only round one, baby," he teased.

"You promise?" He pounded into her, and she cried out loud. "Ahh."

"You have no idea. Plus, you owe me a spanking for coming to get me by yourself."

"What?" Her pussy tightened around him at the thought of it. Sydney submitted to no one....except Kade.

"You heard me." He scraped his sharp teeth across her pale skin. Drawing a bubbling line of blood, he lapped at it with his tongue.

"Yes...please," she cried, the sweet pain of his fangs at her neck.

"I love the sound of you begging," he grunted, slamming into her. Reaching to her breast, he pinched her ripe tip.

"Please, Kade...ahh." The twinge on her nipple sent a jolt straight to her core. She gasped, attempting to stem her orgasm.

"Please what?" He laughed, knowing he couldn't hold back much longer.

"Bite me...Just do it...Please."

"Since you asked so nicely." Without further warning, he struck, his teeth penetrating deep into her shoulder.

Sydney screamed, shuddering as the ripples of ecstasy tore through her. Limp against the wall, she panted; intense spasms consumed her.

Obsessed with her happiness, Kade plunged into his mate. Drinking in her delicious essence, he groaned as he came inside her. As his pulsating release subsided, he rejoiced in victory. His mate reclaimed, life was complete.

⤛⚙· *Chapter Fifteen* ⚙⤜

Sydney stirred in Kade's arms. Asleep, he gently snored and she smiled. Renewed with hope, her chest constricted with love. The man who owned her heart had given her life again, never giving up on her, even when she'd wanted to give up on herself.

She moved to leave the bed, and a gentle arm pulled her back inside the warm confines of the sheets.

"Where do you think you're going?" he asked.

"Nowhere," she giggled.

"Liar."

"I just wanted to see what Tony was doing."

"Ah…leaving me for another man?" His eyes narrowed, but the lilt of his smile told her he was joking.

"Not on your life."

"I couldn't share you." He twirled his forefinger into her hair.

"You don't have to. Our time with Tony…you know how I feel about him, but he's not you." She kissed him lightly on his chest.

"We can still play with him every now and then, though," He raised a playful eyebrow at her. "That is, if that's something you desire."

"You do surprise me, Mister Issacson." Kade had always pushed her sexually, testing the limits of where she'd find her greatest pleasure.

"I enjoy the detective's company. He'll leave us soon, but he was there for you…for me. We owe him," Kade added, his tone serious.

"He's true blue. Always has been," she told him. "But you're right…he's going home soon. We'll need a donor."

"I don't want strangers in between us."

"We can find someone we both like. Many someones, perhaps. But for food only, nothing more."

"Agreed."

"Thank you for understanding." She smiled, relieved that he didn't want to have a sexual relationship with donors. It wasn't as if he'd ever asked. But after what they'd done with Anthony, she'd wondered about his expectations.

A knock sounded and Kade drew the sheet over his mate's bared breasts.

"Come in," he called.

Anthony sheepishly entered the room, his gaze averted. Sydney laughed, realizing he was still unsure of how to proceed with their relationship. She was relieved when Kade broke the ice.

"Come sit, my friend." Anthony went to the chair across the room and

Kade waved him over to the bed and patted the comforter. "Here."

Anthony shook his head and smiled, but acquiesced.

"I, uh, just came to tell you that I'm gonna go by the hospital and see Mya." He sat next to Sydney and put a palm on her covered thigh.

"I have to tell ya, I'm not sure about her," Sydney said. Seeking more of a connection, she placed her hand on top of his. She hadn't seen Anthony since last night. She'd briefly fed from him, without much interaction. It was only later that Kade had told her what he'd done to save him.

"From my perspective, she was in cahoots with Pat and Dominique," Kade speculated. "Granted, I never once saw her downstairs. But I never saw Dominique either."

"Yeah, I dunno. She was loaded up with H," Anthony added. Preliminary blood tests had shown she'd been injected with heroin. "But the docs say she's not an addict. Whatever she had in her, she'd been given in the past forty-eight hours."

"When I met her, she seemed so...I don't know...innocent. I guess my instincts were way off. She did hesitate when she shot me, and the way Pat talked about her, it was as if he knew her."

"Well, we got her covered down at the hospital. The docs called me and said she's coming round. She's starting to talk. I'll go see what she has to say. Given the crime scene in her apartment and indications of possible sexual assault, the DA's probably gonna let her go," Anthony guessed.

"But what if it was staged?" Kade protested.

"What if it wasn't?" he countered. "She was on drugs. With the amount she had in her, coupled with the apparent torture, I don't know. I, of all people, would like to see her go down after what she did to Sydney, but I saw those burns on her neck. I can't imagine her letting someone do that to her willingly. She was barely alive."

"I'll give you all a call when I find out more. So, uh, I was thinking..." Anthony paused, his eyes locked on Sydney's. "You gonna be okay? I mean, I can take some time off if you need me. I kind of wanted to stick around and wrap things up with this case anyway."

"Yeah, I'm fine...thanks to you. You saved me. Saved us." Sydney sat up and kissed his cheek once, her lips inches from his. She turned and smiled at Kade who sensed her arousal. She knew she'd never make love to Anthony, nor would she love him, but if he was willing, she knew for certain, they'd feed with him again. "We'd love to have you stay with us. You're always welcome in our home."

"Did he tell you what he did to me?" Anthony blushed and leaned back onto the heels of his hands.

"He told me you saved him. And for that I'm very, very grateful." She smiled.

"So am I. There's no way we can repay you for what you did," Kade added.

"You don't have to. We're friends. But I meant what I said last night. I'm not going with Luca again. He's kind of a dick."

"Yeah, he can be." Kade laughed.

"He's, um, difficult to get to know," Sydney offered. "Especially when you're a human. You have to give him time to warm up to you."

"Yeah, I can see him warmin' up all right. And then bitin' me like a police dog. No thanks." Anthony stood and brushed his palms down his slacks. "Your girl there seems to have tamed him. You should have seen her barkin' out orders before we went in. She told him right then she was going in alone."

"Yeah, about that," Kade growled. A dangerous smile crossed his face.

Sydney's heart stopped, aware that he was about to do something she might not like.

"Listen, sounds like you two have somethin' to work out. I'll see you guys later. Have fun, Syd." Anthony winked and walked out the bedroom.

"What?" Sydney laughed. "What did I do?"

Kade stripped back the sheets. Gooseflesh rippled across Sydney's exposed skin. The cool air was tempered by the heat that grew between her legs. Like wild prey, she froze. Unsure what he'd do, she tensed in anticipation. A gasp escaped her lips as he reached for her waist, dragging her torso across his legs. Her cheek brushed the soft cotton and she gave a nervous laugh.

"What are you doing? Ahh…" She squirmed as the light touch of his fingers grazed over her hair, trailing between her shoulder blades and onto the small of her back.

"You are a naughty vampire." His hand continued further over her buttocks to the back of her thigh.

"Maybe I like being wicked." She kicked her feet, feigning escape.

"Do you now?" His cock grew thick against the side of her belly.

"Yes, I do. Are you planning on doing something about it?" she goaded. As she went to move, he pressed a firm hand to her shoulder, pinning her still.

"I've been looking forward to this ever since you ran from me back to Philadelphia," he said, a dark tone to his voice. "Then you ran a second time to Embo. And going into danger alone…without Luca? I'm afraid you need a lesson."

"Looking forward to what? Ow…ah," she cried as a hard slap landed on her bottom. *Holy hell.* He'd teased her for months that he'd spank her. He'd even bound her to the bed on occasion, yet the sting of his palm came as an erotic surprise.

"You see," he said, smacking the other cheek. "I know you better than you know yourself. The rush you get from the danger. How do you like it now, my little vamp?"

"I don't know…I…" The wetness in her swollen folds dripped down her thigh and she attempted to conceal her arousal with words. "I don't like…"

He slapped her hard, caressing her reddened flesh. Sydney reached for his cock and swiped her finger across its wet slit. Her ass tingled in sweet pain, yet as she yearned for more, he stopped. She'd hoped that he'd continue, and was taken by surprise when his fingers glided down her crevice. A thick digit plunged deep inside her pussy and she moaned, pressing back into the erotic invasion. Retreating, he coated his fingers in her wetness and entered her again, this time circling her puckered flesh with his thumb.

"Oh God, Kade…what are you…?" With the shock of the intrusion, her fingers loosened around his dick. Unable to move, she did nothing…only felt, immersing herself in the sensation her mate sought to give her.

"You may be a novice, love, but I am a master," he told her.

"Ah…yes." He continued to tease her bottom as his remaining fingers scissored around her swollen lips, pinching her clit, never actually touching her taut nub. Her clit ached in arousal. "I need more…I need…"

"No more running."

"No, no, no," she protested as he removed his fingers from inside her. She gave a muffled whine into the covers. Her hips pumped against his legs seeking relief, but none came. "Ahh…I'm so close."

"I love your body," he said softly. "I love all of you."

"Don't stop…" She grew dizzy with need, his fingers brushing over her clitoris.

"You're so fucking wet." Entering her once again, he allowed the tip of his thumb to press gently into her anus.

"Yes…that feels…it's so wrong, but oh my God. Kade…easy…oh, yes…ah," she cried.

Quivering, her climax slammed into her. Tears brimmed from her lashes as she began to shake. Her fingers fisted his cock as she writhed against his hand. As the spasms subsided, she pushed onto her elbows and knees. Her tousled hair flew in all directions as she whirled between his legs.

Never releasing his swollen flesh, she returned his devious smile as she dipped her head and brought her lips to his cock. Her tongue darted out and lapped at his salty essence. She licked underneath his hard length, and he groaned, hitting his head upon the headboard. Sydney laughed at his response, knowing that despite his declaration that he was the master, she'd mastered him as well. Taking him into her mouth, she sucked and laved at his soft skin. Clutching his hips, she swallowed him down to his root.

His fingers raked into her scalp, guiding her up and down. He lasted only minutes before stopping her, lifting her chin to meet his gaze.

"Come to me," he directed, wiping her lip with his thumb.

She did as he said, climbing atop her mate. Grazing her hands down his ripped abs, she hovered above him, his tip prodding her entrance. He gave her a wicked smile and flipped her onto her back. She squealed in delight as he pinned her arms to the bed.

"Make love to me," she whispered. Her quickening breath struggled to keep up with her heartbeat. She knew what was coming but nothing ever prepared her for his possession.

"For the rest of your life," he promised.

She gasped as he pushed deep inside her, his thick flesh stretching her. As he filled her, she clutched at his shoulders, her fangs dropping. She reveled in the sharp penetration, the walls of her core clamping down around his shaft. He rocked inside her, taking her pink nipple between his lips. Her hips met his, thrust for thrust, his pelvis stroking her clit in a tantalizing rhythm. His sharp teeth descended, piercing her full breast.

An orgasm rolled through her as he sucked her gently. Never giving her quarter, he increased his pace. She rebounded from her climax only to be driven to the precipice of ecstasy once again.

"Kade!" Her head thrashed on the pillow as she screamed.

He bit at her lips, silencing her with his savage kiss. She gave back what she got, biting, their tongues probing each other's. He pounded into her and she rose to meet his need. Moving to accept his cock, she lifted her hips. As he slammed into Sydney, her pussy pulsated around his length. Only the taste of her mate would suffice, and she sought to give him the pleasure he'd given her hundreds of times. He closed the distance, offering her his neck. Without hesitation, she bit down, her fangs slicing into his taut flesh. His powerful blood rushed down her throat, and she came hard, her body shuddering in release.

Kade cried out loud, his explosive orgasm blasting through him. He ground his body against hers. Erupting inside her, he surged into climax. As she laved at the wounds on his skin, he rolled onto his back, never letting her go.

For two hundred years, he'd been alone, and he'd almost lost the love of his life. Two hearts had once again been brought together. The death of her humanity brought to life again, reaffirming their commitment. As she fell asleep on his chest, the emotion he'd held at bay surfaced. He'd never been more grateful for what he'd been given: his soon-to-be wife, a future family. For eternity, they'd be lost in each other's embrace.

◦ Epilogue ◦

Mya smiled as the elevator numbers ticked by above her. She'd easily bypassed the detective in the hospital, her appearance once again altered to suit her purpose. Her only regret was allowing Pat to suck her into his epic fail of a plan to kill Sydney Willows. Not only had she lived, they'd been forced to kidnap the redheaded vampire. Hostages were always a burden. With her still alive, she'd have to deal with her sometime.

Mya reached underneath the floral silk scarf tied stylishly around her neck and fingered the newly healed scabs. She supposed that receiving pain could be a means to an end. A shame it hadn't played out the way Pat had wanted. Mya never played the victim well, though. Pat had known it when he'd asked for her help. She laughed to herself, knowing full well that her sadistic nature would always take precedence over any man's desire to bend her.

As the doors slid open, she smiled. Her plane ride had been filled with delightful dreams of pain. Some would call them nightmares. She'd call them a wet dream laced in blood. She reveled in the fear, excited to share it with her victims.

In truth, they got what they deserved. Nothing was ever as simple as it seemed. No one was one hundred percent innocent nor were they guilty. The spectrum of evil was as wide as the ocean, its waves readying to drown those who stood in its path.

Katrina Livingston, sister of Tristan, Alpha of Lyceum Wolves, would suffer greatly for the sins of others and perhaps her own. Within minutes, Mya would have her to do with as she pleased. As she exited and rolled her red leather carry-on down the hallway, she considered the implements of pain she'd packed for her session.

It only took her seconds to reach the young wolf's apartment. *It's entertaining to play with wolves*, she mused. Vampires were far too easy to kill, taking the thrill out of the hunt. She reached for the welcome heart that hung on the door, tracing her fingers over the last name: *Livingston*. All was well with her life.

With the excitement of New Orleans, she'd almost forgotten her commitment to her new project. She would have loved to have stayed in the south a bit longer. A shame, really, that she'd been caught by the detective.

Her phone buzzed, and she retrieved her purse to view the text message. Pleased, she glanced at the photo and smiled. His caretakers had seen that he stayed just how she'd left him, bound naked in the dark.

She could have left him for weeks, she knew. Immortality was a delicious benefit when torturing supernaturals. Whether it be for revenge or pleasure,

512

with nothing but time, she'd always met her goals, carrying out her devious plans at her leisure. She glanced at the image again, sliding her fingers across the glass to enlarge it. A tingle of delight shivered through her body as she studied his face. His blond hair had grown longer. Through the waterfall of strands covering his face, she could taste the anger emanating from his eyes. She smiled, delighted she'd elicited her intended response.

Unfazed by the Alpha's obvious discomfort, she tossed her cell in her purse. The big bad wolf, Jax Chandler, could wait a bit longer. She knocked on the door, adrenaline rushing through her veins. *Let the fun begin.*

JAX

·❦· *Chapter One* ·❦·

Shackled to the dungeon wall, Jax had never for a second lost focus. *Seized.* *Tortured.* The Alpha would have his revenge. The beast stirred, calculating its escape. Its blood boiled, raging at the monster that had captured him.

Thoughts of the night he'd been kidnapped flashed through his mind. He'd been sitting in his friend, Finn's, nightclub drowning his troubles in a bottle of scotch, mourning the death of his beta, Nick. Getting drunk hadn't dulled his senses enough to curtail his heroic tendencies. When he'd spied a woman falling unconscious on the dance floor, he'd rushed to her side. Stunned, he'd thought he recognized the injured beauty. *Katrina Livingston.*

At one time, the Alpha had suspected she could have been his mate. They'd met at a holiday party. A simple handshake had pricked a sexual awareness that he'd never experienced with another female. The strange sensation had temporarily abated after he'd thought she'd left, and he'd reasoned it'd been a fluke. But later in the evening, he'd found her on the balcony, taking in the sight of winter's first snowflakes, and they'd connected.

Sitting next to the outdoor fireplace, she'd accepted his jacket. Discussing everything from publishing to ice skating, their conversation had lasted nearly two hours. They'd laughed and discovered they both loved visiting New Orleans. An artist, she'd been born and raised in Louisiana, but had moved to Philadelphia with her brother. He'd asked her on a date, wishing to take her on a tour of his city, but she simply smiled, a sad expression washing over her face. When Jax had gone to the bar to get drinks, he'd returned to find that she'd disappeared.

It wasn't as if he'd known for certain she was his future mate, but the nagging suspicion had driven him to track her down in Philadelphia. At first she'd merely refused to talk with him, not answering his calls. In his typical determined style, Jax had taken it further, contacting her brother, Tristan, Alpha of Lyceum Wolves. When he'd accused him of attempting to force a mating, Jax had been confused. While it was true that he'd aggressively pursued Katrina, he'd never in any way attempted to coerce her into his pack. The disagreement had escalated, nearly inciting a war between him and her brother.

He recalled the fateful night at the club. When he'd witnessed someone who looked like Katrina falling ill, he'd gone soft, rushing to her side. Despite everything that had happened, his protective instinct had driven him to remain with her, insisting he accompany her in the ambulance. The hazy memory lingered, and Jax still couldn't be sure what had happened next. Katrina had transformed into something foreign, something evil. The creature wielded dark magick, injecting him with the poison and rendering him unconscious. During his captivity, it had appeared to him as different people, and he'd questioned his sanity.

Jax licked the crust from his lips; the iron-tanged blood only served to remind him of the pain they'd inflicted. All that had been lost. Nick, his beta, had died in battle, his essence soaking into the bayou mud. Despite the tragedy, his freedom robbed, dignity remained wrapped around the Alpha like a steel cloak. Nothing would change the inevitability of the moment or deter him from his task. Every lash of the whip had sharpened his resolve to exact vengeance upon the perpetrator. Deliberate and calm, he'd strategized his attack. Patience had superseded his urge for reprisal. However, today he'd be free. Dying wasn't an option, but killing a necessity.

A faint cry in the distance heightened his senses. It was the first sign of life he'd heard in weeks. The intermittent whimper echoed throughout the stone walls. Jax drew a deep breath, resisting the distraction that called away his focus. The slice of his canines tearing through his gums honed his attention. He'd deliberately starved himself, forcing his feral beast to the surface. It'd be likely he'd lose control, he knew. A risk he'd take; there was no other choice.

His swollen lids opened, taking in the sight of the approaching guard. Adrenaline pumped through his veins; unable to move, he'd have to lure his prey to his side with a split second chance at the kill. The shuffled sound of footsteps resonated in his ears.

Closer...closer...closer. He slowed his heartbeat, eyes staring as if death had come for him. Every cell in his body feigned surrender, conserving energy.

"Wake up, asshole."

Jax ignored the command and lay limp on the floor, his fangs pricking his own lips. The only thing that mattered was the blood he planned to spill. Tonight there'd be no struggle as the silver laced needle came at his skin. Like a lion stalking his prey in the Serengeti, he'd patiently wait for his prize.

Despite his weakened state, he detected the stench of stale cigarettes and whiskey on the human's breath. The kick to his thigh jolted him into battle, and he launched to attack. Ripping into the guard's neck, the Alpha went feral. The first rush of blood was like water to a dying plant. Jax tore at his flesh, swallowing the meat. Aside from a garbled cough, no sound resonated as life drained from the body. Exercising restraint, he ceased the attack to reach into his victim's pockets and search for the key to his shackles. His forefinger scratched along the serrated edge of the tiny metal implement. Yanking it out of the tattered fabric, Jax freed himself within seconds.

Although the blood and flesh of his captor surged his energy, it wasn't nearly enough to satiate his wolf, to force the shift he'd need to heal. Clawing his way up the jagged wall, Jax shoved to his feet. Dizziness threatened to topple him, but he closed his eyes, willing his balance to return.

His beast growled, urging him out of his cell. The musty scent of mold choked him as he made his way through the labyrinth of the tunnels. A pinprick in the distance blossomed into a streak of dusty light, and he stumbled toward the faint hope of freedom. Jax tensed in anticipation of the enemy as a shadow to his right stirred. His vision sharpened on the source, a crumpled feminine form tied to a pole.

Jax dug his claws into the doorjamb, a growl gritted through his teeth. *Fuck me. They'll be here any second. Your priority is getting home to your pack, not her.* Jax had lost count of his days in captivity, but his mind had never stopped worrying about the state of his pack. Although he estimated he'd been missing for weeks, his mind remained clouded from the poison, and it could have been more than a month. With no beta to lead in his absence, battles for dominance would begin. Wolves would die in the process. Weakened and distracted, the pack would be susceptible to attack.

Jax cringed as the cry grew louder. Protective, the instinct of the Alpha roared in protest. He crossed the room, ceding to the wish of his wolf. Jax cautiously sniffed at the battered body, investigating the female. Although the faint recognition of a lupine registered in his mind, she was not of his pack. *Don't fucking do it*, he told himself. *The stray wolf isn't your concern. You don't have time.* Near death, she wouldn't make whatever journey lay ahead beyond liberation.

A whimper escaped into the darkness, stopping him cold. Her pain coiled in his chest as if it was his own, and he sucked a breath. Although his mind told him to run, to leave her behind, his heart disagreed.

Confounded, he sighed and looked over his shoulder to reassure himself that they were alone. The demon would soon discover he was missing. It was just a matter of time before they came for him.

"Please…" the pathetic creature uttered, barely audible.

"Goddammit," Jax cursed under his breath.

Lifting her chin with his finger, he tilted her head upward. Her platinum blonde hair, stained with dirt and blood, fell back onto her shoulders. A thin streak of light painted across her bruised cheek. At the sight of her blackened swollen lids, his gut teemed with anger. *Fucking monsters.* Jax stilled as he studied her face. Recognizing the little wolf, the one who'd both aroused and eluded him, he rushed to free her. *Katrina.*

~◦❀◦ *Chapter Two* ◦❀◦~

Jax questioned his desire to rescue Katrina. Twice burned, he'd be a fucking idiot to think the third time was the charm. There was no such thing as luck. Jax knew better. *Cunning. Timing. Strategy.* These were the factors that contributed to success. Making decisions based on the heart, not facts, would lead to misfortune.

Jax closed his eyes, concentrating on his surroundings. Unable to detect the scent of his captor, the injured wolf was the only blood that registered. He tugged at the handcuffs that had bloodied her wrists. Her fingers had turned white from lack of circulation. The only thing keeping her alive was the magick within her lupine spirit. Jax scanned the room for keys to her shackles. In the corner, he spied a desk littered with papers and metal implements. He reached for a crowbar, and shook his head in frustration. Not exactly the right tool, but given the circumstances, he needed to make this fast.

"Please…," she begged.

"Listen, princess, if you want to get out of here alive you'd better keep it down," he told her, spreading her hands apart onto the floor.

"I'm a wolf…"

"Katrina, I don't have time for games. Just hold still if you want to keep those fingers of yours. This might sting…" Jax's anger boiled up as she countered him.

Jesus Christ, he thought, wishing he could leave her without a shred of regret. But despite his reputation, sometimes well-deserved, for being a dick, he was a man of honor. Oh, he'd rescue her all right, but he swore to the Goddess that when this was all said and done, he'd return her ass to Philadelphia as soon as possible. If he never saw Katrina Livingston for the rest of his immortal life, he'd kiss the ground.

The loud bang reverberated throughout the room as he smashed the bar against the chains, cracking them loose. Sparks flashed in the dim light, the scent of metallic smoke swirling into the air. Jax cast the tool aside and caught Katrina in his arms as she tipped toward the floor. Cognizant that she'd lost consciousness, he hoisted her small frame over his shoulder. With no time to spare, he shoved to his feet, tore through the hallway and burst through the heavy wooden door to freedom.

Sunlight hit his face, and the rush of fresh air choked his shrunken lungs. Jax swiftly shielded her behind a tree, concerned the predator that had taken him was monitoring the exterior. Several seconds ticked by before he peered into the forest, assessing his surroundings. Celebrating the rise of the Alpha, cicadas sang throughout the thick woods. He reached for the ground and scooped at the dirt. With the earth to his nose, he sniffed and exhaled a loud breath in relief. There was no mistaking the rich soil of northern New York.

Who the fuck would kidnap an Alpha in his own territory, his own State? Questions spun in his mind as he wondered if whoever had attacked him was an insider. Retribution would come in due time, but today he'd make it his mission to get home, to rebuild.

A snap of a branch in the distance alerted him to the presence of others. Without hesitation, he took off into the brush. His thighs burned as he pressed upward, heading toward the sound of running water. Thorns sliced into the pads of his bare feet and skin. By the time he'd reached the edge of the rushing water, he'd become aware of the staccato beat on his back. *Katrina.*

"What the hell are you doing?" he snapped, setting her onto her feet. She stumbled backwards and he reached for her.

"Please don't hurt me," she begged, burying her face in her hands.

"Katrina." Jax knelt to her, aware that within seconds, whoever was following him would locate them. "You have to help me here."

"No, no, no," she repeated in a whispered cry. She struggled to cover her tattered bra and panties. "Please…please…"

"Whoever the hell kidnapped us is going to be here in about five minutes. If you shift, you'll feel better. Let's go." Jax stood and stripped off the threadbare boxers he'd been wearing, not bothering to shield his nudity. He closed his eyes, willing his wolf to the surface. Its presence, although sick, snarled in response. As he readied to transform, a whimper distracted him from his task. He blew out a breath and focused on Katrina. "If you're not going to shift, then we've gotta move on foot. Get on with it."

"I'm a wolf but I…" She cowered to the ground, bringing her thighs up to her chest and shaking her head. "Something…there's something wrong with me. Something wrong, wrong, wrong…"

"Jesus, Katrina…we don't have time for this fucking shit. When we get back, I'll hand you over to Tristan and we never have to see each other again. Let's go. Just strip and shift." Jax speared his fingers through his hair, wondering how his instincts about Katrina had been so far off base. She was nothing but trouble with a capital T. Fucked up trouble…the kind you'd find in a back street alley.

"You don't even know what happened to me," she screamed at him, her chin still protectively against her knees.

"I saved your pretty little ass, that's all that matters. But you're not my pack so if you don't shift soon, I can't help you."

"Fuck you," she shot back at the Alpha.

"You'd better stand down, wolf," he ordered.

Jax held his breath, taking in the sight of her battered body. Even though he was tempted to force her to shift, something he knew he could do, it shook him to know someone had beaten her.

"Stay back." With a defiant glare, Katrina pressed to her feet, trembling as she tore off her clothes. Her voice cracked as she fisted her hands and closed her eyes. "And for the record, I'm not doing this because you're an Alpha. I'm doing this for me."

Jax reached for her, having had enough of her antics.

"No, don't…" Katrina attempted to shift. Her eyes rolled up into her head, and she flickered into a transparent state.

Jax fell forward as his hand passed through the air where she'd stood a moment ago. He stumbled, but regained his balance. Shock rolled through him as one of the monsters who'd kidnapped him came into view, black eyes staring back at him. As quickly as it came, it faded.

Katrina eventually transformed to wolf, but was unable to maintain her animal form. She morphed back to human, rolling into the mud and leaves. Naked and shaking, Katrina coughed up blood, her puffy eyes trained on Jax.

"What are you? What?" he asked, stunned at what he'd witnessed.

"Don't." She held a hand up to stop him from touching her.

"Jesus Christ." Jax bent to the ground and scooped her into his arms. "We need to talk about this."

"I told you. I'm a wolf. I'm damaged…broken." A barely audible whisper passed through her lips. "I don't…my name…I don't have a name. Just leave me. I don't blame you."

"What happened to you, Kat?"

"Alpha…" Her head lolled against his chest, warm breath brushing over his skin. "I only know…I know I'm wolf."

"Of course you are." Jax held her tight, cradling her nude body against his.

"You have no responsibility for me…your pack…"

"My pack is not your concern. You may not know who you are, but I do."

Jax had no time to further evaluate what had happened to Katrina. Whatever trauma she'd suffered had affected both her memory and magick. As her tears rolled down his chest, his heart and mind warred. She'd rejected him once, and as Alpha, he owed her nothing. Yet the explosive heat they'd shared long ago was all it had taken to spark his interest. Never mated, Jax knew one day the wolf who completed his soul would come for him. Second chances were opportunities cloaked in failure and as the victor of many a battle, he'd never needed one…until tonight.

"Leave me." Her voice cracked. Contrary to her words, she clutched at his neck, holding on for dear life.

Soft lashes swept butterfly kisses over his skin. Her fear resonated through his wolf, and although he couldn't heal her spirit, Jax refused to let her die. Regardless of *what* she was now, whatever they had done to her, compassion ruled his thoughts.

"We're getting out of here. Sorry, my little wolf. You're stuck with me this time." Jax began running, her body against his. As he leapt over the fallen trees, he took solace in her acquiescence.

From behind, the sound of rustling leaves grew louder and he spied the riverbank to his right. With Katrina unable to run, leveraging nature seemed his best alternative.

"Can you swim?" His eyes darted to the muddy water that swirled downstream.

"What?"

"Don't let go." Instinctively, Jax brushed his lips over her hair, and his stomach clenched as he realized what he'd done. Despite everything she'd said about him, accused him of, there was a weakness she invoked that he'd long forgotten.

The scent of his attackers dusted through the air, grounding his thoughts back into focus. Without further hesitation, Jax plunged into the churning river.

Jax had no choice other than to jump into the freezing water. At first, Katrina had shown signs of lucidity, calling his name in recognition, her eyes lowered in submission. But within minutes, she'd again lost consciousness. If it weren't for his deathly grip around her waist, she'd have drowned. The turbulent ride had lasted more than an hour but they'd eventually settled into a slow-moving current and washed ashore onto a familiar bank.

Trekking the rest of the way by land, Jax carried her until he reached the secluded cabin. He and his beta occasionally spent weekends at the private sanctuary. Although rarely used, the property was closely monitored by pack security. Located in a remote region of the Finger Lakes, it was hours from the city, but Jax knew they'd be alerted to his presence the second he stepped foot through the perimeter's invisible magnetic security system. Thankfully, the biometric lock hadn't been tampered with or changed. It responded to his scans, allowing him access.

By the time he'd reached the master suite, their skin was rippled in gooseflesh. As Jax gingerly laid Katrina onto the mattress, he noted her once healthy olive complexion had been replaced by a pale sallow tone. Without the warmth of his body against hers, she began to violently shiver.

Fucking hell, Jax thought, taking in the sight of Katrina in his bed. He reached for the comforter and tucked it around her, but she continued to shake. His wolf urged him to lie with Katrina, but logic told him to back away. She'd already accused him of trying to force a mating, and he wouldn't give her reason to do so again. Cautious, Jax set his palm onto her back and gently rubbed his hand in circles until she settled into a calming sleep.

"What happened to you?" Jax asked out loud, aware she couldn't hear him. He shook his head, hoping like hell she'd wake and give him answers.

Jax estimated he had exactly four hours before someone from the pack showed up to confront the intruder, maybe less if the pack was out running. Given that the moon was new, he suspected not. But with the sun setting and exhaustion setting in, it made sense to lock up and spend the night in the cabin. Regardless of who showed up to greet him, he planned on returning to the city in the morning.

Jax stood and stole another glance at Katrina. He shouldn't leave her side, he knew, but he needed time to collect his thoughts. *Five minutes. I need a shower.*

"Why the hell am I so worried about her anyway? Look at her, Jax. Never forget. She betrayed you." He raked his fingers through his dirty hair and took off toward the bathroom. "Great, now you're talking to yourself. Get your shit together."

As the hot spray hit his face, Jax contemplated who'd taken over the pack. Although his friend, Finn, was a strong candidate, others would challenge him. It was likely his adversaries had sent wolves in to fight for the territory. With his return, Jax expected that he'd be forced to exert dominance, as they'd test his power, probing for weakness.

Blistering water sluiced over his roughened skin, and he closed his eyes, focusing on his future. At no time during his captivity had his will wavered. Now freed of his shackles, sweet vengeance simmered in the shadows. His wolf raged, demanding retribution. Goddess help the predator who'd attempted to break the Alpha. Death would be welcome by the time he'd finished exacting justice.

⤙❦ *Chapter Three* ❦⤚

Katrina stirred from sleep, her thoughts recalling their escape. Memories slammed into her. *The river.* The ice-cold water had burned her flesh. Struggling for life in the turbulent current, she'd clutched at the sole man who consumed her thoughts. *Jax Chandler.*

She had been kidnapped several times over the past three years, and her attackers had threatened that if she pursued Jax, he'd die. The second she'd met the striking Alpha at the holiday party, their chemistry had combusted and she'd suspected he could be her mate. In an effort to protect him, Katrina had immediately returned to Philadelphia. She'd done everything in her power to thwart his advances, but unrelenting, Jax wouldn't stop calling.

When she'd gone to Tristan for help, he'd misunderstood, believing that Jax had tried to force a mating. The two Alphas had never gotten along, and her request only further incensed Tristan's animosity toward Jax. As much as she hated the spiraling rumor, it was her brother's intervention that had temporarily thwarted Jax's advances. Concerned that Jax would travel to Pennsylvania to find her, she'd left for New Orleans. Putting physical distance between them, she'd hid from the demons. Devastated that she'd shattered his affections, Katrina had taken solace in knowing he'd be safe. Leaving Jax had been the only way to keep him alive.

The familiar sound of a shower pattered in the distance. Katrina jolted upright, and her vision blurred as she opened her eyes. The room spun, and she fell back onto the bed, willing her balance to return.

Katrina's mind raced in panic. The Alpha would seek answers, angered by what she'd done to him. Worse, she'd be helpless to resist the attraction, and the demons had warned her that bonding would destroy him. A tear escaped her lids as she considered his demise. She refused to let it happen.

Regardless, they'd come for her. It wasn't the first time. It wouldn't be the last. Katrina sniffed her palm, scenting the death breeding in her veins. The magick that brought her wolf to the surface had been siphoned once again. Although she'd researched the abductions, seeking a way to eradicate her tormentors, she couldn't be certain she'd survive long enough to stop them from killing her.

Calling on her wolf, a small rush of her shifter magick flickered and Katrina forced herself to shift. Thankful she'd transformed, she conserved her energy. Allowing herself time to rest, she curled into the sheets and prayed Jax would leave her alone. So tired, she had no strength to fight the Alpha. *Stay awake…stay awake and heal,* she repeated, but it was of no use. The seductive darkness called to her like a comforting angel. *Be strong, little wolf, be strong.*

"Katrina, it's okay to be afraid," she heard him say as if she were in a dream. "You can shift back now. I'm not going to let anything happen to you." A strong hand stroked over her pelt, and the power of the Alpha flowed through her.

You'll kill him, they'd told her. *Bond with your mate, and he'll die.* Despite what they'd threatened, none of it made sense to her. *Why had they kidnapped Jax?* She'd heard whispers of his name during her beating. They'd wanted her to hear it, she was certain. Nothing was an accident. Every action they took was deliberate, even if cloaked as coincidence.

But as he continued to pet her, she relaxed, destructive thoughts passing like clouds. The warmth of his touch soothed her soul. Her attraction to Jax was so very difficult to fight. For once, she just wanted to forget, to pretend she could have what would never be hers. Deciding to indulge, she leaned into him. Soon enough she'd attempt to escape.

"I know this feels good, but you can't stay like this forever."

She gave a low growl in response.

"Hey now, you know that's not going to work with me. I can see they did something to you...something awful." Jax hesitated, his voice shaken. He shook his head and continued. "Look, Kat, we can rest for a while like this but sooner or later you're going to have to tell me what happened, what you know. You and I..."

Katrina looked up to the great Alpha, wishing she'd never let the rumors of what had happened between them persist. No matter her good intention, the hurt and anger in his voice was palpable. Some mistakes in life could not be undone.

"I don't know why you said what you said to Tristan...shit, I don't want to talk about this right now. I..." Jax closed his eyes briefly and then opened them, glancing away. "What I need to know is how you got into that pit we were in. I need you to tell me every detail you remember about these assholes."

Katrina struggled to remain awake as he spoke to her. Whatever energy he'd given to her had been absorbed and she soon lost concentration. Just a few more hours of sleep, and she could run.

"All right, little wolf. I see this isn't happening now. You can rest, but our time will come," he promised. "You're not going back to Tristan until I'm satisfied you've told me everything."

Jax's words jumbled in her ears. Unable to keep her eyes open, she fell victim to the drugging exhaustion.

Born of an Alpha, her father's blood ran through her veins. Submission would not come easily for the independent she-wolf. There was only one person she'd ever consider surrendering to…Jax Chandler. It seemed an eternity that she'd denied her carnal craving, but within the safety of her dream, every delicious inch of the Alpha belonged to her. She dragged her tongue over his flesh, tasting her prize. Her wolf rejoiced in response as she owned her mate.

"My Alpha," Katrina moaned, nipping at his skin. Her nipples ached, brushing over his abdomen. As his hardened cock slid between her breasts, his fingers fisted her blonde locks. The sweet twinge of pain to her scalp reminded her of who controlled her, and she smiled.

Katrina's hips straddled his leg as she slowly grazed her lips over his skin. She sought relief for her aching pussy, writhing against his knees, her wetness spreading over his skin. The scent of his masculinity drove her further, her mouth teasing down the muscled ridge leading below his abdomen.

"No, no, no, little wolf." A low growl warned her to stop. Her teeth met his skin in response, unwilling to accept his dismissal.

"Not today, baby," the commanding voice ordered. Katrina sucked a breath as her head was tugged upward by the strong hand wrapped around her hair. "As much as I want you, it's not going to be like this. Call me old-fashioned, but I like my women lucid."

Her eyes flew open in shock as she woke, stunned to see Jax smiling down on her. *What the hell did I do?* She'd thought it all an erotic dream, but as his dick prodded her chest, she realized what she'd done. Katrina attempted to push away with her arms but he held tight.

"Jax," she breathed. "I'm sorry. What did I…oh, Jesus."

"You can call me Alpha." His smile turned cold and Katrina's heart pounded in her chest. She could sense his anger. "I want answers."

"Jax…" she began.

"Alpha." His voice boomed throughout the room.

"Let me go…Alpha," she demanded under her breath. Her hand caught his wrist, tearing it away.

Rolling over onto her back, she pulled at the sheets, attempting to conceal her bare skin. Jax made no move to stop her but neither did he cover his own nudity. Her eyes skimmed over his chest down to his erection and then back to his eyes. She turned her head away, her cheeks heating in embarrassment. Not only had she almost sucked his cock, she'd been unable to resist ogling his gorgeous male form. She'd never seen him nude before, hadn't recalled what he'd looked like when he'd stripped in the woods. But the memory of her night with the charismatic Alpha had been permanently etched in her mind.

As surprised as she'd been to wake with her lips pressed to his flesh, the burning desire for him never faltered. She could escape, move a thousand miles away and the yearning for Jax would never cease. It was a nightmare she couldn't shake. The only resolution was finding a cure to her affliction...one she'd either find or die trying.

Jax shifted onto his side, and Katrina's eyes flashed to his. As much as she wanted to hide, she owed him the truth. Her stomach churned; she was terrified he'd never believe her excuse for why she'd rebuked his advances, for the rumors that had started.

After she left for New Orleans, Jax helped Tristan locate a wolf that had attacked his mate, and the two Alphas had come to a truce. By the time she returned to Philadelphia rumblings about Jax Chandler had ceased within the Lyceum Wolves. She'd decided at that time not to reopen old wounds, and didn't discuss it further with Tristan.

"You ready to try this again?" he asked, bringing her thoughts back to focus. His piercing stare bored into her, the power of the Alpha filtered throughout the room. "What happened to you?"

"It's complicated." Katrina rolled over to face him, curling onto her side.

"I want to talk about what happened in that prison. I want to know what those things are and why you were there."

"But what I just did..." Katrina's eyes fell to his chest but she refused to look any lower. She averted her gaze, and took a deep breath.

"Oh, don't you worry, Kat. We're going to discuss that, too." He shot her a wicked smile that quickly faded. "But right now, I need to know what I'm dealing with...those things..."

"Demons." Katrina's voice cracked. At the mention of the creatures, she fought the threatening nausea, the stench of their putrid breath fresh in her memory. No matter how many times they came for her, she never got used to the abuse. "I'm not sure exactly what they are. Maybe they're not demons per se. Sometimes...the magick...it feels like witches. I don't know for sure."

"In the days, weeks...shit, I don't even know how long they had me...I just know they looked different. The one that lured me," he paused as if he were embarrassed to admit what he'd seen, then continued, "it came to me in Finn's night club. I thought it was you."

"It looked like me?" she asked, surprise in her voice. Guilt rolled through her at his confession. They'd used her to lure the Alpha.

"Yeah. The strength of these things," he sighed. "That night, she was stronger than a human. They used silver to take me down, keep me down. My power had no influence on them."

"It doesn't," Katrina interrupted. She tucked the covers under her chin and stared blankly ahead. "That's why I think it's some kind of magick. They want our power."

"Wolves?"

"I think so." A tear rolled down her cheek and she didn't move to wipe it away. "Usually, it's just me. The times they've taken me..."

"Wait, are you telling me they've taken you more than once?" Jax's voice grew soft and he slid his hand across the sheets toward Katrina.

She nodded in silence.

"Jesus Christ. Does Tristan know?"

As Jax's fingers touched her cheek, Katrina began to softly cry. *My fault. I should have been smarter. I should have figured out a way to kill them by now.*

"Hey, it's going to be okay. I swear to you."

"No, Jax. You don't understand." Her wet lashes fluttered open and she licked her lips. "These things. There's something about me they want, they've always wanted. I've been trying for so long to make it stop. You don't know how hard I've tried over the years."

"Years?" He shook his head in disbelief.

"Yes, years. A couple now. Their power is stronger every time. They've stolen…" Katrina sucked back a sob. "My magick. In the woods, you saw what happened. Something's happening to me. I'm not right. And my wolf? She's slowly dying. If I don't find a way to kill them…I'm going to die."

"No, that can't be."

"Yes." Katrina shoved up to sit, and brushed both hands over her face and through her hair. She took a deep breath and blew it out, distraught with the agonizing situation. "Look Jax, I've got to go. Just being here now with you is putting you in danger. I'm like poison to you."

"What the hell are you talking about? You were just all over me five minutes ago and believe me, the way it felt…you weren't exactly killing me. What is going on with you?"

Katrina registered the disappointment crossing Jax's face, his lips drawn tight in anger. He'd never forgive her for what she'd done and she didn't blame him.

"Alpha," she began, and lowered her eyes in submission. "I'm grateful you saved me but I have to go."

"No fucking way, Kat. Not this time. I feel like I'm going crazy here. You and me…Jesus Christ, what you told Tristan. And then just now, you weren't faking that. You may have been sleeping but that was real. What the fuck is going on?"

"Nothing. I need to do this on my own and you can't help me. The longer I'm around you…"

"What? Please enlighten me, would you? What the hell do you think is going to happen? You could have been killed back there, and I saved your ass. You're in the middle of New York. Where exactly are you going to go?" Jax sat up and raked his fingers through his tousled hair.

"I don't know. I just know I have to get out of here. You're in danger as long as I'm here." Katrina pushed off the bed to leave and Jax leapt onto her. His body crushed against hers as he pinned her arms down against the mattress. Like a startled rabbit, she froze. The warmth and strength of her Alpha emanated from his skin to hers and she fought the arousal that she'd buried.

"No running," he told her, bringing his lips within inches of hers. "I will never hurt you, little wolf. But I'm done playing games. You. Will. Not. Leave."

"Jax..." Katrina's chest rose, her eyes locked on his.

"We need to work together to defeat these demons, witches. Whatever the hell they are, I cannot allow you to go alone. Tristan hasn't protected you." His forehead pressed to hers. "I don't know why you said the things you did."

"You'll never know how sorry I am." The whisper passed through her lips, finally a truth. "I don't ever want to hurt you again. Please."

"Don't fight me, Kat. This thing between us..."

"That night at the party..." Katrina struggled to continue as the heat grew between her legs. Ever since that night, she'd kept track of the Alpha, followed him on social media, cried herself to sleep knowing she'd be alone forever. Watching him from afar through a looking glass while he'd dated woman after woman had crushed her heart.

"Your body knows mine, little wolf." Jax leaned in to sniff her neck, his tongue darted out along the hollow of her throat. He growled as she turned her head in submission, giving him access. "We can't ignore this. No fucking way. Do you know why I'm Alpha?"

"You're strong." Katrina ached in desire as he slid the tip of his tongue along her skin. Her chest heaved for breath; she couldn't resist him. Her body lit on fire as his lips pressed to her neck.

"Raw instinct. Knowing when to trust what your gut is telling you. And do you know what it tells me about you?"

"What?" she moaned. Her skin broke out in gooseflesh, his warm breath on her ear.

"When I wake up with your sweet body against mine, you tasting of my flesh, calling my name...that is as real as it gets. But at the same time, I cannot ignore what you've done. Accusing me of forcing a mating? Tell me, why does a wolf do such a thing?" Jax whispered. "I should hate you, despise you for what you've done. But I don't. No, I believe this is a puzzle. None of it makes sense right now, but I will have answers. I always get what I want, Katrina."

"I had to protect you. You and Tristan have never got along, you know that. I needed you to leave me alone, and he misunderstood what I told him. But I swear to you, I never meant to hurt..." She shuddered in arousal as he took her earlobe between his teeth. Katrina cursed her body as she arched up into him. "Ah...Jax."

"This is why I'm Alpha. Instinct tells me I can't ignore this. There's something between us, a reason we're brought together. You and I have things to work out, and you're staying with me for as long as it takes."

"Please, Jax. I'm not good for you," she protested. Her heart fluttered as Jax raised his head to pin her with his gaze.

"What secrets are you keeping? Your lips may lie." His knees pressed her legs open, and he settled between them. "Hmm…your body tells me the truth."

"I want to tell you, but…please…" Katrina tilted her hips upward, his hardened dick prodded her belly.

"Tell me you'll stay, help me find who did this to you…to me…my pack."

Katrina registered the desperation in his words. The desire to be with Jax was overwhelming. Any rational arguments had been slayed by the primal attraction that sizzled over her skin. Her spiraling thoughts justified reasons to stay within the arms of her Alpha. Jax had unlimited resources at his disposal to research the dark society. If they went to New Orleans, it could buy them the time they needed to discover a way to destroy them. Before she had a chance to think any further about the implications, her heart had won the argument.

"Yes." She closed her eyes, the word barely audible on her lips.

As his mouth captured hers, her wolf cried in celebration. Her tongue swept against his as she reveled in the moment she'd dreamed about for years. Never had she imagined it would be under these circumstances. Rescued and enchanted by the Alpha, Katrina lost herself in his touch. She wrapped her legs around his waist, pulling him toward her.

"What is it about you?" Jax asked, sucking her bottom lip.

"I'm sorry…" Katrina gasped as he kissed her again, this time with a passion that speared through her from her head to her toes.

Consumed by lust, she was barely aware of the footsteps coming down the hallway. As Jax tore his lips from hers and shoved her to the back of the bed, she panted for air, her chest heaving.

"Stay back," he warned.

A creak of the door was all the warning she had before it flew open, strangers looming in the hallway. As the Alpha shifted into his powerful black wolf, Katrina's eyes lit in reverence. The majestic beast snarled, its tail up, standing tall in a show of aggression.

Katrina attempted to shift, but her magick faltered; a flicker of her wolf appeared only to disappear. As the intruders approached the threshold, she scanned the room for a weapon. Wrapping her fingers around the base of a brass lamp, she ripped its cord from the wall. Katrina didn't hesitate as she launched the heavy object at the red-haired stranger. The base nicked him in the head and he fell to his knees.

"Jesus Christ, Jax. Get your girl under control," he called, holding a hand to his bleeding scalp.

"Katrina?" She froze as she registered the sound of the familiar voice.

Jax flashed to his familiar form, towering above them all. His loud growl blasted through the room, silencing the din.

"Finn, rise," Jax commanded. "What's he doing here?"

"Saving your sorry ass," Jake quipped, lifting his gaze to meet Jax's.

"Watch your words, wolf," Jax warned.

"Are you hurt?" Jake asked, his voice tense.

"I'm all right," Katrina replied, giving him a small smile. The last time she'd been in Louisiana, she and Jake had grown close, becoming good friends. Although Katrina considered going to him, she cautiously remained on the bed, her focus drawn to the angry Alpha.

"Stay back," Jax snarled. He eyed the wolf, assessing the situation.

"It's, um…it's okay, Jax…" Katrina regarded his pensive expression, but continued, hoping to soothe his concern. "I know Jake. We're friends."

"What the hell happened?" Without asking for the Alpha's permission, Jake intrepidly crossed toward Katrina.

Jax stepped to block his path, and Katrina reached for his hand. Running the pad of her thumb over his palm, she attempted to assuage the protective Alpha. She suspected Jax remained unaware of their connection, yet his actions spoke volumes.

"He won't hurt me." She lifted her gaze to meet Jax's, noting the vulnerability in his eyes.

"Jax. Please. It's okay. We're just friends. I'm not leaving you." As the words left her lips, she knew she'd said it in all honesty. She'd have to tell him sooner or later about the prophesy. If they completed the bond, he'd die, but it was a conversation to be had in private.

She smiled as Jax leaned in and brought her hand to his cheek. The soft skin of his lips at her palm tickled her skin and she gave a small laugh.

"I need to talk to Finn," Jax told her.

Katrina nodded in acknowledgment and wrapped the sheet around her body. As he dropped her hand and stepped aside, her eyes never left his. Her heart pounded, the loss of his touch leaving her with an odd sense of emptiness.

"How did you end up here? Did he hurt you?" Jake glared at Jax as he passed to his right.

"I'm okay. Really, Jake." Katrina assured him as he wrapped his arms around her. "Jax helped me escape."

"Not again?"

"Yes, again." Jake had seen her struggle to shift on more than one occasion and was one of the few people she'd confided in about the abductions.

"We've got to get you out of here. Somewhere safe. I'll take you back to Logan…protect you. You should have never left New Orleans."

As Katrina pulled out of his embrace, she shook her head. *No more running.*

"I'm going to stay with Jax." She tried to ignore the look of surprise on Jake's face as she spoke, and although scared about hurting Jax, she couldn't leave him again.

"Now hold on one fucking minute." Jake's voice grew louder. "First of all, Tristan is your Alpha. Second of all, you know you're safer in New Orleans with us. Look, I know this assho…" His eyes darted to Jax and he rephrased. "This Alpha. He likes to shoot off orders like he owns the entire world. You have a home and it's not here."

"Jake, please. I know I said I'd…"

"You'll never be safe here. They'll come again. You know it's true."

"She stays with me," Jax asserted.

"Alpha, I think we'd better talk," Finn interrupted. "We've been searching for you for over a month."

"They're here," Jax commented. "You," he pointed to Finn, "come with me. Jake stays." His eyes focused in on Katrina who held the covers against her chest. "Do not leave the cabin. This is none of your concern."

Katrina sensed their presence. *Wolves*. Although they weren't of her pack, the hum of their magick grew thick in the air. Instinct told her to go with Jax, but his command to remain with Jake took precedence. Before she had a chance to speak, the Alpha shifted, and within a blink of an eye, he'd gone out the door.

You'll kill him, they'd told her. For so long, she'd believed their words. Deliberately avoiding Jax, she'd thought she'd protected him. Katrina brought her fingers to her mouth, his searing kiss lingering on her lips, and she began to question everything she'd thought to be true. No matter her fear, her heart had won; she'd chosen to stay with the one man who she believed was her mate.

◆◈· *Chapter Four* ·◈◆

Jax pushed thoughts of Katrina to the recesses of his mind as his pack came into view. He'd expected the infighting. A wave of agitation rippled through his psyche, confirming the instability. He scanned the woods but didn't sense any intruders or newcomers to their clan. Yet as he transformed, he took notice of several young males stepping closer, tipping their hands in confrontation.

He waved Finn behind him, happily surprised the experienced wolf had stepped in to lead. While they'd been close at one time, their lives had taken separate paths. Jax had recruited Finn to work with him at his magazine, ZANE. A photographer, he'd been an integral player, creating high profile spreads that brought a unique perspective to the publication. Although talented, Finn chose to leave New York City. He'd gone to Ireland to settle a dispute within his mother's pack. Upon returning, he'd refused to return to ZANE, giving up his artistic passion. Jax had argued with Finn, insisting he was throwing away his life, but supported him when he'd created a New York City night club that catered to supernaturals.

As he looked into the eyes of his old friend, Jax recognized the blood-thick loyalty that stood the test of time. He considered everything that had transpired over the years, their friendship and the greater good of the pack. Prior to his abduction, Jax had been devastated by Nick's death. He'd grown despondent and refused to name another beta. He couldn't fathom another wolf taking his best friend's place. Yet as Jax stood before his pack, he reached inside himself, drawing on the wisdom that only an Alpha could possess. It was his duty to protect his wolves, no matter what turbulence affected his own life. With the decision made, he'd bury the pain and announce his edict.

"Agrestis Wolves, I stand before you today as your Alpha," Jax addressed them. He waited patiently as they flickered back into their human forms. A glint of moonlight appeared as silver shadows on their skin. "You are not without your leader."

"You were captured?" a voice called out.

"Yes, I was attacked, but I prevailed and stand before you today." Jax sought to ease their concerns, mindful they'd be shaken. It wasn't as if dangerous supernatural beings didn't exist, but it was rare one was powerful enough to kill an Alpha.

"And what about Nick? He's dead. You didn't protect him," he charged.

Jax's eyes flickered red with rage as the brawny wolf, Arlo, spoke Nick's name. On the verge of losing his temper, the Alpha forced his pulse to steady.

Jax had long recognized Arlo's antagonistic nature, but this was the first time he'd been aggressive enough to challenge the Alpha. As the pack stirred, Jax sensed their acceptance of the defiant wolf. In the Alpha's absence, he'd assumed a position of authority.

"Shut the fuck up about Nick." Jax's voice boomed throughout the forest. Several wolves reverted to their animal form out of fear, cowering in submission. "What happened in New Orleans was a battle. People die in battle."

"Maybe you should care a little more about what happens here in your own pack," Arlo countered. He stepped forward, fisting his meaty hands. Dirt clung to his sweat-covered flesh.

"We've gotten along without you," Easton, a second wolf, yelled. He, too, eyed Jax and made a move toward the porch.

In his peripheral vision, Jax spied Finn stripping down. The sight of the strong redheaded male preparing for a fight gave confidence to the Alpha's choice. Jax stared down his pack and set forth with his announcement.

"Agrestis Wolves. I hereby name Finn Cavanagh as my beta." His eyes darted over to his friend, who remained impassive. If it weren't for the tick in his forehead, his somber expression would have concealed his irritation. "This is my pack and mine alone. If you challenge me, do it now, but there will be no discourse."

"I smell the bitch." Arlo stroked his flaccid cock and sniffed up into the air. "That's right, Chandler. Her scent is in the wind. You going to let us all have a go?"

"You'd leave your own wolves to go fuck a Lyceum whore?" Easton laughed.

A surge of rage exploded within as the Alpha shifted. The threat toward Katrina had been the trigger; his reaction swift and forceful. Lurching forward, Jax attacked. Although Easton had managed to transform, Jax pounced onto the grey wolf, slicing his teeth into his neck. Blood rushed into his mouth, feeding his fury. The whimpering wolf rolled onto its back in submission, its paws drawn tight to its body. Despite his frenzied state, Jax maintained control. Granting the wolf mercy, he turned his focus to Arlo, whose teeth were firmly embedded into his hackles.

Forcing his body backward, Jax slammed the large brown wolf into the dirt. Arlo had always been a skilled fighter, but he was no match for the powerful Alpha. Jax had ruled for over thirty years, and he'd demonstrate his dominance yet again. In the heat of battle, no compassion would be granted to the wolf who threatened his rank. The Alpha never took killing lightly. Yet tonight death would blanket the forest, its foul stench a reminder to those who challenged him, of who exactly led Agrestis Wolves.

Growling, saliva and blood sprayed into the air as Jax secured his hold. Arlo snapped in an attempt to dislodge the fierce Alpha. Unrelenting, Jax pierced his fangs deep into his opponent's fur, shredding the skin. The tenacious wolf shoved upward, refusing to submit. With his forepaws, Jax pinned the wolf immobile and lodged his jaws further into Arlo's neck. Releasing the supreme strength of an Alpha, Jax vigorously shook his challenger. Bones snapped as he crushed its spine, the sanguine essence rushing down his throat.

Jax absorbed the magick as the life drained from the wolf. Raging, he shifted to human and sprang to his feet. A mournful, triumphant howl tore from the Alpha's lungs, and his wolves rose to meet his call. Overcome with emotion, he both celebrated his victory and grieved the loss of a pack member. For the greater good, blood had been spilled to protect them all. Jax wiped tears from his face, satisfied when Finn nodded and joined him. *My new beta.* No longer divided, Agrestis Wolves were united once again. *The Alpha had risen.*

Jax shoved the cabin door open, and Finn followed. They'd run with the pack for over an hour and had returned exhilarated but exhausted. Although Jax had known leaving Katrina was a risk, his wolves took priority over the woman who'd nearly started a territorial war. The attraction between them was undeniable, but he struggled to reconcile his feelings with what she'd done in the past. No matter how beautiful she was, he didn't yet trust her. Instinct may have urged him to keep her close, but logic told him to question whether she was friend or foe.

The attractive little wolf caused him angst, an emotion he was not at all used to feeling. A curious pang of jealousy had stabbed through him when he'd observed the interaction between Katrina and Jake. His gut twisted as he speculated on the nature of their relationship. She'd told him that they were friends, but was she telling the truth?

Jake was a good friend to his sister Gillian's mate, Dimitri. He'd shown aggressive tendencies from the moment Jax had met him in New Orleans. While Jake displayed irritation toward him, it was clear the young wolf hadn't tried to establish himself as Alpha nor had he challenged Finn. On the contrary, his new beta appeared entirely comfortable with the Acadian wolf, welcoming him as a guest.

Jax turned on the kitchen sink spigot and submerged his head in the flowing water. The icy stream did little to thwart the churning thoughts of Katrina, Jake and the challenge. Jax reasoned he'd need a long shower to wash away the death lingering on his skin. Finn's rough voice drew him out of his contemplation. He jerked his head upward, droplets spraying throughout the kitchen.

"Jesus Christ, Jax. Do you think you could have taken five fucking minutes to ask me to take Nick's place?" Finn glared at his Alpha.

Jax caught the look of disgust that crossed his beta's face and shrugged. While the debonair Alpha was usually the epitome of a gentleman, he had trouble shaking off the feral tendencies the challenge had brought forth.

"This shouldn't be a surprise." Jax grabbed a dishtowel and wiped his face. "You're my beta."

"What the hell is going on with you?" Finn gestured to the wet tiles.

"What?" Jax glanced to the floor and chose to ignore the mess. "It's just water."

It had been over a year since Jax had visited his private home. While the décor of the cabin was upscale, its exposed beams and soapstone kitchen counters gave it a slightly rustic feel. The great room, with its vaulted ceilings and skylights, soaked in the light of the moon. Despite not visiting there often, he'd utilized a service to keep the home well stocked with supplies.

Naked, Jax strode across the room to the bar, where he reached for a bottle of Lagavulin. Setting four glasses onto the smooth surface, he uncorked the scotch and began to pour.

"Seriously. Have you lost your shit?" Finn snatched a throw blanket off the sofa and wrapped it around his waist.

"What is wrong with you?" The caustic liquor burned his throat as he downed a shot and poured another glass. Offering Finn a tumbler, he handed it off and fell back down onto the black leather sofa.

"Really, you gonna just lie there? Letting it all hang out?" Finn took a swig and wiped his mouth with the back of his hand.

"What do you want me to say?" Jax closed his eyes and opened them, taking a deep breath. His mood grew dark and he continued. "It had to be done. I could not allow Arlo to challenge me further."

Jax lifted his gaze to meet Finn's. He wasn't waiting for judgment. They both knew what he'd done was in the best interest of the pack.

"I'm not talking about that. He was an asshole. He's been fighting me since the day you went missing, but Jax…fuck. How was I supposed to take over?"

"Did Tristan show his face?" the Alpha asked, stretching his neck from side to side.

"You kiddin' me? After what went down with Katrina, you think I was going to tell him who I saw in the club? Fuck no. If he was lookin' for her, I wasn't volunteering information. He would have been up here tearing the entire city apart."

"Smart move." Even though Jax and Tristan had established peace, a truce of sorts, the issue with Katrina had never been resolved. He still believed that Jax had gone after his sister.

"It was Logan who called. Gillian was behind it. Holy shit, man. I'd call her a pit bull but that would be an insult to the breed. The tiger in her…she would not give up. She kept calling here for you and next thing I knew, I had the Alpha of Acadian Wolves threatening me."

"She's my sister. The Alpha genes are strong in that one. She won't submit, you know that, right? Dimitri's got his hands full with her but I can't help but be proud. She doesn't take any shit."

"Yeah well, tiger girl got Logan involved and before I knew it, Jake was here. Between the two of us, we were able to manage things, but Jax…" Finn took a deep draw and coughed. "What happened to you…you've got no idea how fucking happy I am you're back. But tonight…"

"Ah, the beta thing…" Jax swirled his drink, taking note as the legs ran down the sides of the glass.

"Yeah, that." Finn shook his head and threw it back against the back of his chair.

"You would have been my choice of beta if you hadn't left." Jax lofted the statement in silence, waiting for Finn to acknowledge it, to finally tell him what had happened over in Ireland that had kept him from coming home. He'd never been the same.

"Look, you know I had to go. And hell, I've been back for a while now. But your beta?"

"It's done. Nick was my best friend, you know that. He, uh…" Jax's voice cracked as his sorrow rose to the surface. He swallowed the last of his scotch and choked back his emotions. "He's gone. I love him, but there's no going back."

"He was a great guy."

"And so are you. What's done is done. Finn, this makes sense. You're the only one I can trust. We've been friends a long time. It was the right decision."

"You could have told me. To just put it out there like that. It's not like I wasn't ready to fight tonight. Seriously, I was ready to tear the shit out of Easton and Arlo. Those dickheads have been challenging me since the day you left, but hell, to just do it like that…not tell me."

"How long have you known me?" Jax stood and went to the bar.

"A long fucking time, that's how long." Finn stared at his Alpha, his eyes bloodshot.

"This is why I'm Alpha. I make decisions. There is no wavering. It's what I do." Jax didn't expect others to always understand his responsibility. It was the ultimate burden and opportunity. The lives of hundreds of wolves and the future of their pack rested in his hands.

"I can see you're going to give me more of your Alpha mumbo jumbo, so let's move to the next topic. What the fuck is up with your, uh," Finn gestured to his friend's dick. His mouth curled up in a half grin, "your lack of clothes? Because I know Jax Chandler, and this is not him."

"Perhaps I don't give a fuck what anyone thinks tonight. I'm going back to my nature. I'm raw." Jax pounded on his chest with a closed fist. The killing had surged a virile energy within him that he struggled to contain.

His thoughts turned to Katrina. The fresh scent of coconut shampoo lingered in the air and he wondered where Jake was. Had he watched her while she ran the soap over her smooth skin? An unfamiliar possessive urge crawled inside his belly and his lips drew tight in agitation. He didn't want to care who she fucked or what she did.

Jax curled his fingers into the mahogany bar, his claws scratching the wood. *Fuck it all, I need to see her now*, he thought.

"Jax." He heard her voice softly call to him. As he raised his eyes to hers, the beast inside stirred. *Mine.*

-⟨⟩⟨⟩⟨⟩⟨⟩ *Chapter Five* ⟨⟩⟨⟩⟨⟩⟨⟩-

The sight of Katrina standing in the hallway took his breath away. She appeared fragile, her wet hair combed behind her shoulders. Her once brunette locks had turned blonde, and he wondered if the change was related to her abduction. His eyes darted to Jake as he brushed by Katrina, giving her a small hug as he passed. The brief but intimate interaction reminded him that no matter his visceral attraction, he didn't trust her.

"Everything all right?" Jake asked.

"Kat." Jax ignored the question, his eyes locked on Katrina's.

"Everything's great, Jake. Thanks for taking care of my pack while my sorry ass was captured, Jake." The Acadian wolf gave a smirk, his voice laden with sarcasm. He snatched a tumbler and poured a scotch. "You're welcome, Alpha. No problem, Alpha."

"Sometimes showing trust is a form of appreciation." Jax gave a brief smile to Jake and turned his attention back to Katrina.

As he drew closer to the she-wolf, he noted no other scent on her. As much as Jake grated on his nerves, the confirmation he hadn't touched Katrina ameliorated the Alpha's concerns. After Jax had fought to save Dimitri and Gillian, he considered that Logan had returned the favor by sending an honorable wolf to help Finn watch over his pack.

"Sometimes a simple thank you works too, but whatever." Jake stole a glance at Jax's bare ass. His eyes darted to Finn, who laughed in response. "And sometimes...just putting on some clothes is a great way to show appreciation. You look like you work out. I'll give you that. But dude, I don't need to see your junk all day long. How 'bout some threads?"

Before Jax had a chance to retort, Katrina approached, distracting him. Her petite form swam in his black cashmere bathrobe. The lapels drifted open, and his eyes fell to the swell of her breasts. A warm hand on his roughened cheek stunned him into silence. His eyes lifted to meet hers.

"Clothes do not make the man. The Alpha can do as he wishes." Katrina smiled.

"Don't listen to her, Finn. She grew up with Tristan. That one never gets dressed either," Jake retorted.

Katrina glared over to Jake for only a second. Jax never lost focus as she spoke to him. Although he towered over her, she commanded his attention.

"Death is never easy," she told him.

"I'm fine," he began.

"I smell it on you. Never forget, Jax. I am an Alpha's daughter. An Alpha's sister. A death within the pack destroys a wolf to renew the lives of many. The wolves…they're settled now?"

"Yes. And you are…" He leaned into her touch, within inches of her lips. Jax's cock jerked as he breathed in her scent. A devious smile crossed his face. "You smell delicious."

Jax's chest tightened as Katrina's expression grew somber. He wanted to trust her. He'd never thought it possible that anyone besides another Alpha could understand what it was like for him to kill during a challenge, yet she stood before him unafraid, undaunted by the fatality he'd caused. There had only been a handful of occasions when he'd been forced to take the life of a brother. Each time it came with a price, and the cost was high on his soul. Yet this was the responsibility of a leader, and the pack rejoiced in the peace and stability of an established Alpha. They'd mourn the loss, perhaps some would harbor resentment, the family and friends of the deceased, but they'd also come to acceptance. It was the culture of the wolves: their past, their future, how it always would be.

"I know I said I'd stay, but maybe Jake is right. Maybe I should go. After what I did to you…your wolves…they won't understand," Katrina explained, her voice gentle.

Her soft palm on his skin soothed the bitterness of the past. Confused by his mixed emotions, he blinked and the memory of what she'd done flashed through his mind. A fresh surge of anger surfaced. Until she confessed what had happened, why she did what she'd done, he couldn't forgive her. His hardened dick told him to forget about it, but reason prevailed. *Don't let the temptress fool you.* Jax wrapped his hands around her wrists, closed his eyes and shook his head.

"We need to clear the air." He lifted his gaze to meet hers, his brow furrowed and tense. He forced himself to remember everything that had happened, and his tone grew firm. "Until I know everything, and I mean every last fucking detail about what is going on with these demons, you aren't leaving. Consider yourself a guest. Or a hostile witness. Whichever you prefer…doesn't matter, because you're not leaving."

"You can't keep me against my will."

"Oh, I can and I will. What you did…" he growled.

"Things aren't how they seem," she offered.

"And just how are they?" Finn rose and approached them. "You accused Jax of forcing you to mate with him."

"I told you…" Katrina's eyes darted from Finn to Jax. "You have to believe me. I never told Tristan you tried to force me to mate with you. But I was trying to get you to stop coming after me. I was trying to protect you from these things. You and Tristan…you've never gotten along. When I told him that you wouldn't stop coming after me, the rumors started. I know I should have stopped it but then Marcel died. It was just easier. You left me alone. You were safe. I'm sorry, Jax. But it's not what you think."

"Really? Because people almost got killed over your little accusation. Who does that?" Finn asked.

"Someone who's desperate, that's who," Jake interjected, crossing the room to Jax and Katrina.

"How would you know? You were down in NOLA. It's not like you were here when it happened," Finn countered.

"I know Kat and there's no way she'd do that without a reason." His eyes went to Jax. "Let her go."

"Really, just how well do you know her?" Finn questioned, his question laced with implication. "Are you lovers? Friends with benefits? Fuck buddies? Do tell, wolf."

"Enough!" Jax yelled, without letting go of Katrina.

"You know her presence in this cabin causes trouble in the pack as we speak. It's part of the reason Arlo is dead," Finn said accusingly.

"What?" Katrina's eyes widened. Unsuccessfully, she attempted to break free of Jax's hold.

"That's right, baby. They could smell you on him." Finn poured a shot and downed it. "They were going after you. And he defended your pretty little ass."

"No...Jax...please...you have to let me go." Katrina shook her head, continuing to tug her wrists from his grip.

"I said enough!" Jax yelled. "All of you. You will not blame her for Arlo's death."

"Please just let me go. I'm not good for you," she protested.

"Finally, someone in this goddamned room sees reason. I don't know why you are so set on keeping her. It's like you aren't even thinkin' straight." Finn tunneled his fingers through his ginger locks. In a moment of recognition as to what was happening to his Alpha, his eyes landed on Jake, who shook his head no.

"I need to go back to New Orleans. I'll find answers there. They won't stop. If I stay here..."

"I'm warning you. Do not challenge me," Jax commanded. Although he'd loosened his grip, he hadn't released her. "I already told you earlier, we're going to work things out between us. What happened in that cave and when you went to shift, no...this is fucked up. I saw what happened. That night in the club, the person who kidnapped me looked like you, but it wasn't. In the ambulance...they changed. I want to know what the hell we are dealing with. Why are they after you? Why me?" Jax released Katrina and threw his hands up in frustration. She rubbed her wrists, tears brimming in her eyes. Her rage emanated from her like a beacon, stabbing through his chest. "No, you're not leaving New York until I have answers, and if there's something in New Orleans that you know about that's going to help us, then I'm going with you."

"Jax..." Katrina's shoulders slumped in defeat. She looked to Jake for help but he shrugged, deferring to the Alpha.

"We can't stay here. I've got to get back to the city, check on ZANE. Fuck." Jax blew out his breath, the realization that his multi-billion dollar corporation, while probably still running, had been ignored. Assuring the publication subsidiaries were still intact was a priority. "Finn. I need you to round everyone up. We're going back home."

Jax turned away from Katrina, needing space. As he strode down the hallway to go shower, guilt rushed through him. Jesus Christ, she was pushing him to his limits. He wanted to fuck her senseless until they both couldn't breathe. She'd kill them both. The way she tested him drove him insane, yet his beast celebrated her defiance. When his wolf demanded her submission, she'd give it freely and the moment would be all the more sweet.

Jax stepped into the shower, letting the cold spray pelt his skin, and prayed his body's reaction would subside. He hadn't wanted to escalate the argument further. If she hadn't lied to Tristan, why had she allowed her brother to continue to think he'd attempted a forced mating? Although her excuses were like poison on her lips, the woman's compassion touched his soul. He despised that she appeared to care, that her touch calmed his wolf in a way that no other woman had. Jax glanced to his erection, and cursed it. With his arm leveraged across the tile, he tugged at his cock and stroked himself. Like a punishment, he pumped it with vigor, angry that she did this to him, enraged he'd lost control. *Goddamned, motherfucking…*As his seed erupted, he cried out in frustration and smashed his fist against the wall. The crack of the tiles did nothing to change his decision. When they got to New York, he'd interrogate her to his satisfaction and send her home to NOLA with Jake.

-·❧ *Chapter Six* ❧·-

Katrina stared out the tinted window of the limo and wondered how the hell she'd survived the past three days. After they'd returned to the city, Jax had insisted she stay in his home. She'd argued, unsuccessfully, that she'd be safer in a hotel, when in truth it would be Jax who'd be safe from her.

Her guest room, located on the first level of the three-story Central Park West penthouse, had become a prison cell. She'd considered escaping, but Finn had been assigned to guard her. While he'd initially spoken to her with contempt, he'd softened toward her after he'd found her crying on the balcony. A weakened moment, she acknowledged. Katrina didn't usually lose her composure. But the sand in the hourglass was spilling out fast; soon they'd be out of time.

Jax had isolated himself on the third floor, ignoring her but to say good morning and good night. When she'd attempted a conversation, he'd summarily dismissed her, claiming he was needed in a meeting. The more time she spent away from Jax, the more her magick dissipated. If the demons didn't make a move to abduct her, she suspected she'd die anyway.

Earlier in the day, Katrina had called Tristan to explain that she'd gone to New York and had been in contact with Jax. As much as she loved her brother, she almost felt relieved when she'd found out he was out of town, traveling to an emergency meeting in Seattle to help settle a dispute among allied Alphas. Over the past couple of years, she'd told Tristan about her kidnappings, but there'd never been enough evidence for them to find a perpetrator. Until recently, she'd always been able to immediately shift. Healing quickly, no physical evidence remained of her abduction. When she'd asked Tristan to help keep Jax away, he'd been quick to assume that he'd attempted to force a mating. Although she'd denied it, the rumor had settled within the pack. When she'd left for New Orleans, their relationship faltered. Soon after, her brother Marcel, died, leaving Katrina devastated. Despite moving back to Philadelphia to be with Tristan, they'd grown further apart.

Their phone conversation had been brief but she assured him that she was safe. Tristan, however, insisted he'd be flying home within the day. Regardless, Katrina knew the only place she'd ever felt remotely safe had been New Orleans. But she knew Jax would never let her go nor would he be satisfied until he had the answers he sought.

As they stopped in midday traffic, Katrina smoothed the silky printed fabric over her thighs. She wondered if Jax had selected the stylish wrap dress himself or had simply hired a personal shopper. The day after she arrived, her closet had been filled with a selection of clothing, all in her size. Food of her liking was cooked by his personal chef, delivered by butlers. He'd spared no expense seeing to her comfort. In her gilded cage, she grew miserable, desperate for his touch.

The car lurched forward, reminding her of their final destination. Jake called her name, interrupting her contemplation.

"You okay?" he asked.

"I'm fine," she lied. Her stomach clenched in anticipation of seeing Jax. "I don't get why I have to meet him here. He comes home at night. We've been in New York for days."

"He's busy. The business, it hasn't been doing as well without him," Finn offered. "Nick was in charge of operations. So now Jax has been training someone to take over but it's intensive work. Most of his established corporations are doing well, but ZANE...the magazine is a delicate operation. It was Nick's baby. It's important to Jax that it doesn't tank."

"Is it in trouble?"

"He's been gone for a month and a half. It's doing okay but Jax doesn't settle for mediocre."

As they came to a red light, Jake moved over to sit next to Katrina and took her hand in his. "Listen Kat," he began. "All this shit you've been through over the past couple of years, we're going to find a way to make it stop."

Katrina looked out the window and took a deep breath. No words could fix the situation. They needed to get to New Orleans and search for a spell, a weapon against her attackers.

"Look, I know what's happening between you and Jax. I'm not sure why you've fought so hard to stay away from him. But I've spent time with you. Long nights in the bayou. You're the real deal. Lying isn't your style. So whatever reason you've got going on for putting distance between you and Jax..."

Katrina's eyes flashed to his. She sighed, considering his point, but didn't answer.

"You need to talk to him. You know I give Jax a hard time. There are times when the two of us butt heads. He can be a son of a bitch, for sure. But he's Alpha of this pack for a reason. He was there for Gillian. He helped her shift to a wolf for the first time. I saw him fight down in New Orleans. He would have given his life to protect any one of us, a pack that isn't even his. And Nick paid the price. What happened to Nick..." Jake's mouth drew tight as he recalled what had happened. "Fuck, he didn't deserve any of it."

Katrina glanced up at Finn, who appeared stunned by Jake's account of the night his friend had died. It hadn't occurred to her that his wolves hadn't known the details about the death of their beta.

"So my point is, he might be an asshole at times but you can trust him with whatever you have brewing. I can feel your magick draining. Maybe Jax hasn't been around you enough to feel it but he damn sure will. Let him help you."

Katrina, at a loss for words, nodded in agreement. She closed her eyes, searching for her wolf. No longer could she hide the truth. Denying her mate, her Alpha, would torture her. But if they could find a way to destroy the demons, bring them down one by one, they'd both have a chance of living.

You can do this, Katrina told herself, rehearsing her speech. For fifteen minutes she'd worn a hole in the carpet of the spacious office. Located atop the Midtown Manhattan skyscraper, floor to ceiling windows lined the walls of the octagonal-shaped room.

Katrina ran her fingers over his sleek desk, noting how not even a pen was out of order. How could she be the mate of such a highly organized person? She laughed, recalling how her office was littered with pens of every color and half-filled sketch pads. Creative, she drew, painted and created. In Philadelphia, she'd been involved in the arts, and had opened a salon, enjoying doing the hair and makeup of local celebrities. But after her last abduction, being forced to return to New Orleans, she'd opened a gallery featuring several of her own paintings as well as work from local artists.

The door creaked open, and Katrina jumped. She cursed her jittery nerves, but her attention was soon distracted by the laughter of a female. Katrina turned to find the source running her hands over Jax's forearms. Her wolf snarled, and she fought to maintain an impassive expression as they entered the office. Jax faced Katrina, his eyes locking on hers. In a suit and tie, he was every bit as spectacular as he'd been raw and naked in the bedroom. For a brief second, she imagined tearing off his tie, ripping the buttons off his shirt so she could continue what she'd started in the cabin.

Katrina swore she felt his fierce beast growl. With her palms flattened against the window, she struggled to stand as his power washed over her. She couldn't be sure if he was deliberately exerting control or if somehow, in her weakened state, she was unconsciously absorbing his magick. She sucked a breath, and blinked, attempting to remain upright.

"Katrina, hey." Jax reached for her arm, and slid his hand behind her back, supporting her. "It's okay. I've got you."

As the warmth of his breath brushed her cheek, Katrina thought she'd melt. The draw of the Alpha was impossible to fight. As Jax set her down into a chair, he broke contact. Her heart pounded in her chest, and she inhaled, attempting to regain her composure. *I can't do this*, she thought. *I need this man, in my life, in my bed.* None of it made any sense, she knew. She had to confess everything before she gave in to the urge to run out of his office.

"I'm okay," she managed, staring up into his blue eyes.

"Jax," the woman interrupted, annoyance in her tone.

"You scared me," he admitted, never taking his sight off Katrina.

"Jax," she repeated, louder this time. "The upcoming photo shoot. Are we going with five girls or—"

"Later," he dismissed her.

"But sir, the models will be here in an hour."

"London, go find Adam. He'll help you with the details. You're ready to prep this one on your own. I'll be down in an hour."

"But I thought—"

"Discussion's over. Go find Adam. Now."

His focus on Katrina never wavered as he sat on the edge of his desk. Katrina unconsciously reached for his hand, the urge to touch him overwhelming.

"Yes sir." The staccato beat of heels echoed in the distance, and Katrina startled in her seat as the door smacked shut. Although the woman hadn't slammed it, she'd closed it with enough force to make a point, demonstrating her irritation. Katrina fought the envy that flittered in her mind.

"What's wrong?" Jax asked, his tone soft but firm.

"I'm fine."

"No. More. Lies."

Katrina shuddered as his voice boomed around her, his power washing over her like a tidal wave.

"I told you before." She lowered her eyes. While she didn't intend to imply submission, her body hummed with the energy of the Alpha. Breathing deeply, she sought to control what was happening to her. "My magick...they've stolen it. I can't...please stop."

"Stop what?" Jax asked as he walked to the bar. He retrieved a bottle of water from the refrigerator, opened it and offered it to Katrina. "Drink this."

Katrina defiantly met his gaze, her lips pursed in anger. How could he not know what he was doing? She'd known Tristan could release his power on a whim, influencing the pack.

"It's overpowering me...your energy."

"Drink it." Jax nodded, waiting on her to obey. "Not a request."

Katrina brought the rim to her lips and did as he told her. Jesus almighty, if she'd felt better, she'd have knocked this Alpha on his ass. It wasn't as if she hadn't gone head to head with Tristan on occasion. Torn between ripping off his clothes and dousing him with the contents of the bottle, she silently counted to ten.

"Your energy. Control it," she told him in the most even tone of voice she could conjure. "I don't know what's going on. I told you...they've done something to me."

"I'm not deliberately sending it to you, Kat." A curious expression crossed his face as if he didn't believe her. "I'm not saying it's not possible. I'm saying that I'm not trying to hurt you. Believe me, if I were forcing it on you, you'd know it."

Katrina's eyes flashed in recognition of his threat. Today, they'd have it out and one way or another, she'd move on.

"Why are we doing this here?" Katrina scanned the room, and brushed a lock of her hair behind her ear. "I've been at your house for days and I've barely seen you."

"Because." Jax paused. As he rounded behind her, Katrina stilled, frozen like a frightened deer. The wolf towered above her, the heat of his body emanating onto her skin. Firm hands rested on her shoulders, and she closed her eyes, as he continued. "This is where I attend to my business matters, and as much as I want you for pleasure, and make no mistake, I do...you're currently business. You see, negotiations are a tricky thing. Much like poker, the players conceal their weakness, their strengths. At home, you have me at a disadvantage. I seem to have trouble controlling myself around you."

Katrina gasped as his lips brushed her ear, her nipples stabbing through the silk.

"I..." At a loss for words, she opened her eyes, afraid to make a move.

"That's right, my sweet little wolf, you're in my world now. And while I still find it difficult to resist you, I will have answers. The truth. All of it."

Jax stood and walked away, leaving Katrina's body on fire with arousal.

"My company. My office. My rules. I can't tell you how much I'd love to punish you for your indiscretions. Ah, to spank your ass while you scream for mercy....well, that does sound lovely. Not today, though." He smiled and sniffed the air.

Katrina tightened her legs together, aware he'd scent her desire. It wasn't as if it was a secret she was attracted to him, but hell, just imagining his firm hand on her cheek, the loud slap to her flesh, provoked wetness. Embarrassed by her own fantasy, she averted her gaze.

"You are a naughty one, aren't you?" he teased knowingly. "Don't you worry, I promise someday, just not today. No, today is for discovering truth."

Katrina fought a small smile, wanting so badly to take him up on his offer. But if they made love, it would only be a matter of time before their instinct drove them to mate.

"Feeling better?" He raised an eyebrow at her and extended his hand. "Take it."

Jax was in his element. Katrina knew not to test him as she placed her small hand in his. He led her around the large black desk, and while curiosity urged her to ask what he was doing, she resisted talking. *Answers. The truth. It's all he's ever wanted.* He'd either believe her or not, but the exhaustion of protecting him could no longer be sustained. One thing was certain; challenging the Alpha wasn't in her best interest.

"Like this," he told her, reaching for her hips.

Her face registered surprise as he backed her up against the edge. When his firm hands went to her waist, she held her breath.

"Up you go. Business first, then play."

"What are you doing?" Katrina's hands went to his shoulders as he lifted her up onto the flat surface.

"Very nice." He gave a wicked grin as he ran his fingers down her arms. His soft touch left a trail of delight on her skin. Taking her wrists, he carefully set her palms flat onto the surface so she leaned back at an angle. Katrina went to move, and he placed his hands on top of hers. With a tilt of his head, he warned her. "Don't move."

"What are you doing? Why am I on your desk?" Katrina's pulse raced as he sat back into his chair, studying her like she was on display at a museum.

"I'm leveling the playing field. Something about you," he drawled. Removing his suit jacket, he hung it on the back of his chair. "It distracts me. I simply cannot have it. I won't fall victim to the half-truths that spill from those luscious lips of yours. No, I can think of much more pleasant things that should be coming out of your mouth."

"Jax…" A picture of Jax's chiseled abdomen flashed into Katrina's mind. Recalling how his cock pressed to her skin, she imagined sucking him down her throat. A new wave of desire rushed over her, and her face flushed.

"That's right. I'm very much looking forward to having you on your knees." He smiled as if he'd read her mind. "But first, we talk."

"What are you…?" As his hands glided over her thighs, her skin rippled in gooseflesh.

"We shall start at the beginning. Why, dear Katrina, did you tell your brother that I tried to force a mating?" Jax pinned her with his stare, his voice low and firm. Despite the lingering fingertips atop her knees, Katrina heard this question as an order; the request came from the Alpha, not a lover.

"I already told you the truth. I asked Tristan to help me keep you away. You wouldn't leave me alone. Once you called him, it just confirmed it. He was angry at you, and it all just spiraled out of control. I'm sorry I let it go so far, but I was trying to protect you," she explained, her body tense with arousal. He silently listened without interrupting, so she continued. "These…demons. The things that have taken me. It's happened six times over the past three years. At first," Katrina paused and looked out the window. A firm hold on her chin directed her gaze back to Jax and her heart raced. "They told me that my mate, an Alpha…that I'd kill him. What they've done to me, they'll take it from my mate too. They've been waiting, hoping for it to happen."

Katrina lifted her hands, and was swiftly reprimanded.

"Do. Not. Move," Jax ordered as his hands moved to her knees. Katrina's heart slammed against her ribs as he spread her legs. His fingers lingered on her inner thighs, but all the while, he never took his eyes off hers. "You have one chance to set things right with us. This is it. Don't you dare lie to me."

"I'm not," Katrina protested. She refused to cry, no matter the desperation that bubbled in her chest. "I know you think I'm crazy. Why do you think I haven't told anyone? Tristan suspects I've lost my mind."

"That doesn't make sense. He's your brother. Why doesn't he know what's going on with you?"

"It's not like Tristan can't feel if I'm in trouble, but every time they took me, I wasn't gone for long. I never had trouble shifting. I'd recover quickly. This time, though, things are different. It's a total loss of time…loss of magick."

"If you never lied to Tristan about me, why let the rumor continue? How exactly could you protect me by staying away from me?"

"Because, Jax…" Katrina shook her head, exhausted with keeping secrets. "You're an Alpha. You are *the* Alpha. *My* Alpha."

"Are you trying to say that we're mates? How would you know for certain? We've never made love."

"Between my father and Tristan, I've attended summits, met nearly every standing Alpha in the country. It wasn't Logan. I mean, I spent enough time with him when he was my brother's beta. No…the night we met…"

"The party?"

"Yes. I'd known about you for some time."

"You stalked me?" he asked, amusement in his question.

"Not really." Katrina rolled her eyes, a small smile formed on her lips. "Maybe a little cyber stalking, okay? But what was I supposed to do? Put yourself in my shoes. You know how it is for wolves. We have no idea who our mate is, let alone if we'll ever even meet them. And then this 'thing' tells me I have one and that when I meet him, I'm going to kill him. I suspected it was you. There's part of me…I still don't know for sure."

"Let me get this straight, some sicko abducts you, beats you, steals your magick and you believe some mumbo jumbo they tell you?"

"And this is exactly why I didn't tell you." Katrina seethed. She'd had enough of his games. If he didn't believe her, he could go to hell. She'd find a way to kill these demons on her own. As her hands flew up off the desk, he struck as fast as a cobra, snatching her wrists out of the air. Desperate, she screamed at him. "You want the truth? I'll give you the fucking truth. I didn't stop Tristan when he misunderstood. I let them continue believing the lie so you'd stay far away from me. That night at the party? I wanted you so bad I couldn't breathe. But I left anyway. I did all this to save you from me…me, the person who will ultimately kill the great Alpha. The one who might be my mate."

"Put your hands back where I told you, now." Jax loosened his hold, returning her hard glare.

"Make me," she challenged.

"Hands on the desk," he growled.

"I'm only doing this to prove a point." Katrina yanked her arms away from him and set her palms flat. "Do not misread this as my submission."

"Believe me, little wolf, when you submit, we'll both know it." Jax slid his hands underneath the hem of her skirt, slowly grazing his fingers up to her hips. His expression softened as he spoke. "This thing between us…ah, Kat. I wanted you too. And when I thought you'd lied. I was so angry. Confused. I've dated a lot of women, but that night…it was like there was no one else."

"Jax…" Katrina licked her lips, recalling his searing kiss. She could no longer abide her craving for the one man she'd gone so long without. But neither could she give in to him without him acknowledging the truth, believing her words. "You have no idea how much I've wanted to be with you. I'm sorry I left. I really am so sorry, but…I don't want to hurt you…I won't hurt you. I don't know why this is happening to me. But I'm trying to fix it…looking for a way to stop them."

Jax paused, his eyes locked on hers. Katrina's stomach fluttered as she waited on his words.

"I sure as hell wish you'd told me what was happening instead of running. But are we really mates? Meant for each other? There's only one way to find out. You know it. And I know it." Jax's lips hovered inches over her knee, his warm breath on her skin. "I should send you back to Tristan, but I just can't."

Katrina hissed as his lips brushed her inner thigh. She knew why he wouldn't let her go; for the same reason she hadn't run. As the tip of his nose edged under her dress, she took pause, aware that she wasn't a hundred percent certain he was indeed her mate. After all she'd done to protect him from the curse, what if she was wrong?

"These things…these demons…they're going to have to go through me if they think they're taking you again. You need to learn to trust me." Jax raised his eyes, pinning her with his stare. In silence, his fingers hooked around her panties.

"I never meant to hurt you…" Katrina tilted her hips, allowing him to remove her underwear. As the cool air hit her damp pussy, she arched her chest.

"Time for pleasure, my little wolf. I've waited so long to have you…open your dress," Jax told her.

Barely cognizant of her surroundings, Katrina scanned the office. Although alone inside, employees milled about outside his door. She focused back on Jax, his wolfish grin greeting her.

"That's right. Someone could see us."

Katrina sighed, her desire spiking as he flittered his fingers over her mound.

"Do it now," he ordered, pushing the fabric over her hips, exposing her pussy.

Katrina smiled. Her Alpha wanted to play, to test her limits. While it would take more than teasing to make her submit, she'd give him what he asked. Sliding her palm over her breast, she reached for the buttons, slowly opening her dress. Without waiting for instruction, she brushed the sleeves down her arms and peeled off her bra, baring herself to him.

"You're more beautiful than the first time I saw you," he groaned.

Katrina yelped as he cupped her ass, pulling her toward him. She cried out loud as he took her breast in his mouth. Spearing her fingers through his hair, she guided his head. Her nipple swelled in response, his bite nipping its tip.

"Jax," she breathed.

"You...are exquisite." His fingers slid through her wet folds and flicked at her clit. "Hmm...is this what you want?"

"Ah, yes." Katrina's energy surged. As his mouth went to her other breast, her pussy ached with need. So long she'd waited for his touch, and now she was certain she'd never be able to leave him.

Jax caressed her ripe flesh in his hand, and captured her mouth with his. As his tongue brushed against hers, Katrina tasted her mate, allowing her mind to calm, to forget all the trauma she'd suffered. His strong lips overpowered her own, and she relented, reveling in his devastating kiss.

"Please, Jax..." she cried as he drove two fingers inside her readied core. She gasped as his lips moved down over her chin, peppering kisses down her neck.

"From this moment, things will never be the same," she heard him mumble. "Open for me, little wolf."

Katrina leaned back, doing as directed. The slick stone cooled her pussy as he pressed her knees wider still. Her patience wore thin as he brought his head between her legs, blowing air over her taut nub. As he dragged his tongue through her labia, Katrina moaned his name. His fingers curled inside her and she nearly flew off the desk.

"Jesus, you taste better than I ever imagined," he spoke into her lips, gently lapping at her sensitive hooded bead. "Tell me you'll never lie to me."

"Jax..." Katrina heaved for breath. For years she'd avoided the man she'd desperately craved. Coming alive for the first time in her life, she'd give him anything he wanted.

"Say it," he pressed. Sucking her clit between his lips, he drank of her essence.

"I swear it. I swear to you. But we can't bond...I won't hurt you." Tears streamed from her eyes, her gut torn with the guilt that she could destroy him.

"Never," he repeated.

"Ahh...please..." Katrina's orgasm crashed around her and she cried for mercy, shuddering with every lash of his tongue. She wrapped her legs around his shoulders as she exploded in pleasure and fell back on to her elbows. She screamed, forgetting where they were, and jolted back into reality as she heard the crash of a door slamming open.

"What the fuck is...?" Finn asked.

Katrina lifted her head forward to see Jax smiling from between her legs.

"Out," he ordered.

She closed her eyes, and for the first time that she could remember, she laughed. Katrina scented both Jake and Finn at the entrance but chose to ignore them. Instead of being embarrassed, a sense of liberation washed over her.

"You'd think those two would know not to come in here." Jax pressed his lips to the top of her bared mound, and withdrew his fingers.

"Maybe they like to watch," she suggested with a sexy smile.

"Something you're interested in, perhaps?"

As he brought his wet fingers to her mouth, she smiled, neither confirming nor denying his provocative question. He cupped her chin, sliding his thumb into her mouth. Katrina moaned, tasting herself, nipping at his fingertip. With the softest touch, he rose to kiss her, and she opened to him. As his lips took hers, gently sucking and biting, Katrina softened into his strong embrace, his power rejuvenating her wolf, infusing her with his magick.

She opened her eyes as his lips lost contact. Her Alpha gazed at her with the possession she'd expect from her mate. Although Jax hadn't admitted the connection, his kiss was all she'd needed to confirm her suspicion. It both thrilled and scared her that Jax Chandler, one of the most dangerous and cunning Alphas in existence, was destined to be hers. But if they didn't find a way to destroy the demons, she'd be the wolf who exacted his demise.

❧ *Chapter Seven* ❧

Jax had always suspected that Katrina Livingston could be his mate. After he'd met her in New York, he'd gone feral with lust for the one woman he couldn't have. Unable to stop thinking of her and desperate to get in contact, he'd called Tristan. But after she'd leveled accusations, Jax swore that no woman could do that to him and still be his mate. His instincts had always been dead on until that moment in time.

But her claim that she'd never told Tristan he'd forced a mating resonated as truth. Jax and Tristan had a turbulent past. His father had never favored Tristan's more liberal views regarding supernaturals and humans. A brutal ruler, he'd deliberately incited wars with Lyceum Wolves. When Jax assumed the position of Alpha, he quickly learned that Tristan would never trust him. The tension never dissipated after his father died. Occupying bordering territories, the two Alphas reluctantly coexisted.

With Katrina in his home and office, exposed to his satisfaction, his emotions swirled inside his chest like a tornado. From the second he'd met her, Katrina had incited his beast's hunger like no other. There was no denying how responsive she was to his touch. Feasting between her legs, his cock turned to concrete, her essence bringing him to life. Like the devil himself, she tempted him and he fantasized, looking forward to seeing how far he could take her.

When his office door had opened and they'd been interrupted by Finn and Jake, she'd simply laughed, altogether focused on him. As he looked up into her eyes and caught the flicker of delight, his heart seized, cognizant that no matter what had transpired, he'd give her a second chance. Unable to control the explosive chemistry between them, his wolf sure as hell wasn't going to let her walk out of his life again.

As he broke their kiss, he inwardly reprimanded himself for his lack of discipline. It wasn't as if he'd planned to fuck her on his desk. *Jesus, I'm losing it.* The sugary taste of her pussy on his lips left him wanting more, and he fought the craving. A soft brush of her fingertips to his cheek broke his contemplation, and he placed his palm over her hand.

"This thing between us…" At a loss for words from desire, he forced his concentration to business. His comfort zone lay with strategy, planning the attack. "I need to know everything you know about these things…this society. What do they do when they take you? Do you ever go anywhere else? How many of them?"

"I, ugh…well, sometimes it's hard to remember," she answered, her voice soft.

Jax knew he'd taken her off guard. As he shifted from lover to inquisitor, he sensed the change in her demeanor. She withdrew her hand, and his wolf recoiled at the loss of her touch.

"Even if it's small, it could be important," Jax answered.

His eyes fell to her glistening mound, and his painful erection strained against his trousers. He'd never wanted to make love to anyone more in his life than at that moment, and it took every ounce of self-control he possessed to tug at the hem of her dress, covering her bare skin.

Jax shook his head, both irritated and aroused. Attempting to shake the lustful haze from his mind, he stood and crossed to the window, leaving her alone at his desk. With his palm glued to the glass, he scanned the cityscape. He was a cold bastard, he knew, for walking away, but if he didn't put some distance between them, he'd be buried inside her for hours.

"A few months ago, there was a vampire…" she began.

"A vampire?" Jax kept his response calm even though the hairs on the back of his neck pricked in alertness. Out of the corner of his eye, he spied her sliding her arms into sleeves. Averting his gaze, he forced his line of vision back out the window.

"Yes, he was only there for a few hours. He's very strong."

"You spoke to him?" Jax turned to face Katrina. Conflicted, he knew they needed to focus on a solution to the demons that'd kidnapped them, but as he registered the hurt in her eyes, he changed the subject back to their relationship. "Kat…what just happened with us…this isn't finished. I have a shoot to go to…" *Fuck, you sound like an inarticulate fool. Look at what she does to you.* He took a deep breath and attempted a recovery. "Please don't take this the wrong way, but if we are mates, and I'm not saying that we are, we need more time. I need more time."

"I'm fine," she replied, her fingers nervously sliding down her lapel as she adjusted her dress.

Jax plowed his fingers over his impeccably coiffed hair. He took note of her somber expression. She'd interpreted his actions as rejection. Holy shit, he didn't think he could screw something up more than he already had. Yet the more words that spewed from his lips, the more he managed to fuck up the situation.

Katrina's presence in his life threw him off balance. Feelings and emotions were not something Jax did well, and clearly Katrina fell into that category. Deciding to avoid the conversation that would inevitably come, his thoughts drifted back to the vampire.

"Tell me about the vamp."

"I told you, he's strong," she replied.

"They're all strong."

"No, he's the strongest. More than Léopold."

"You know Léopold?" Jax didn't conceal the surprise in his question. Léopold Devereoux, one of the most dangerous vampires on the east coast, was ancient and ruthless. He'd been known to kill all creatures, including wolves.

"Yes," Katrina answered without hesitating. "He's an ally to the Acadian Wolves. Jake knows him."

His wolf grew agitated at the mention of the virile, unmated wolf who'd become Katrina's confidant. Jax suspected she'd baited him, and shoved the distracting thought away. Focused on acquiring information, he'd ignore it…for now.

"Does the vampire have a name?" he pressed.

"Quintus. His name is Quintus." Katrina's eyes flashed in fear. "But Jax, I don't think we should go after him."

Jax heard the quiver in her voice, and appreciated her apprehension. *Quintus Tullius.* A mercenary over the centuries, the elusive vampire was a force unto himself within the supernatural community. Guarded and lethal, he'd exiled himself underground. The seductive vampire was well known for his sexual exploits.

"Tell me." Jax approached Katrina. She blinked up at him, stoic in her composure, as if they'd never touched. With the scent of sex fresh in the air, his wolf stirred, yearning to inflame her cool demeanor. Jax restrained the urge to rip off her clothes and claim her. He balled his hands, straining to concentrate. "Did he touch you?"

"Whatever does that have to do with anything?"

"Because I know Quintus. I'm asking you again," he said, slow and deliberate. "Did. He. Touch. You?"

Katrina's hand reached for her neck, and Jax's stomach dropped. He couldn't be sure if they'd made love, but with her silent gesture, he was certain Quintus had bitten her. His beast raged at the thought of it and threatened to snap. Desperately trying to remain rational, Jax turned on his heel and took a deep breath.

"You want to know if he touched me?" Katrina asked in confusion. "Where are you going with this?"

When Katrina's hand reached for his arm, he froze. The woman had him torn up inside. He needed to get his shit together before he made yet another mistake.

"Yes, yes…he bit me, okay? But it was nothing. He was weak. And I needed to get the hell away from those things. I fed him. What is wrong with you?"

As Jax turned, his gaze on hers, he noted the innocence in her words and shook his head.

"What? Wait, you thought I…" She gave a half smile. "I'm not saying I haven't been with other men, but never Quintus. I only met him once."

"But he's tasted you?" Jax pressed.

"Yes, and I'm not sorry for it. It helped him heal, and we escaped. I won't say he's not attractive, because that would be a lie and I think we just established," her gaze went to the desk and back to Jax, "that I'm not going to lie to you anymore. But I won't feel guilty for saving myself. Or him. Now that being said, Quintus…even though he was nice to me that day, he can be dangerous…unpredictable."

"Indeed." Jax restrained his anger. When he questioned Quintus, he'd discover if he'd taken advantage of Katrina. "What was he doing in that hellhole?"

"I don't know. Like I said, he was only there for a few hours." She paused in contemplation. "They were foolish to leave me with him. He could have killed me if he'd wanted to, but he didn't. He saved my life," she admitted. Katrina fingered her skin and shivered. "You know vampires, Jax. They only have two ways. Pain or pleasure. And all I'm going to say about it is that he didn't hurt me."

"We'll go see him." Jax reached for his jacket and slipped it on. Retrieving his cell phone from its inner pocket, he slid his fingers across the glass.

"Do you really think this is such a great idea? No one even knows where he is. Besides, I just told you that he's dangerous. If you confront him, he'll see you as a threat. He might even try to hurt you."

Jax glanced up at Katrina, giving her an amused smile. She had no idea just how powerful he really was. Returning to his task, he scrolled through his contacts.

"What's so funny?" Katrina asked, her hands on her hips. "I can assure you that there's nothing funny about Quintus. I get that you're Alpha but he's really old. He can do everything Léopold can do plus a host of other things we can't conceive of. This isn't a good idea. We should leave him be. I have contacts in New Orleans."

"And we'll use those as well, but Quintus? We're going to see him. You must learn to trust your Alpha, little wolf."

"You're not my Alpha yet."

"I will be," he replied with confidence.

As he sent the text message, his spirits lifted. Whatever had stolen away Katrina's magick, it had to be destroyed and he was one step closer to annihilating it. He glanced at Katrina, and his beast stirred once again. He knew he'd have to have her soon.

The truth. Today, for the first time, he'd heard it from her lips. One small step toward trusting her again. But first, she'd have to learn how to trust him, and he looked forward to teaching her.

·❦· *Chapter Eight* ·❦·

"Quintus Tullius?" Jake asked.

"Right pocket." Finn aimed at the shiny blue ball. He pecked at it, and it went careening into the hole.

"Tell me why we're doing this again? I've been around Léo and let me tell you, he's one badass vamp. If this guy made him, he must be a real prize."

"I'm the king." Finn fisted a hand into the air.

"Yeah, yeah. How is it that you make it every single time?" Jake smiled and shook his head.

"Because I'm the king." The ginger beta eyed the billiards table, scouting his shot.

"Sure you are, big guy." Although Jake was six-three, Finn had him by a few inches, his muscles bulging. "Look, I'm not saying we shouldn't go but I'm just sayin' maybe we should at least call Léo before we do this."

"I only take orders from one wolf. No offense, dude, but it ain't you. Jax wants to go see this vamp? I'm there. This pack has been through hell the past month and there's no way I'm challenging him. Not happenin'. So you can either come with us or go back to New Orleans." Finn rounded the corner, attempting to case a better view. He tilted his head and pointed to his next target. "One ball. Get ready to bow to the king."

"You suck." Jake took a swig of his beer and set it on the bar, watching his opponent sink another ball. "For the record, I think Katrina should stay back here."

"You'll get no argument from me. But Jax seems to have other plans." Finn shook his head and chalked his stick. "Look, I know you're friends with Kat, but this thing with her and Jax…"

"Red, let me give you a bit of advice. I think we both know what's happening here between them. I can't say I'm thrilled about how this is goin' down, but I can say that number one, this mating shit…I'm going to run like hell if it happens to me. It's messy, complicated stuff. You do not want to even try to understand it. And number two, you need to stay clear of Kat until they actually do mate, because until they do, Jax is going to be one possessive son of a bitch. Oh, but it will happen. The easy way. Or the hard way. I'm not willing to take bets as to when."

"How the hell can't he see what's going on? And why the fuck did Kat go and tell her brother he was forcing a mating, when they are mates? It makes no fuckin' sense. Orange stripe. Center pocket."

"It sounds to me as though she went running to Tristan and then somehow this whole thing got blown out of proportion. She's protecting Jax from something," Jake noted. "But I can't say exactly what's going on."

"Well, that's a helluva way to do it. We all were confused because none of us had ever even seen her except for that one party."

As the ball sunk into the leather catch, Jake rolled his eyes. "I refuse to call you King but you're pretty damn good at this."

"I'm the king all right," Finn laughed.

"Kat's not what she seems. Down in the bayou, she, uh, she just had a way about her. You know she paints. Sculpts too. She's really talented. She started working with all the kids, teaching art clubs, giving back to the pack. I wish she'd stayed."

"Sounds like maybe you like her. Did you guys ever…?" Finn left the question open ended and held the pool stick up suggestively.

"Fuck no. I mean, yeah, if she had wanted to, I would have, but no, we never got that far. And besides, things were already complicated enough for her. You know, she came back down to New Orleans with Luca. But nothing was going on between them at that point."

"A vampire, huh?" Finn laughed. "Now, that's interesting."

"She's all wolf. Trust me. I've seen her. I think she was just doing it to keep Jax away."

"Well, it appears she has a mate now."

"That she does."

"One who may go down kicking and screaming."

"Wait up. I don't get that. Didn't he call Tristan about her?"

"He did, but I think he just wanted to see her again. Then all these allegations got stirred up and you know how that story ended. It was a serious no go after that. The man didn't skip a beat. It's not like he's pussy deprived. He's an Alpha. More women after him than he knows what to do with. Some who aren't going to be very happy when they find out about Kat."

"I guess she's not going to go over too well with his pack," Jake surmised.

"Like a lead fucking balloon." Finn pointed to the eight ball and smiled. "Hearts are going to break. Maybe some heads. Before it's all said and done, I think you can expect a fight. I mean, not only do some of these women think he's theirs, well, they just don't like Kat after what happened. It's messy."

"Good times ahead." As the black ball disappeared, Jake held a congratulatory palm up in the air. "One of these times, I will win, you know."

"Ah, but for now…" Finn smiled and slapped his opponent's hand. "Crown me, baby."

"I'm gonna warn ya, I'm not going to let anything happen to her. It's why I'm still here. And as for Jax? Yeah, I busted his balls down in New Orleans. But after what happened to Nick, seeing the Alpha fight…" The memory of watching Nick die washed over Jake and guilt settled in his gut. "The bottom line is that whatever these things are, they came after him too. No way am I leaving him hangin' either. I've seen a lot of shit over the years. Witches.

Magick. Demons. But Jax is tough. He's got this."

"I appreciate your support." Jax rounded the corner, a small smile crossing his face.

"Hey now, don't go getting a big head." Jake rolled his eyes.

"You just remember who's Alpha and we'll get along fine."

"You take care of Kat and we will," Jake responded, the smile gone from his face.

"You like her?" Jax picked a marble ball up off the table, tossed it in the air and caught it.

"I do like her. She may not be my mate but she's my friend." Jake eyed the confident wolf. His commanding presence thickened the air, his power rolling off him in waves. "We do this together. I don't want her hurt."

"Don't get in my way, my friend. Like I said, just remember who's Alpha and all will be well." Jax set the orb on the table and rolled it forward.

"You don't get what she is to you, do you?" Jake pressed.

"Katrina?" Jax paused and smiled. "There's something between us. She told me she was trying to protect me. That I'm her mate. These things, the demons...they told her if we mated, I'd die."

"I knew there was some reason she'd gone to Tristan." Jake said. "But let's say they told her they'd kill you, why would she believe these things?"

"Good question. Tell me, Jake. If you were an Alpha, what would you do?" Jax posed the question rhetorically and continued. "I'd like to think she was scared. They only abducted her for short periods of time, never long enough for Tristan to notice she was missing. It's not like she's a child. She goes weeks at a time without seeing him. Eventually when she tells him what's happening, she has no proof. To be fair to Tristan, without evidence, this can be a difficult situation. Does he divert resources to a crime where there's no evidence except for maybe her bruises? But even then, she's shifted, healed. As it is, Katrina's finding it hard to grasp what's happening to her."

"She's alone," Jake added.

"Or she perceives she's alone? Doesn't think Tristan believes her."

"They threaten her and go through with it."

"Yes, they steal her magick. So then when they threaten me?"

"She believes they'll go through with attacking you," Jake concluded.

"I think that's exactly what happened. Think about this. If they've threatened to kill her only potential mate, she's going to do what she has to do to protect me. Of course this gets tricky. Does she know for sure I'm her mate? No, but she suspects it. Same is true for me. Do we absolutely know yet? No, but sometimes our instinct is all we have. Would you risk the life of your mate even if you didn't know for sure? I wouldn't. So now we have some decisions to make. Mating is serious business. To deny one's mate, it can be done, but not easily."

"Hey man, I'm not mated, but Dimitri? Logan? It was pretty intense. I've never seen a wolf deny their mate. So if that's what you are looking to do, I can't help you there. And honestly…" Jake blew out a breath. After everything that had happened with Nick, he felt indebted to Jax. The Alpha had suffered a great loss to help his own pack. "I think you need to explore this thing with Kat. I won't lie, I care about her a lot. But she's not mine. And denying her as yours, I think it could hurt you every bit as much as it would hurt her."

"I never said I planned to deny her. But what Finn said is true. My pack, they'll resist her. She'll have to earn her way. I cannot do this for her."

"Kat's strong. You need to give her a chance to show you what she's made of."

"It's true she has Alpha blood in her veins. I suspect she's every bit as difficult as my sister." Jax gave a small chuckle.

"Yeah, well, Gillian doesn't really do submission." Jake laughed.

"She'll fight me on this." Jax smiled as if he'd enjoy finding out if she'd submit to him. "But I cannot compromise who I am."

"If you're worried about her ability to establish rank, she's tough. It's not like she didn't take out a few wolves in New Orleans and that wasn't even her pack. You already said it all. She's Alpha born."

"We need to discuss Quintus. You must let me deal with him tonight, do you both understand?" Jax changed the subject abruptly. "It concerns me that he's tasted of Katrina. He's deadly. Could kill both of you in a blink. Don't fuck with him. Stay close to me and keep your dick in your pants. This place," Jax paused, a serious expression washing across his face, "it's dark. Seductive. Everything Quintus enjoys. Remember at all times that this is the vampire who created Léopold. Whatever happens, do not engage with him. Follow my lead, even if it is in opposition to what you believe is right. I'm not your Alpha, Jake. But I will send you home if you challenge me tonight. I'd prefer not to send you home in a body bag."

Jake nodded, hearing Jax's words, surmising that the Alpha had had previous interactions with the dangerous vampire.

The sound of footsteps in the hallway alerted Jake to Katrina's presence, and his eyes locked on Jax, who smiled with his typical cool confidence. As she rounded the corner, all attention went to the radiant she-wolf.

ᴥ Chapter Nine ᴥ

Katrina contemplated what had happened in Jax's office. Having told him the truth, she finally felt free. She wasn't certain he'd believed her but it didn't matter. For the first time in years, hope penetrated her thoughts. She considered how he'd blasted her with his energy and then denied it. The sensation had left her invigorated yet confused as to what had really occurred.

His seductive interrogation rocketed her into ecstasy, but when he'd withdrawn, she'd been disappointed. Although she'd always known that her actions would have long-term consequences, she still wasn't prepared for the distance he tried so hard to put between them. Her wolf couldn't accept it, and even though she'd spent so much time avoiding Jax, her thoughts were consumed with the Alpha.

Conflicted, she prayed that what the demons had told her wasn't true. *Could they have lied to me about Jax? Why do they care if I mate with him?* There was no denying that being intimate with the Alpha had supplemented her own magick. Feeling energized, she was ready for whatever battle lay ahead.

Quintus. In truth, she'd never expected to see him again. The captivating vampire had treated her with both compassion and respect during their short time together. When he'd bitten her, she'd come undone but in spite of her induced state of arousal, he'd never taken advantage. With her blood in his veins, he recovered within minutes.

She recalled the dizziness that ensued as he transported them out of their prison. It'd been the only time in her life that she'd experienced materialization, the intense magick overwhelming her body and mind. A kiss to her forehead was all she remembered when she later awoke inside her condo. It was only afterward that she'd discovered how deadly the ancient vampire truly was, and she considered herself lucky that she hadn't ended up dead.

Katrina scanned her elegant guest bedroom, appreciating how opulent Jax's lifestyle was in comparison to hers. It wasn't as if she didn't have money. On the contrary, she'd been gifted a considerable trust. But not wishing for unwanted attention, she'd chosen to live modestly. Her simple two bedroom condo in the city had always been enough for her, and when she moved to New Orleans, she took up residence in an apartment in the French Quarter situated over her newly renovated art gallery.

As she turned off the light, and went in search of Jax, butterflies fluttered in her stomach. Katrina couldn't be certain the kindness Quintus had shown her still existed. Or perhaps he'd be utterly ruthless, the stone-cold killer his reputation portrayed him to be.

Voices filtered through the hallway, and she caught her name on Jax's lips. Committed to her sworn honesty, she'd never lie to him again. She'd admitted the vampire had tasted her blood, and she'd known it would draw the Alpha's ire. She couldn't be sure if he was jealous or if he simply thought less of her for feeding Quintus, but she refused to be ashamed of what she'd done; she'd survived.

As expected, their conversation quieted as she entered the billiards room. Although she was aware of both Finn's and Jake's eyes on her, Jax was the only one who commanded her attention. His black t-shirt hugged his contoured pecs, jeans hung low on his hips. Katrina noted how his typically Nordic blond hair had darkened to a light shade of brown. Unconsciously, she fingered her own locks, reminded of the power of the demons and how they'd changed her.

Her eyes went to his lips, which curled up in a sexy smile. Confident and casual, Jax was sex personified. The Alpha's gaze upon her skin made her feel as if she wasn't wearing any clothes. She brushed her palms over her white tank top, assuring herself that she was dressed. The memory of what he'd done to her in his office flashed in her mind. She struggled to thwart her arousal and crossed her arms over her chest, hoping to hide the hardened peaks that strained against her bra.

Jax approached, his expression serious and sensual. As he reached for her hand, his touch seared her flesh. He brushed his lips to her cheek, and she closed her eyes, inhaling his masculine scent. Acutely aware of the rush of his power, she accepted it, reveling in his strength.

"You ready to go see Quintus?" Katrina heard him ask, his breath on her ear. Her chest rose slowly and she attempted to focus, to shake the desire that Jax incited.

"I'm not convinced he can help us," she responded, avoiding his question. As he stepped away from her, Katrina bit her lip, anxious about seeing the vampire.

"If there's one thing I know, it's that if Quintus was bested by these things, he's going to want revenge. And I can sure as hell guarantee that he knows more than we do." Jax brushed a hand over his hair, certitude in his eyes. "Stay with me. Understand? You belong to me in this place."

"But I... it's not true," she refuted him.

"You're under my protection, therefore you're mine. Do not give him any indication otherwise." Jax took out his cell phone and tapped against the glass. "Cael's got the limo ready."

Mine. Katrina's face heated as he said the words, her emotions already turbulent. He hadn't acknowledged her as his mate, but as his hand grazed the small of her back, she saw the smile on his lips and her heart caught. Jax Chandler was a force unto himself, one that, try as she might to control his influence on her, she was struggling to contain. Drawing on her inner strength, she steeled her nerves. Not convinced she belonged to the cunning

Alpha, she'd hold her own in the presence of Quintus. If he truly held the keys to her freedom, she'd play the game to discover his secrets.

As they pulled into Central Park, Katrina struggled to see where they were going. Of all the places in the city, she couldn't fathom how Quintus could remain undetected in one of the most vibrant sections of the park. The driver opened the door, and in silence they exited the car. Although it was nearly midnight, and the crowds had long since dissipated, she sensed a few stray humans roaming the grounds.

The limo's headlights flashed off, and Katrina adjusted her vision. The Angel of the Waters stood majestically guarding Bethesda Terrace, the reflection of the moon in the rippling lake. Katrina peered down the stone staircase, its arches leading into tunnels through to the fountain. In the safety of daylight, she suspected not a soul would give the area a second glance except to marvel at the beauty of the attraction.

Jax held a finger to his lips, silencing their small party. He stilled as they came up to a large stone pillar. A carved owl had been etched into its center. The three-dimensional bird stood proudly as if it could come alive at any moment. Small bats on either side kept company, their ominous blank eyes staring out onto the trespassers.

"Remember what we discussed," Jax told them, reaching his hand behind the chiseled figure.

As his fingers entered the recess, Katrina's pulse raced in anticipation and she inhaled deeply, attempting to slow her heartbeat. Her eyes darted to Jake and back to Jax as a small glow the size of a firefly appeared. A grinding rumble commenced, the pillar cracking wide open, revealing a staircase.

Jax gestured for them to descend, and Katrina looked up to him, uncertainty registering in her expression. In her human form, as lupine, she could see in the darkness, but she'd never willingly step into a pitch black cavern, one that appeared as ancient as the vampire they were going to visit. Trusting the Alpha, she followed him into the confined space, startled as the exit sealed shut behind them. With her hands on Jax's shirt, she blindly put one foot in front of the other.

The sound of the heavy bass alerted her that they were no longer alone. A splash of scarlet-red light appeared as they stepped into a vestibule. Katrina took in the sight of the black granite lobby. White silk fabric lined with strings of lights hung in columns from the ceiling. A clatter echoed in the foyer as a thin tall man passed through a waterfall of iridescent glass beads. Dressed only in black satin pants, his pale skin appeared translucent. He addressed Jax, but made no eye contact with Katrina. Black and silver flecks floated in his red irises. As he spoke, he licked at the crusted brown substance in the corners of his mouth. He shot her a vile smile, and she noted the black lines running down his teeth.

Katrina didn't scare easily. Over the years she'd been exposed to many different creatures in her brother's nightclub. From vampires to witches, she'd interacted with both good and evil. But as she watched the creature speak to Jax, the hair stood up on the back of her neck, chills rolling over her skin. Sensing an otherworldly vibe from the maître d, she wondered if he'd been possessed. Her hand found its way to Jax's shirt. Seeking contact with her protector, she breathed out the dread that had crept over her. Comforted by the warmth of Jake at her back, she never took her sight off of the macabre greeter.

"He's expecting you, Mr. Chandler."

"Indeed," Jax replied.

"This way." The thin man granted Katrina a sinister stare before turning back through the beaded entryway.

"Stay close," Jax whispered in her ear, taking her hand.

Katrina nodded, suspecting that whatever lay in the other room would be both dark and abominable. She caught a glimpse of Jake's tense expression, but Finn remained impassive. With her curiosity piqued after Jax had easily gained them entry, Katrina resisted asking how well he knew Quintus.

Her questions faded as they pressed through the shimmering baubles and entered the bar. The pulsing bass of techno music resonated under the soles of her boots. Unshaken, Katrina scanned the club for the vampire. Brick walls adorned with rusty hooks and chains surrounded a triangular bar, its shiny tinned surface littered with glasses and ashtrays.

Patrons of various ages ignored their entrance. Katrina noted that most of the women wore little clothing, baring their breasts, and the men followed suit. Her attention went to a woman who stood spread eagled atop bar stools. With her hands bound to the ceiling, each high-heeled foot was set firmly onto a seat. Men took turns licking between her legs. A trickle of blood ran down her thigh, a vampire at her hips. Screaming in ecstasy, she writhed toward the waiting mouths.

They weaved their way throughout the sea of dancing bodies. As they approached the back of the club, a woman, perched on her hands and knees, grunted, her fangs solidly embedded into the arm of a waif who lay dazed on a red velvet sofa. From behind her, a man buried his cock into the vampire, his eyes glazed over in a hedonistic frenzy.

Katrina's heart pounded against her ribs, her breath quickening. A firm stroke of Jax's thumb to her palm told her he sensed her unease. He responded with a wave of power, reminding Katrina that he'd protect her. Whatever happened, Jax Chandler was every bit as deadly as the creatures that slithered in the night.

In an instant, the music rolled back into a quiet thump, and flaring lights blinded Katrina. Disoriented, she held tight to Jax, immediately detecting the vampire's presence. *Quintus.*

"Jax," Katrina heard a distinctive male voice call. The familiar Italian accent caught her attention.

Jax released her hand, readying to approach the dark figure. He nodded to Finn and Jake, who immediately flanked Katrina, taking her hands.

As his face came into view, Katrina recognized the attractive vampire. Dressed in black leather, he appeared larger than life. His beard had been trimmed close, the penetrating gaze of his black eyes bored into her. She noted the brief glint of recognition that flashed right before he diverted his focus to Jax. Despite the tension, instinct told her he wouldn't hurt her.

"Quintus," Jax nodded, acknowledging his presence.

"Fucking with demons isn't good for your health, my friend," Quintus commented, his attention darting to Katrina and back to the Alpha.

"I hear they captured you as well," Jax countered.

"It's been a long time, Alpha." A corner of his mouth ticked upward.

"That it has. Perhaps this time, we work together?" Jax glanced to Katrina, who tore her hand from Jake's.

"Ah, Katrina, my lovely little savior." Quintus smiled.

"She's mine, Quint. These things…" Jax stepped in front of Katrina, blocking her view, "…they must be stopped."

"You'll get no argument from me. However, my existence is unaffected by their actions. It seems to me that you're the one with the problem. You see," Quintus gave Jax a slick grin, easing toward Katrina, "it's the Alpha's sister they want. She's special."

Katrina's heart raced as he brushed his roughened finger over her cheek. Before she could respond, Jake had shoved her out of the way, clutching Quintus' arm. She screamed as the vampire took Jake into his grip. With his arm around the wolf's neck, he dragged his fangs over his throat, drawing a bubbling line of blood.

"No!" she screamed. Katrina attempted to rush to Jake's aid, but was restrained by Finn. "Get off me."

"Quintus, no," Jax ordered.

"This wolf," Quintus stated, licking the sanguine fluid over his lips. "He's not yours. His Acadian blood…how I do love the taste of a virile wolf."

"Leave him be," Jax insisted. "He's learning, testing his new role. It's Katrina. He's protective of her. Please, show mercy so we can continue."

"Don't hurt him," Katrina cried. With a strength she didn't realize she possessed, she elbowed Finn, breaking free of his hold. But as she went to run to Jake, Jax commanded her.

"Do. Not. Move." Jax held his hand out to stop her.

The rush of his command slammed into Katrina, and she heaved for breath. She'd never experienced the negative energy that could be utilized by an Alpha. Clutching her gut, her eyes teared. Despite the passion she'd felt earlier for Jax, she hated him for attempting to force her submission. Refusing to lower her eyes, she glared at Jax in defiance.

"No, Jax." Katrina stopped cold, her voice a shaken whisper. Although he'd overpowered her, she refused to submit when Jake's life was at stake. "Maybe I was wrong about…"

"Don't interfere," Jax warned.

"Quintus." Katrina's scolding tone morphed into a soft plea, begging for mercy. "Please. Jake is my friend. He meant no harm."

"Ah, bella, what they did. I could not let them have you." Quintus' hold on Jake loosened and the wolf gasped for breath.

"I never expected you to save me that day." Katrina wiped the moisture from her cheek as she recalled what had happened. "I just knew I had to save you. One of us had to get out of there."

"Cara mia, I was a fool. I should've known when I saw her…it was too good to be true." Quintus shoved Jake to the floor, and took a seat in a large leather chair.

Katrina noted the change in the vampire's demeanor and speculated that he spoke of someone he'd lost long ago. Slowly, she backed away, noting that Jake was unhurt. Jax's eyes narrowed on her, his displeasure evident.

"I need your help, Quint," Jax stated, his gaze remaining locked on Katrina. "*We* need your help. This thing, these demons, whatever the fuck they are…they're trying to kill her."

"I see, and your interest in her?" Quintus spread his legs open, lounging backward. He paused, contemplating his words, and stroked his beard. "What is she to you? Don't fuck with me, Jax."

"Why do you need to know? Katrina's relationship to me is no concern of yours," Jax growled.

"Interesting," Quintus mused with a small smile. "Why does the great Alpha answer my question with a question?"

"All you need to know is that she's mine. She belongs to me."

Katrina seethed at his statement. After tonight, their future was uncertain. She would not mate with an Alpha who could not trust her, one who'd use his power to force her into submission.

"We've been friends a long time," Quintus continued and barked a laugh. "Maybe that's a stretch. Perhaps, we have a mutually beneficial relationship. Regardless of what you call it, I know you, Chandler…perhaps better than you think."

"Then you'll tell me everything you know?" he pressed.

"Sit." Quintus pointed to the chair next to him. "These two," he gestured to Jake and Finn, "we talk alone."

"Go get a drink. Don't leave her alone," Jax ordered.

Jake's mouth closed tight, his lips pursed in anger. Finn's temple pulsed in concern but he didn't challenge his Alpha. Finn gestured for Katrina to follow Jake.

Jax expected her to obey, to allow them to talk without her. Katrina's anxiety rose as she debated her next action. Defying Jax twice would further anger the Alpha. Quintus called her name, requesting her presence, and without asking, she stepped forward.

"She stays. Tell them, Alpha."

Katrina noted the amusement in Quintus' eyes even though his mouth revealed no emotion. Jax nodded in acknowledgement, his eyes going to hers. Although he didn't speak, she sensed his irritation with the vampire.

"I'm fine," she assured Jake, in the hopes he'd go willingly with Finn.

Jax sat next to Quintus, in a set of matching intricately carved mahogany chairs. The plush leather seats, embroidered with fleur-de-lis, reminded her of New Orleans. With no room to sit, she stood in front of the small round coffee table, protectively crossing her arms.

"Shall we begin again?" Quintus tapped the wood with his fingers and smiled up at Katrina. "Which one of you would like to tell me the nature of your relationship? How exactly does the sister of the Lyceum Wolves' Alpha come into the company of Jax Chandler?"

"Katrina and I are together because we both were kidnapped," Jax explained.

"That may be true but there is something else. Now what could that be?" Quintus extended his hand to Katrina. "Come, bella."

Afraid to look to Jax for approval, she allowed the vampire to take her palm in his. As he pressed his cool lips to her skin, her wolf growled in warning. Katrina attempted to jerk her arm away but he held tight.

"Quid pro quo, my friends. I shall help you in exchange for the truth. And," he gazed at Katrina and then to Jax, "a taste of her blood."

"No fucking way." Jax lurched to his feet. "We're leaving."

"Jax, please. We need to know. We need his help," Katrina pleaded.

"Have you lost your mind?" Jax gritted out, his eyes flared in rage.

"I can tell you about the demons who seek to steal her magick." Both Jax and Katrina were silenced by his statement, and focused on him. "That's right, my friend. Her magick." Quintus brought her palm to his nose and sniffed. "She's strong this evening, but she's filled with *your* energy."

"No, that can't be," Jax protested.

"Ah, it's true, isn't it? You've been feeding on his strength, haven't you? Maybe unable to control it? You're sucking it up like a beautiful little sponge, but sadly," he reflected, "your own magick, the very essence that makes you shift, come alive into the beautiful creature you are... it's weak."

Katrina's eyes blurred with tears as Quintus confirmed what she'd suspected. She'd felt stronger but it was Jax who'd invigorated her being. She drew on his power, and without him, she'd be unable to sustain her own magick.

"I don't know what's happening," she admitted, her response quiet.

"No, don't listen to him, Kat. He just wants to feed from you."

"Indeed I do," Quintus quipped. "She's lovely."

"She's my mate," Jax declared.

Katrina shook her head no, wishing he hadn't provided the information to Quintus.

"Really now?" Quintus laughed in amusement. "But you haven't mated? She's unmarked. You didn't claim her right away. Hmm...well, now, what does that say?"

"It says nothing." Jax shook his head in annoyance. "It says we're still trying to figure out what in the hell is going on. Look, Quint, if you can't give us answers, we're done here."

"No," Katrina interrupted. If they didn't get the answers they sought, they might never be free. Even in New Orleans, where she'd been less visible to the demons, she suspected they'd eventually find her.

"I said, no. We're leaving," Jax replied.

Quintus released a hearty laugh. "The Alpha has indeed met his match. Refreshing to see the almighty Jax Chandler challenged by such a lovely creature. This tells me she must be deadly." His expression went serious as his gaze washed over Katrina. "You must be careful, my friend. Like many of the world's most beautiful plants, she could be lethal."

"This is over. Come on, Kat. We'll go to New Orleans." Jax stood.

"No, please." Katrina tugged her hand away from Quintus and slowly reached for Jax. By the time her palm touched his face, her body hummed with his energy. "He's right about me. This is your magick you feel, not mine. I need answers. We're running out of time. Let him bite me. Anything I feel, I will only ever feel for you. It's not real."

"I can't let you do this." His forehead pressed to hers.

"That's the thing, Jax....you don't *let* me do anything. As much as I want you to be, you aren't my Alpha yet. I know you don't want me to get hurt, but I can't let these things kill you or me. We need answers. And if that means sacrificing, then I need to do this. Please understand."

"This isn't a good idea." Jax's focus went to the vampire as he considered her argument.

"I want to be free," she maintained.

"Jesus, this isn't right. But if we do this, I'm going to be right here with you."

Katrina gave Jax a small smile as he reluctantly granted his permission.

"Quintus, I give you my blood only. Nothing else, do you understand? Don't force me to shift," Katrina warned, unsure what would happen if she panicked. The demons had changed her, and the incident in the woods with Jax served to remind her that they'd infused her with whatever evil they held.

"Jax, you can't let her do this," Jake called, hearing every word of their conversation. Finn held him back, and while she understood his concern, there was no turning back.

"Jake, stop." Katrina held her hand up to him, and focused on Jax. "Stay with me. Don't leave my side. Quintus won't hurt me." Katrina paused, catching the delight in the vampire's dark smile. "Will you?"

"As a man of honor, I swear it. There's one thing you should know about me, and I'd think my friend Jax would know this by now; no action is without reason. And your blood," Quintus reached for her wrist and brought it to his nose, "it's no different. You saved me once and I save you in return, bella."

"Tell me now. How do we kill these things?" she asked.

"We're agreed, Alpha? Knowledge for blood?" Quintus asked, continuing to press his nose to Katrina's skin.

"Katrina…" Jax began.

Katrina sensed his hesitation. As her eyes locked on his, she attempted to push her magick back at him. Hoping he could feel her strength, she prayed he'd trust her. Although not marked nor bonded as mates, she knew his wolf would likely go feral having any man touch her. But with little choice, desperation sliced through her chest.

"It's just blood," she said, her tone confident. No matter how shaken she was inside, she'd never show fear.

"Just blood," Jax confirmed. "Do not touch her, Quint. It will be the last thing you feel before you die."

"Agreed?" the vampire asked, raising an eyebrow.

"Yes," Jax bit out. "Go. What do you know?"

"Circe," Quintus stated.

"What?" Katrina asked, confused.

"It's a who. Greek mythology," Jax responded, his focus trained on the vampire.

Quintus laughed. "Ah, I always knew you were a smart one."

"A goddess," Jax continued.

"Of magick. It was said she turned men into animals. Which is interesting, as you shifters are animals." Quintus smiled up at Katrina and licked his lips.

"Would you stop with the cryptic answers," Jax demanded.

"Circe worshippers. They harbor magick, stealing it."

"But why would anyone do that? Why not just go to witches? They conjure it naturally, both good and bad."

"Who's to say they aren't witches? Some say witches. Some say demons. Not much is known. What you see is an illusion. They shift, indulging in the deception. The torture they practice, the pain and fear, the energy it elicits. They use it."

"What in the hell for?" Jax asked, scrubbing his chin.

"They have a dark master, one who hasn't been able to break free of the underworld."

"Circe? But she can't be real," Katrina countered.

"I cannot say one way or another." Quintus' tone resounded low and rough. "Whispers. Rumors. Blah. In the end, all the three of us know to be true is what we saw in there. And even then, the illusions…they're so very real."

Katrina's arm broke out in gooseflesh as the chilling tone of Quintus' voice rolled over her. "Why take me? I'm just a wolf."

"An Alpha's daughter," Quintus told them, his words slow and deliberate. "An Alpha's sister."

"An Alpha's mate," Jax finished his sentence.

"But that happens sometimes. It's not unusual to be all three," Katrina stated.

"An Alpha's daughter or sister? Yes, that's fairly common. But for you also to be the mate of an Alpha? All three? Not so much," Jax countered.

"There may be something else. Something about you. Assuming there are others, why do they come for you? Why Jax, for that matter?" Quintus pondered. "Perhaps your family hides secrets."

"Tristan wouldn't do that. I've told him what happened," she protested.

"But he hasn't stopped it, now has he?" Quintus pointed out.

"My brother's a busy man. He has many things to attend to on any given day. Tris might not have completely believed me, but he'd never lie to me."

"Well, now, I'm no expert on Tristan Livingston. But I saw you the night I was captured. I saw what they did to you. The bruises," Quintus reflected with a lilt of compassion in his words. "No one could withstand what they'd done to you. Yet not only did you survive, you fed me."

"I'd shift," Katrina argued. "I was never gone for long. A day at most. Sometimes only hours."

"Something about your magick. It's special to them. Potent." The vampire once again reached for her hand and turned it over, inspecting her palm.

"Why let me go then? Why not drain me dry?" Katrina questioned. Her voice grew louder as she tried to contain her panic.

"Because they are letting you heal," Jax told her.

"They sow the field and wait for it to grow again. Then they come back to yield the crop. But like an overplanted field, your ability to replenish grows weak. But there is something unusual about the Alpha. Why do they attack him? Why risk the wrath of his pack?"

"How do we kill them?" Jax interrupted.

"Tricky business. I suppose you must figure out a way to stop them from sucking away her essence."

"You mean like a vampire?" Jax raised an accusing eyebrow at him.

"Now, now...no need to toss around insults." Quintus brushed the back of Katrina's palm over his beard. "We are not so different, after all. You know full well that vampires are born of the same magick as wolves. Immortality. Our ability to transform. Unlike wolves, who thrive on the cycles of the moon, vampires drink the blood of humanity itself. Their magick, however, is neither good nor evil. It simply exists."

"So what are these things? Like drones?" Jax growled, his eyes on Katrina's hand. "Get to the short of it."

"Testy aren't we, Alpha?" Quintus laughed and continued. "My guess is that they're like mages, driven by the demon itself, working collectively to escape. They seek the assistance of witches who need favors."

"What kind of favors?"

"The kind of favors that lie deeply entrenched in black magick. Spells that are so very difficult on their own, they seek the help of the demon. The price is high, I imagine."

"What kind of a demon has the power to control these things from the underworld?" Katrina asked, as a chill ran up her spine.

"That is the question, my sweet dove. Something strong. Destructive."

"Something or someone," Jax added. "What's your part in this? Why were you there with Katrina?"

"Simply put, I danced with a witch, a very nasty one. But that's neither here nor there. The creature that appeared to me that night..." His voice trailed off, and Katrina noted the sadness that flushed his expression. As if someone had slapped his face, he blinked and continued. "She appeared...it appeared as someone I'd known long ago. I should've known better but sometimes matters of the heart can obscure reason."

"What's the name of the witch? Who did you fuck with, Quint?"

"Doesn't matter," he grumbled. "No need to speak her name. The last time I saw her in New Orleans..."

Katrina startled as Quintus jerked her arm; her feet stumbled back.

"I'm afraid we're out of time." The ancient vampire's eyes flashed red, his voice lowered into a whisper. "Your Katrina is like a beacon. They're coming."

"What do you mean, 'they're coming?'" Jax rushed to Katrina, wrapping his hand around her waist.

"No more time, Alpha. I need her blood now. I will get us out of here."

"How are you going to do that?" Katrina yelled. "What is happening?"

"They're here. Come. I'll get you out. But first...her blood?" Quintus sought the approval of the Alpha.

The room began to quake, and Katrina fell back onto Quintus' lap. Bits of cracked bricks sprayed from the ceiling in the far corner, and a small tunnel of light poured onto the dirty stone floor. Jax fell to his knees in front of her, and his eyes met the vampire's.

"Do not touch her. Blood only," Jax repeated.

Katrina's pulse raced at the realization that they'd come for her again. *You can't have me again.* She tore at her blouse and ripped the fabric, exposing her shoulder. With her gaze locked on Jax, she grabbed tight to his hands.

"Do it now!"

She screamed as the vampire's fangs pierced her flesh. The room spun, suction at her neck. The searing pain transposed into desire. With her hands on her mate, she moaned in ecstasy.

"Jax," she cried. "Please help me."

Clutching at his lapel, she pulled him to her. As his lips met hers, her world went dark.

➤ᵉ⊛ *Chapter Ten* ⊛ᵉ➤

Jax fought the nausea as they materialized onto his bedroom floor. He blinked, and checked his surroundings, quickly realizing that Quintus had transported them back to his penthouse. Although the shifty vampire had saved their lives, his fangs remained lodged in Katrina's shoulder.

"Get the fuck off her!" As Quintus raised his head, Jax's fist landed directly on the vampire's nose. The vampire hissed, bringing his hand to his face. Blood sprayed onto the cherry hardwood floor. "Jesus fucking Christ."

"What the hell is wrong with you? I just saved your goddamned ass. Fuck me." He licked at his lips.

"I'll tell you what's wrong. Look at what you just did to her." Jax scooped Katrina in his arms and inspected her skin. Two tiny red bumps protruded from her pale flesh, the wounds healing. Jax sighed, shaking his head. Katrina's head lolled in the crook of his arm, and he glared at Quintus. "What's wrong with her? What did you do?"

"You're an ungrateful asshole. Same as all those years ago," Quintus spat, leveraging the bed to shove to his feet.

"Really? Are we back to that? She never wanted you anyway." Jax blew out a frustrated breath.

He'd known Quintus for over fifty years. They'd fought off the rise of a human sect that sought to destroy all supernaturals. Allies, they'd survived battles, shared meals and women, but one woman had come between them. *Margot Tremainne.* At the time, Jax had been a neophyte Alpha, seeking to assert his role. He'd thought it a game to best Quintus, winning the affection of the flirty French mistress.

"Si, amico mio. It's about trust."

Jax laughed. When his friend reverted to speaking Italian, he knew he was in trouble.

"Jesus, Quint. I'm sorry, okay. Fuck. It was a long time ago. I was a dick, is that what you want to hear?"

"Si. You are." Quintus brushed the dirt off his leathers. "Those shitheads made a mess."

"What did you do to Kat?" Jax pressed his cheek to hers. Despite her being unconscious, she appeared well, her heartbeat strong, her breathing normal.

"She'll be fine."

"Does she look all right to you?" Guilt flooded Jax; he'd allowed him to bite her.

"You know damn well that dematerializing isn't easy, even for someone as good as me. I had to take both of you. That takes a lot of magick, and I needed nourishment, if you will. Katrina's blood," he paused as if he'd enjoyed a meal at a five star restaurant, "she's the very best. Must be the Alpha in her. I'm not quite sure but si, she's delicious."

"You seriously need to get the fuck out of here before I stake your ass."

"Jealousy is an ugly emotion."

"You hurt her."

"Pfft. She's fine. Just resting. You're well aware that materializing is difficult on you wolves. And the humans?" He rolled his eyes and checked his hair in the mirror, smoothing a strand back into place. "Don't even get me started. So weak. They're pathetic. I will not apologize for saving you both. I would have never been able to get you both out at the same time if I hadn't drank from her."

"Yeah right, like I'm supposed to believe that shit." Jax brushed his lips to her forehead, and pulled the fabric of her shirt together, shielding her bra from Quintus' view.

"Believe what you want. One thing is certain, you must find a way to stop these demons."

"Tell me the name of the witch. Who did you screw with?"

"Why do you want to know so badly? I escaped, didn't I?"

"Yeah, but you needed her." Jax glanced to Katrina and sighed. "Just tell me. I need a starting point. Whoever the witch is, she knows more about these things than we do. If I know what I'm dealing with, I can destroy it."

"Fine, but it's your funeral. Her name's Ilsbeth. The bitch…"

"Ilsbeth," Jax interrupted with a disgusted laugh. "It fucking figures."

The powerful witch had last been seen in New Orleans. After casting a spell on Dimitri, robbing him of his ability to shift, she'd disappeared. Logan had suspected that Léopold had killed her.

"Si. She's not one to be trifled with."

"Yeah, well, she's dead."

"Has this been confirmed?" Quintus asked in surprise.

"One could wish. But no." Jax slid his arms underneath Katrina. Cradling her to his chest, he pressed to his feet. "After tonight, it's obvious we need to get to New Orleans sooner rather than later. Logan will help me. He owes me."

A pang of grief stabbed at him, the mention of the debt cleaved through the thin veil of his healed emotions. He'd protected his sister, fought alongside of Acadian wolves, but it was his brother who had died.

"Ah, I heard about Nick. Sorry, amico." The sympathy in Quintus' statement was evident, but out of respect, the vampire remained far away from the Alpha's mate.

"Look Quint. I've gotta take care of Katrina. Jake and Finn…"

"They'll be home safely. They're after her, not them." Quintus turned to leave. He paused, looking over his shoulder. "This demon, it grows stronger.

Finding her tonight, it broke through my wards. New Orleans is safer. With all the witchcraft buzzing in the Quarter, it may have a harder time finding her."

"My home is always protected with wards, but I agree...we'll leave tomorrow."

"If you need me...you know where to find me."

"Hey, Quint," Jax called as the ancient vampire passed through the doorway.

"Yeah?"

"Thanks, man."

Quintus nodded and gave a wave in silence as he dematerialized.

Jax glanced down to Katrina, his heart heavy. The great Alpha had failed those closest to him, and a seed of doubt crept into his mind as he wondered if he could keep her safe. He studied her face, noting how her pink lips curled into a smile even in her sleep. She moaned and buried her nose into his shirt, her hand traveling over his shoulder. His cock stirred in response, and he knew he was in trouble.

What the hell was I thinking? Jax settled into the oversized tub, adjusting his steel-hard dick. *Clean her off. Get her into bed. We'll all get a good rest and leave in the morning.* It all had seemed a good idea when he was formulating his plan. After he'd run the soap over her arms, he'd grown aroused. With her head lying flat on his shoulder, he held a firm hand around her waist, contemplating his next move.

Taking a deep breath, he closed his eyes, reflecting on the scene in the club. He'd considered refusing Quintus her blood. But not only did they desperately need information, he'd known the vampire wouldn't hurt Katrina. The bastard may have held a grudge but they'd been through enough battles for him to know that he could trust him. Although he'd been grateful to Quintus for saving them, the memory of his teeth embedding in her creamy skin made him sick. *Mine*, his beast growled in disagreement, but human reason had agreed to the act.

Is she really my mate? The question danced in his mind. Instinct told him she was but until they made love, he couldn't be completely certain. It was getting more difficult to deny his wolf's craving. It bared its fangs, warning him not to wait. *Take her now*, it urged. Although Jax had always been a patient man, her slick nude form against his left little room for restraint.

Katrina's eyes fluttered open, and he breathed a sigh of relief.

"Jax," she whispered, licking her lips.

"Shh, little wolf, I've got you. You're safe." Brushing a stream of warm water over her belly, he stroked her skin.

"But Quintus." Panic laced her words. "He bit me…"

"You must learn to obey your Alpha." His dominance rose to the surface. A soft hand grazed over his thigh, and his cock swelled in response.

"Why are we in water?" she asked, ignoring his statement. As she went to sit up, Jax held her tight to him.

"Because we were covered in dirt and you were unconscious. Seemed the easiest way to clean us both." Jax gave a small laugh.

"Hmm…that's it, huh?" Her hand reached for his. "I guess I can think of worse ways to wake up."

As she wove her fingers through his, Jax smiled. When he'd stripped her bare to bathe her, he'd known it could go one of two ways. She'd either be as aroused as he was, or she'd come out scratching like a wildcat. But it was apparent from her reaction that she, too, continued to fall victim to the unrelenting attraction.

"We need to talk about what happened tonight." If she was his mate, she'd have to submit; there was no other way.

"What?" she asked innocently.

"Kat," he gritted out as her bottom slid over his hardened dick. "Tonight with Quintus…you could have been killed."

"Me? He was about to kill Jake," Katrina responded with a demure tone. She pressed her thumb into his palm and teased the soft skin between their fingers. "Did you expect me to stand by and watch? I had to do something. I know what you did. Your power…"

"I won't apologize. I wasn't going to let anything happen to you."

"But Quintus…"

"Quintus is a friend, but he's dangerous. I'm well aware of how lethal he is which is exactly why I ordered you, forced you back."

Jax reached into her hair, gently pulling her head to one side, revealing her creamy white neck. Her lips parted, and he couldn't tell if it was in arousal or surprise. With his eyes on hers, he grew serious.

"You will learn not to test me." Jax grazed his nose over her skin, letting her scent infiltrate his mind. His wolf snarled, demanding submission.

"You can't change who I am. Jax…I…" she breathed. Her back arching, the rosy tips of her nipples broke through the bubbles.

Jax lost control, and with the speed of his animal, he flipped her over onto her back. The sound of splashing water resounded throughout the dimly lit room. Swirling puffs of eucalyptus-scented steam floated into the air, and Jax delighted in the gasp that escaped from Katrina's lips.

He pinned her arms to the flattened surface surrounding the tub. With his chest pressed to hers, their wet skin sizzled with the heat of passion. The tip of his cock pressed through her folds, teasing her nub. She moaned as he licked the hollow of her neck.

"I will have all of you or none at all, Katrina," he told her, his lips at her neck. "You know our ways. You were raised as one of us. Why do you continue to challenge me?"

"You need to understand. I've been on my own a long time. Aside from Tristan, I don't take orders from anyone. What you're asking…it won't be easy. Ah…" she cried as he dragged his tongue up over her skin.

"Are you mine?" he asked.

"I…I…" she stuttered.

Jax lifted his head, meeting her gaze. "Are you mine? It's simple. You feel this."

Jax took her lips with his, passionately demanding her decision. His tongue sought hers. She wrapped her legs around his waist, bringing him closer. His wolf roared, yearning for her submission, but with his control weak, the urge to be buried deep inside her superseded all else.

Shadows danced in the candlelight as he shoved out of the stone tub, water dripping off their silky flesh. Making his way into the bedroom, Jax groaned as she bit at his lips. His calves brushed the mattress, and he tore his mouth from hers. Gripping her waist, he tossed her onto the bed. The fire in her eyes drilled through him as she backed up on her elbows, her swollen pink mouth parted.

"Are you mine?" he asked again. The planes of his muscled physique tensed, his cock jerking as blood rushed into it.

"I…I…I want to say yes…" Her hand brushed her long mane out of her eyes.

His eyes drank in the sight of her bared on his bed, the beaded moisture rolling down her abdomen. She licked her lips and brought her hand to her breast, teasing her nipple between her fingers.

"Say yes to what…that you belong to me?" Jax pounced on the bed. She startled only slightly but continued to caress her tip. On his knees, he straddled her torso. His tight balls brushed over her stomach, and he took his cock into his hand, stroking it. "That you're mine?" He inched forward, and grazed the tip of his seeping head through the valley of her breasts. She released her nipple, and her hands crept up the front of his thighs. Her sexy smile drove him to press her further. "That you'll fuck me? Which is it, princess? Because this is happening tonight."

"You know I want you," she breathed, never taking her eyes off the Alpha. "But I won't hurt you, Jax. I can't make promises I can't keep. Not now…not until we have answers."

Although he knew why she hesitated, he was convinced more than ever that whatever they'd told her about her killing him was bullshit. The more he was around Katrina, the stronger their connection grew.

Jax pumped his hardened dick through the swell of her mounds. Her hips lifted, and he knew she sought relief for the ache between her legs. She'd admit she was his before he gave her what she needed.

"Is this what you want? My cock inside you?" Jax smiled, brushing the crown over her nipple. He delighted as the ripple of her shiver grazed his inner thighs.

"You're torturing me…making me wait."

Jax eyed the seductive beauty. Goddammit, she was going to drive him fucking crazy. With his skin against hers, his wolf howled, recognizing his mate. The Alpha needed to hear the words from her lips, that she felt it too, that she was his.

"Say yes, Katrina. Say it. Say you belong to me. Or I swear, I will get up and walk away right now." He slid closer, thumbing his seed over his shaft.

"Jax…please." Katrina blinked, running her hands up his ripped abs. "Please…yes. Yes, I belong to you."

Jax knew she was scared of hurting him, would resist the bonding until she knew otherwise. His hunger had reached a precipice. The dam broke, the Alpha's power burst, and he fought to retain the tendrils of energy that threatened to spiral from his body.

Guiding his glistening head toward her mouth, he swiped it over her lower lip. Her pink tongue darted out and swept over its slit, eliciting a tremor through his body.

"Suck it," he told her, his eyes locked on hers.

Her lips opened at his request and he pressed into her wet mouth. The suction around his shaft increased and his hands went to the headboard. Clutching onto the wood, he plunged into her warmth. She hummed, the vibrations traveling from his tip to his root, and he cursed.

"Fuck, yeah." As he continued to pump in and out of her, his wolf claimed her as his own. Resounding and unequivocal, the call for his mate registered. No male would touch her without his permission; she'd be his for all of time.

A small purr came from her throat, and he hissed as she dug her fingernails into his ass. He laughed, noting her aggression. Her tongue twirled over his head, and he fought the urge to erupt.

"Oh no, I'm not coming in your mouth. I've gotta be inside you." She released a small whine as he withdrew.

"No…" she protested.

"See that's the thing, baby. This wolf is your Alpha, not the other way around and…" He paused. Sitting back on his knees, he spread her legs wide open, and admired her slick mound, her lips swollen in arousal. "…this pussy." He ran his crown through her slippery folds, brushing it over her blossoming clit, its shiny bulb beckoning to him. "Oh, shit, yeah. See how wet you are for me." Pressing his cock to her entrance, he lifted her legs. "My woman. My mate."

"Yes," she cried.

Plunging inside Katrina, Jax grunted, sheathing himself fully. Her quivering channel pulsed around his shaft, and he sucked a deep breath, willing himself not to come.

Palming his cheeks, she pressed her fingers into his mouth. Jax sucked her, tasting, feeling, consumed with his mate. His wolf celebrated, urging the

Alpha to bite her. He rocked in and out of her, all the while licking at her thumb. He'd thought he'd take her roughly, but as he descended into rhythmic thrusts, he gently spread her knees to the side. Seeking her mouth, he brought his lips to hers. With each long stroke, he kissed her, desperate to claim her. His hand found her breast, caressing her soft swell.

Together they moved in harmony, and all Jax could think about was how he'd never in his life been with someone who challenged him, met his dominance with vigor and passion. His wolf called to him to mark her. He tunneled his fingers into her hair, and she gave a small squeak as he wrapped them around her locks.

With his eyes locked on hers, his gut clenched as she willfully bared her neck to him. Although her sign of submission registered, Jax wasn't foolish enough to interpret it as her embracing their mating. His wolf, on the other hand, feral for his mate, lost control. Jax pounded into her, accepting the consequences of his actions. Katrina Livingston may have once drawn both his lust and ire, but tonight in his arms and bed, she willingly gave herself to him.

As his fangs descended, he allowed his beast the control it sought, biting into the soft flesh of her neck. With the only shred of restraint he possessed, Jax resisted drawing blood, which he knew would initiate bonding. He heard her cry his name as he held her in place, his teeth marking her skin. Katrina convulsed underneath him in orgasm.

"Mate," Jax grunted, stiffening as his release tore through him.

"Yours." Katrina shuddered with ecstasy, clutching to her Alpha.

"I've wanted you forever," she admitted. "I can't lose you."

"I'm here, baby. It's going to be okay," he promised. Warm tears brushed his cheek, and his heart melted. A rush of emotion coiled in his chest. "I'll keep you safe. I swear it."

No matter what she'd been told by the demons, he knew in his heart that she could never destroy him. Her sacrifice in keeping them apart had crushed her spirit, denied her wolf. In his arms, her energy splintered apart. Like fireworks, she'd come alive.

Jax rolled to his back, bringing her with him. Her small sob quieted and he wrapped both his arms around her, cradling her to his chest.

"Katrina, this is meant to be. Fighting it, running from it like you've done…it limits your strength, expends energy you need to conserve."

"If something happens to you…" she began.

"Let me worry about that now, will you? The rush you've felt; maybe you are absorbing my power, but I feel stronger than ever. And just now," Jax wiped a tear from her cheek with his thumb, "my wolf is calm, content that his mate is claimed."

"I can't believe you marked me." Her small fingers grazed over his chest, her voice shaky.

"I'm not going to fight nature when we have other things to fight. We need to do this together. I'm not buying this shit about you hurting me. I don't know why those assholes told you that, but I'm telling you that I feel amazing."

"I never knew what it would be like. Making love to you…my wolf, she claims you as her own." Katrina pressed her lips to his chest.

"I wasn't sure either. But that first time we met our connection was so strong. I suspected. It's why I kept calling. Talked to your brother. I couldn't just let you go. But when you ran and I thought you'd lied, well, hell. I know mates don't always get along but that made me question my sanity." Jax speared his fingers through his hair. "I've been Alpha a long time. I trust my instincts. And my instincts told me that you could be mine. So to have them be so far off base…and now, together like this? It makes so much sense to be with you. Look." Jax lifted her chin with a finger, exposing her neck. "It's unbelievable."

"What?" she asked, her eyes lighting up.

"My mark on you, it's ever so slight but it's there."

"Really?" She smiled.

"Really. And it's beautiful…like you." Jax brushed his lips to the top of her head. "But do be warned, little wolf."

"Hmm…what?" Katrina's words grew sleepy, her thigh coming up over his legs.

"I wasn't joking earlier. You'll learn to obey me within my pack. There is no other way."

"I love the way you feel inside me," she responded without acknowledging his statement.

Jax gave a small smile, aware that she'd ignored his statement. But Katrina underestimated the determination of her Alpha. She'd learn to trust him. While she'd bared her neck, he suspected that she'd test him the first chance she had. His cock twitched, as he fantasized about the erotic ways he'd teach his little wolf to embrace her submission.

Within his arms, Katrina succumbed to slumber, and he prayed to the Goddess that he could keep her safe. With dawn approaching, he'd have just enough time to assign Finn to watch over his anxious pack. As he drifted off to sleep, Quintus' words played through his mind. *New Orleans*. Tomorrow they'd depart for the Big Easy, and search for the keys that would unlock their future. They'd finally get answers, seeking a weapon against the enemy that never rested. The demons had found her tonight; time was running out. *Tick tock. Tick tock.*

Chapter Eleven

"What did you do?" Finn asked, staring at the inside of the refrigerator.

"Nothing. Not a damn thing," Jax lied.

"I may have been your beta for all of fucking two days, but I know you. We grew up together, remember?" He reached for a carton of milk, opened and sniffed it.

"I haven't known him for as long as you, but something is up," Jake commented, smearing cream cheese on his bagel. He took a bite and smiled. "Only in New York."

"What the hell is with you two anyway? I come out here to get some coffee and you've taken over my house. Why don't you tell me how you got home?"

"Nice, by the way." Jake pointed his pastry at the Alpha. "Whatever...just disappear. And letting Quintus bite Kat? Don't even get me started."

"I wouldn't go there if I were you," Finn warned.

"Oh I'm goin' there. He let that vamp bite her right there in front of everyone." He swallowed, and waved his butter knife in the air as he spoke.

"I'm in a moderately good mood this morning, Jake. Let's not ruin it." Jax smiled and held his nose to his latte, inhaling its delicious aroma. He opened the lid and peered inside. "Don't you love how they make these cool little hearts?"

"He did not just say that." Finn rolled his eyes and snatched a bagel out of the bag. He threw it onto the black and white speckled granite countertop.

"Hearts? No, no I did not notice. You're joking, right?" Jake shoved the round dough into his mouth, continuing to talk as he chewed. "Please tell me he's joking."

"What?" Finn rummaged through a drawer and slammed it shut. Scanning the kitchen, he spied a serrated knife from the wooden block and retrieved it. "We got back fine, by the way. I can see you cared so much about what happened."

"These things are after Katrina, not the two of you. Besides, you're no worse for wear. You even had time to bring by breakfast, which was very thoughtful, by the way," Jax commented.

"You're welcome." Finn sawed through the bread.

"You're a tough guy, and him," Jax's eyes darted over to Jake and then fell back onto his drink, "he's preparing for his own time."

"Preparing for his own time?" Jake asked. "What the hell is that even supposed to mean? Have you been drinking?"

"No, my friend. Just observant." Jax smiled as he took a long sip of his coffee. "Hmm, I missed these."

"What's wrong with him?" Jake glanced to Finn.

"Did you know that Alphas sometimes run in families?" Jax reached for his iPad that he'd set on the counter, and joined Jake at the kitchen table. He gazed out the floor to ceiling window which looked out onto Central Park, and smiled. He loved his city more than ever, and it'd be here he'd rule with his mate.

"No shit," Jake replied, his answer laden with sarcasm.

"But sometimes, it doesn't. Sometimes an Alpha is just born. He's made." Jax slid his fingers across the glass, opening his email, then paused. "I cannot bring you the answers you seek. I can only guide you."

"Look, I don't even know what that means. All I'm sayin' is that you let Quintus bite…"

"Enough." Jax waved a dismissive hand in the air.

"She must not really be your mate, because damn, if she didn't challenge you right there," Finn noted.

"Oh, she's my mate." Jax laughed. She'd kill him, but she was indeed his. Her true submission would be sweet when it came but it would not happen easily.

"She sure as hell didn't act like it last night. Who the hell thinks she can go up against someone like Quint?"

"Someone who's desperate, that's who." Jake nodded at Jax as if to give him support. "Someone who was trying to save me. She's brave."

"See there, he also has instinct," Jax noted with a smile.

"Instinct? I think the both of you have lost it over that she-wolf." Finn attempted to stuff the bagel into the toaster, but it wouldn't fit. "Fuck."

"Katrina is tough. As wolf, she's one of the strongest I've seen. I'm talking 'Gillian strong'. She's pretty badass." Jake shrugged and gave a nod.

"Her father was an Alpha. Her brothers." Jax blew out a breath and looked over to Finn. "And her mate as well. There's something extraordinary about her."

"By extraordinary, do you mean crazy? Because she's kind of crazy for challenging an Alpha. That's special all right. The pack is going to have a field day if you don't get her under control." Finn managed to insert the bagel into the slot. His finger sizzled and he jumped. "Shit. That's fucking hot."

"Yes, genius. It's a toaster," Jake jibed.

"Fuck off."

"Cold water," Jax suggested.

"Ice," Jake told him.

"Cold water," Jax repeated. "Or shift."

"He's going to shift over a boo-boo on his little finger?" Jake gave a small chuckle.

"You're both assholes." Finn toggled on the spigot and shoved his finger under the stream. "It's cold water, by the way."

"Whatever." Jake reached for his orange juice and took a swig.

"The Alpha is always right." Jax laughed and focused back on his screen. "Tell me about last night."

"Nothing happened. You three vaped out of the basement and the earthquake stopped. Whatever was on its way in must've sensed you were gone. After that, we left the same way we came in. The place was a disaster, but we got home, that's all that counts." Jake leaned back in his chair and stared out onto the city. "Nice place, by the way."

"Thanks. It's home. Speaking of which…today we're going to New Orleans."

"What about the pack?" Finn asked.

"You're in charge while I'm gone. I should only be a few days."

"What about Katrina?" Finn wiped his hands dry on a towel.

"She's going with us." Jax trained his vision on Jake, who met his hard stare. "Ilsbeth. We're going to find her. I don't know exactly what happened between her and Quint, but she's wrapped up in this shit storm."

"There was a time," Jake reflected, "she wasn't all that bad. But what she did to Dimitri, to his wolf? When I think back on it, I just don't get it. I know she wanted D, but there are rules we all play by. The witches? The vamps? They all know the score with us wolves. We can't commit to others who aren't our breed."

"Friend em'. Fuck em' at your own risk, but emotions? It's trouble," Finn added.

"It's none of my concern why she did what she did. I just need to know how she knew about the demons. So we're going back to New Orleans." Jax's voice grew contemplative. Returning to the city would bring up memories of Nick's death, but he had no choice.

"Hey Jax, you know Nick, he, uh…that night." Jake paused and rubbed his chin. "Chaz, he'd hurt your sister…would have killed her. He's a hero. He died protecting her."

"That night you almost died too, my friend," Jax noted. "I took Nick's death hard. But I can't lose control of my emotions again. You both know that the pack, the energy of an Alpha, it affects everyone. When I was missing, I'm sure all hell broke loose. I took no pleasure killing Arlo."

"He was a dick anyway," Finn began.

"Perhaps, but that wolf…he was a brother. An uncle. A son. Killing during a challenge? The death it brings. It always comes at a cost, don't ever think it doesn't. But this is our responsibility. To lead. There is no other path for us." Although Jax dare not speak the truth of his suspicion regarding the young wolf, he hoped someday Jake would realize his destiny. "I've already called Logan. He knows we're coming and why. Jake will remain at my side. Finn. You're needed here."

"You still haven't told us about Katrina. The pack…" Finn shook his head, hesitating.

"She's my mate." Jax shoved out of his chair, and moved to stand at the window.

When he'd woken, he'd found her quietly sleeping on his chest, wrapped around him like a blanket. With their turbulent past, he didn't expect an easy road to their mating. He needed to convince her that bonding wouldn't hurt him. But with his mark blossoming on her skin, his wolf celebrated, content she'd been claimed.

A laugh drew Jax out of his contemplation and he turned to see both Finn and Jake, shaking their heads.

"What's so funny?" Jax asked.

"I just never thought I'd see the almighty Jax Chandler fall so hard. All the women over the years? Shit, I remember that little vamp from LA you dated. She had her fangs into you…literally." Finn laughed. "And London? Holy hell. She's going to lose it when she finds out you've found a mate."

"You one hundred percent sure you guys are mates?" Jake asked.

"Of course he is." Katrina stood in the entryway to the kitchen, a sheet wrapped around her.

Jax smiled, unsure of what to say. A laugh escaped his lips, as he thought about how she'd turned his life upside down in two days. The articulate Alpha had been rendered speechless. As he took in the sight of her bright eyes, her tousled hair, his cock jerked. Holy hell, he was in trouble.

"He marked me. Can you see it?" she asked, trailing her fingertips over her neck. She blinked and gave Jax a sexy sleepy smile.

He went to her, setting his coffee on the table. Jax ran the pads of his fingers over the lines. The quarter-sized intricate design had grown a deeper shade of pink.

"It's beautiful. How do you feel, baby?"

"Baby, my ass…" Finn commented under his breath.

Jax ignored him, cupping her cheek. She turned into his touch, her lips brushing over his skin.

"Come here," he told her, bringing her into his arms.

"Hmm…" Katrina nuzzled against his chest.

"Jake and Finn brought breakfast." The Alpha spoke into her hair, inhaling her scent. A mixture of coconut infused with mango still remained and he recalled their interaction in the tub. Lifting his head, he met her gaze and trailed his thumb along her bottom lip.

"Sounds good." She snuggled into his embrace.

"Hungry?" His dick tented the thin fabric of his pajama pants, detecting her arousal.

"Yes," she purred, her palm sliding over his bare chest.

"Really, people? We're right here," Finn pointed out. "Maybe you all need to go get a room, as they say."

"Hey, speak for yourself." Jake leaned back in his chair with a wide grin. "Kat. Jax. Don't listen to the big guy over there. I'm up for a show."

Jax caught the amusement on Jake's face and knew he was only half kidding. He'd heard from Gillian how she'd helped him heal after he'd been shot, having made love to both Dimitri and Jake. While he couldn't be certain he'd share his mate, he'd happily let him watch. Jax suspected her interest in the idea, pushing the envelope sexually. Undressed in his office, his little wolf had responded with arousal to the intrusion. Jax had always been sexually adventurous, and after making love to Katrina, he looked forward to exploring her fantasies.

"Seems we have an audience this morning," Jax laughed.

"Ah," Katrina peeked around his shoulder and winked at Jake. "It appears we do."

Jax put his arm around her and ushered her to the table, unfazed about revealing his erection to the others. Some things were meant to be concealed, but his sexual prowess and his interest in his mate wasn't one of them.

"Finn, call a pack meeting. Announce that I've left for New Orleans on official business. Meeting with Logan and my sister."

"And if they ask about Kat?" Finn stood from the table, combing his hair back with his fingers.

"Tell them she's a person of interest in custody with our pack." Jax smiled at Katrina, who laughed. "Tell them I'm interrogating her, ensuring she provides us with information leading to the capture of my kidnappers."

"Interrogating, huh?" Finn shook his head and gave a lopsided grin.

"He certainly has perfected the craft." Jake smiled at Katrina and Jax. "I mean, all that *interrogating* he did in the office yesterday and then last night obviously led to more *interrogating*, hence the marking. The Alpha's been busy."

"You guys aren't going to make this easy on me, are you?" Jax asked, picking up his coffee.

"Nope. Not even a little bit." Jake pressed his lips together, stifling his laugh.

"Yeah, no, not going to happen," Finn agreed with a smirk. "Hey, don't feel too bad, Alpha. While you were doing all that *interrogating*, Jake and I were bonding."

"You got it, brother. We had to save ourselves."

"You two are hilarious." Jax shook his head and sighed.

"They are pretty funny," Katrina admitted. She reached for a pastry, her eyes on Jake.

"Go tell the pack. Also, do me a favor and call the helicopter. I want to skip the traffic. I've already texted Rhys and called up the plane."

"Okay, I'm outta here." Finn began to walk toward the foyer but stopped and paused. "You gonna be okay without me? The last time..."

"I'm not going to tell you that we aren't going to run into trouble. But Jake's going with me. Logan and Dimitri are there too. I've gotta find out what Ilsbeth knew. If I find the witch, I have a better shot figuring out how to stop these things." Jax blew out a breath and pinched the bridge of his nose. "I really need you up here, Finn. The pack has been through enough shit the past month. One of us has to stay to keep order, and that, my man, is you. I'm trusting you to do this."

"I got it. I'll text you later with a status." His new beta gave a wave and turned on his heel, leaving the room.

Jake gave a sideways glance to Katrina and back to Jax. "So, uh, just to recap about last night. Everything's okay? Quintus looked like he bit you pretty hard."

"My mate doesn't listen well." Jax slowly spread the cheese onto the bread, his eyes trained on his knife.

"You're both overreacting. I'm perfectly fine." Katrina unconsciously reached behind her neck, where Quintus had bitten her.

"Very soon she'll experience a lesson that she will not forget," Jax warned. His eyes went to Jake, who nodded his head in agreement.

"I'm sorry but I wasn't going to let Quint kill Jake," she replied.

"You know I love ya, Kat, but Jax is right. There's a reason he's the Alpha of this pack. You can't just ignore him when he tells you what to do in these situations," Jake asserted. "It's worse that you challenged him. You're his mate."

"We're not bonded yet," she contended.

"We will be soon." Katrina's words cut through Jax, and he couldn't identify the emotion that followed. Anger? Arousal? The growl of his wolf reverberated in his mind, urging him to take her again. While he hadn't known her long enough to fall in love, the commitment would come in time.

"You know what will happen if we mate. I can't risk anything happening to you." Katrina pursed her lips and set her food on a plate. "And as far as me not listening, as you put it. I've lived a long time on my own with no master. I'm an Alpha's daughter, a sister. Tristan doesn't force me into antiquated rules. What makes you think submission to your will is in my blood?"

"Because, my little wolf…" Jax didn't miss a beat as he drove his fingers through her hair at the nape of her neck. Tugging her locks, he tilted her head backward, exposing her throat. He leaned in, his lips inches from hers. "That little mark on your neck is mine. You are mine. Our mating will happen. Don't. Test. Me."

The tense whisper of his statement died as Jax captured her lips. His bruising kiss was met with passion. Katrina gasped into his mouth, returning his advance, biting and sucking at her mate. Fingernails raked down over his shoulder, tearing at his skin, and the sting reminded him that Katrina harbored a wild nature, one that might be impossible to tame.

"And I think that's my cue to leave." Jake laughed and pushed up from the table. "As much as I enjoy a good show, I can't figure out if this is going to be super-hot or more like gladiators. Yeah, I'll catch up with you guys later."

As Jake left the kitchen, Jax forced his libido under control. He'd torn his lips away from his mate, frustrated with her refusal to accept her fate, their mating. After making love with her, there was no doubt in his mind that the bond would make them stronger. But without her trust, he'd need proof before she'd consent.

Jax heard the water running, and was reminded that Katrina had gone to shower. His cock hardened as the image of her perfect nipples dripping with water formed in his mind. *Goddammit. For the next year, I'm going to have a perpetual hard-on.* He adjusted his erection, but resisted the urge to stroke it. As much as he loved that the Goddess had given him an attractive mate, it was going to make it damn hard to concentrate on business.

The doorbell rang, breaking his concentration. On any other day, he'd have his staff attend to it, but he'd dismissed his butler and the rest of the staff, unwilling to risk Katrina's safety or theirs. As he opened the door, he sensed London's presence. He waved her into the foyer and retreated into the great room.

"Why are you here?" Jax had been grooming her to take over day to day operations. London had been working with Nick for several years and knew the company inside and out.

"Finn said…well, if you're leaving, I need to get your input on these first." She sat on the sofa and flipped open her tablet.

"I just sent you my feedback. We didn't have to do this in person. Go with the black and white on the cover. Follow up with the color spread."

"I just thought…"

"Why are you really here?" Jax asked, already suspecting why she'd insisted on visiting him at his penthouse.

By now, the pack already had their suspicions about Katrina's role in his life. After their romantic interlude on his desk, half the company probably had heard her scream in orgasm. Although he'd found his mate's lack of inhibition refreshing, he'd thought better of what he'd done afterward. He needed more time to work through Katrina's introduction to the pack. Going down on her with the office door swinging wide open wasn't exactly the optimal way to do it.

Jax ignored London, who slowly put her things back into her bag. With thick raven hair, green eyes and a razor-sharp mind, she'd caught the attention of many men, humans and supernaturals alike. Although Jax hadn't slept with her, they'd shared an intimate moment. In a moment of weakness after Nick's death, they'd kissed in the nightclub. Despite the fiery interaction, he hadn't expected more than a fling. Despite not being his mate, the females in his pack often sought the attention of the Alpha.

As he leaned back on the sofa, he pretended to be engrossed in his email.

With Katrina already vulnerable, he wasn't ready to divulge information to his pack.

"There are rumors," he heard her say. Jax kept his head down but lifted his gaze to meet hers.

"You shouldn't believe everything you hear."

"Everyone knows she's here." London scooted toward the Alpha, closing the distance. "So she isn't staying? That bitch from Lyceum wolves is finally going home?"

"You need to check yourself." Jax's eyes flared in anger and he struggled to conceal his irritation. "Katrina. That's her name. I suggest you use it. Not a request. And yes, she's staying here. For as long as I say she stays."

"Jax, please." London's voice softened as she edged closer, her knee brushed his. "We haven't talked about what happened. The night you disappeared. At the club. Our kiss." She closed her eyes and drew a breath, her chest rising and falling slowly. Gradually she opened them, and continued. "There's something between us. I don't know what it is. I know I was with Nick before and maybe that's an issue, but he's gone."

"I don't want to talk about Nick. I don't want to talk about that night. It was a kiss. It was nothing more. I'm sorry, London." Jax shook his head and set his iPad aside. Jesus, he hadn't expected this conversation today. In the distance, he noted the shower had stopped running.

"Then maybe…" London gently laid her things on the table. "You need to give us a chance."

Before Jax knew what was happening, the brunette had swung her thigh over his. Straddling him, she pressed her groin to his.

"What the hell?" Jax exclaimed. Because Katrina hadn't claimed him, her wolf would lose it if she saw him with another woman. "You need to get off me right now."

"That night…you kissed me. I'll never forget it. If you just give us a chance I know…"

Jax sensed the second Katrina entered the room, but it was the growl that drew his attention. The small white wolf bared her teeth. With her hackles raised, she gave no doubt as to her intention to attack London.

"Get off me right now. Easy now." Jax lifted her by the waist and tossed her onto the sofa. He held up his hands defensively, aware that Katrina had gone feral. "Nothing's going on here, Kat. London's just confused. She's missing Nick."

"What the hell is wrong with her?" London backed into the corner of the couch, pulling her knees to her chest. "Really? She wants a challenge? I'm not shifting right now."

"No one is shifting. Get your things off the table and slowly walk out of the house."

London moved to collect her tablet and Katrina stalked toward her, continuing to growl.

"Kat. This is not what it seems. You need to trust me." A rush of satisfaction filled his chest, observing his mate possessively claim him. But he couldn't let her kill London. "You need to back off. Let her leave. She's got to get back to the office."

"I can't believe you let her in here," London lamented.

"Let her go," Jax commanded.

Katrina whined. Her fangs exposed, she settled to the floor. Although she hadn't ceased her aggression, it would have to be sufficient. Jax's gaze moved to London, who'd already begun to stand. "Move slowly and get out now. Keep moving. And not a word to the pack, London."

"Seriously?" London asked.

"I'll be back in a few days and if I hear you've been talking, your employment will be in jeopardy. Leave here and go back to the office. Go now!"

Jax towered above the petite wolf, breathing a sigh of relief as London slammed the door behind her. He looked to Katrina, who continued to show the whites of her teeth.

"What you just saw here," Jax held his palms upward and swiveled, looking around the condo, "this was nothing. A misunderstanding. My pack...they don't know about you, baby."

Katrina transformed into her human form. Standing bare, she glared at Jax.

"This thing between us...you know we both have pasts. You can't go around trying to kill every woman I ever dated." Jax laughed. "You haven't even marked me yet. Your wolf, she's not going to be very happy until she gets what she wants."

"Who is she?"

"No one. We work together."

"You fucked her?"

"No, but I did kiss her. Jesus, why am I even explaining myself to you? You know what, Kat? You're going to have to learn how to trust me."

"Really? You do realize you just had a woman straddling you, right?"

"And you need to learn how to listen." Jax drank in the sight of his mate standing nude before him. From her fierce eyes to her full breasts down to her cream-colored painted toenails, she exuded sexuality. She brushed her long blonde mane behind her ears, and licked her lips. The defiance caused his dick to thicken.

"Are you kidding me?" she continued. "You were the one with a female in your lap."

"And you," Jax approached her within two broad steps and gave her a devious grin, "are the one who continues to challenge me."

He wasn't sure whether it was the tip of her pink tongue brushing over her swollen lip or the way she crossed her legs, attempting to conceal her own arousal, but he lost control. Katrina squealed as he placed his fingers on her waist and hoisted her over his shoulder.

"What the hell are you doing? Put me down."

"My dear, dear, Katrina." Jax ran a strong palm over the back of her thigh. "I realize we don't know each other very well yet, but you, my lovely mate, you must learn to trust me."

"I do trust you." Katrina didn't fight as he lifted her and set her in front of the back of the sofa.

"Really? Because on more than one occasion I've given an order and you not only ignored it, you fought me. And this," Jax smiled as he turned her around, her bottom brushing over the front of his thighs, "is the perfect opportunity for us to have this discussion."

His cock lengthened as he ran through the scenario he planned. He'd always enjoyed a little bondage. Today, he'd test Katrina's limits. The defiant little wolf needed a lesson and she'd learn why he was Alpha.

⟐ Chapter Twelve ⟐

Katrina yelped as Jax bent her over the sofa. He spread her legs wide open, the cool air rushing over her pussy. She reached to balance herself, her palms flat on the soft leather.

"What do you think you're doing?" she asked, her emotions vacillating between pissed as hell and aroused. A smooth palm cupped her ass and she sighed, deciding on the latter. "Just because my body responds to you, that doesn't mean I'm forgetting that bitch you let in here."

"Trust," he began.

Katrina gasped as his warm breath teased her bottom. His fingers dug into her hips.

"Even animals born without the magick to shift understand that trust is essential to life. You should know better. There's structure within our lives that protects all of us. Without it, there is chaos. So this is why our wolves value order. Challenges to my position aren't tolerated." Jax slid his grip over her smooth ass and squeezed gently. "Disobedience…"

"I know full well what it's like to live within a pack, but this situation isn't life and death." Katrina's pussy ached as his soft fingers traced a line down between her legs, grazing over the outside of her labia. Growing wet, she shifted her position, attempting to move. Her action was rewarded with a firm slap to her bottom, the sting leaving her skin tingling. "Hey…"

"As I was saying, disobedience is not tolerated. Wolves, they choose willingly to submit to their Alpha, accepting their position within the pack. Because they know…" He paused and smacked his palm against her other cheek.

"You can't just spank me," she protested. Guilt rose as arousal flooded between her legs. She'd never allowed a man to spank her, yet the twinge on her skin left her wanting more.

"The pack knows," he continued, ignoring her statement. He trailed a finger through her wet slit, eliciting a moan, "that by giving their submission, they're protected. As a whole, we are stronger than individuals. We cannot do that without collaboration. This is what unites us."

"I don't know what you want from me," she sighed. Her aching clit swelled as he brushed over it. Katrina pushed up on her toes, but was unable to move, as his hands held her firmly in place.

"You're not going anywhere." The Alpha bit gently at his mate.

"What do you want from me? Ah…" Katrina sucked a breath as his teeth nipped at her flesh, leaving her quivering with pleasure and pain. "You could die if we…Jax…"

591

"What do I want?" he growled. His warm breath teased her skin. "I want everything. You. Us. This."

"I can't…" Soft lips brushed over her bottom, silencing her. Painfully aroused, she knew it'd be minutes before she was begging him to fuck her.

"You can feel it, can't you?" He cupped her mound, tapping his fingers over its smooth surface. "Your Alpha knows you better than you know yourself. That is part of my responsibility. To care for you…to protect you."

"Jax, please…" Katrina tilted her hips, seeking relief.

"That's much better, my sweet little wolf. I love to hear you beg." Jax rose, nestling his erection into the crevice of her ass. Sliding a hand down her back, he fisted her hair and tilted her head up until her gaze met his. "I've got a little surprise for you."

"But…oh Jesus, you can't leave me here like this." Katrina's heart pounded against her ribs. Whatever he was planning couldn't be good and with her body already on fire, she breathed through her unmet need. She considered running, escaping the dominant Alpha, but the truth was that she couldn't resist his challenge. Whatever erotic game he planned, she'd play, but true submission wasn't a prize she was willing to give just yet. Her wolf paced, urging her to mark him, and she shook her head, refusing the demand. The desire to protect her mate outweighed the possessive need to claim him as her own.

A rush of cold air caressed her skin, making her aware he'd left her.

"Don't move," he warned, his voice low and commanding. A shiver of anticipation ran over her body.

"What are you doing?"

"I want you exposed and open to me. You don't seem to listen very well and I can tell you're thinking of challenging me right now."

"How do you know what I'm thinking?"

"No lies." He arched an eyebrow at her in warning. "Wolves…we choose our Alpha. Our pack. We choose to submit for the greater good. Even the strongest wolves, they do not challenge for the sake of challenging. This brings discord. It puts us all in danger. Last night…"

"We needed to get the information. He was going after Jake," she began, but went silent as he settled pillows underneath her torso, supporting her weight.

"It was dangerous. You didn't know what Quintus would do. I happen to know him very well. He's an old friend."

"But you didn't tell me that. How was I supposed to know?" Katrina hugged the cushions, unsure whether she wanted to let Jax proceed. Her heart raced as she caught sight of the black cuffs and dangling brass chain.

"Trust, Kat. Because I'm your mate and Alpha. You can always be assured that I will protect you and do what is in the best interest of this pack." Jax gave her a devious smile as he reached for her wrist and began to fasten the soft leather. "You understand I would never hurt you?"

Katrina had never let anyone restrain her, but found herself nodding as he asked the question. Jax had never given her reason not to trust him. It wasn't as if Katrina didn't understand his argument. She'd never directly challenged Tristan, but her brother didn't push her the way Jax did. Katrina had lived for decades independently of pack politics and did what she pleased.

As he fastened the leather to her wrists, his eyes never left hers. *I must be crazy*, she thought. *Why on earth am I letting him do this?* Deep within her soul she yearned for what he demanded. Although the Alpha drove her wolf wild, it was the woman who couldn't resist his test.

"The point of this is that you are making a decision to listen to me." Jax eyed the legs of the heavy marble coffee table and deftly wrapped the cord around the base and secured the clasp.

"Is this really necessary?" She laid her cheek onto the soft pillow, resting her head.

"Yes, because this is your choice. We both know full well that you could shift and escape if you wanted." He ran his finger over her cheek, his lips hovering over hers. "You are choosing to stay here, because you want this."

Katrina's heart caught. His mouth crushed onto hers, and she tugged on her restraints. Her sensitive nipples grazed over the chenille fabric as she wriggled against it. Katrina moaned as his tongue gently swept against hers. His hand stroked over her hair, and she blinked up at him, objecting when he tore his lips away. She heaved for breath, her body igniting with desire.

"Do you have any idea how much I've wanted you? How much my wolf needs you?" he asked.

"Oh Goddess…" Katrina's thoughts spun, regretting how much time she'd lost with her mate. She knew damn well how hard it had been for her to not only leave Jax, but to force herself to date other people, to escape all the way to New Orleans. A slow form of torture, she'd unsuccessfully attempted to put him out of her mind. No matter how many times she told herself she was protecting him, her heart ached to see him again.

Under his touch, she could no longer deny the raw emotion, the chemistry that churned with every word he spoke. Her Alpha commanded her, she knew. Admitting his victory, however, would be difficult. It meant she'd agreed to the mating, that she'd given in to her wolf's desire to claim him as her own. If she lost control, she feared she'd do more than mark him. Her fangs ached, yearning to slice through his skin, allowing the magick of his blood to flow into her, solidifying the bond.

The soft brush of the head of his cock against her bottom broke her contemplation. Her skin pricked in awareness as he slid it down the cleft, teasing her entrance.

"This," he slapped her cheek again, and Katrina cried aloud, "will be mine, and do you know why?"

"No, Jax…don't say it." As he spanked her again, her pussy tightened. "I can't…"

"You're a difficult one. But look how responsive you are to this." The sound of a crack rang out in the room as he delivered another blow. "Tell me why…why will you be mine?"

"Because," she whispered. She'd give her soul to surrender to the mating, but refused to hurt him.

"Ah…" Fingers slid between her folds, brushing over her clitoris.

"You fight your own happiness." Jax pressed a finger inside her slippery core and she clenched down on him.

"I can't do this…"

"Fuck, you're beautiful." Jax reached around her neck, sliding his thumb over her bottom lip. "So stubborn. But do you want me to stop, Katrina?"

"No, no, no," she told him as he plunged in and out of her heated channel. She parted her lips, sucking a breath.

"This moment. Look at you. You choose submission. You display your trust. Why do you deny me otherwise?"

"You know why," she breathed, her lips wet with saliva. As he added another finger inside her, she quivered around him. "Don't stop."

"Don't you dare come," he warned, withdrawing his hand. "Why do you submit to me here?"

Katrina's body shivered as he retreated. Her wolf howled, begging her to claim him, to say the words. In her heart, she knew she couldn't go without him another day.

"Because…" As he slammed his fingers back inside her pussy, applying pressure to her clit, she came apart. "You're my mate. Please Jax…I don't want to ever hurt you, but fuck…ah yes, don't stop…you're my mate."

"Your Alpha." Jax removed his fingers and slammed his cock into Katrina.

"Yes, yes, yes," she cried, as his shaft entered her from behind.

All Katrina could smell, feel, and see was Jax. As he stretched her wide, she dug her fingers into the couch, bracing herself as he pounded into her tight channel. She shuddered as his fingers found her swollen nub.

"You are everything I need, Katrina. Do you hear me?" he told her.

"Jax I…" she panted, her body alive with energy. The strength of his magick filtered through her veins. As she felt the pad of his thumb circle her puckered flesh, she tensed.

"You need to trust me," she heard him tell her. The pressure built as he slid over her skin, igniting a dark arousal she'd never experienced. "No challenging."

"I promise. Yes, ah, yes, oh…please, please," she repeated as he slid it into her back hole.

Full with pleasure, she embraced his erotic touch. Katrina screamed Jax's name as her climax crashed down on her. She splintered into a thousand pieces. Quivering in ecstasy, her toes dug into the carpet. His fingers moved to her hips, and she heard him grunt, giving a final thrust.

"Kat," Jax cried, pressing his lips to her neck.

Katrina went limp, floating within the relaxation of her submission. His kiss, his touch, it was all she'd ever needed. Surrendering to the Alpha, she prayed she wouldn't destroy him.

Within seconds, her hands were freed and he lifted her, cradling her against his chest. As they fell onto an adjoining sofa and she rested within his arms, Katrina grazed her lips to his chest.

"My Alpha," she whispered. With her heart and soul, she swore she'd fight to keep him, not just for a night, but forever.

·❧· *Chapter Thirteen* ·❧·

My Alpha. Jax closed his eyes, his mind whirling with emotion. He'd never understood how a mate could take a man's world, shatter everything he thought he knew and then end up molding it all together in a spectacular masterpiece.

When Katrina walked in on him and London, Jax had known she'd lose control. No matter the control she'd exercised, until she'd marked Jax, her wolf wouldn't accept another woman touching him. The instinct to own her mate would far exceed any rational thoughts. Although they'd explored her submission and she'd said the words out loud, her fears about losing him drove her to resist mating.

He hadn't planned on cuffing her to the table. Although he'd used the restraints on occasion, the act had been more than simple bedroom play. She could have shifted, broken free at any point. He knew it. She knew it. But she'd chosen to stay within his confines, accepting the situation on his terms. It was a lesson she'd need to learn out of the bedroom as well.

Jax buried his nose into her hair, pleased with his scent on her skin. He weaved his fingers through hers, and brought her palm to his lips. His heart squeezed in his chest and in that moment he realized how vulnerable he'd become. Upon Nick's death, his emotional reserve had been depleted. Without knowing that day who he had rescued, Jax had found Katrina. She'd begun to heal the cavern in his heart that had been left in the wake of Nick's passing.

Katrina curled against his body, bringing his hands into the warmth of her breasts. Adrift within a peaceful haze, she moaned, and it reminded him that she hadn't fallen asleep.

"Jax," she whispered.

"Hmm…are you okay?"

"Very okay." She laughed. "More than okay."

"Me too," he agreed with a kiss to her head.

"My wolf knows. She knows you are her mate," she admitted quietly.

"And you?" He forced himself to breathe calmly as he waited on her answer. After everything they'd just experienced, he hoped the lesson had taken hold.

"I'm sorry for challenging you. The vampire…I didn't know you knew him. I know that's not reason enough, but you must know I'm desperate. If he'd killed Jake? I couldn't live with myself. He's protective of me. But it's more than that. I just feel so out of control."

Jax stroked her hair gently and inhaled.

"When I'm with you, your magick…I can feel it. You make me feel whole again. They've changed me, though. Remember in the woods?"

"Yes."

"My magick, they siphon it, poison it with whatever evil they manage to get from this thing they worship. I don't think they just want my magick, though. I think they want me. They want me to be like them."

Katrina shivered against his chest. Although he suspected it was the topic causing her to shudder, not the temperature, he reached for a throw blanket and spread it over her.

"Whatever this is, the only way we can fight it is together. I know you're tough, Katrina, and I'm glad you are." He gave a small laugh. "Well, of course, I'd have a mate to match me. It's not like I don't understand why you've done some of the things you've done. I get you want control because control's been taken from you. But you need to let me help."

"Jax…that night we met at the party." Katrina blinked, her lashes tickling his chest. "I knew. I saw you across the room. When you touched me…it's so stupid. I didn't think it would be like that. I just knew you were my mate."

"I remember that night. I won't ever forget it."

"I've never felt that way. Just this immediate connection with you. I can't explain it." She shook her head and reflected. "You know, I'm not a young wolf. I was born in the early 1800s. I've lived through many bad times. These things, yeah, they hurt me, but it's not the first time I've been tortured."

"I didn't realize…" Jax attempted to conceal his shock at her confession.

"No, it's okay. It was a long time ago. There was this woman, Simone. She, uh, got off on killing women. Was into some kind of black magick. Tristan had to go to Kade Issacson and Luca Macquarie for help." Katrina's voice grew serious, her eyes focused on their intertwined fingers. "They both found me."

"I'm so sorry, Kat." Jax reasoned that if her brother had been forced to seek assistance from the New Orleans vampires, it had to have been a dire situation.

"The things I saw Simone do? I just…it's not right." Katrina closed her eyes and sighed.

"Jesus, I wish I'd been able to protect you. Things will be different. I promise you."

"It wasn't until recently…these things came for me. Of course, when they told me I'd meet an Alpha, my true mate…I didn't believe them at first. I mean, when so many years pass, you just stop believing that it will happen. You take lovers, try not to get too involved because you know if you meet your mate, you will hurt the other person. But that night, everything changed."

"I know what you mean. I've been around for quite a while too." Like Katrina, Jax had lived a long time, experienced the loneliness. He'd casually dated. Sex was easy. Relationships, however, were entirely too complicated.

Unable to mate with humans or witches, he'd kept his interactions to one night stands. Within the confines of wolves, he'd grown close to few females. They understood the inevitability that would come for all wolves. If another met his or her mate, they'd better accept the situation when they were forced to separate. "Something about your eyes. Your smile."

"My smile?"

"Yes, do you remember what we talked about?" he asked, wrapping a single strand of her soft hair around his finger.

"Ice skating. You were trying to talk me into going to Rockefeller Center."

Jax laughed. "You told me you were an Olympic champion."

"Give me a few more years and I might be."

"What happened to your hair?" Jax regretted asking the question as soon as it left his lips. He suspected it had to do with her abductions. The impulsivity of his comment was evidence that he'd lost the ability to restrain himself around his mate. "Sorry, I didn't mean to ask."

"No, it's okay. This last time…I wasn't there that long. You saw me. It's not just about beating me, forcing me to submit. It's about their chanting…like spells or whatever. It feels like…" Katrina brought his hand to her chest. Her voice trembled. "My hair isn't the same. What they are doing is changing me from the inside out."

"You don't have to talk about it."

"I want to tell you, but it's hard to explain. It's like a drill in my chest…the noise of their words. I want to cover my ears but I can't. It gets louder and louder and it feels like my blood is draining out. But it's not my blood. It's my magick…it pours out of me. I can't control it. And now…"

"What?"

"When we were in your office, your power overwhelmed me. It was almost like when an Alpha gets angry. You know how it works. You can push out your emotions, your power. Force wolves to submit."

"I can control the flow of my magick. As my mate, you may have some of the same influence I have. You know that, right? Your energy…the pack will sense you. Us together, how we are feeling affects everyone."

"I think it's what Quint said. Maybe somehow because I'd lost my magick, and now, because you're my mate, I take yours. All these years I've waited." Katrina stifled the tears which filled her eyes. "And when I think back to when I first met you. How you made me feel? To know it could be real, that I had this mate? I was overwhelmed."

"Happy?" he asked with a kiss to the top of her head.

"So happy," she agreed. "And you were funny. I wasn't expecting that. You weren't this arrogant man that they write about in the headlines."

"They say that? No, I've never heard that before," he joked, trying to lighten her mood.

"I know, hard to believe, right?" She gave a small laugh. "Seriously, going home…asking Tristan to help keep us apart? I'm telling you, it broke my heart. But I couldn't risk hurting you."

"We're compatible." He changed the subject. "You seemed to enjoy your little lesson tonight."

"I've never done that before," she admitted.

"Hmm…in two hundred years you never had a little spanking?"

"Truth?" Katrina pushed up onto his chest, meeting his gaze.

"Yeah." Jax brushed a hair behind her ear, surprised she didn't immediately agree.

"I've been with other guys, but not many. And I haven't ever let anyone tie me up. Oh, no. To let someone do that? First of all, even though I could have easily gotten out of the restraints, it takes a lot of trust to let someone do that. And second, well, as you've already noticed, I'm not necessarily submissive. But when I'm with you? It's like I want to do all kinds of things I've never done. You make me feel free. You should know, though, Jax, I have been bitten before, and not just by Quintus."

Jax held his tongue, attempting to remain calm. It had been bad enough that Quintus had tasted of his mate. The act of drawing blood, allowing someone to drink from her was extraordinarily intimate.

"Luca…he…it's never been serious. He's just a friend." Katrina hesitated. "But back to your original question, no I've never been spanked. Nor have I ever let anyone tie me up. Not until you."

"I'll push you further," Jax responded. Katrina may not have been with many others but he suspected his little wolf enjoyed experimenting as much as he did.

"Seeing you with that other woman tonight…I'm hanging on by a thread. We need to find answers, because, Jax," her eyes fell, sorrow washing across her face, "I almost lost control tonight and bit you."

"It's natural. She wants to claim her Alpha. I know it took a little lesson to get you there, but…" His cock hardened as he recalled how she'd screamed his name as he slammed into her pussy.

"No, Jax. Not just mark you. My wolf…she wants your blood…to complete the bond."

Jax smiled, his chest tightening with emotion at her statement. Their connection grew stronger, weaving itself together. The way she'd protested bonding, he hadn't considered how strongly the instinct to mate would affect her. She'd restrained her beast for too long, denying it the craving it sought.

"I keep going back to this, Kat. And I know it's hard for you to just blindly trust me, but you have to learn, or at least try." Katrina flashed her eyes at him, her cheeks still flushed from lovemaking. Jax cupped her chin, tracing his thumb under her swollen lower lip. "I wasn't fooling around when I told you about instincts. It's one of the benefits of being an Alpha. The chemistry involved in mating is strong, and I'd be naïve to think it isn't influencing my desire to keep you in my life. I know what these things told you, but I don't want you to be afraid of mating, completing the bond. I'm telling you, when I'm around you, I've never felt stronger in my life. Whatever power or energy you're getting from me, I don't know…maybe it's just that we somehow are working together. But the longer you hold off on marking me, the harder it will be for you. It's natural that your wolf is not just going to want to mark me, but bond with me. But no matter how I feel about this, I'm not going to force you. Your wolf, on the other hand, she may have the last word."

"I want to believe you. To have a chance at a life with you? To be mated? You don't know how many times I had to stop myself from dreaming about it. It just hurts too much."

"It's okay to dream, baby." Jax leaned toward Katrina. His eyes went to her lips and then met her gaze. Every second he spent with her, he grew more determined that he needed her in his life. "We're going to find answers in New Orleans. If I have to search every inch of this earth to find that damn witch, I will."

She gave him a small smile, and it was enough to tell him that a seed of hope had been planted. Trust would come in time and so would her submission to their mating. If he could keep them both alive and destroy the evil that came for them, they'd have a future together.

Jax peered up at the once majestic Garden District mansion. The clean slate staircase had been obscured by overgrown Oleander hedges. Although it had been nearly two months since Ilsbeth had gone missing, the coven home had quickly fallen into disrepair. The enormous pentagram perched above the main entrance was draped in fine white webbing. It was as if death itself emanated from the house.

Jax had crossed paths with the infamous witch a few times over the years. He'd been wise not to ask for any favors, aware that she always expected a greater one in return. Over the years Ilsbeth had grown powerful, establishing her influential coven. Until recently, the witch had been relatively benevolent to most creatures. However, her bitter jealousy led to dark magick and lies. Believing she was deeply in love with Dimitri, she'd become convinced that if he was no longer a wolf, he'd never mate. The despicable act had nearly cost Dimitri his life.

Jax called Logan on the flight down to New Orleans. Rumors of shape shifters had twisted through supernatural circles but no one had actually claimed to have seen one. Although Dimitri and Gillian had insisted on coming with him to Ilsbeth's home, he'd refused, and had sought Logan's order to keep them at home. Whatever information Jax sought was his responsibility alone. He would not risk the life of his sister and her mate.

Luca stood waiting on their arrival. His wife, Samantha, who belonged to Ilsbeth's coven, had agreed to assist them in their search for the manipulative sorceress.

A squeeze to his hand brought his focus to Katrina. She gave him a warm smile, and crossed her long slender legs. Tucking a stray hair into her casual bun, she removed the sunglasses that had been pushed up onto her head. He inwardly laughed, thinking about how ridiculous it was that they were about to go into a dangerous situation and all he could think about was fucking his mate. Her black cotton dress rode up her thigh tempting him further, and he reasoned he'd be lucky if he didn't bond with her before the week was through.

His eyes darted to Jake, who watched them in the rearview mirror. The car came to a stop and he turned his attention back to his little wolf.

"You ready to do this?"

"I think so. I know I'm ready to get answers, that's for sure." Her eyes lit up as she caught sight of Luca and Samantha. "They're here."

"Gilly wanted to come but there was no way I was letting her get hurt. Not after last time," he told her, his focus distracted by the vampire.

Jax observed Luca's expression. The corners of his mouth had been drawn tight with tension. He didn't blame him for not wanting to be in the middle of witchcraft central. But Jax suspected that the vampire's cool demeanor had more to do with his presence.

"Hey, are you going to be okay?" Her voice softened as she ran her hand over Jax's cheek.

"Yes." Jax buried his emotions, taking notice as Katrina smiled at Luca through the glass.

Although she'd told him about their relationship, their silent interaction gnawed at his gut. This man had been with his mate, tasted of her blood. Until Katrina, he'd never been possessive of a woman. He didn't want to ask, but couldn't stop the question before it left his lips. "Are you and Luca still good friends?"

"Well, yes, somewhat, but he's…" The engine cut off, and Katrina was silenced as the door swung open, and a large masculine hand reached to assist her.

"You don't know how to stay out of trouble, do you?" a deep Australian accent asked.

Jax tensed as she exited, falling into the arms of the imposing vampire. He exchanged glances with a petite redheaded woman who was burgeoning with child. Katrina, as if realizing her actions, broke free of the embrace and extended a hand to the witch.

"Samantha. You look beautiful."

"Thank you." Samantha smiled warmly.

"Luca. Samantha. This is Jax Chandler." Katrina hesitated and looked up into his eyes. "My mate."

"Oh my. Congratulations," Samantha exclaimed.

"When I heard you were coming, and with who," Luca said, his tone serious, "I know you've wanted this, but Kat, are you sure? Did you complete the bond?"

"Luca," Samantha reprimanded him, a gentle slap to his arm. "What kind of question is that? They're wolves. I may not have been around very long but even I know how it works. They have no choice."

"Not true," Jake interjected.

"Jake." Luca nodded.

"It's so good to see you again." Samantha took his hand in hers and gave it a squeeze.

"Hey, Luca. I'd say it's nice to see you...but yeah, I know you're not exactly a fan. No offense, Sam, but the big guy here can be a bit...particular."

Samantha and Katrina laughed in response.

"What you call particular, I call civilized. Stripping off my clothes and turning into an animal for fun? Let me just say I can think of a hundred other things I'd like to do." Luca sniffed.

"As I was saying," Jake continued, ignoring the cantankerous vampire. "Although wolves are given a mate, the ultimate choice is ours and ours alone. Should we choose to ignore fate, it's painful, nearly impossible, but it can be done. That being said, I've known a few wolves who managed to refuse the mating. Wasn't pretty."

"Sometimes we learn through pain," Luca commented, giving Jax a hard stare.

"It's none of your concern," the Alpha replied.

"That's where you're wrong. You listen to me, Kat here is my..."

"Luca, please." Katrina placed her hand onto his arm and kept her voice soft. "So many years. Goddess knows I wouldn't be here without you, but you must let us try. You know what I did was wrong."

"You survived. How is that wrong? Jesus, we both lied to Tristan."

"We didn't lie. Granted, we could have tried to tell him otherwise. But you and I both know that Tristan never liked Jax. My brother's smart. It's possible he even knew the rumors weren't true, and thought it best that I stay away from him for other reasons. Tristan knew and we both knew that sending me to New Orleans was the right decision at the time. What's done is done."

"Maybe you're right, but you and I..."

"This isn't the place to talk about this." Katrina's eyes went to Samantha, who gave her a sympathetic smile. "We don't need to rehash history."

"Samantha knows everything. There're no secrets between us." Luca glared at Jax. "Can you say the same about you and the wolf?"

"It's not that simple. You know that it's not. Jax and I have only been together a few days." Katrina closed her eyes and took a deep breath. Opening them, she pinned her eyes on Luca. "I love you, you know that, right?"

"Yeah," he agreed with a heavy sigh.

"I've been alone forever. You need to let me have this." Katrina's voice wavered as moisture brimmed her eyes. "As much as I tried to deny what's going on between Jax and me to protect him, it's simple, I don't want to anymore. I want him in my life. Every second I'm with Jax, I'm more convinced that he's the only one who can save me. These things are trying to kill me. It's not just about them stealing my magick. This is about my life. Please understand," she begged.

"The bottom line here is that you have no say in our relationship. Discussion's over," Jax interrupted, glaring at Luca. He didn't wish to hurt him, especially considering he was expecting a child, but neither would he tolerate another male interfering with their bond. Without giving him time to argue further, he took Katrina's hand in his and stepped toward the mansion. "Let's get going. We need to get in the house. Samantha? Did you open up the wards?"

"I removed them temporarily. But once you leave, you won't be able to get back in the house. The wards will go back in place, and it'll be locked up," Samantha warned.

"Wasn't this a coven house?" Katrina asked, glancing up to the huge stone mansion. "Where are all the witches?"

Samantha's gaze went to Luca. He nodded and she turned her attention back to Jax and Katrina.

"After Ilsbeth disappeared, there was a bit of infighting. There's another house in the French Quarter. It's where I trained. This place," Samantha gestured to the porch, "this was Ilsbeth's home. She held parties here for special occasions and holidays. She usually only let a couple of others stay with her."

"So you just closed it up?" Jax asked. "Has anyone else been inside?"

"Not exactly. There's a warlock. He's taken over."

"Goes by the name of Mick Germaine," Luca added.

"He asked me to set wards to keep others out. I figured since this belonged to Ilsbeth, it was the right thing to do."

"I can't imagine the other witches are happy about that," Jax speculated.

"Well, yes, some weren't pleased. But they had no choice. Mick…he's very powerful." Samantha nervously stroked a hand over her belly as Luca wrapped a protective arm around her.

"A few of the witches still live in the Quarter but most have moved out of the city. Mick's got a setup there." Luca hesitated, his eyes darted to the mother of his child and back to Jax. "Look, I'm not saying the guy's evil, but you should know he's being watched. Kade and I keep tabs on him."

"I try to stay away from the conflict. Negativity isn't good for the baby. She needs peace," Samantha told them.

"When are you due?" Jax asked. He caught a glint of pain in Katrina's eyes, and he took note to explore that further.

"This month. Any day." She laughed. "Honestly not many people know vampires who've had children. So we're kind of playing this by ear."

"Anything else we should know about this place?"

"I'd go in with you but…" Samantha shrugged.

"No way," Luca growled.

"Thank you for doing this." Katrina smiled. "We really appreciate you coming today, helping us."

"I'm glad to help." Samantha reached for Katrina's palm. Her eyes widened as she wrapped her fingers around her hand. She gasped, refusing to release Katrina. "What happened to you?"

"Oh God…let me go. I don't want to hurt you." Katrina's voice rose with panic as Samantha's grip tightened.

"What the hell?" Luca grabbed both of their wrists and attempted to separate them, but Samantha held up a silencing hand.

"No. I'm fine. Leave me be."

Jax rushed behind Katrina, and slid his hands around her waist. The irises of Samantha's eyes swirled in shades of silver and he grew concerned that whatever had taken Katrina was hurting the witch.

"Your magick…it's not like a wolf. No, no, no…how can this be?" Samantha sucked a deep breath and blew it out.

"I…they did something to me," Katrina admitted softly. As Samantha released her arm, she snapped it into her chest. "Did I hurt you?"

"No, not at all. But Kat…I've never felt anything like you. You're almost like a…but no…that can't be." She shook her head in confusion.

"Almost like a what?" Jax asked.

"Her magick, it's so strong. But not like a wolf. Whatever these things are doing…they're changing you. Your hair." Samantha brushed her hand over Katrina's head. "This isn't of your doing."

"No. The last time…well, if Luca told you everything, you know…they're taking my magick. Once it comes back, they take me again. Something about this last time. I don't know. It felt different. I didn't recognize Jax. I didn't know who I was."

"I think it's best we let you look through the house." Samantha slowly backed away from Katrina, holding onto Luca. "I've got to go call Mick and let him know you're here."

Jax studied the witch, aware she'd sensed something about Katrina that frightened her. It worried him that she'd suggested his mate was anything other than wolf. Aside from the incident in the woods, her difficulty shifting, she'd been stronger than ever. With his mark on her skin, even her scent grew more like his. Despite his desire to ignore the witch, deny her suspicion, instinct told him that she had no motive to lie. He glanced over to Jake, who scrubbed his chin in worry, and he knew he wasn't alone in his thoughts.

Luca and Samantha gave them a parting wave before they settled into their car, and Jax's attention went to Katrina, who appeared preoccupied.

"You sure you want to do this?" he asked, gently brushing his hand over the small of her back. "You don't need to go in. Jake and I can handle this."

"No." She took a deep breath and exhaled. Driving her fingers into the back of her hair, she grimaced. "Samantha knew something just now. Don't tell me you didn't believe her, either. I don't know what the hell's going on but I'll be damned if I'm going to lie back and take this shit. No way. If Ilsbeth sent Quintus to that prison, she had to have known something. She's tied in with these things. She fed him to them. We have to find her and make her tell us what she knows."

"Let's do this, then." Jax weaved his fingers into hers and brought the back of her hands to his lips.

As they made their way up the stairs, Jax prayed like hell there weren't any surprises inside Ilsbeth's funhouse. He wrapped his fingers around the cold metal door knob, the loud click confirming the home was unlocked. Jake flanked Katrina and pushed the door wide open.

The musty air rushed outside, causing them to cover their noses with their hands. A streak of light shone through the doorway, illuminating dancing specks of dust that swirled in its stream. Jax reached for Katrina as she rushed to enter, but she slipped through his fingertips. Both he and Jake followed in after her, but stopped dead in their tracks. The loud screech forced them to put their hands over their ears. Jax wore a confused expression as he glanced to Jake, who shrugged in response.

"Do you hear it?" Katrina asked. She spun in a circle, her hands outward as if she was catching the luminous rays. "It's beautiful."

·❧· *Chapter Fourteen* ·❧·

Katrina's magick ruptured, flowing through her fingertips as the classical music filled her chest. She twirled in the midst of the symphony around her. Caught up in the wave, she reveled in the cacophony.

"Where is it coming from?" she yelled. Katrina turned to find both Jax and Jake on their knees, holding their palms over their ears. They grunted, doubled over as the music grew louder.

Katrina couldn't fathom why the concerto wasn't affecting her in kind. Her wolf threatened to shift as her mate agonized on the floor, and she attempted to calm her own magick. Closing her eyes, she concentrated, absorbing the harmonic tones. The sweet melody continued and she suspected that Ilsbeth had set a spell. A scream tore out of her lungs, calling on the witch who had set the trap. "Stop it, now!"

"Holy shit," Jax exclaimed.

"Fuck me." Racked with dizziness, Jake tumbled over, and the Alpha caught him in his arms.

"Jax! Are you okay?" Katrina knelt and put a hand to Jax's forehead, his skin heating her palm.

"Yeah, but he doesn't look too good. What did you do?" Jax coughed and inspected Jake's eyes.

"I didn't do anything. I think it was a spell or something. It was…it sounded magnificent."

"Why'd you run in here?"

"I don't know. I was outside and then I saw the sunlight coming through the stained glass. I just…something just drew me in. I can't explain it." Katrina's chest tightened in guilt. She didn't even know Ilsbeth but when the door opened, a force called to her and before she knew what she was doing she was inside, dancing. Demanding the witch cease her attack had been as natural as breathing.

"Jesus, Kat." Jax wiped the sweat from his brow, and locked his eyes on hers. "This isn't good. You know that, right?"

"I…I don't know what to say. It just happened." Jax's penetrating stare told her they'd discuss what had happened later.

"Hey sweetheart." Jake stirred and he blinked, smiling up at Katrina. His eyes darted to Jax. "You too, big boy. I'm feeling loved."

"Yeah, right." Jax went to push him off but hesitated as Jake groaned.

"Are you all right?" Katrina asked Jake. "Do you think you can walk?"

"I was just enjoying that righteous rock concert. Must have passed out. Waking up to your beautiful face, though? Worse places to be. Just sayin'."

He winked and brought his hand to his head. "Fuck, that hurt."

"Okay, smartass, you ready to get up now?" Jax glanced around the foyer, its cathedral ceiling adorned in hanging crystals of various shapes and colors.

"I don't know. I kind of like being held. I'm reliving my childhood."

"Goddammit, Jake." Jax shoved him away, and stood. He extended a hand to Katrina, who brushed a kiss to Jake's forehead before she accepted his assistance.

"You saw what she did?" Jake pushed onto his knees and blew out a breath, steadying himself before getting to his feet. "Not the kiss. Although that was nice. Very nice. I mean the other thing."

"Yeah, I saw it all right and I don't like it one damn bit." Jax walked toward the staircase, and scanned the room.

"I didn't do it on purpose." Katrina stifled the panic that rose in her throat. Never in her life had she controlled magick outside her own wolf, nor had she conjured psychic connections with physical objects. But there was no doubt in her mind that her command had ceased the music.

"It was kinda cool if you think about it." Jake shrugged and patted her on the shoulder.

"Scary? Yes. Cool? Not so much," Jax disagreed.

"Hey Alpha, did you ever hear that expression, 'look on the bright side of life?'" Jake winked at Katrina and brushed the dust off of his jeans. "You gotta loosen up, man."

"I'm just tryin' to keep us alive. I know you're used to all this voodoo shit down here, but I prefer my mate to be a wolf," Jax replied. "No offense, Kat."

"I am a wolf. Just what the hell are you trying to say? You believe Samantha?" Katrina tore her hand from his and put her hands on her hips. *I knew it. He thinks something is wrong with me.*

"I'm sorry. I didn't mean it like that. It's just that…" Jax sighed and exhaled loudly. "Look, something just happened here and I don't know what it was. I know you're a wolf but I don't have a good feeling about this. I really don't want anything happening to you."

"Let's just look for whatever we came for," Katrina told him, hurt that he doubted her. Granted, she knew what she had done wasn't normal but it wasn't as if she didn't have a wolf inside her. Since being with Jax, she'd felt stronger than ever.

Katrina stared up at the spectacular curved staircase. Streaks of sunlight reflected off its mahogany banister.

"This place is huge. Where should we search?" Jake asked.

"Everywhere," Jax responded.

"It's somewhere in here." Katrina ran her palm along the wall, its rectangular insets appeared in an artistic geometric pattern. The cool wood tingled her skin, and as much as she didn't want it to be true, a voice inside her head told her the mystery would be found within the grand home. "I want to see Ilsbeth's bedroom."

"So did a lot of people. Dimitri used to joke that was where the magick really happened," Jake laughed.

"That turned out well," Jax noted.

"No, he's right." Katrina started up the stairs.

"Where the hell are you going?" Jax asked.

"To get answers." She stopped on the third stair and turned back toward Jake and Jax. "Where do women keep all their secrets? We keep them close to us. If it's not in the bedroom, my guess is that it's somewhere special to her. She was passionate."

"Crazy is more like it." Jake gave a smirk.

"She was a lover spurned. Fueled by passion," she surmised. "Sometimes when a person is desperate, they're not thinking clearly."

"Hey, I'd like to give that bitch the benefit of the doubt as much as the next person, but seriously? She almost killed Dimitri's wolf. He would have lost everything, including his pack. She might as well have just killed him." Jake shook his head. "No, I'm sorry. Sometimes you cross a line and you can't go back. You say something, in her case, do something, something really, really shitty and you can't just call 'take backs'. Not buyin' it."

"Sometimes people are redeemable, Jake. Sometimes we do things for reasons people don't always understand." Katrina's eyes met Jax's. "And we deserve forgiveness."

"I know you're talking about what went down with you and Jax, but this is different. You didn't try to kill Jax. I knew Ilsbeth over the years, yeah, sure there were times when she'd get her freak on or help people out, but she was one fucking scary witch. You did not want to get in her way. I'm sorry, Kat, but we're just going to have to agree to disagree on this one."

"Don't you want to find her?" Katrina felt the energy emanating through her palm as she caressed the railing. A dynamic vibration hedging between benevolence and anger reverberated within its otherwise lifeless timber and Katrina pulled her hand away. Concealing her reaction from Jax, she wasn't ready to disclose what she'd sensed. She prayed whatever supernatural phenomenon she was experiencing in the house didn't follow her home.

"We all want to find her," Jax agreed, following her up the steps.

"I don't," Jake admitted.

Katrina caught the hard stare of disbelief Jax gave him.

"We do want to find her. And so do you," Jax told him. "Ilsbeth has answers. Who knows what we're going to find here today? All I know is that it would be a helluva lot easier if we could just ask her about what she did to Quintus instead of playing Sherlock Holmes."

"I get your point, oh-great-one, but after what went down with D, I'm good without seeing her again."

Katrina heard Jax growl under his breath as they ascended. A hum sounded in her ears, and neither male took notice. The closer they came to the bedroom, the stronger it became. She found it ironic that, for the first time, her body and mind were responding to a witch she'd never known. Despite rumors of Ilsbeth's death, Katrina knew in her heart that she was alive. Whether she was well or not was another question entirely, but her vibrant spirit filtered through the hallways. As she opened the mistress's bedroom door, she became more convinced her salvation lay hidden within the mystical estate.

Upon first glance, nothing appeared sinister. To the contrary, the well-decorated room gave off an air of comfort. The room's amethyst-colored walls were offset by pale bamboo hardwood floors. A circular bed with a satin padded headboard sat in the center of the pentagram-shaped room. Above it, a web of beaded crystals hung from a chandelier, its strands connecting to each of the corners. A life-sized painting of a nude mermaid covered one of the walls. Its sparkled canvas flickered in the waning sunset.

Along the far side of the room, a built-in bookshelf was filled with hundreds of books. Katrina scanned the collection, running her fingers over the spines. From Shakespeare to romances, it appeared Ilsbeth was an avid reader.

Katrina considered the impeccable state of the bedroom and noted how everything appeared in its place. The witch had been particular, she speculated. From the brush and mirror set on the dresser to the matching floral notebook and pen sitting on her desk, its perfect décor could have been found within a design magazine.

Spying a closet door, Katrina crossed the room and turned its handle. She flipped on the light switch and stepped into the large walk-in wardrobe. To the left, an entire wall of neatly stacked shoes sat on wooden shelves. She glanced to the right, finding racks of clothing, sorted by colors. An enormous bronze floor mirror rested along the far wall. A garland of dried pink roses draped over its grand arch, bringing a sense of nostalgia to the room. Everything had been properly arranged, including a set of matched luggage in one of the corners, which further convinced Katrina the witch hadn't planned on leaving.

She heard a laugh come from the bedroom and peered through the door to find Jake dangling a pair of black panties from his finger. He stood in front of the chic dresser, its drawers opened. Katrina almost felt guilty for rummaging through Ilsbeth's things but self-preservation prevailed. The only way to find clues to the witch's whereabouts was to thoroughly search everything.

"D always said she wasn't exactly vanilla. He sure as hell enjoyed the kinky witch before all the shit went down." Jake inspected the delicate lace and ran his finger through its seam. "Oh, yeah. Crotchless. And beaded. Nice. That's one way to get a wolf."

"Seriously?" Katrina rolled her eyes.

"Hey, am I lying?" Jake laughed and gestured with the undergarment up into the air toward Jax.

"I'm with Jake on this one. Sexy. Easy access." Jax shrugged and gave a smirk.

"Maybe you need to get Kat a pair," Jake suggested, holding them to his nose. "Hmm…smells nice. Gardenias. No, wait. Lavender."

Jax sniffed. "Definitely, lavender."

"Maybe I don't need him to buy me anything. Maybe," Katrina paused and cocked her head to the side, giving Jake and Jax a wicked smile, "I already own a pair. Maybe a couple of pairs."

"Oh, yeah…now that I'd like to see." Jake tossed the underwear back into the drawer, closed it and opened another one.

"Not going to happen." Jax combed through the desk and flipped through some loose papers.

"I've already seen her au natural." Jake retrieved a pair of handcuffs and waved them at Katrina.

"Ah, but that's not the same," Jax countered.

"Jax is right. Shifting doesn't count." Katrina shook her head and laughed.

"How's that?"

"It's the allure of the chase. Sometimes what we can't see is far more arousing than what we can." Jax smiled at Katrina, who winked at him.

"Maybe if you're a good Alpha, I'll give you something to chase later," she teased. Katrina studied the intricate pattern of the wallpaper. The seams appeared to come together in the shape of a door. "Hey, look at this."

Katrina ran her finger over the brass circle. Jax reached for it, admiring its intricate pattern.

"I'm not sure what it is. Hold up. Wait." He extended and inserted a long claw into an edge and it clicked open, revealing a solid ring. "It looks like a door knocker. Now what the hell would that be doing here?"

"Hey, it's in the bedroom. Looks like you could clip something to it. Maybe it was for BDSM play. You could definitely tie something onto it."

"Yes, you could," Jax responded. "But I don't know. It's in an odd location. If you were going to install these in the bedroom, you'd want them higher up."

"And you would know this because?" Jake laughed.

"It's a door." Katrina glided her palm downward, kneeling onto the floor. Jake followed her action, while Jax continued to manipulate the metal.

"She's right. It's cold. There's definitely something here." Jake rapped his knuckles on the wood.

"There's something else…" Katrina felt more than just air. A twinge of magick seeped through and she shivered in response. "We have to get inside."

"You sure that's a good idea? Secret door. Bondage ring. I have a bad feeling about this." Jake watched as Jax tugged on the ring. "I've seen a lot of horror movies and this doesn't usually turn out well."

"Maybe there's a key?" she asked.

"Here…let me try," Jake suggested.

"Be my guest, but I'm telling you I just almost yanked the thing out of the wall and it's not budging." Jax pounded on the wall with his fist and although a hollow sound resonated, the sturdy surface didn't budge. "I think Katrina's right. There must be a key or something."

"We haven't searched the rest of the house. Maybe we should just move on to another room." Jake grunted, pulling and pushing on the brass sphere. It made no movement, but he stepped up his efforts, and continued. "I've been here a couple of times, and there're other places we should look. The office, for one, is a place we should search. She's got an entire wall with nothing but ingredients. I'm talkin' a huge antique apothecary cabinet. I bet the thing has dried worms from the 1700s along with ashes from the French Revolution. She once took blood from a naiad right in front of Léo. Dimitri even gave her his wolf hair." Jake gave a great heave and snapped his fingers away. "Goddammit."

"I don't know." Jax speared his fingers through his hair. "We all know there's something back there."

"Jax." Katrina removed her hand and stood. Besides the magick, there was nothing else she could detect. "Whoever would have gone to such lengths to build some kind of secret wall surely has something hidden behind it. Maybe we could find a tool in the basement to open it up."

"We could check out the garage," Jax suggested.

"After we get done breaking into the super-secret playroom, can we please go downstairs?" Jake asked, his voice laden with sarcasm. "Seriously. That set up she has, it's the real deal. Hundreds of drawers."

"Maybe he's right. I'm sure she does have stuff down there," Katrina reluctantly agreed, frustrated the door wouldn't open. "But I want in here."

"How about you stay here with Jax and I'll go look in the garage for something to open it? I've been in there, too. It's mostly tools and stuff."

"It's beautiful, though." Katrina observed the ring. Her eyes were drawn to the antique object. She hadn't noticed it at first, but what she'd thought were geometric shapes were miniscule horse heads intertwined, fitting perfectly together.

"What is it?" Jax asked.

"Do you see it? They look like little ponies…" Katrina's fingers drifted to the object, and a jolt of preternatural energy ripped through her body. As if she'd been electrocuted, she stood frozen, unable to move her hand. She felt the pinch of Jax's fingers wrapped around her wrist, his loud voice telling her to let go. But the longer she touched it, the stronger the draw to unlock it. A click sounded in her ears, the door falling free of her palm.

Katrina sucked a breath, willing her dizziness to end. Strong arms caught her as her legs gave out, and she breathed in the scent of her mate. Her eyes blinked open and she deliberately attempted to slow her pulse.

"Hey, baby." Jax pressed his lips to her forehead. "You okay? You scared me."

"Scared us," Jake exclaimed. "I'm shitting my pants right now. How the hell did you do that? Both Jax and I tried to open that thing and you just…"

Katrina caught the glare Jax shot Jake, and she knew it was because he didn't want to address the elephant in the room. For some unexplainable reason, Ilsbeth's magick was influencing her. As much as Katrina wanted to believe it was just the house, the shock on Samantha's face and her foreboding words warned her that something more insidious was happening.

But given the urgency, they didn't have time to speculate. As the door swung wide open, it occurred to Katrina that if it had opened that quickly, it could shut and lock as well. She forced herself to wake up from the spell, and right herself.

"Where are you going?" Jax asked, refusing to let her go.

"The door. We need to get going."

"Maybe you need to rest a minute. I'm not going to pretend to know what just happened here, but it obviously did something to you. You almost fell."

"I gotta go with Jax on this one. What the hell is going on? First the music. Now this." Jake held the door with his foot.

"I don't know. I…" Katrina stuttered. How could she explain what had happened when she had no idea what was affecting her? She accepted Jax's assistance and held his hand as she regained her balance.

"How can't you know? You saw what just happened, right?" Jake pressed.

"Let her be," the Alpha growled. "We'll discuss it later. The sooner we find something, the sooner we get out of here."

"Fine. But I'm just sayin' it's not natural."

"Leave it," Jax told him.

"You know I'm right," Jake insisted.

"Just stop." Katrina had had enough. The air in the room thickened, making it difficult for her to breathe, and she suspected that whatever was inside the house, it was forcing her to move. She put her hand on her chest, and took a step toward the dark entrance. As she ventured into the darkness, the pressure lifted and she couldn't be sure in that moment whether the flutter in her stomach was caused by relief or dread.

Katrina breathed in the scent of sage as she entered the great room. Awestruck, she held tight to the railing as they made their way toward the wooden spiral staircase. Floor to ceiling built-in bookshelves circled the oval balcony. She stopped momentarily to gaze up at the stars through the cathedral ceiling that was made entirely of glass. Katrina wondered why it couldn't be seen from the front of the home, but guessed that Ilsbeth had enacted a spell, creating the illusion of solid stone, which had hidden it.

"This is unbelievable." Jake ran his hand over the books. "Now this is what I call a library."

"It must be some kind of a ceremonial room," Jax noted.

Katrina remained silent as she glanced down into the space, empty save for an altar.

"I'm pretty sure Ilsbeth held coven gatherings out in the gardens, but y'all know it rains quite a bit in New Orleans."

"Sure does. This place looks pristine, though." Jax led their party down the steps. He held his arm out, keeping both Katrina and Jake behind him. "Not only that. Do you see any other exits or entrances?"

"No way in or out but through the portal," Jake agreed.

"It's special," Katrina told them. As Jax stepped onto the granite floor, she brushed past him and moved into the center, taking in the sight of her surroundings. "It's a perfectly closed oval."

Antique velvet-covered sofas and chairs were set around its perimeter. The scarlet-colored walls on the lower level gave a warm contrast to the cool stone beneath her feet. Katrina approached one of the many paintings adorning its walls.

"I can't believe this. No, these can't be real." Her heart pounded with excitement, noting the canvas that had been set into an ornate filigree gold frame.

"Gauguin," Jax acknowledged.

"Monet," Jake called from across the room.

"It's quite the private collection." Katrina slid a finger across its border, but unlike what had happened in the bedroom, she felt nothing. She turned her attention to the altar that faced the north side of the hall. Her eyes darted to Jax, who gestured with his hand as if reading her mind.

"Look at all the granite." Jake slid his toe across the floor. "Some religions consider it sacred. It has magnetic properties."

"I always thought witches preferred limestone," Katrina said, approaching the wooden structure.

"Ilsbeth never did anything small. She's been around for hundreds of years." Jake came up behind Jax and Katrina and sighed.

"Everything in her bedroom was unique. This hall. The furniture. The paintings. It's all very personal." Katrina pointed to the altar cloth. Its detailed embroidery depicted naked women; one in particular was a larger size. Her platinum blonde hair fell to her feet.

"She's one of a kind. And this place? It looks like no one has ever even been in here," Jax surmised.

"Maybe." Jake nodded. "We can check with Dimitri and Leo to see if they know anything else, but neither one of them has ever mentioned this place to me. The only times I've been to her house, we either met in the yard or her office."

"I've been around plenty of witches over the years," Jax told them.

"Bet you're bummed you missed out on Ilsbeth." The corner of Jake's mouth curled, but his eyes remained on alert.

"What she did to my sister's mate is unforgiveable." Jax picked up a candle, studied it and set it down. "But I suspect like with many people, she's neither all good nor all evil. Witches, wolves, vampires…they often skate the edge of both."

"I don't know how you could say that after what happened to…" Jake began. Katrina shot him a glare and shook her head no.

"What happened to Nick wasn't Ilsbeth's fault entirely," Jax continued.

"They attacked Dimitri, and he was unable to shift. I saw what she did to him," Jake countered

"True, but he may never have met Gillian otherwise. My sister is formidable." Jax fingered through a brass incense bowl and sniffed it.

"I didn't know Ilsbeth, but the feelings I'm getting from being in this house, from touching her things…" Katrina paused and caught the wide-eyed expression of both Jake and Jax. "What? Can we just acknowledge that something is off with me and leave it at that? I'm not saying I'm some kind of psychic, but I'm not going to lie to either one of you. Maybe Ilsbeth has some kind of spell set so she can make contact with us?"

"I don't like it." Jake picked up a copper disc and observed its pentagram design.

"A pentacle," Jax noted.

"How come you're so willing to give Ilsbeth the benefit of the doubt after what she did to Dimitri? And Quintus for that matter?" Jake tossed the object not so delicately back onto the table. "You don't seem like the forgiving type."

"Because, my friend, Alphas learn to be the judge, the jury and executioner. We must be prudent in our interpretation of the facts. Sometimes things aren't as they appear. Take Quint." Jax lifted a small bronze statue of a horned woman and inspected it. "We've been friends a long time. Long enough for me to know he wasn't going to kill my mate. But he's impulsive. He's not always a nice guy. In fact, he can be a very nasty vampire at times."

"Are you honestly trying to tell me that he deserved what Ilsbeth did to him?"

"No, what I am saying is that he may have done something equally as atrocious to Ilsbeth and without knowing all the details, I can't judge. For all I know, his actions may have been even more egregious than hers. So in the absence of facts, an Alpha must rule on the side of caution. You need to evaluate all the evidence and should it be missing, you can decide whether or not you will take action."

"Well, I'm not the Alpha. All I know is that she fucked with D. Therefore, ipso facto, evil bitch."

"All I can say is that you'll learn what it's like someday."

"Many witches are benevolent with their spells. But these horns?" Katrina gestured to the large headdress that sat in the center of the altar. A pair of antlers extended from the headband. "It gives me the creeps."

"She's the high priestess," Jax answered. "They belong to her."

"Not anymore. There's a new sheriff in town," Jake said in his best western accent. "Mick Germaine. That should be interesting. Would love to get Logan's thoughts on that."

"How's that?" Jax asked.

"Nothin'," Jake sighed.

"Doesn't sound like nothing." Katrina reached for a small silver bell, but paused as Jax cocked his head and made an observation.

"Now that's interesting."

"What?" she asked

"That bell there…"

"Yeah?" Katrina pinched its tip and rang it; the audible chime sounded loudly. She looked inside and ran her finger against the smooth metal before setting it down.

"Well, there's only supposed to be one of those. I've been to a few ceremonies. Granted they weren't typical, in that it was a special occasion, but the bell? I recall them ringing it at the beginning and end. That there," Jax pointed to an object. Its oxidized metal finish bubbled in shades of red, "that looks like another bell."

"Well this one here is just an ordinary bell. And this one…it looks…it's an antique. Maybe it's why she has two." Katrina reached for it, and the second her skin touched its surface, the energy hummed through her hand. "Oh my God…"

"Let go," she heard Jax order but compelled, she held tight.

Katrina gave a firm shake and although nothing sounded, a small item fell onto the cloth below. The rusty article, smaller than a quarter, rolled toward Jake, who snapped it up with his fingers. As Katrina released the bell, it dropped onto a knife handle, the tip of which tipped upward, slicing her finger.

"Ow." Katrina snatched her hand away from the altar.

"What the hell?" she heard Jake exclaim.

She turned her attention back to the table. The sickle-shaped instrument glowed where her blood had stained its shiny blade.

"Are you okay?" Jax asked. He tore off a piece of his t-shirt and reached for her hand.

"It's just a tiny cut." Katrina bit her lip, the sharp pain resonating up her arm. "What is that thing?"

"It's a boline," Jax commented, tending to her wound.

"I thought they used an athame?" Jake lifted the knife into the air, where the color slowly returned to its original state.

"It's not used for the same purpose. They use it for cutting things other than flesh. You okay?" Jax wrapped the torn cloth tightly around her pinkie.

Katrina nodded and brought her bandaged hand to her chest. "What fell out of the bell?"

"It's a ring." Jake inspected the rusty metal object. "I'm pretty sure it's a poison dispenser."

"What would that be doing on the altar?" Katrina's heart raced. "Something about these things...we need to figure out what's going on. I could feel the energy in it."

"They go back to the medieval times. Pretty clever really." Jake fingered the ring. "This one? My guess is early fifteenth century."

"But why would Ilsbeth own one of those? It's so...*human*. She's a powerful witch. She could probably poison someone much more easily with a spell." Jax pinched the bridge of his nose. "This isn't making sense."

"True, and look at this house. Ilsbeth has money. I was in her closet. Designer clothes. Every last shoe in its place. I can't exactly see her wearing that ring," Katrina said.

"Maybe she didn't wear it." Jake attempted to jar the circular bulb, using his nail to scrape away the dirt. "Like everything else in this damn place, not opening."

"Maybe she collected it like the paintings, but after what just happened here, my gut's telling me it's important. Jake, get the boline and the bell too. We've already been in here an hour and we still need to search the rest of the house." Jax turned to Katrina and gave her a sympathetic smile. "You sure you don't want to go sit in the car? I'm almost afraid to see what other tricks this witch has going on in here. I don't want you to get hurt."

"No. After what happened in the foyer, I don't think it's a good idea for me to leave you guys alone." Katrina scanned the room one more time, almost expecting Ilsbeth to materialize before them. "This house. I don't know why, but I'm meant to be here. It wants me here."

They exited in silence, and Katrina suspected both of them thought she was losing her mind. Although they'd had the decency not to comment further about how the magick affected her, she grew convinced that she was connected to the witch. Despite what Ilsbeth had done to Dimitri, Katrina didn't sense malevolence within her home. These objects, the music, even her spilled blood had been an intentional act, one designed to communicate.

As they entered the secret passageway, Katrina gave a parting glance to the special place Ilsbeth had taken great care to create, and she wondered what other secrets lay within the walls of the mansion. The energy she'd felt previously had dissipated, but they were one step closer to finding answers. Through the tunnel, the exit into the bedroom was revealed, the last streams of light from the sun lancing through the darkness. With salvation on the horizon, she breathed in hope that one day she'd awaken in the arms of her mate, free from the evil that plagued them.

·❦· *Chapter Fifteen* ·❦·

Jax palmed the tarnished piece of jewelry and considered what had transpired at Ilsbeth's mansion. For over three hours, they had searched. Jake had been correct about the office contents. From everyday herbs and crystals to more rare substances such as a vampire fang, the apothecary contained Ilsbeth's treasured ingredients. But Katrina hadn't experienced any other psychic connections after they'd left the bedroom.

On the short ride back to his Burgundy Street home in Quarter, they'd sat in silent contemplation. Jax had bought the recently renovated early nineteenth century mansion sight unseen, but justified the purchase with the intention of spending more time with Gillian. He surveyed the empty living room, admiring the hand-carved cream-colored crown molding. The plaster walls had been painted a distinctive robin's-egg blue. Matching silk curtains hung perfectly from the twelve-foot-high ceiling. A grand fireplace sat against the wall to the right and Jax set the ring and other items they'd collected on its mantle. He reached for the switch, igniting the gas, and watched as the flames roared to life.

A rattle overhead told him Katrina had turned on the shower. He'd resisted pressing her about what had happened at the house. In the pit of his stomach a nagging thought persisted. What if his mate was changing? What if she changed into something to the point where they'd be unable to bond? Samantha's shocked expression was all he needed to tell him that something was terribly wrong with Katrina's magick, more than he'd suspected. While she no longer experienced trouble shifting, her behavior and experiences in Ilsbeth's mansion had bordered on the inconceivable.

Jax attempted to shake the troubling thoughts from his mind and made his way into the kitchen. With no time to decorate, the only furniture he'd ordered had been for the master bedroom and a kitchen table and chairs. Jax searched through the cabinets, thankful he'd had the forethought to ask his butler to stock the home with food and drinks. Snatching a couple of snifters off the shelf, he set them on the counter. He reached for the bottle of cognac and uncorked it, the classic notes of vanilla and cinnamon wafting into his nostrils. Jax held the tumbler up to the light, swirling the well-aged liquor.

Like its circular motion, his mind spun, strategizing. They needed a witch to help them figure out the significance of the poison ring. He'd texted Luca on the ride home, but the vampire steadfastly refused to let him see Samantha again. Jax didn't blame Luca for not wanting his pregnant fiancée involved in their business. They'd all seen how the black magick was affecting Katrina. Bringing the mystical objects to Samantha and possibly risking her baby's safety was not an option.

If you want something done right, take it to the boss. Unfortunately, the boss, Mick Germaine, was an unknown player in the convoluted supernatural world. Unlike his acclaimed counterpart, Ilsbeth, the warlock hadn't impressed Kade as ally or adversary. Luca told him that Mick had left New Orleans, taking up residence an hour outside of the city toward Bayou Goula in Iberville parish. Jax had convinced the vampire to set up a meeting with the head priest. Tomorrow night they'd go see the warlock.

Tonight, however, Jax would tend to his mate. His wolf had grown anxious, yearning to taste her again. Katrina's tenacity never ceased to amaze him. He shook his head and gave a small laugh. She fought him at every turn, yet he'd caught her every glance, watching him.

As he put the rim to his lips and let the spicy tonic flow over his tongue, Jax decided to test his little wolf further. There would be no secrets between them, nor any limits he didn't test. He gathered the glasses and set forth to the bedroom, looking forward to the pleasure he'd find within the arms of his mate.

Stalking his prey, Jax quietly cracked open the bathroom door. In contrast to his ultra-modern New York City penthouse, everything about his new home was ingrained with a classic elegance. Mini brass gas lamp sconces illuminated the walls. The enormous shower sat center, its clear walls in a perfect square. Exposed copper piping emerged from the floor, curving into the oversized circular showerhead.

Jax sipped his cocktail and kicked off his shoes, observing the way her back arched as she ran water through her long hair. With one hand, he yanked his t-shirt over his head and tossed it aside. Katrina pretended not to notice him as he circled the steam-filled enclosure. Her eyes closed, she teased him, running her hands down over her breasts. *Ah, how my mate enjoys being watched.* Perhaps he'd give her the opportunity to do so for Jake, he mused with a small smile.

He unzipped his jeans and shrugged out of them. The sound of Katrina's sigh told him she was every bit aware of what he was doing. Her arousal filtered into the air, and he lost patience. Jax set the drinks on the counter and took his dick into his hands. Unable to wait a second longer, he paced toward the door.

Steam swirled around him as he stepped into the glass-encased shower. He came up behind Katrina, the warm mist brushing over his face. His cock brushed the small of her back and he slipped his arms around her. Her head fell back onto his shoulder and he heard a soft moan.

"Hmm…Jax."

"You were expecting someone else?" He held her close, his hands sliding over her stomach.

"Why is it that, in such a short time, I'm starting to feel like I've never been without you?"

"Because we've known each other our whole lives. Our wolves, their minds have always been one. It is us who have to learn to adjust. They simply do what nature has taught them."

"How is it you know everything?"

"How come you answer questions with a question?"

"Have you ever been in love?" she asked.

Jax's chest tightened at the question. So many years had passed, but he'd thought he'd been in love only once.

"I thought so," he replied.

"You have?" she asked, a lilt of surprise in her voice.

Jax detected pain in her response and he knew he shouldn't have said anything. But given he expected the truth from her, he wouldn't lie.

"It was a long, long time ago. There was a girl. I was just a teenager. Foolish."

"We all do things in our youth we regret."

"Some later in life," he noted. "But what I did? We mustn't pretend we can marry humans. It is not our way."

"You broke her heart?"

"My father insisted." Jax grew silent. Aside from Gillian and Nick, he hadn't discussed his family with anyone.

"I see." Katrina's arms wrapped over his.

"Have you been in love?" Jax diverted attention away from his own situation. In truth, he sought answers about the vampire.

"I've had lovers, but I've never been in love."

"And Luca?"

"Luca? It's complicated," she sighed.

"It always is. But, my mate, I want to know what I'm dealing with. Do I have competition?" he half joked, wrapping her wet hair around his hand.

"I told you that Luca rescued me." Katrina blinked away the moisture. With her head tilted backwards, she met Jax's gaze. "Sometimes, for whatever reason, you meet someone and there's just this connection. We've been lovers on and off over the years, but was I in love with him? Not really. Not like you mean. We're just friends."

"He still cares about you," Jax observed, selfishly relieved that she hadn't fallen in love with the vampire.

"I care about him, too. Samantha, she's been good for him. Softens him up a bit. He can be a bit cranky." She laughed. "He's not exactly fond of humans...as in not at all. Frankly, I'm surprised he bonded with a witch. I only say that because he's not tolerant of other supernaturals. He cooperates with them only because Kade's his maker. He makes him help the wolves at times. But he and I? I don't know. He was never like that with me. When we first met, he was unjaded. We were both still very young."

"I want you to know that even though I said I thought I was in love," Jax paused and carefully selected his words, "I've never felt this attraction, not like what I feel when I'm with you. When I first heard you laugh, I just…if you hadn't left, I would have chased you for the rest of the night. And now that I actually have you? I'm never letting go."

"I don't want you to let go."

"We'll get answers tomorrow from the warlock. This thing is far from over." Jax traced his finger over his mark and his lips tightened in determination.

"We may be out of time," she whispered. "Samantha. She knows."

"Knows what?" he asked, aware of what she was insinuating.

"I'm changing. I can still shift, but inside," Katrina brought her fist to her chest, "something is happening. Tonight at the house…I don't know how I did what I did. I've never even met Ilsbeth. But the magick? It's almost as if she knew me."

"It's going to be all right, Kat." Jax spoke with conviction. It terrified him that something evil had rooted inside his mate, but he wouldn't let her see his trepidation. "Tonight…all I want to do is be with you."

Jax's hand found her breast. He took a slippery tip in between his fingers and let his other hand dip in between her legs.

"Jax…I want…this," she breathed.

"I need to be in you again," Jax admitted. Claiming her hadn't been nearly enough to sate his wolf. He yearned to make love to her over and over, marking her with his scent, his touch.

Katrina cried out loud as he slid a finger deep inside her core. Her head lolled forward and she braced her arm against the glass.

Jax smiled. He'd never been with a woman so responsive to his touch. Made for him and him alone, his mate shuddered in pleasure. Her breath quickened and he knew she was close. Driving two more fingers deep inside her channel, he pumped into her, his thumb circling her clit. He wrapped his hand under her chin, and she parted her lips, her tongue laving at his thumb.

Jax's shaft strained against the crevice of her ass. The thought of fucking her, taking her in every conceivable way hardened his cock to concrete. Nothing would be off limits with Katrina, and the excitement of exploring how far they could go sent shivers through his body.

A small whimper escaped her lips as her core spasmed. He didn't relent as she came, plunging his fingers in and out of her pussy.

"Yes, yes…that's it, baby. Let go. You don't need to hide from me," he encouraged her, as her small cry became a scream.

"Yes, yes, yes…" Katrina's voice echoed in the shower.

Jax withdrew and spun her around toward him. Lifting her by the waist, he grazed his cock through her wet folds. He stumbled backward, his back slamming into the side wall. Katrina held tight around his neck and slipped her hand down between them. Jax hissed as she took his shaft into her hand and stroked it.

"Mine," she whispered in his ear and guided it into her pussy.

"Fuck, yeah," Jax grunted as he drove up into her. Her channel fisted him and he sucked a breath, the sensation quivering over his sensitive skin. "No, no, no…don't move, don't move."

"You feel so good inside me. Please, I need this. I need you," she told him.

The bite of her nails digging into his shoulders took the edge off and he slowly withdrew and rocked inside her again. Moving together as one, they made love. Water dripped down their faces, their lips crushing together. He'd never get enough of this woman, he knew. Tonight was just the beginning. Every time she revealed a slight vulnerability, she countered with a strength that could only be found within the arms of an Alpha's mate.

His tongue swept against hers and he drank in her loving kiss. As she sucked his bottom lip ever so gently, he increased his pace. Thrusting up into her, he grazed his pelvis against hers, and felt her shake beneath him.

"Oh, Jax!" Her deafening calls urged him and he pounded up into her.

"That's it. Fucking come, baby. Oh shit," Jax cursed. From his root to its tip, her sheath tightened around him, and he called out her name as he came deep inside her.

Her teeth scraped down over his shoulder, and he noted how she'd been careful to avoid marking him. Despite her control, he suspected she'd snap soon, marking him regardless of whether she intended it or not. Her wolf would have its due.

As he slipped out of his mate, and gently set her on her feet, he locked his eyes on hers. Jax recognized the tears brimming on her lashes, and his heart caught as she wrapped her arms around him tightly, holding on for dear life.

"I don't want to give you up," she whispered.

"It's going to be all right, Kat." Jax meant the sentiment even if he hadn't figured out how to make it happen yet. In time, he'd find answers. In time, she'd be his forever. No one would take her away from him, not when he'd just found her.

Jax reached for the spigot and shut off the water. Not willing to break contact, he simply stood, letting the heat from their bodies warm them. Katrina went to pull away and he cupped her cheek. She closed her eyes, resting her head in his palm.

"As long as I'm alive, I'll protect you with my life. This thing…whatever it is, we'll face it together. You're not alone anymore."

She blinked her eyes open, and gave him a small smile. A flicker of hope flashed in her eyes, and he knew that was all people sometimes needed to keep going. No one had said finding and keeping his mate would be easy, only that it would happen.

Jax held tight to her hand and opened the door. He grasped the edge of the towel and wrapped the cottony fabric around Katrina. She went to take it from him but he shook his head no. Without argument, Katrina allowed him to do as he wished.

Here and now, he'd tend to his mate. Jax patted the moisture from her chest and pressed his lips to hers, sucking the stray droplets into his mouth. Silence filled the room save for her gasp as he kissed along her collarbone, carefully drying her. Gentle swipes over her arms were met with moans, his lips finding her breast. He continued slowly, tasting her and moving the towel over her hips.

Stopping to lift his gaze to hers, he knelt before her, bringing the fabric down over the swell of her ass, then weaving it through her legs. As he glided it over her thighs, he exposed her bare mound. She whimpered as his lips brushed over her inner thigh, leaving her shivering in anticipation.

Her fresh arousal drifted throughout the room, her sweet scent tempting him. Jax ran his palms up the back of her thighs until her fleshy globes rested in his hands. Breaking eye contact, he brought his face to her abdomen. He inhaled deeply, hearing the rush of air escape from her lips in response.

"You're beautiful," he breathed, his lips ever so slightly grazing her pussy. "From the minute I saw you and now…"

"Ah…Jax." Katrina's muscles tensed as he teased her with his touch.

"So perfect." He dragged the tip of his tongue through her slit, flicking it over her swollen nub. Her honeyed essence coated his lips and he hummed in delight. "Perfectly made for me."

Jax smiled as she raked her fingers into his hair, fisting it. The prick on his scalp heightened his arousal, and as she tilted his head upward, he momentarily allowed her indulgence to take control. Her heated stare confirmed what he'd known. His little mate not only wanted to be watched but she loved watching his mouth on her.

With a growl, he drove his tongue through her folds. She cried out but held tight to his head. His hands dropped to her pussy and he used his thumbs to spread her labia wide open, granting him access to his prize. But instead of sating her yearning, he mercilessly teased her, licking along the sides of her clit, but never providing her the full friction she sought.

"Jax…please. I can't wait," Katrina panted. "In me…please, I need you in me now."

Jax heard the soft thud as her head rested back onto the wall. Her hands fell to his shoulders and she widened her stance.

He smiled and rewarded her by sucking her clitoris between his lips. As she went onto her tiptoes, quivering with pleasure, he spoke into her wetness.

"Easy, baby…hold on, now."

"Jesus, Jax…please…oh God…" Katrina lost her words as Jax stretched her open further with his fingers and drove his tongue up into her core.

Jax stroked her sensitive ridged channel and delighted as her sweet juice coated his lips. She writhed onto his face, quivering under his touch. Struggling to breathe, Jax didn't relent as he applied pressure with his thumb to her clit. She rocked atop him, heaving for breath. A scream tore from her lips as she convulsed, her orgasm slicing through her. With her palms pressed flat against the glass, she attempted to brace herself against the onslaught of spasms rippling through her.

Jax sprang to his feet, his mouth capturing hers. He wanted her to taste herself on his lips, to savor the exquisite flavor of her arousal. As the Alpha possessed his mate, she returned his branding kiss with fervor. Never in his life had he been more terrified and exhilarated at the same time. His mate, Katrina, owned his soul.

Chapter Sixteen

Katrina's heart pounded as if she'd run a marathon. Her thoughts spiraled as he picked her up off her feet and carried her to the bed. When they'd returned from Ilsbeth's, she'd grown contemplative within her own reflections on the experience. But from the second her mate stepped into the bathroom, the concerns about everything they'd found, her future, all of it, if for only a brief respite, disappeared. Her emotions were replaced with arousal.

She felt his eyes on her, watching and waiting as she washed her hair, bubbles sluicing down her back and over her breasts. Like a lover's hands, she'd cupped her breasts, tweaking her tips into swollen points. After he'd made love to her in the shower, emotions surfaced once again. The magnificent man who'd taken her completely was so much more than a passing phase. As each intimate second passed, she'd exercised every last shred of self-control not to mark him as her own. As thoughts of losing him rushed back into her mind, she was unable to contain the tears that escaped.

But once again, he'd assured her he'd protect her. Yearning to hear the words, she wanted more than anything to believe him. Spoken with conviction, nothing but truth resounded in his statement.

When he'd fallen to his knees in front of her, the sight of her great Alpha took her breath away. His long locks fit perfectly into her hands, guiding his mouth to her pussy. Both vulnerable and ripe with a strength she'd never known a man to possess, he played her body, the maestro leading her in a symphony of pleasure.

She attempted to focus and catch her breath as he set her on the bed. The fire in his eyes told her he was far from finished making love. Her chest rose and fell in anticipation as she watched him stalk to the dresser and retrieve items. *I'll test your limits*, he'd told her and she expected nothing less from the commanding wolf.

Although the lights were dimmed, she caught the blur of an object in his hand. She shivered in excitement, her fingers drifting over her stomach.

"I want you. All of you, Katrina." His low and sensual voice washed over her as he climbed up onto the bed and straddled her legs. Her eyes darted to the item he held behind his back.

"Presents? And it's not even my birthday." She licked her lips and gave a nervous laugh, as a wicked smile crossed his face.

"You could say that. Do you like surprises?" His head dipped to her breast. She arched her back and mewled as his rough tongue swept around her areola. Without warning, he drove two thick fingers into her pussy. "Hmm…I see you do."

Katrina gasped at the intrusion and moaned as her channel quivered around him.

"Jax…what are you…?" Katrina lost her thought as his teeth tugged on her nipple, the pleasurable sting bringing her attention to his mouth.

"You make me lose control, woman," he growled. His fingers slowly pressed in and out of her slick core. "Everything about you…"

Katrina smiled as he lifted his head and she caught the mischievous glint in his eyes. His thickened shaft lay heavy on her thigh, and her pussy clenched around him. As much as she wanted to move, to seek his penetrating arousal, she thought better of it. Her palms moved to cup his unshaven cheeks and he turned his lips to her fingers, sucking them as if he were making love to them. His eyes never left hers as his tongue swirled over them, nipping softly as he let them slip from his mouth.

"I'm going to make love to you," he promised. Katrina nodded as he withdrew his fingers and pressed his thick head to her entrance.

Jax smiled, and she gazed into his penetrating eyes. The sight of her magnificent Alpha stirred excitement throughout her body. Katrina had waited a lifetime to feel this way about someone. To be so utterly consumed by a man, his kiss meant more than breathing. Hundreds of years had passed and no one mortal or wolf had possessed her the way Jax Chandler had in a matter of days.

Seconds felt like hours as his lips hovered above hers, his warm breath on her mouth. His whispered name was all she managed before he kissed her. Melting underneath him, she brushed her tongue against his, reveling in the taste of her mate. His rough whiskers brushed her face, reminding her of the wild soul that lurked within his gentle kiss.

Her legs wrapped around his waist as he slid inside her core, inch by inch, slowly filling her. She protested as he tore his mouth from hers. His weight rested on her and he braced himself up onto his elbow, spearing his fingers into her hair. Her eyes blinked open and she caught him staring at her, his heated gaze causing her heart to flip.

"Don't be afraid," he told her, and she knew he was referring to losing him.

"I…I…Jax." Katrina tilted her hips up as he rocked in and out of her.

"You can't deny your wolf forever."

"I can't resist much longer." She didn't want to say the words out loud. She suspected that she'd mark him soon, unable to resist the lure of her mate.

"This, us, it's everything."

"I want to…" Katrina's words faltered as he increased his pace, and she lost herself within his eyes. *Her lover. Her mate. Her Alpha.*

Before she knew what was happening Jax withdrew and rolled her on her stomach. Katrina squealed as he lifted her bottom into the air. She braced herself on her elbows and heard him command her.

"Like this," he told her. "Hands and knees, princess."

"Jax, please." She wiggled and a firm slap to her bottom rewarded her sass. "Ah...yes."

"Time to play, little wolf."

"Please, just..." Katrina breathed as he slid his ridged shaft into her glistening pussy, stretching her open as he filled her.

"Don't move even a little bit," Jax grunted.

Katrina's head rolled forward and she moaned, her sheath contracting around his rock-hard cock. She heard him exhale, and startled as the cool gel dripped down her cleft.

"I told you not to move," he warned, gliding his palm down over her cheek. His thumb circled her puckered flesh, igniting every cell of her body with desire. "Right here, Katrina. I'm going to have you soon. But first..."

Katrina heard his soft chuckle. She turned her head and caught a glimpse of his devious smile as he waved a shiny gold object in the air, holding it by its looped handle.

"A new toy just for my mate. I told you in New York when I had you indisposed," he paused and laughed, "tied up so nicely. Jesus, it makes me want to fucking come just thinking about it. Hmm. But I digress. As I was saying, I told you I planned to push you, my sweet wolf. My tastes...they aren't exactly vanilla. And I suspect that yours aren't either."

Katrina sucked a breath as the smooth metal surface brushed over her bottom. Although she'd fantasized over the years, there'd been no one she'd trusted to indulge. Tonight, she'd give herself over to her commanding Alpha, the one who'd settle for nothing less than raw honesty.

"I've always wanted..." She stilled as he probed her back hole, the tight ring resisting its entrance.

"Easy, now. Relax and trust me, Kat. I'd never hurt you." Jax removed the tip and replaced it with his thumb. Wiggling it slowly, he pressed it into her bottom, stretching her muscle. "We've got to move slowly."

Katrina closed her eyes, allowing him to prepare her. Her hips rocked forward and back, sliding him in and out of her pussy. Ripe with arousal, she moaned, "More."

"There you go. See how good that feels. That's a girl. Just push back. Look how amazing you are," Jax praised. He withdrew his finger and gently inserted the plug. "I can't wait to fuck you in your beautiful little ass."

"Ah...slow...slow...oh..." A tiny twinge was soon replaced by a delightful fullness that she'd never experienced. "That feels...ah yes. Don't stop."

"It's almost all the way in. You're doing great," he praised. "Just feel me. Let this happen. Let us happen."

Katrina relaxed into the dark intrusion, accepting a pleasure she'd only ever allow her mate to give her. She reached for the headboard of the canopied bed and braced herself as he withdrew his cock and penetrated her core.

"Jax…so full. Please, yes," she cried.

"You feel so good…" Jax muttered. "You're so tight around me."

Katrina gripped the wood, unable to think of anything but the pleasure rippling through her body. Strong fingers grazed through her slick folds, and she gasped. As he stroked her clitoris, Katrina shook, losing control. The most violent, mind-numbing release of her life crashed over her, leaving her body tingling all over. Her core contracted, fisting Jax, bringing him with her. She moaned as he clutched her shoulders and slammed inside her pussy. A triumphant call tore from his lips as he gave one last forceful thrust.

Katrina panted, her body going limp as he removed the toy. They fell onto their sides and he immediately wrapped his arm over her, his lips gently peppering her collarbone with his kisses. She breathed into his embrace as his leg draped over her hip. Katrina's heart crushed, her wolf crying into the night, begging to mark her mate.

She'd opened her body and mind to Jax but still held the tiniest but most precious sliver of herself back. Without a doubt, she could fall hard and fast for the wolf who'd exposed her secret desires and accepted her for everything she was. But until she knew for certain that she couldn't hurt him, she'd never claim him as her own. As she drifted off to sleep, a solitary tear ran down her cheek and over her lips, the taste of regret bitter on her tongue.

Although the heaviness of slumber called her to curl into the sheets, the warmth encasing her body had cooled. *Jax.* Katrina blindly swept her hand across the bed, grasping the blanket. Her eyes went to the large antique wooden wall clock, its brass pendulum reflecting the street light. It was nearly four thirty in the morning and she wondered where Jax had gone.

Giving a yawn, she shoved up to sit on the bed and glanced around the bedroom. Katrina peered through the cream-colored translucent fabric that hung from the rungs overhead, and smiled. Her Alpha had chosen a romantic décor for his elegant home. It reminded her that there was so much to learn about her mate. In spite of their heated sexual tryst, only time would unravel his mysteries.

A shiver ran over her arms, the air conditioning cooling her skin. Instead of searching for clothes, she simply tugged at the sheet and wrapped it around her body. Katrina swung her legs over the bed, and steadied her feet onto the cold hardwood floors. As she made her way down the hallway, a flicker of light reflecting into the walls told her Jax had gone downstairs.

She padded down the grand stairway and her thoughts drifted to another era. Having grown up in the early 1800s, she recalled long ago when a home would be lit by candles, the warm breeze of spring pouring through the windows. Although there had been no modern conveniences, it had been a simpler time in many respects.

Rustling papers drew her out of her contemplation and as she rounded a corner, she spotted Jax sitting on an area rug in front of the fireplace. Wearing only a pair of jeans, her shirtless Alpha appeared lost in rumination. He held a small wooden frame in his hand; a large cardboard box sat next to him. Afraid to startle him, she kept quiet. She smiled when he whispered her name, realizing he'd sensed her presence.

"Katrina." Jax set the picture into the box and patted the floor.

"Whatcha doing?" She eyed the container.

"I couldn't sleep, so I thought I'd check things out."

"Everything okay?"

"Everything's great. This place," he glanced around the empty room, "I bought it after seeing it online." He laughed, his eyes meeting hers. "I called my realtor and told her I wanted it. Never even stepped inside it until today. Pretty crazy, huh?"

"It must have been special," she commented, trailing her fingers over his shoulder.

"Maybe. Not really. It wasn't so much the house. It was Gillian. This is going to sound strange, because my pack is my family. But to have a blood member? It changed everything for me. My mother and father…they aren't alive anymore." Jax shook his head, his face pensive. "When Gilly came into my life, I swore I wouldn't be some long distance relative who sent holiday cards twice a year. No, that isn't going to happen. I want to be close to her. I want her close to me. I want…"

"A family?" Katrina's heart broke for him, sensing how lonely he'd been. It wasn't as if she didn't understand the anguish of solitude. After decades of watching others find their partners and have children, she'd buried the painful dream of finding her mate, forced to accept her solitary existence.

"Yes, a family." He reached for her hand and covered it with his. "I don't want to scare you, Kat. I mean, shit, it's not like we have exactly had an easy go of things. We aren't even bonded yet but you need to know…"

"Jax…I can't promise you forever, because I don't know what will happen to me. But I'm your mate. I belong to you. I'm your family now." Katrina gave him a warm smile.

"I already told you, I'm not letting you go," he replied and changed the subject. "This box. I guess Samuel sent these things here before I went missing."

"Things?"

"Yeah, you know. Family photos, stuff I've collected over the years. Gillian stayed with me for a while after Nick died. We went through some of it. As you can imagine, I have a lot of shit." He blew out a breath and picked up a well-worn cream-colored domino. He fingered it, running his pad over the blackened dimples. "Samuel got some of my family things mixed up with Nick's."

"You need help sorting them?"

"Nah, not right now." He held the trinket up to the light. "It's made of bone. Wood on the bottom."

"Yours?" She smiled.

"Yes and no. Nick collected them over the years. This one's an antique. We used to play…a whole lifetime really. Nick loved these damn things." He reached for her hand and tugged her toward him. "Come join me."

Katrina settled next to him, and picked up the frame he'd set back into the box. She studied the black and white photograph. A young woman stood stoically, her long dress brushing the ground. Katrina recalled owning a similar garment in the 1840s. The dress she'd worn had been fashioned in a royal blue damask fabric. Although it had revealed her bare shoulders, the long sleeves covered her arms.

"Who is she?" While the girl didn't smile, Katrina noted a glint of happiness in her eyes.

"Phoebe." Jax gave a regretful smile and retrieved it from her hands.

"A friend?" *A lover?* Katrina sensed the sorrow from her mate as if it was her own, and she realized that from now on, his wellbeing would be tied to hers. Her fingers once again traveled to her shoulder, his mark tingling on her skin.

"I thought I was in love." He laughed and shook his head. "So young. I must've been around seventeen. I might as well have been a baby."

"She was human?" Katrina's wolf let out a low growl, and she stifled the displeasing emotion. To be jealous of a dead girl was ridiculous, she knew. But with her Alpha unclaimed, the irrational thought surfaced.

"Yes."

"Things were different back then." Katrina recalled her mother's warning to stay within their pack. When Tristan became Alpha, he'd been a more progressive leader, allowing interaction with humans. Regardless, wolves learned to be cautious of falling in love with others, expecting they'd someday meet their mate.

"My father was a strict man. He, uh," Jax sighed, "he didn't tolerate any breaking of rules. It was more than just submission. My mother, she doted on him like a king. It was never enough. That day…"

"What happened?"

"He'd caught me with her. I was foolish. I knew better. We'd never even had sex, you know. Just kissed. But it was enough. He scented her on my clothes. He beat me that day."

"Oh, Goddess…" Katrina caressed his back. The thought of any father abusing his child made her sick to her stomach. But to know her mate had been mistreated; she wished she could go back in time and kill his father herself.

"He got the best of me. He knew that I was growing stronger, that the Alpha within my soul was strong. Sometimes I think it was the only way he thought he could survive. I'd either have to leave the pack or challenge him."

"What happened?"

"My mother, she went into a depression after that day. She took care of my bruised body, but she couldn't repair the damage that had been done to our family. She'd begged me to submit, to accept that no matter what my father asked, I'd have to give in. But that's the thing, Kat, when you're Alpha, you don't get a choice. You are born Alpha and when the opportunity comes, you seize it."

"But Logan, he didn't challenge anyone. He was Tris' beta for so many years. Granted he was a leader but I never expected he'd take over Acadian Wolves."

"Tristan knew. I guarantee it. We all can sense the Alpha within others. Now it's true that some wolves suppress it. Something in their lives happens and they just decide life is better without responsibility. But for most of us, it's an overwhelming call. We cannot deny it, any more than we can deny breathing." Jax scrubbed his palm over his tousled hair and shrugged. "But Phoebe? She never asked for any of this. Hell, she didn't even know I was a wolf."

"You stopped seeing her?" Katrina asked.

"That's the thing. I didn't stop seeing her. I wasn't going to let that bastard tell me who I could or couldn't see. He'd been telling me my whole damn life what to do. I'd watched him lead, he bullied pack members. And the girl? I wanted her more than anything. Jesus, when I think about it…shit, I was just like any other teenager."

"Horny?" She gave a small laugh.

"Hell, yes. She was beautiful and just the sweetest girl in town. And I was an asshole, a selfish prick who should have known better."

"No, don't say that. There's no way you could have known anything. We all were teenagers once."

"I killed her." Jax's voice grew soft and he traced his finger along the rim of the frame.

"What? No." Katrina's eyes widened, her heart rate sped up at his declaration. There was no doubt in her mind that her Alpha could kill, she'd witnessed the aftermath at the cabin. But deliberately murder an innocent? No way.

"My father ordered her death and his beta killed her. No one suspected anything. Her body was found in the woods a week later. He made it look like she'd been mauled. Her fault, they'd said. Stupid girl had gone where she shouldn't have. But I knew better. My whole pack knew."

"Oh Jax," she gasped. "I'm so sorry."

"It was my fault. Her blood," Jax extended his palms and stared at them as if they were dripping before him, "it's on my hands."

"No, Jax. You didn't…"

"Yes, Kat. It was my first lesson in being an Alpha. Patience. Restraint. These qualities of mind are every bit as important as the brute strength and cunning needed to win a challenge. I," he paused, brushing both of his hands over his head, "did not have the patience. Nor did I consider the consequences of my actions. I underestimated the power of my opponent. Had I had patience, I would have waited for the day when I would become Alpha. My self-indulgence cost Phoebe her life."

"You were just a kid." Katrina fought the tears, choosing to be strong for her mate. "I'm not going to pretend that you haven't been carrying around this guilt for a long time, but you need to let it go. Your father sounds like an awful person, a complete psychopath. I know you know this. I've watched you lead. I've been on the end of some of your 'lessons'. There's a difference between teaching and punishing. And there sure as hell is a difference between punishing a teenager and murdering an innocent girl who did nothing more than fall in love with a boy."

"My mother had already been hanging on by a thread. She, uh, only lived a few more years. You know, they talk about the spirit within us. I'm pretty sure it's what killed her will to live." Jax set his eyes on Katrina, who took his hand in hers. "The day she died, I left the pack. I only returned later…when I was stronger. After Gillian had been born…"

"Does Gillian know about your father? What he did?"

Jax shook his head no.

"You didn't tell her?" Katrina eyed him with concern.

"It's not like I didn't want to tell her but hell, I'd just reconnected with Gilly. How am I supposed to tell her that her father, this great warrior, just so happened to be a ruthless murderer? From what I can tell, Mirabel, her mother, hasn't told her either. She managed to escape. When I came back to the pack, things had only grown worse. He'd stolen her tiger. Pack members were terrified. We were on the verge of territorial wars with others because his behavior had become more aggressive. He didn't exactly believe in diplomacy."

"You returned? What happened?" Katrina instinctively knew what words he'd confess even before he said them and she'd already made the decision to support him. No man deserved what his father had done to him.

"I killed him." Jax closed his eyes and blew out a deep breath before continuing, his voice calm and low. "I'd had enough. Someone had to stop him. And I was Alpha. I am Alpha."

"A challenge?"

"Yes. I almost died that day. But I wasn't going to give up. Not for one second. Even as blood was pouring out of me, my flesh in his claws and teeth, my conviction never wavered. This face," his eyes went to the photo, "she was in my mind. That day, she was avenged. Her blood may be on my hands but I did what I had to do to set it right. I am not my father."

"No, you're nothing like him at all."

"Tristan doesn't think so. You know that's why he doesn't trust me. I don't blame him. But Phoebe? I didn't mean to get her killed."

"Come here." Katrina brought Jax into her embrace, his face rested on her breast. As she cradled his head and caressed his hair, she felt the stress drain from his muscles. Her heart broke for her great Alpha. "None of this is your fault, Jax. Do you hear me? You are nothing like your father. Nothing at all. You may have been born of an Alpha, but you grew into the leader you are today. I watched my father. Marcel. Hunter. Tristan. Great men make mistakes and learn from them. I'll tell you this." She pressed her lips to his head and spoke softly. "*You* are an amazing man. You're honorable. Courageous. Compassionate. And you're mine. I am your family. Me. You're not alone."

Jax raised his gaze to meet hers and Katrina cupped his cheeks. He'd bared his heart and soul, trusting her. She leaned in and kissed away the moisture on his lashes. She'd always known Jax was a striking if not beautiful man but it was his sensitive heart and mind that took her breath away.

She grazed her lips down his cheek, finally settling on his mouth. As the sheet fell away and she gave herself to him, the decision not to claim him became all the more difficult. Falling for Jax Chandler was as inevitable as the sun rising, and she was helpless to control it.

Chapter Seventeen

Jax blinked his eyes open, smiling as the sight of Katrina resting on his chest came into view. Although his wolf stirred, restless she hadn't claimed him, the man delighted in the peaceful bliss. Confessing the nature of Phoebe's death and the beating at the hands of his father had incited a cathartic awakening. Not only had Katrina soothed his battered soul, she'd accepted him for who he was and who he would become.

It was true that living pack members had witnessed the challenge, with some holding him in a higher reverence. Newer members, however, hadn't lived through the bitter history, the significance of what had occurred lost on them. He knew he'd have to tell Gillian the truth someday but it'd have to wait. His sister had already texted him five times since he'd arrived, and he'd insisted she stay clear of him until it was safe. He hoped Dimitri had resumed some control over his mate but suspected it was unlikely, given her nature.

A stream of sunlight stabbed at his eyes and he yawned. He glanced at the time, and wasn't surprised they'd slept until three in the afternoon. A loud bang sounded from afar, and he cursed under his breath. *What the ever loving fuck?* He'd given Jake the security code so he could come over whenever he was ready. But listening to the racket coming from downstairs, he couldn't fathom what the damn wolf was doing.

He pressed a soft kiss to Katrina's forehead and carefully peeled her off him. She mewled as he tucked the blanket around her, and he smiled in response. Jax brushed away a hair from her cheek and took a long minute to drink in the sight of his mate. Her swollen pink lips curled into a small smile and he hoped she was having the best dream of her life. Although she'd been pale, she'd developed a tiny hue of color in her cheeks after only being in the sun for the day. Her long blonde hair spilled out over the black sheets like a majestic waterfall, tempting him to wake her just so he could run his fingers through the silky strands.

After using the bathroom and throwing on a pair of jeans and a t-shirt, he padded down the hallway in his bare feet. The ruckus filtered throughout the house as he descended the steps, the spicy scent of pepper filling his nostrils. By the time he reached the landing, the melodic beat of zydeco grew louder.

"Hey, bro," Jake called from the kitchen.

"What the hell?" Jax's eyes went to the sink, which was filled with half a dozen bowls. A large cauldron boiled on the gas stove.

"Mudbugs, man."

"What?" Jax reached for a cabinet door, opening and shutting three of them before he found the mugs. "Have you lost your goddamned mind?"

"Mudbugs. Crawfish, Yankee boy."

"What?"

"Got a boil goin' baby. Secret family recipe. Oh, yeah." Jake waved his wooden spoon in the air, and gave a hip roll to the music. He laughed and turned to his concoction.

"I'm going to wake up from this nightmare." Jax scanned the room and made a beeline for the coffee machine. "Have you been drinking? Please tell me you've been drinking, because I don't think there is any other reason for your babble."

"As a matter of fact, I've got a pitcher of Bloody Marys ready to go, my friend."

"You do realize I just woke up?" Jax poured his coffee, sniffed it and took a sip.

"Uh, that falls in the category of don't care. I've been up for a while now." Jake picked up a loaf of flaky French bread and pointed it at Jax. "While you've been gettin' busy, I went and got myself a good rest. Being that my ass has been in Cali and New York for the past two months, I'm missing my roots."

"There's something wrong with you, you know that?"

"I'm hungry and you're grumpy. Want some?" He tore off a chunk and crumbs flew up into the air.

"You're a slob."

"You love me and you just can't admit it, can you, Alpha?" Jake joked.

"Toss me the bread." Jax gave him a smirk and caught the loaf as it flew across the room, white flecks spraying everywhere. "I'm not cleaning this up."

"As if you would clean? Let's get real. I'm sure Samuel is on his way down here now."

"No, he isn't, smartass. I told him to stay home."

"Backup maid?" Jake smiled broadly and nodded.

"I'll text him." Jax retrieved his phone and sent a message to his butler. He hoped he could find someone to tend to the mess after they'd left the house.

"Good deal. You're going to love me big time in a few minutes," Jake promised.

"Crawfish for breakfast? I highly doubt it. Are you always this cheery in the morning?" Jax sipped his drink.

"It's technically the afternoon but yes and yes. Positive attitude. It's what it's all about."

"Really? Is that what you demonstrated yesterday?"

"Hey, easy there. First of all, that witch is one scary bitch. You don't even know the half of it. And second of all, Kat's reaction to that house...well, that kind of speaks for itself. We all may have pretended like it didn't happen, but you know that shit's not right. And that redheaded witch knew the score. Fucking Luca, man. He's got a stick so far up his ass he's like one of those marionettes."

"He's not going to let us see her, so just give it up. Mick's next on the list."

"Are you sure you really wanna go there? I like running in the bayou at night as much as the next wolf, but I'm not so sure about this freak fest this warlock has going on." Jake sat down at the table with Jax and tapped a beat on it with his spoon, then paused. "I've met Mick before, ya know? He's, uh, how should I put this? He's kind of a free spirit. If you'd met him, you would never think he was some big and powerful warlock. He's a player."

"A player?"

"Yeah, you know. A player. With the ladies," Jake sang, a lilt of amusement in his tone. "And I'm not just talking witches. He's charismatic. Really good-looking."

Jax raised a questioning eyebrow at him in silence.

"For a guy." Jake glanced to his steaming pot and then focused back on the Alpha. "My point is that we better have a plan B. It's not that I doubt what Samantha's sayin'. Logan confirmed that Mick has taken most of the coven outside of the city. But from what I gather, it's more like a big ole voodoo orgy. There's magick happenin' all right, if you know what I mean?"

"So he's a flake? It's better than hearing we're going out to talk to some mage who practices black magick." Jax shrugged. It wasn't the best situation but it wasn't the worst. In the end, it didn't matter, because he was going to get answers if it was the last thing he did.

"I'm just setting expectations is all, which are pretty low."

"It's quite simple. If Mick doesn't have answers, I'm going to Logan and there'll be an all-out war with the vamps. Because that will mean that Samantha really is the only one who might be able to help. Granted, I get why Luca doesn't want her around this black magick stuff. Or Katrina right now for that matter. I don't want her or her baby hurt. But I'm not buying that she doesn't know what we found. And even though she may be a new witch, she must be pretty damn influential if she has the keys to Ilsbeth's private home. I wonder if she's even taking orders from Mick." Jax reached for the butter and sliced off a slab, smearing it onto the bread.

"You can be stone cold sometimes, you know that, right?"

"You misinterpret things, Jake. Come on, you've been around Logan and other Alphas, right? It's not your first time at the rodeo."

"Yeah, but they're not as bold as you, no offense."

"None taken." Jax bit into the bread.

"I'm not sayin' this is a bad thing, it's just that you are a little more intense than most Alphas. That's all." Jake shoved out of his chair, and went to the refrigerator to retrieve the pitcher. He set it on the table and searched the cabinets until he found glasses.

"What you describe as intense, I would describe as thoughtful. I've learned the hard way not to be impulsive. At the same time, as Alpha, one must be decisive." Jax shrugged. "You'll see."

The young wolf had no idea of his own power, Jax mused. From the second he'd met Jake, he'd known he was special. Yet, Jax resisted telling him. *All things in good time.* Until there was a need, it would be best for Jake to learn on his own.

"And," Jake pointed his glass at the Alpha, before setting it in front of him. "You're a cryptic son of a bitch. You wouldn't happen to be related to Léo, would ya?"

"A vampire? Ha. Ha. You're hilarious." Jax's stomach growled and he peered around Jake to eye the pot on the stove. "That done yet?"

"Ah, ha! I knew it. You gettin' ready to show my cookin' some love?" Jake poured the thick red liquid over some ice and inserted a crisp celery stalk.

"Maybe." Jax laughed and reached for the cocktail. "Don't tell anyone, though. I'd hate to ruin my rep."

"You're badass. I don't think a little happy time with my mudbugs is going to make people think you've gone soft." Jake focused on his meal and didn't hesitate, changing the topic. "So, uh, speaking of soft, how's Katrina?"

"Nice segue."

"Hey, I try." He laughed.

"She's good."

"Good? Trouble in paradise already?"

"It's complicated." Jax coughed and set the glass down. "Damn, these are strong. What the hell did you put in them?"

"Again. Secret recipe. Besides, it's good for you. Veggies. Kinda like a salad in a glass."

"That would be a smoothie."

"Close enough. So what's the deal with Kat?"

"It's nothing really." Jax sighed, contemplating how much to share with the wolf who was becoming a friend. He enjoyed Jake's company, his continual petty challenges akin to a puppy biting at his heels. He saw a more innocent version of himself and hoped that with guidance, he and Logan could give Jake what he needed to be a great leader.

"You know I love Kat, I mean like a friend," Jake was quick to qualify, "but she's been on the run for a long time."

Jax nodded.

"She acts strong. Hell, she is strong, but she's scared."

"She won't mark me." Jax's eyes met Jake's as he confided in him. "Fucking demons, whatever they are. She's convinced she's going to hurt me."

"I don't know much about mating, but watching D...let's just say it doesn't seem like you get a whole lot of choice. I mean he was resisting it, worried he'd kill Gilly's tiger and then the next day? Boom. They're mated. Now, this thing with her magick…it's not right."

"I know. I can feel it. Sometimes," Jax paused, and glanced over his shoulder. He heard water running upstairs, which told him she was awake. "Her magick, it can be strong, just like it should be for someone who's an Alpha's mate. But then, there are other times when it just feels different. I mean, we both know wolves aren't mediums. They don't touch objects and *feel* something. We're wolves. We shift. Yes, the pack can sense me and my feelings, and I can get a general vibe on my pack, but this is completely different." Jax sighed and swirled the celery around the spicy mixture before extracting it. "I don't know if it's Katrina and what they did to her? Or maybe somehow Ilsbeth did something and it's just that house? Maybe she set up a spell so that only Katrina could find the clues?"

"Let's say that's the case. That would mean that Ilsbeth somehow knew about what was happening to Kat. Someone would have had to have told her, because Kat never even met Ilsbeth."

"You said D was sleeping with her?"

"Yeah, but he's true blue with the pack, man. He'd never let secrets slip out over pillow talk."

"Ilsbeth knew about these things, because she sent Quint to the prison. And so that means she probably knew about them before Kat ever came down to New Orleans."

"How would she know what was going on in New York?"

"Because she's like Léopold. She travels a lot. I've met her several times at charity functions in Manhattan."

"You've met, huh?" Jake raised a suspicious eyebrow at the Alpha.

"What?" Jax shook his head and took a bite of celery.

"Just how many times have you met her?"

"What the fuck is that supposed to mean? I don't know. A few times. A half dozen times tops."

"Just wondering why you're so willing to forgive the bitch. Oh, did I just say that?" Jake held his finger to his mouth, his eyes wide. "Sorry, I meant witch."

"We've been through this, okay? I get what she did to Dimitri. I'm just saying, and this is the Alpha speaking, got me? The Alpha can see the big picture. Ilsbeth has done some good things over the years. She's helped Kade. Even Léopold. Granted they're vampires, but she performed tasks in goodwill. So that tells me that on occasion, she can take the right path. Now as Gilly's brother, I want to kill her for what she did. It's fucked up." Jax sipped his drink and blew out a breath. "But that's the thing, as Alpha, I don't just get to be her brother. I must see the big picture. And it tells me that she's not all bad."

"She's not all good," Jake countered.

"True. But what happened last night? Something…instinct is telling me that Ilsbeth is trying to help us. Maybe something bad happened to her."

"One can only hope." Jake threw a stack of newspapers on the table. "Can you spread those out for me?"

"What?"

"Spread em' out. On the table. Bugs are up." Jake slid oven mitts onto his hands and lifted the metal colander out of the boiling pot.

Jax unfolded the papers and continued his train of thought. "I'm just saying, maybe she went away to lick her wounds…"

"Or hide because D was going to kick her ass from here to the moon."

"More like Gilly. Stop interrupting." Jax gestured to the covered surface. "This good?"

"Yeah, thanks."

"The thing is, just because Kat didn't know her doesn't mean she didn't know Kat. She's shrewd. She might have known what was going down. Maybe she even knew that she'd need Katrina to help bring these assholes down."

"Heads up, Sherlock," Jake instructed, dumping a steaming pile of red crustaceans onto the papers. "Look at that! That's a slice of heaven right there."

"I'm just sayin'. You need to learn to look at the big picture, Jake. Jesus, those things do smell good."

"Told ya."

"Not as good as…" Jax turned to find Katrina standing in the doorway.

Wearing nothing but his white dress shirt, his mate smiled at him and shifted her weight from one hip to another, inadvertently flashing a hint of inner thigh. He made a mental note to thank Samuel for making sure his closet had been stocked with his clothing. *She's the only sustenance I need, not a damn crawfish.*

"Hey, Kat." Jax inwardly laughed, realizing how nothing else seemed to exist in her presence. Pushing onto his feet, he reached for her hand. She giggled as he took her into his embrace. Although she'd showered, he could still smell his scent all over her skin and his cock hardened in response.

"Hey," she responded back, her voice soft and husky.

Her smooth palm ran under the fabric of his shirt, grazing over his abs. She gazed up into his eyes and brushed her thumb over his flat nipple. Jax lost his words, and his eyes fell to her lips. Smiling, his mouth descended on hers.

The kiss was gentle, like a soft breeze in summertime. More than aroused, he was comforted by the support she'd given him when he'd told her about what had happened with Phoebe and his father. His heart tightened as she relaxed into his arms. He could fall for this woman, and although he'd known it would happen, the rush of adrenaline running through him confirmed how much he cared about her, about his future with Katrina.

"You guys are killin' me, ya know that, right?" Jake teased.

Jax smiled into her lips and slowly opened his eyes, pleased with the come-fuck-me-now expression his mate wore. A pity it had to wait. But the way his thick shaft strained like a steel beam against his zipper, breakfast would have to be fast. A set of fingernails combed down his back, and he sucked a breath as they delved down inside his pants, cupping his ass.

"Hmm…now that's the way I like to wake up," Katrina purred.

"Baby, you're tempting me." Jax laughed as her other hand glided down between his legs and gripped his straining erection, stroking it through the denim. "Ah, shit. Not fair."

"Who said life is fair, Alpha?" Katrina pressed a kiss to his cheek and glanced to Jake, who shook his head.

"Really? I am right here." Jake gestured to his chest.

"Hmm…I think Jake likes to watch," she quipped.

"You're wicked." *My little minx wants some public fun, does she?* Jax hadn't thought it was possible, but her statement sent a fresh rush of blood to his already painfully erect cock.

As she spun in his arms to open a cabinet, he gave a devious smile to Jake.

"Let me help you," Jax said sweetly. Without releasing her waist, he came up behind Katrina and lifted her shirt, exposing her bare bottom.

"What are you doing?" She laughed. As she reached for a coffee cup, she jumped as he roughly clasped a rounded cheek.

"My mate is very poorly behaved, don't you think? Teasing you like she did." Jax looked over his shoulder to Jake. "I think it's my little wolf who likes being watched. Perhaps you should come see her?"

Jax knew he was playing with fire, inviting him to play. Allowing Jake to bring Katrina pleasure wasn't an option. His wolf would lose it, and he risked shifting. Unmated, his wolf growled in warning, but the Alpha's pulsing dick won the battle.

"You're serious?" Jake shot him a look of surprise, and dropped the pot holders onto the counter.

"Did you know that my mate enjoys being spanked?"

"Jax," Katrina hissed, wiggling under his touch.

"Isn't it amazing how the Goddess sees fit to give me such an adventurous mate?" Jax nuzzled his nose into her thick locks and teased the back of her neck with his lips. The fresh scent of her coconut-scented shampoo reminded him of her wild nature. "You know, my sweet princess…the sooner we complete our mating, the sooner we can explore all the possibilities."

As Jax kissed her skin, he sensed her wolf yearning to claim him. Although Katrina kept her restrained, the tether strained tight, fraying apart where he'd worn it thin. Like a game of chess, he'd strategically play his new mate, breaking her will until she set her wolf free. He suspected when she finally did, they'd bond.

"She's always been beautiful." Jake cautiously approached.

The Alpha lifted his head, meeting his gaze. As expected, the young wolf knew better than to reach for her.

"She," Jax smacked her ass, the slap sounding throughout the kitchen. As he expected, Katrina moaned in arousal, not making an effort to move, "is amazing. And very, very hot."

Jax's fingers grazed down her cleft until he cupped her mound, giving it a light tap.

"Jax...we shouldn't do this," she panted.

"Jake was nice enough to make us breakfast." He winked and gave a small chuckle. "And you came down here teasing us with something far more delicious. Should we give him a taste?"

"I...I..." Katrina's gaze went to Jake. "Ah..."

"Hmm? What was that? I can't hear you." Jax plunged two thick fingers into her, causing her to cry out in pleasure. He marveled at how aroused she'd become at having an audience. "She's dripping wet. And such a naughty wolf. You like him watching, don't you? Tell him, Kat."

"Jax...just...oh please," she breathed. Bracing her arms on the outside of the cabinet, she spread her legs wider, giving him better access.

"You need to answer when I ask you a question. Seeing that my hands are busy, would you mind assisting me in teaching Katrina how to answer me?" Jax glanced to her ass and nodded at Jake.

Taking his guide, Jake gave him a grin. "Yes, Alpha."

As Jake slapped Katrina, her tight channel clenched around Jax's fingers. "Oh yeah, she likes that, all right. Don't you, Kat?"

Her hips began to thrust forward seeking relief, and Jax thought he'd come from the sound of her moaning. Jake spanked her again and she yelped.

"Yes, goddammit, I like it. Please...I can't take this. Fuck me." Katrina bit at her own skin and squirmed as Jax withdrew his fingers.

Jake fell back against the granite counter as Jax moved behind his mate, and unzipped his jeans. His eyes went to Jake, who undressed.

"Look at Jake. Look what you do to him." Although unsure if he'd ever share his mate fully, the idea of making Jake watch turned him on as well. Jax slid his palm over his thick cock. Thumbing its slit, he brushed his seed over his shaft. He lifted her shirt once again and positioned himself, pressing his crown to her entrance.

"Oh my God..." Katrina grunted as Jax plunged into her.

Sliding a hand up under the flowing cotton, he reached for her breast. His other hand reached around between her legs, his middle finger spreading through her labia.

Her pussy pulsated around him as he rocked in and out of her slick core. Katrina glanced to Jake, who stroked his dick. Jax gave her a wicked smile as her gaze finally drifted to him. He never took his eyes off of her as he increased the pace. In all his days, he'd never been so impulsive. Fucking her in the kitchen, let alone in front of Jake, had been the furthest thing from his mind when he'd woken up, but there was no way he was stopping now.

"Fuck me...harder, Jax, harder," she urged.

Taking her clit between his fingers, he gently pinched, gradually tightening his hold. The sound of his flesh smacking against hers rang in his ears as he thrust into his mate. Jax bit his lip, struggling to keep his orgasm at bay. Her tight channel spasmed around his rigid length, hurling him into release. He erupted, a loud grunt tearing from his lips. Katrina screamed in ecstasy, repeatedly saying his name. Spent, Jax collapsed against his mate and wrapped his arms around her, pressing his lips to her shoulder.

In a short time, his entire life had become about Katrina and her only. If she liked being watched, he'd give her anything and everything she wanted. She was like a force of nature that had swept him off his feet, spinning him up into a cyclone, and he didn't want to set his feet on the earth again. Her terrific storm had smashed apart his reality, setting forth a new world where he did nothing without her.

A warm washcloth touched his hand and he accepted it, cleaning both himself and Katrina. He tossed it into the laundry room, but never lost contact with his mate. She slowly turned in his arms and fell into his embrace. The soft rise and fall of her chest synched against his. Both were left breathless from their heated encounter. He smiled, kissing her hair, blissfully aware that he'd lost complete control of the situation.

For the first time as an Alpha, he realized that from here on out, there was one part of his life he no longer ruled. When it came to Katrina, she drove him over the edge, testing his judgment, but there was no denying his mate would bring him to new levels of pleasure he'd never known.

Jax tore the tail off the tiny crawfish and glanced to Jake and then back to Katrina. *Sex in the kitchen?* Par for the course. *Swallowing the innards of a small crustacean?* Uncivilized.

"Just do it," he heard Katrina tell him.

"It tastes good," Jake coaxed.

"I've lived a long time. Hunted as a wolf. Eaten all kinds of delicacies. Sushi? Yes. Escargot? Yes. Shrimp brains? Uh..." He sighed and looked at the tiny antennae. Its eyes stared up at him, and they weren't screaming 'eat me'. *Why did I let them talk me into this?* "Can't I just eat the tail? It's how I get them at home."

"Don't be a baby. Just suck it." Jake laughed.

"Don't rush me."

"You already did the hard part. Now just suck." Katrina brought the little red head to her lips and slurped. "Hmm...see? It's good."

"That's right. Your woman knows how to suck a head."

"Fuck you." Without dropping the slippery treat, Jax punched Jake on his arm, who feigned injury.

"He's getting violent," Jake teased.

"Duh, he's an Alpha." Katrina's voice softened, and she gave him a warm smile. "You can do this, dear."

"You two must have been barracuda shifters in another life, because you're both relentless." Jax stared at the crawfish and shook his head. "Sorry, little guy, but they say you taste good." He quickly brought the shell to his lips and sucked the fluid down.

"Yay!" Katrina clapped as Jake broke out in a hearty laugh. "He did it!"

"So?"

"I won't lie." Jax paused. He fought a smile, attempting to fool them. "It was...great. Spicy, like liquid fire. What the hell is in that stuff, anyway?"

"Secret recipe." Jake winked at Katrina.

"Load me up." Jax handed his plate to his friend, who shoveled the tiny red creatures onto it.

"So...tonight. Do you think we'll find out anything from this warlock?" Katrina asked.

Her question immediately broke the humorous mood that had followed their erotic interlude. Jax's gaze went to Jake, who deferred to the Alpha. Although instinct told him that tonight they'd get answers, he couldn't be certain of the situation they'd encounter.

"The weather's supposed to be bad. Rain," Jake noted.

"We'll take the SUV." Jax peeled away a shell.

"Sometimes the roads get shut down. We should leave early."

"What kind of place is this?" Katrina asked. Her eyes darted to Jake.

"I told Jax already. Mick's kind of a free spirit. I'm actually pretty surprised that he's the cream that rose to the top." He stood and began to crumple up the used newspaper. "But it is what it is."

"There're many different kinds of witchcraft. Just because Ilsbeth chose to run her coven a certain way, that doesn't mean the witches agreed. I've seen it happen before. You know, something happens to the high priestess and pandemonium lets loose." Jax shrugged.

"I guess it's not that much different than wolves. While you were away..." Jake hesitated. "Well, no use in rehashing that. It wasn't pretty."

"And that's how it's always been. It can happen with the vampires too. For as long as I can remember, Kade's been down in New Orleans. But in Philly? Alexandra was the queen bee until Tristan shut her down." Katrina stood and began to clear the dishes. "What a bitch that one is."

"She is a piece of work," Jax commented, raising an eyebrow.

"But now he has his hands full with them in his club. They fight over the humans, with no one to put an end to it. From what I hear, Léo's trying to intervene." Kat rummaged through the drawers, finally retrieving a dish towel.

"So you can see how tonight could be unpredictable." Jake turned on the sink faucet and began to wash dishes.

"I'll dry," Katrina added.

"Yep, Alexandra was a sick one, all right. But on the flip side, she kept her vamps in check. Léo will take care of it eventually." Jax sighed and took in the sight of the mess all around him. He considered that this was the first time in months that he'd gone for any length of time without thinking of Nick's death, and now both Jake and Katrina had given him that gift. A simple meal had brought them together.

Even in the midst of a bad situation, the universe always had a way of working out the details. Nick had passed, and the devastation that followed hadn't been pretty. But as he watched the young wolf and his mate at the counter, she turned and gave him a smile that would melt a glacier. In that instant, he knew that life was coming full circle.

Chapter Eighteen

Katrina's nerves danced as they pulled up the long winding driveway. The row of Southern live oak trees greeted them, Spanish moss hanging from the branches. Hundreds of glowing orbs speckled the lawn. The luminaries flickered with candlelight, their illumination brightening as they approached the buildings. To the side a dilapidated plantation house sat in need of repair, its wooden porch appearing to sag in one corner. Yet the shadows in the windows told her that its inhabitants hadn't abandoned the deteriorating structure.

A thunderbolt rocked the car and Katrina stifled the shiver that ran through her body. As they drew closer to the valet, she rubbed her hands together. The tingling in her fingertips traveled up her arms and over her scalp. As during her experience at Ilsbeth's, she sensed the magick in the air. Although she'd thought to keep the disturbing sensation to herself, she chose to disclose it. Tonight they entered as a team and secrets could cost them their lives.

"Jax." She never took her eyes off the entrance as she placed her palm on her mate's shoulder.

"You okay?"

"Remember what happened to me at Ilsbeth's? I feel something in my hands. It's not my wolf either. It's something else."

What's going on?" Jax immediately turned to face her from the passenger seat and took her fingers in his.

"Just kind of this thing. I don't know how to explain it." Katrina withdrew her hands and stared down at her palms, her expression serious. "It, uh, it feels warm. Almost like caterpillars. Goddess, that sounded stupid."

"Whatever's in you, Kat…I'm not going to lie and tell you it's nothing to worry about. But you haven't been weak since we got to New Orleans. No episode like in the woods that day." Jax brushed his knuckles over her cheek and she closed her eyes, relaxing into his touch. "The good news is that both of us are still strong, and I've marked you."

"But I haven't claimed you yet. My wolf…" Katrina knew she wouldn't last much longer. She suspected her wolf would take over her will, outweighing her humanity. Every time they made love, she grew one step closer to making him her own. If her teeth sliced open his skin and she drank of his blood, the bonding would commence.

"She's stronger than ever." Katrina noted the flicker of happiness in Jax's eyes, and it broke her heart that she'd waited so long. But she'd die first before she hurt Jax. She held a silencing finger to his lips. "I know what you're going to say. Don't you ever think I don't want this, because I do...you..." Moisture rose to her eyes along with her emotion. "You've changed everything. I just can't do it until I know you're going to be safe. It's killing me not to claim you."

"It's going to be all right, baby. I promise you. All of this. You. Me. Your magick. Remember what I told you about instinct. We're about to pick up another puzzle piece, and very soon it's all going to come together."

"Hey guys, I don't mean to break up this special moment, but I think our main man just came out to say hello."

Jake turned into a grand arched car port. The elaborate cedar structure had been carved with intricate patterns. As Katrina zeroed in on it, tiny skulls, chiseled into the wooden beams, in different sizes and patterns alike, came together like a fine painting. Although it struck her as creepy, the arrangement did have an artistic flair.

For but a second she reminisced, missing her gallery, being able to freely create without fear of abduction. The vehicle jolted to a stop and her focus was drawn to the man who stood watch over them at the entrance. Bright lights in hues of purple streamed around the stranger. He had the appearance of a tall, thin angel, and a shiny translucent fabric hung loosely from his outspread arms.

The car door clicked open, and she took Jax's hand. The rush of his power flowed through her skin. He winked, and she knew he'd deliberately sent the calming energy to her. No matter what happened in the next hour, she'd be with her Alpha.

"Welcome, welcome, welcome," The violet-colored stream morphed to lavender, finally dissipating as the warlock came into view.

Mick Germaine. Wearing a long silver robe embroidered with silver sequins, the shirtless mystic smiled broadly. Katrina studied the handsome stranger. She considered that he looked like he could have been one of the models in Jax's magazine. His piercing gray eyes drew her focus, accentuating his chiseled jawline. The sides of his head had been shaved, his long dark hair brushed up into a ponytail. Barefoot, his tanned legs peeked through his holed jeans.

"Come, come." He gestured toward the door, and then extended a hand to Jax. "Alpha, I am humbled by your visit to my Shangri-La."

Katrina held tight to the crook of Jax's arm. Waves of energy poured over her. As if she were standing in a waterfall of flowing magick, it rained down from above. The humming power whirled around her, and she struggled to concentrate. Inhaling, she breathed out the tension, allowing her body and mind to adjust to the increased activity. Jax's low, commanding voice brought her attention back to the conversation as she heard him introduce her.

"This is my mate, Katrina Livingston." Jax stood protectively in front of her but she managed to extend a hand.

"Ah…Kitty Kat," Mick trilled. As she placed her hand in his, she watched his eyes light up in surprise at her touch. "You're in transition, I see. Come. Let's talk inside."

Katrina's palm sizzled within his grasp and she snatched her hand back to her body. "Thank you, but I'll stay with my mate."

"But is he now?" Mick challenged. With an outstretched arm, he ushered them into the building. With the body of a well-trained athlete, he conveyed deliberate strength with every step.

Katrina reached for Jax, and took in the sight of the great room. Its brick walls rounded upward, wooden beams spearing up into an apex. Streaming swatches of red and black velvet draped from the ceiling. Shelves of various heights supported thick candles, which illuminated the room in a dim sensual light. Scantily clad women and men danced to a slow rhythmic beat upon a limestone dance floor. As if in a trance, the mass of zombie-like witches swayed, their bodies moving in a well-rehearsed ballet.

As they weaved their way through the sea of people, Katrina held tight to Jax. Mick led them through a pair of heavy swinging Cyprus doors, and as they shut, the din ceased behind them. The small circular foyer appeared to break off into two hallways. Katrina strained to see where they led as Mick turned to address their group.

Her focus drifted to the enormous chandelier that hovered above them. The hand-blown glass fixture took on the appearance of a modern octopus. White extensions radiated from its striking royal-blue interior. Having spent hours in antique and specialty stores over the years, Katrina estimated the piece to be well over five thousand dollars. Although Mick had retained the rustic nature of the building, it was apparent that he'd infused opulence in the details of the décor.

"As much as I'm looking forward to our little chat, I do believe I should be a good host and show you around my new spread." He gave a broad smile and lowered his voice. "This is a very special place."

"Look Mick, we appreciate you meeting with us, but y'all know it's about to get to stormin' out there. And we'd like to get back home," Jake told him.

"We don't want to get stuck out here," Jax added.

"No one gets *stuck* in paradise, my friends. You see, when Ilsbeth went walkabout, I was forced to take on her coven. This, as you know," he nodded toward Jax, "is a great responsibility."

"Mick, please, we just need…" Katrina began, but was interrupted.

"Patience is a virtue. It's part of the reason we're in the bayou. Back to nature where we belong." He took a dramatic breath and flicked his ponytail. "I did not ask to become a high priest. Oh no, no, no. But all these bitches are far too weak to take over. So when Ilsbeth left, I thought to myself, 'self, where should you go to be one with nature? Where should you go to commune and get back to your roots?' and my meditations led me here."

"Why leave the city?" Jake asked.

"Because our very essence comes from the soil. The air. The water that falls upon us tonight. And the great blazing sun of Louisiana. Oh yes," Mick held his palms up to the air as if in worship, "the city, I am afraid, while ripe with magick, is polluted." He held out his fingers and counted off his reasons. "The ground. The air. The water. This is where the coven is meant to be."

"We're just gonna have to agree to disagree there, warlock, because I think it's pretty damn fine where it was," Jake countered.

Jax shot Jake a look of irritation for engaging with the eccentric witch. Jake rolled his eyes in response.

"This coven is for the pure of heart. For those looking for happiness within nature." Mick gave Katrina a wicked smile.

Although he was attractive, Katrina's keen sense warned her away. She found herself moving closer against Jax, and tugged on the back of his shirt. Mick's eyes painted over her from head to toe, undressing her. Under the black light, the tattoos over his body danced. An illusion, perhaps, a flock of birds along his flank of muscular abs flapped their wings.

He smiled at her, and her eyes flared in acknowledgement. Her wolf went on alert, unsure of what he'd do next. Katrina concentrated on calming her beast. The magick inside her teetered on explosive, and she grew concerned that if she shifted, it wouldn't be her wolf that appeared.

"Ah...I know you sense my energy, Kitty, but it is not me you have to fear," he blithely commented.

Before Katrina had a chance to respond, he waved a hand and a chart appeared on the wall, its lettering stenciled in calligraphy. From one to thirty, rooms were labeled in order with a notation of occupied or vacant.

"The city is stifling. Here in the woods we can conjure the pure magick that Mother Nature provides. And what is the most potent of all energy?" he asked rhetorically, giving a maniacal laugh. "Sex. Love. Hate, of course, however that is not the kind of negativity I wish to bring into my circle. My counterpart, the great Ilsbeth, she had a much more traditional approach. And as you know, she was quite the destructive force. I choose benevolence."

Jax rolled his eyes. Katrina interrupted, aware her Alpha was losing patience with the warlock.

"Mr. Germaine, we need your assistance with..."

"Ah, so the dear, sweet Samantha has told me. I'll never know how such a darling witch could marry that overbearing set of fangs." He sniffed. "To each her own, I suppose. First the tour, Kitty. Then we chat. As you have noticed, the weather grows turbulent. Excellent energy for our celebration but as you've pointed out, we get to havin' travel issues out here. And seeing as how you arrived by car this evening, you may be spending the night with us."

"That's not happening," Jax countered.

"Alpha, you're not from the south, so please defer to the experts." He gestured to his chest and laughed. "As I was saying, my barn…my special place…I've created rooms for my coven as well as guests. The left side is reserved for my witches. The right, where you are standing now, is for guests. Follow me."

Katrina shook her head at Jax, whose mouth had drawn tight. His jaw ticked in anger, but given no choice, he followed. Through a labyrinth of darkened hallways, they eventually passed several closed doors. Mick paused at an empty room; a flicker of candlelight danced inside it.

"And this, my friends, is where our guests can rest for a few hours or for the entire evening. I present to you the Voodoo room. A bit cliché, I know, but I thought the Alpha would enjoy it." Mick laughed and continued walking. "This here is our looking-glass room. As you can see, this offers entertainment for our voyeurs. Tell me, Kitty," the warlock turned to Katrina and gave her a sensual smile, "do you like to watch?"

"It's none of your business," she snapped. Her eyes darted to the window display. A foursome inside paid their party no mind as they made love. A woman lay on her back sucking her partner's cock, while another woman attended to her pussy. A second man fucked her from behind.

"Tsk, tsk…that answer won't do at all," he sneered. "Negative thoughts are not welcome in my space. I'm afraid if you want answers, tit for tat."

"Now just wait a damn minute," Jax began.

"Yes, but you won't ever be involved," Katrina spat. "Now can we hurry up? I am aware of how the weather is down here and we're running out of time."

"Ha! Very good, Kitty. You like to watch…hmm…I knew it!" Mick turned on his heel, squealing in delight as if he'd been given a birthday gift. "And this is another play room. Of course I have my own private dungeon but we must make sure our guests have options."

Katrina peered inside at the various instruments of pleasure and pain. A St. Andrew's cross rested in the corner, and the thought of tying up her Alpha flashed in her mind. As much as she'd enjoyed submitting to Jax in bed, she imagined she'd enjoy dominating given how out of control her life had been. She caught Jax staring at her and wondered if he could read her thoughts. Averting her gaze, she looked to Mick, who waved them into an office, where a perky brunette greeted them.

"Come in, come in. 'Tis time for business. This is Avery. She's one of my very special witches." He blew her a kiss, which she caught in the air and pretended to bring to her mouth. She moaned as her fingers seductively trailed between her breasts, her eyes set on Jax.

Katrina's instinct to attack was thwarted by both Jake and Jax who reached for her wrists. The silent cue interrupted her vicious thoughts. She looked to Jax, but he shook his head, warning her back. With a huff, she yanked her arms free and glared at the witch.

"Kitty doesn't like to share? What a shame. You wolves are very possessive creatures, almost as bad as the bloodsuckers. Sit. Please." Mick gestured to a set of scarlet crushed velvet sofas. Rounding his swirled marble desk, he threw himself into a white leather chair. He propped his feet up onto the edge and steepled his fingers.

Katrina reluctantly sat, taking in her surroundings. Brick walls adorned with antique farm tools were countered by the modern technology that rested along an extended console. She detected the faint scent of coumarin. The herbaceous odor lingered in the air, and she spied a small bowl of black tonka beans on the end table.

A giggle bubbled behind her and Katrina's eyes flew to Avery. Dressed in a black see-through corset, she slinked over to Mick. The opaque stripes trailing down over her breasts did little to cover the rosy nipples that strained through the mesh fabric. Garters snapped tight to her thigh-high stockings, long legs pinned into patent leather pumps. Her eyes locked on Katrina, and she pursed her cherry-stained lips at Jax.

Rooting her feet to the ground, Katrina struggled to stay calm. Jake mouthed the word 'no' from across the room. Her wolf growled, urging her to attack. Her hands fisted in frustration but she knew losing control within a love shack of witches was a bad idea. Silently counting to ten, she prayed the meeting would be over within the hour. Mick cleared his throat and her focus was brought back to the warlock.

"Boring you, am I?"

"I'm sorry, what?" she asked.

"You need to claim him, you know?" he responded.

"How do you know I haven't already?" Katrina's heart pounded in her chest; she had not expected to discuss the topic with Mick.

"Running, running, running. Don't think Ilsbeth didn't take notice, ah, because she did. These things…they've always been troublesome."

"What do they want?" As Katrina's pulse raced faster, her curiosity bloomed. Until now, no one had had answers.

"Demons, quite a bother really. Always trying to escape as such. There're many levels. Some walk among us, simply bringing negativity. Others possess the bodies of the dying. And some…" Mick paused, his eyes narrowed in concern. Gone was the flighty host, replaced by a more serious individual, who appeared concerned for his own wellbeing. His voice rasped in both a cold and thoughtful tone. "They want to possess the living. But you see, they are not meant to do so. They reap pestilence and death, and once allowed to walk among us, they'll take over this realm. So you understand how it is imperative to stop them."

"Yes, I heard these tales as a child, but these things, the ones that kidnapped me, they take new forms."

"It's true. We don't know much. The Méchants. The 'evil ones', loosely translated. I can smell their influence on you." His gaze went to Katrina. "But back to your mating. Now what did they tell you?"

Katrina hesitated. Jax nodded and took her hand in his. "It's okay, Kat. Tell him."

"They told me." Katrina swallowed. A gentle squeeze of her hand from her Alpha imbued her with the warmth and confidence to continue. It had sounded ridiculous, but she'd believed them. "I didn't know at the time about Jax. I mean, they just said my mate would be an Alpha. But there aren't many Alphas and some are already mated. I'd been following Jax."

"You stalked him? That's lovely." Mick clapped his hands.

"No, I just, I don't know...I was attracted to him. I'd seen his pictures. Then one night. Happenstance really..."

"There are no coincidences," Jax commented.

"Your Alpha is correct," Mick acknowledged.

She returned Jax's warm smile and continued. "The second we met...I suspected he was the one. I wouldn't be able to resist mating with him. I could kill him. Running was the only way to protect him from me." She sighed and shook her head, lifting her eyes to meet Mick's. "This thing. It changed me. When we escaped, I shifted. But it wasn't me. I was weak, and even now, I know it's Jax who fills me with strength."

"They have done this to you on purpose," he told her. "They confuse you. They've opened a portal to your essence, your energy. And each time they take you, they harvest the spirit of an Alpha's lineage, sucking it out of you like a farmer milks the cow. But, my dear, they cannot close the hole. It's like a flat tire after being punctured by a nail, it closes tight, but not quite tight enough. The air slowly leaks. It's the same with your magick."

"But why do they need her magick? Why not just take any wolf? You'd think they'd be getting a fresh wolf instead of using her over and over," Jake asked.

"Why not just kill me?"

"How much do they need?" Jax went solemn, as if he'd come to a revelation.

A shiver ran down Katrina's arm, and she sucked a quiet breath. *What the hell is coming for us all?*

"Let me start with the why. Well, three is of significance. Unlike what you might think, not many are born of an Alpha, sister and mate. That is quite obvious. But a better guess is that one or both of your parents has a tie to this demon. A favor, perhaps?"

"How can that be? Tristan would have known if our family owed a demon. If it weren't for Jax actually being there..." She gave an exhausted sigh. "I can ask Tristan again."

"Do ask quickly, Kitty. You're running out of time." Mick leaned over his desk toward them. "The hole...the very one I told you about. You must feel it. Your magick leaks...and your mate," his eyes trained on Jax, "your Alpha, he fills you with his."

"But I don't feel weak," Jax said in denial. "I'll admit I can feel the slight transfer but nothing is wrong with me."

"But your mate? She doesn't just have your magick. Something grows within her, it eats at yours. They want to use her."

"They implanted a chip in her?" Jake asked. "Or is this more like one of those amoebas that eats away at you?"

"What the fuck?" Jax scolded him.

"What? I'm just sayin'. Tell me you haven't watched the videos where they extract the bug that laid eggs inside of someone's skin."

"Really? You had to go there?" Mick shook his head.

"Ew, no, that did not happen," Katrina protested, and rubbed her arms. The thought that something else could be inside her made her nauseous.

"No, my dear." Mick glared at Jake. "You wolves can be so uncouth at times. I'm all about nature, but seriously?"

"Say what you want, witch-boy, but if she's got somethin' growin' inside her, well…my mind jumps to larvae."

"Don't listen to him," Jax told her, and pinned his eyes on Jake, who shrugged. "Shut it now."

"Katrina has something inside her. Not a bug per se." Mick shook his finger at Jake. "A seedling of dark magick. Something that only witches have. Mages. The ability to change form? Demons have long been able to do that nifty trick."

"And how do you know all this shit anyway? You seem to know an awful lot about demons and Katrina." Jake leaned back into his chair.

"He has a good point. How do we know you're not involved?" Jax asked.

"Very good question. I can only offer you my honesty, and have no proof of my innocence. I do know that the high priestess had interactions over the years with the Méchants. Favors here, favors there. Ilsbeth's magick was not without reproach. Take for example," he paused and leaned back in his chair, "Dimitri. One does not steal magick easily. And in doing so…there's a price."

"I imagine a very high price," Jax added.

"Indeed," Mick agreed.

"So wait." Jake leaned forward, shook his head and scrubbed both hands through his hair. "Are you telling us that not only did Ilsbeth try to kill Dimitri's wolf, but that she did it by getting help from these things?"

"There are only so many things we can do with our magick. At some point, we require special ingredients. It's no secret that she was known for her collection of elements. A menagerie if you will."

"I hope that bitch is burning in hell as we speak." Jake crossed his arms across his chest.

"Look, we get that Ilsbeth took unconventional paths to get her way, but at the end of the day, all I care about is my mate."

"As you should. So, first things first. How do we fix Kitty?" Mick set his sights on Katrina. "These demons…you know they will lie. So let's start with the obvious. Mating will not hurt your Alpha. I cannot be one hundred percent certain, but I have done my research. No need to thank me," he buffed his long fingernails upon his pants and then admired them, "but this leak. I'm afraid this is a problem."

"What makes you think I can...?" Katrina began.

"This leak. This energy. The sexual essence that is generated between beings. It can purify." Mick stood and made a sweeping gesture with his palm. "But you must have the assistance of an Alpha."

"Wait." Jax shook his head. "Are you saying what I think you are saying?"

"Are you saying I have another mate? No, that's not possible," Katrina insisted.

"I'm saying exactly what I said. It's an energy healing. Nothing more. Nothing less. But, as you pointed out or should I say, may have guessed, the Alpha can help to prepare her for her true goal."

"Dimitri and Gillian healed me," Jake blurted out.

"I don't want to hear this." Jax stared at the wall, refusing to look at him. It wasn't as if he didn't know what happened between Gillian, Jake and Dimitri, but he preferred not to discuss his sister's sex life, let alone in front of the warlock.

"Jax, come on. You know how wolves are. Don't even try to tell me that you and Nick didn't share," Jake challenged him.

The statement pierced through Katrina like a knife in her gut. Her claws dug into the couch, tearing at the fabric. The idea of Jax being intimate with another woman sent her wolf into a frenzy.

"First, don't bring up his name here," Jax told him. "Second, I just don't see how this will work to help us. And third, where the fuck am I supposed to find another..."

Katrina's eyes went wide as Jax's voice trailed off. She couldn't tell where his thoughts had gone but she suspected he'd found a solution, one she couldn't be certain she'd like.

"Once Katrina has stopped siphoning your magick and leaking her own, you both will be strong enough to face them, to use whatever you brought me to defeat them." Mick smacked his hands onto his desk. "So let's see it then. Show and tell. I've told you what you need to do and now it's time for show."

Katrina's head spun, wondering how the hell they'd be able to carry out his instructions. She'd known something was off with her own magick, but the solution Mick proposed seemed ludicrous.

"Before we show you what we found, I think it's important to note that Katrina," Jax's eyes darted to his mate and then back to the warlock, "she had some unusual experiences in the house. It was almost like Ilsbeth or the house was trying to communicate."

"Hmm...interesting." Mick smiled up at Avery and feverishly rubbed his hands together. "Come on now, the suspense is killing me."

"There is a ring. It was inside this bell." Jax retrieved the rusty items from his pocket, and set them on the desk. "There's a boline, too. I know it looks normal, but it accidentally nicked Kat and her blood smeared onto it. And then the damn thing glowed. You could see something written on it. It made no sense."

Katrina slipped her hand into the purse that was strapped against her shoulder and carefully removed the sickled blade. She'd been afraid to touch the ring since the incident at the mansion. Although she'd been cut by the knife, the coldness of the object elicited no energy or emotion. She unwrapped the cloth napkin and carefully set it down on the marble.

Mick lifted the jewelry into the light. Sliding open his drawer, he retrieved a magnifying glass and studied it. "It's a poison ring. Very clever."

"Fifteenth century," Jake added.

The warlock shot him a questioning look.

"History. It's kind of my thing." Jake gave a half smirk.

"The vampires always underestimate wolves, but never me. Oh, no." He took a deep breath and sighed, placing it on the desk. Mick's attention went to the knife. "Looks like a simple boline to me." Holding the hilt he spun it around, examining all the sides. "You say it glowed, huh? A simple spell. But what is not known is whether or not Katrina's blood did this alone? Or does it work for everyone? Just wolves?"

"We don't know."

"Did you find anything else?"

"Just the bell, but otherwise, no," Jax answered.

"When I was there…" Katrina's eyes widened as she recalled the experience, how the electricity had hummed through her hands. She held her palms upward and stared at them, "…it was just this feeling. Like a tingling. That bell. I couldn't let go of it until the ring fell out. Ilsbeth wanted me to have it."

"We don't know for sure what's happening," Jax added.

"You don't have to believe me. I may not have known Ilsbeth but I know as sure as I'm sitting here that she wanted me to have that ring. She wanted me in her house. And that knife there. It may be used for cutting herbs or whatever, but it means something."

"I suppose, but you haven't tested the theory," Mick told her. "It's true your magick has changed; you're more like a witch now."

Jax shot Mick a glare.

"What?" The warlock rolled his eyes. "It's true. Pfft. As I was saying, you may be able to trigger whatever spell has been infused into the object."

Katrina's stomach sank at his statement, her patience wearing thin. She didn't have time to theorize. Irritated, she snatched the boline.

"What are you doing?" Jax asked, his words slow and deliberate.

"We can't just sit here and speculate. I'm using this thing now. I want to know if it'll work again and what it all means. We're here with Mick. There's no time like the present to figure out what's going on." She held the point to her palm.

"Just wait a second. Don't do this, Kat."

Katrina had grown tired of everyone telling her what she could or could not do. *Lost magick. Demons. Mating.* With every breath she took, she lost control of her own life. Rage surfaced fast and hot, and she considered all she'd been through. A survivor, she deserved more than empty questions and 'what ifs'.

"I'm sorry. This is all about instinct. And mine tells me to survive." Slicing the sharp edge across her palm, she cringed, the white hot pain stabbing up her forearm. She swiped her thick blood across its blade. Satisfaction filled her chest as lettering appeared in its wake.

"Read this," she demanded. With a loud clank, Katrina dropped the boline onto Mick's desk. Scarlet drops sprayed across the white stone surface.

Jax accepted tissues from Avery and grabbed Katrina's wrist. His eyes narrowed in on her, angry she'd challenged him.

"I'm fine," she insisted, yanking her hand from Jax. He asked her to trust him, to follow his lead, but he couldn't trust her in return to know her own body and mind. Wrapping her palm, she stemmed the blood flow. She caught the look of disgust that crossed Mick's face, displeased she'd marred his furniture. Ignoring his concern, she gestured to the knife. "Hurry before it disappears."

"You didn't need to make such a mess." Mick allowed Avery to wipe around the object, absorbing the fluid. "Well, this is interesting. A message from Ilsbeth."

"How do you know?"

"Ilsbeth has a Nordic ancestry. She was always fond of tricking people with her use of other languages. While French is often spoken in the bayou, Swedish is less known."

"What does it say?" Katrina pressed.

"Där de döda lögnen och vattnet stiger vi möter. Dolda men sett, hitta förtrollningen som du söker. Of course this is much more of a rhyme in English. Where the dead lie and the water rises, we meet. Hidden but seen, find the spell you seek."

"Seriously?" Jake rose and rubbed his eyes. "This whole damn area is filled with water."

"Lake Ponchartrain?" Katrina guessed. "It can be dangerous."

"True, but so can the river," Jax countered.

"The river?" Jake asked.

"Yes. The river," Jax repeated. "The last time I was down in New Orleans I was in this bar having a drink."

"You and half the world," Mick commented.

"Are you going to listen? Because I'm in no mood."

"Proceed." Mick gave a broad gesture with his palm outstretched.

"It was around Mardi Gras. I'm sitting there, and the bartender starts telling me about how once a year people are allowed to dump the remains of their loved ones in the river. That people wait all year long."

"Start with the Quarter," Katrina suggested.

"How the hell are we supposed to find something down there? We don't even know what it is or where it could be. I guess we could start with the river banks, but some are covered with hundreds of stones. Are we planning on looking under every one? Not to mention the steps, docks, boats. It could be any damn place," Jake pointed out.

"We do it the same way we did it at Ilsbeth's. Look, I'm not even sure how or why, but she wants me to find this. I think there is something about this ring, maybe this knife…we're supposed to do something with them," Katrina asserted.

"Destroy the demons?" Mick suggested, wearing an impassive expression.

"Maybe. Maybe not. We shouldn't assume Ilsbeth is trying to help us. For all we know we're bringing these assholes some kind of gift. But whatever it is, Kat's right. We need to go find what Ilsbeth wanted us to find. We'll figure it out from there," Jax told them.

"Before you leave, I'd like to have a moment with my little Kitty Kat." Mick bowed to Jax, bending his arm over his stomach. "Please, indulge me, Alpha."

"I'll be all right," Katrina assured Jax.

"Are you sure about this? I think maybe I should…" Jax began, but hesitated as Katrina nodded, her expression tense but certain. Before turning toward the door, he collected the items they'd brought off the desk and shot Mick a glare. "Let me be clear. While I appreciate your input today, I'd better not find out you're lying. You get five minutes. You hurt my mate and you're dead." Jax reached for Katrina, and squeezed her hand. "I'll be right here in the hallway. He does anything and I'll know."

"Thanks. I promise I'll be okay," she responded.

"You're just going to leave her alone with the magick man?" Jake asked.

"I'm not going anywhere. The door stays open. Understand?" Jax growled.

"But of course I will maintain the fine lady's reputation." Mick gave a furtive smile and turned to Avery. "Sorry, darling, but this is private. Please see to all the needs of the Alpha and his friend."

"I'd absolutely love to," she mewled, her palms adjusting her cleavage. She licked her lips and reached for the crook of Jax's arm.

Katrina clutched at the desk, restraining her urge to attack the flirty witch. Her wolf scratched and whined, warning her not to let him go alone. Hearing voices in the hallway, she was assured that Jax had not gone far, but it did little to assuage her beast.

A hand tugged at her palm, uncurling her fingers. She stared up into icy eyes that appeared to swirl into infinity. The limitless depth of the warlock's pupils caught her focus, and she wondered if he wore contact lenses.

"Look at how well you heal, even without shifting." Mick uncapped a bottle of water and poured it onto a clean tissue. "May I?"

"Um, what?" Katrina averted her gaze, afraid he possessed some sort of hypnotic power. "Oh yes, sorry. Yeah. My hand's fine, really."

"Beautiful skin. Such a shame you are to be mated. Had we met in another time, perhaps we would have celebrated life's pleasures," he drawled. "But alas, I fear it is not to be."

"Mr. Germaine…"

"Mick…please. We're almost family." He carefully stroked her skin dry.

"Not exactly, but…" Katrina gasped as her palm came into view. No scar or line remained; the cut had completely disappeared. "How did you…"

"Magick. I'm not the high priest for nothing. You may think me peculiar, but I assure you my intentions are altruistic."

"How do I know that?" Despite Mick's statement to the contrary, she didn't trust his motives for helping them.

"Conjuring demons is a messy business." He ignored her question. "You see, demons aren't content to stay in the netherworld. They seek the life they cannot have. The devil has long possessed humans. This world," he paused and lifted her hand in his, bringing it inches from his lips, "it must have balance. This is one point on which Ilsbeth and I agreed. Imbalance brings chaos. Turmoil. Imagine the implications if demons have the power to become wolves? To create their own pack? The very existence of wolves is at stake."

With an ethereal presence, waves of energy radiated off the mystical warlock. He lifted her hand and kissed the back of it, startling Katrina. Disturbed by his words and actions, she tugged away and crossed her arms, feigning confidence. No matter how much she wanted to run from his office, she forced herself to listen to his oration, gleaning every last bit of information he shared.

"Once your portals close, you may be able to save your own magick, but the witchcraft imposed on you will forever leave its mark. You've been branded by the demon. I'm afraid you cannot remove what has been done. Ilsbeth, she is neither all saint nor all sinner. But I believe she has touched you. Somewhere along the line, she gifted you with a sliver of her power, and now my dear, you must go use it. Find what she wishes you to find."

Awestruck, Katrina stared at Mick, her body relaxing into the trance he'd evoked. She vacillated between believing every single word he spoke and dismissing the entire evening as a hallucination. He smiled at her, his effervescent laughter erupted, and she blinked, woken from her dream.

"I, um, thank you." Katrina flexed her fingers as the suggestive laugh of a female caught her attention. Her Alpha's voice followed, sparking a hot wave of jealousy in her chest. "I have to go."

Without saying goodbye, Katrina took off out of Mick's office into the dark hallway. As promised, Jax had not gone far, but nor had the seductive witch. Her Alpha stood backed against a wall, his hands wrapped around her wrists. The sight of Avery's palms flattened on Jax's shoulders incited her beast into a rage.

"You! Get the hell off of him, now!" Katrina stalked toward them.

"Hmm….why won't you share?" A wicked smile crossed Avery's face and she waggled her eyebrows at Katrina. "He's delicious. I can feel every last hard ridge." As she attempted to slide her hands lower, Jax lifted her arms away.

"Hey, sorry, Kat, I…this," he stuttered, swiveling his head. "I'm telling you this isn't what it looks like. Where the hell did Jake go?"

"You have three little precious seconds to get away from Jax before I shift and rip out your throat," Katrina growled. She kicked off her shoes and tore off her dress, readying to shift. "One. Two. Three."

Avery threw her hands up and spun in circles away from Jax. With an evil laugh, she reached into her pocket and blew purple and silver sparkles up into the air. "You need happy dust."

Katrina glared at Avery, who continued to smile at them. Her beast threatened to shift, urging her to kill the witch. "You touch him again, and it will be the last thing you ever do with those pretty little nails of yours."

"It's okay, Katrina," Jax coaxed, his voice calm. "Believe me, I get what's going on here. Your wolf, you've been holding her back for a long time and she's not happy. You need to leave the witch alone, though. No matter what your wolf is telling you, you can't just kill her."

Katrina sniffed into the air and grazed her nose into his chest, scenting the witch on his clothing, and growled. Her hand reached between his legs and grabbed his half-hard dick. Although a sliver of her humanity registered the fact that they were inside of a coven, her wolf inside demanded she claim him. Feral, she ignored logic, which told her to wait until they returned home.

Jax gave a small chuckle as Katrina grabbed his wrist and kicked open a door with her foot. She slammed it behind her, paying little attention to the room she'd entered. Set in a seventies theme, plastic beads covered the walls. Prismatic light splintered from a spinning mirrored ball overhead. A kaleidoscope of colors mottled over the shag carpet and furniture.

Katrina stared up into his blue eyes, her gorgeous Alpha looming over her. Stabbing her fingers into Jax's chest, she directed him backward until his calves touched the mattress. She fisted his shirt at the collar, holding it out from his neck. Jax made no move to stop her as she clawed at the fabric with her nails. Tearing it apart at the seams, she discarded it on the floor. With her gaze locked on his, she dragged her tongue over his flat nipple. As he went to embrace her, she bit him hard in warning.

"Don't move," she growled. Wild, her beast ran free. She'd have her way with her Alpha and by the time she was done, no one would ever have him again.

Jax hissed as Katrina raked her fingernails down his chest, marking his skin with fine red trails. Her hands drifted to his belt, and she unbuckled it. With a swift tug, she whipped it out and dangled it from her fingers. As she unzipped his pants and tugged down the denim, Katrina caught the glint of excitement as his eyes went to the leather.

"Off," she ordered, her eyes intense as he complied, kicking off the jeans.

Katrina smiled, soaking in the spectacular sight of her mate. From the hard lines of his masculine form to his hardened arousal, she sought to own every inch of him. She reached for his dick and stroked it, gliding her thumb over his weeping slit.

"Ah...what are you doing with that belt, Kat?" he groaned, not making an attempt to move.

"This?" She held it up in the air, giving a small smile. Katrina had never indulged as a dominant yet she'd detected his curiosity to explore the unknown. In the split second that she sensed his interest, she fell into her role, determined to push his limits. *Pain. Pleasure.* Her Alpha had sexual tastes that ran the gamut, and she was about to discover how far he'd go. "Is this what you want? You've been a very bad Alpha."

"I'm warning you, you best not go there," he breathed.

"Why's that? Because you might like it?" Katrina released him and reached behind her back, unsnapping her bra. She cupped a firm breast, teasing its tip into a taut peak. "Remember our little deal? Honesty. We're mates, after all."

"You haven't claimed me yet," he baited her.

Katrina gave a small chuckle, cognizant he'd challenged her on purpose. She was well aware that although he indulged her, allowing her to dominate, her submission to her Alpha was imminent. Feral with sexual energy, Katrina proceeded to tease him.

Standing at a distance from her mate, she smiled as he patiently waited, hunger flaring in his eyes. Holding the strap, she hooked a thumb into the side of her panties and tugged them away. As if her lover's hands were on her body, her fingers glided over her breasts and traveled slowly down her stomach. Slipping them through her slippery folds, she cried out in pleasure as she brushed over her clit.

With his eyes locked on hers, Jax stood perfectly still as Katrina approached. She lifted her hand to his mouth and dragged her cream along his lips. He sucked her fingers, and her pussy dampened. She studied her beautiful mate, his teeth nipping at her thumb. A small grin emerged on his face, and her heart pounded against her ribs. This man would break her, and the whole time she'd beg for more.

Jax's eyes went to the leather in her hand, reminding her of her intent. His sexy smile, wrapped around her like an embrace, had distracted her from her task. She moved to his side and widened her stance. Taking his steel-hard cock into her hand, she gripped him. With each stroke, her hips tilted forward. Her wet folds grazed his thigh and she bit her lip. Holding the strap, her eyes went to his and he nodded.

"This is happening now. I'm going to mark you tonight. And do you know why, Alpha? Because you're mine." Wielding the leather, she slapped it across his ass and he grunted in arousal. "My mate."

Jax fisted his hands as his head lolled back. "Again," he begged.

Katrina's breath caught at the sight of her Alpha embracing the stinging punishment. She swatted him again and he began to furiously thrust his stiffened cock into her hand.

"Don't you dare come," she demanded. Jax panted, sweat beading across his brow, but did as Katrina instructed. "On the bed now. After tonight there will be no doubt who you belong to."

Jax fell back into bed, grinning up at her, and her heart melted. A true dominatrix she was not. But as he let her direct him, she suspected, like everything else he did in his life, he'd done it on purpose. He'd given her the confidence she needed, her wolf needed. Years of being out of control were erased as she descended onto her Alpha. She climbed atop him, straddling his waist and gave him a smile. "Your hands."

She stifled a laugh as he put his wrists out to her, but quickly resumed her work. Binding him with only a buckle, she knew he'd quickly escape. But the act was symbolic of his trust in her. She gently slid her hands up his hardened abs, admiring every little ridge under her fingertips. When she reached his chest, she gently lifted underneath his arms, brushing her palms up along the sensitive inner skin.

Pressing his wrists over his head, she bent forward and deliberately slid her ripened tips across his face. His lips caught her nipple, and she sucked a breath. Although his hands were restrained, he'd taken control, teasing her peak into a sensitive bundle of nerves. Desire jolted through her body and she writhed her hips, not yet touching him. Aching with need, she tugged her breast from his mouth and slithered down his abdomen.

Torturing him had evolved into a painful exercise for her as well. Denying her own orgasm, she seated herself between his legs, letting her warm breath wash over his shaft. Her lips parted, and she gently lapped at his crown, his salty-tasting essence coating her tongue. His thighs tensed around her torso as she swallowed him down her throat. As she sucked, his head teased her palate, his hips lifting to meet her rhythm.

Katrina studied the contours of his beautiful cock as it disappeared, his smooth skin on her lips. Withdrawing his magnificent erection, she stroked it with her hand and set her attention on his balls. Taking his velvety sac into her mouth, she extended her hand underneath his ass. Her fingers traveled down his cleft, teasing his puckered flesh.

His breath grew ragged as she released his testicle with a pop. Taking him deep into her mouth, she pressed a finger into his back hole.

"Ah, Christ," he cried, but made no protest.

Delving deeper, she touched over his sensitive area of nerves. He jolted his hips upward as she discovered his hidden spot.

"Kat. Oh fuck." Jax pounded his hands into the headboard. "I'm going to…"

He was close, she knew, but once again, she'd deny him his orgasm. She withdrew her hand, ceasing her delightful assault. Grazing her teeth ever so slightly down his shaft, she removed it and laved her tongue over its head.

"Please…Jesus, don't stop."

Like a phoenix, she rose up on her forearms, and crawled her way up his body. She brushed her clit over his balls, still stroking his dick. Katrina took in the sight of her virile mate. A fine sheen coated his skin, his heavy eyes lifting to meet hers.

"No more games, Alpha."

"Holy shit, Kat. You're killin' me here. I can't take much more. I need to be inside you. Like fucking now."

"Is this what you need?" she asked, swiping his head through her swollen labia. As his hardness brushed over her clitoris, she moaned. Blood rushed through her veins, arousal thrashing through every pore of her body. His hungry eyes devoured her as she directed his crown into her wet entrance. Unable to wait one second longer, she impaled herself on his ridged flesh.

"Fuck yes," he grunted.

"Jax. Oh my God…" A slight twinge passed quickly as her readied core accommodated her mate, his cock stretching her open.

Katrina rocked forward, her hips against his. The release she'd held at bay crashed over her as she leaned forward, her fingers crushing into his pecs. Her palm went to his cheek and she held his chin in place. Her mouth descended on his, biting and sucking at his lips.

The honeyed taste of her mate drove her wild. *Claim him.* The words resounded in her head. The gorgeous male beneath her body belonged to her and her alone. Commanding and compassionate, the New York Alpha was the only person in the world who could complete her wolf.

He slammed his cock up into her, his dominance rearing. Within seconds, he'd brand her, reminding her of who was really in control. But first her beast would have its due, seeking the unbreakable bond. As she tore her lips from his, she knew marking him would never be enough.

Her fangs distended, and like lightning she struck, her teeth slicing into his shoulder. She heard a faint cry as his powerful blood rushed down her throat. Before she knew what was happening, he'd broken free of his leather bonds and flipped her onto her back.

"Forever," he repeated as he pounded into her. "You're mine. Fovever."

Jax pinned her arms to the bed, demanding her submission. Releasing his flesh, her glistening lips parted. She tilted her head, baring her throat to her Alpha, acquiescing to his command. As his canines punctured her skin, magick ruptured, her essence absorbed by her mate. Her wolf danced in the abyss of her mind, finally sated.

"My Alpha," she breathed as he ground his pelvis against hers. The friction to her clit pushed her over the edge and she screamed his name as the hardest orgasm of her life seized her body.

"Say it again," he ordered, punishing her with his rough thrusts.

"My Alpha. I'm yours..." was all she could manage. Tiny specks of light danced before her eyes, her release filtering through her every nerve.

"That's right, baby. That's right..." His lips crushed over hers, and she surrendered to his will, relinquishing her body, soul and mind to her mate.

Jax grazed his hips over her sensitized flesh, milking every last spasm. With a final thrust, he groaned and erupted deep inside her. As he slowed his pace, he delicately sucked at her lips, making love to her mouth as he'd done to her body.

Connected with her mate, the fiery culmination of their bond enveloped Katrina. All fears vanished within Jax's embrace. For the first time in two hundred years, Katrina's wolf slept calmly, peace filtering throughout her consciousness.

"Jax." As their lips separated, air rushed into her lungs. A whisper of his name escaped. Emotion coiled in her chest and Katrina struggled to articulate her thoughts.

"Kat, ah baby, I'm sorry," he began, giving a ragged sigh.

"Sorry for...are you okay?" Panic set in and she pushed at his chest with her palms.

"Easy, little wolf." Jax shifted onto his back, bringing her with him.

Strong arms surrounded her, his warmth radiating through her skin. Despite the comfort, she grew concerned that their mating had harmed him like she'd been told. *Selfish, selfish, selfish.* The temptation of seeing him with the witch had spurred her frenzy. Guilt for initiating the mating took hold.

"Hey, stop." Jax's lips touched her forehead and he spoke softly against her brow. "I'm fine. I only said I was sorry because, well, look where we are."

Desperate for her Alpha, obscured in passion, she'd forgotten they'd made love inside the coven. She sighed at the realization that probably every witch within a mile had heard their antics.

"I'm the one who should be sorry, Jax. I just lost it out there."

"Don't you dare go there. Ever since I marked you, I've wanted this so bad. It's not the most romantic setting, but I don't regret it for a second."

"This place is crazy." Katrina's eyes went to the peace sign that hung on the wall. It struck her as funny and she began to laugh.

"You do know who you're mated to, right?" Jax asked as he glanced to the brightly colored plaid sofa in the corner.

"You mean *the* Mr. Jax Chandler? Devastatingly handsome. Sophisticated." She drew circles on his muscular chest with the pad of her finger. "Or do you mean the powerful Alpha? I heard he's lethal."

"Is that how you see me?" he asked.

"The Alpha I'm mated to is caring." Katrina pressed upward so she could look into his eyes. Carefully constructing her thoughts, her voice softened. "He's also vulnerable. Knows what it's like to be hurt. He's protective of those he cares about. Willing to put his own life on the line for his wolves, for his mate. He's…amazing. He's mine."

Katrina resisted expressing the feelings that grew exponentially every second she spent in his presence. Love wasn't something that always occurred between mates. Chemistry drew mates together in a juncture of destiny, a formidable force to deny. Only through a serendipitous occurrence would two wolves grow to truly love each other. Despite rationalizing away the feelings that brewed inside her, Katrina had to admit her thoughts bordered on obsession.

"I…you have no idea how much this meant. I can feel you all around me," he responded. "It's like nothing I've ever experienced."

"I feel it too." She paused. "Jax, I want you to know that even though the witch may have pushed my wolf, I've wanted this since the second I met you. I feel like such an idiot for believing their lies. I'm sorry I waited so long. Being with you is everything to me."

As Katrina disclosed her confession, she buried her face in Jax's chest, unable to reveal how deeply their mating had affected her, how much he meant to her. So many years, she'd lived a cold, lonely existence. She'd closed her heart, a deliberate effort to thwart feelings for other men. Everything she'd ever known had been destroyed, replaced by the realization that she cared more for Jax than she'd ever thought possible. The altruistic effort to save him by denying their connection had morphed into a desperate mission to claim their life together.

The gentle brush of his lips on her skin relaxed her mind and she suspected he'd read her emotion. The strength of the bond would keep them in sync, but her magick would continue to weaken, replaced by a perversion of the true spirit of the wolf. Mick's warning played in her mind. More determined than ever, she'd trust her mate to keep her safe as they continued to search for a way to destroy the demons.

◈ *Chapter Nineteen* ◈

"Why the hell is it that we always have to look for this shit at night?" Jake picked up a rock and threw it into the Mississippi. "Nope. Can't be the day. Witchy, spooky-ass message has to be found at night. Of course it does. Nothing is ever easy."

"Who knows. Maybe it's because it glows, or, as you put it, something witchy is about to go down," Jax replied. "It's easier this way anyway. Less people around."

"Don't be a baby. Besides, look at the city all lit up. It's gorgeous." Katrina leaned back onto the metal railing, admiring the lights flickering over the cityscape. A trumpet played in the distance, its rich tones resonating up to the river walk.

"You two...seriously. I love you both, but you're more annoying than ever," Jake huffed. "I'm going to check over there." He pointed to a set of wide boardwalk stairs that led down to the river's edge. Two young homeless men shared a cigarette, their dog lay at their feet.

"We'll be down in a minute," Jax replied, giving it his best effort to concentrate on their task.

He wrapped his arm around Katrina's waist and tugged her close. Her giggling was music to his ears, happiness evident in her laughter. His nose brushed into her hair, the delicious scent of his mate consuming his thoughts.

It had been over twenty-four hours since they'd mated and with every glance, every touch of their skin, the bond deepened. Making love to her at the coven, letting her dominate and fuck him, had been impulsive. Although he'd suspected Katrina's wolf wouldn't be deterred much longer, he hadn't anticipated the witch's advances. Jax speculated that perhaps she'd deliberately incited Katrina over the edge, but her motives for doing so remained a mystery. Regardless, Jax celebrated the glorious outcome.

After a short respite, they'd dressed and managed to find Jake dancing with a set of twins. Thankfully, the rain had let up and they were able to drive home without incident. Before they returned, the warlock had wished them well, and gave them a final instruction to search at dusk. However, they still had no idea exactly what they were looking for, besides a promise of another clue.

It concerned Jax that Katrina's magick continued to be compromised. Although Mick had advised him to use another Alpha to strengthen her wolf, he struggled with the idea of sharing his mate. He'd never made love to a woman with another Alpha. Both his touch and raging power were to be wielded with caution. He recalled a time when he and Nick indulged, taking a woman together. The experiences had been pleasurable, but his beta had always submitted and neither had claimed the chosen female.

With his wolf sated, Jax considered he'd be less likely to attack another male. On a visceral level, however, the idea of letting another Alpha touch her provoked possessive emotions. *Mine*, he told Katrina and he'd meant it. No other male would command his mate.

As he observed Jake's agile run down the stairs, he knew what needed to be done. An Alpha, the young wolf still hadn't suspected his true nature. But Jax suspected he'd be the one to help him heal Katrina. They'd already successfully experimented. Their sexual interlude in the kitchen had been primal, and Jake had willingly deferred to him, careful not to cross the line. He couldn't be sure if either of them would agree, but the discussion needed to happen sooner rather than later if they were going to help Katrina seal her magick.

"Kat," Jax began, hoping his mate would be open to his proposal. She swiveled her body, facing the river, and snuggled into his side. "How're you feeling?"

"I'm feeling amazing," she breathed.

"I mean your power. Has it changed since we mated?"

"I'm not going to lie to you. After everything," she sighed and tilted her head up toward him, "it feels about the same. I don't feel weak, if that's what you mean. But it still feels like if I'm not around you for any amount of time, I get drained. Like this morning, for example. You were downstairs, and just that hour or whatever when you were away, I could feel it slipping. Then I start to panic. I'm thinking, 'what if I can't shift? What if I turn into something else?' Ugh, I hate this." She shook her head and stared out to the Mississippi, city lights reflecting on its surface. "It's like a bathtub. You know, you fill it up but you can't get the stopper just right. So you lie back and just when you think you are about to relax, half the water is gone and you're freezing cold."

As serious as the situation was, the image of Katrina lying wet and naked in his bath caused his cock to stir. He shoved the picture to the back of his mind, admonishing the thought. *Focus, Jax.*

"Whatever we find tonight, I have a feeling it will be because of your magick." Jax hated that they'd hurt his mate. She curled against his body, reminding him that she was as much a part of him as the arm that held her.

"It's not my magick. I don't know why Ilsbeth chose me," she pondered, her lips tight. "But I guess it doesn't matter. I just want to find this thing...the spell or whatever it is and get it over with. I want to be free."

"You will, Kat. I promise you," he told her. With his lips pressed to her hair, he continued. "The thing is that when we go back to New York, you need to be strong."

"I know."

"What did you think of what Mick said?" Jax hesitated, almost afraid to speak the words. He would never force Katrina into being with another man. If she agreed, it would be her decision. "About needing another Alpha to help us?"

"Jax, I..." Katrina stuttered, and turned to face him, her eyes on his. "I need to tell you something."

"What?"

"It's about an Alpha. My brother. I called Tristan today. I asked him about my mom and dad. But also...I told him we mated."

"You should have told me before you did that, Kat." Jax shook his head, frustrated she hadn't asked him first. Tristan's incendiary reaction would come swiftly, probably assuming he'd forced her to mate.

"You don't understand. He already knows I'm with you. I think he was okay with everything until I mentioned we mated." She cringed and gave a half smile. "Please don't be mad. I needed to talk to him. I had to ask if something happened to me when I was a child...anything that my parents could have done to bring this demon to my feet."

"It's not that I don't understand, but Tristan? It's going to take time for him to accept us, after everything that happened." Jax's mind spun with possible ways of handling the situation. If he called Tristan, he might make it worse, because he'd likely tell him to fuck off if he challenged their mating. "We've got to get home as soon as possible. Your brother is going to be pissed."

"More like, 'is pissed'."

"We'll deal with this together. The bottom line is that he has no choice but to accept the situation. He's not your father and even if he was, it's what you want that matters. He'll get over it." Jax tilted his head and smiled down at Katrina. "He has to. Because there is no way I'm giving you up."

"I'm not giving you up either." She embraced him, laying her head against his chest. "Tristan doesn't know anything anyway. After this mess is over, we'll go see him and make peace."

"Kat, we need to talk about the warlock. What he said about finding another Alpha...I don't think he meant Tristan." Jax let the silence linger between them, waiting for her to draw a conclusion.

"If you're suggesting we find an Alpha just so I can..." She averted her gaze and shook her head. "I don't want to be with anyone else but you. I just found you. Besides, I can't just have sex with anyone. No, I'll just have to face these things with my magick as it is."

"That's not what I'm saying at all. I want you to remember something, little wolf. No matter how bad you think it is, you can always trust me." A stone skipped across the river, and Jax's attention went to the wolf, who gave him a curt wave. "What about Jake?"

"What about him?" She glanced over to Jake and back to Jax.

"Hear me out, okay? We never really talked about what happened in the kitchen. I'll be honest. I wasn't sure how I'd feel about it when he slapped your ass. But your reaction said it all. The whole thing with him there? I enjoyed it and I know you did too. It was hot."

"Yeah it was. And if you don't stop talking about this, you're going to have to fuck me right here on the dock, because you're making me horny. You know that, right?" She laughed.

"You're aroused just talking about it? What do you think it does to me?" Jax brought her hand between his legs to cup his straining erection.

"I love it when you're hard like this…do you know how much I want this right now?" She gave him a flirty smile.

"Not as much as me. Now come on…stay on topic, woman." He laughed.

"How the hell am I supposed to do that?" She stroked him, stealing a glance behind her to make sure no one saw them.

"We're talking about Jake." He coughed. "You keep doing that and I'm going to come."

"Ah…Jax," she sighed. "Do I want to play with him? With the three of us? Yes, someday." Katrina gritted her teeth and shook her head, blowing out a breath. She removed her hand and faced her mate. "Look, what we did the other day was great, but given a choice, like if all this wasn't going on? I just want to be with you."

"Jake's going to be an Alpha. Someday he'll lead his own pack." Jax's expression flattened as he told her what he suspected.

"Jake? But he…he's not even beta."

"It's the reason he and I go at it sometimes. I've been trying, in a most subtle way, to prepare him. When I came back, I was surprised to see him. Logan had sent him to San Diego, and I thought for sure he'd end up staying, taking over that pack."

"Maybe in some ways he did what you thought he'd do, though," she mused.

"How's that? He was with Finn."

"Exactly. Finn wasn't running the pack. Jake was there for him." She shrugged.

"Just think about it, Kat. I won't ask you or make you do anything you don't want to do. It's just that I'm worried about you. I know you feel stronger, but I also know the reality of the situation."

Jax caught Jake watching them out of the corner of his eye and hoped he hadn't overheard their conversation. Taking Kat into his arms, he gazed down into her eyes and his heart caught. The unfamiliar yearning in his chest was so much more than lust and he struggled to accept the emotions that rooted in his chest.

"I want you to know…this thing between us." His eyes darted to the glistening water and back to Katrina. "I told you that night we met…I've never met anyone like you. I meant that. I mean it even more now. You're determined. Strong. I'm not sure what I'm trying to say, but…" *Goddess, I sound like a fool. Get your shit together.* He gave a small laugh, realizing that for the first time in his life a woman was making him nervous. "I care about you. A lot. I won't do anything to jeopardize our future. As much as I want you completely healed, the ball is in your court. We...us...our relationship is more important. We'll figure out a way to deal with things, okay?"

A broad smile broke across Katrina's face upon his revelation. Her palm cupped his unshaven cheek and she rose to her tiptoes.

"I care about you too. More than you know."

Jax gave in to desire, and kissed his mate. Nothing mattered but Katrina, her happiness and their new journey. He almost wished he had the control to stop thinking about her, but relenting to the overwhelming need to be with her was impossible to resist.

The rolling waves lapped against the dock, drawing his attention back to their task and he begrudgingly broke contact. Jax opened his eyes, still focused on his mate. In his peripheral vision, he caught sight of Jake holding his palms upward, mouthing the words, 'what the fuck?', and he laughed in response.

"I think that our friend is getting pissed at us."

Katrina glanced at Jake and smiled. "He's patient. I'll give him that."

"Let's go. This could be a long night."

Jax took Katrina's hand and led her down the steps. He turned to the strangers and growled, his eyes flashing red. Amid their screams and the dog barking, Katrina's voice cut into the night.

"What are you doing?" she asked.

"We don't need an audience. Plus, I don't want anyone else getting hurt. I don't know what's down here. Maybe something bad. Maybe nothing." Jax waited until the area cleared before meeting Jake at the bottom. "Okay, you're the local. Where do you think most people throw ashes?"

"Well on Mardi Gras day they usually come on up here with the parade...you know, through Jackson Square to the river. But shit, I mean you know people probably do it other times. That's a human thing. Us wolves...we've got our own rituals. Puff and flush isn't one of them."

"Jake," Katrina admonished him.

"I'm sorry. I'm just sayin' you know we don't do this kind of thing. Back in the old days, who the hell knows what they did?"

Jax and Katrina rolled their eyes at each other, aware that Jake truly had no idea how long they'd lived. She shook her head, smiling, as he continued.

"Take the yellow fever epidemic of 1853, this city was filled with hundreds of dead people. They didn't know what to do with the bodies. Some of them just rotted away in the houses until the stench could be smelled through the burning tar." He sighed. "The cemeteries were full. But hell, I'm sure that through the years, people saw fit to make enemies wear cement boots, if ya know what I mean. And then you have the swimmers. I read just last week that someone died."

"But for the sake of this message," Katrina interrupted. "Ilsbeth did this. I'm pretty sure she's older than even we are. She's old school."

"Traditional," Jax added.

"I'd go with Mardi Gras. The coven house isn't too far from here either. Dumaine Street. So let's say someone—"

"Or something?" Jax interjected.

"Or something came after her. I mean she could get up to the riverfront fairly easily on foot." Jake scanned the area. "She's not going to hide something on a boat."

"No, she needs a safe place. Somewhere not many people go." Katrina bent down and ran her fingers over a smooth gray stone.

"Well, where we're standing right now. It's easy access to the river, but this place is usually loaded with people during the day."

"Supernaturals?" Jax scrubbed his hand through his hair.

"Mostly humans," Jake replied. "They play music. Sleep. Just kind of hang out here."

"Okay, well, assuming I'm human, I'm not going to go to certain places," Katrina surmised. She swiveled her head around, examining the area. "Dark places."

"Dangerous places." Jax honed in on the docks. Several sets lined the river's edge.

"That one." Jake pointed to a large pier, much wider than the others. "Under there."

"If I were a human there's no way I'd go underneath there. It's dark. Dirty." Katrina nodded in agreement. "Maybe I'd venture in to go to the bathroom or something, but it's not safe under there."

Jax took stock of the iron girders that emerged from the rocks. As on the steps, graffiti splattered their rust-covered surfaces. White drainage pipes caged the entrance but gave a wide berth for access. The gray blocks were littered with trash, clothing and other odd items. A cemetery of sorts, nothing living emerged. In contrast, the cemented river walk above teemed with life.

"We go in and get out. I told Kat that I think whatever we're looking for, it may show itself to just her."

"If Ilsbeth was in a hurry, she may have just stashed it," Jake guessed.

"But she'd planned for me to find the ring. The knife. I was the only one to feel those things. It was my blood. The message told us where to go. Why wouldn't she have planned this too?"

"Maybe." Jax sighed, and reached for her hand. "Or maybe she planned to put it here but ran out of time."

"We could be wrong about all of this, you know," Jake pointed out. "Are you feeling anything," he paused, incredulous he was even asking, "witchy? You know...any tingles?"

"No, smartass. I don't feel anything. I think we have to err on the side of logic."

"Kat?" Jake called to her.

"Yeah?" she asked.

"Sorry about the witchy thing. I know it's not really funny. I'm just frustrated."

"It's okay. And I wouldn't expect you to treat me any different."

"There's only one way to find out what's under here." As much as Jax loathed the idea of exploring the filthy underbelly, they had little choice. "You ready to roll?"

"Yep." Katrina gave him a small smile and squeezed his hand.

"Right behind ya," Jake called over to them.

"Watch your step," Jax warned. "There's broken glass all over the place."

The Alpha ducked as he stepped underneath the pipes. The stench of mold and stale water filled his nostrils, and he heard Katrina cough in response. He thanked the Goddess for his night vision, otherwise they'd be walking blind. Twenty feet into the cavern, he stopped to investigate the grotto. He ran his fingers over the peeling rust, and brushed it off on his jeans. A noise caught his attention. Focusing in, he observed an empty trashcan tossed about in the current that slapped against a wooden piling.

Reluctantly he let go of Katrina's hand as she tugged it away. Scanning the darkened abyss, he reasoned Ilsbeth could have hidden an object practically anywhere. Heavy tires, steel beams and hundreds of mildew-covered rocks blanketed the ground.

"We need a plan," Jax noted. "Jake, why don't you search near the water? Kat and I will look up here."

"Maybe we need to think about Ilsbeth," Katrina suggested.

"How do you mean?" Jake asked.

"Well, let's assume, giving her the benefit of the doubt, that she was trying to help us."

"That's a big assumption, Kat." Jake picked up a stone and threw it into the water. "I know you guys think I'm coming down hard on her but you don't know what it was like for D. She put him through hell. Jax, think about it, you know as an Alpha. What would happen to a wolf who could no longer shift? It's kind of presumed that if you can't shift, your beast is dead or doesn't exist. He would lose his pack. His family."

"True," Jax acknowledged. It was a hard reality. Dimitri would have been an outcast. A friend of the pack perhaps, but he'd no longer be allowed to participate in pack activities. His entire life would have been destroyed.

"I'm not asking you to forgive her, Jake. And I'm certainly not saying that Ilsbeth is innocent." Katrina's attention went to the far corner of the dock and then back to her wolves. "I'm just saying that in this situation maybe she chose to do the right thing. There have been times that she's helped people."

Jax didn't blame him for harboring resentment. The witch had cursed Dimitri in a most heinous fashion, one that could have resulted in his demise. Yet his mate's words rang true. Jax had already tried on one occasion to get

Jake to understand that without the facts surrounding Quintus, there was no way to judge the circumstances of her actions.

"As much as I hate what she did, because it was disgusting, I think we have to also be logical," Jax insisted, his tone serious. "The more I think about this, the more I'm leaning toward her helping us. If Ilsbeth had meant us harm, I'm pretty sure we wouldn't have made it out of that house. No, I have to believe that for whatever reason, she wants us to find something that will help us stop these demons."

"All right. Let's say she was helping. Something attacks her at the coven," Jake theorized.

"Or maybe she knew it was coming?" Jax guessed.

"Ilsbeth wasn't tall. Maybe five three? I'm not aware of her ability to levitate. Demons? Maybe. Not witches. So that doesn't leave her a lot of options if she came down here on her own." Katrina licked her lips and pursed them in thought.

"Even if she climbed up on here," Jake kicked one of the concrete bases that surrounded the beam, "she's not tall enough to reach up in there."

"So either she hid it under one of these rocks or she hid it where she could reach," Katrina concluded.

Jax squatted, picked up a rock and set it aside. "The ground's not safe. Granted, a storm could take it all, but the water could wash it away more easily down here."

"So we're back to the idea that she hid it where she could reach." Katrina raised her hands and began to pace toward the land. By the time her fingers brushed the girders, both Jax and Jake had caught up, flanking her.

"It could be anywhere above us. Spread out," Jax instructed.

"I wish we knew what we were looking for." She sighed.

"It has to be a spell or instructions on how to get rid of these things."

"So, uh, and please don't take this the wrong way," Jake's eyes went to Jax, "but exactly who is supposed to do a spell here? It sure as hell isn't you or me."

Silence lingered, and Jax hesitated to point out the obvious. Although Katrina was still a wolf, her magick had taken on properties of other supernatural beings. He suspected that whatever the demon had seeded had faltered, yet the essence of witchcraft had set hold in her soul. Katrina's voice echoed in the darkness, and his suspicion was confirmed.

"I think it's me." She shrugged, continuing to search. "We already know that whatever they did changed me. I'm not sure why I can feel Ilsbeth, but she knew about me. I'm sure of it. We know that she knew about the demons, and supposedly asked for their help. I don't ever remember seeing Ilsbeth but maybe she *was* there. And Samantha," Katrina paused, "she knows I'm not right. I could see it in her eyes. It scared her. Because she knows it's unnatural."

"Yeah, well, Samantha shouldn't judge. You do know she wasn't born a witch," Jake asserted. "A mage did that to her."

"But Samantha was human. Weak. Katrina's nature is strong; her beast will fight the intrusion," Jax argued.

"What Mick said about Ilsbeth is true." Jake ran his fingers underneath the girder. "Aside from her bedroom antics, she was old school. Traditional. Now I know she helped Léo to get rid of a demon once, but to help one stay? I'm not sayin' she didn't do it, but it just doesn't all add up, why she would bring something here that didn't belong. It's out of sorts with how she was. She was all about getting power for herself, not giving it to someone or something else. Sorry, but that queen bee wasn't giving up the throne to no one, no how."

"Regardless of her involvement, she knew about me and obviously she knows about them. I mean she sent Quint..." Katrina's voice trailed away.

"What is it?" Jax ran to Katrina's side. Jake quickly followed.

"There." She pointed to the left, to where the concrete met the beam. "Do you see how it's cracked? It's almost as if..."

"It's not sealed. The cement's loose." Jax studied the rough surface and swiped his hand over it. Although it had been caked with mud, a crevice outlining a breakage surfaced.

Extending a claw, he skewered it into the dirt and scraped the crusty flecks until the visible rectangular perimeter had been exposed. Inserting his fingers into the fissure, he tugged at the jagged stone and it crumbled away. Reaching inside, he retrieved a rectangular tin box. The partially rusted container sat easily in his palm. Brushing the dust away, he inspected its red lettering.

"Family medicine?" Jake read the label.

"Aids digestion?" Katrina sighed with disappointment. "It's junk."

"It's an antique quack box. It was pretty easy to fool people back then, but when you think about it, not much has changed. Look." Jake pointed to the writing. "Chocolate coated. Guaranteed to work."

"Well it makes sense," Jax said.

"How's that?' Katrina asked.

"You saw that set up she had going in her office. The collections of novelties. All used for spells. She's been around for a long time. This box is simple," he explained.

"Classic," Jake agreed.

"Like Ilsbeth," Katrina whispered. "Open it."

Jax carefully removed the top and set it on the ledge. A single sheet of perfumed paper sat unharmed in the center of the box. A floral motif adorned the heading. As he lifted it out, the familiar scent of lavender drifted into the air. Jax exchanged a quick glance with Jake, and stared at the nearly black surface. A series of dashes and dots read across the page: -.....-.. --- -- - -.. / .-.. .. -. --. .-.-.- / -... . ... - .-. --- -.-- / - ..... / ....--. .... --- -. .-.-.- .

"What the hell is this?" Jax tilted his head from side to side, stretching the stress out of his muscles.

"That's Morse code, man," Jake laughed. "Now of all the things I expected to see in a witch's fun box, that was not one of them."

"What does it say?" Katrina grazed the pad of her finger over its surface. "You were in the navy, right?"

"Hell, yeah." Jake smiled. "It says…shit, she's as cryptic as ever."

"What does it say?" Jax asked, his voice terse. He grew impatient with not only Jake but the entire situation. The stench underneath the docks intensified. The putrid scent of a dead animal permeated the air, and his instinct told him they should leave.

"It says, 'Blood ring. Destroy the siphon.'…whatever the hell that's supposed to mean."

"We'll figure it out back at the house. Let's get going. Something's not right here. Can you smell that?" Jax glanced behind him, searching for its source.

"Yeah, I thought it was the river," Jake replied.

"It's awful." Katrina coughed.

Jax set the note back into the box. Not wanting Katrina to sense his disappointment, he threaded his fingers through hers and began to lead her back out toward the river walk. Jax startled as Katrina tugged her hand out of his and ran back to where they'd found the box. He called for her to return, but it was too late.

‒✺· *Chapter Twenty* ·✺‒

Katrina froze as she laid her hand over the forgotten tin cover, which was blanketed in frost. She went still, the apparition appearing before her. As it solidified, she swore her eyes were playing tricks. The beautiful vampire she'd met once long ago laughed, stretching out her arms. Her tight red dress strained against her wiry muscles. Contrasting with her alabaster skin, her red hair had been swept up into a perfectly coiffed French twist. She smiled, revealing her bloodstained fangs.

"Katrina, darling, there you are. You can run but you'll be with us soon enough." Her voice trilled, sickeningly sweet as if she'd been poisoned with saccharin.

"Dominique? What are you doing here?" Katrina blinked. Confused, she turned to Jax. Her vision tunneled and he dwindled into a speck in the distance. "Does Kade know what you're doing?"

"Your magick grows strong. Soon you'll be ripe once again." Dominique's booming voice shook the ground.

Katrina screamed as the gorgeous vampire transformed into a creature she recalled from her nightmares. Like a scorpion, its tail whipped through the wind. The long piercing weapon slashed at the air, preventing Jax and Jake from reaching her. Its feminine hands and feet sprouted hooves while its face remained a perverted image of a human. Bald, its eyes glazed over, the red hue so piercing it caused her to squint. The unrecognizable mouth distorted into a massive cavern, a black pit of death.

It let out an ear-deafening screech as its tail scored the rafter of beams, setting off sparks. The scent of burnt metal wafted into the air. Smoke thickened underneath the dock until she could barely see through the black fog. She caught a glint of the bladed tail as it whizzed toward her. Darkness claimed Katrina, and the familiar touch of her mate comforted her. She would not die alone.

Katrina snuggled against Jax, dreams afloat in her mind. She stirred and pressed her lips to his skin. The hazy cloud began to lift and she ran her fingers over the familiar grooves of his abdomen. Even with her eyes closed, she recognized the distinctive scent of her mate, his soothing masculine essence cloaked around her.

Memories of the incorporeal being she'd encountered at the dock flooded back, and she struggled to remember how she'd returned safely to their bed. Katrina had met the ginger vampire at a party once. While she'd been a snarky aggressive female, one not to be trifled with, Dominique had never struck her as ill-willed. Devoted to Kade, she'd served him well. The savage monstrosity that had emerged out of the ghostly form shocked Katrina, and she wondered if she'd hallucinated. The illusion had seemed so real, but confusion persisted.

Jax's soft voice drew her out of her contemplation, and Katrina's eyelids fluttered open.

"Hey, baby, you okay?"

"Hmm…that thing," she began.

"I saw the vampire, but she disappeared."

"What? No." Katrina shook her head, disoriented. "The thing. It was a demon. Its tail. You saw it, right?"

Her question was returned by silence and Katrina's eyes filled with tears. *I'm losing my mind.* As if it wasn't bad enough that her magick had changed, that she sensed things at Ilsbeth's house, had been told by the warlock she'd been contaminated, she now questioned her sanity.

"It's okay, Kat. Please," Jax said, holding her tighter still. "I did see Dominique…if that was Dominique. I don't know what the hell it was. So if you saw something else, believe me, both Jake and I saw you. You were frozen, then started screaming and collapsed."

"I'm scared," she admitted. Katrina's strength had been surging ever since their mating, yet it had splintered apart in the presence of her perpetrator.

"What did you see?" Jax asked.

"It was this thing. A monster. This sounds crazy." She sighed.

"I've seen things, Kat. When they captured me," Jax said. "You know I'm a strong wolf. But the beatings, I don't even remember what they looked like…the attackers. At times they looked human. Other times, they looked like something out of hell. So whatever you saw last night, I believe it. Don't go doubting yourself."

"It was so real."

"Black magick can be powerful. That night in the club, when I thought it was you, I touched you and you were as real to me as you are now. If they can fool me into thinking that was you, whatever they are doing is serious."

"I just want to be done with this. I want a normal life. I want to take you to my gallery. I want to show you my paintings and run with you in the pack. I want to be free again. Not just free," she smiled up at him, "but I want to be with you. I was alone for so long."

"Tell me about your mom and dad," Jax asked, attempting to distract her thoughts from what had happened under the docks. He knew that she'd been raised in New Orleans, but there was so much to discover about his mate.

"My mom is strong-willed." Katrina laughed. "And my dad has a hard time keeping up with her. He stepped down as Alpha a while ago, let Marcel run the pack. Tristan had gone to Philadelphia. Hunter left for Wyoming. They wanted to travel, and if you're gone six months out of the year, it's kind of hard to lead a pack."

"How long was he Alpha?" Jax ran his fingers through her hair and brought a strand to his nose.

"He ran it for two hundred years, give or take. Right now, they're in some remote part of the Amazon. My mom is a scientist, so to speak. Looks for rare species and sometimes gives her findings to research companies. And Dad likes to explore with her, so he goes along for the ride. I wish they were here, though. Because then we could ask them if they know something, *anything* about what happened that would cause them to come after me."

"Still, what Mick said is true. It's rare for one to have so many connections to Alpha blood. Your father. Your brothers. And now your mate."

"My mate." She gave a small laugh. Her thigh draped across his waist, brushing over his dick.

"What's so funny, woman?" He noted that she'd changed the subject, but with his hand finding its way to her breast, he lost focus. Caressing it gently, he circled her areola with the pad of his finger.

"I can't believe it. I know you don't realize how much of a crush I had on you. It's embarrassing," she admitted.

"Embarrassing, huh? Sounds pretty awesome to me."

"I loved fantasizing about you." She smiled and flashed her eyes at him. "But the real thing is so much better."

"Fantasies, huh? Now we're getting to the good part. Let's hear it. Ah," Jax groaned as she cupped his testicles, smoothing her thumb over the crinkled skin. His length thickened as her fingers lightly teased his shaft.

"Let's hear what?" Her lips curled against his skin as she took his nipple between her teeth.

"What did you fantasize about? Like what would happen?"

"Are you serious? I can't tell you that."

"It's making me hard just thinking about it. Tell me, ah shit, yes," Jax cried as she fisted his cock.

"My Alpha," she growled, her tongue laving his chest. "You really want to hear about it? All right. I'd fantasize that I'd be at a museum. Maybe a party. I'd see you across the dance floor."

"Dancing is good. Foreplay."

"Hmm…but soon I'd be the only one there, and you'd…" She giggled.

"Don't stop," Jax breathed, unsure whether he was referring to her story or the fact that she'd tightened her grip.

"You'd undress me right there. No one would be there, but it was the thrill of knowing that anyone could see us."

"What happens next?" He smiled.

"Nothing," she lied.

"Do we need another lesson, my little wolf?" he questioned, sensing she hadn't told him the truth.

"We'd run away together and fall madly in love." Her voice trailed into a whisper as the words lingered in the silence of the night. Still unsure of Jax's feelings, her heart crushed, exposing her raw emotions.

Love. It had once seemed as elusive as catching a ray of a rainbow. Yet as she opened to Jax, becoming more vulnerable than she'd ever let herself be, she discovered the freedom in speaking the secret she'd never told anyone. In the bed of her mate, she no longer dreamed of making love. She dreamed of Jax loving her the way she'd fallen for him.

Jax delighted in Katrina's playful squeal as he turned the tables on his mate, rolling her onto her back. As he lay between her legs, supporting his weight on his forearms, his steel-hard shaft prodded her core. If only for a few heated seconds, he resisted burying himself deep inside her.

Katrina's sensual confession had turned heartfelt, revealing more than a passing lust. It exposed an exceptional future, one he craved more than the air he breathed. Jax couldn't say he ever thought he'd fall in love. But the raging emotion taking hold of his heart healed his broken world.

"I like your fantasy." Jax gazed into her eyes, a smile crossing his face.

"Jax…I…what about yours?" She blinked.

"You're it, baby. I'm living mine." Jax's lips captured Katrina's as he thrust inside her.

Her mouth parted, gasping for breath, as his cock speared inside her. They gazed into each other's eyes, the sensual urgency palpable. With every ounce of passion he possessed, his lips caressed hers, and she responded in kind. His simple kiss spoke the intense emotions he couldn't yet articulate. Rocking in and out of Katrina, he grazed her pelvis against his. As she arched upward, taking him deeper, he increased the pressure against her clit.

"That's it, Kat. Just feel me…feel how much you mean to me," he told her, his lips hovering above hers.

"Jax…yes…there…" Her eyes widened as her head tilted back toward the headboard.

Never had he made love with a woman the way he'd done with Katrina. The passion in her eyes as she reached climax tore at his heart, the raw intimacy exposed. Her breath was ragged as she came, her gaze focused on Jax. Fingernails stabbed his shoulders, and he reveled in the pain, her body shuddering underneath his.

As her pussy fisted his cock, the quivering vise ripped his orgasm from his soul. He stiffened against her, whispering her name. Jax's mouth grazed her temple, the salt of her tears on his lips.

Katrina completed his life, and the great Alpha knew that his beast had, in its own way submitted, to nature, to his mate. Falling for the little wolf, a new Alpha was born, and he would give his own life to protect her.

Jax scanned the courtyard, pleased that he'd purchased the Vieux Carré mansion. Gas lamp sconces flickered alongside hundreds of tiny white lights that ran up the side of a massive wall of ivy. In the corner, an iconic three-tiered fountain sat majestically, its gentle stream of water babbled, the calming waterfall echoing through the silence. Potted Palmetto palms lined a brick walkway that ran along the perimeter of the outdoor space. He glanced to Katrina, who enjoyed a swim in the large rectangular pool, and dreamed of a day when their vacation home would be filled with only joy.

Jax's attention was drawn to Jake's voice. They'd been sitting outdoors, discussing the contents of the tin box they'd discovered. *Blood ring. Destroy the siphon.*

"So what do you think it means?" he asked.

"I think we do what it says. I haven't even brought this up with Katrina, but I'm pretty sure she has to do something with that damn ring. My best guess is that she uses the boline to bleed onto it. But honestly, it looks like a piece of junk. I just don't get how this is going to do anything at all."

"Let me see it." Jake picked up the antique piece of jewelry. He ran his finger over its octagonal crown, scraping bits of dirt away from the top, revealing a dark blue sapphire. "Ah, look at Daddy's little pretty."

"Humans are particularly vulnerable to poison. Think about it. Going all the way back in time, nature has always provided means of death long before weapons were designed." Jax studied the object as Jake rolled it in his fingers. "Leaves. Berries. Naturally occurring substances to chemical derivatives. Modern drugs, even."

"This baby makes it easy to commit murder. Suicide, too. It's easily concealed and often undetectable. But there's a catch, using a ring." He held up the object to the candlelight. "If you're going to kill, you have to get close to your victim."

"True. The murderer would have to dispense it into a drink. But that's not possible with a supernatural. When we confront these things, they aren't going to just drink it."

"Maybe it has to go into them another way. It seems to me that all these things are basically living on borrowed time. They're essentially dead, using the same black magick to shift and get around."

"So what are you thinking? You get one, you get them all?" Jax's lip tugged to the side in thought, and he pinched the bridge of his nose. "But still, what do you do with it?"

"Not sure."

"The whole purpose of a poison ring is to use it. To conceal the murder weapon. Throughout time people have used all kinds of things to poison people. Darts. Knives."

"Really anything can be used if you're injecting it." Jake flicked the side of the ring. "There's something here. Here, feel this."

"I don't want to break it by forcing it open." Jax took it from Jake, and skimmed his thumb along its surface.

"Or worse, spill whatever is in it out."

"Grab me a glass off that tray, would ya?" Jax picked at the rust until it revealed a tiny ridge. As he inspected it, the fine lines of a hinge appeared.

Jake retrieved one and set it in front of Jax.

"Thanks." His eyes went to Jake's as he flicked the small attached lever. "If it releases the poison, we'll catch it."

Jax held his breath as he worked, giving it a strong shove with his finger. The metal popped as a tiny lancet ejected.

"And the plot thickens," Jake mused.

"Yes it does. So maybe you don't drink anything," Jax surmised. "Maybe you put the poison on this and stab the person. A little bit will do ya, as they say."

"The question is, how is the blood used? Let's assume it's Kat's blood, because let's face it, she's the one who has the craft flowing through her like a river. Does she just open the ring? Mix her blood with the poison?"

"Well, until she actually opens it, I'm going to go with all of the above. I'm curious about what's inside, but I really don't think we should open it here. Instinct tells me that it's best we leave it closed until it's time for the show."

"Yeah, I hear you. It's like opening a tube of toothpaste. Whatever's in there could be much more than just powder. Might not be able to get it back in. Knowin' Ilsbeth, she's got a surprise stuffed in here."

"Let's just keep this under wraps for a while, okay? Tomorrow we'll jet home and talk about it to Kat on the plane. Right now, I just want her to relax." Jax's focus went to his mate, who rested her arms and head on the edge of the pool.

"Is she okay? You guys didn't get up until late."

"She doesn't remember what happened at the dock," Jax disclosed. "And we're not going to tell her."

When Katrina asked him if he'd seen another creature under the dock, he hadn't completely told her the truth. While he'd seen something that appeared as if it were Dominique, what he hadn't shared was how Katrina had changed. Transforming from solid into a mass of splintered lights, she'd convulsed in a translucent state.

He hadn't thought twice about running to her, and by the time she'd fully materialized, she jolted violently toward the ground. If he hadn't been there to catch her, she'd have cracked her head open on the rocks. She'd remained unconscious until they returned home, scaring the shit out of him. Exhausted, she'd only spoken a few words, before falling into a deep slumber. After sleeping most of the day, she'd finally awoken, but seemed to have no recollection of the entire incident.

"You sure about not telling her what we saw?" Jake tilted his head in question.

"As much as I hate keeping secrets from Kat, I don't see any benefit in telling her tonight. She's already upset that she saw something we didn't. She says she saw some kind of demon thing. Last night, it shook me up seeing her like that."

"Yeah, that was kind of fucked up. Scared me, too."

"We're gonna have to work as a team. I want to get home and get this shit done. We'll bring the pack. I'm going to call Quint in too." Jax reached for his beer. "Tonight we rest. Tomorrow we fight."

"I have to say that Katrina looks no worse for wear. She actually looks happy," Jake observed.

"Yeah, she does. It's not that she doesn't know what's going down, she's just centered." Jax watched as Katrina swam back and forth in the pool, her creamy bottom breaching the surface.

"A late night swim is most definitely a good idea." Jake gave Jax a devious smile.

"She's pretty amazing, huh?" Jax still couldn't believe how hard he was falling for Katrina. The sight of his beautiful mate caused his heart to pause. Katrina completed his life, made him whole. If he died today, this would be enough.

"Look at you," Jake teased.

"What?"

"Hey, I don't blame you. Kat, she's a terrific person." Jake picked up his glass and took a swig of the ale. "You don't know. When she first came down here. She'd been in Philly a good part of the past hundred years. But she fit right in, ya know? Just like she'd never left. Marcel? If anyone messed with his sister, look the fuck out. He didn't fool around when it came to her. When he died, she was devastated. The past couple of years haven't been easy on her."

"She's resilient."

"It's gotta be scary for her to have all this shit going down with her magick, but she doesn't give up. A lot of wolves would have just said, 'fuck it'. But she's tough. She's got that Alpha blood in her, all right."

"Yeah, she does," Jax agreed.

"I just have to ask you something." Jake hesitated and scrubbed his fingers over his hair. "I know it's none of my business, but when it comes to Kat...I can see she's falling for you. So I don't know what your intentions are, but you were kind of a playboy in New York. It's not like some guys just give up that lifestyle. Some wolves, even after they're mated, act like bastards."

"What are you trying to get at?"

"Don't hurt her. It's as simple as that." Jake stared out over the veranda to the cabana on the far side of the pool. "If you do...hey, I know we've kind of become," he half coughed and gave a smirk, "what I think I'd say is friends, but I'll kick your ass all the same."

"I imagine you think you will." Jax laughed. He found it humorous to hear Jake challenge him in such an affectionate manner.

"I'm not kidding."

"I know you're not." Jax took a deep breath and considered his next words. "Jake…I think we need to talk about something."

"Yeah."

"You and I. Remember the first time we met? How you felt about me?"

"Do I need to get a box of tissues for this convo? I'm starting to get the feels." Jake smiled.

"Do you need to be such a jackass? Don't answer that. I already know the answer." Jax shot him a side glance and mindlessly dragged his thumb over the raised lettering on his beer bottle. "I'm trying to be serious here. Do you remember?"

"What about it? We met in New Orleans. You were an asshole. We fought. Saw you again in New York. Still kind of an asshole." He laughed. "Okay, maybe less of an asshole, but still. That kind of makes a nice fairytale, huh?"

"Fuck you."

"I'm still looking for my happy ending." He winked. "What do you say, Alpha?"

"Can you be serious for one fucking second?"

"What?"

"Did you ever stop and consider why you have this incessant need to challenge me?"

"Um, was I not clear about the asshole part?" he joked.

Jax shook his head and glared at him.

"Come on, Jax. What? I don't know. You're just kind of different than most Alphas I've been around."

"You've been around who? Marcel? Tristan? Logan? Am I right?"

"Yeah."

"Tell me what happened in San Diego."

"Why are you asking me this?" Jake's expression turned somber. He rimmed the edge of his glass with his finger.

"Just tell me," Jax pressed.

"After we killed Chaz, you know Logan sent me out there. It was a mess."

"Challenges?"

"Yeah, it's not like they threw me a parade. How would you feel if some strange wolf you didn't know came in and beat the shit out of every male in the pack and declared himself king of the kingdom? They didn't know me. And I didn't know them either. But hey," he exhaled and shrugged, "it didn't matter. I had a job to do. I know what it's like to follow orders, Jax. When you're in the military, you do what you're told. Sure, you may give leeway here and there, but you don't argue. You're an Alpha. You tell your wolves what to do and they'd better damn well do it."

"And you left because?" Jax left the question hanging.

"I left because I needed to help your sorry ass. Granted, things weren't exactly under control when you got home but Finn and I did our best."

"What about San Diego?"

"What about it? I chose a person who seemed decent enough to run the pack and I left." Jake sighed. "Okay, what's with all this cryptic shit? Why does it matter why I left? I'm an Acadian wolf. Always have been, always will be."

"That's true, but you know, sometimes our nature guides us outside our pack. Before you say another word," Jax held up a silencing hand, "just hear me out. I've been Alpha for a long time. Longer than any of the other Alphas you've known. Unlike Marcel, Tristan and Logan, you didn't know me, so our first meeting was a little rough, but," he laughed, "it's to be expected, given the situation. Look, Jake, under different circumstances, I'd keep quiet, let you navigate this by yourself, because I believe you truly will work things out. But given this situation with Kat…"

"What does she have to do with anything?" he interrupted.

"The fact of the matter is that you went to San Diego because you were sent there. That's all well and true. But once you got there you fought. By virtue of that, you became Alpha. Not just an assigned Alpha."

"That's different…"

"No, Jake. It's not. You may have been sent to do a job but you did it in a way that earned you that rank. I suspect that when Logan sent you, he knew what I knew." Jax glanced to his alluring mate and back to Jake. "You've always had the capability to be an Alpha. We're born that way. Programmed to lead. And if we get the opportunity, we snatch the brass ring."

"I belong here," Jake insisted, his jaw tensed.

"Maybe. Maybe not. Hey, I'm not telling you what to do. I'm just explaining the reality of the situation. You can joke all you want but it doesn't negate what happened in San Diego."

"Yeah, well, you're right about one thing. It's not your decision what I do."

"But when it comes to Kat…"

"Wait a second. Does this have something to do with what that damn warlock said?" Jake closed his eyes and blinked them open, registering where the conversation was going. "What we did yesterday in the kitchen, that was fun and all but I'm not going to get in your way. I know you guys are mated. I just want to see her be happy."

"I appreciate that." Jax locked his eyes on Jake's. "Yeah. Yesterday was cool. And it's part of the reason why I think we can take things further, help Kat."

"Take things further? As in you, me…Kat?"

"Here's the deal. Even though you left your pack, the power you have inside you, that raw energy that only an Alpha possesses, it's there. Do I believe every word Mick is telling me? Hell, fucking no. There's something that rubs me the wrong way about him. But I do believe that if we work together," Jax's focus went to Kat and he smiled at her, "I think we might be able to seal up whatever magick gets in and out of her. Tomorrow, we all have to go back and face these things. She needs to be as strong as possible."

"And you really think that if we do this, it'll help her?"

"I know it will. It's not going to change the fact that they messed with her. Hell, she may go the whole rest of her life affected by the witchcraft, for all I know. But I don't give a shit. As long as she can shift, she's going to be okay."

"You sure about this? The three of us? You know I've always loved Kat. Well, not love love, but you know what I mean," Jake explained, his voice strained.

"Calm down, Jake. Yeah, I'm as sure as I'm going to get. In the end, it's up to Kat though."

"I know better than anyone that she's not going to go doing something she doesn't want to do." Jake gazed to Katrina, who had turned her attention to her phone. "Hey, man. Does Logan really know?"

"About you? I'm sure he does. But it's like you pointed out. This is your choice. You've established yourself as an Alpha. I understand your reasons for leaving. Helping me and my pack was a convenient reason to leave San Diego. It made it easy. But I'm challenging you now…challenging you to consider what's going to happen to the wolves you left behind. Maybe after this is all over you might want to take some time off to think about what you want to do. How will it feel as the years go by and your natural tendency to lead pushes Logan's limits? Your own limits?"

Jake drifted into silent contemplation as he brought his drink to his lips. Jax set a hand onto his shoulder, and stood, giving him space. The Alpha respected the young wolf more than he knew. The night of Nick's death, Jax had observed through blurred grief how Jake fought for his own life. Jake had battled valiantly to save his sister. Two wolves had almost died that night.

Jax set his attention on his mate, crossing the patio to the edge of the pool. As his eyes went to Katrina, he knew full well that the connection between him and Jake would intensify, not only by making love to her, but fighting once again, side by side, in battle. He considered that besides Finn, he hadn't opened himself to another friend since the fateful night his beta died.

But as Katrina smiled up at him, his heart tightened and he knew he'd do anything for her. A war would come tomorrow. Losing Katrina or Jake wasn't an outcome he could conceive of nor accept. He'd gladly die first before letting anything happen to either of them.

"You okay?" Katrina asked.

"I was just about to ask you the same thing." Jax knelt down to her. His eyes drifted to her rosy tips. They jutted through the brightly lit water and quickly disappeared underneath.

"Swim with me?" She smiled.

"You know neither of us just answered that question." A small smile formed on his lips. Droplets of water beaded on her chest, tempting him further.

"Maybe it's because we already know the answer. We're both doing pretty well as long as we have each other," she replied. Her gaze darted to Jake and back to her mate. "Is he okay?"

"Yeah, I think he'll be all right." Jax settled onto the concrete, dipping his feet into the water. Her hands glided up his calves, and his arousal spiked. He laughed to himself, thinking that he hadn't been this horny since he was a teenager. All she had to do was smile at him and his dick turned to stone.

"So we go back to New York tomorrow, huh?"

"Once we get back, we'll go meet the pack out in the country. I'm thinking we'll take the ATVs. Trek the rest. Some of us will go wolf." Jax had already strategized the attack in his mind. "How about for the rest of tonight we just relax? Watching you here in the pool...you know you have me worked up."

"Hmm...do I now?" she flirted. "You know, I really could use a lifeguard. Someone to give me mouth to mouth."

"I'm highly trained." He winked.

"Really?"

"Spent my summers at the Jersey shore."

"Should I be jealous?" She smiled, her fingers traveling underneath the hem of his shorts.

"Never, baby."

"So tell me, Mr. Lifeguard," Katrina purred. She withdrew her fingers and reached for his waistband. Unbuttoning and unzipping him, she freed his erection into her waiting hands. "Do you always go commando? Because I kinda like that."

"Yeah, ya never know when you gotta strip down and run." Jax sucked a deep breath and edged toward her.

"Don't you mean swim?"

"Run? Swim? Whatev... Kat," he gasped as Katrina licked the tip of her tongue over his crown.

Jax leaned back onto his palms and took in the sight of his mate. Mesmerized, he froze as she swallowed him into her warm mouth. Her tongue caressed his cock, and his legs tensed as arousal threaded through his body. He closed his eyes, savoring the sensation and groaned when she sucked hard, a twinge of pain running up through his testicles.

Controlling him with only her mouth, she slid her hands around his hips.

Jax sucked a breath as she stabbed her nails into his ass, leveraging herself so she could take his entire shaft down her throat. Her teeth teased his sensitive skin as she withdrew and then plunged him back through her lips. She moaned, humming and sucking him, and he arched up inside her.

Holy fuck, I'm going to come. "No, no, no…Kat. I want to be in you." Jax took a deep breath, stemming the explosion that teetered so close to climax. He gave a small laugh as she released him and licked her lips like a kitten with milk. "Enjoying yourself?"

"Hmm…yes." She fisted his shaft and continued to deliver deliberate slow strokes.

"You're trouble." Jax leaned forward. Reaching underneath her arms, he lifted her up out of the pool and shoved to his feet. "The best kind."

She giggled, wrapping her legs around him. Jax kicked off his shorts and crushed his lips onto hers. The cool water soaked through his shirt, her hands tugging at the fabric. Their desperate kiss was interrupted as they heard the sound of a chair grate against the patio.

With his mouth on hers, he gave a sideways glance to Jake, who stopped briefly to give him a small smile. Katrina's line of vision followed his until their lips slowly separated.

"It's up to you," he whispered in her ear.

Sharing Katrina would not come without consequence nor would it come without a price. He'd considered the implications. Over the past week, he'd opened his heart to not only Katrina but Jake as well. His mate gave him a renewed strength, and his budding friendship with the wolf reminded him of the bond he'd had with Nick. Caring for both of them energized his soul, yet it also introduced a new level of vulnerability. If anything happened to either of them, he doubted he'd recover.

His focus went to Katrina, whose expression registered a common understanding. Both excitement and arousal coursed through his veins, and he gave her a small nod in acknowledgement. Bonded with his mate, he knew the power of another Alpha would help protect her in battle.

As Katrina extended her palm to Jake, Jax's cock thickened. Jake never made a move, his eyes locked on hers.

"Come," she called, her voice soft and husky.

"Be good to her," Jax warned.

Aware that Jake would never touch her without his permission, Jax gestured for him to join them. He'd invite Jake to infuse Katrina with the power of an Alpha, but he knew they'd only go so far, that he wouldn't share all of her with him. He planned to carefully control their sensual play, directing their erotic interlude.

Without waiting, he carried Katrina to the cabana and laid her on the bed. She smiled up at him and her happiness resonated deep within his chest. Water droplets glistened across her slick skin. His palms wet from touching her, he stroked his cock. Sensing Jake's presence, he turned to the wolf.

"You sure you guys are okay with this?" Jake asked.

"Isn't my mate beautiful?" the Alpha responded, ignoring his question. Jax wasn't sure if he could honestly answer yes, but his wolf didn't protest. His sole concern was Katrina and Katrina alone.

"She's amazing," Jake replied.

"Come to me, my Alpha," Katrina whispered, reaching for Jax. "So close to the full moon. My wolf, she yearns to run free. I need you."

"We can't exactly run in the city but we can make love in the moonlight," he responded.

Jax climbed atop the mattress, and smiled at her. He settled between her legs, spreading her thighs wide. Her chest rose and fell in anticipation of his touch, and he scented her desire.

In his peripheral vision he caught a glimpse of Jake tugging his shirt over his head. The sight of his bare chest surged his excitement; the anticipation of watching Katrina explore her secret fantasies within the safety of their bond spiked his arousal. He suspected Katrina would enjoy being with two wolves far more than she'd ever expected.

"Come," he told Jake, a devilish flare in his eyes. Positioned between her thighs, Jax pressed his lips to her stomach.

Jake's legs brushed his shoulder as he went to lie next to Katrina. Although the wolf's erection jutted at her hip, Jax sensed his apprehension.

"Touch her," the Alpha directed. Katrina sighed as Jake caressed her with his hand. Taking a ripe tip between his fingers, he rolled the swollen peak. "Yes, just like that. Her breasts...they're so soft. You like that, baby, don't you?"

"Hmm...yes." Katrina arched into Jake's touch, tilting her hips toward Jax. Jake kept his eyes locked on the Alpha, seeking guidance.

"Tell him what you want, Kat," Jax instructed, his lips peppering kisses over her hip.

"Kiss me," she breathed, her eyes set on Jax's. "Ah..."

Jake's gaze went to Kat's, and his mouth captured her nipple. Taking both breasts in his hands, he laved at the pink treasures. Both she and her Alpha watched in fascination as Jake attended to his task, sucking and licking them into hard points.

"That's it. See how much she enjoys your mouth on her? Tonight is all about Katrina," he told him. "We're going to make you feel so good."

Jax slid his thumbs down through her slick seam, and opened her wide. As he dipped his head between her legs, he smiled at Jake. His cock stiffened at the sight of him making love to Katrina. His mouth descended onto her pussy, his tongue darting over her clit. He delighted as she shivered underneath him.

Desire coursed through him, and he sent his power flowing through her. The sweet surrender of sharing was transforming into one of the most intimate experiences of his life. Having bonded with Katrina and now connecting to Jake, he reveled in the moment. With his heart mended, he wondered if it wasn't him who had needed healing.

Chapter Twenty-Two

Katrina's heart pounded in her chest with the anticipation of giving herself to both wolves. The sight of her striking Alpha taking control caused her to flood in arousal. Although Jax's commanding nature was possessive, she caught the savage desire in his smile as he watched Jake pleasuring her. Wolves were more sexually open than other species, but she'd never thought he'd accept another male in their bed. Given their new bond, she knew that the only reason he was doing it was for her, to strengthen her magick. Selfless, her loving Alpha had seeded the idea yesterday. Although she'd always been attracted to Jake, and he'd become a good friend, she'd never taken him as a lover...until now.

Her body sizzled as both men put their lips to her skin. Their raw power infiltrated her soul. Katrina gasped as Jake sucked her ripe tips, making love to her breasts. Jax drove a thick finger into her core, and she moaned, rocking her pelvis into his touch. Every last cell ignited on fire as his delicious tongue rasped back and forth over her clitoris, delivering erotic laps to her pussy. Ripples of pulsating waves speared through her, and she wrapped her thighs around his torso, bringing him closer to her. Raking her fingers into Jake's dark brown hair, she lifted his head, catching his heated gaze. His mouth descended gently upon hers, and she pinned her eyes on Jax as he sucked her swollen nub between his lips.

"Jax," she cried, as her mate's teeth grazed over her clit. Her orgasm lingered in the distance and she raised her hips, seeking more.

"You taste so good, baby. Fuck yeah." He speared three fingers inside her, giving no quarter. "I need you, Jake. Come here."

"No, no, no," Katrina protested as Jax withdrew. "I'm so close, I'm so close...ah...."

She fought for breath, clutching at the bed. Jax raised her leg, catching it under her knee.

"Lick her pussy." Tapping her mound with his cock, Jax directed Jake.

"Jax...I..." she panted.

"I want you to taste how delicious she is." Jax gave her a wicked smile as Jake brought his tongue to her clit. "That's it. Lick her just like that. Look at how pink and wet she is."

"Hmm... holy hell," she cried as Jake used his fingers to spread her labia open, gaining better access to her hidden pearl.

"Hold on, little wolf. Things are about to get interesting." He laughed.

"Jax...oh..." Katrina inhaled loudly as her mate sheathed himself inside her. Inch by inch, his enormous cock filled her tight channel. The sweet twinge she experienced as he stretched her open was offset by Jake flicking over her swollen nub.

Jax secured her thighs, hoisting her legs over his shoulders, rocking in and out of her. Katrina lost a sense of who was touching her. Clutching at Jake's back, she sighed as he sucked her into his mouth, the tip of his tongue ruthlessly laving her clitoris. As Jax pounded in and out of her, she was helpless but to accept the mind-numbing pleasure they lavished upon her.

"I can feel your pussy tighten all around me, baby," Jax grunted. "Oh yeah, she's so close, Jake. Let's do this."

Jax gave a hard thrust, his crown grazing her sensitive band of nerves. Jake increased the pressure on her hooded bead and Katrina screamed, coming hard. She shuddered uncontrollably, her head thrashing from side to side as her orgasm ripped through her.

"Yes...so good. Please, please, please," she panted. Incoherent, she trembled as the last waves of her climax claimed her.

Struggling to catch her breath, she gave a squeak as Jax pulled out and flipped her onto her stomach. Katrina rubbed her face into the bed, still tingling all over her body. Stretching out her palms, she raised her bottom, presenting to her mate. She quivered as he ran his palms up her inner thighs, tracing his fingers lightly through the crease between her legs.

"Hmm...Jake sure does know what he's doing, huh?" he commented with a wink to his friend. "Do you want to suck his cock? I think I'd like to hear him scream."

She was taken off guard; no one had ever talked so dirty to Katrina. Exposing her inner desires, her Alpha continued to push her, giving her permission to enjoy parts of her sexuality she wasn't ready to admit she enjoyed.

"Get in front of her," Jax ordered.

Leaning onto her elbows, Katrina set her vision on Jake as he settled himself against the back of the bed. He stroked his shaft, running his thumb over the wet opening. Katrina's lips parted, hungry to taste him.

"Don't move," Jax told her. She gasped as he slid his finger inside her core and removed it. "You're so fucking wet. Taste how sweet you are."

Guiding his hand to her mouth, he skimmed his thumb over her lips, parting them. As she nipped at her mate's fingertips, Katrina watched Jake fist his dick. Licking and sucking, she moaned as he pleasured himself.

"You make me so fucking hard. Watching him do that to you? Jesus, you're hot," Jax praised her. "You ready for Jake, now?"

"Hmm." She nodded. Katrina reached for Jake but Jax stopped her.

"No, baby. I'm controlling this show," he told her, his voice low and rough.

Katrina's pulse raced as she caught the interaction between the two males. Jake lay back, submitting to the Alpha. The intense stare between them turned heated as Jax reached for Jake's cock. Jake grunted as Jax gave it a firm stroke before he set its crown to Katrina's lips. She closed her eyes as he swiped her mouth open with the hardened shaft. Katrina lapped at his head, the taste of his salty essence teasing her tongue.

Putting her hand over Jax's, together they guided Jake's cock into her warm mouth. She relaxed, opening her throat, and swallowed him. Jake moaned, and the sound of his pleasure drove her to take him deeper.

Jax retreated and dragged his hard length down the cleft of her bottom, teasing her wet opening. As he entered her from behind, she gasped, but never let go of Jake. He slowly slid inside, and her core tightened with each slow thrust.

As they made love, a surge of their power rippled through her. The added unfamiliar energy of Jake took her by surprise. Her magick intertwined with theirs. Like an orchestra, the individual instruments brought a unique quality to the piece they created together. The weakened portals in her psyche weaved together, fortifying and sealing the breach that had allowed her magick to seep away.

"Yes..." she breathed as fingers teased open her back hole. Releasing Jake, she stroked him as Jax pounded into her from behind.

"I'm going to take you here right now, Kat. Do you understand?" he asked, his tone demanding.

"I...I'm not sure if I can do this." Despite her words, Katrina had already decided to submit to her Alpha's darkest fantasies. She yearned to embrace every erotic lesson he sought to teach her.

She turned her head back to Jax. He withdrew quickly and reached for his shorts. Retrieving a small tube, he returned, and she knew he'd planned this, regardless of Jake's participation. Her Alpha was calculating, a man who always took what he wanted. Possessing her, he'd claim every inch of her body and she was certain she'd enjoy every second.

Katrina shivered, waiting for him to fill her. As the cool gel dripped down her crevice, she inhaled in anticipation, his head brushing over her back hole.

"You're gorgeous, Kat." Jake gently caressed her hair, gazing into her eyes.

"I'm going to go gently, baby. Just relax into me, and push back," Jax instructed. "Breathe."

"Ah...Jax." Katrina's lips parted, and she did as he said. A slight twinge rippled through her as he entered her tight band of muscle.

"Don't tense. Just let me in. That's a girl. Oh yes...just a little more." His fingers circled her clit, and as he settled in further, pain was replaced by saturating pleasure.

"So full," she cried, patiently waiting for him to move. But he remained still inside her, giving her time to adjust to his dark intrusion.

"Ah fuck. Just give me a second," he pleaded.

"Please...Jax." Katrina sucked a breath, her nerves on fire with desire.

"Easy now." Slowly, Jax pulled out and rocked inside her, all the while caressing her swollen nub.

Jake held her hair as she slid him into her mouth. Overwhelmed with arousal, she laid her head on Jake's thigh as she sucked his cock. Moving in a simultaneous rhythm, Jax penetrated her. He increased his speed and intensity, plunging in and out, until they both shivered on the precipice of orgasm.

"Ah, I'm so close. Please, Kat," Jake begged.

"See what you're doing to him…"

Katrina barely heard her wolves, the rush of her climax teetering on the edge. She tightened her grip on Jake's shaft, fisting him, and still sucking. Jake's hips arched up into her mouth, his body shaking.

"No, no…I'm going to…" Jake tried to pull away, but she held tight.

The power of her Alphas surged through her body. Unable to hold back her release, she removed Jake from her lips.

"My Alpha…" Screaming Jax's name, a wave of ecstasy slammed into her.

"Oh yeah, Kat, fuck yes," Jake grunted, his milky essence spilling onto her breasts.

"That's it. Yes, yes…" Jax gave a final thrust, groaning, his glorious cry slicing through the air. "Ahh!"

Katrina's body went limp as the last remnants of her release rushed through her, the electricity of their explosive energy humming in her body. She'd experienced Jax's extraordinary power, but with Jake's added, her magick spiraled out of control. A warm washcloth on her skin lasted only a minute, before Jax swept her up into his arms. Cradled against his chest, she scented her mate. A peaceful sensation settled around her, the love of her Alpha rooted deep in her soul.

Love. Never in her life had she told someone she loved them. Until now, letting someone inside her heart had never been an option. Waiting over two hundred years for her mate, she'd denied herself precious intimacy. Her perfect match, Jax pushed her limits and gave of himself so she'd be healed, strong enough to fight for both of them.

In her mind's eye, her wolf ran to his, together at last. In the morning they'd face reality, but for tonight, she closed her eyes, content to be within his embrace. *Loving her Alpha.*

⁓✣ *Chapter Twenty-Three* ✣⁓

Jax's heart contracted as he watched Katrina sleep. Teasing her hair into his fingers, he considered the feeling that proliferated inside his chest. As a boy, he'd thought he'd fallen in love with the human girl. As a man, his juvenile crush paled in comparison to the emotions he held for Katrina. He'd always wondered what it would be like to be mated. While it was true that his wolf's need to bond had been sated, it was his human need for intimacy that surprised him most. More than content, he couldn't stop from smiling.

"*I love you,*" he whispered, the words true to his heart. Saying it out loud exhilarated him. He considered telling her when she woke, but he didn't want to scare her with his confession nor did he want her to think he'd said it because of their dire situation.

His thoughts drifted to their interlude at the pool. Making love with her and Jake had been incredible. Connecting with Jake filled him with a deep sense of satisfaction. Their friendship, because of both the situation and Kat, had deepened to a level he hadn't thought he'd experience again with another male.

Although he'd felt his own power mesh with Jake's, he was unsure how it affected Katrina. He suspected it strengthened her, but it remained to be seen. They might not know for sure until they were confronted with the demons.

Jax glanced to the clock. In another five hours, they'd board the plane for New York. He planned to hold a pack meeting and announce his mating before they returned to the dungeon. He'd need the support of his wolves going into battle. Although Katrina would have to earn her right to remain in the pack, Jax was confident of her ability to lead with him as part of the Alpha pair.

A loud bang to the door jolted him upright. He jumped out of bed and shoved into a pair of jeans. Jax quickly covered Katrina and took off down the stairs to address the source of the menacing noise. The incessant knocking intensified, and as he swung open the door, he was confronted with the angry vampire.

"What the hell did you do?" Luca accused. He barreled toward Jax, shoving his chest with both his hands.

"Out of courtesy to my mate, I'm going to give you one warning. Calm down. Put your hands on me again, and you'll regret it," Jax growled.

"I'm sick of you fucking wolves…" Luca charged, raising a fist.

With preternatural speed, Jax snatched his arm out of the air. Twisting it behind his back, he shoved him up against the wall, and jammed his face between the stair rails. Jax reached for a wooden spindle and snapped off a shard, stabbing it between Luca's shoulder blades.

"You know, I really tried to be nice, but you're lacking manners." Jax's eyes darted to Jake, who walked through the threshold. Holding a white paper bag and cardboard beverage carrier, Jake stopped and assessed the situation.

"Hey, no one told me we were having a barbeque. Are we making shish-kabob?" Jake gave Jax a sly smile. "I brought café-au-lait. Sorry I didn't bring enough for everyone...didn't know you were expecting company."

"Funny thing, neither did I." Jax dragged the point of the stake over Luca's shirt, tearing through the fabric.

"Beignets though? Got plenty of those." Jake set the drinks onto the floor. He slid behind the steps and dangled the pastry bag under Luca's nose. "If you're a good vamp, I might let you have one. But something here tells me you're messin' with my boy."

"Fuck you," Luca spat. "Where is she?"

"See?" Jax commented. "No manners at all."

"Did you ever hear that expression, 'you catch more flies with honey'?" Jake reached into the sack and retrieved a powdery beignet. He took a bite and smiled at Jax. "I think he may have missed that one."

"Here's your choice, Luca. Because clearly we got off on the wrong foot. I can release you and we can discuss this like adults. Or," Jax paused.

"I think you might want to listen to this part, big fella. Bite?" Jake held the pastry to Luca's lips. "No? Okay, suit yourself but they're delish."

"I could take this stake and drive it right through your rude ass. Because honestly, I have a lot of my own shit going on right now, and this? Yeah, I don't need this right now."

"You'd better tell me where she is. I told you that she wasn't allowed around you or Katrina, and now..." Luca unsuccessfully struggled to free himself.

"Um, Jax..." Jax peered up to Katrina, who stood at the top of the steps wearing his t-shirt. Despite the serious situation, the sight of her warmed his heart and he smiled up at his mate.

"What's going on?" She yawned.

"Nothing, baby. Luca here...well, you see, it seems like he didn't get his coffee this morning."

"You know what that does to vamps. It's terrible," Jake added with a laugh. "Just can't do a thing until he gets his joe. Cranky pants."

"Okay, let's try this." Katrina padded down the steps until she was at eye level with Luca. Setting her gaze on him, she brushed back her hair, twisting her ponytail. "What's going on, Luca? And why is my Alpha holding a stake to your back?"

"Samantha," he breathed. Luca shook his head in frustration. "She's been missing since last night."

"Jax, let him go. Please," she pleaded.

"Only if he says he'll behave. Otherwise, I'm good with killing him."

"Jax, come on." She turned to Jake, who rolled his eyes and gave another chuckle.

"Beignet?" He offered her the bag.

"Thank you, no." Katrina stepped around him, making her way to the landing. Standing next to Luca, she put her palm on Jax's arm and leaned to speak to her friend. "Luca, you know we're friends, but you can't just come into an Alpha's home and threaten him. You may be old and strong but Jax is just as old, and please don't take this the wrong way, but Jax will kick your ass. He's Alpha for a reason, sweetie. Now I'm really sorry that Samantha is missing but we had nothing to do with it. You need to calm down so we can talk. Can you do that?"

Luca blew out a ragged breath, and set his sight on Katrina. "Fine."

"See." Katrina's eyes darted to Jax and then back on Luca. She spoke to him softly and slowly as if he were a child. "Now take a few deep breaths and relax. Count to ten. Come on, do it."

Katrina looked to Jax and mouthed the words, 'Put that away', glancing at the stake. The Alpha shook his head no. "Please."

Jax's body surged with anger for the asshole in his hold. The vampire had crossed a line by coming into his home and attacking him. If it had been any other person, they'd be dead already. The only thing saving his sorry ass was the fact he'd been friends with Katrina. Inwardly Jax laughed, considering how his mate was already changing his actions.

"Are you going to behave?" Katrina placed her hand onto Luca's shoulder and he nodded. "Promise. I cannot protect you if you break my trust."

"I promise," he spat.

"Jax, please let him go," she asked.

"I'm telling you right now, asshole. You're extremely lucky that you have such a pretty friend. But if you go after me again, even she can't save you." Jax shoved him one last time before releasing him. He sighed as Katrina rushed into his arms.

"You know, you wake up and you think, 'I'll go get some breakfast.' But you just never expect this kind of shit at seven in the morning. It was exciting, though. I was kind of hoping for shish-kabobs. Guess not," Jake joked.

Luca stumbled back against the wall, and brought his hands to his face. Jax held tight to Katrina, sensing she was about to go to him. It wasn't as if he didn't care that Samantha was missing but the vampire had no right accusing him of wrongdoing, let alone attacking him.

"What happened?" Jax asked.

"Avery called the house last night." Luca closed his eyes slowly then opened them again. Holding his hand to his forehead, he continued. "I didn't want her to go, but you know these witches...everything's been a mess with

Ilsbeth gone. She, uh, she was a difficult woman, but she kept her coven out of trouble. This Mick fucker, he's out partying in the middle of nowhere. That might be fine for some of the witches but there's a lot of them who are more traditional. They stay in town. Last night, Avery called. Said she'd decided to move back to the Quarter and wanted Sam's help getting situated."

"Did she go alone?" Katrina inquired.

"No, I dropped her off at the coven house...like I've done a million fucking times before. I told her I'd be back in a few hours...which I was."

"How does she just go missing?" Jax threaded his fingers through Katrina's.

"I went to pick her up and they said she left with Avery to get some supplies. That's not out of the ordinary, so at first, I didn't think much of it. There're a couple of stores in town where they get things for spells and so forth."

"But she never came back," Jax concluded.

"No. I went and tore up the coven house looking for them and there was no sign of either of them. So I drove all the way out to Mick's. He wasn't there but I searched the whole place. I mean," Luca sighed, "I could tell she wasn't there. I didn't even scent her but I had to look."

"So you decided to come here?" Jake asked

"Yes. Look, the other day...at Ilsbeth's." Luca's eyes went to Katrina. "Samantha told me things."

"Like what?" Katrina's tone was terse, and Jax squeezed her hand, reminding her he was there for her.

"Jesus Christ, Katrina. We've known each other forever." Luca paced, avoiding eye contact. "But she said you had magick in you. Not the kind you're supposed to have. She said when she touched you, your aura...this is going to sound crazy."

"Just say it," Katrina pressed.

"She said, ah fuck," he stopped to look at her. "She said you felt like Ilsbeth. Now like I said, you and I, we go way back. If you were Ilsbeth, I think I'd damn well know. But you scared her, okay?"

"I'm not Ilsbeth." Katrina broke free of Jax and crossed to Luca. She reached for his hand. "I'm still me, but Sam is right. They did something to me. There's magick inside me that isn't mine. Something about Ilsbeth's house the other day...it affected me....spoke to me. I don't know why it's happening, but I can tell you that we had nothing to do with Samantha disappearing. I swear it."

"But we will help you find her." Jax approached Luca, setting his palm onto Katrina's lower back. "There's one thing we agree on. This thing with Avery is suspicious and Mick is the only one who might have an answer. We're going back to New York today, but first, I think we should pay Mick a visit before we leave."

"I'll call the chopper," Jake told him.

"But I was already at Mick's place. I told you that she wasn't there. I couldn't even find him."

"Maybe you couldn't find him. Or maybe he was hiding? Or maybe he just was off in the woods? Regardless, I think we should give it a try. Between Katrina's magick and us scenting as wolf…if he's there, we'll find him. My guess is that the warlock knows exactly where Avery went," Jax surmised.

"But Samantha would have never gone with her. She would have called me by now," Luca explained.

"If Avery is a player in this circus, we have to find out."

"Seems like she was his toy," Jake noted. "A mistress, I'd bet."

"More like a prize student," Katrina added.

"Here's the plan. Let's get dressed and we'll copter back to Bayou Goula." Jax reached for his back pocket and checked the time on his cell phone. He pecked at the glass. "Jake, call the pilot and have him shift the departure time to New York. I'm texting Finn to let him know we're going to be late, but he'll have the pack together by the time we get there."

"Are we meeting in the city or how's this working?" Jake asked.

"We'll fly into Newark and take the chopper up to the Finger Lakes. There's a pack house a few hours outside of where they held us. Once we get there, we have to work fast. For whatever reason, these things seem to have better radar on Kat when she's not in New Orleans."

"Could have to do with Ilsbeth," Katrina guessed.

"Maybe. This place is loaded with wards, every which way you turn. At home, you're much more exposed."

"This is our home." Katrina smiled at Jax, who gazed up at her from his cell.

"Yeah, I guess it kind of is now, isn't it?" Jax acknowledged. He glanced to the empty living room and made a mental note to ask her to help him decorate. Although he loved New York City, this was Katrina's birthplace. She had friends and family in the Big Easy, as well as her own gallery. It wasn't lost on him that she hadn't asked to visit it, but he suspected she didn't want to put her employees or neighbors in danger by doing so.

"I have to find her." Luca's voice wavered as he spoke. "Our baby…she's due any day now. She's been through so much. Dominique…"

At the mention of the vampire, Jax's eyes darted to Jake then to Kat, before settling back on Luca. He hadn't planned on mentioning the incident at the docks. But Jax had heard that Dominique had kidnapped Samantha a few months ago, almost killing her. After having experienced shape shifting first hand, thinking he'd seen Katrina in the club when he hadn't, he doubted more than ever that they'd truly seen Dominique. It was much more likely that they'd seen an apparition or a glamour created by witchcraft.

"Luca, I wasn't going to tell you this, but the other night," Jax paused and glanced to Katrina, "we all saw something that looked like Dominique."

"What?" Luca exhaled loudly and closed his eyes, an expression of shock washing across his face.

"Just hold up there, okay? Before you think it was her that kidnapped Samantha again, I've got to tell you, we don't think it was her. This thing looked like her, but that's where it ends."

"What are you saying? It was someone dressed like her? She's been missing for months."

"Just what I said…it looked like her. These things…demons, witches, whatever they are, they're using some kind of magick to make themselves look like other beings. But they haven't been successful with wolves."

"Demons have always been able to possess humans. They're weak," he noted.

"Yeah, well. Apparently they've replicated their little trick with some vampires too," Jake told him.

"I don't know what started them down this path, but Mick seems to think they are looking to take over packs. I personally don't believe one hundred percent of what comes out of his mouth, but that day they took me…that woman on the floor looked like Katrina. In her human form anyway. We don't know if they can transform into animals yet."

"This is too much to process. Does Kade know?"

"No, I haven't told him. Been kind of busy here. You're welcome to text him, but the fact of the matter is that we don't know exactly how or why this is happening. Somehow the witches are involved. I'm pretty sure Ilsbeth had a hand in this somehow. All we know for sure is they've been stealing Katrina's magick over the past three years. What they're really planning long term is anyone's guess."

"I want to help, Kat, but my priority right now is Sam. We've got to find her." Luca paced, his hands on his forehead.

"Let's go get dressed." Jax reached for Katrina's hand and led her toward the staircase. "Jake, you mind keeping watch on the vamp?"

"You got it, boss." Jake gave a small smile and eyed Luca.

As the Alpha ascended the steps, he glanced back to the vampire and shook his head. Before Luca had had a chance to ask for help, Jax had already decided to search for the redheaded witch. With child, she'd never survive the kind of torture the demons had inflicted on him.

He racked his brain, attempting to put together the pieces of the puzzle. Nothing was an isolated incident as far as he was concerned. *His own kidnapping. Dimitri losing his wolf. Ilsbeth disappearing afterwards. Katrina's infusion of witchcraft. The warlock. Avery's role in Samantha's disappearance.* His mind churned the facts, and although he couldn't definitively find the correlation between them, he was becoming more convinced Ilsbeth had instigated a chain reaction of mayhem. Maybe she'd meant to do it, maybe not. At this point, it mattered little. A demagogue, she was powerful enough to spark the trail of destruction.

Jax took Katrina into his arms, kissing her hair. A scant scent of chlorine from her midnight swim still remained and he smiled, thinking about making love with her. Determined to find and destroy the demons, he swore to the Goddess that today would be the day. Their nefarious existence was coming to an end.

Headphones muffled the deafening sound of the whirling blades. Jax concealed his shock as they circled the scene. From the air, he viewed the incinerated remains of the building. Red-hot embers kindled, wispy tendrils of smoke spiraled toward white puffy clouds. The odor of the charred wood seeped into the aircraft cabin.

As they descended, Jax observed a small group of witches on the front porch of the original mansion. He found it interesting that it had gone untouched while the newer structure had completely burned to the ground.

"What the hell happened here?" Jax heard Jake ask as the helicopter touched down.

"I doubt the magick man torched it himself," Jax responded. "But then again, who knows?"

"That guy is an asshole," Luca spat. "Don't get me wrong. Duplicity was Ilsbeth's middle name. But we could count on her to help keep things under control. This guy? He says he's about 'going back to nature' but it's all a bunch of fuzzy bullshit. He's more interested in fucking than developing the coven. He left Samantha and the other witches in the Quarter to fend for themselves. It's been a shit show."

"Couldn't Samantha or someone else have taken over? Kicked him out?" Jake asked.

"Ever since I was turned, Ilsbeth's been in charge. I love Sam, but before I knew her, I wasn't terribly fond of witches."

"Or wolves," Kat added.

"Or humans." Jake smiled.

"Oh please. Vampires are far superior creatures. Humans are...well, they are interesting but I tire of their weak nature." Luca sighed. "My point is that I have come to respect the witches. Samantha...she's strong. An amazing woman. Her power is growing, no doubt, but she's pregnant."

"Back to Jake's question, wasn't there anyone else who challenged him? I find it hard to believe that Ilsbeth hadn't groomed any other witches," Jax pressed, sensing that he withheld information,

"At this time, there is no one who can fight Mick," Luca hedged. "His party slash feel good style approach of running the coven appealed to several of the witches who'd grown tired of living under Ilsbeth's iron fist."

"Luca, you search the house. Kat and I will question Mick. You're too upset right now to do it. I have a feeling you might drain him before we get answers. The last time we were here he seemed to be in a sharing mood. We don't have time to get into a pissing match." Jax turned to Jake. "Go wolf. Run the woods and see if you can scent Samantha. Let's be as fast as we can. If Sam's not here, we've got to look elsewhere."

"You got it," Jake answered, peeling off his clothes.

"Are we on the same page?" Jax asked, pinning his gaze on Luca.

"Yeah," he grumbled.

"Don't fuck it up. Get your shit together for your witch. We're going to find her."

Not waiting for the pilot, Jax wrapped his fingers around the handle and shoved open the door. He stretched out his hand to Katrina and helped her step onto the gravel driveway. Out of the corner of his eye, he caught Jake leaping out of the helicopter, his tail wagging behind him. Jax gave Luca a nod of warning.

The warlock approached, this time wearing only shorts and a fitted yellow t-shirt with a smiley face on it. His face, marred by soot, wore a somber expression.

"Alpha. You'll understand if I don't extend a greeting." He held up his blackened palms. "My wonderland has been ruined."

"I see." Jax hesitated, deciding not to apologize. "Luca needs to search for Samantha. She's missing."

"Yeah, I heard that he came lookin' for her earlier. But Sam hasn't been here. This isn't her scene."

"All the same to you, we need to search. I'd very much appreciate your cooperation." *Or I'll force you, and it won't be pretty.* Jax gave a cool smile, hoping the warlock understood the implications of his choice should he refuse the request.

Mick's eyes darted to the vampire and back to Jax, his lips tense with anger. "But of course. Search away."

"Thank you. I knew you'd understand." Jax gestured to Luca, who set off toward the dilapidated home.

"If you don't mind me asking, what makes you think Sam would be here?" Mick scrubbed a dirtied hand through his hair.

"Avery. She was at the coven house," Katrina explained.

"We'd like to talk to her," Jax told him.

"Avery, Avery, Avery. Fucking turncoat bitch. You think you can trust someone," he sneered.

"Trouble in paradise?" Jax raised a questioning eyebrow.

"She gave me a hard time about being with Elsie."

"Elsie?" Katrina asked.

"Yeah, Elsie. Well, Elsie and Amber...Natalie, too. Look, I'm not tied to one witch. That's the beauty of what I preach here. But Avery, she thought she was my girlfriend." He put his hands on his hips and shook his head, rolling his eyes. "This...this fire. She did this. I know it. Jealousy is a very ugly emotion. Coveting what others have. No, my love is free. It always has been. She didn't understand."

"You had a fight last night?" Jax asked.

"Yes, it's why I sent her away. She's no longer welcome here. Of course I didn't have the heart to kick her out of New Orleans. This is her home after all. I could be a hard-ass but it's not like I'm channeling Ilsbeth. That's not my style. Fuck, if you pissed off Ilsbeth, you'd find yourself at the end of a nasty spell, like waking without a hard-on for the rest of your supernatural life. Either that or she'd ban you from the entire state of Louisiana. I'm better than her. I'm a compassionate leader," he professed.

"Yeah, I'm sure you're a real Mother Teresa." Jax wasn't buying the warlock's song and dance. Something about the story didn't ring true, yet he couldn't prove it false. "Avery had a hand in Samantha's disappearance. So if you know where your girlfriend likes to hang out, it's time to spill."

"Are you hard of hearing? I just told you she's not my goddamned girlfriend." Mick raised his voice, a tick in his temple visibly pulsated as sweat beaded on his forehead. He took a deep breath, his demeanor switching back to his previously calm state. "Forgive me. Avery is a free spirit. She could be anywhere in the bayou, but I suspect she's held up in a vampire bar in the Quarter. I'm afraid I cannot help you."

"Got a text number?" Jax pressed.

"Yeah, give me your phone."

Jax took out his cell, bringing up the contacts. He handed it to Mick, who pecked out the digits into the directory. Jax accepted it back and pressed send.

"Direct to voicemail," he commented and proceeded to tap out a text message to Avery.

"Doesn't surprise me she's not answering. Always forgets to turn on her phone," the warlock told them. "Look, I've got nothing else to tell you. But please, feel free to join the vampire. And when I say feel free, I mean, go find him. I've worked hard to keep this a no fang zone, and I'm sure the girls aren't very happy he's sniffing through their things."

Jax didn't bother saying thank you as he took off with Katrina toward the house. After his interaction with Avery, he'd witnessed her mischievous nature. She'd taken great pleasure in making Katrina jealous, deliberately coming on to him. But at no point had he sensed malevolent intentions from the witch.

The warlock, on the other hand, presented as a ditzy mess of a leader. In all his years, Jax had never met a high priest who loosely attended to coven members the way Mick did. The flare of anger the warlock had displayed may have been a natural reaction to the destruction of his club, but was contrary to how he'd acted in the past. Jax doubted that Ilsbeth had ever groomed him, and he wondered who else was strong enough to lead the witches in

New Orleans or who might be vying to be a high priestess. Even though Mick had taken over since Ilsbeth's disappearance, it was likely others were staging a coup.

Noting the rotted wooden step, Jax tested it with his foot before ascending. It crackled underneath his shoe but held. Two women wearing colorful sundresses rocked back and forth in a vintage porch swing, unfazed by the creaking of the rusted chains that secured it to the peeling ceiling above. They gave him a small smile, and Jax thought their placid disposition odd, given the fire.

Instead of making casual conversation, he ignored them and reached for the screen door. He peered inside, scanning the area before allowing Katrina to follow him into the foyer. The stale odor of musty carpets saturated the air, and he noted a faint scent of cat urine. The walls, covered in textured wallpaper, had been partially scraped, revealing teal-colored paint. Large bins filled with debris sat stacked in a corner along with several paint rollers.

"Luca!" Jax kept his sight trained on Katrina, who inspected items that rested on a wooden curio table.

"Looks like they're renovating. Sage," she speculated, picking up a clump of herbs and holding it to her nose.

"Apparently so. Guess it's good they have a place to live."

"You think she did it?" Katrina asked.

"Avery?" Jax shrugged, his eyes inspecting a large antique chandelier that hung precariously from the second floor ceiling. The hundreds of crystals dripped from the light fixture like pearl necklaces.

"She seemed to enjoy causing trouble the other night. But it doesn't quite make sense." She paused and set her focus on Jax. "Why hit on you if she's in love with Mick?"

"Exactly." Jax loved how his mate's mind worked, as he'd been thinking exactly the same thing. "Do you hear him?"

"Upstairs," she responded. "Luca!"

"Let's go up…" Jax stilled, as his cell phone buzzed in his back pocket. Retrieving it, he slid his finger across the glass and froze as the image appeared. Although he was hesitant to show Katrina, he wasn't about to keep this secret from her. "Kat, I need you to come see this. We're going to find her."

"Oh Goddess, no," Katrina exclaimed.

Jax immediately recognized the location, its brownish stone walls stained with the blood of its victims. Sitting, she appeared calm, despite the flecks of fear in her eyes. Her mouth had been duct taped shut, he presumed to keep her from uttering spells. With manila rope bound around her wrists, her hands rested on her swollen belly. *Samantha*.

Chapter Twenty-Four

Jax weaved his way through the crowd, making a concerted effort to personally greet every wolf in the pack. With over a hundred adult members in attendance, he'd been acutely aware of every precious second that passed. Although he knew they sensed his bond, and quite possibly scented her in the building, introducing Katrina as his mate required patience.

Through the A-frame wall-to-ceiling windows of the ballroom, dusk fell over the shimmering lake. While Jax generally retreated to his private luxury cabin, he'd built the mansion for pack meetings and company events. The two hundred and ninety acre property housed a boat house, three swimming pools, a basketball court and a bowling alley. With over thirty rooms, it easily accommodated groups of out of town guests.

What Jax hadn't anticipated was fighting an enigmatic adversary on his own turf. While they'd fought the occasional territorial war over the years, wolf against wolf, he'd known his enemy's weaknesses and strengths. Tonight, however, they were going in on a wing and a prayer. A medieval ring coupled with the promise of a cryptic message. At best, they were theorizing that Katrina would have the power to ameliorate the demons, using the slice of the ring and her blood. At worst, Ilsbeth had set them up for failure, a cruel joke added to the damage she'd already inflicted on Dimitri.

Calming Luca down after he'd seen the image of Samantha had been no small feat. The vampire had been on the edge of losing it completely, and Jax had considered leaving him in New Orleans. A loose cannon, Luca could be more of a detriment than a help if he decided to go rogue. Only after gaining Kade's assurance that the vampire agreed to defer to the Alpha's orders had Jax allowed him to come to New York.

On the flight up to New York, Luca had disclosed Samantha's rapid rise within the coven. Trained under Ilsbeth, she'd hidden her abilities from other witches, concerned that her power would be misinterpreted as threatening. Luca and Samantha had discussed the possibility of her becoming high priestess after Ilsbeth had disappeared, but they'd decided it wasn't in the best interest of the baby to cause any conflict within the coven. With child, she'd retreated, only practicing her craft within the safety of her home. They expected a daughter, and it was foretold she'd be a witch.

Tonight they'd work together to destroy the demons. Freeing Samantha was critical, not only to ensure the safety of her child but for her to help fight the black magick. Jax knew as well as Luca that it was a miracle she was even pregnant. A rare phenomenon; vampires didn't have children. It was only through the magick of his mate that they'd conceived.

As Jax approached the podium, the room went quiet, and he sensed her presence. *Katrina*. Planned to the second, she'd arrived exactly on time. Luca, Finn and Jake protectively surrounded her as she approached. Even though they'd been together just hours before, his heart caught, seeing her. Her long blonde hair had been braided down her back. Jeans and a black leather jacket presented an edgy exterior but he knew in their private moments, his mate softened, fit him comfortably and perfectly.

Intrepid and confident, she smiled at him. Goddess, he loved her. Revealing the secrets in his heart would come soon, he knew. But when he did it, he planned to make it special. No demons or witchcraft, fear of death or war would be involved when the words were spoken. The memory of their love would be an extraordinary, unforgettable moment.

Silence in the crowd morphed into a low roar and Jax tapped the microphone. Katrina, Jake, Finn and Luca joined him on stage. He gave them a small nod before he began.

"Agrestis Wolves. Today is a beginning and an end. An evil has been brought to New York. This enemy, these creatures are responsible for my abduction. They practice and utilize an insidious form of black magick, the likes of which I've never seen. The demons, they seek to shift into wolves." Jax inhaled, pleased his pack had snapped back into obedience, listening attentively. Despite Katrina's presence, they hadn't challenged her...yet. "Their goal is to steal the magick that belongs only to wolves. They don't wish to only replicate our human forms. They seek our beasts. The animals that run free within our souls. They seek to infiltrate our packs."

Jax paused to allow the message to take hold, then he continued.

"They have the ability to cause illusions. They lie. And they're here in our state. Our territory. Our woods. Where we run. Where we raise our pups."

As he expected, muffled whispers rumbled through the crowd. He held up a silencing hand.

"They've taken Luca Macquarie's fiancée, Samantha...a witch who's with child. They're also responsible for impersonating and kidnapping Katrina Livingston." Jax drew a breath and reached for his mate, who placed her hand in his. "You may ask, why should I care about Katrina, a Lyceum wolf?"

Jax brought her to his side and wrapped his arm around her waist.

"As many of you know, Agrestis Wolves have endured a contentious past with Lyceum Wolves. My father...some of you lived under his savage reign. You watched as he incited territorial wars, brutalized wolves and humans alike. You watched as he beat his own son. You watched as I returned to challenge him, to kill him, to lead Agrestis Wolves as your Alpha. However, you were not the only wolves who took notice of my father's sins. Tristan Livingston has been rightfully cautious of me over the years. While I have never been my father, nor will I ever be, his heinous acts continue to leave a blemish upon my reputation. So when these demons lied to Katrina, she asked her brother to keep me away from her. Although the untrue rumors proliferated, Katrina only sought to protect me from what she thought would be my certain death. But the fact of the matter is that you cannot deny what nature demands. If it is meant to be, destiny will bring two individuals back together. That's exactly what happened the day I rescued her. You see, Katrina," he smiled at her and turned his focus back to the pack, "she's my mate. The bond is complete."

Silence blanketed the room at his announcement. After he had killed Arlo earlier in the week, most would think twice about challenging his mating. However, when they shifted to wolf, Katrina would have to establish her own dominance.

"I know this may come as a surprise to some of you, given past events, but I can assure you that her heart is true. Our bond is strong. Unbreakable. I'm giving you fair warning that my mate is tenacious. So should any of you choose to challenge her or our bond, it will not end well."

Jax caught the ire that flared in London's eyes. He'd anticipated that quite a few females wouldn't accept their mating and wished to be clear about the situation.

As expected, Katrina remained quiet, deferring to him. At some point, she too, as part of the mated Alpha pair, would direct the pack. Although Katrina was typically friendly, he predicted she'd kill before letting another female take her place at his side.

"Tonight most of you are running wolf. Some of us are taking the ATVs so we can go human when we get there. Finn's going to break you up into teams. I'll need several of you to stay here to mind the pups and protect the pack house," he directed, his voice serious. "These demons and whatever witchcraft is driving these things will die tonight. It is the only acceptable outcome. Be mindful of the vampire who chooses to fight with us. As I mentioned, Samantha, the redheaded witch, is pregnant. If..." He turned to Luca, and restated, "...When we find her, I expect you to protect her as you would one of your own. She can help us fight these things but only if she is allowed to speak. Okay, let's do this shit. I'm ready to get on with leading this pack and I want these fucking things dead and out of my State."

Diabolical energy whipped through the wind, and Jax struggled to concentrate. As they'd journeyed through the forest's edge, Katrina had warned him of the impending storm, but he hadn't asked how she'd known. She appeared unaffected, her arms wrapped around his waist. Ever since their encounter with Jake, her magick had grown more stable. No longer did it seep away, causing her weakness, or to doubt her ability to shift. But neither did it negate the witchcraft that had broken through her psyche.

Thunder rumbled, and Jax gripped the handlebars. He swerved right, as lightning struck a massive white oak tree and uprooted it. It crashed to the ground, and Jax swiveled his head to check that Luca, who had followed his path, was unharmed. The vampire, undeterred, continued to trail behind him. Ahead, Jake and several other pack members trekked as wolf from the north. Finn headed up a second group, intersecting with them from the south.

Jax geared down the engine and slowed as they approached. He suspected whatever was inside the cave would sense their arrival. Both he and Katrina had discussed their experiences and had no recollection of the entrance. They only remembered the general location of where they'd escaped. Jax suspected the dungeon had more than one entry point. He recalled seeing multiple passageways and theorized that in addition to the torture chamber and adjoining cells, they'd discover a room of worship.

The quad came to a stop, and Jax turned to Katrina. She gave him a small smile, pressed her lips to his and jumped off the ATV. He followed her and scanned the area. Through the tainted air, he sensed his pack. His eyes darted back to Luca, who was already off his bike, his fangs extended.

As they approached the cave, the familiar door he'd shoved through to freedom came into view. Set into a thirty foot vertical cliff, the entrance was partially concealed by hanging vines. Although not visible, the whoosh of roaring rapids reminded him that the river flowed not too far away from where they stood.

"Do you feel that?" Katrina asked, gripping her jacket collar tight around her neck.

"Someone's not too happy to see us," Jax replied. Breaking limbs sounded behind him, and he caught sight of Jake and Finn padding toward him.

"Jake, you come with us. Finn, I need you to stay with the pack. There's got to be more than one entrance and exit from this place. I want you guys to find them. Once you do, set up guard."

Finn howled in response and Jake took his place next to Jax.

"Kat, you ready to go with the ring?" On the flight up to New York, they'd discussed how to utilize the items they'd found at Ilsbeth's house. As much as he loathed the idea of letting Katrina get close to the demon, they all suspected that only her magick would kill it. If it weren't for her, they'd have never discovered the mystical objects.

"As ready as I'm ever going to be." She retrieved the antique band from her front jeans pocket and slid it onto her finger.

"If for some reason taking one down doesn't take them all out, then this is going to be a whole helluva lot harder, but either way, we've got this. If we need back up, I'll call on the pack but I don't want to expose them to these things."

"She's here," Luca grunted, his palms pressed flat to the gritty stone. "Oh Jesus, no!"

"What's wrong?" Katrina ran to his side, settling her hands on his shoulders. He trembled beneath her fingertips.

"Sam's in labor. The baby," he screamed. "I've got to get inside."

Jax swung open the heavy door, easily passing into the tunnel. But as Luca went running toward the entrance, he slammed into an invisible barrier. His nose bloodied, he pounded it with his fists, to no avail.

"Wards," Jax noted.

"For Luca?" Katrina asked.

"I don't know. Could be for him or could be all vampires? Or maybe they're only letting us in because they want us here." Jax glanced down the dark passage, and heard the faint whimper of a female. Although he sympathized with Luca's anguish, time was of the essence. If they could free Samantha, it was possible she could release whatever wards had been set up to prevent his entry. "We've gotta go. We'll find her. She and the baby will make it out of here, Luca. Hang tight and keep trying to break through. If we can get to her, she may be able to help us, or when we kill these things, maybe the walls will come down."

"Swear to me." Luca's voice wavered, his eyes closing tight in frustration. Blood ran down his face and he made no move to wipe it clean.

"I swear to you. We'll get her. Just do what I say. We're running out of time." Jax tore off his shirt, readying to shift to wolf. He reached for Katrina's hand, his energy accelerating through his body in tandem with adrenaline. "Let's kill these things."

Chapter Twenty-Five

Katrina breathed in the dank air and fought the fear that threatened her courage. While Jax stripped off his pants and shifted to wolf, she'd peered inside an empty cell and recalled the times she'd been captured, reliving both her fear and rebellion. Never once had she given in, allowed them to break her. Exhausted and racked with pain, she'd endured. Despite the tendrils of trepidation coiling in her chest, she celebrated the chance to mete out justice.

A muffled sob echoed in the distance, and they both took off toward its source. Following Jax, she cautiously navigated the labyrinth. Her steps quickened, seeking the tormented witch who writhed in labor.

As the decades passed, Katrina's dreams of a family had become a painful indulgence, forcing her to accept her childless existence. Admittedly, she'd been envious when she'd first heard Luca and Samantha had conceived. Not only had he fallen in love but he'd been blessed with a family. However, she'd quickly buried the ugly emotion, electing to be happy for her friend. With the child's birth imminent, Katrina was determined to see her safely born into this world. *Samantha can't lose her baby.*

A pinprick of light flared in the distance, and Katrina's lungs burned as she sprinted toward the fluorescent rainbow. Jax and Jake ran ahead, barking in warning. As she stepped into the enormous stone cavern, she squinted, the luminous bursts ceding. Although confused as to what had caused the temporary explosion, Katrina concentrated on her task: finding Samantha.

She stepped carefully into the atrium, taking in her surroundings. Candlelit luminaries flickered, illuminating magnificent hovering stalactites. Like ominous spears of death, the sharp limestone dripped from the ceiling. In the center of the room, she caught sight of a darkened pit. Katrina spied a glass-encased cell, with a crumpled form lying in the corner. At first she thought it was the witch but as she approached she noticed the emaciated figure couldn't possibly be pregnant.

A moan stole her attention, and Katrina's chest tightened as she caught sight of Samantha agonizing on the bedrock floor. Wide tear-filled eyes stared back at her and she dropped to her knees. Reaching for the duct tape, Katrina attempted to remove it gently. Samantha's hands were bloodied from clutching at the dirt. Jax's familiar black wolf padded toward the witch and licked at her brow. Transforming to his human form, he knelt beside her.

"Sam, it's okay," Katrina lied, concerned they were far from safe. As she sat at her feet, the black magick spun in the air and she was certain the demons would soon show themselves.

"The baby," Samantha cried. She clutched at her belly, doubling over as a contraction seized her body.

"We should get you out of here." Jax brushed her hair from her eyes.

"No, no, no…too late…ahh!" Samantha released an ear-piercing scream as the pain tore through her. "I'm going to die."

"Listen to me, Sam. I've lived a long time. I've seen babies born before, and we're going to do this together. You and your baby are going to be fine. You understand?" Katrina locked her eyes on Jax in silent understanding. It had been years since she'd witnessed a birth, but given the circumstance, they had no choice. She glanced to Samantha, waiting for Jax to send her his energy. The power of an Alpha could usually only be felt by wolves, but she hoped for the best as Jax put his hands on her shoulders. "I'm just going to check you here, okay? Just let me have a peek and see how far you are along."

"Where's Luca? I can feel him. Oh Goddess, he needs to be here. I need him. Help me," Samantha cried. "She's coming."

"Yes, she is. She's going to be strong and beautiful, just like her mamma." Katrina lifted Samantha's skirt, taking note that she was almost fully dilated. "This baby is going to be coming any minute."

"Luca? Where is he?"

"There's wards. He's locked out."

"Oh Goddess. It's a trap. It's a trap," Samantha panted. "He's here."

"It's going to be all right."

"Jax!" Jake's voice boomed across the cave.

"Kind of busy here," Jax replied.

"Dominique. She's in this…uh." Jake rapped on the glass with his fist. "It's some kind of a cage. I can't tell if she's dead or not."

"Sam, are you with me?" Katrina asked. It wasn't as if she didn't care about the female vampire, but a new soul was about to be born, and the child was her first priority. "I'm going to need you to push soon. Jax, just, I don't know….can you keep her head off the ground? Whatever you're doing with your energy, keep doing it. She seems calmer. Okay, let's get ready…" Katrina's voice died away as a flash burst from the center of the room.

Samantha rolled to her side, and Jax shifted back to his wolf. Katrina caught a glimpse of Avery teetering across the rocky surface. While she'd known the witch probably had something to do with Samantha's disappearance, her eye had been blackened and she appeared to be more of a victim than a perpetrator.

"Leave her alone," Avery spat at the cloud of dust that began to take form.

Katrina coughed, fine particulates drifting up into the air. She stretched the edge of her t-shirt over her nose and mouth, using it as a mask. Flecks of light danced, a human shape constructing itself before their eyes.

"So nice of you to join us, Kitty Kat," it cackled.

Mick. Katrina's stomach clenched, nausea setting in as she realized what was happening. The warlock spun in a circle, holding his palms upward; bolts of electricity fired up toward the ceiling, causing rocks to tumble down onto them. Shirtless and barefoot, he wore only black slacks.

"You should see the look on your face." Mick slowed his pace, spewing maniacal laughter. Abruptly, he went quiet and faced Avery, his eyes blazing in anger. "This is none of your concern."

"You promised. You said you wouldn't hurt her." As if she were drunk, Avery's footing slipped, weaving as she walked toward Samantha.

"What the fuck are you doing?" Katrina screamed at him.

As Mick set his sights on the females, Jax and Jake attacked. The warlock whispered, flinging his hands toward them, causing a mesh of silver netting to fall from above. Both wolves shifted to their human forms, groaning as they attempted to dislodge the web of toxic metal. Katrina's heart dropped as Jax struggled. He shook his head at her, warning her off. In response to his command, she stayed put.

Samantha released a blood-curdling screech, and Katrina focused on the witch. The baby's head was exposed, crowning the birth canal; the child would be born any minute.

"Sam, I need you to push," Katrina told her in a gentle tone of voice, forced to ignore her mate's capture.

"That's right, push, push away, witch," Mick hissed, hovering above them.

"Stay away from us," Katrina ordered, giving him a brief glare.

"There was a time I was happy partying in the bars, fucking whoever I wanted," he pondered, pacing back and forth. "But Ilsbeth, she helped me see the light."

"Don't touch her," Jax grunted, weakened from the silver.

"You see, the greedy little bitch had to have Dimitri. Yeah, he fucked her good, all right. She couldn't stop talking about him." Mick paused to pick up a sharp rock and hurled it at Jake. "What she saw in him, I'll never know. You wolves are so self-righteous with your pack mentality. The challenges. Submission. The brutality of it all. So uncivilized." He sighed and rolled his eyes, continuing. "Ilsbeth always wanted what she couldn't have. She couldn't handle the fact that he'd find his mate. She was desperate. Pathetic."

"That's it, Sam. Don't hold your breath. Take a breath and blow it out. You've got this." Katrina tried to ignore his oration, but she'd always known this had been tied to Ilsbeth.

"But to steal magick from wolves," Mick kicked Jax in the stomach, pleased as the Alpha spat blood, "it's not very simple. No, no, no. One must find alternatives to spells. In my defense, she asked for my assistance. She needed a very special kind of ingredient to kill Dimitri's wolf. So you see…. demons, they can be very useful at times."

Katrina concentrated on the baby as her shoulders breached.

"It's interesting, that saying, 'be careful what you wish for'. Ilsbeth got what she wanted. She almost was successful too. But I've always been one to make the most of a party. Of course the demon wanted something from me in return. A vessel. But I'm no fool. I'd never let that happen. I didn't need another master, and demons don't exactly take orders from witches. They can, however, be tricked into teaching us their secrets. Ah….what I learned to do…" He laughed and danced in celebration. "I have learned how to transform myself. Others, too. Sometimes it's an illusion, sometimes it's as real as I'm standing here. The vampire," he pressed a palm to the glass cell and gave a depraved smile, "she was my first. It was so easy to steal her magick. The demon taught me well. Little experiments here and there. I was even able to turn little Avery here into a human, to have her do my bidding. She always enjoyed the fine art of torture. The last time she came for you. Ah, how she loved to hear you scream. Too bad she's been such a disappointment as of late."

"Ilsbeth caught you." Jax clawed at the netting, scraping a section away from his arm.

"Perhaps. But she started it all. I did what she asked. She got what she wanted. Dimitri. The thing is, she didn't care for my methods. When I showed her all that could be done here," Mick gestured to Dominique, "she wasn't as enamored with what I'd created, my transformation. So you can imagine when she saw Katrina. That day, oh, the lecture she gave. I suspect that's when she gave you a slice of her magick. She retreated into the boring purist bullshit she loved so much. A sly little spell, I'll give her that. That ring she gave you…"

"Belongs to me," Katrina retorted.

"Not for long, my dear. How I do wish I could have taken it from you in New Orleans, but her magick is strong. Ilsbeth cursed it."

"Protected it," Jax countered.

"You say tomato, I say fucking bitch…blah, blah, blah," he trilled. "Clever priestess. You would have known if I'd tried to steal it. I could feel Ilsbeth's vibe all over it. So of course, I imparted wisdom that day. Because I'm helpful like that. And the filthy animals you are, you think only of sex…the bonding. It's like training dogs."

"Why let us bond? You knew it would strengthen me," Katrina asked.

"The demon, let's not speak its name, shall we? Its energy…it feels *so* good." Mick ran his fingers down his chest, waggling his shoulders in a delightful shiver. "You know what it's like, don't you, Kitty Kat? Because I put a little of it in you. Took me a few times of capturing you before I realized how to perfect my magick. But I've had one tiny problem. It's like a beer tap. Tap on. Tap off. Well, I suppose it didn't work as well as I planned, because even though you sucked magick from the Alpha, it leaked like piss. But seeing you with your Alphas…ah, all the pieces came together. Your leak has stopped, hasn't it?"

Katrina turned her head, averting her gaze. She wouldn't give him the gratification of telling him that what he'd suggested had worked.

"No need to answer. I can already feel it."

"She's almost here." Katrina blinked, eyeing Mick out of her peripheral vision as he approached from behind.

"But the wolves, shifting into an animal is quite difficult. It takes a great deal of magick. Alpha magick. It's not easy to kidnap and keep an Alpha, as proved the case with Jax. But Katrina? You've been so easy to catch. Like a little fishy, I capture and release, capture and release. The only trouble is…ah, Katrina, these past couple of years…must you have been so difficult?"

Mick yanked her braid, jerking her head backward so he could glare into her eyes. The stinging pain to her scalp came swiftly. Her eyes widened in disgust as his lips crushed on hers. The stench of his rancid breath rushed into her nostrils, the sour taste of him choking her as he forced his tongue into her mouth. She shoved at his chin with the heel of her hand, thrusting him away, but not before his teeth bit at her lip, drawing blood. She thought to use the ring to slash at him but Samantha wailed, diverting her attention.

"Get your fucking hands off of her," Jax growled, his body half freed.

Mick's evil laughter echoed in her ears, and she willed herself not to cry. Unwilling to give him the satisfaction of her tears, Katrina spat iron-tinged saliva onto the dirt, and focused on her task, carefully guiding the baby into the world.

"Don't worry, Kitty Kat. You'll die soon enough. I think, maybe I'll fuck you first. After seeing your little display at the club, I've got some plans for you. That's right, you know I'm good at the torture. I was very satisfied up until recently." He cast an ugly stare at Avery, who clutched at the wall for support. "I can think of at least a half dozen things I'd like to do with that pussy of yours before I kill you." Mick glared at Katrina, his eager eyes watching as the witch labored. "I've always planned on killing you, but then sometimes a plan comes together perfectly. My dear Samantha, you're ripening for me. Birthing a first witch. So I thought 'why just take Katrina and the Alphas when I can kill the child and take her magick too?'"

"Don't listen to him, Sam," Katrina said, her voice strong and calm. She'd die before allowing this asshole to take the child.

Samantha quietly chanted as she pushed.

"Your spells won't work here, witch. The only reason I taped that pretty little mouth shut was so I didn't have to hear you cry." He sniffed. "After tonight, I will have all the magick I ever needed to be able to shift into a wolf. A true wolf, not just their human form. Whenever I want, wherever I want, I will run as beast. Taking over the packs will be a challenge but as I teach other worthy mages, it will happen. Humans. Vampires. Witches. Wolves. There will be no domain that is not under my control."

"You'll never get away with it." Jax struggled for freedom, his legs twitching.

"Let's see." Mick tilted his head and held two fingers to his temple. "I've located a very special wolf. The daughter, sister and mate of an Alpha. I've stolen her magick…learned how to siphon it and store it. Now, I've captured two Alphas and a witch. I'm able to transform into multiple beings at once."

In a flash, seven men appeared. All different ages and races, their eyes empty orbs, black pits. *Demons*. He snapped his fingers and they dissipated. Katrina fought the bile that rushed up her throat. The beings that had tortured her were all part of Mick.

"That's right, Kat. I've become very powerful."

"Neat trick, asshole, but tonight you're going to die," Jax yelled, attempting to redirect his focus away from Katrina.

Samantha gave a final guttural scream, and Katrina eased the baby into her arms, tears streaming down her face. In the midst of evil, the child's newfound magick thrummed, the innocence in her energy rushing through her skin.

"You did it, Sam. Oh Goddess, she's so beautiful." Katrina cleared the infant's mouth with her fingers, and she began to cry for her mother.

As she leaned to put the newborn into Samantha's outstretched arms, Mick stomped toward them. Katrina quickly rested the child onto the witch's chest, and moved to place herself in front of them. Fumbling with the ring, she never took her eyes off of Mick. She flicked at the latch and released the small lancet. *You want me, bastard? Come closer.*

Unexpectedly, Avery ran to Mick and shoved at him with her palms. "No. You promised to leave the baby alone. You swore, just the wolves. Just the wolves!"

Katrina screamed as Mick transformed into the scaly creature she'd witnessed under the docks. Its shiny bladed tail whizzed through the air, slicing straight through Avery's frail neck. Her head whirled across the cavern, blood spraying in a circular motion. The sanguine flecks splattered across Katrina's cheek.

Her eyes widened in amazement as the ancient vampire flashed into view. Katrina jumped to her feet and tore off her jacket, waving it at Mick. Diverting the creature's attention, she lured it toward her, its clawed feet scraping the rocks.

"About fucking time," Jax grumbled.

"Sorry, amico." Quintus reached for the silver netting with his gloved hands and shoved it aside, freeing Jax and then Jake. "Wasn't a picnic getting in here. Lucky for you I'm smooth with the ladies."

"Fuck," the Alpha breathed and promptly shifted, needing to clear the poison from his system.

"Well, yes. Fucking is usually how it's done, but sometimes I can just ask nicely. Some witches can be quite friendly," the vampire quipped.

"Hey, over here, asshole," Katrina yelled at Mick. Slicing the blade down her hand, she concealed the pain. She fingered the gem until it flipped open and smeared the white powdery substance inside over her palms and the knife.

The creature turned its head, realizing the Alpha had been freed. Its tail whipped toward the wolves, and Katrina seized the moment, lunging at its back. Wrapping her legs around the creature, she held tight and brought the ring to its neck. The small but deadly lancet carved through the rough scales like a laser. Katrina slid the ring off her finger, embedding it deep into the beast's throat. It screeched in pain and bucked at the intrusion, flinging her into the air. She landed on the dirt with a thud. Her lungs burned as she shook off the shock, but was given no reprieve as it lunged for her.

Jax leapt onto the demon, his jaws lodging into its neck, tearing at its flesh. It retaliated, scoring the Alpha's back with its talons. Jax howled in pain but refused to let it attack Katrina. Jake struggled to embed his fangs in its legs, and it whipped its tail at the wolf's paw, forcing him to release.

Katrina screamed in horror as its razor sharp tail slashed past Jake, narrowly missing his neck. The savage beast hissed as the poison took hold. Wheezing and spurting blood, it swung its tail at Katrina. Although she'd partially shifted, it caught her torso, slicing its blade clean through her abdomen.

Struck by the searing demon, she stumbled back onto the rocks and fell to the ground. Her magick leaked out with her blood, and she surrendered, helpless to fight as Mick siphoned her essence away. Despite the demon's attempt to heal itself with her energy, it continued to thrash, its form shifting from beast to man and back to beast once again. Lying immobile, Katrina blinked, watching in fascination as the creature squealed in agony. Splintering, it crumbled into hundreds of pieces, falling into the pit. She smiled as Jax's familiar blue eyes came into view.

"Kat, baby. No, don't leave me…I need you. I love you. Please Goddess, no," she heard him tell her.

Don't cry, my Alpha, she thought, his tears warming her face. With no discernible spirit inside her wolf, Katrina submitted to the inevitable. Death beckoned, its peaceful blanket embracing her in its arms.

"I love you," she whispered.

Final words, she would never regret giving her life for her Alpha, for the child. As the light called for her, she prayed Jax would find love again.

Chapter Twenty-Six

Jax gingerly placed Katrina's body onto the grass and cradled her head to his chest. The turbulent spring weather had calmed, the sky clearing, stars shining bright. His wolf howled uncontrollably as the grief crushed his chest. Being Alpha was all Jax had known up until the moment he'd met Katrina Livingston. He'd never anticipated the soulful connection he'd forge with his mate. A life-altering experience, the incredible female now consumed his thoughts.

"I love you so much." Numb, he rocked Katrina, whispering in her ear as if she were still alive. Her wolf completely gone, there was no detectable magick left within her beautiful spirit. Ignoring Jake's plea to release her, he'd lost track of time, refusing to let her body go.

A baby's cry broke his trance, and he lifted his gaze to the redheaded witch his mate had died saving. Samantha carefully knelt beside him, Luca supporting her arms as she joined him. Wrapped in Katrina's leather jacket, the infant quieted in his presence.

"She needs her," Samantha stated.

"Kat's gone." Jax turned his focus back to his mate, brushing his lips to her cool forehead.

"Kate. We named her after Katrina," she told him.

Jax sucked back a sob. While he appreciated the gesture, he couldn't bring himself to say a word. His thoughts spiraled. After he buried his mate, he'd step down as Alpha and become a lone wolf. There was nothing left for him to give anyone. Not his friends, not his pack.

"Katrina needs her. Please Jax," Samantha pressed.

"I...I can't right now," Jax managed. His bloodshot eyes met hers, tears fresh on his face.

"Her magick..."

"It's gone. She's gone," he cried. "Sam, look, I need to be alone with her and say goodbye. Please..."

"Katrina needs Kate," Samantha repeated.

With no fight left, confusion twisted through him as she reached for Katrina's hand. Her limp arm rolled onto the grass and he choked as her lifeless fingers touched the ground.

"No...what are you doing? You need to leave her alone," Jax pleaded.

"Just please, let me do this," Samantha told him, her voice calm.

Jax licked the salty moisture from his lips, perplexed by her actions. She unwrapped the child and kissed her forehead. Samantha smiled up at Luca and gently placed the baby onto Katrina's chest. As the infant cooed against his mate, he immediately sensed the surge of magick tingling through Katrina's fingertips.

"What is she doing?" He wore a stunned expression, his eyes widening at the sensation.

"Our little Kate is very powerful, much more powerful than most witches suspect. But Mick, he must have done his research. He knew what kind of magick our special miracle would bring to this world." Samantha set her palm to the Alpha's cheek. "It's true that Katrina's magick was siphoned. But our little Kate, she didn't let him have it. She took it. It's inside her. And now," she smiled to Katrina, whose chest rose in a shallow breath, "her magick has been restored."

Jax, too tired to argue with Samantha, closed his eyes. Emotionally and physically exhausted, he threaded his fingers through Katrina's, a scant quiver of life flittering over his skin. Jax jolted upright, observing his mate's eyelids flutter.

"Jax," Katrina breathed, a loud gasp escaping her lips.

"Kat," Jax cried. His palm grazed over the baby's back in amazement. "How did she do that?"

"She's a very special child. A first witch. An old soul." Samantha scooped the infant into her arms, giving him a broad knowing smile. "Luca and I are going to have our hands full with little Kate."

"Sam…tell me this is real," Jax blinked, terrified to believe his own ears and eyes.

"It's okay, Jax. She needs to shift. You're her Alpha. Call to her." Samantha focused on her infant, playing with her tiny fingers.

"Baby, can you hear me?" Jax gave a small laugh as Katrina squeezed his hand. A small smile formed on her lips. "That's it. Oh Goddess…"

"My Alpha…" She wheezed, a hand moving to her bloodied abdomen. "I feel awful."

"You need to shift," he told her.

"Help me," she managed.

Jax carefully removed her clothing. Shocked Katrina was alive, he lifted her into his embrace. Skin to skin, their energies merged. He smiled as she opened her eyes, his chest tightening in emotion.

"Let's go for a run, little wolf." With a gentle kiss, he breathed in relief as Katrina shifted. The small white wolf gave a bark and he laughed.

"You're beautiful," he told her and transformed, freeing his beast.

Elated, he sprinted, quickly catching up to Katrina. Full of life, she pranced under the moon, her shiny coat reflecting its light. Within seconds the pack surrounded them, and concern they'd challenge her so soon after her recovery surfaced. Establishing her rightful rank within the group, Katrina stared down each and every member. Her ears and tail erect, she stood firm, refusing to back away. Asserting her dominance, she ran a circle around her mate. Jax gave a bark and was pleased as his wolves lowered their bodies in submission to their Alpha pair.

Satisfied, he howled in celebration, but his exhilaration was short-lived as an unfamiliar wolf answered. Katrina took off toward the rustling leaves, in search of the intruder. He cursed, promising to continue her lessons in submission. Within seconds, he surpassed her stride, and was not surprised at his first scent of the wolf. *Tristan.*

Jax hesitated, seeing the great brown wolf tear through the forest. Although Tristan was formidable, the Alpha knew he'd crush him. Jax glanced back to Katrina. The joy in her eyes was soon replaced with fear as her brother ran directly toward her mate, and she realized he planned on attacking.

The black Alpha growled in warning but it didn't deter Tristan. The Lyceum wolf lunged at Jax, and they both barreled down an embankment. As they settled at the creek's edge, Jax's nature demanded he take action. Tristan attempted to lodge his teeth into the Alpha's neck, but Jax easily maneuvered out of reach. Refusing to back down, Jax had little choice but to force him into submission. Leveraging a strong paw into Tristan's flank, he shoved his opponent into the mud, his fangs settling into the soft fur of his throat. Katrina would never forgive him if he killed her brother. He exercised restraint and snarled rather than tearing open his skin.

"Let him go!" Jax heard the panicked voice of his mate call to him.

His eyes darted up to Katrina, who had taken on her human form. Wolves from both packs stood on alert, but didn't dare to intervene.

"Tristan, stop this. He's my mate." Katrina cautiously walked toward them and held her hand to her brother's snout. Tristan sniffed and licked at her fingers, and she fell to her knees, placing her palms on each wolf. "Our mating is meant to be…Goddess, please stop."

Sensing the shift in Tristan as the Lyceum wolf calmed, Jax released him. Waiting for him to shift first, he followed as Tristan shoved to his feet.

"I'm not going to let him do this to you, Kat," Tristan began.

"Tris…I already explained this to you when I called. I know you haven't gotten along with Jax. Please. The past is the past. He doesn't run his pack like his father. He's not like that." Katrina glanced to her Alpha and back to her brother. "I love you, but I'm not letting Jax go. You need to accept this. This male is mine. He belongs to me."

It was a serious moment, but it struck Jax as funny how bluntly she spoke to Tristan. Unable to restrain his emotion, he laughed and shook his head at her words. *This woman is going to kill me, and I'm going to love every goddamned minute,* he thought. Her dominance would not be mistaken by a single wolf in either pack. An Alpha's mate through and through, she spoke her mind with truth and conviction and no one would mess with her.

"What's so fucking funny?" Tristan asked, smearing the mud from his eye.

"Apple. Tree." Jax shrugged and winked at Katrina. "Or in this case.

Apple." He pointed to Tristan and then his mate. "Apple. She's pretty awesome, isn't she?"

"What kind of mate did you think you'd end up with, my Alpha?" she purred with a sexy smile.

"Ah fuck." Tristan sighed and threw his head backward, his hands on his hips.

"What?" Katrina pressed.

"You really are mated for real, aren't you?"

"Yes, of course I am." She laughed. "I keep trying to tell you that."

"I've only ever wanted to see you happy," Tristan insisted.

"I love you, Tris. I'm sorry for everything that happened. You need to know that Jax isn't his father. I love him."

Tristan stared at Jax for a long minute and extended his hand. "Don't hurt her."

"I will protect her with my life. I promise you." Jax clasped his palm, giving it a firm shake, but his attention was quickly drawn to his mate.

A broad smile crossed his face, his heart pounding so hard he thought it'd explode. *I love her so much.* Strong and compassionate, she professed her feelings for him, her statement spoken loud enough for every wolf to hear.

Without a care as to what anyone thought, Jax released Tristan and reached for Katrina, pulling her into his embrace. Passion for his mate flooded his chest as his lips captured hers. The sound of wolves serenading echoed through the trees, and Jax lost himself in the moment, so in love with the little wolf who owned his heart.

~ Chapter Twenty-Seven ~

Katrina took a deep breath, willing the butterflies in her stomach into submission. She glanced in the long mirror, and adjusted the edge of the plunging neckline. Sleeveless, the black ribbing fit her like a glove, the silver pleated skirt flowed easily, its hem brushing her calves. She reached for her lipstick, and smiled, pleased that her auburn locks had returned. Upon Mick's death, fully healed, she no longer experienced the foreign magick.

Twisting the gloss upward, she gently applied it to her lips, grateful that she'd not only met her mate but that they'd both made it out of that hellhole alive. It wasn't until after she'd quelled her brother's fears that they'd returned to the cave. Jake, not belonging to either pack, had stayed to watch over Dominique. The extent of her friend's compassion never ceased to amaze Katrina. Despite his misgivings, he'd fed the vampire, assuring her survival. While his blood had instantly regenerated her body, Dominique remained despondent.

Because she was sired of Kade Issacson, he'd been contacted right away. But it was Quintus who'd offered to return her to New Orleans. Under any other circumstances, she and Jax might not have agreed to the transportation arrangement. Given her condition, however, Jax permitted the ancient vampire to assist them.

As planned, Jake had set off the C-4 explosives, collapsing the entrances to the cavern. Without inspection, it was difficult to ascertain the condition of the interior, but the former Navy SEAL assured them no one would ever be able to enter. Katrina prayed to the Goddess that whatever demon Mick had summoned had been entombed forever.

The reality was that if he'd allowed it to breach the earthly realm once to grant favors, there was no guarantee it hadn't escaped. A deal with the devil was not one where the debtor set the terms. It was likely he'd overestimated his ability, bringing a great atrocity into the world. At Jax's request, they'd conducted an ecumenical service to bless the land and restore it. The ministers, from both human and supernatural religions, had assured them the area had been cleaned. Cautiously optimistic, Jax had allowed wolves to run on the property.

Thoughts of Ilsbeth haunted Katrina. Although her magick no longer sang in her body, she couldn't help but wonder what had happened to the witch. Mick had never disclosed what he'd done to her but whatever it was, Katrina suspected she'd met a torturous existence. Not convinced Ilsbeth was dead, she'd hired a private detective to search for the witch.

Neither Jax nor Jake had been pleased, but they'd accepted that Katrina sought closure. Despite the high priestess's heinous attack on Dimitri, she'd gone to great lengths to help Katrina, which had led to Mick's demise. Convinced the witch regretted her actions, she wished she could thank her.

Katrina's mind drifted to Jake, who'd asked to stay in Jax's remote cabin. While she'd thought it odd he didn't immediately return to New Orleans, she suspected Jax had influenced his decision. An Alpha, Jake would have to decide his own fate. Now that Jax had called him out on leaving his San Diego pack, he'd been given confirmation of what he'd probably known all along. Katrina understood the conflict, having grown up in New Orleans. It had been difficult moving to Philadelphia. Taking her rightful place with her Alpha in New York City, she drew comfort from knowing they'd visit and stay in their French Quarter home on occasion.

Katrina dabbed her lips with a tissue, and wondered what Jax had planned. They'd been home for a week, and he'd worked nonstop, catching up on business. When she'd come home from her new gallery, she'd found a note on the bed instructing her to meet him on the roof at seven. It was the one place in the penthouse he hadn't allowed her to see yet, and she suspected he'd been planning something special ever since they'd returned to the city.

Remarkably adventurous, her Alpha had a delightful habit of taking her off guard. She'd learned not to expect anything but the unexpected. Falling for the charismatic wolf had been easy, but since the night of her death, they hadn't professed their love to each other. Although disappointed they hadn't exchanged the sentiment, she'd never doubted his commitment. Aware of how Nick's death had affected Jax, she'd patiently wait for him to open his heart fully. There was no place else on the entire Earth she'd rather be than in his arms.

Wearing the dress he'd laid out for her, Katrina stepped into the elevator and pushed the button. As she arrived and the door slid open, she smiled, hearing Mozart play into the night air. The sight of her Alpha took her breath away. Katrina's eyes were drawn to his clean-shaven face. Sophisticated and debonair, he'd dressed in a suit and tie, his hair once again styled short.

"My queen." Jax extended his hand with a broad smile.

As Katrina placed her palm in his, she gave a nervous laugh. The sexual tension sizzled between them as her skin touched his. Her face heated, and she brushed her fingertips over her cheek. As he led her out onto the veranda, she smiled, taking in the gorgeous scene.

White cushioned outdoor furniture sat adjacent to a stone column corner fireplace. The spectacular space had been designed with a modern flair yet the potted trees and plants gave a warm impression. Her heels tapped along the marble floor, and she noted a section of grass on the far side of the patio. In the center, a rectangular pool sparkled, a series of fountains dancing upward.

Her eyes went to a set table, and she smiled, realizing he'd planned dinner.

As she turned to Jax, she accepted a glass of champagne.

"A toast?" His eyes darted to the string quartet. "The classics always were my favorite. Eine Kleine Nachtmusik."

"A Little Night Music. It's beautiful," she replied.

"We think alike, my sweet mate." He held his glass to the air. "To a thousand more nights together."

"I'm looking forward to it." She gave a sexy smile, the effervescent drink bubbling over her tongue.

"Come." Jax winked as he took her glass, setting it aside.

Katrina breathed deeply. Aroused simply from being in his presence, she couldn't conceal her attraction.

As he swept her into his arms, she sighed. Within his embrace, she rested her head onto his chest, breathing in the masculine scent of her mate. His freshly showered skin registered first, a faint touch of cologne detectible, its mint and lemon scent adding to his allure. She resisted the urge to rub against him as his hand caressed her lower back, teasing her bottom. Dancing slowly, offbeat to the music, her body ignited in desire.

"Jax." She lifted her head to make eye contact with her sexy wolf. "This is beautiful."

"I wanted it special for you…for us." He glanced to the fountains. "The pool has always been here, but the rest? I worked on it this week."

"What?" Her eyes widened at his confession.

"This place…uh, Nick and I…we used to come up here. We'd have a drink. A cigar. Guy stuff." Jax looked to the furnishings and back to Katrina. "It was time for a change. You deserve a home, Kat."

"We'll make a home together." Katrina's breath caught as he turned serious.

"Everything I have. Everything I ever will be…it's yours. Always."

"Jax…I…"

"Katrina," Jax paused and gestured to the musicians. They ceased playing, but within minutes of them leaving, the music continued, filtering through speakers. Her Alpha took her hand and placed her palm to his chest, his eyes locked on hers. "You are everything to me. How I feel…" He laughed and continued. "I feel amazing. I never knew what it would be like to find you. When we first met…that rush? I can still remember feeling obsessed. And when you didn't want me, I was so angry. I couldn't understand how it could be possible to have this chemistry with someone…it was so strong. It didn't make sense that you couldn't be my mate."

"I'm sorry…"

"Making love with you. Finding out you are my mate. Getting to know you…falling for you…I told you when you were sleeping." He smiled. "When you died."

"Told me what?"

"I love you, Kat. I've never met anyone like you and I never will. I love you more than I ever thought was possible."

"Jax…" She smiled, her heart melting.

"I should have told you I loved you when we got back but I just wanted it to be special. I wanted you to remember this moment forever. No death. No evil. Just you and me." He glanced to the cityscape and back to Katrina. "I want to share my life with you."

"I love you, too." Katrina's eyes fell to his lips then returned to his eyes. "You are the only one I've ever loved…will ever love."

"I love you." Jax leaned in toward her, closing the distance between them.

"Jax…" her words were silenced as his lips took hers.

Katrina wrapped her arms around his neck, drowning in his passionate kiss. His soft mouth made love to hers, his tongue seeking and tasting. Breathless, she gasped as he broke contact, his heated gaze undressing her.

Without speaking he led her over to the edge of the lawn, and circled around her to her back. His strong hands weighed down onto her shoulders, his fingertips stroking the hollow of her neck.

"You look stunning tonight."

Katrina went still, recognizing the dominant tone in his voice, his erection brushing her bottom. His warm breath teased her ear.

"I love this dress on you, but there's a problem with it, I'm afraid."

"What…I…" The sound of her zipper being undone silenced her. She smiled, aware of what her devious wolf had planned.

"Your skin…it's," Jax trailed his tongue behind her ear, eliciting a barely audible moan, "delicious."

Gooseflesh broke over her skin as he peppered kisses onto her neck and hooked his thumbs over the thin straps, drawing the fabric away. The cocktail dress pooled at her feet. Bared, her nipples hardened into points, the cool evening air caressing them like a lover.

"No bra?" he growled, nipping her shoulder. "And what is this fine surprise?"

A broad smile broke across Katrina's face. She'd bought the panties especially for her Alpha. A thong designed of delicate crystals hung low on her hips by black satin ribbons, adorning her as if she were wearing a necklace.

Like a panther he stalked around Katrina, and drank in the sight of his mate. The feral look in his eyes sent a jolt to her pussy and her thighs tensed.

"For me?" He smiled and raised a questioning eyebrow at her.

"Only for you," she responded, her voice breathy.

She sighed as he cupped her cheeks, his thumb tracing over her bottom lip. Darting her tongue over his fingers, she sucked it.

"You are a naughty, little wolf, aren't you?"

"On the contrary, Alpha. I'm very, very good."

"I'm not sure about that. After all, you have caused our dinner to be delayed."

"Hungry?"

She gasped, as his hands moved to her waist. With lightning-fast speed, he pressed his lips between her breasts.

"Jax, ah…"

"I'm ravenous." Taking her swollen peak between his teeth, he tugged it.

Katrina cried out. The sweet pain morphed to pleasure, his tongue laving and sucking. He focused his attention on her other breast and she stabbed her fingers through his hair.

"And this…"

She sucked a breath as he tugged on the strings, and the gems pattered against the stone floor. He dropped to his knees, and she blinked, never once caring that she stood bare in the night.

"No clothing will ever be as beautiful as this," he told her.

Katrina's head lolled back as Jax dragged his tongue through her wet slit.

"That feels…yes," she managed. Wearing only her heels, she widened her stance, seeking his touch.

"So fucking sexy," he hummed. "And this…"

"Ahh…" Katrina tightened her grip on his hair. Her clit tingled as he sucked it into his mouth, and her body quivered in response.

"I love every single part of you, baby. You taste," he drove two thick fingers up inside her, "so good."

Unrelenting, his wicked tongue lashed over her swollen nub. As his fingers curled inside her, grazing the thin strip of nerves, Katrina screamed in ecstasy. Her release came fast and strong. She teetered in her pumps, struggling to remain balanced. Jax's hand clutched her hip, steadying her.

She heaved for breath, her heart pounding in her chest like she'd run a marathon. As he raised his eyes to meet hers, she shivered, watching in fascination as he smiled. With slow deliberation, he dragged his tongue up through her seam, pressing his lips to her mound.

"Jax…make love to me," she breathed.

He pushed to his feet, taking her in his arms. His mouth descended on hers, and their lips collided in a desperate attempt to become one. Their tongues intertwined, and Katrina swore she could feel his love through every cell of her body. His savage kiss drove her wild, and she tore at his jacket, tossing it to the floor. Within seconds, she'd removed his tie. Desperate to have him inside her, she tore at his shirt, buttons scattering across the tiles.

They fell to their knees onto the soft grass, and he kicked off his pants. She reached for her prize, gripping his hard cock in her hand.

"Katrina," he called into her lips as she stroked him.

Taking control, Jax flipped her onto her back. A small cry escaped her as he settled between her thighs, his broad head prodding her core. She wrapped her legs around his, urging him to take her. As he slammed inside, she moaned, her fingers clawing down his back.

"Ah, Kat," Jax laughed into her mouth. "You're a dangerous woman."

"You feel so good."

Jax rocked out and thrust back inside her slick channel. "I fucking love you."

"I love you too...don't stop...just like that...keep going. Ah..."

"Hmm...bossy little mate."

"Fuck me." Katrina smiled in his lips as he plunged inside her, increasing his pace. "Yes, yes..."

Jax tore his mouth from hers to gaze into her eyes. He wrapped his fist into her loose locks that had come undone. The twinge of pain focused her attention and she tilted her hips up to his. Thrust for thrust, his pelvis grazed over her clit, her orgasm building. Feral, she dug her nails into his ass and he cried out. The sound of flesh smacking flesh echoed in her ears as he fucked her even harder.

With each forceful stroke, Jax pounded into her, hurling her over the edge. Helpless to fight the wave of ecstasy, she surrendered. Trembling, her thighs tightened around him, bringing him deeper inside her.

With a guttural cry, her Alpha stiffened against her. He slowly made love to her lips, refusing to separate from his mate. Katrina reveled in his branding kiss, a reminder that she belonged to him. Infinitely connected, their energy merged, forever as one.

"I love you," she whispered, her voice cracking with emotion. She smiled against his bare chest, her heart bursting with happiness.

Jax Chandler. Her dominant, loving Alpha commanded her heart and soul. She'd waited centuries to find him and had almost lost it all...her life, her mate. Within his arms, Katrina smiled up at the stars, her love for Jax certain and true. *My Alpha.*

Jax smiled as Katrina cuddled into his embrace, his heart crushing with emotion. He breathed in the ambrosial scent of his mate and pressed his lips to her hair. Intoxicated with love, he accepted the loss of control that came with loving someone so completely.

A lifetime of thinking he'd happily go through life unmated had been proven utterly ridiculous. He inwardly laughed, realizing that as Alpha he'd insisted on her submission, all the while knowing that she'd done the same to him. Fiery and tenacious, Katrina completed him. Exuberant that he'd found his mate, the beast celebrated its glorious bond.

She stirred in his arms and he peered into her eyes, still laden with passion.

"I could sleep here all night," she told him, her small hand caressing his chest.

"Hmm...me too. You can't see the stars as well as in the country, though," he noted. "We never did eat dinner."

"Why did you put in all this grass? It's super soft."

"You mean it wasn't obvious?"

"Somehow I don't think you planned for us to make love on it."

"I had every intention of making it though dinner." Jax laughed. A romantic evening was as far as he'd thought. Telling her he loved her had been special but he should have anticipated that he wouldn't have been able to control his libido around his mate. She'd looked spectacular in the dress he'd bought for her, but hell, she'd looked even more amazing wearing only heels. "Did I tell you how beautiful you are?"

"Hmm…I love you in that suit. So handsome," she purred. "Seeing how hot you look, I might have to make you go to the office in gym shorts. Those girls go crazy over you, I'm sure."

"Is my mate jealous?"

"Never," she denied with a small chuckle.

"There's only one woman for me and she's in my arms. And as for this grass…" Jax hesitated, unsure if he should divulge the real reason he'd had it installed. But he'd decided long ago that they'd never again have secrets. "Truth?"

"Truth." Katrina pressed up onto his chest, catching his gaze.

"I love you. You and I," he sighed, "we've been alone a long time. You're my family now. And I'm not talking about the pack. Yeah, that counts, but you're my blood. I know we haven't talked about kids but…"

"You want to have a child?" Katrina asked.

Jax nodded, detecting her heartbeat race at his revelation. Concerned he'd scared her, he decided to back off and let her know that regardless of her desire to have children, she alone fulfilled his dreams.

"Kat, we don't have to…"

"Yes," she interrupted, a small smile forming on her lips.

"Yes?" he asked, excitement in his eyes.

"Yes." She laughed and hugged him. "My big silly Alpha…you put in the grass for our kids?"

"Yes…it's crazy, right?"

"Not at all. It's brilliant. Our pups need a place to run."

"Pups?" His voice went up an octave in surprise.

"Pup. Pups. Whatever." She laughed.

"I love you, baby. So much."

"I love you, too," she whispered, her voice sleepy.

Jax smiled as slumber claimed his mate. With her in his arms, he relaxed into a blissful state of contentment. Loving Katrina had nearly broken him. Losing her, even if only for minutes, had been devastating. His little wolf, the one who'd denied and protected him, had stolen his heart.

Jake raced through the woods, his wolf agitated. Ever since his talk with Jax, a gnawing guilt had eaten at his gut. *Alpha.* Becoming a true Alpha didn't sit well with him. He didn't even know anyone well enough in California to call them a friend, let alone consider them family. When he'd left, his conscience had been clear. It hadn't mattered that he'd fought and won every single challenge in San Diego. Loyalty meant everything to him, and he owed everything to his pack, the Acadian Wolves.

Fucking Jax Chandler. *Asshole. Mentor. Friend.* Jake couldn't stop thinking about what the Alpha had told him, his words playing in his mind, confirming that he'd earned his right as Alpha. It wasn't as if he hadn't always known about the aggression that lurked inside him. He'd concealed it well from everyone. In the navy, he'd let it loose, rewarded for his remarkable fighting and shooting skills. After several years, he'd returned home, only to retrain his mind.

Jake never imagined living anywhere else but New Orleans. He'd deliberately subdued the will of his wolf, burying his desire to dominate. Challenging Logan would bring certain death, and there was no way in hell he'd ever hurt his friend.

Conflicted, he'd grown used to going off for long periods of time in the bayou. Resting his mind had become his only coping mechanism to sate the wolf that sought submission. In his solitude, his beast calmed, accepted his fate.

But in the presence of others, it took all his energy to pretend to be something he wasn't: a follower. He'd succeeded in his masquerade until he'd met Jax. The more experienced Alpha pushed his buttons, seemingly challenging him on purpose. At the same time, his wolf submitted to Jax, sensing the overwhelming power the older wolf possessed.

Forging a deep friendship with the Alpha had been both unexpected and surprisingly comforting. No longer did he have to hide his true nature. Jax hadn't pressured him into making a decision. Rather, he offered words of acknowledgement, imparting his vast wisdom about what it meant to be Alpha.

Making love with Jax and Katrina had been an extraordinary experience, but he needed time to think about his future. Alone once again, his wolf ran free, content to be without others. Jax had given him full access to his cabin and Jake planned on staying for as long as it took to clear his head. Although spring, the morning air remained crisp, winter lingering on its heels. The foliage, waking from its frozen slumber, sprouted buds, birds serenading above.

His ears pricked in awareness, detecting a human presence, and Jake crouched down in the bushes. Through the thicket, he spied a reflection in the water. He patiently listened. The sound of rushing water swooshed over the rocks. In the absence of voices, Jake's curiosity piqued.

He caught a glimpse of movement behind the waterfall, and instinct drove him to investigate. His stealthy strides through the muddied creek went unnoticed as he approached. The small figure made no move to escape, and he went still, peering behind the trailing water.

Jake shifted as she came into sight. *What the fuck?* Shocked, he rubbed the moisture from his eyes. The emaciated female shook uncontrollably, shivering on the rocks. Her arms clutched protectively around herself, shielding her bareness. He called to her but she didn't respond. Burning hate was soon replaced with an uneasy compassion as she stared through him as if she'd lost all memory of who he was.

Conflicted, Jake despised her, but knew he had no other choice as he took action. A small whimper was the only sound she made as he scooped her into his arms. Taking her back to New Orleans wouldn't be easy. When it came to her, nothing ever was. The female had nearly ruined his friend, yet she'd saved another. With her skin against his, no magick emanated from the pathetic creature. She'd been evil. She'd been kind. She'd been powerful. She was *the* witch. *The* high priestess. *Ilsbeth.*

Romance by Kym Grosso

The Immortals of New Orleans

Kade's Dark Embrace
(Immortals of New Orleans, Book 1)

Luca's Magic Embrace
(Immortals of New Orleans, Book 2)

Tristan's Lyceum Wolves
(Immortals of New Orleans, Book 3)

Logan's Acadian Wolves
(Immortals of New Orleans, Book 4)

Léopold's Wicked Embrace
(Immortals of New Orleans, Book 5)

Dimitri
(Immortals of New Orleans, Book 6)

Lost Embrace
(Immortals of New Orleans, Book 6.5)

Jax
(Immortals of New Orleans, Book 7)

Club Altura Romance

Solstice Burn
(A Club Altura Romance Novella, Prequel)

Carnal Risk
(A Club Altura Romance Novel, Book 1)

Wicked Rush
(A Club Altura Romance Novel, Book 2) Coming 2016

About the Author

Kym Grosso is the New York Times and USA Today bestselling and award-winning author of the erotic romance series, *The Immortals of New Orleans* and *Club Altura*. In addition to romance, Kym has written and published several articles about autism, and is a contributing essay author in *Chicken Soup for the Soul: Raising Kids on the Spectrum*.

Kym lives with her family in Pennsylvania, and her hobbies include reading, tennis, zumba, and spending time with her husband and children. She loves traveling just about anywhere that has a beach or snow-covered mountains. New Orleans, with its rich culture, history and unique cuisine, is one of her favorite places to visit.

• • • •

Social Media/Links:

Website: http://www.KymGrosso.com
Facebook: http://www.facebook.com/KymGrossoBooks
Twitter: https://twitter.com/KymGrosso
Pinterest: http://www.pinterest.com/kymgrosso/

Sign up for Kym's Newsletter to get Updates and Information about New Releases:
http://www.kymgrosso.com/members-only

Made in the USA
Middletown, DE
15 May 2023

30589382R00406